THE
RINCEWIND
TRILOGY

THE RINCEWIND TRILOGY

Terry Pratchett

GOLLANCZ

London

First published as one volume in Great Britain 2001

Gollancz
An imprint of the Orion Publishing Group
Orion House, 5 Upper St Martin's Lane, London WC2H 9EA

A CIP catalogue record for this book is available
from the British Library

ISBN 0575 072369

Typeset at the Spartan Press Ltd,
Lymington, Hants

Printed in Great Britain by
Clays Ltd, St Ives plc

SOURCERY

DEDICATION

Many years ago I saw, in Bath, a very large American lady towing a *huge* tartan suitcase very fast on little rattly wheels which caught in the pavement cracks and generally gave it a life of its own. At that moment the Luggage was born. Many thanks to that lady and everyone else in places like Power Cable, Neb., who don't get nearly enough encouragement.

This book does not contain a map. Please feel free to draw your own.

There was a man and he had eight sons. Apart from that, he was nothing more than a comma on the page of History. It's sad, but that's all you can say about some people.

But the eighth son grew up and married and had eight sons, and because there is only one suitable profession for the eighth son of an eighth son, he became a wizard. And he became wise and powerful, or at any rate powerful, and wore a pointed hat and there it would have ended . . .

Should have ended . . .

But against the Lore of Magic and certainly against all reason – except the reasons of the heart, which are warm and messy and, well, *unreasonable* – he fled the halls of magic and fell in love and got married, not necessarily in that order.

And he had seven sons, each one from the cradle at least as powerful as any wizard in the world.

And then he had an eighth son . . .

A wizard squared. A source of magic.

A sourcerer.

Summer thunder rolled around the sandy cliffs. Far below, the sea sucked on the shingle as noisily as an old man with one tooth who had been given a gobstopper. A few seagulls hung lazily in the updraughts, waiting for something to happen.

And the father of wizards sat among the thrift and rattling sea grasses at the edge of the cliff, cradling the child in his arms, staring out to sea.

There was a roil of black cloud out there, heading inland, and the light it pushed before it had that deep syrup quality it gets before a really serious thunderstorm.

He turned at a sudden silence behind him, and looked up through tear-reddened eyes at a tall hooded figure in a black robe.

IPSLORE THE RED? it said. The voice was as hollow as a cave, as dense as a neutron star.

Ipslore grinned the terrible grin of the suddenly mad, and held up the child for Death's inspection.

'My son,' he said. 'I shall call him Coin.'

A NAME AS GOOD AS ANY OTHER, said Death, politely. His empty sockets stared down at a small round face wrapped in sleep. Despite rumour, Death isn't cruel – merely terribly, terribly good at his job.

'You took his mother,' said Ipslore. It was a flat statement, without apparent rancour. In the valley behind the cliffs Ipslore's homestead was a smoking ruin, the rising wind already spreading the fragile ashes across the hissing dunes.

IT WAS A HEART ATTACK AT THE END, said Death. THERE ARE WORSE WAYS TO DIE. TAKE IT FROM ME.

Ipslore looked out to sea. 'All my magic could not save her,' he said.

THERE ARE PLACES WHERE EVEN MAGIC MAY NOT GO.

'And now you have come for the child?'

NO. THE CHILD HAS HIS OWN DESTINY. I HAVE COME FOR YOU.

'Ah.' The wizard stood up, carefully laid the sleeping baby down on the thin grass, and picked up a long staff that had been lying there. It was made of a black metal, with a meshwork of silver and gold carvings that gave it a rich and sinister tastelessness; the metal was octiron, intrinsically magical.

'I made this, you know,' he said. 'They all said you couldn't make a staff out of metal, they said they should only be of wood, but they were wrong. I put a lot of myself into it. I shall give it to him.'

He ran his hands lovingly along the staff, which gave off a faint tone.

He repeated, almost to himself, 'I put a lot of myself into it.'

IT IS A GOOD STAFF, said Death.

Ipslore held it in the air and looked down at his eighth son, who gave a gurgle.

'She wanted a daughter,' he said.

Death shrugged. Ipslore gave him a look compounded of bewilderment and rage.

'What *is* he?'

THE EIGHTH SON OF AN EIGHTH SON OF AN EIGHTH SON, said Death, unhelpfully. The wind whipped at his robe, driving the black clouds overhead.

'What does that make him?'

A SOURCERER, AS YOU ARE WELL AWARE.

Thunder rolled, on cue.

'What is his destiny?' shouted Ipslore, above the rising gale.

Death shrugged again. He was good at it.

Sourcerers make their own destiny. They touch the Earth lightly.

Ipslore leaned on the staff, drumming on it with his fingers, apparently lost in the maze of his own thoughts. His left eyebrow twitched.

'No,' he said, softly, 'no. I will make his destiny for him.'

I advise against it.

'Be quiet! And listen when I tell you that they drove me out, with their books and their rituals and their Lore! They called themselves wizards, and they had less magic in their whole fat bodies than I have in my little finger! Banished! *Me*! For showing that I was human! And what would humans be without love?'

Rare, said Death. Nevertheless—

'Listen! They drove us here, to the ends of the world, and that killed her! They tried to take my staff away!' Ipslore was screaming above the noise of the wind.

'Well, I still have some power left,' he snarled. 'And I say that my son shall go to Unseen University and wear the Archchancellor's hat and the wizards of the world shall bow to him! And he shall show them what lies in their deepest hearts. Their craven, greedy hearts. He'll show the *world* its true destiny, and there will be no magic greater than his.'

No. And the strange thing about the quiet way Death spoke the word was this: it was louder than the roaring of the storm. It jerked Ipslore back to momentary sanity.

Ipslore rocked back and forth uncertainly. 'What?' he said.

I said no. Nothing is final. Nothing is absolute. Except me, of course. Such tinkering with destiny could mean the downfall of the world. There must be a chance, however small. The lawyers of fate demand a loophole in every prophecy.

Ipslore stared at Death's implacable face.

'I must give them a chance?'

Yes.

Tap, tap, tap went Ipslore's fingers on the metal of the staff.

'Then they shall have their chance,' he said, 'when hell freezes over.'

No. I am not allowed to enlighten you, even by default, about current temperatures in the next world.

'Then,' Ipslore hesitated, 'then they shall have their chance when my son throws his staff away.'

NO WIZARD WOULD EVER THROW HIS STAFF AWAY, said Death. THE BOND IS TOO GREAT.

'Yet it is possible, you must agree.'

Death appeared to consider this. *Must* was not a word he was accustomed to hearing, but he seemed to concede the point.

AGREED, he said.

'Is that a small enough chance for you?'

SUFFICIENTLY MOLECULAR.

Ipslore relaxed a little. In a voice that was nearly normal, he said: 'I don't regret it, you know. I would do it all again. Children are our hope for the future.'

THERE IS NO HOPE FOR THE FUTURE, said Death.

'What does it contain, then?'

ME.

'Besides you, I mean!'

Death gave him a puzzled look. I'M SORRY?

The storm reached its howling peak overhead. A seagull went past backwards.

'I meant,' said Ipslore, bitterly, 'what is there in this world that makes living worth while?'

Death thought about it.

CATS, he said eventually, CATS ARE NICE.

'Curse you!'

MANY HAVE, said Death, evenly.

'How much longer do I have?'

Death pulled a large hourglass from the secret recesses of his robe. The two bulbs were enclosed in bars of black and gold, and the sand was nearly all in the bottom one.

OH, ABOUT NINE SECONDS.

Ipslore pulled himself up to his full and still impressive height, and extended the gleaming metal staff towards the child. A hand like a little pink crab reached out from the blanket and grasped it.

'Then let me be the first and last wizard in the history of the world to pass on his staff to his eighth son,' he said slowly and sonorously. 'And I charge him to use it to—

I SHOULD HURRY UP, IF I WERE YOU . . .

'—the full,' said Ipslore, 'becoming the mightiest—'

The lightning screamed from the heart of the cloud, hit Ipslore on the point of his hat, crackled down his arm, flashed along the staff and struck the child.

The wizard vanished in a wisp of smoke. The staff glowed green, then white, then merely red-hot. The child smiled in his sleep.

When the thunder had died away Death reached down slowly and picked up the boy, who opened his eyes.

They glowed golden, from the inside. For the first time in what, for want of any better word, must be called his life, Death found himself looking at a stare that he found hard to return. The eyes seemed to be focused on a point several inches inside his skull.

I did not mean for that to happen, said the voice of Ipslore, from out of the empty air. *Is he harmed?*

No. Death tore his gaze away from that fresh, knowing smile. HE CONTAINED THE POWER. HE IS A SOURCERER: NO DOUBT HE WILL SURVIVE MUCH WORSE. AND NOW – YOU WILL COME WITH ME.

No.

YES. YOU ARE DEAD, YOU SEE. Death looked around for Ipslore's wavering shade, and failed to find it. WHERE ARE YOU?

In the staff.

Death leaned on his scythe and sighed.

FOOLISH. HOW EASILY COULD I CUT YOU LOOSE.

Not without destroying the staff, said the voice of Ipslore, and it seemed to Death that there was a new, thick, exultant quality to it. *And now the child has accepted the staff you cannot destroy it without destroying him. And that you cannot do without upsetting destiny. My last magic. Rather neat, I feel.*

Death prodded the staff. It crackled, and sparks crawled obscenely along its length.

Strangely enough, he wasn't particularly angry. Anger is an emotion, and for emotion you need glands, and Death didn't have much truck with glands and needed a good run at it to get angry. But he was mildly annoyed. He sighed again. People were always trying this sort of thing. On the other hand, it was quite interesting to watch, and at least this was a bit more original than the usual symbolic chess game, which Death always dreaded because he could never remember how the knight was supposed to move.

YOU'RE ONLY PUTTING OFF THE INEVITABLE, he said.

That's what being alive is all about.

BUT WHAT PRECISELY DO YOU EXPECT TO GAIN?

I shall be by my son's side. I shall teach him, even though he won't know it. I shall guide his understanding. And, when he is ready, I shall guide his steps.

TELL ME, said Death, HOW DID YOU GUIDE THE STEPS OF YOUR OTHER SONS?

I drove them out. They dared to argue with me, they would not listen to what I could teach them. But this one will.

IS THIS WISE?

The staff was silent. Beside it, the boy chuckled at the sound of a voice only he could hear.

There was no analogy for the way in which Great A'Tuin the world turtle moved against the galactic night. When you are ten thousand miles long, your shell pocked with meteor craters and frosted with comet ice, there is absolutely nothing you can realistically be like except yourself.

So Great A'Tuin swam slowly through the interstellar deeps like the largest turtle there has ever been, carrying on its carapace the four huge elephants that bore on their backs the vast, glittering, waterfall-fringed circle of the Discworld, which exists either because of some impossible blip on the curve of probability or because the gods enjoy a joke as much as anyone.

More than most people, in fact.

Near the shores of the Circle Sea, in the ancient, sprawling city of Ankh-Morpork, on a velvet cushion on a ledge high up in the Unseen University, was a hat.

It was a good hat. It was a *magnificent* hat.

It was pointy, of course, with a wide floppy brim, but after disposing of these basic details the designer had really got down to business. There was gold lace on there, and pearls, and bands of purest vermine, and sparkling Ankhstones[*], and some incredibly tasteless sequins, and – a dead giveaway, of course – a circle of octarines.

Since they weren't in a strong magical field at the moment they weren't glowing, and looked like rather inferior diamonds.

Spring had come to Ankh-Morpork. It wasn't immediately apparent, but there were signs that were obvious to the cognoscenti. For example, the scum on the river Ankh, that great wide slow waterway that served the double city as reservoir, sewer and frequent morgue, had turned a particularly iridescent green. The city's drunken rooftops sprouted mattresses and bolsters as the winter bedding was put out to air in the weak sunshine, and in the depths of musty cellars the beams twisted and groaned when their dry sap

[*] Like rhinestones, but different river. When it comes to glittering objects, wizards have all the taste and self-control of a deranged magpie.

8

responded to the ancient call of root and forest. Birds nested among the gutters and eaves of Unseen University, although it was noticeable that however great the pressure on the nesting sites they never, ever, made nests in the invitingly open mouths of the gargoyles that lined the rooftops, much to the gargoyles' disappointment.

A kind of spring had even come to the ancient University itself. Tonight would be the Eve of Small Gods, and a new Archchancellor would be elected.

Well, not exactly *elected*, because wizards didn't have any truck with all this undignified voting business, and it was well known that Archchancellors were selected by the will of the gods, and this year it was a pretty good bet that the gods would see their way clear to selecting old Virrid Wayzygoose, who was a decent old boy and had been patiently waiting his turn for years.

The Archchancellor of Unseen University was the official leader of all the wizards on the Disc. Once upon a time it had meant that he would be the most powerful in the handling of magic, but times were a lot quieter now and, to be honest, senior wizards tended to look upon actual magic as a bit beneath them. They tended to prefer administration, which was safer and nearly as much fun, and also big dinners.

And so the long afternoon wore on. The hat squatted on its faded cushion in Wayzygoose's chambers, while he sat in his tub in front of the fire and soaped his beard. Other wizards dozed in their studies, or took a gentle stroll around the gardens in order to work up an appetite for the evening's feast; about a dozen steps was usually considered quite sufficient.

In the Great Hall, under the carved or painted stares of two hundred earlier Archchancellors, the butler's staff set out the long tables and benches. In the vaulted maze of the kitchens – well, the imagination should need no assistance. It should include lots of grease and heat and shouting, vats of caviar, whole roast oxen, strings of sausages like paperchains strung from wall to wall, the head chef himself at work in one of the cold rooms putting the finishing touches to a model of the University carved for some inexplicable reason out of butter. He kept doing this every time there was a feast – butter swans, butter buildings, whole rancid greasy yellow menageries – and he enjoyed it so much no-one had the heart to tell him to stop.

In his own labyrinth of cellars the butler prowled among his casks, decanting and tasting.

The air of expectation had even spread to the ravens who inhabited the Tower of Art, eight hundred feet high and reputedly the oldest building in the world. Its crumbling stones supported

9

thriving miniature forests high above the city's rooftops. Entire species of beetles and small mammals had evolved up there and, since people rarely climbed it these days owing to the tower's distressing tendency to sway in the breeze, the ravens had it all to themselves. Now they were flying around it in a state of some agitation, like gnats before a thunderstorm. If anyone below is going to take any notice of them it might be a good idea.

Something horrible was about to happen.

You can tell, can't you?

You're not the only one.

'What's got into them?' shouted Rincewind above the din.

The Librarian ducked as a leather-bound grimoire shot out from its shelf and jerked to a mid-air halt on the end of its chain. Then he dived, rolled and landed on a copy of *Maleficio's Discouverie of Demonologie* that was industriously bashing at its lectern.

'Oook!' he said.

Rincewind put his shoulder against a trembling bookshelf and forced its rustling volumes back into place with his knees. The noise was terrible.

Books of magic have a sort of life of their own. Some have altogether too much; for example, the first edition of the *Necrotelicomicon* has to be kept between iron plates, the *True Arte of Levitatione* has spent the last one hundred and fifty years up in the rafters, and *Ge Fordge's Compenydyum of Sex Majick* is kept in a vat of ice in a room all by itself and there's a strict rule that it can only be read by wizards who are over eighty and, if possible, dead.

But even the everyday grimoires and incunabula on the main shelves were as restless and nervy as the inmates of a chicken-house with something rank scrabbling under the door. From their shut covers came a muffled scratching, like claws.

'What did you say?' screamed Rincewind.

'Oook!'*

---

* A magical accident in the Library, which as has already been indicated is not a place for your average rubber-stamp-and-Dewey-decimal employment, had some time ago turned the Librarian into an orang-utan. He had since resisted all efforts to turn him back. He liked the handy long arms, the prehensile toes and the right to scratch himself in public, but most of all he liked the way all the big questions of existence had suddenly resolved themselves into a vague interest in where his next banana was coming from. It wasn't that he was unaware of the despair and nobility of the human condition. It was just that as far as he was concerned you could stuff it.

'Right!'

Rincewind, as honorary assistant librarian, hadn't progressed much beyone basic indexing and banana-fetching, and he had to admire the way the Librarian ambled among the quivering shelves, here running a black-leather hand over a trembling binding, here comforting a frightened thesaurus with a few soothing simian murmurings.

After a while the Library began to settle down, and Rincewind felt his shoulder muscles relax.

It was a fragile peace, though. Here and there a page rustled. From distant shelves came the ominous creak of a spine. After its initial panic the Library was now as alert and jittery as a long-tailed cat in a rocking-chair factory.

The Librarian ambled back down the aisles. He had a face that only a lorry tyre could love and it was permanently locked in a faint smile, but Rincewind could tell by the way the ape crept into his cubbyhole under the desk and hid his head under a blanket that he was deeply worried.

Examine Rincewind, as he peers around the sullen shelves. There are eight levels of wizardry on the Disc; after sixteen years Rincewind has failed to achieve even level one. In fact it is the considered opinion of some of his tutors that he is incapable even of achieving level zero, which most normal people are *born* at; to put it another way, it has been suggested that when Rincewind dies the average occult ability of the human race will actually go up by a fraction.

He is tall and thin and has the scrubby kind of beard that looks like the kind of beard worn by people who weren't cut out by nature to be beard wearers. He is dressed in a dark red robe that has seen better days, possibly better decades. But you can tell he's a wizard, because he's got a pointy hat with a floppy brim. It's got the word 'Wizzard' embroidered on it in big silver letters, by someone whose needlework is even worse than their spelling. There's a star on top. It has lost most of its sequins.

Clamping his hat on his head, Rincewind pushed his way through the Library's ancient doors and stepped out into the golden light of the afternoon. It was calm and quiet, broken only by the hysterical croaking of the ravens as they circled the Tower of Art.

Rincewind watched them for a while. The University's ravens were a tough bunch of birds. It took a lot to unsettle them.

On the other hand—

—the sky was pale blue tinted with gold, with a few high wisps of fluffy cloud glowing pinkly in the lengthening light. The ancient chestnut trees in the quadrangle were in full bloom. From an open window came the sound of a student wizard practising the violin, rather badly. It was not what you would call ominous.

Rincewind leaned against the warm stonework. And screamed.

The building was shuddering. He could feel it come up through his hand and along his arms, a faint rhythmic sensation at just the right frequency to suggest uncontrollable terror. The stones themselves were frightened.

He looked down in horror at a faint clinking noise. An ornamental drain cover fell backwards and one of the University's rats poked its whiskers out. It gave Rincewind a desperate look as it scrambled up and fled past him, followed by dozens of its tribe. Some of them were wearing clothes but that wasn't unusual for the University, where the high level of background magic does strange things to genes.

As he stared around him Rincewind could see other streams of grey bodies leaving the University by every drainpipe and flowing towards the outside wall. The ivy by his ear rustled and a group of rats made a series of death-defying leaps on to his shoulders and slid down his robe. They otherwise ignored him totally but, again, this wasn't particularly unusual. Most creatures ignored Rincewind.

He turned and fled into the University, skirts flapping around his knees, until he reached the bursar's study. He hammered on the door, which creaked open.

'Ah. It's, um, Rincewind, isn't it?' said the bursar, without much enthusiasm. 'What's the matter?'

'We're sinking!'

The bursar stared at him for a few moments. His name was Spelter. He was tall and wiry and looked as though he had been a horse in previous lives and had only just avoided it in this one. He always gave people the impression that he was looking at them with his teeth.

'Sinking?'

'Yes. All the rats are leaving!'

The bursar gave him another stare.

'Come inside, Rincewind,' he said, kindly. Rincewind followed him into the low, dark room and across to the window. It looked out over the gardens to the river, oozing peacefully towards the sea.

'You haven't been, um, overdoing it?' said the bursar.

'Overdoing what?' said Rincewind, guiltily.

'This is a building, you see,' said the bursar. Like most wizards when faced with a puzzle, he started to roll himself a cigarette. 'It's not a ship. There are ways of telling, you know. Absence of porpoises frolicking around the bows, a shortage of bilges, that sort of thing. The chances of foundering are remote. Otherwise, um, we'd have to man the sheds and row for shore. Um?'

'But the rats—'

'Grain ship in harbour, I expect. Some, um, springtime ritual.'

'I'm sure I felt the building shaking, too,' said Rincewind, a shade uncertainly. Here in this quiet room, with the fire crackling in the grate, it didn't seem quite so real.

'A passing tremor. Great A 'Tuin hiccuping, um, possibly. A grip on yourself, um, is what you should get. You haven't been drinking, have you?'

'No!'

'Um. Would you like to?'

Spelter padded over to a dark oak cabinet and pulled out a couple of glasses, which he filled from the water jug.

'I tend to be best at sherry this time of day,' he said, and spread his hands over the glasses. 'Say, um, the word – sweet or dry?'

'Um, no,' said Rincewind. 'Perhaps you're right. I think I'll go and have a bit of rest.'

'Good idea.'

Rincewind wandered down the chilly stone passages. Occasionally he'd touch the wall and appear to be listening, and then he'd shake his head.

As he crossed the quadrangle again he saw a herd of mice swarm over a balcony and scamper towards the river. The ground they were running over seemed to be moving, too. When Rincewind looked closer he could see that it was because it was covered with ants.

These weren't ordinary ants. Centuries of magical leakage into the walls of the University had done strange things to them. Some of them were pulling very small carts, some of them were riding beetles, but all of them were leaving the University as quickly as possible. The grass on the lawn rippled as they passed.

He looked up as an elderly striped mattress was extruded from an upper window and flopped down on to the flagstones below. After a pause, apparently to catch its breath, it rose a little from the ground. Then it started to float purposefully across the lawn and bore down on Rincewind, who managed to jump out of its way just in time. He heard a high-pitched chittering and caught a glimpse of thousands of determined little legs under the bulging fabric before it hurtled onward. Even the bedbugs were on the move, and in case they didn't

13

find such comfortable quarters elsewhere they were leaving nothing to chance. One of them waved at him and squeaked a greeting.

Rincewind backed away until something touched the back of his legs and froze his spine. It turned out to be a stone seat. He watched it for some time. It didn't seem in any hurry to run away. He sat down gratefully.

There's probably a natural explanation, he thought. Or a perfectly normal unnatural one, anyway.

A gritty noise made him look across the lawn.

There was no natural explanation of *this*. With incredible slowness, easing themselves down parapets and drainpipes in total silence except for the occasional scrape of stone on stone, the gargoyles were leaving the roof.

It's a shame that Rincewind had never seen poor quality stop-motion photography, because then he would have known exactly how to describe what he was seeing. The creatures didn't exactly move, but they managed to progress in a series of high speed tableaux, and lurched past him in a spindly procession of beaks, manes, wings, claws and pigeon droppings.

'What's happening?' he squeaked.

A thing with a goblin's face, harpy's body and hen's legs turned its head in a series of little jerks and spoke in a voice like the peristalsis of mountains (although the deep resonant effect was rather spoiled because, of course, it couldn't close its mouth).

It said: 'A Ourcerer is umming! Eee orr ife!'

Rincewind said 'Pardon?' But the thing had gone past and was lurching awkwardly across the ancient lawn.*

So Rincewind sat and stared blankly at nothing much for fully ten seconds before giving a little scream and running as fast as he could.

He didn't stop until he'd reached his own room in the Library building. It wasn't much of a room, being mainly used to store old furniture, but it was home.

Against one shadowy wall was a wardrobe. It wasn't one of your modern wardrobes, fit only for nervous adulterers to jump into when the husband returned home early, but an ancient oak affair, dark as night, in whose dusty depths coat-hangers lurked and bred; herds of flaking shoes roamed its floor. It was quite possible that it

---

*The furrow left by the fleeing gargoyles caused the University's head gardener to bite through his rake and led to the famous quotation: 'How do you get a lawn like this? You mows it and you rolls it for five hundred years and then a bunch of bastards walks across it.'

was a secret doorway to fabulous worlds, but no-one had ever tried to find out because of the distressing smell of mothballs.

And on top of the wardrobe, wrapped in scraps of yellowing paper and old dust sheets, was a large brass-bound chest. It went by the name of the Luggage. Why it consented to be owned by Rincewind was something only the Luggage knew, and it wasn't telling, but probably no other item in the entire chronicle of travel accessories had quite such a history of mystery and grievous bodily harm. It had been described as half suitcase, half homicidal maniac. It had many unusual qualities which may or may not become apparent soon, but currently there was only one that set it apart from any other brass-bound chest. It was snoring, with a sound like someone very slowly sawing a log.

The Luggage might be magical. It might be terrible. But in its enigmatic soul it was kin to every other piece of luggage throughout the multiverse, and preferred to spend its winters hibernating on top of a wardrobe.

Rincewind hit it with a broom until the sawing stopped, filled his pockets with odds and ends from the banana crate he used as a dressing table, and made for the door. He couldn't help noticing that his mattress had gone but that didn't matter because he was pretty clear that he was never going to sleep on a mattress again, ever.

The Luggage landed on the floor with a solid thump. After a few seconds, and with extreme care, it rose up on hundreds of little pink legs. It tilted backwards and forwards a bit, stretching every leg, and then it opened its lid and yawned.

'Are you coming or not?'

The lid shut with a snap. The Luggage manoeuvred its feet into a complicated shuffle until it was facing the doorway, and headed after its master.

The Library was still in a state of tension, with the occasional clinking* of a chain or muffled crackle of a page. Rincewind reached under the desk and grabbed the Librarian, who was still hunched under his blanket.

'Come on, I said!'

'Oook.'

'I'll buy you a drink,' said Rincewind desperately.

The Librarian unfolded like a four-legged spider. 'Oook?'

Rincewind half-dragged the ape from his nest and out through the

---

*In most old libraries the books are chained to the shelves to prevent them being damaged by people. In the Library of Unseen University, of course, it's more or less the other way about.

door. He didn't head for the main gates but for an otherwise undistinguished area of wall where a few loose stones had, for two thousand years, offered students an unobtrusive way in after lights-out. Then he stopped so suddenly that the Librarian cannoned into him and the Luggage ran into both of them.

'Oook!'

'Oh, gods,' he said. 'Look at that!'

'Oook?'

There was a shiny black tide flowing out of a grating near the kitchens. Early evening starlight glinted off millions of little black backs.

But it wasn't the sight of the cockroaches that was so upsetting. It was the fact that they were marching in step, a hundred abreast. Of course, like all the informal inhabitants of the University the roaches were a little unusual, but there was something particularly unpleasant about the sound of billions of very small feet hitting the stones in perfect time.

Rincewind stepped gingerly over the marching column. The Librarian jumped it.

The Luggage, of course, followed them with a noise like someone tapdancing over a bag of crisps.

And so, forcing the Luggage to go all the way around to the gates anyway, because otherwise it'd only batter a hole in the wall, Rincewind quit the University with all the other insects and small frightened rodents and decided that if a few quiet beers wouldn't allow him to see things in a different light, then a few more probably would. It was certainly worth a try.

That was why he wasn't present in the Great Hall for dinner. It would turn out to be the most important missed meal of his life.

Further along the University wall there was a faint clink as a grapnel caught the spikes that lined its top. A moment later a slim, black-clad figure dropped lightly into the University grounds and ran soundlessly towards the Great Hall, where it was soon lost in the shadows.

No-one would have noticed it anyway. On the other side of the campus the Sourcerer was walking towards the gates of the University. Where his feet touched the cobbles blue sparks crackled and evaporated the early evening dew.

*

It was *very* hot. The big fireplace at the turnwise end of the Great Hall was practically incandescent. Wizards feel the cold easily, so the sheer blast of heat from the roaring logs was melting candles twenty feet away and bubbling the varnish on the long tables. The air over the feast was blue with tobacco smoke, which writhed into curious shapes as it was bent by random drifts of magic. On the centre table the complete carcass of a whole roast pig looked extremely annoyed at the fact that someone had killed it without waiting for it to finish its apple, and the model University made of butter was sinking gently into a pool of grease.

There was a lot of beer about. Here and there red-faced wizards were happily singing ancient drinking songs which involved a lot of knee-slapping and cries of 'Ho!' The only possible excuse for this sort of thing is that wizards are celibate, and have to find their amusement where they can.

Another reason for the general conviviality was the fact that no-one was trying to kill anyone else. This is an unusual state of affairs in magical circles.

The higher levels of wizardry are a perilous place. Every wizard is trying to dislodge the wizards above him while stamping on the fingers of those below; to say that wizards are healthily competitive by nature is like saying that piranhas are naturally a little peckish. However, ever since the great Mage Wars left whole areas of the Disc uninhabitable[*], wizards have been forbidden to settle their differences by magical means, because it caused a lot of trouble for the population at large and in any case it was often difficult to tell which of the resultant patches of smoking fat had been the winner. So they traditionally resort to knives, subtle poisons, scorpions in shoes and hilarious booby traps involving razor-sharp pendulums.

On Small Gods' Eve, however, it was considered extremely bad form to kill a brother wizard, and wizards felt able to let their hair down without fear of being strangled with it.

The Archchancellor's chair was empty. Wayzygoose was dining alone in his study, as befits a man chosen by the gods after their serious discussion with sensible senior wizards earlier in the day. Despite his eighty years, he was feeling a little bit nervous and hardly touched his second chicken.

In a few minutes he would have to make a speech. Wayzygoose had, in his younger days, sought power in strange places; he'd

---

[*] At least, by anyone who wanted to wake up the same shape, or even the same species, as they went to bed.

wrestled with demons in blazing octagrams, stared into dimensions that men were not meant to wot of, and even outfaced the Unseen University grants committee, but nothing in the eight circles of nothingness was quite so bad as a couple of hundred expectant faces staring up at him through the cigar smoke.

The heralds would soon be coming by to collect him. He sighed and pushed his pudding away untasted, crossed the room, stood in front of the big mirror, and fumbled in the pocket of the robe for his notes.

After a while he managed to get them in some sort of order and cleared his throat.

'My brothers in art,' he began, 'I cannot tell you how much I – er, how much . . . fine traditions of this ancient university . . . er . . . as I look around me and see the pictures of Archchancellors gone before . . .' He paused, sorted through his notes again, and plunged on rather more certainly. 'Standing here tonight I am reminded of the story about the three-legged pedlar and the, er, merchant's daughters. It seems that this merchant . . .'

There was a knock at the door.

'Enter,' Wayzygoose barked, and peered at the notes carefully.

'This merchant,' he muttered, 'this merchant, yes, this merchant had three daughters. I think it was. Yes. It was three. It would appear . . .'

He looked into the mirror, and turned round.

He started to say, 'Who are y—'

And found that there are things worse than making speeches, after all.

The small dark figure creeping along the deserted corridors heard the noise, and didn't take too much notice. Unpleasant noises were not uncommon in areas where magic was commonly practised. The figure was looking for something. It wasn't sure what it was, only that it would know it when it found it.

After some minutes its search led it to Wayzygoose's room. The air was full of greasy coils. Little particles of soot drifted gently on the air currents, and there were several foot-shaped burn marks on the floor.

The figure shrugged. There was no accounting for the sort of things you found in wizards' rooms. It caught sight of its multi-faceted reflection in the shattered mirror, adjusted the set of its hood, and got on with the search.

Moving like one listening to inner directions, it padded noise-lessly across the room until it reached the table whereon stood a tall, round and battered leather box. It crept closer and gently raised the lid.

The voice from inside sounded as though it was talking through several layers of carpet when it said, *At last. What kept you?*

'I mean, how did they all get started? I mean, back in the old times, there were real wizards, there was none of this levels business. They just went out and – did it. Pow!'

One or two of the other customers in the darkened bar of the Mended Drum tavern looked around hastily at the noise. They were new in town. Regular customers never took any notice of surprising noises like groans or unpleasantly gristly sounds. It was a lot healthier. In some parts of the city curiosity didn't just kill the cat, it threw it in the river with lead weights tied to its feet.

Rincewind's hands weaved unsteadily over the array of empty glasses on the table in front of him. He'd almost been able to forget about the cockroaches. After another drink he might manage to forget about the mattress, too.

'Whee! A fireball! Fizz! Vanishing like smoke! Whee! – Sorry.'

The Librarian carefully pulled what remained of his beer out of the reach of Rincewind's flailing arms.

'Proper magic.' Rincewind stifled a belch.

'Oook.'

Rincewind stared into the frothy remnants of his last beer, and then, with extreme care in case the top of his head fell off, leaned down and poured some into a saucer for the Luggage. It was lurking under the table, which was a relief. It usually embarrassed him in bars by sidling up to drinkers and terrorising them into feeding it crisps.

He wondered fuzzily where his train of thought had been derailed.

'Where was I?'

'Oook,' the Librarian hinted.

'Yeah.' Rincewind brightened. '*They* didn't have all this levels and grades business, you know. They had sourcerers in those days. They went out in the world and found new spells and had adventures—'

He dipped a finger in a puddle of beer and doodled a design on the stained, scratched timber of the table.

One of Rincewind's tutors had said of him that 'to call his

understanding of magical theory *abysmal* is to leave no suitable word to describe his grasp of its practice'. This had always puzzled him. He objected to the fact that you had to be good at magic to be a wizard. He *knew* he was a wizard, deep in his head. Being good at magic didn't have anything to do with it. That was just an extra, it didn't actually *define* somebody.

'When I was a little boy,' he said wistfully, 'I saw this picture of a sourcerer in a book. He was standing on a mountain top waving his arms and the waves were coming right up, you know, like they do down in Ankh Bay in a gale, and there were flashes of lightning all round him—'

'Oook?'

'I don't know why they didn't, perhaps he had rubber boots on,' Rincewind snapped, and went on dreamily, 'And he had this staff and a hat on, just like mine, and his eyes were sort of glowing and there was all this sort of like *glitter* coming out of his fingertips, and I thought one day I'll do that, and—'

'Oook?'

'Just a half, then.'

'Oook.'

'How do you pay for this stuff? Every time anyone gives you any money you eat it.'

'Oook.'

'Amazing.'

Rincewind completed his sketch in the beer. There was a stick figure on a cliff. It didn't look much like him – drawing in stale beer is not a precise art – but it was meant to.

'That's what I wanted to be,' he said. 'Pow! Not all this messing around. All this books and stuff, that isn't what it should all be about. What we need is real wizardry.'

That last remark would have earned the prize for the day's most erroneous statement if Rincewind hadn't then said:

'It's a pity there aren't any of them around any more.'

Spelter rapped on the table with his spoon.

He was an impressive figure, in his ceremonial robe with the purple-and-vermine[*] hood of the Venerable Council of Seers and the yellow sash of a fifth level wizard; he'd been fifth level for three

---

[*] The vermine is a small black and white relative of the lemming, found in the cold Hublandish regions. Its skin is rare and highly valued, especially by the vermine itself; the selfish little bastard will do anything rather than let go of it.

years, waiting for one of the sixty-four sixth level wizards to create a vacancy by dropping dead. He was in an amiable mood, however. Not only had he just finished a good dinner, he also had in his quarters a small phial of a guaranteed untastable poison which, used correctly, should guarantee him promotion within a few months. Life looked good.

The big clock at the end of the hall trembled on the verge of nine o'clock.

The tattoo with the spoon hadn't had much effect. Spelter picked up a pewter tankard and brought it down hard.

'Brothers!' he shouted, and nodded as the hubbub died away. 'Thank you. Be upstanding, please, for the ceremony of the, um, keys.'

There was a ripple of laughter and a general buzz of expectancy as the wizards pushed back their benches and got unsteadily to their feet.

The double doors to the hall were locked and triple barred. An incoming Archchancellor had to request entry three times before they would be unlocked, signifying that he was appointed with the consent of wizardry in general. Or some such thing. The origins were lost in the depths of time, which was as good a reason as any for retaining the custom.

The conversation died away. The assembled wizardry stared at the doors.

There was a soft knocking.

'Go away!' shouted the wizards, some of them collapsing at the sheer subtlety of the humour.

Spelter picked up the great iron ring that contained the keys to the University. They weren't all metal. They weren't all visible. Some of them looked very strange indeed.

'Who is that who knocketh without?' he intoned.

'*I do.*'

What was strange about the voice was this: it seemed to every wizard that the speaker was standing right behind him. Most of them found themselves looking over their shoulders.

In that moment of shocked silence there was the sharp little snick of the lock. They watched in fascinated horror as the iron bolts travelled back of their own accord; the great oak balks of timber, turned by Time into something tougher than rock, slid out of their sockets; the hinges flared from red through yellow to white and then exploded. Slowly, with a terrible inevitability, the doors fell into the hall.

There was an indistinct figure standing in the smoke from the burning hinges.

'Bloody hell, Virrid,' said one of the wizards nearby, 'that was a good one.'

As the figure strode into the light they could all see that it was not, after all, Virrid Wayzygoose.

He was at least a head shorter than any other wizard, and wore a simple white robe. He was also several decades younger; he looked about ten years old, and in one hand he held a staff considerably taller than he was.

'Here, he's no wizard—'

'Where's his hood, then?'

'Where's his *hat*?'

The stranger walked up the line of astonished wizards until he was standing in front of the top table. Spelter looked down at a thin young face framed by a mass of blond hair, and most of all he looked into two golden eyes that glowed from within. But he felt they weren't looking at him. They seemed to be looking at a point six inches beyond the back of his head. Spelter got the impression that he was in the way, and considerably surplus to immediate requirements.

He rallied his dignity and pulled himself up to his full height.

'What is the meaning of, um, this?' he said. It was pretty weak, he had to admit, but the steadiness of that incandescent glare appeared to be stripping all the words out of his memory.

'I have come,' said the stranger.

'Come? Come for what?'

'To take my place. Where is the seat for me?'

'Are you a student?' demanded Spelter, white with anger. 'What is your name, young man?'

The boy ignored him and looked around at the assembled wizards.

'Who is the most powerful wizard here?' he said. 'I wish to meet him.'

Spelter nodded his head. Two of the college porters, who had been sidling towards the newcomer for the last few minutes, appeared at either elbow.

'Take him out and throw him in the street,' said Spelter. The porters, big solid serious men, nodded. They gripped the boy's pipestem arms with hands like banana bunches.

'Your father will hear of this,' said Spelter severely.

'He already has,' said the boy. He glanced up at the two men and shrugged.

'What's going on here?'

Spelter turned to see Skarmer Billias, head of the Order of the Silver Star. Whereas Spelter tended towards the wiry, Billias was expansive, looking rather like a small captive balloon that had for some reason been draped in blue velvet and vermine; between them, the wizards averaged out as two normal-sized men.

Unfortunately, Billias was the type of person who prided himself on being good with children. He bent down as far as his dinner would allow and thrust a whiskery red face towards the boy.

'What's the matter, lad?' he said.

'This *child* had forced his way into here because, he says, he wants to meet a powerful wizard,' said Spelter, disapprovingly. Spelter disliked children intensely, which was perhaps why they found him so fascinating. At the moment he was successfully preventing himself from wondering about the door.

'Nothing wrong with that,' said Billias. 'Any lad worth his salt wants to be a wizard. I wanted to be a wizard when I was a lad. Isn't that right, lad?'

'Are you puissant?' said the boy.

'Hmm?'

'I said, are you puissant? How powerful are you?'

'Powerful?' said Billias. He stood up, fingered his eighth-level sash, and winked at Spelter. 'Oh, pretty powerful. Quite powerful, as wizards go.'

'Good. I challenge you. Show me your strongest magic. And when I have beaten you, why, then I shall be Archchancellor.'

'Why, you impudent—' began Spelter, but his protest was lost in the roar of laughter from the rest of the wizards. Billias slapped his knees, or as near to them as he could reach.

'A duel, eh?' he said. 'Pretty good, eh?'

'Duelling is forbidden, as well you know,' said Spelter. 'Anyway, it's totally ridiculous! I don't know who did the doors for him, but I will not stand here and see you waste all our time—'

'Now, now,' said Billias. 'What's your name, lad?'

'Coin.'

'Coin *sir*,' snapped Spelter.

'Well, now, Coin,' said Billias. 'You want to see the best I can do, eh?'

'Yes.'

'Yes *sir*,' snapped Spelter. Coin gave him an unblinking stare, a stare as old as time, the kind of stare that basks on rocks on volcanic islands and never gets tired. Spelter felt his mouth go dry.

Billias held out his hands for silence. Then, with a theatrical flourish, he rolled up the sleeve of his left arm and extended his hand.

The assembled wizards watched with interest. Eighth-levels were above magic, as a rule, spending most of their time in contemplation – normally of the next menu – and, of course, avoiding the attentions of ambitious wizards of the seventh level. This should be worth seeing.

Billias grinned at the boy, who returned it with a stare that focused on a point a few inches beyond the back of the old wizard's head.

Somewhat disconcerted, Billias flexed his fingers. Suddenly this wasn't quite the game he had intended, and he felt an overpowering urge to impress. It was swiftly overtaken by a surge of annoyance at his own stupidity in being unnerved.

'I shall show you,' he said, and took a deep breath, 'Maligree's Wonderful Garden.'

There was a susurration from the diners. Only four wizards in the entire history of the University had ever succeeded in achieving the complete Garden. Most wizards could create the trees and flowers, and a few had managed the birds. It wasn't the most powerful spell, it couldn't move mountains, but achieving the fine detail built into Maligree's complex syllables took a finely tuned skill.

'You will observe,' Billias added, 'nothing up my sleeve.'

His lips began to move. His hands flickered through the air. A pool of golden sparks sizzled in the palm of his hand, curved up, formed a faint sphere, began to fill in the detail . . .

Legend had it that Maligree, one of the last of the true sourcerers, created the Garden as a small, timeless, private self-locking universe where he could have a quiet smoke and a bit of a think while avoiding the cares of the world. Which was itself a puzzle, because no wizard could possibly understand how any being as powerful as a sourcerer could have a care in the world. Whatever the reason, Maligree retreated further and further into a world of his own and then, one day, closed the entrance after him.

The garden was a glittering ball in Billias's hands. The nearest wizards craned admiringly over his shoulders, and looked down into a two-foot sphere that showed a delicate, flower-strewn landscape; there was a lake in the middle distance, complete in every ripple, and purple mountains behind an interesting-looking forest. Tiny birds the size of bees flew from tree to tree, and a couple of deer no larger than mice glanced up from their grazing and stared out at Coin.

Who said critically: 'It's quite good. Give it to me.'

He took the intangible globe out of the wizard's hands and held it up.

'Why isn't it bigger?' he said.

Billias mopped his brow with a lace-edged handkerchief.

'Well,' he said weakly, so stunned by Coin's tone that he was quite unable to be affronted, 'since the old days, the efficacity of the spell has rather—'

Coin stood with his head on one side for a moment, as though listening to something. Then he whispered a few syllables and stroked the surface of the sphere.

It expanded. One moment it was a toy in the boy's hands, and the next . . .

. . . the wizards were standing on cool grass, in a shady meadow rolling down to the lake. There was a gentle breeze blowing from the mountains; it was scented with thyme and hay. The sky was deep blue shading to purple at the zenith.

The deer watched the newcomers suspiciously from their grazing ground under the trees.

Spelter looked down in shock. A peacock was pecking at his bootlaces.

'—' he began, and stopped. Coin was still holding a sphere, a sphere of air. Inside it, distorted as though seen through a fish-eye lens or the bottom of a bottle, was the Great Hall of Unseen University.

The boy looked around at the trees, squinted thoughtfully at the distant, snow-capped mountains, and nodded at the astonished men.

'It's not bad,' he said. 'I should like to come here again.' He moved his hands in a complicated motion that seemed, in some unexplained way, to turn them *inside out*.

Now the wizards were back in the hall, and the boy was holding the shrinking Garden in his palm. In the heavy, shocked silence he put it back into Billias's hands, and said: 'That was quite interesting. Now I will do some magic.'

He raised his hands, stared at Billias, and vanished him.

Pandemonium broke out, as it tends to on these occasions. In the centre of it stood Coin, totally composed, in a spreading cloud of greasy smoke.

Ignoring the tumult, Spelter bent down slowly and, with extreme care, picked a peacock feather off the floor. He rubbed it thoughtfully back and forth across his lips as he looked from the doorway to the boy to the vacant Archchancellor's chair, and his thin mouth narrowed, and he began to smile.

An hour later, as thunder began to roll in the clear skies above the city, and Rincewind was beginning to sing gently and forget all about cockroaches, and a lone mattress was wandering the streets, Spelter shut the door of the Archchancellor's study and turned to face his fellow mages.

There were six of them, and they were very worried.

They were so worried, Spelter noted, that they were listening to him, a mere fifth level wizard.

'He's gone to bed,' he said, 'with a hot milk drink.'

'Milk?' said one of the wizards, with tired horror in his voice.

'He's too young for alcohol,' explained the bursar.

'Oh, yes. Silly of me.'

The hollow-eyed wizard opposite said: 'Did you see what he did to the door?'

'I know what he did to Billias!'

'*What* did he do?'

'I don't want to know!'

'Brothers, brothers,' said Spelter soothingly. He looked down at their worried faces and thought: too many dinners. Too many afternoons waiting for the servants to bring in the tea. Too much time spent in stuffy rooms reading old books written by dead men. Too much gold brocade and ridiculous ceremony. Too much fat. The whole University is ripe for one good push . . .

Or one good pull . . .

'I wonder if we really have, um, a problem here,' he said.

Gravie Derment of the Sages of the Unknown Shadow hit the table with his fist.

'Good grief, man!' he snapped. 'Some child wanders in out of the night, beats two of the University's finest, sits down in the Archchancellor's chair and you wonder if we have a problem? The boy's a natural! From what we've seen tonight, there isn't a wizard on the Disc who could stand against him!'

'Why should we stand against him?' said Spelter, in a reasonable tone of voice.

'Because he's more powerful than we are!'

'Yes?' Spelter's voice would have made a sheet of glass look like a ploughed field, it made honey look like gravel.

'It stands to reason—'

Gravie hesitated. Spelter gave him an encouraging smile.

'Ahem.'

The ahemmer was Marmaric Carding, head of the Hoodwinkers. He steepled his beringed fingers and peered sharply at Spelter over the top of them. The bursar disliked him intensely. He had considerable doubt about the man's intelligence. He suspected it might be quite high, and that behind those vein-crazed jowls was a mind full of brightly polished little wheels, spinning like mad.

'He does not seem overly inclined to use that power,' said Carding.

'What about Billias and Virrid?'

'Childish pique,' said Carding.

The other wizards stared from him to the bursar. They were aware of something going on, and couldn't quite put their finger on it.

The reason that wizards didn't rule the Disc was quite simple. Hand any two wizards a piece of rope and they would instinctively pull in opposite directions. Something about their genetics or their training left them with an attitude towards mutual co-operation that made an old bull elephant with terminal toothache look like a worker ant.

Spelter spread his hands. 'Brothers,' he said again, 'do you not see what has happened? Here is a gifted youth, perhaps raised in isolation out in the untutored, um, countryside, who, feeling the ancient call of the magic in his bones, has journeyed far across tortuous terrain, through who knows what perils, and at last has reached his journey's end, alone and afraid, seeking only the steadying influence of us, his tutors, to shape and *guide* his talents. Who are we to turn him away, into the, um, wintry blast, shunning his—'

The oration was interrupted by Gravie blowing his nose.

'It's not winter,' said one of the other wizards flatly, 'and it's quite a warm night.'

'Out into the *treacherously changeable spring weather*,' snarled Spelter, 'and cursed indeed would be the man who failed, um, at this time—'

'It's nearly summer.'

Carding rubbed the side of his nose thoughtfully.

'The boy has a staff,' he said. 'Who gave it to him? Did you ask?'

'No,' said Spelter, still glowering at the almanackical interjector.

Carding started to look at his fingernails in what Spelter considered to be a meaningful way.

'Well, whatever the problem, I feel sure it can wait until morning,' he said in what Spelter felt was an ostentatiously bored voice.

'Ye gods, he blew Billias away!' said Gravie. 'And they say there's nothing in Virrid's room but soot!'

'They were perhaps rather foolish,' said Carding smoothly. 'I am sure, my good brother, that you would not be defeated in affairs of the Art by a mere stripling?'

Gravie hesitated. 'Well, er,' he said, 'no. Of course not.' He looked at Carding's innocent smile and coughed loudly. 'Certainly not, of course. Billias was very foolish. However, some prudent caution is surely—'

'Then let us all be cautious in the morning,' said Carding cheerfully. 'Brothers, let us adjourn this meeting. The boy sleeps, and in that at least he is showing us the way. This will look better in the light.'

'I have seen things that didn't,' said Gravie darkly, who didn't trust Youth. He held that no good ever came of it.

The senior wizards filed out and back to the Great Hall, where the dinner had got to the ninth course and was just getting into its stride. It takes more than a bit of magic and someone being blown to smoke in front of him to put a wizard off his food.

For some unexplained reason Spelter and Carding were the last to leave. They sat at either end of the long table, watching each other like cats. Cats can sit at either end of a lane and watch each other for hours, performing the kind of mental manoeuvring that would make a grand master appear impulsive by comparison, but cats have got nothing on wizards. Neither was prepared to make a move until he had run the entire forthcoming conversation through his mind to see if it left him a move ahead.

Spelter weakened first.

'All wizards are brothers,' he said. 'We should trust one another. I have information.'

'I know,' said Carding. 'You know who the boy is.'

Spelter's lips moved soundlessly as he tried to foresee the next bit of the exchange. 'You can't be certain of that,' he said, after a while.

'My dear Spelter, you blush when you inadvertently tell the truth.'

'I didn't blush!'

'Precisely,' said Carding, 'my point.'

'All right,' Spelter conceded. 'But you think you know something else.'

The fat wizard shrugged. 'A mere suspicion of a hunch,' he said.

'But why should I *ally*,' he rolled the unfamiliar word around his tongue, 'with you, a mere fifth level? I could more certainly obtain the information by rendering down your living brain. I mean no offence, you understand, I ask only for knowledge.'

The events of the next few seconds happened far too fast to be understood by non-wizards, but went approximately like this:

Spelter had been drawing the signs of Megrim's Accelerator in the air under cover of the table. Now he muttered a syllable under his breath and fired the spell along the tabletop, where it left a smoking path in the varnish and met, about halfway, the silver snakes of Brother Hushmaster's Potent Asp-Spray as they spewed from Carding's fingertips.

The two spells cannoned into one another, turned into a ball of green fire and exploded, filling the room with fine yellow crystals.

The wizards exchanged the kind of long, slow glare you could roast chestnuts on.

Bluntly, Carding was surprised. He shouldn't have been. Eighth-level wizards are seldom faced with challenging tests of magical skill. In theory there are only seven other wizards of equal power and every lesser wizard is, by definition – well, lesser. This makes them complacent. But Spelter, on the other hand, was at the fifth level.

It may be quite tough at the top, and it is probably even tougher at the bottom, but halfway up it's so tough you could use it for horseshoes. By then all the no-hopers, the lazy, the silly and the downright unlucky have been weeded out, the field's cleared, and every wizard stands alone and surrounded by mortal enemies on every side. There's the pushy fours below, waiting to trip him up. There's the arrogant sixes above, anxious to stamp out all ambition. And, of course, all around are his fellow fives, ready for any opportunity to reduce the competition a little. And there's no standing still. Wizards of the fifth level are mean and tough and have reflexes of steel and their eyes are thin and narrow from staring down the length of that metaphorical last furlong at the end of which rests the prize of prizes, the Archchancellor's hat.

The novelty of co-operation began to appeal to Carding. There was worthwhile power here, which could be bribed into usefulness for as long as it was necessary. Of course, *afterwards* it might have to be – discouraged . . .

Spelter thought: patronage. He'd heard the term used, though never within the University, and he knew it meant getting those above you to give you a leg up. Of course, no wizard would normally dream of giving a colleague a leg up unless it was in order to catch them on the hop. The mere thought of actually encouraging a competitor . . . But on the other hand, this old fool might be of assistance for a while, and *afterwards*, well . . .

They looked at one another with mutual, grudging admiration and unlimited mistrust, but at least it was a mistrust each one felt he could rely on. Until afterwards.

'His name is Coin,' said Spelter. 'He says his father's name is Ipslore.'

'I wonder how many brothers has he got?' said Spelter.

'I'm sorry?'

'There hasn't been magic like that in this university in centuries,' said Carding, 'maybe for thousands of years. I've only ever read about it.'

'We banished an Ipslore thirty years ago,' said Spelter. 'According to the records, he'd got married. I can see that if he had sons, um, they'd be wizards, but I don't understand how—'

'That wasn't wizardry. That was sourcery,' said Carding, leaning back in his chair.

Spelter stared at him across the bubbling varnish.

'Sourcery?'

'The eighth son of a wizard would be a sourcerer.'

'I didn't know that!'

'It is not widely advertised.'

'Yes, but – sourcerers were a long time ago, I mean, the magic was a lot stronger then, um, men were different . . . it didn't have anything to do with, well, *breeding*.' Spelter was thinking, eight sons, that means he did it eight times. At least. Gosh.

'Sourcerers could do everything,' he went on. 'They were nearly as powerful as the gods. Um. There was no end of trouble. The gods simply wouldn't allow that sort of thing any more, depend upon it.'

'Well, there was trouble because the sourcerers fought among themselves,' said Carding, 'But one sourcerer wouldn't be any trouble. One sourcerer correctly advised, that is. By older and wiser minds.'

'But he wants the Archchancellor's hat!'

'Why can't he have it?'

Spelter's mouth dropped open. This was too much, even for him.

Carding smiled at him amiably.

'But the hat—'

'It's just a symbol,' said Carding. 'It's nothing special. If he wants it, he can have it. It's a small enough thing. Just a symbol, nothing more. A figurehat.'

'Figurehat?'

'Worn by a figurehead.'

'But the gods choose the Archchancellor!'

Carding raised an eyebrow. 'Do they?' he said, and coughed.

'Well, yes, I suppose they do. In a manner of speaking.'

'*In a manner of speaking*?'

Carding got up and gathered his skirts around him. 'I think,' he said, 'that you have a great deal to learn. By the way, where is that hat?'

'I don't know,' said Spelter, who was still quite shaken. 'Somewhere in, um, Virrid's apartments, I suppose.'

'We'd better fetch it,' said Carding.

He paused in the doorway and stroked his beard reflectively. 'I remember Ipslore,' he said. 'We were students together. Wild fellow. Odd habits. Superb wizard, of course, before he went to the bad. Had a funny way of twitching his eyebrow, I remember, when he was excited.' Carding looked blankly across forty years of memory, and shivered.

'The hat,' he reminded himself. 'Let's find it. It would be a shame if anything happened to it.'

In fact the hat had no intention of letting anything happen to it, and was currently hurrying towards the Mended Drum under the arm of a rather puzzled, black-clad thief.

The thief, as will become apparent, was a special type of thief. This thief was an artist of theft. Other thieves merely stole everything that was not nailed down, but this thief stole the nails as well. This thief had scandalised Ankh by taking a particular interest in stealing, with astonishing success, things that were in fact not only nailed down but also guarded by keen-eyed guards in inaccessible strongrooms. There are artists that will paint an entire chapel ceiling; this was the kind of thief that could steal it.

This particular thief was credited with stealing the jewelled disembowelling knife from the Temple of Offler the Crocodile God during the middle of Evensong, and the silver shoes from the Patrician's finest racehorse while it was in the process of winning a race. When Gritoller Mimpsey, vice-president of the Thieves' Guild, was jostled in the marketplace and then found on returning home that a freshly-stolen handful of diamonds had vanished from their place of concealment, he knew who to blame.* This was the

---

* This was because Gritoller had swallowed the jewels for safe keeping.

type of thief that could steal the initiative, the moment and the words right out of your mouth.

However, it was the first time it had stolen something that not only asked it to, in a low but authoritative voice, but gave precise and somehow unarguable instructions about how it was to be disposed of.

It was that cusp of the night that marks the turning point of Ankh-Morpork's busy day, when those who make their living under the sun are resting after their labours and those who turn an honest dollar by the cold light of the moon are just getting up the energy to go to work. The day had, in fact, reached that gentle point when it was too late for housebreaking and too early for burglary.

Rincewind sat alone in the crowded, smoky room, and didn't take much notice when a shadow passed over the table and a sinister figure sat down opposite him. There was nothing very remarkable about sinister figures in this place. The Drum jealously guarded its reputation as the most stylishly disreputable tavern in Ankh-Morpork and the big troll that now guarded the door carefully vetted customers for suitability in the way of black cloaks, glowing eyes, magic swords and so forth. Rincewind never found out what he did to the failures. Perhaps he ate them.

When the figure spoke, its husky voice came from the depths of a black velvet hood, lined with fur.

'Psst,' it said.

'Not very,' said Rincewind, who was in a state of mind where he couldn't resist it, 'but I'm working on it.'

'I'm looking for a wizard,' said the voice. It sounded hoarse with the effort of disguising itself but, again, this was nothing unusual in the Drum.

'Any wizard in particular?' Rincewind said guardedly. People could get into trouble this way.

'One with a keen sense of tradition who would not mind taking risks for high reward,' said another voice. It appeared to be coming from a round black leather box under the stranger's arm.

'Ah,' said Rincewind, 'that narrows it down a bit, then. Does this involve a perilous journey into unknown and probably dangerous lands?'

'It does, as a matter of fact.'

'Encounters with exotic creatures?' Rincewind smiled.

'Could be.'

'Almost certain death?'

'Almost certainly.'

32

Rincewind nodded, and picked up his hat.

'Well, I wish you every success in your search,' he said, 'I'd help you myself, only I'm not going to.'

'What?'

'Sorry. I don't know why, but the prospect of certain death in unknown lands at the claws of exotic monsters isn't for me. I've tried it, and I couldn't get the hang of it. Each to their own, that's what I say, and I was cut out for boredom.' He rammed his hat on his head and stood up a little unsteadily.

He'd reached the foot of the steps leading up into the street when a voice behind him said: 'A *real* wizard would have accepted.'

He could have kept going. He could have walked up the stairs, out into the street, got a pizza at the Klatchian takeaway in Sniggs Alley, and gone to bed. History would have been totally changed, and in fact would also have been considerably shorter, but he would have got a good night's sleep although, of course, it would have been on the floor.

The future held its breath, waiting for Rincewind to walk away.

He didn't do this for three reasons. One was alcohol. One was the tiny flame of pride that flickers in the heart of even the most careful coward. But the third was the voice.

It was beautiful. It sounded like wild silk looks.

The subject of wizards and sex is a complicated one, but as has already been indicated it does, in essence, boil down to this: when it comes to wine, women and song, wizards are allowed to get drunk and croon as much as they like.

The reason given to young wizards was that the practice of magic is hard and demanding and incompatible with sticky and furtive activities. It was a lot more sensible, they were told, to stop worrying about that sort of thing and really get to grips with Woddeley's *Occult Primer* instead. Funnily enough this didn't seem to satisfy, and young wizards suspected that the real reason was that the rules were made by old wizards. With poor memories. They were quite wrong, although the real reason had long been forgotten: if wizards were allowed to go around breeding all the time, there was a risk of sourcery.

Of course, Rincewind had been around a bit and had seen a thing or two, and had thrown off his early training to such an extent that he was quite capable of spending hours at a time in a woman's company without having to go off for a cold shower and a lie-down. But that voice would have made even a statue get down off its pedestal for a few brisk laps of the playing field and fifty press-ups. It was a voice that could make 'Good morning' sound like an invitation to bed.

The stranger threw back her hood and shook out her long hair. It was almost pure white. Since her skin was tanned golden the general effect was calculated to hit the male libido like a lead pipe.

Rincewind hesitated, and lost a splendid opportunity to keep quiet. From the top of the stairs came a thick trollish voice: ''Ere, I *thed* you can't go fru dere—'

She sprang forward and shoved a round leather box into Rincewind's arms.

'Quick, you must come with me,' she said. 'You're in great danger!'

'Why?'

'Because I will kill you if you don't.'

'Yes, but hang on a moment, in that case—' Rincewind protested feebly.

Three members of the Patrician's personal guard appeared at the top of the stairs. Their leader beamed down at the room. The smile suggested that he intended to be the only one to enjoy the joke.

'Don't nobody move,' he suggested.

Rincewind heard a clatter behind him as more guards appeared at the back door.

The Drum's other customers paused with their hands on assorted hilts. These weren't the normal city watch, cautious and genially corrupt. These were walking slabs of muscle and they were absolutely unbribable; if only because the Patrician could outbid anyone else. Anyway, they didn't seem to be looking for anyone except the woman. The rest of the clientele relaxed and prepared to enjoy the show. Eventually it might be worth joining it, once it was certain which was the winning side.

Rincewind felt the pressure tighten on his wrist.

'Are you mad?' he hissed. 'This is messing with the Man!'

There was a swish and the sergeant's shoulder suddenly sprouted a knife hilt. Then the girl spun around and with surgical precision planted a small foot in the groin of the first guard through the door. Twenty pairs of eyes watered in sympathy.

Rincewind grabbed his hat and tried to dive under the nearest table, but that grip was steel. The next guard to approach got another knife in the thigh. Then she drew a sword like a very long needle and raised it threateningly.

'Anyone else?' she said.

34

One of the guards raised a crossbow. The Librarian, sitting hunched over his drink, reached out a lazy arm like two broom handles strung with elastic and slapped him backwards. The bolt rebounded from the star on Rincewind's hat and hit the wall by a respected procurer who was sitting two tables away. His body-guards threw another knife which just missed a thief across the room, who picked up a bench and hit two guards, who struck out at the nearest drinkers. After that one thing sort of led to another and pretty soon everyone was fighting to get something – either away, out or even.

Rincewind found himself pulled relentlessly behind the bar. The landlord was sitting on his moneybags under the counter with two machetes crossed on his knees, enjoying a quiet drink. Occasionally the sound of breaking furniture would make him wince.

The last thing Rincewind saw before he was dragged away was the Librarian. Despite looking like a hairy rubber sack full of water, the orang-utan had the weight and reach of any man in the room and was currently sitting on a guard's shoulders and trying, with reasonable success, to unscrew his head.

Of more concern to Rincewind was the fact that he was being dragged upstairs.

'My dear lady,' he said desperately. 'What do you have in mind?'

'Is there a way on to the roof?'

'Yes. What's in this box?'

'Shhh!'

She halted at a bend in the dingy corridor, reached into a belt pouch and scattered a handful of small metal objects on the floor behind them. Each one was made of four nails welded together so that, however the things fell, one was always pointing upwards.

She looked critically at the nearest doorway.

'You haven't got about four feet of cheesewire on you, have you?' she said wistfully. She'd drawn another throwing knife and was throwing it up and catching it again.

'I don't think so,' said Rincewind weakly.

'Pity. I've run out. Okay, come on.'

'Why? I haven't done anything!'

She went to the nearest window, pushed open the shutters and paused with one leg over the sill.

'Fine,' she said, over her shoulder. 'Stay here and explain it to the guards.'

'Why are they chasing you?'

'I don't know.'

'Oh, come on! There must be a reason!'

'Oh, there's plenty of reasons. I just don't know which one. Are you coming?'

Rincewind hesitated. The Patrician's personal guard was not known for its responsive approach to community policing, preferring to cut bits off instead. Among the things they took a dim view of was, well, basically, people being in the same universe. Running away from them was likely to be a capital offence.

'I think maybe I'll come along with you,' he said gallantly. 'A girl can come to harm all alone in this city.'

Freezing fog filled the streets of Ankh-Morpork. The flares of street traders made little yellow haloes in the smothering billows.

The girl peered around a corner.

'We've lost them,' she said. 'Stop shaking. You're safe now.'

'What, you mean I'm all alone with a female homicidal maniac?' said Rincewind. 'Fine.'

She relaxed, and laughed at him.

'I was watching you,' she said. 'An hour ago you were afraid that your future was going to be dull and uninteresting.'

'I *want* it to be dull and uninteresting,' said Rincewind bitterly. 'I'm *afraid* it's going to be short.'

'Turn your back,' she commanded, stepping into an alley.

'Not on your life,' he said.

'I'm going to take my clothes off.'

Rincewind spun around, his face red. There was a rustling behind him, and a waft of scent. After a while she said, 'You can look round now.'

He didn't.

'You needn't worry. I've put some more on.'

He opened his eyes. The girl was wearing a demure white lace dress, with fetchingly puffed sleeves. He opened his mouth. He realised with absolute clarity that up to now the trouble he had been in was simple, modest and nothing he couldn't talk his way out of given a decent chance or, failing that, a running start. His brain started to send urgent messages to his sprinting muscles, but before they could get through she'd grabbed his arm again.

'You really shouldn't be so nervous,' she said sweetly. 'Now, let's have a look at this thing.'

She pulled the lid off the round box in Rincewind's unprotesting hands, and lifted out the Archchancellor's hat.

The octarines around its crown blazed in all eight colours of the spectrum, creating the kind of effects in the foggy alley that it would take a very clever special effects director and a whole battery of star filters to achieve by any non-magical means. As she raised it high in the air it created its own nebula of colours that very few people ever see in legal circumstances.

Rincewind sank gently to his knees.

She looked down at him, puzzled.

'Legs given out?'

'It's – it's the hat. The *Archchancellor's* hat,' said Rincewind, hoarsely. His eyes narrowed. 'You've stolen it!' he shouted, struggling back to his feet and grabbing for the sparkling brim.

'It's just a hat.'

'Give it to me this minute! Women musn't touch it! It belongs to wizards!'

'Why are you getting so worked up?' she said.

Rincewind opened his mouth. Rincewind closed his mouth.

He wanted to say: It's the Archchancellor's hat, don't you understand? It's worn by the head of all wizards, well, on the head of the head of all wizards, no, metaphorically it's worn by all wizards, potentially, anyway, and it's what every wizard aspires to, it's the symbol of organised magic, it's the pointy tip of the profession, it's a symbol, it's what it means to all wizards . . .

And so on. Rincewind had been told about the hat on his first day at University, and it had sunk into his impressionable mind like a lead weight into a jelly. He wasn't sure of much in the world, but he was certain that the Archchancellor's hat was important. Maybe even wizards need a little magic in their lives.

Rincewind, said the hat.

He stared at the girl. 'It spoke to me!'

'Like a voice in your head?'

'Yes!'

'It did that to me, too.'

'But it knew my name!'

Of course we do, stupid fellow. We are supposed to be a magic *hat, after all.*

The hat's voice wasn't only clothy. It also had a strange choral effect, as if an awful lot of voices were talking at the same time, in almost perfect unison.

Rincewind pulled himself together.

'O great and wonderful hat,' he said pompously, 'strike down this impudent girl who has had the audacity, nay, the—'

Oh, do shut up. She stole us because we ordered her to. It was a near thing, too.

'But she's a—' Rincewind hesitated. 'She's of the female persuasion . . .' he muttered.

So was your mother.

'Yes, well, but she ran away before I was born,' Rincewind mumbled.

Of all the disreputable taverns in all the city you could have walked into, you walked into his, complained the hat.

'He was the only wizard I could find,' said the girl, 'He looked the part. He had "Wizzard" written on his hat and everything.'

Don't believe everything you read. Too late now, anyway. We haven't got much time.

'Hold on, hold on,' said Rincewind urgently, 'What's going on? You *wanted* her to steal you? *Why* haven't we got much time?' He pointed an accusing finger at the hat. 'Anyway, you can't go around letting yourself be stolen, you're supposed to be on – on the Archchancellor's head! The ceremony was tonight, I should have been there—'

Something terrible is happening at the University. It is vital that we are not taken back, do you understand? You must take us to Klatch, where there is someone fit to wear me.

'Why?' There was something very strange about the voice, Rincewind decided. It sounded impossible to disobey, as though it was solid destiny. If it told him to walk over a cliff, he thought, he'd be halfway down before it could occur to him to disobey.

The death of all wizardry is at hand.

Rincewind looked around guiltily.

'Why?' he said.

The world is going to end.

'What, again?'

I mean it, said the hat sulkily. *The triumph of the Ice Giants, the Apocralypse, the Teatime of the Gods, the whole thing.*

'Can we stop it?'

The future is uncertain on that point.

Rincewind's expression of determined terror faded slowly.

'Is this a riddle?' he said.

Perhaps it would be simpler if you just did what you're told and didn't try to understand things, said the hat. *Young woman, you will put us back in our box. A great many people will shortly be looking for us.*

'Hey, hold on,' said Rincewind. 'I've seen you around here for years and you never talked before.'

I didn't have anything that needed to be said.

Rincewind nodded. That seemed reasonable.

'Look, just shove it in its box, and let's get going,' said the girl.

'A bit more respect if you please, young lady,' said Rincewind haughtily. 'That is the symbol of ancient wizardry you happen to be addressing.'

'You carry it, then,' she said.

'Hey, look,' said Rincewind, scrambling along after her as she swept down the alleys, crossed a narrow street and entered another alley between a couple of houses that leaned together so drunkenly that their upper storeys actually touched. She stopped.

'Well?' she snapped.

'You're the mystery thief, aren't you?' he said, 'Everyone's been talking about you, how you've taken things even from locked rooms and everything. You're different than I imagined . . .'

'Oh?' she said coldly. 'How?'

'Well, you're . . . shorter.'

'Oh, come *on*.'

The street cressets, not particularly common in this part of the city in any case, gave out altogether here. There was nothing but watchful darkness ahead.

'I said come on,' she repeated. 'What are you afraid of?'

Rincewind took a deep breath. 'Murderers, muggers, thieves, assassins, pickpockets, cutpurses, reevers, snigsmen, rapists and robbers,' he said. 'That's the *Shades* you're going into!'*

'Yes, but people won't come looking for us in here,' she said.

'Oh, they'll come in all right, they just won't come out,' said Rincewind. 'Nor will we. I mean, a beautiful young woman like you . . . it doesn't bear thinking about . . . I mean, some of the people in there . . .'

'But I'll have you to protect me,' she said.

Rincewind thought he heard the sound of marching feet several streets away.

'You know,' he sighed, 'I knew you'd say that.'

Down these mean streets a man must walk, he thought. And along some of them he will break into a run.

*

*The Ankh-Morpork Merchants' Guild publication *Wellcome to Ankh-Morporke, Citie of One Thousand Surprises* describes the area of Old Morpork known as The Shades as 'a folklorique network of old alleys and pictureques streets, wherre exitment and romans lurkes arounde everry corner and much may be heard the traditinal street cries of old time also the laughing visages of the denuizens as they goe about their businesse private.' In other words, you have been warned.

It is so black in the Shades on this foggy spring night that it would be too dark to read about Rincewind's progress through the eerie streets, so the descriptive passage will lift up above the level of the ornate rooftops, the forest of twisty chimneys, and admire the few twinkling stars that manage to pierce the swirling billows. It will try to ignore the sounds drifting up from below – the patter of feet, the rushes, the gristly noises, the groans, the muffled screams. It could be that some wild animal is pacing through the Shades after two weeks on a starvation diet.

Somewhere near the centre of the Shades – the district has never been adequately mapped – is a small courtyard. Here at least there are torches on the walls, but the light they throw is the light of the Shades themselves: mean, reddened, dark at the core.

Rincewind staggered into the yard and hung on to the wall for support. The girl stepped into the ruddy light behind him, humming to herself.

'Are you all right?' she said.

'Nurrgh,' said Rincewind.

'Sorry?'

'Those men,' he bubbled, 'I mean, the way you kicked his . . . when you grabbed them by the . . . when you stabbed that one right in . . . who *are* you?'

'My name is Conina.'

Rincewind looked at her blankly for some time.

'Sorry,' he said, 'doesn't ring a bell.'

'I haven't been here long,' she said.

'Yes, I didn't think you were from around these parts,' he said. 'I would have heard.'

'I've taken lodgings here. Shall we go in?'

Rincewind glanced up at the dingy pole just visible in the smoky light of the spitting torches. It indicated that the hostelry behind the small dark door was the Troll's Head.

It might be thought that the Mended Drum, scene of unseemly scuffles only an hour ago, was a seedy disreputable tavern. In fact it was a *reputable* disreputable tavern. Its customers had a certain rough-hewn respectability – they might murder each other in an easygoing way, as between equals, but they didn't do it vindictively. A child could go in for a glass of lemonade and be certain of getting nothing worse than a clip round the ear when his mother heard his expanded vocabulary. On quiet nights, and when he was certain the Librarian wasn't going to come in, the landlord was even known to put bowls of peanuts on the bar.

40

The Troll's Head was a cesspit of a different odour. Its customers, if they reformed, tidied themselves up and generally improved their image out of all recognition might, just might, aspire to be considered the utter dregs of humanity. And in the Shades, a dreg is a dreg.

By the way, the thing on the pole isn't a sign. When they decided to call the place the Troll's Head, they didn't mess about.

Feeling sick, and clutching the grumbling hatbox to his chest, Rincewind stepped inside.

Silence. It wrapped itself around them, nearly as thickly as the smoke of a dozen substances guaranteed to turn any normal brain to cheese. Suspicious eyes peered through the smog.

A couple of dice clattered to a halt on a tabletop. They sounded very loud, and probably weren't showing Rincewind's lucky number.

He was aware of the stares of several score of customers as he followed the demure and surprisingly small figure of Conina into the room. He looked sideways into the leering faces of men who would kill him sooner than think, and in fact would find it a great deal easier.

Where a respectable tavern would have had a bar there was just a row of squat black bottles and a couple of big barrels on trestles against the wall.

The silence tightened like a tourniquet. Any minute now, Rincewind thought—

A big fat man wearing nothing but a fur vest and a leather loincloth pushed back his stool and lurched to his feet and winked evilly at his colleagues. When his mouth opened, it was like a hole with a hem.

'Looking for a man, little lady?' he said.

She looked up at him.

'Please keep away.'

A snake of laughter writhed around the room. Conina's mouth snapped shut like a letterbox.

'Ah,' the big man gurgled, 'that's right, I likes a girl with spirit—'

Conina's hand moved. It was a pale blur, stopping *here* and *here*: after a few seconds of disbelief the man gave a little grunt and folded up, very slowly.

Rincewind shrank back as every other man in the room leaned forward. His instinct was to run, and he knew it was an instinct that would get him instantly killed. It was the Shades out there. Whatever was going to happen to him next was going to happen to him here. It was not a reassuring thought.

A hand closed around his mouth. Two more grabbed the hatbox from his arms.

Conina spun past him, lifting her skirt to place a neat foot on a target beside Rincewind's waist. Someone whimpered in his ear and collapsed. As the girl pirouetted gracefully around she picked up two bottles, knocked out their bottoms on the shelf and landed with their jagged ends held out in front of her. Morpork daggers, they were called in the patois of the streets.

In the face of them, the Troll's Head's clientele lost interest.

'Someone got the hat,' Rincewind muttered through dry lips, 'They slipped out of the back way.'

She glared at him and made for the door. The Head's crowd of customers parted automatically, like sharks recognising another shark, and Rincewind darted anxiously after her before they came to any conclusion about him.

They ran out into another alley and pounded down it. Rincewind tried to keep up with the girl; people following her tended to tread on sharp things, and he wasn't sure she'd remember he was on her side, whatever side that was.

A thin, half-hearted drizzle was falling. And at the end of the alley was a faint blue glow.

'Wait!'

The terror in Rincewind's voice was enough to slow her down.

'What's wrong?'

'Why's he stopped?'

'I'll ask him,' said Conina, firmly.

'Why's he covered in snow?'

She stopped and turned around, arms thrust into her sides, one foot tapping impatiently on the damp cobbles.

'Rincewind, I've known you for an hour and I'm astonished you've lived even that long!'

'Yes, but I have, haven't I? I've got a sort of talent for it. Ask anyone. I'm an addict.'

'Addicted to what?'

'Life. I got hooked on it at an early age and I don't want to give it up and take it from me, this doesn't look right!'

Conina looked back at the figure surrounded by the glowing blue aura. It seemed to be looking at something in its hands.

Snow was settling on its shoulder like really bad dandruff. *Terminal* dandruff. Rincewind had an instinct for these things, and he had a deep suspicion that the man had gone where shampoo would be no help at all.

They sidled along a glistening wall.

'There's something very strange about him,' she conceded.

'You mean the way he's got his own private blizzard?'

'Doesn't seem to upset him. He's smiling.'

'A frozen grin, I'd call it.'

The man's icicle-hung hands had been taking the lid off the box, and the glow from the hat's octarines shone up into a pair of greedy eyes that were already heavily rimed with frost.

'Know him?' said Conina.

Rincewind shrugged. 'I've seen him around,' he said. 'He's called Larry the Fox or Fezzy the Stoat or something. Some sort of rodent, anyway. He just steals things. He's harmless.'

'He looks incredibly cold.' Conina shivered.

'I expect he's gone to a warmer place. Don't you think we should shut the box?'

It's perfectly safe now, said the hat's voice from inside the glow. *And so perish all enemies of wizardry.*

Rincewind wasn't about to trust what a hat said.

'We need something to shut the lid,' he muttered. 'A knife or something. You wouldn't have one, would you?'

'Look the other way,' Conina warned.

There was a rustle and another gust of perfume.

'You can look back now.'

Rincewind was handed a twelve-inch throwing knife. He took it gingerly. Little particles of metal glinted on its edge.

'Thanks.' He turned back. 'Not leaving you short, am I?'

'I have others.'

'I'll bet.'

Rincewind reached out gingerly with the knife. As it neared the leather box its blade went white and started to steam. He whimpered a little as the cold struck his hand – a burning, stabbing cold, a cold that crept up his arm and made a determined assault on his mind. He forced his numb fingers into action and, with great effort, nudged the edge of the lid with the tip of the blade.

The glow faded. The snow became sleet, then melted into drizzle.

Conina nudged him aside and pulled the box out of the frozen arms.

'I wish there was something we could do for him. It seems wrong just to leave him here.'

'He won't mind,' said Rincewind, with conviction.

'Yes, but we could at least lean him against the wall. Or something.'

Rincewind nodded, and grabbed the frozen thief by his icicle arm. The man slipped out of his grasp and hit the cobbles.

Where he shattered.

Conina looked at the pieces.

'Urg,' she said.

There was a disturbance further up the alley, coming from the back door of the Troll's Head. Rincewind felt the knife snatched from his hand and then go past his ear in a flat trajectory that ended in the doorpost twenty yards away. A head that had been sticking out withdrew hurriedly.

'We'd better go,' said Conina, hurrying along the alley. 'Is there somewhere we can hide? Your place?'

'I generally sleep at the University,' said Rincewind, hopping along behind her.

You must not return to the University, growled the hat from the depths of its box. Rincewind nodded distractedly. The idea certainly didn't seem attractive.

'Anyway, they don't allow women inside after dark,' he said.

'And before dark?'

'Not then, either.'

Conina sighed. 'That's silly. What have you wizards got against women, then?'

Rincewind's brow wrinkled. 'We're not supposed to put anything against women,' he said. 'That's the whole point.'

Sinister grey mists rolled through the docks of Morpork, dripping from the rigging, coiling around the drunken rooftops, lurking in alleys. The docks at night were thought by some to be even more dangerous than the Shades. Two muggers, a sneak thief and someone who had merely tapped Conina on the shoulder to ask her the time had already found this out.

'Do you mind if I ask you a question?' said Rincewind, stepping over the luckless pedestrian who lay coiled around his private pain.

'Well?'

'I mean, I wouldn't like to cause offence.'

'Well?'

'It's just that I can't help noticing—'

'Hmm?'

'You have this certain way with strangers.' Rincewind ducked, but nothing happened.

'What are you doing down there?' said Conina, testily.

'Sorry.'

'I know what you're thinking. I can't help it, I take after my father.'

'Who was he, then? Cohen the Barbarian?' Rincewind grinned to show it was a joke. At least, his lips moved in a desperate crescent.

'No need to laugh about it, wizard.'

'What?'

'It's not my fault.'

Rincewind's lips moved soundlessly. 'Sorry,' he said. 'Have I got this right? Your father really is *Cohen the Barbarian*?'

'Yes.' The girl scowled at Rincewind. 'Everyone has to have a father,' she added. 'Even you, I imagine.'

She peered around a corner.

'All clear. Come on,' she said, and then when they were striding along the damp cobbles she continued: 'I expect your father was a wizard, probably.'

'I shouldn't think so,' said Rincewind. 'Wizardry isn't allowed to run in families.' He paused. He knew Cohen, he'd even been a guest at one of his weddings when he married a girl of Conina's age; you could say this about Cohen, he crammed every hour full of minutes. 'A lot of people would like to take after Cohen, I mean, he was the best fighter, the greatest thief, he—'

'A lot of *men* would,' Conina snapped. She leaned against a wall and glared at him.

'Listen,' she said, 'There's this long word, see, an old witch told me about it . . . can't remember it . . . you wizards know about long words.'

Rincewind thought about long words. 'Marmalade?' he volunteered.

She shook her head irritably. 'It means you take after your parents.'

Rincewind frowned. He wasn't too good on the subject of parents.

'Kleptomania? Recidivist?' he hazarded.

'Begins with an H.'

'Hedonism?' said Rincewind desperately.

'*Herrydeterry*,' said Conina. 'This witch explained it to me. My mother was a temple dancer for some mad god or other, and father rescued her, and – they stayed together for a while. They say I get my looks and figure from her.'

'And very good they are, too,' said Rincewind, with hopeless gallantry.

She blushed. 'Yes, well, but from *him* I got sinews you could moor a boat with, reflexes like a snake on a hot tin, a terrible urge to steal things and this dreadful sensation every time I meet someone that I should be throwing a knife through his eye at ninety feet. I can, too,' she added with a trace of pride.

'Gosh.'

'It tends to put men off.'

'Well, it would,' said Rincewind weakly.

'I mean, when they find out, it's very hard to hang on to a boyfriend.'

'Except by the throat, I imagine,' said Rincewind.

'Not what you really need to build up a proper relationship.'

'No. I can see,' said Rincewind. 'Still, pretty good if you want to be a famous barbarian thief.'

'But not,' said Conina, 'if you want to be a hairdresser.'

'Ah.'

They stared into the mist.

'*Really* a hairdresser?' said Rincewind.

Conina sighed.

'Not much call for a barbarian hairdresser, I expect,' said Rincewind. 'I mean, no-one wants a shampoo-and-beheading.'

'It's just that every time I see a manicure set I get this terrible urge to lay about me with a double-handed cuticle knife. I mean sword,' said Conina.

Rincewind sighed. 'I know how it is,' he said. 'I wanted to be a wizard.'

'But you *are* a wizard.'

'Ah. Well, of course, but—'

'Quiet!'

Rincewind found himself rammed against the wall, where a trickle of condensed mist inexplicably began to drip down his neck. A broad throwing knife had mysteriously appeared in Conina's hand, and she was crouched like a jungle animal or, even worse, a jungle human.

'What—' Rincewind began.

'Shut up!' she hissed. 'Something's coming!'

She stood up in one fluid movement, spun on one leg and let the knife go.

There was a single, hollow, wooden thud.

Conina stood and stared. For once, the heroic blood that pounded through her veins, drowning out all chances of a lifetime in a pink pinny, was totally at a loss.

'I've just killed a wooden box,' she said.

46

Rincewind looked round the corner.

The Luggage stood in the dripping street, the knife still quivering in its lid, and stared at her. Then it changed its position slightly, its little legs moving in a complicated tango pattern, and stared at Rincewind. The Luggage didn't have any features at all, apart from a lock and a couple of hinges, but it could stare better than a rockful of iguanas. It could outstare a glass-eyed statue. When it came to a look of betrayed pathos, the Luggage could leave the average kicked spaniel moping back in its kennel. It had several arrowheads and broken swords sticking in it.

'What is it?' hissed Conina.

'It's just the Luggage,' said Rincewind wearily.

'Does it belong to you?'

'Not really. Sort of.'

'Is it dangerous?'

The Luggage shuffled round to stare at her again.

'There's two schools of thought about that,' said Rincewind. 'There's some people who say it's dangerous, and others who say it's very dangerous. What do you think?'

The Luggage raised its lid a fraction.

The Luggage was made from the wood of the sapient peartree, a plant so magical that it had nearly died out on the Disc and survived only in one or two places; it was a sort of rosebay willowherb, only instead of bomb sites it sprouted in areas that had seen vast expenditures of magic. Wizards' staves were traditionally made of it; so was the Luggage.

Among the Luggage's magical qualities was a fairly simple and direct one: it would follow its adopted owner anywhere. Not any-where in any particular set of dimensions, or country, or universe, or lifetime. *Anywhere*. It was about as easy to shake off as a head cold, and considerably more unpleasant.

The Luggage was also extremely protective of its owner. It would be hard to describe its attitude to the rest of creation, but one could start with the phrase 'bloody-minded malevolence' and work up from there.

Conina stared at that lid. It looked very much like a mouth.

'I think I'd vote for "terminally dangerous",' she said.

'It likes crisps,' volunteered Rincewind, and then added, 'Well, that's a bit strong. It *eats* crisps.'

'What about people?'

'Oh, and people. About fifteen so far, I think.'

'Were they good or bad?'

'Just dead, I think. It also does your laundry for you, you put your clothes in and they come out washed and ironed.'

'And covered in blood?'

'You know, that's the funny thing,' said Rincewind.

'The funny thing?' repeated Conina, her eyes not leaving the Luggage.

'Yes, because, you see, the inside isn't always the same, it's sort of multidimensional, and—'

'How does it feel about women?'

'Oh, it's not choosy. It ate a book of spells last year. Sulked for three days and then spat it out.'

'It's horrible,' said Conina, and backed away.

'Oh, yes,' said Rincewind, 'absolutely.'

'I mean the way it stares!'

'It's very good at it, isn't it?'

We must leave for Klatch, said a voice from the hatbox. *One of these boats will be adequate. Commandeer it.*

Rincewind looked at the dim, mist-wreathed shapes that loomed in the mist under a forest of rigging. Here and there a riding light made a little fuzzy ball of light in the gloom.

'Hard to disobey, isn't it?' said Conina.

'I'm trying,' said Rincewind. Sweat prickled on his forehead.

Go aboard now, said the hat. Rincewind's feet began to shuffle of their own accord.

'Why are you doing this to me?' he moaned.

Because I have no alternative. Believe me, if I could have found an eighth level mage I would have done so. I must not be worn!

'Why not? You are the Archchancellor's hat.'

And through me speak all the Archchancellors who ever lived. I am the University. I am the Lore. I am the symbol of magic under the control of men – and I will not be worn by a sourcerer! There must be no more sourcerers! The world is too worn out for sourcery!

Conina coughed.

'Did you understand any of that?' she said, cautiously.

'I understood some of it, but I didn't believe it,' said Rincewind. His feet remained firmly rooted to the cobbles.

They called me a figurehat! The voice was heavy with sarcasm. *Fat wizards who betray everything the University ever stood for, and they called me a figurehat! Rincewind, I command you. And you, madam. Serve me well and I will grant you your deepest desire.*

'How can you grant my deepest desire if the world's going to end?'

The hat appeared to think about it. *Well, have you got a deepest desire that need only take a couple of minutes?*

'Look, how can you do magic? You're just a—' Rincewind's voice trailed off.

I AM magic. Proper magic. Besides, you don't get worn by some of the world's greatest wizards for two thousand years without learning a few things. Now. We must flee.

But with dignity, of course.

Rincewind looked pathetically at Conina, who shrugged again.

'Don't ask me,' she said. 'This looks like an adventure. I'm doomed to have them, I'm afraid. That's genetics* for you.'

'But I'm no good at them! Believe me, I've been through dozens!' Rincewind wailed.

Ah. Experience, said the hat.

'No, really, I'm a terrible coward, I always run away.' Rincewind's chest heaved. 'Danger has stared me in the back of the head, oh, hundreds of times!'

I don't want you to go into danger.

'Good!'

I want you to stay OUT of danger.

Rincewind sagged. 'Why me?' he moaned.

For the good of the University. For the honour of wizardry. For the sake of the world. For your heart's desire. And I'll freeze you alive if you don't.

Rincewind breathed a sigh almost of relief. He wasn't good on bribes, or cajolery, or appeals to his better nature. But threats, now, threats were familiar. He knew where he was with threats.

The sun dawned on Small Gods' Day like a badly poached egg. The mists had closed in over Ankh-Morpork in streamers of silver and gold – damp, warm, silent. There was the distant grumbling of springtime thunder, out on the plains. It seemed warmer than it ought to be.

Wizards normally slept late. On this morning, however, many of them had got up early and were wandering the corridors aimlessly. They could feel the change in the air.

---

*The study of genetics on the Disc had failed at an early stage, when wizards tried the experimental crossing of such well known subjects as fruit flies and sweet peas. Unfortunately they didn't quite grasp the fundamentals, and the resultant offspring – a sort of green bean thing that buzzed – led a short sad life before being eaten by a passing spider.

The University was filling up with magic.

Of course, it was usually full of magic anyway, but it was an old, comfortable magic, as exciting and dangerous as a bedroom slipper. But seeping through the ancient fabric was a new magic, saw-edged and vibrant, bright and cold as comet fire. It sleeted through the stones and crackled off sharp edges like static electricity on the nylon carpet of Creation. It buzzed and sizzled. It curled wizardly beards, poured in wisps of octarine smoke from fingers that had done nothing more mystical for three decades than a little light illusion. How can the effect be described with delicacy and taste? For most of the wizards, it was like being an elderly man who, suddenly faced with a beautiful young woman, finds to his horror and delight and astonishment that the flesh is suddenly as willing as the spirit.

And in the halls and corridors of the University the word was being whispered: *Sourcery!*

A few wizards surreptitiously tried spells that they hadn't been able to master for years, and watched in amazement as they unrolled perfectly. Sheepishly at first, and then with confidence, and then with shouts and whoops, they threw fireballs to one another or produced live doves out of their hats or made multi-coloured sequins fall out of the air.

Sourcery! One or two wizards, stately men who had hitherto done nothing more blameworthy than eat a live oyster, turned themselves invisible and chased the maids and bedders through the corridors.

Sourcery! Some of the bolder spirits had tried out ancient flying spells and were bobbing a little uncertainly among the rafters. Sourcery!

Only the Librarian didn't share in the manic breakfast. He watched the antics for some time, pursing his prehensile lips, and then knuckled stiffly off towards his Library. If anyone had bothered to notice, they'd have heard him bolting the door.

It was deathly quiet in the Library. The books were no longer frantic. They'd passed through their fear and out into the calm waters of abject terror, and they crouched on their shelves like so many mesmerised rabbits.

A long hairy arm reached up and grabbed *Casplock's Compleet Lexicon of Majik with Precepts for the Wise* before it could back away, soothed its terror with a long-fingered hand, and opened it under 'S'. The Librarian smoothed the trembling page gently and ran a horny nail down the entries until he came to:

Sourcerer, *n. (mythical). A proto-wizard, a doorway through which new majik may enterr the world, a wizard not limited by the physycal capabilities of hys own bodie, not by Destinie, nor by Deathe. It is written that there once werre sourcerers in the youth of the world but not may there by nowe and blessed be, for sourcery is not for menne and the return of sourcery would mean the Ende of the Worlde . . . If the Creator hadd meant menne to bee as goddes, he ould have given them wings. SEE ALSO: thee Apocralypse, the legende of thee Ice Giants, and thee Teatime of the Goddes.*

The Librarian read the cross-references, turned back to the first entry, and stared at it through deep dark eyes for a long time. Then he put the book back carefully, crept under his desk, and pulled the blanket over his head.

But in the minstrel gallery over the Great Hall Carding and Spelter watched the scene with entirely different emotions.

Standing side by side they looked almost exactly like the number 10.

'What is happening?' said Spelter. He'd had a sleepless night, and wasn't thinking very straight.

'Magic is flowing into the University,' said Carding. 'That's what sourcerer means. A channel for magic. Real magic, my boy. Not the tired old stuff we've made do with these past centuries. This is the dawning of a . . . a—'

'New, um, dawn?'

'Exactly. A time of miracles, a . . . a—'

'*Anus mirabilis?*'

Carding frowned. 'Yes,' he said, eventually, 'something like that, I expect. You have quite a way with words, you know.'

'Thank you, brother.'

The senior wizard appeared to ignore the familiarity. Instead he turned and leaned on the carved rail, watching the magical displays below them. His hands automatically went to his pockets for his tobacco pouch, and then paused. He grinned, and snapped his fingers. A lighted cigar appeared in his mouth.

'Haven't been able to do that in years,' he mused. 'Big changes, my boy. They haven't realised it yet, but it's the end of Orders and Levels. That was just a – a rationing system. We don't need them any more. Where is the boy?'

'Still asleep—' Spelter began.

'I am here,' said Coin.

He stood in the archway leading to the senior wizard's quarters, holding the octiron staff that was half again as tall as he was. Little veins of yellow fire coruscated across its matt black surface, which was so dark that it looked like a slit in the world.

Spelter felt the golden eyes bore through him, as if his innermost thoughts were being scrolled across the back of his skull.

'Ah,' he said, in a voice that he believed was jolly and avuncular but in fact sounded like a strangled death rattle. After a start like that his contribution could only get worse, and it did. 'I see you're, um, up,' he said.

'My dear boy,' said Carding.

Coin gave him a long, freezing stare.

'I saw you last night,' he said. 'Are you puissant?'

'Only mildly,' said Carding, hurriedly recalling the boy's tendency to treat wizardry as a terminal game of conkers. 'But not so puissant as you, I'm sure.'

'I am to be made Archchancellor, as is my destiny?'

'Oh, absolutely,' said Carding. 'No doubt about it. May I have a look at your staff? Such an interesting design—'

He reached out a pudgy hand.

It was a shocking breach of etiquette in any case; no wizard should even think of touching another's staff without his express permission. But there are people who can't quite believe that children are fully human, and think that the operation of normal good manners doesn't apply to them.

Carding's fingers curled around the black staff.

There was a noise that Spelter felt rather than heard, and Carding bounced across the gallery and struck the opposite wall with a sound like a sack of lard hitting a pavement.

'Don't do that,' said Coin. He turned and looked through Spelter, who had gone pale, and added: 'Help him up. He is probably not badly hurt.'

The bursar scuttled hurriedly across the floor and bent over Carding, who was breathing heavily and had gone an odd colour. He patted the wizard's hand until Carding opened one eye.

'Did you see what happened?' he whispered.

'I'm not sure. Um. What did happen?' hissed Spelter.

'It bit me.'

'The next time you touch the staff,' said Coin, matter-of-factly, 'you will die. Do you understand?'

Carding raised his head gently, in case bits of it fell off.

'Absolutely,' he said.

'And now I would like to see the University,' the boy continued. 'I have heard a great deal about it . . .'

Spelter helped Carding to his unsteady feet and supported him as they trotted obediently after the boy.

'Don't touch his staff,' muttered Carding.

'I'll remember, um, not to,' said Spelter firmly. 'What did it feel like?'

'Have you ever been bitten by a viper?'

'No.'

'In that case you'll understand exactly what it felt like.'

'Hmm?'

'It wasn't like a snake bite at all.'

They hurried after the determined figure as Coin marched down the stairs and through the ravished doorway of the Great Hall.

Spelter dodged in front, anxious to make a good impression.

'This is the Great Hall,' he said. Coin turned his golden gaze towards him, and the wizard felt his mouth dry up. 'It's called that because it's a hall, d'you see. And big.'

He swallowed. 'It's a big hall,' he said, fighting to stop the last of his coherence being burned away by the searchlight of that stare. 'A great big hall, which is why it's called—'

'Who are those people?' said Coin. He pointed with his staff. The assembled wizards, who had turned to watch him enter, backed out of the way as though the staff was a flamethrower.

Spelter followed the sourcerer's stare. Coin was pointing to the portraits and statues of former Archchancellors, which decorated the walls. Full-bearded and point-hatted, clutching ornamental scrolls or holding mysterious symbolic bits of astrological equipment, they stared down with ferocious self-importance or, possibly, chronic constipation.

'From these walls,' said Carding, 'two hundred supreme mages look down upon you.'

'I don't care for them,' said Coin, and the staff streamed octarine fire. The Archchancellors vanished.

'And the windows are too small—'

'The ceiling is too high—'

'Everything is too *old*—'

The wizards threw themselves flat as the staff flared and spat. Spelter pulled his hat over his eyes and rolled under a table when the very fabric of the University flowed around him. Wood creaked, stone groaned.

Something tapped him on the head. He screamed.

53

'Stop that!' shouted Carding above the din. 'And pull your hat up! Show a little dignity!'

'Why are you under the table, then?' said Spelter sourly.

'We must seize our opportunity!'

'What, like the staff?'

'Follow me!'

Spelter emerged into a bright, a horrible bright new world.

Gone were the rough stone walls. Gone were the dark, owl-haunted rafters. Gone was the tiled floor, with its eye-boggling pattern of black and white tiles.

Gone, too, were the high small windows, with their gentle patina of antique grease. Raw sunlight streamed into the hall for the first time.

The wizards stared at one another, mouths open, and what they saw was not what they had always thought they'd seen. The unforgiving rays transmuted rich gold embroidery into dusty gilt, exposed opulent fabric as rather stained and threadbare velvet, turned fine flowing beards into nicotine-stained tangles, betrayed splendid diamonds as rather inferior Ankhstones. The fresh light probed and prodded, stripping away the comfortable shadows.

And, Spelter had to admit, what was left didn't inspire confidence. He was suddenly acutely aware that under his robes – his tattered, badly-faded robes, he realised with an added spasm of guilt; the robes with the perforated area where the mice had got at them – he was still wearing his bedroom slippers.

The hall was now almost all glass. What wasn't glass was marble. It was all so splendid that Spelter felt quite unworthy.

He turned to Carding, and saw that his fellow wizard was staring at Coin with his eyes gleaming.

Most of the other wizards had the same expression. If wizards weren't attracted to power they wouldn't be wizards, and this was real power. The staff had them charmed like so many cobras.

Carding reached out to touch the boy on the shoulder, and then thought better of it.

'Magnificent,' he said, instead.

He turned to the assembled wizardry and raised his arms. 'My brothers,' he intoned, 'we have in our midst a wizard of great power!'

Spelter tugged at his robe.

'He nearly killed you,' he hissed. Carding ignored him.

'And I propose—' Carding swallowed – 'I propose him for Archchancellor!'

There was a moment's silence, and then a burst of cheering and shouts of dissent. Several quarrels broke out at the back of the crowd. The wizards nearer the front weren't quite so ready to argue. They could see the smile on Coin's face. It was bright and cold, like the smile on the face of the moon.

There was a commotion, and an elderly wizard fought his way to the front of the throng.

Spelter recognised Ovin Hakardly, a seventh-level wizard and a lecturer in Lore. He was red with anger, except where he was white with rage. When he spoke, his words seared through the air like so many knives, clipped as topiary, crisp as biscuits.

'Are you mad?' he said. 'No-one but a wizard of the eighth level may become Archchancellor! And he must be elected by the other most senior wizards in solemn convocation! (Duly guided by the gods, of course.) It is the Lore! (The very idea!)'

Hakardly had studied the Lore of magic for years and, because magic always tends to be a two-way process, it had made its mark on him; he gave the impression of being as fragile as a cheese straw, and in some unaccountable way the dryness of his endeavours had left him with the ability to pronounce punctuation.

He stood vibrating with indignation and, he became aware, he was rapidly standing alone. In fact he was the centre of an expanding circle of empty floor fringed with wizards who were suddenly ready to swear that they'd never clapped eyes on him in their life.

Coin had raised his staff.

Hakardly raised an admonitory finger.

'You do not frighten me, young man,' he snapped. 'Talented you may be, but magical talent alone is not enough. There are many other qualities required of a great wizard. Administrative ability, for example, and wisdom, and the—'

Coin lowered his staff.

'The Lore applies to all wizards, does it not?' he said.

'Absolutely! It was drawn up—'

'But I am not a wizard, Lord Hakardly.'

The wizard hesitated. 'Ah,' he said, and hesitated again. 'Good point,' he said.

'But I am well aware of the need for wisdom, foresight and good advice, and I would be honoured if you could see your way clear to providing those much-valued commodities. For example – why is it that wizards do not rule the world?'

'What?'

'It is a simple question. There are in this room—' Coin's lips moved for a fraction of a second—' four hundred and seventy-two

55

wizards, skilled in the most subtle of arts. Yet all you rule are these few acres of rather inferior architecture. Why is this?'

The most senior wizards exchanged knowing glances.

'Such it may appear,' said Hakardly eventually, 'but, my child, we have domains beyond the ken of the temporal power.' His eyes gleamed. 'Magic can surely take the mind to inner landscapes of arcane—'

'Yes, yes,' said Coin. 'Yet there are extremely solid walls outside your University. Why is this?'

Carding ran his tongue over his lips. It was extraordinary. The child was speaking his thoughts.

'You squabble for power,' said Coin, sweetly, 'and yet, beyond these walls, to the man who carts nightsoil or the average merchant, is there really so much difference between a high-level mage and a mere conjuror?'

Hakardly stared at him in complete and untrammelled astonishment.

'Child, it's obvious to the meanest citizen,' he said. 'The robes and trimmings themselves—'

'Ah,' said Coin, 'the robes and trimmings. Of course.'

A short, heavy and thoughtful silence filled the hall.

'It seems to me,' said Coin eventually, 'that wizards rule only wizards. Who rules in the reality outside?'

'As far as the city is concerned, that would be the Patrician, Lord Vetinari,' said Carding with some caution.

'And is he a fair and just ruler?'

Carding thought about it. The Patrician's spy network was said to be superb. 'I would say,' he said carefully, 'that he is unfair and unjust, but scrupulously even-handed. He is unfair and unjust to everyone, without fear or favour.'

'And you are content with this?' said Coin.

Carding tried not to catch Hakardly's eye.

'It's not a case of being content with it,' he said. 'I suppose we've not given it much thought. A wizard's true vocation, you see—'

'Is it really true that the wise suffer themselves to be ruled in this way?'

Carding growled. 'Of course not! Don't be silly! We merely tolerate it. That's what wisdom is all about, you'll find that out when you grow up, it's a case of biding one's time—'

'Where is this Patrician? I would like to see him.'

'That can be arranged, of course,' said Carding. 'The Patrician is always graciously pleased to grant wizards an interview, and—'

'Now *I* will grant *him* an interview,' said Coin. 'He must learn that wizards have bided their time long enough. Stand back, please.'

He pointed the staff.

The temporal ruler of the sprawling city of Ankh-Morpork was sitting in his chair at the foot of the steps leading up to the throne, looking for any signs of intelligence in intelligence reports. The throne had been empty for more than two thousand years, since the death of the last of the line of the kings of Ankh. Legend said that one day the city would have a king again, and went on with various comments about magic swords, strawberry birthmarks and all the other things that legends gabble on about in these circumstances.

In fact the only real qualification now was the ability to stay alive for more than about five minutes after revealing the existence of any magic swords or birthmarks, because the great merchant families of Ankh had been ruling the city for the last twenty centuries and were about as ready to relinquish power as the average limpet is to let go of its rock.

The current Patrician, head of the extremely rich and powerful Vetinari family, was thin, tall and apparently as cold-blooded as a dead penguin. Just by looking at him you could tell he was the sort of man you'd expect to keep a white cat, and caress it idly while sentencing people to death in a piranha tank; and you'd hazard for good measure that he probably collected rare thin porcelain, turning it over and over in his blue-white fingers while distant screams echoed from the depths of the dungeons. You wouldn't put it past him to use the word 'exquisite' and have thin lips. He looked the kind of person who, when they blink, you mark it off on the calendar.

Practically none of this was in fact the case, although he did have a small and exceedingly elderly wire-haired terrier called Wuffles that smelled badly and wheezed at people. It was said to be the only thing in the entire world he truly cared about. He did of course sometimes have people horribly tortured to death, but this was considered to be perfectly acceptable behaviour for a civic ruler and generally approved of by the overwhelming majority of citizens.*

The people of Ankh are of a practical persuasion, and felt that the Patrician's edict forbidding all street theatre and mime artists made

---

*The overwhelming majority of citizens being defined in this case as everyone not currently hanging upside down over a scorpion pit.

up for a lot of things. He didn't administer a reign of terror, just the occasional light shower.

The Patrician sighed, and laid the latest report on top of the large heap beside the chair.

When he had been a little boy he had seen a showman who could keep a dozen plates spinning in the air. If the man had been capable of working the same trick with a hundred of them, Lord Vetinari considered, he would just about begin to be ready for training in the art of ruling Ankh-Morpork, a city once described as resembling an overturned termite heap without the charm.

He glanced out of the window at the distant pillar of the Tower of Art, the centre of Unseen University, and wondered vaguely whether any of those tiresome old fools could come up with a better way of collating all this paperwork. They wouldn't, of course – you couldn't expect a wizard to understand anything as basic as elementary civic espionage.

He sighed again, and picked up the transcript of what the president of the Thieves' Guild had said to his deputy at midnight in the soundproof room hidden behind the office in the Guild headquarters, and . . .

Was in the Great Ha . . .

Was *not* in the Great Hall of Unseen University, where he had spent some interminable dinners, but there were a lot of wizards around him and they were . . .

. . . *different.*

Like Death, which some of the city's less fortunate citizens considered he intimately resembled, the Patrician never got angry until he had time to think about it. But sometimes he thought very quickly.

He stared around at the assembled wizards, but there was something about them that choked the words of outrage in his throat. They looked like sheep who had suddenly found a trapped wolf at exactly the same time as they heard about the idea of unity being strength.

There was something about their eyes.

'What is the meaning of this outr—' he hesitated, and concluded, 'this? A merry Small Gods' Day prank, is it?'

His eyes swivelled to meet those of a small boy holding a long metal staff. The child was smiling the oldest smile the Patrician had ever seen.

Carding coughed.

'My lord,' he began.

'Out with it, man,' snapped Lord Vetinari.

Carding had been diffident, but the Patrician's tone was just that tiny bit too peremptory. The wizard's knuckles went white.

'I am a wizard of the eighth level,' he said quietly, 'and you will not use that tone to me.'

'Well said,' said Coin.

'Take him to the dungeons,' said Carding.

'We haven't got any dungeons,' said Spelter. 'This is a university.'

'Then take him to the wine cellars,' snapped Carding. 'And while you're down there, build some dungeons.'

'Have you the faintest inkling of what you are doing?' said the Patrician. 'I demand to know the meaning of this—'

'You demand nothing at all,' said Carding. 'And the meaning is that from now on the wizards will rule, as it was ordained. Now take—'

'*You?* Rule Ankh-Morpork? Wizards who can barely govern themselves?'

'Yes!' Carding was aware that this wasn't the last word in repartee, and was even more alive to the fact that the dog Wuffles, who had been teleported along with his master, had waddled painfully across the floor and was peering short-sightedly at the wizard's boots.

'Then all truly wise men would prefer the safety of a nice deep dungeon,' said the Patrician. 'And now you will cease this foolery and replace me in my palace, and it is just possible that we will say no more about this. Or at least that you won't have the chance to.'

Wuffles gave up investigating Carding's boots and trotted towards Coin, shedding a few hairs on the way.

'This *pantomime* has gone on long enough,' said the Patrician. 'Now I am getting—'

Wuffles growled. It was a deep, primeval noise, which struck a chord in the racial memory of all those present and filled them with an urgent desire to climb a tree. It suggested long grey shapes hunting in the dawn of time. It was astonishing that such a small animal could contain so much menace, and all of it was aimed at the staff in Coin's hand.

The Patrician strode forward to snatch the animal, and Carding raised his hand and sent a blaze of orange and blue fire searing across the room.

The Patrician vanished. On the spot where he had been standing a small yellow lizard blinked and glared with malevolent reptilian stupidity.

Carding looked in astonishment at his fingers, as if for the first time.

'All *right*,' he whispered hoarsely.

The wizards stared down at the panting lizard, and then out at the city sparkling in the early morning light. Out there was the council of aldermen, the city watch, the Guild of Thieves, the Guild of Merchants, the priesthoods . . . and none of them knew what was about to hit them.

It has begun, said the hat, from its box on the deck.

'What has?' said Rincewind.

The rule of sourcery.

Rincewind looked blank. 'Is that good?'

Do you ever understand anything anyone says to you?

Rincewind felt on firmer ground here. 'No,' he said. 'Not always. Not lately. Not often.'

'Are you sure you *are* a wizard?' said Conina.

'It's the only thing I've ever been sure of,' he said, with conviction.

'How strange.'

Rincewind sat on the Luggage in the sun on the foredeck of the *Ocean Waltzer* as it lurched peacefully across the green waters of the Circle Sea. Around them men did what he was sure were important nautical things, and he hoped they were doing them correctly, because next to heights he hated depths most of all.

'You look worried,' said Conina, who was cutting his hair. Rincewind tried to make his head as small as possible as the blades flashed by.

'That's because I am.'

'What exactly *is* the Apocralypse?'

Rincewind hesitated. 'Well,' he said, 'it's the end of the world. Sort of.'

'Sort of? *Sort of* the end of the world? You mean we won't be certain? We'll all look around and say "Pardon me, did you hear something?"?'

'It's just that no two seers have ever agreed about it. There have been all kinds of vague predictions. Quite mad, some of them. So it was called the Apocralypse.' He looked embarrassed. 'It's a sort of apocryphal Apocalypse. A kind of pun, you see.'

'Not very good.'

'No. I suppose not.'*

---

* Wizards' tastes in the matter of puns are about the same as their taste in glittery objects.

Conina's scissors snipped busily.

'I must say the captain seemed quite happy to have us aboard,' she observed.

'That's because they think it's lucky to have a wizard on the boat,' said Rincewind. 'It isn't, of course.'

'Lots of people believe it,' she said.

'Oh, it's lucky for other people, just not for me. I can't swim.'

'What, not a stroke?'

Rincewind hesitated, and twiddled the star on his hat cautiously.

'About how deep is the sea here, would you say? Approximately?' he said.

'About a dozen fathoms, I believe.'

'Then I could probably swim about a dozen fathoms, whatever they are.'

'Stop trembling like that, I nearly had your ear off,' Conina snapped. She glared at a passing seaman and waved her scissors. 'What's the matter, you never saw a man have a haircut before?'

Someone up in the rigging made a remark which caused a ripple of ribald laughter in the topgallants, unless they were forecastles.

'I shall pretend I didn't hear that,' said Conina, and gave the comb a savage yank, dislodging numerous inoffensive small creatures.

'Ow!'

'Well, you should keep still!'

'It's a little difficult to keep still knowing who it is that's waving a couple of steel blades around my head!'

And so the morning passed, with scudding wavelets, the creaking of the rigging, and a rather complex layer cut. Rincewind had to admit, looking at himself in a shard of mirror, that there was a definite improvement.

The captain had said that they were bound for the city of Al Khali, on the hubward coast of Klatch.

'Like Ankh, only with sand instead of mud,' said Rincewind, leaning over the rail. 'But quite a good slave market.'

'Slavery is immoral,' said Conina firmly.

'Is it? Gosh,' said Rincewind.

'Would you like me to trim your beard?' said Conina, hopefully.

She stopped, scissors drawn, and stared out to sea.

'Is there a kind of sailor that uses a canoe with sort of extra bits on the side and a sort of red eye painted on the front and a small sail?' she said.

'I've heard of Klatchian slave pirates,' said Rincewind, 'but this is a big boat. I shouldn't think one of them would dare attack it.'

'One of them wouldn't,' said Conina, still staring at the fuzzy area where the sea became the sky, 'but these five might.'

Rincewind peered at the distant haze, and then looked up at the man on watch, who shook his head.

'Come on,' he chuckled, with all the humour of a blocked drain. 'You can't really see anything out there. Can you?'

'Ten men in each canoe,' said Conina grimly.

'Look, a joke's a joke—'

'With long curvy swords.'

'Well, I can't see a—'

'—their long and rather dirty hair blowing in the wind—'

'With split ends, I expect?' said Rincewind sourly.

'Are you trying to be funny?'

'Me?'

'And here's me without a weapon,' said Conina, sweeping back across the deck. 'I bet there isn't a decent sword anywhere on this boat.'

'Never mind. Perhaps they've just come for a quick shampoo.'

While Conina rummaged frantically in her pack Rincewind sidled over to the Archchancellor's hatbox and cautiously raised the lid.

'There's nothing out there, is there?' he asked.

How should I know? Put me on.

'What? On my head?'

Good grief.

'But I'm not an Archchancellor!' said Rincewind. 'I mean, I've heard of cool-headed, but—'

I need to use your eyes. Now put me on. On your head.

'Um.'

Trust me.

Rincewind couldn't disobey. He gingerly removed his battered grey hat, looked longingly at its dishevelled star, and lifted the Archchancellor's hat out of its box. It felt rather heavier than he'd expected. The octarines around the crown were glowing faintly.

He lowered it carefully on to his new hairstyle, clutching the brim tightly in case he felt the first icy chill.

In fact he simply felt incredibly light. And there was a feeling of great knowledge and power – not actually present, but just, mentally speaking, on the tip of his metaphorical tongue.

Odd scraps of memory flickered across his mind, and they weren't any memories he remembered remembering before. He probed gently, as one touches a hollow tooth with the tongue, and there they were—

Two hundred dead Archchancellors, dwindling into the leaden, freezing past, one behind the other, watched him with blank grey eyes.

That's why it's so cold, he told himself, the warmth seeps into the dead world. Oh, no . . .

When the hat spoke, he saw two hundred pairs of pale lips move.

Who are you?

Rincewind, thought Rincewind. And in the inner recesses of his head he tried to think privately to himself . . . help.

He felt his knees begin to buckle under the weight of centuries.

What's it like, being dead? he thought.

Death is but a sleep, said the dead mages.

But what does it *feel* like? Rincewind thought.

You will have an unrivalled chance to find out when those war canoes get here, Rincewind.

With a yelp of terror he thrust upwards and forced the hat off his head. Real life and sound flooded back in, but since someone was frantically banging a gong very close to his ear this was not much of an improvement. The canoes were visible to everyone now, cutting through the water with an eerie silence. Those black-clad figures manning the paddles should have been whooping and screaming; it wouldn't have made it any better, but it would have seemed more appropriate. The silence bespoke an unpleasant air of purpose.

'Gods, that was awful,' he said. 'Mind you, so is this.'

Crew members scurried across the deck, cutlasses in hand. Conina tapped Rincewind on the shoulder.

'They'll try to take us alive,' she said.

'Oh,' said Rincewind weakly. 'Good.'

Then he remembered something else about Klatchian slavers, and his throat went dry.

'You'll – you'll be the one they'll really be after,' he said. 'I've heard about what they do—'

'Should I know?' said Conina. To Rincewind's horror she didn't appear to have found a weapon.

'They'll throw you in a seraglio!'

She shrugged. 'Could be worse.'

'But it's got all these spikes and when they shut the door—' hazarded Rincewind. The canoes were close enough now to see the determined expressions of the rowers.

'That's not a seraglio. That's an Iron Maiden. Don't you know what a seraglio is?'

'Um . . .'

She told him. He went crimson.

'Anyway, they'll have to capture me first,' said Conina primly. 'It's you who should be worrying.'

'Why me?'

'You're the only other one who's wearing a dress.'

Rincewind bridled. 'It's a robe—'

'Robe, dress. You better hope they know the difference.'

A hand like a bunch of bananas with rings on grabbed Rincewind's shoulder and spun him around. The captain, a Hublander built on generous bear-like lines, beamed at him through a mass of facial hair.

'Hah!' he said. 'They know not that we aboard a wizard have! To create in their bellies the burning green fire! Hah?'

The dark forests of his eyebrows wrinkled as it became apparent that Rincewind wasn't immediately ready to hurl vengeful magic at the invaders.

'Hah?' he insisted, making a mere single syllable do the work of a whole string of blood-congealing threats.

'Yes, well, I'm just – I'm just girding my loins,' said Rincewind. 'That's what I'm doing. Girding them. Green fire, you want?'

'Also to make hot lead run in their bones,' said the captain. 'Also their skins to blister and living scorpions without mercy to eat their brains from inside, and—'

The leading canoe came alongside and a couple of grapnels thudded into the rail. As the first of the slavers appeared the captain hurried away, drawing his sword. He stopped for a moment and turned to Rincewind.

'You gird quickly,' he said. 'Or no loins. Hah?'

Rincewind turned to Conina, who was leaning on the rail examining her fingernails.

'You'd better get on with it,' she said. 'That's fifty green fires and hot leads to go, with a side order for blisters and scorpions. Hold the mercy.'

'This sort of thing is always happening to me,' he moaned.

He peered over the rail to what he thought of as the main floor of the boat. The invaders were winning by sheer weight of numbers, using nets and ropes to tangle the struggling crew. They worked in absolute silence, clubbing and dodging, avoiding the use of swords wherever possible.

'Mustn't damage the merchandise,' said Conina. Rincewind watched in horror as the captain went down under a press of dark shapes, screaming, 'Green fire! Green fire!'

64

Rincewind backed away. He wasn't any good at magic, but he'd had a hundred per cent success at staying alive up to now and didn't want to spoil the record. All he needed to do was to learn how to swim in the time it took to dive into the sea. It was worth a try.

'What are you waiting for? Let's go while they're occupied,' he said to Conina.

'I need a sword,' she said.

'You'll be spoilt for choice in a minute.'

'One will be enough.'

Rincewind kicked the Luggage.

'Come on,' he snarled. 'You've got a lot of floating to do.'

The Luggage extended its little legs with exaggerated nonchalance, turned slowly, and settled down beside the girl.

'Traitor,' said Rincewind to its hinges.

The battle already seemed to be over. Five of the raiders stalked up the ladder to the afterdeck, leaving most of their colleagues to round up the defeated crew below. The leader pulled down his mask and leered briefly and swarthily at Conina; and then he turned and leered for a slightly longer period at Rincewind.

'This is a robe,' said Rincewind quickly. 'And you'd better watch out, because I'm a wizard.' He took a deep breath. 'Lay a finger on me, and you'll make me wish you hadn't. I warn you.'

'A wizard? Wizards don't make good strong slaves,' mused the leader.

'Absolutely right,' said Rincewind. 'So if you'll just see your way clear to letting me go—'

The leader turned back to Conina, and signalled to one of his companions. He jerked a tattooed thumb towards Rincewind.

'Do not kill him too quickly. In fact—' he paused, and treated Rincewind to a smile full of teeth. 'Maybe . . . yes. And why not? Can you sing, wizard?'

'I might be able to,' said Rincewind, cautiously. 'Why?'

'You could be just the man the Seriph needs for a job in the harem.' A couple of slavers sniggered.

'It could be a *unique* opportunity,' the leader went on, encouraged by this audience appreciation. There was more broad-minded approval from behind him.

Rincewind backed away. 'I don't think so,' he said, 'thanks all the same. I'm not cut out for that kind of thing.'

'Oh, but you could be,' said the leader, his eyes bright. 'You could be.'

'Oh, for goodness sake,' muttered Conina. She glanced at the men on either side of her, and then her hands moved. The one stabbed with the scissors was possibly better off than the one she raked with the comb, given the kind of mess a steel comb can make of a face. Then she reached down, snatched up a sword dropped by one of the stricken men, and lunged at the other two.

The leader turned at the screams, and saw the Luggage behind him with its lid open. And then Rincewind cannoned into the back of him, pitching him forward into whatever oblivion lay in the multidimensional depths of the chest.

There was the start of a bellow, abruptly cut off.

Then there was a click like the shooting of the bolt on the gates of Hell.

Rincewind backed away, trembling. 'A unique opportunity,' he muttered under his breath, having just got the reference.

At least he had a unique opportunity to watch Conina fight. Not many men ever got to see it twice.

Her opponents started off grinning at the temerity of a slight young girl in attacking them, and then rapidly passed through various stages of puzzlement, doubt, concern and abject gibbering terror as they apparently became the centre of a flashing, tightening circle of steel.

She disposed of the last of the leader's bodyguard with a couple of thrusts that made Rincewind's eyes water and, with a sigh, vaulted the rail on to the main deck. To Rincewind's annoyance the Luggage barrelled after her, cushioning its fall by dropping heavily on to a slaver, and adding to the sudden panic of the invaders because, while it was bad enough to be attacked with deadly and ferocious accuracy by a rather pretty girl in a white dress with flowers on it, it was even worse for the male ego to be tripped up and bitten by a travel accessory; it was pretty bad for all the rest of the male, too.

Rincewind peered over the railing.

'Showoff,' he muttered.

A throwing knife clipped the wood near his chin and ricocheted past his ear. He raised his hand to the sudden stinging pain, and stared at it in horror before gently passing out. It wasn't blood in general he couldn't stand the sight of, it was just his blood in particular that was so upsetting.

The market in Sator Square, the wide expanse of cobbles outside the black gates of the University, was in full cry.

It was said that everything in Ankh-Morpork was for sale except for the beer and the women, both of which one merely hired. And most of the merchandise was available in Sator market, which over the years had grown, stall by stall, until the newcomers were up against the ancient stones of the University itself; in fact they made a handy display area for bolts of cloth and racks of charms.

No-one noticed the gates swing back. But a silence rolled out of the University, spreading out across the noisy, crowded square like the first fresh wavelets of the tide trickling over a brackish swamp. In fact it wasn't true silence at all, but a great roar of anti-noise. Silence isn't the opposite of sound, it is merely its absence. But this was the sound that lies on the far side of silence, anti-noise, its shadowy decibels throttling the market cries like a fall of velvet.

The crowds stared around wildly, mouthing like goldfish and with about as much effect. All heads turned towards the gates.

Something else was flowing out besides that cacophony of hush. The stalls nearest the empty gateway began to grind across the cobbles, shedding merchandise. Their owners dived out of the way as the stalls hit the row behind them and scraped relentlessly onwards, piling up until a wide avenue of clean, empty stones stretched the whole width of the square.

Ardrothy Longstaff, Purveyor of Pies Full of Personality, peered over the top of the wreckage of his stall in time to see the wizards emerge.

He knew wizards, or up until now he'd always thought he did. They were vague old boys, harmless enough in their way, dressed like ancient sofas, always ready customers for any of his merchandise that happened to be marked down on account of age and rather more personality than a prudent housewife would be prepared to put up with.

But these wizards were something new to Ardrothy. They walked out into Sator Square as if they owned it. Little blue sparks flashed around their feet. They seemed a little taller, somehow.

Or perhaps it was just the way they carried themselves.

Yes, that was it . . .

Ardrothy had a touch of magic in his genetic makeup, and as he watched the wizards sweep across the square it told him that the very best thing he could do for his health would be to pack his knives, spices and mincers in his little pack and have it away out of the city at any time in the next ten minutes.

The last wizard in the group lagged behind his colleagues and looked around the square with disdain.

'There used to be fountains out here,' he said. 'You people – be off.'

The traders stared at one another. Wizards normally spoke imperiously, that was to be expected. But there was an edge to the voice that no-one had heard before. It had knuckles in it.

Ardrothy's eyes swivelled sideways. Arising out of the ruins of his jellied starfish and clam stall like an avenging angel, dislodging various molluscs from his beard and spitting vinegar, was Miskin Koble, who was said to be able to open oysters with one hand. Years of pulling limpets off rocks and wrestling the giant cockles in Ankh Bay had given him the kind of physical development normally associated with tectonic plates. He didn't so much stand up as unfold.

Then he thudded his way towards the wizard and pointed a trembling finger at the ruins of his stall, from which half a dozen enterprising lobsters were making a determined bid for freedom. Muscles moved around the edges of his mouth like angry eels.

'Did you do that?' he demanded.

'Stand aside, oaf,' said the wizard, three words which in the opinion of Ardrothy gave him the ongoing life expectancy of a glass cymbal.

'I hates wizards,' said Koble. 'I really hates wizards. So I am going to hit you, all right?'

He brought his fist back and let fly.

The wizard raised an eyebrow, yellow fire sprang up around the shellfish salesman, there was a noise like tearing silk, and Koble had vanished. All that was left was his boots, standing forlornly on the cobbles with little wisps of smoke coming out of them.

No-one knows why smoking boots always remain, no matter how big the explosion. It seems to be just one of those things.

It seemed to the watchful eyes of Ardrothy that the wizard himself was nearly as shocked as the crowd, but he rallied magnificently and gave his staff a flourish.

'You people had better jolly well learn from this,' he said. 'No-one raises their hand to a wizard, do you understand? There are going to be a lot of changes around here. Yes, what do you want?'

This last comment was to Ardrothy, who was trying to sneak past unnoticed. He scrabbled quickly in his pie tray.

'I was just wondering if your honourship would care to purchase one of these finest pies,' he said hurriedly. 'Full of nourish—'

'Watch closely, pie-selling person,' said the wizard. He stretched out his hand, made a strange gesture with his fingers, and produced a pie out of the air.

It was fat, golden-brown and beautifully glazed. Just by looking at it Ardrothy knew it was packed edge to edge with prime lean pork, with none of those spacious areas of good fresh air under the lid that represented his own profit margin. It was the kind of pie piglets hope to be when they grew up.

His heart sank. His ruin was floating in front of him with short-crust pastry on it.

'Want a taste?' said the wizard. 'There's plenty more where that came from.'

'Wherever it came from,' said Ardrothy.

He looked past the shiny pastry to the face of the wizard, and in the manic gleam of those eyes he saw the world turning upside down.

He turned away, a broken man, and set out for the nearest city gate.

As if it wasn't bad enough that wizards were killing people, he thought bitterly, they were taking away their livelihood as well.

A bucket of water splashed into Rincewind's face, jerking him out of a dreadful dream in which a hundred masked women were attempting to trim his hair with broadswords and cutting it very fine indeed. Some people, having a nightmare like that, would dismiss it as castration anxiety, but Rincewind's subconscious knew being-cut-to-tiny-bits-mortal-dread when it saw it. It saw it most of the time.

He sat up.

'Are you all right?' said Conina, anxiously.

Rincewind swivelled his eyes around the cluttered deck.

'Not necessarily,' he said cautiously. There didn't seem to be any black-clad slavers around, at least vertically. There were a good many crew members, all of them maintaining a respectful distance from Conina. Only the captain stood reasonably close, an inane grin on his face.

'They left,' said Conina. 'Took what they could and left.'

'They bastards,' said the captain, 'but they paddle pretty fast!' Conina winced as he gave her a ringing slap on the back.

'She fight real good for a lady,' he added. 'Yes!'

Rincewind got unsteadily to his feet. The boat was scudding along cheerfully towards a distant smear on the horizon that had to be hubward Klatch. He was totally unharmed. He began to cheer up a bit.

The captain gave them both a hearty nod and hurried off to shout orders connected with sails and ropes and things. Conina sat down on the Luggage, which didn't seem to object.

'He said he's so grateful he'll take us all the way to Al Khali,' she said.

'I thought that's what we arranged anyway,' said Rincewind. 'I saw you give him money, and everything.'

'Yes, but he *was* planning to overpower us and sell me as a slave when he got there.'

'What, not sell me?' said Rincewind, and then snorted, 'Of course, it's the wizard's robes, he wouldn't dare—'

'Um. Actually, he said he'd have to give you away,' said Conina, picking intently at an imaginary splinter on the Luggage's lid.

'*Give* me away?'

'Yes. Um. Sort of like, one free wizard with every concubine sold? Um.'

'I don't see what vegetables have got to do with it.'

Conina gave him a long, hard stare, and when he didn't break into a smile she sighed and said, 'Why are you wizards always nervous around women?'

Rincewind bridled at this slur. 'I like that!' he said, 'I'll have you know that – look, anyway, the point is, I get along very well with women in general, it's just women with swords that upset me.' He considered this for a while, and added, 'Everyone with swords upsets me, if it comes to that.'

Conina picked industriously at the splinter. The Luggage gave a contented creak.

'I know something else that'll upset you,' she muttered.

'Hmm?'

'The hat's gone.'

'What?'

'I couldn't help it, they just grabbed whatever they could—'

'The slavers have made off with the hat?'

'Don't you take that tone with me! *I* wasn't having a quiet sleep at the time—'

Rincewind waved his hands frantically. 'Nonono, don't get excited, I wasn't taking any tone – I want to think about this . . .'

'The captain says they'll probably go back to Al Khali,' he heard Conina say. 'There's a place where the criminal element hang out, and we can soon—'

'I don't see why we have to do anything,' said Rincewind.

'The hat wanted to keep out the way of the University, and I shouldn't think those slavers ever drop in there for a quick sherry.'

'You'll let them run off with it?' said Conina, in genuine astonishment.

70

'Well, someone's got to do it. The way I see it, why me?'

'But you said it's the symbol of wizardry! What wizards all aspire to! You can't just let it go like that!'

'You watch me.' Rincewind sat back. He felt oddly surprised. He was making a decision. It was his. It belonged to him. No-one was forcing him to make it. Sometimes it seemed that his entire life consisted of getting into trouble because of what other people wanted, but this time he'd made a decision and that was that. He'd get off the boat at Al Khali and find some way of going home. Someone else could save the world, and he wished them luck. He'd made a decision.

His brow furrowed. Why didn't he feel happy about it?

Because it's the wrong bloody decision, you idiot.

Right, he thought, I've had enough voices in my head. Out.

But I belong here.

You mean you're me?

Your conscience.

Oh.

You can't let the hat be destroyed. It's the symbol . . .

. . . all right, I know . . .

. . . the symbol of magic under the Lore. Magic under the control of mankind. You don't want to go back to those dark Ians . . .

. . . What? . . .

Ians . . .

Do I mean aeons?

Right. Aeons. Go back aeons to the time when raw magic ruled. The whole framework of reality trembled daily. It was pretty terrible, I can tell me.

How do I know?

Racial memory.

Gosh. Have I got one of those?

Well. A part of one.

Yes, all right, but why me?

In your soul you know you are a true wizard. The word 'Wizard' is engraved on your heart.

'Yes, but the trouble is I keep meeting people who might try to find out,' said Rincewind miserably.

'What did you say?' said Conina.

Rincewind stared at the smudge on the horizon and sighed. 'Just talking to myself,' he said.

★

Carding surveyed the hat critically. He walked around the table and stared at it from a new angle. At last he said: 'It's pretty good. Where did you get the octarines?'

'They're just very good Ankhstones,' said Spelter. 'They fooled you, did they?'

It was a *magnificent* hat. In fact, Spelter had to admit, it looked a lot better than the real thing. The old Archchancellor's hat had looked rather battered, its gold thread tarnished and unravelling. The replica was a considerable improvement. It had style.

'I especially like the lace,' said Carding.

'It took ages.'

'Why didn't you try magic?' Carding waggled his fingers, and grasped the tall cool glass that appeared in mid-air. Under its paper umbrella and fruit salad it contained some sticky and expensive alcohol.

'Didn't work,' said Spelter. 'Just couldn't seem, um, to get it right. I had to sew every sequin on by hand.' He picked up the hat-box.

Carding coughed into his drink. 'Don't put it away just yet,' he said, and took it out of the bursar's hands. 'I've always wanted to try this—'

He turned to the big mirror on the bursar's wall and reverently lowered the hat on to his rather grubby locks.

It was the ending of the first day of the sourcery, and the wizards had managed to change everything except themselves.

They had all tried, on the quiet and when they thought no-one else was looking. Even Spelter had a go, in the privacy of his study. He had managed to become twenty years younger with a torso you could crack rocks on, but as soon as he stopped concentrating he sagged, very unpleasantly, back into his old familiar shape and age. There was something elastic about the way you were. The harder you threw it, the faster it came back. The worse it was when it hit, too. Spiked iron balls, broadswords and large heavy sticks with nails in were generally considered pretty fearsome weapons, but they were nothing at all compared to twenty years suddenly applied with considerable force to the back of the head.

This was because sourcery didn't seem to work on things that were intrinsically magical. Nevertheless, the wizards had made a few important improvements. Carding's robe, for example, had become a silk and lace confection of overpoweringly expensive tastelessness, and gave him the appearance of a big red jelly draped with antimacassars.

'It suits me, don't you think?' said Carding. He adjusted the hat brim, giving it an inappropriately rakish air.

Spelter said nothing. He was looking out of the window.

There had been a few improvements all right. It had been a busy day.

The old stone walls had vanished. There were some rather nice railings now. Beyond them, the city fairly sparkled, a poem in white marble and red tiles. The river Ankh was no longer the silt-laden sewer he'd grown up knowing, but a glittering glass-clear ribbon in which – a nice touch – fat carp mouthed and swam in water pure as snowmelt.*

From the air Ankh-Morpork must have been blinding. It gleamed. The detritus of millennia had been swept away.

It made Spelter strangely uneasy. He felt out of place, as though he was wearing new clothes that itched. Of course, he was wearing new clothes and they did itch, but that wasn't the problem. The new world was all very nice, it was exactly how it should be, and yet, and yet – had he wanted change, he thought, or had he only wanted things rearranged more suitably?

'I said, don't you think it was made for me?' said Carding.

Spelter turned back, his face blank.

'Um?'

'The hat, man.'

'Oh. Um. Very – suitable.'

With a sigh Carding removed the baroque headpiece and carefully replaced it in its box. 'We'd better take it to him,' he said. 'He's starting to ask about it.'

'I'm still bothered about where the real hat is,' said Spelter.

'It's in here,' said Carding firmly, tapping the lid.

'I mean the, um, real one.'

'This *is* the real one.'

'I meant—'

'This is the Archchancellor's Hat,' said Carding carefully. 'You should know, you made it.'

'Yes, but—' began the bursar wretchedly.

'After all, you wouldn't make a *forgery*, would you?'

'Not as, um, such—'

'It's just a hat. It's whatever people think it is. People see the Archchancellor wearing it, they think it's the original hat. In a

---

*Of course, Ankh-Morpork's citizens had always claimed that the river water was incredibly pure in any case. Any water that had passed through so many kidneys, they reasoned, had to be very pure indeed.

certain sense, it *is*. Things are defined by what they do. And people, of course. Fundamental basis of wizardry, is that.' Carding paused dramatically, and plonked the hatbox into Spelter's arms. '*Cogitum ergot hatto*, you might say.'

Spelter had made a special study of old languages, and did his best.

' "I think, therefore I am a hat?" ' he hazarded.

'What?' said Carding, as they set off down the stairs to the new incarnation of the Great Hall.

' "I considered I'm a mad hat?" ' Spelter suggested.

'Just shut up, all right?'

The haze still hung over the city, its curtains of silver and gold turned to blood by the light of the setting sun which streamed in through the windows of the hall.

Coin was sitting on a stool with his staff across his knees. It occurred to Spelter that he had never seen the boy without it, which was odd. Most wizards kept their staves under the bed, or hooked up over the fireplace.

He didn't like this staff. It was black, but not because that was its colour, more because it seemed to be a moveable hole into some other, more unpleasant set of dimensions. It didn't have eyes but, nevertheless, it seemed to stare at Spelter as if it knew his innermost thoughts, which at the moment was more than *he* did.

His skin prickled as the two wizards crossed the floor and felt the blast of raw magic flowing outwards from the seated figure.

Several dozen of the most senior wizards were clustered around the stool, staring in awe at the floor.

Spelter craned to see, and saw—

The world.

It floated in a puddle of black night somehow set into the floor itself, and Spelter knew with a terrible certainty that it *was* the world, not some image or simple projection. There were cloud patterns and everything. There were the frosty wastes of the Hublands, the Counterweight Continent, the Circle Sea, the Rimfall, all tiny and pastel-coloured but nevertheless real . . .

Someone was speaking to him.

'Um?' he said, and the sudden drop in metaphorical temperature jerked him back into reality. He realised with horror that Coin had just directed a remark at him.

'I'm sorry?' he corrected himself. 'It was just that the world . . . so beautiful . . .'

'Our Spelter is an aesthete,' said Coin, and there was a brief chuckle from one or two wizards who knew what the word meant, 'but as to the world, it could be improved. I had said, Spelter, that everywhere we look we can see cruelty and inhumanity and greed, which tell us that the world is indeed governed badly, does it not?'

Spelter was aware of two dozen pairs of eyes turning to him.

'Um,' he said. 'Well, you can't change human nature.'

There was dead silence.

Spelter hesitated. 'Can you?' he said.

'That remains to be seen,' said Carding. 'But if we change the world, then human nature also will change. Is that not so, brothers?'

'We have the city,' said one of the wizards. 'I myself have created a castle—'

'We rule the city, but who rules the world?' said Carding. 'There must be a thousand petty kings and emperors and chieftains down there.'

'Not one of whom can read without moving his lips,' said a wizard.

'The Patrician could read,' said Spelter.

'Not if you cut off his index finger,' said Carding. 'What happened to the lizard, anyway? Never mind. The point is, the world should surely be run by men of wisdom and philosophy. It must be guided. We've spent centuries fighting amongst ourselves, but together . . . who knows what we could do?'

'Today the city, tomorrow the world,' said someone at the back of the crowd.

Carding nodded.

'Tomorrow the world, and—' he calculated quickly – 'on Friday the universe!'

That leaves the weekend free, thought Spelter. He recalled the box in his arms, and held it out towards Coin. But Carding floated in front of him, seized the box in one fluid movement and offered it to the boy with a flourish.

'The Archchancellor's hat,' he said. 'Rightfully yours, we think.'

Coin took it. For the first time Spelter saw uncertainty cross his face.

'Isn't there some sort of formal ceremony?' he said.

Carding coughed.

'I – er, no,' he said. 'No, I don't think so.' He glanced up at the other senior mages, who shook their heads. 'No. We've never had one. Apart from the feast, of course. Er. You see, it's not like a coronation, the Archchancellor, you see, he leads the fraternity of wizards, he's,' Carding's voice ran down slowly in the light of that

75

golden gaze, 'he's, you see . . . he's the . . . first . . . among . . . equals . . .'

He stepped back hurriedly as the staff moved eerily until it pointed towards him. Once again Coin seemed to be listening to an inner voice.

'No,' he said eventually, and when he spoke next his voice had that wide, echoing quality that, if you are not a wizard, you can only achieve with a lot of very expensive audio equipment. 'There will be a ceremony. There must be a ceremony, people must understand that wizards are ruling, but it will not be here. I will select a place. And all the wizards who have passed through these gates will attend, is that understood?'

'Some of them live far off,' said Carding, carefully. 'It will take them some time to travel, so when were you thinking of—'

'They are wizards!' shouted Coin. 'They can be here in the twinkling of an eye! I have given them the power! Besides,' his voice dropped back to something like normal pitch, 'the University is finished. It was never the true home of magic, only its prison. I will build us a new place.'

He lifted the new hat out of its box, and smiled at it. Spelter and Carding held their breath.

'But—'

They looked around. Hakardly the Lore master had spoken, and now stood with his mouth opening and shutting.

Coin turned to him, one eyebrow raised.

'You surely don't mean to close the University?' said the old wizard, his voice trembling.

'It is no longer necessary,' said Coin. 'It's a place of dust and old books. It is behind us. Is that not so . . . brothers?'

There was a chorus of uncertain mumbling. The wizards found it hard to imagine life without the old stones of UU. Although, come to think of it, there was a lot of dust, of course, and the books were pretty old . . .

'After all . . . brothers . . . who among you has been into your dark library these past few days? The magic is inside you now, not imprisoned between covers. Is that not a joyous thing? Is there not one among you who has done more magic, *real* magic, in the past twenty-four hours than he has done in the whole of his life before? Is there one among you who does not, in his heart of hearts, truly agree with me?'

Spelter shuddered. In his heart of hearts an inner Spelter had woken, and was struggling to make himself heard. It was a Spelter who suddenly longed for those quiet days, only hours ago, when magic was gentle and shuffled around the place in old slippers and always had time for a sherry and wasn't like a hot sword in the brain and, above all, didn't kill people.

Terror seized him as he felt his vocal chords twang to attention and prepare, despite all his efforts, to disagree.

The staff was trying to find him. He could feel it searching for him. It would vanish him, just like poor old Billias. He clamped his jaws together, but it wouldn't work. He felt his chest heave. His jaw creaked.

Carding, shifting uneasily, stood on his foot. Spelter yelped.

'Sorry,' said Carding.

'Is something the matter, Spelter?' said Coin.

Spelter hopped on one leg, suddenly released, his body flooding with relief as his toes flooded with agony, more grateful than anyone in the entire history of the world that seventeen stones of wizardry had chosen his instep to come down heavily on.

His scream seemed to have broken the spell. Coin sighed, and stood up.

'It has been a good day,' he said.

It was two o'clock in the morning. River mists coiled like snakes through the streets of Ankh-Morpork, but they coiled alone. Wizards did not hold with other people staying up after midnight, and so no-one did. They slept the troubled sleep of the enchanted, instead.

In the Plaza of Broken Moons, once the boutique of mysterious pleasures from whose flare-lit and curtain-hung stalls the late-night reveller could obtain anything from a plate of jellied eels to the venereal disease of his choice, the mists coiled and dripped into chilly emptiness.

The stalls had gone, replaced by gleaming marble and a statue depicting the spirit of something or other, surrounded by illuminated fountains. Their dull splashing was the only sound that broke the cholesterol of silence that had the heart of the city in its grip.

Silence reigned too in the dark bulk of Unseen University. Except—

Spelter crept along the shadowy corridors like a two-legged spider, darting – or at least limping quickly – from pillar to archway, until he reached the forbidding doors of the Library. He peered nervously at the darkness around him and, after some hesitation, tapped very, very lightly.

Silence poured from the heavy woodwork. But, unlike the silence that had the rest of the city under its thrall, this was a watchful, alert silence; it was the silence of a sleeping cat that had just opened one eye.

When he could bear it no longer Spelter dropped to his hands and knees and tried to peer under the doors. Finally he put his mouth as close as he could to the draughty, dusty gap under the bottommost hinge and whispered: 'I say! Um. Can you hear me?'

He felt sure that something moved, far back in the darkness.

He tried again, his mood swinging between terror and hope with every erratic thump of his heart.

'I say? It's me, um, Spelter. You know? Could you speak to me, please?'

Perhaps large leathery feet were creeping gently across the floor in there, or maybe it was only the creaking of Spelter's nerves. He tried to swallow away the dryness in his throat, and had another go.

'Look, all right, but, look, they're talking about shutting the Library!'

The silence grew louder. The sleeping cat had cocked an ear.

'What is happening is all wrong!' the bursar confided, and clapped his hand over his mouth at the enormity of what he had said.

'Oook?'

It was the faintest of noises, like the eructation of cockroaches.

Suddenly emboldened, Spelter pressed his lips closer to the crack.

'Have you got the, um, Patrician in there?'

'Oook.'

'What about the little doggie?'

'Oook.'

'Oh. Good.'

Spelter lay full length in the comfort of the night, and drummed his fingers on the chilly floor.

'You wouldn't care to, um, let me in too?' he ventured.

'Oook!'

Spelter made a face in the gloom.

'Well, would you, um, let me come in for a few minutes? We need to discuss something urgently, man to man.'

'Eeck.'

'I meant ape.'

'Oook.'

'Look, won't you come out, then?'

'Oook.'

78

Spelter sighed. 'This show of loyalty is all very well, but you'll starve in there.'

'Oook oook.'

'*What* other way in?'

'Oook.'

'Oh, have it your way,' Spelter sighed. But, somehow, he felt better for the conversation. Everyone else in the University seemed to be living in a dream, whereas the Librarian wanted nothing more in the whole world than soft fruit, a regular supply of index cards and the opportunity, every month or so, to hop over the wall of the Patrician's private menagerie.* It was strangely reassuring.

'So you're all right for bananas and so forth?' he inquired, after another pause.

'Oook.'

'Don't let anyone in, will you? Um. I think that's frightfully important.'

'Oook.'

'Good.' Spelter stood up and dusted off his knees. Then he put his mouth to the keyhole and added, 'Don't trust anyone.'

'Oook.'

It was not completely dark in the Library, because the serried rows of magical books gave off a faint octarine glow, caused by thaumaturgical leakage into a strong occult field. It was just bright enough to illuminate the pile of shelves wedged against the door.

The former Patrician had been carefully decanted into a jar on the Librarian's desk. The Librarian himself sat under it, wrapped in his blanket and holding Wuffles on his lap.

Occasionally he would eat a banana.

Spelter, meanwhile, limped back along the echoing passages of the University, heading for the security of his bedroom. It was because his ears were nervously straining the tiniest of sounds out of the air that he heard, right on the cusp of audibility, the sobbing.

It wasn't a normal noise up here. In the carpeted corridors of the senior wizards' quarters there were a number of sounds you might hear late at night, such as snoring, the gentle clinking of glasses, tuneless singing and, once in a while, the zip and sizzle of a spell gone wrong. But the sound of someone quietly crying was such a novelty that Spelter found himself edging down the passage that led to the Archchancellor's suite.

---

* No-one ever had the courage to ask him what he did there.

79

The door was ajar. Telling himself that he really shouldn't, tensing himself for a hurried dash, Spelter peered inside.

Rincewind stared.

'What *is* it?' he whispered.

'I think it's a temple of some sort,' said Conina.

Rincewind stood and gazed upwards, the crowds of Al Khali bouncing off and around him in a kind of human Brownian motion. A temple, he thought. Well, it was big, and it was impressive, and the architect had used every trick in the book to make it look even bigger and even more impressive than it was, and to impress upon everyone looking at it that they, on the other hand, were very small and ordinary and didn't have as many domes. It was the kind of place that looked exactly as you were always going to remember it.

But Rincewind felt he knew holy architecture when he saw it, and the frescoes on the big and, of course, impressive walls above him didn't look at all religious. For one thing, the participants were enjoying themselves. Almost certainly, they were enjoying themselves. Yes, they must be. It would be pretty astonishing if they weren't.

'They're not dancing, are they?' he said, in a desperate attempt not to believe the evidence of his own eyes. 'Or maybe it's some sort of acrobatics?'

Conina squinted upwards in the hard, white sunlight.

'I shouldn't think so,' she said, thoughtfully.

Rincewind remembered himself. 'I don't think a young woman like you should be looking at this sort of thing,' he said sternly.

Conina gave him a smile. 'I think wizards are expressly forbidden to,' she said sweetly. 'It's supposed to turn you blind.'

Rincewind turned his face upwards again, prepared to risk maybe one eye. This sort of thing is only to be expected, he told himself. They don't know any better. Foreign countries are, well, foreign countries. They do things differently there.

Although some things, he decided, were done in very much the same way, only with rather more inventiveness and, by the look of it, far more often.

'The temple frescoes of Al Khali are famous far and wide,' said Conina, as they walked through crowds of children who kept trying to sell Rincewind things and introduce him to nice relatives.

'Well, I can see they would be,' Rincewind agreed. 'Look, push off, will you? No, I don't want to buy whatever it is. No, I don't want to meet her. Or him, either. *Or* it, you nasty little boy. Get *off*, will you?'

The last scream was to the group of children riding sedately on the Luggage, which was plodding along patiently behind Rincewind and making no attempt to shake them off. Perhaps it was sickening for something, he thought, and brightened up a bit.

'How many people are there on this continent, do you think?' he said.

'I don't know,' said Conina, without turning round. 'Millions, I expect?'

'If I were wise, I wouldn't be here,' said Rincewind, with feeling.

They had been in Al Khali, gateway to the whole mysterious continent of Klatch, for several hours. He was beginning to suffer.

A decent city should have a bit of fog about it, he considered, and people should live indoors, not spend all their time out on the streets. There shouldn't be all this sand and heat. As for the wind . . .

Ankh-Morpork had its famous smell, so full of personality that it could reduce a strong man to tears. But Al Khali had its wind, blowing from the vastness of the deserts and continents nearer the rim. It was a gentle breeze, but it didn't stop and eventually it had the same effect on visitors that a cheesegrater achieves on a tomato. After a while it seemed to have worn away your skin and was rasping directly across the nerves.

To Conina's sensitive nostrils it carried aromatic messages from the heart of the continent, compounded of the chill of deserts, the stink of lions, the compost of jungles and the flatulence of wild-ebeest.

Rincewind, of course, couldn't smell any of this. Adaptation is a wonderful thing, and most Morporkians would be hard put to smell a burning feather mattress at five feet.

'Where to next?' he said. 'Somewhere out of the wind?'

'My father spent some time in Khali when he was hunting for the Lost City of Ee,' said Conina. 'And I seem to remember he spoke very highly of the *soak*. It's a kind of bazaar.'

'I suppose we just go and look for the second-hand hat stalls,' said Rincewind. 'Because the whole idea is totally—'

'What I was hoping was that maybe we could be attacked. That seems the most sensible idea. My father said that very few strangers who entered the *soak* ever came out again. Some very murderous types hang out there, he said.'

Rincewind gave this due consideration.

'Just run that by me again, will you?' he said. 'After you said we should be attacked I seemed to hear a ringing in my ears.'

'Well, we want to meet the criminal element, don't we?'

'Not exactly *want*,' said Rincewind. 'That wasn't the phrase I would have chosen.'

'How would you put it, then?'

'Er. I think the phrase "not want" sums it up pretty well.'

'But you agreed that we should get the hat!'

'But not die in the process,' said Rincewind, wretchedly. 'That won't do anyone any good. Not me, anyway.'

'My father always said that death is but a sleep,' said Conina.

'Yes, the hat told me that,' said Rincewind, as they turned down a narrow, crowded street between white adobe walls. 'But the way I see it, it's a lot harder to get up in the morning.'

'Look,' said Conina, 'there's not much risk. You're with me.'

'Yes, and you're looking forward to it, aren't you,' said Rincewind accusingly, as Conina piloted them along a shady alley, with their retinue of pubescent entrepreneurs at their heels. 'It's the old herrydeterry at work.'

'Just shut up and try to look like a victim, will you?'

'I can do that all right,' said Rincewind, beating off a particularly stubborn member of the Junior Chamber of Commerce, 'I've had a lot of practice. For the last time, I don't want to buy *anyone*, you wretched child!'

He looked gloomily at the walls around them. At least there weren't any of those disturbing pictures here, but the hot breeze still blew the dust around him and he was sick and tired of looking at sand. What he wanted was a couple of cool beers, a cold bath and a change of clothing; it probably wouldn't make him feel better, but it would at least make feeling awful more enjoyable. Not that there was any beer here, probably. It was a funny thing, but in chilly cities like Ankh-Morpork the big drink was beer, which cooled you down, but in places like this, where the whole sky was an oven with the door left open, people drank tiny little sticky drinks which set fire to the back of your throat. And the architecture was all wrong. And they had statues in their temples that, well, just weren't suitable. This wasn't the right kind of place for wizards. Of course, they had some local grown alternative, enchanters or some such, but not what you'd call *decent* magic . . .

Conina strolled ahead of him, humming to herself.

You rather like her, don't you? I can tell, said a voice in his head.

Oh blast, thought Rincewind, you're not my conscience again, are you?

Your libido. It's a bit stuffy in here, isn't it? You haven't had it done up since the last time I was around.

Look, go away, will you? I'm a wizard! Wizards are ruled by their heads, not by their hearts!

And I'm getting votes from your glands, and they're telling me that as far as your body is concerned your brain is in a minority of one.

Yes? But it's got the casting vote, then.

Hah! That's what you think. Your heart has got nothing to do with this, by the way; it's merely a muscular organ which powers the circulation of the blood. But look at it like this – you quite like her, don't you?

Well . . . Rincewind hesitated. Yes, he thought, er . . .

She's pretty good company, eh? Nice voice?

Well, of course . . .

You'd like to see more of her?

Well . . . Rincewind realised with some surprise that, yes, he would. It wasn't that he was entirely unused to the company of women, but it always seemed to cause trouble and, of course, it was a well known fact that it was bad for the magical abilities, although he had to admit that his particular magical abilities, being approximately those of a rubber hammer, were shaky enough to start with.

Then you've got nothing to lose, have you? his libido put in, in an oily tone of thought.

It was at this point Rincewind realised that something important was missing. It took him a little while to realise what it was.

No-one had tried to sell him anything for several minutes. In Al Khali, that probably meant you were dead.

He, Conina and the Luggage were alone in a long, shady alley. He could hear the bustle of the city some way away, but immediately around them there was nothing except a rather expectant silence.

'They've run off,' said Conina.

'Are we going to be attacked?'

'Could be. There's been three men following us on the roof-tops.'

Rincewind squinted upwards at almost the same time as three men, dressed in flowing black robes, dropped lightly into the alley-way in front of them. When he looked around two more appeared from around a corner. All five were holding long curved swords and, although the lower halves of their faces were masked, it was almost certain that they were grinning evilly.

83

Rincewind rapped sharply on the Luggage's lid.

'Kill,' he suggested. The Luggage stood stock still for a moment, and then plodded over and stood next to Conina. It looked slightly smug and, Rincewind realised with jealous horror, rather embarrassed.

'Why, you—' he growled, and gave it a kick – 'you *handbag.*'

He sidled closer to the girl, who was standing there with a thoughtful smile on her face.

'What now?' he said. 'Are you going to offer them all a quick perm?'

The men edged a little closer. They were, he noticed, only interested in Conina.

'I'm not armed,' she said.

'What happened to your legendary comb?'

'Left it on the boat.'

'You've got nothing?'

Conina shifted slightly to keep as many of the men as possible in her field of vision.

'I've got a couple of hairgrips,' she said out of the corner of her mouth.

'Any good?'

'Don't know. Never tried.'

'You got us into this!'

'Relax. I think they'll just take us prisoner.'

'Oh, that's fine for you to say. You're not marked down as this week's special offer.'

The Luggage snapped its lid once or twice, a little uncertain about things. One of the men gingerly extended his sword and prodded Rincewind in the small of the back.

'They want to take us somewhere, see?' said Conina. She gritted her teeth. 'Oh, no,' she muttered.

'What's the matter now?'

'I can't do it!'

'What?'

Conina put her head in her hands. 'I can't let myself be taken prisoner without a fight! I can feel a thousand barbarian ancestors accusing me of betrayal!' she hissed urgently.

'Pull the other one.'

'No, really. This won't take a minute.'

There was a sudden blur and the nearest man collapsed in a small gurgling heap. Then Conina's elbows went back and into the stomachs of the men behind her. Her left hand rebounded past

Rincewind's ear with a noise like tearing silk and felled the man behind him. The fifth made a run for it and was brought down by a flying tackle, hitting his head heavily on the wall.

Conina rolled off him and sat up, panting, her eyes bright.

'I don't like to say this, but I feel better for that,' she said. 'It's terrible to know that I betrayed a fine hairdressing tradition, of course. Oh.'

'Yes,' said Rincewind sombrely, 'I wondered if you'd noticed them.'

Conina's eyes scanned the line of bowmen who had appeared along the opposite wall. They had that stolid, impassive look of people who have been paid to do a job, and don't much mind if the job involves killing people.

'Time for those hairgrips,' said Rincewind.

Conina didn't move.

'My father always said that it was pointless to undertake a direct attack against an enemy extensively armed with efficient projectile weapons,' she said.

Rincewind, who knew Cohen's normal method of speech, gave her a look of disbelief.

'Well, what he *actually* said,' she added, 'was never enter an arse-kicking contest with a porcupine.'

Spelter couldn't face breakfast.

He wondered whether he ought to talk to Carding, but he had a chilly feeling that the old wizard wouldn't listen and wouldn't believe him anyway. In fact he wasn't quite sure he believed it himself . . .

Yes he was. He'd never forget it, although he intended to make every effort.

One of the problems about living in the University these days was that the building you went to sleep in probably wasn't the same building when you woke up. Rooms had a habit of changing and moving around, a consequence of all this random magic. It built up in the carpets, charging up the wizards to such an extent that shaking hands with somebody was a sure-fire way of turning them into something. The build up of magic, in fact, was overflowing the capacity of the area to hold it. If something wasn't done about it soon, then even the common people would be able to use it – a chilling thought but, since Spelter's mind was already so full of chilling thoughts you could use it as an ice tray, not one he was going to spend much time worrying about.

85

Mere household geography wasn't the only difficulty, though. Sheer pressure of thaumaturgical inflow was even affecting the food. What was a forkful of kedgeree when you lifted it off the plate might well have turned into something else by the time it entered your mouth. If you were lucky, it was inedible. If you were *unlucky*, it was edible but probably not something you liked to think you were about to eat or, worse, had already eaten half of.

Spelter found Coin in what had been, late last night, a broom cupboard. It was a lot bigger now. It was only because Spelter had never heard of aircraft hangars that he didn't know what to compare it with, although, to be fair, very few aircraft hangars have marble floors and a lot of statuary around the place. A couple of brooms and a small battered bucket in one corner looked distinctly out of place, but not as out of place as the crushed tables in the former Great Hall which, owing to the surging tides of magic now flowing through the place, had shrunk to the approximate size of what Spelter, if he had ever seen one, would have called a small telephone box.

He sidled into the room with extreme caution and took his place among the council of wizards. The air was greasy with the feel of power.

Spelter created a chair beside Carding and leant across to him.

'You'll never believe—' he began.

'Quiet!' hissed Carding. 'This is amazing!'

Coin was sitting on his stool in the middle of the circle, one hand on his staff, the other extended and holding something small, white and egg-like. It was strangely fuzzy. In fact, Spelter thought, it wasn't something small seen close to. It was something *huge*, but a long way off. And the boy was holding it in his hand.

'What's he doing?' Spelter whispered.

'I'm not exactly sure,' murmured Carding. 'As far as we can understand it, he's creating a new home for wizardry.'

Streamers of coloured light flashed about the indistinct ovoid, like a distant thunderstorm. The glow lit Coin's preoccupied face from below, giving it the semblance of a mask.

'I don't see how we will all fit in,' the bursar said. 'Carding, last night I saw—'

'It is finished,' said Coin. He held up the egg, which flashed occasionally from some inner light and gave off tiny white prominences. Not only was it a long way off, Spelter thought, it was also extremely heavy; it went right through heaviness and out the other side, into that strange negative realm where lead would be a vacuum. He grabbed Carding's sleeve again.

'Carding, listen, it's important, listen, when I looked in—'

'I really wish you'd stop doing that.'

'But the staff, his staff, it's not—'

Coin stood up and pointed the staff at the wall, where a doorway instantly appeared. He marched out through it, leaving the wizards to follow him.

He went through the Archchancellor's garden, followed by a gaggle of wizards in the same way that a comet is followed by its tail, and didn't stop until he reached the banks of the Ankh. There were some hoary old willows here, and the river flowed, or at any rate moved, in a horseshoe bend around a small newt-haunted meadow known rather optimistically as Wizards Pleasaunce. On summer evenings, if the wind was blowing towards the river, it was a nice area for an afternoon stroll.

The warm silver haze still hung over the city as Coin padded through the damp grass until he reached the centre. He tossed the egg, which drifted in a gentle arc and landed with a squelch.

He turned to the wizards as they hurried up.

'Stand well back,' he commanded. 'And be prepared to run.'

He pointed the octiron staff at the half-sunken thing. A bolt of octarine light shot from its tip and struck the egg, exploding into a shower of sparks that left blue and purple after-images.

There was a pause. A dozen wizards watched the egg expectantly.

A breeze shook the willow trees in a totally unmysterious way.

Nothing else happened.

'Er—' Spelter began.

And then came the first tremor. A few leaves fell out of the trees and some distant water bird took off in fright.

The sound started as a low groaning, experienced rather than heard, as though everyone's feet had suddenly become their ears. The trees trembled, and so did one or two wizards.

The mud around the egg began to bubble.

And exploded.

The ground peeled back like lemon rind. Gouts of steaming mud spattered the wizards as they dived for the cover of the trees. Only Coin, Spelter and Carding were left to watch the sparkling white building arise from the meadow, grass and dirt pouring off it. Other towers erupted from the ground behind them; buttresses *grew* through the air, linking tower with tower.

Spelter whimpered when the soil flowed away from around his feet, and was replaced by flagstones flecked with silver. He lurched as the floor rose inexorably, carrying the three high above the treetops.

The rooftops of the University went past and fell away below them. Ankh-Morpork spread out like a map, the river a trapped snake, the plains a misty blur. Spelter's ears popped, but the climb went on, into the clouds.

They emerged drenched and cold into blistering sunlight with the cloud cover spreading away in every direction. Other towers were rising around them, glinting painfully in the sharpness of the day.

Carding knelt down awkwardly and felt the floor gingerly. He signalled to Spelter to do the same.

Spelter touched a surface that was smoother than stone. It felt like ice would feel if ice was slightly warm, and looked like ivory. While it wasn't exactly transparent, it gave the impression that it would like to be.

He got the distinct feeling that, if he closed his eyes, he wouldn't be able to feel it at all.

He met Carding's gaze.

'Don't look at, um, me,' he said. 'I don't know what it is either.'

They looked up at Coin, who said: 'It's magic.'

'Yes, lord, but what is it made of?' said Carding.

'It is *made* of magic. Raw magic. Solidified. Curdled. Renewed from second to second. Could you imagine a better substance to build the new home of sourcery?'

The staff flared for a moment, melting the clouds. The Discworld appeared below them, and from up here you could see that it was indeed a disc, pinned to the sky by the central mountain of Cori Celesti, where the gods lived. There was the Circle Sea, so close that it might even be possible to dive into it from here; there was the vast continent of Klatch, squashed by perspective. The Rimfall around the edge of the world was a sparkling curve.

'It's too big,' said Spelter under his breath. The world he had lived in hadn't stretched much further than the gates of the University, and he'd preferred it that way. A man could be comfortable in a world that size. He certainly couldn't be comfortable about being half a mile in the air standing on something that wasn't, in some fundamental way, there.

The thought shocked him. He was a wizard, and he was worrying about magic.

He sidled cautiously back towards Carding, who said: 'It isn't exactly what I expected.'

'Um?'

'It looks a lot smaller from up here, doesn't it.'

'Well, I don't know. Listen, I must tell you—'

'Look at the Ramtops, now. You could almost reach out and touch them.'

They stared out across two hundred leagues towards the towering mountain range, glittering and white and cold. It was said that if you travelled hubwards through the secret valleys of the Ramtops you would find, in the frozen lands under Cori Celesti itself, the secret realm of the Ice Giants, imprisoned after their last great battle with the Gods. In those days the mountains had been mere islands in a great sea of ice, and ice lived on them still.

Coin smiled his golden smile.

'What did you say, Carding?' he said.

'It's the clear air, lord. And they look so close and small. I only said I could almost touch them—'

Coin waved him into silence. He extended one thin arm, rolling back his sleeve in the traditional sign that magic was about to be performed without trickery. He reached out, and then turned back with his fingers closed around what was, without any shadow of a doubt, a handful of snow.

The two wizards observed it in stunned silence as it melted and dripped on to the floor

Coin laughed.

'You find it so hard to believe?' he said. 'Shall I pick pearls from rim-most Krull, or sand from the Great Nef? Could your old wizardry do half as much?'

It seemed to Spelter that his voice took on a metallic edge. He stared intently at their faces.

Finally Carding sighed and said rather quietly, 'No. All my life I have sought magic, and all I found was coloured lights and little tricks and old, dry books. Wizardry has done nothing for the world.'

'And if I tell you that I intend to dissolve the Orders and close the University? Although, of course, my senior *advisors* will be accorded all due status.'

Carding's knuckles whitened, but he shrugged.

'There is little to say,' he said. 'What good is a candle at noonday?'

Coin turned to Spelter. So did the staff. The filigree carvings were regarding him coldly. One of them, near the top of the staff, looked unpleasantly like an eyebrow.

'You're very quiet, Spelter. Do you not agree?'

No. The world had sourcery once, and gave it up for wizardry. Wizardry is magic for men, not gods. It's not for us. There was something wrong with it, and we have forgotten what it was. I liked wizardry. It didn't upset the world. It fitted. It was right. A wizard was all I wanted to be.

He looked down at his feet.

'Yes,' he whispered.

'Good,' said Coin, in a satisfied tone of voice. He strolled to the edge of the tower and looked down at the street map of Ankh-Morpork far below. The Tower of Art came barely a tenth of the way towards them.

'I believe,' he said, 'I believe that we will hold the ceremony next week, at full moon.'

'Er. It won't be full moon for three weeks,' said Carding.

'Next week,' Coin repeated. 'If I say the moon will be full, there will be no argument.' He continued to stare down at the model buildings of the University, and then pointed.

'What's that?'

Carding craned.

'Er. The Library. Yes. It's the Library. Er.'

The silence was so oppressive that Carding felt something more was expected of him. Anything would be better than that silence.

'It's where we keep the books, you know. Ninety thousand volumes, isn't it, Spelter?'

'Um? Oh. Yes. About ninety thousand, I suppose.'

Coin leaned on the staff and stared.

'Burn them,' he said. 'All of them.'

Midnight strutted its black stuff along the corridors of Unseen University as Spelter, with rather less confidence, crept cautiously towards the impassive doors of the Library. He knocked, and the sound echoed so loudly in the empty building that he had to lean against the wall and wait for his heart to slow down a bit.

After a while he heard a sound like heavy furniture being moved about.

'Oook?'

'It's me.'

'Oook?'

'Spelter.'

'Oook.'

'Look, you've got to get out! He's going to burn the Library!'

There was no reply.

Spelter let himself sag to his knees.

'He'll do it, too,' he whispered. 'He'll probably make *me* do it, it's that staff, um, it knows everything that's going on, it knows that I know about it . . . please help me . . .'

'Oook?'

'The other night, I looked into his room . . . the staff, the staff was *glowing*, it was standing there in the middle of the room like a beacon and the boy was on the bed sobbing, I could feel it reaching out, teaching him, whispering terrible things, and then it noticed me, you've got to help me, you're the only one who isn't under the—'

Spelter stopped. His face froze. He turned around very slowly, without willing it, because something was gently spinning him.

He knew the University was empty. The wizards had all moved into the New Tower, where the lowliest student had a suite more splendid than any senior mage had before.

The staff hung in the air a few feet away. It was surrounded by a faint octarine glow.

He stood up very carefully and, keeping his back to the stonework and his eyes firmly fixed on the thing, slithered gingerly along the wall until he reached the end of the corridor. At the corner he noted that the staff, while not moving, had revolved on its axis to follow him.

He gave a little cry, grasped the skirts of his robe, and ran.

The staff was in front of him. He slid to a halt and stood there, catching his breath.

'You don't frighten me,' he lied, and turned on his heel and marched off in a different direction, snapping his fingers to produce a torch that burned with a fine white flame (only its penumbra of octarine proclaimed it to be of magical origin).

Once again, the staff was in front of him. The light of his torch was sucked into a thin, singing stream of white fire that flared and vanished with a 'pop'.

He waited, his eyes watering with blue after-images, but if the staff was still there it didn't seem to be inclined to take advantage of him. When vision returned he felt he could make out an even darker shadow on his left. The stairway down to the kitchens.

He darted for it, leaping down the unseen steps and landing heavily and unexpectedly on uneven flags. A little moonlight filtered through a grating in the distance and somewhere up there, he knew, was a doorway into the outside world.

Staggering a little, his ankles aching, the noise of his own breath booming in his ears as though he'd stuck his entire head in a seashell, Spelter set off across the endless dark desert of the floor.

Things clanked underfoot. There were no rats here now, of course, but the kitchen had fallen into disuse lately – the

University's cooks had been the best in the world, but now any wizard could conjure up meals beyond mere culinary skill. The big copper pans hung neglected on the wall, their sheen already tarnishing, and the kitchen ranges under the giant chimney arch were filled with nothing but chilly ash . . .

The staff lay across the back door like a bar. It spun up as Spelter tottered towards it and hung, radiating quiet malevolence, a few feet away. Then, quite smoothly, it began to glide towards him.

He backed away, his feet slipping on the greasy stones. A thump across the back of his thighs made him yelp, but as he reached behind him he found it was only one of the chopping blocks.

His hand groped desperately across its scarred surface and, against all hope, found a cleaver buried in the wood. In an instinctive gesture as ancient as mankind, Spelter's fingers closed around its handle.

He was out of breath and out of patience and out of space and time and also scared, very nearly, out of his mind.

So when the staff hovered in front of him he wrenched the chopper up and around with all the strength he could muster . . .

And hesitated. All that was wizardly in him cried out against the destruction of so much power, power that perhaps even now could be used, used by him . . .

And the staff swung around so that its axis was pointing directly at him.

And several corridors away, the Librarian stood braced with his back against the Library door, watching the blue and white flashes that flickered across the floor. He heard the distant snap of raw energy, and a sound that started low and ended up in zones of pitch that even Wuffles, lying with his paws over his head, could not hear.

And then there was a faint, ordinary tinkling noise, such as might be made by a fused and twisted metal cleaver dropping on to flagstones.

It was the sort of noise that makes the silence that comes after it roll forward like a warm avalanche.

The Librarian wrapped the silence around him like a cloak and stood staring up at the rank on rank of books, each one pulsing faintly in the glow of its own magic. Shelf after shelf looked down[*] at him. They had heard. He could feel the fear.

The orang-utan stood statue-still for several minutes, and then

[*] Or up, or obliquely. The layout of the Library of Unseen University was a topographical nightmare, the sheer presence of so much stored magic twisting dimensions and gravity into the kind of spaghetti that would make M. C. Escher go for a good lie down, or possibly sideways.

appeared to reach a decision. He knuckled his way across to his desk and, after much rummaging, produced a heavy key-ring bristling with keys. Then he went back and stood in the middle of the floor and said, very deliberately, 'Oook.'

The books craned forward on their shelves. Now he had their full attention.

'What is this place?' said Conina.

Rincewind looked around him, and made a guess.

They were still in the heart of Al Khali. He could hear the hum of it beyond the walls. But in the middle of the teeming city someone had cleared a vast space, walled it off, and planted a garden so romantically natural that it looked as real as a sugar pig

'It looks like someone has taken twice five miles of inner city and girdled them round with walls and towers,' he hazarded.

'What a strange idea,' said Conina.

'Well, some of the religions here – well, when you die, you see, they think you go to this sort of garden, where there's all this sort of music and, and,' he continued, wretchedly, 'sherbet and, and – young women.'

Conina took in the green splendour of the walled garden, with its peacocks, intricate arches and slightly wheezy fountains. A dozen reclining women stared back at her, impassively. A hidden string orchestra was playing the complicated Klatchian *bhong* music.

'I'm not dead,' she said. 'I'm sure I would have remembered. Besides, this isn't *my* idea of paradise.' She looked critically at the reclining figures, and added, 'I wonder who does their hair?'

A sword point prodded her in the small of the back, and the two of them set out along the ornate path towards a small domed pavilion surrounded by olive trees. She scowled.

'Anyway, I don't like sherbet.'

Rincewind didn't comment. He was busily examining the state of his own mind, and wasn't happy at the sight of it. He had a horrible feeling that he was falling in love.

He was sure he had all the symptoms. There were the sweaty palms, the hot sensation in the stomach, the general feeling that the skin of his chest was made of tight elastic. There was the feeling, every time Conina spoke, that someone was running hot steel into his spine.

He glanced down at the Luggage, tramping stoically alongside him, and recognised the symptoms.

'Not you, too?' he said.

Possibly it was only the play of sunlight on the Luggage's battered lid, but it was just possible that for an instant it looked redder than usual.

Of course, sapient pearwood has this sort of weird mental link with its owner . . . Rincewind shook his head. Still, it'd explain why the thing wasn't its normal malignant self.

'It'd never work,' he said. 'I mean, she's a female and you're a, well, you're a—' He paused. 'Well, whatever you are, you're of the wooden persuasion. It'd never work. People would talk.'

He turned and glared at the black-robed guards behind him.

'I don't know what you're looking at,' he said severely.

The Luggage sidled over to Conina, following her so closely that she banged an ankle on it.

'Push off,' she snapped, and kicked it again, this time on purpose.

Insofar as the Luggage ever had an expression, it looked at her in shocked betrayal.

The pavilion ahead of them was an ornate onion-shaped dome, studded with precious stones and supported on four pillars. Its interior was a mass of cushions on which lay a rather fat, middle-aged man surrounded by three young women. He wore a purple robe interwoven with gold thread; they, as far as Rincewind could see, demonstrated that you could make six small saucepan lids and a few yards of curtain netting go a long way although – he shivered – not really far enough.

The man appeared to be writing. He glanced up at them.

'I suppose you don't know a good rhyme for "thou"?' he said peevishly.

Rincewind and Conina exchanged glances.

'Plough?' said Rincewind. 'Bough?'

'Cow?' suggested Conina, with forced brightness.

The man hesitated. 'Cow I quite like,' he said, 'Cow has got possibilities. Cow might, in fact, do. Do pull up a cushion, by the way. Have some sherbet. Why are you standing there like that?'

'It's these ropes,' said Conina.

'I have this allergy to cold steel,' Rincewind added.

'Really, how tiresome,' said the fat man, and clapped a pair of hands so heavy with rings that the sound was more of a clang. Two guards stepped forward smartly and cut the bonds, and then the whole battalion melted away, although Rincewind was acutely conscious of dozens of dark eyes watching them from the surrounding foliage. Animal instinct told him that, while he now appeared to be alone with the man and Conina, any aggressive moves on his part would suddenly make the world a sharp and painful place. He tried to radiate tranquillity and total friendliness. He tried to think of something to say.

'Well,' he ventured, looking around at the brocaded hangings, the ruby-studded pillars and the gold filigree cushions, 'you've done this place up nicely. It's—' he sought for something suitably descriptive – 'well, pretty much of a miracle of rare device.'

'One aims for simplicity,' sighed the man, still scribbling busily. 'Why are you here? Not that it isn't always a pleasure to meet fellow students of the poetic muse.'

'We were brought here,' said Conina.

'Men with swords,' added Rincewind.

'Dear fellows, they do so like to keep in practice. Would you like one of these?'

He snapped his fingers at one of the girls.

'Not, er, right now,' Rincewind began, but she'd picked up a plate of golden-brown sticks and demurely passed it towards him. He tried one. It was delicious, a sort of sweet crunchy flavour with a hint of honey. He took two more.

'Excuse me,' said Conina, 'but who are you? And where is this?'

'My name is Creosote, Seriph of Al Khali,' said the fat man, 'and this is my Wilderness. One does one's best.'

Rincewind coughed on his honey stick.

'Not Creosote as in "As rich as Creosote"?' he said.

'That was my dear father. I am, in fact, rather richer. When one has a great deal of money, I am afraid, it is hard to achieve simplicity. One does one's best.' He sighed.

'You could try giving it away,' said Conina.

He sighed again. 'That isn't easy, you know. No, one just has to try to do a little with a lot.'

'No, no, but look,' said Rincewind, spluttering bits of stick, 'they say, I mean, everything you touch turns into *gold*, for goodness sake.'

'That could make going to the lavatory a bit tricky,' said Conina brightly. 'Sorry.'

'One hears such stories about oneself,' said Creosote, affecting not to have heard. 'So tiresome. As if wealth mattered. True riches lie in the treasure houses of literature.'

'The Creosote *I* heard of,' said Conina slowly, 'was head of this band of, well, mad killers. The original Assassins, feared throughout hubward Klatch. No offence meant.'

'Ah yes, dear father,' said Creosote junior. 'The *hashishim*. Such a novel idea.* But not really very efficient. So we hired Thugs instead.'

'Ah. Named after a religious sect,' said Conina knowingly.

Creosote gave her a long look. 'No,' he said slowly, 'I don't think so. I think we named them after the way they push people's faces through the back of their heads. Dreadful, really.'

He picked up the parchment he had been writing on, and continued, 'I seek a more cerebral life, which is why I had the city centre converted into a Wilderness. So much better for the mental flow. One does one's best. May I read you my latest oeuvre?'

'Egg?' said Rincewind, who wasn't following this.

Creosote thrust out one pudgy hand and declaimed as follows:

'A summer palace underneath the bough,
A flask of wine, a loaf of bread, some lamb couscous with courgettes, roast peacock tongues, kebabs, iced sherbet, selection of sweets from the trolley and choice of Thou,
Singing beside me in the Wilderness,
And Wilderness is—'

He paused, and picked up his pen thoughtfully.

'Maybe cow isn't such a good idea,' he said. 'Now that I come to look at it—'

Rincewind glanced at the manicured greenery, carefully arranged rocks and high surrounding walls. One of the Thous winked at him.

'This is a Wilderness?' he said.

'My landscape gardeners incorporated all the essential features, I believe. They spent simply ages getting the rills sufficiently sinuous. I am reliably informed that they contain prospects of rugged grandeur and astonishing natural beauty.'

'And scorpions,' said Rincewind, helping himself to another honey stick.

'I don't know about that,' said the poet. 'Scorpions sound *unpoetic* to me. Wild honey and locusts seem more appropriate, according to the standard poetic instructions, although I've never really developed the taste for insects.'

'I always understood that the kind of locust people ate in wild-

*The Hashishim, who derived their name from the vast quantities of *hashish* they consumed, were unique among vicious killers in being both deadly and, at the same time, inclined to giggle, groove to interesting patterns of light and shade on their terrible knife blades and, in extreme cases, fall over.

ernesses was the fruit of a kind of tree,' said Conina. 'Father always said it was quite tasty.'

'Not insects?' said Creosote.

'I don't think so.'

The Seriph nodded at Rincewind. 'You might as well finish them up, then,' he said. 'Nasty crunchy things, I couldn't see the point.'

'I don't wish to sound ungrateful,' said Conina, over the sound of Rincewind's frantic coughing. 'But why did you have us brought here?'

'Good question.' Creosote looked at her blankly for a few seconds, as if trying to remember why they were there.

'You really are a most attractive young woman,' he said.

'You can't play a dulcimer, by any chance?'

'How many blades has it got?' said Conina.

'Pity,' said the Seriph, 'I had one specially imported.'

'My father taught me to play the harmonica,' she volunteered.

Creosote's lips moved soundlessly as he tried out the idea.

'No good,' he said. 'Doesn't scan. Thanks all the same, though.' He gave her another thoughtful look. 'You know, you really are most becoming. Has anyone ever told you your neck is as a tower of ivory?'

'Never,' said Conina.

'Pity,' said Creosote again. He rummaged among his cushions and produced a small bell, which he rang.

After a while a tall, saturnine figure appeared from behind the pavilion. He had the look of someone who could think his way through a corkscrew without bending, and a certain something about the eyes which would have made the average rabid rodent tiptoe away, discouraged.

That man, you would have said, has got Grand Vizier written all over him. No-one can tell him anything about defrauding widows and imprisoning impressionable young men in alleged jewel caves. When it comes to dirty work he probably wrote the book or, more probably, stole it from someone else.

He wore a turban with a pointy hat sticking out of it. He had a long thin moustache, of course.

'Ah, Abrim,' said Creosote.

'Highness?'

'My Grand Vizier,' said the Seriph.

—thought so—, said Rincewind to himself.

'These people, why did we have them brought here?'

The vizier twirled his moustache, probably foreclosing another dozen mortgages.

'The hat, highness,' he said. 'The hat, if you remember.'

'Ah, yes. Fascinating. Where did we put it?'

'Hold on,' said Rincewind urgently. 'This hat . . . it wouldn't be a sort of battered pointy one, with lots of stuff on it? Sort of lace and stuff, and, and—' he hesitated – 'no-one's tried to put it on, have they?'

'It specifically warned us not to,' said Creosote, 'so Abrim got a slave to try it on, of course. He said it gave him a headache.'

'It also told us that you would shortly be arriving,' said the vizier, bowing slightly at Rincewind, 'and therefore I – that is to say, the Seriph felt that you might be able to tell us more about this wonderful artifact?'

There is a tone of voice known as interrogative, and the vizier was using it; a slight edge to his words suggested that, if he didn't learn more about the hat very quickly, he had various activities in mind in which further words like 'red hot' and 'knives' would appear. Of course, all Grand Viziers talk like that all the time. There's probably a school somewhere.

'Gosh, I'm glad you've found it,' said Rincewind, 'That hat is gngngnh—'

'I beg your pardon?' said Abrim, signalling a couple of lurking guards to step forward. 'I missed the bit after the young lady—' he bowed at Conina – 'elbowed you in the ear.'

'I think,' said Conina, politely but firmly, 'you'd better take us to see it.'

Five minutes later, from its resting place on a table in the Seriph's treasury, the hat said, *At last. What kept you?*

It is at a time like this, with Rincewind and Conina probably about to be the victims of a murderous attack, and Coin about to address the assembled and cowering wizards on the subject of treachery, and the Disc about to fall under a magical dictatorship, that it is worth mentioning the subject of poetry and inspiration.

For example, the Seriph, in his bijou wildernessette, has just riffled back through his pages of verse to revise the lines which begin:

> 'Get up! For morning in the cup of day,
> Has dropped the spoon that scares the stars away'

—and he has sighed, because the white-hot lines searing across

98

his imagination never seem to come out exactly as he wants them.

It is, in fact, impossible that they ever will.

Sadly, this sort of thing happens all the time.

It is a well-known and established fact throughout the many-dimensional worlds of the multiverse that most really great discoveries are owed to one brief moment of inspiration. There's a lot of spadework first, of course, but what clinches the whole thing is the sight of, say, a falling apple or a boiling kettle or the water slopping over the edge of the bath. Something goes click inside the observer's head and then everything falls into place. The shape of DNA, it is popularly said, owes its discovery to the chance sight of a spiral staircase when the scientist's mind was just at the right receptive temperature. Had he used the lift, the whole science of genetics might have been a good deal different.*

This is thought of as somehow wonderful. It isn't. It is tragic. Little particles of inspiration sleet through the universe all the time, travelling through the densest matter in the same way that a neutrino passes through a candyfloss haystack, and most of them miss.

Even worse, most of the ones that hit the exact cerebral target hit the *wrong* one.

For example, the weird dream about a lead doughnut on a mile-high gantry, which in the right mind would have been the catalyst for the invention of repressed-gravitational electricity generation (a cheap and inexhaustible and totally non-polluting form of power which the world in question had been seeking for centuries, and for the lack of which it was plunged into a terrible and pointless war) was in fact had by a small and bewildered duck.

By another stroke of bad luck, the sight of a herd of white horses galloping through a field of wild hyacinths would have led a struggling composer to write the famous *Flying God Suite*, bringing succour and balm to the souls of millions, had he not been at home in bed with shingles. The inspiration therefore fell to a nearby frog, who was not in much of a position to make a startling contribution to the field of tone poetry.

Many civilisations have recognised this shocking waste and tried various methods to prevent it, most of them involving enjoyable but illegal attempts to tune the mind into the right wavelength by the use of exotic herbage or yeast products. It never works properly.

---

* Although, possibly, quicker. And only licensed to carry fourteen people.

And so Creosote, who had dreamt the inspiration for a rather fine poem about life and philosophy and how they both look much better through the bottom of a wine glass, was totally unable to do anything about it because he had as much poetic ability as a hyena.

Why the gods allow this sort of thing to continue is a mystery.

Actually, the flash of inspiration needed to explain it clearly and precisely has taken place, but the creature who received it – a small female bluetit – has never been able to make the position clear, even after some really strenuous coded messages on the tops of milk bottles. By a strange coincidence, a philosopher who had been devoting some sleepless nights to the same mystery woke up that morning with a wonderful new idea for getting peanuts out of bird tables.

Which brings us rather neatly on to the subject of magic.

A long way out in the dark gulfs of interstellar space, one single inspiration particle is clipping along unaware of its destiny, which is just as well, because its destiny is to strike, in a matter of hours, a tiny area of Rincewind's mind.

It would be a tough destiny even if Rincewind's creative node was a reasonable size, but the particle's karma had handed it the problem of hitting a moving target the size of a small raisin over a distance of several hundred lightyears. Life can be very difficult for a little sub-atomic particle in a great big universe.

If it pulls it off, however, Rincewind will have a serious philosophic idea. If it doesn't, a nearby brick will have an important insight which it will be totally unequipped to deal with.

The Seriph's palace, known to legend as the Rhoxie, occupied most of the centre of Al Khali that wasn't occupied by the wilderness. Most things connected with Creosote were famed in mythology and the arched, domed, many-pillared palace was said to have more rooms than any man had been able to count. Rincewind didn't know which number he was in.

'It's magic, isn't it?' said Abrim the vizier.

He prodded Rincewind in the ribs.

'You're a wizard,' he said. 'Tell me what it does.'

'How do you know I'm a wizard?' said Rincewind desperately.

'It's written on your hat,' said the vizier.

'Ah.'

'And you were on the boat with it. My men saw you.'

'The Seriph employs slavers?' snapped Conina. 'That doesn't sound very *simple*!'

'Oh, I employ the slavers. I am the vizier, after all,' said Abrim. 'It is rather expected of me.'

He gazed thoughtfully at the girl, and then nodded at a couple of the guards.

'The current Seriph is rather *literary* in his views,' he said. 'I, on the other hand, am not. Take her to the seraglio, although,' he rolled his eyes and gave an irritable sigh, 'I'm sure the only fate that awaits her there is boredom, and possibly a sore throat.'

He turned to Rincewind.

'Don't say anything,' he said. 'Don't move your hands. Don't try any sudden feats of magic. I am protected by strange and powerful amulets.'

'Now just hold on a minute—' Rincewind began, and Conina said, 'All right. I've always wondered what a harem looked like.'

Rincewind's mouth went on opening and shutting, but no sounds came out. Finally he managed, 'Have you?'

She waggled an eyebrow at him. It was probably a signal of some sort. Rincewind felt he ought to have understood it, but peculiar passions were stirring in the depths of his being. They weren't actually going to make him brave, but they were making him angry. Speeded up, the dialogue behind his eyes was going something like this:

Ugh.

Who's that?

Your conscience. I feel terrible. Look, they're marching her off to the harem.

Rather her than me, thought Rincewind, but without much conviction.

Do something!

There's too many guards! They'll kill me!

So they'll kill you, it's not the end of the world.

It will be for me, thought Rincewind grimly.

But just think how good you'll feel in your next life—

Look, just shut up, will I? I've had just about enough of me.

Abrim stepped across to Rincewind and looked at him curiously.

'Who are you talking to?' he said.

'I warn you,' said Rincewind, between clenched teeth, 'I have this magical box on legs which is absolutely merciless with attackers, one word from me and—'

'I'm impressed,' said Abrim. 'Is it invisible?'

Rincewind risked a look behind him.

'I'm sure I had it when I came in,' he said, and sagged.

It would be mistaken to say the Luggage was nowhere to be seen. It was somewhere to be seen, it was just that the place wasn't anywhere near Rincewind.

Abrim walked slowly around the table on which sat the hat, twirling his moustache.

'Once again,' he said, 'I ask you: this is an artifact of power, I feel it, and you must tell me what it does.'

'Why don't you ask it?' said Rincewind.

'It refuses to tell me.'

'Well, why do you want to know?'

Abrim laughed. It wasn't a nice sound. It sounded as though he had had laughter explained to him, probably slowly and repeatedly, but had never heard anyone actually do it.

'You're a wizard,' he said. 'Wizardry is about power. I have taken an interest in magic myself. I have the talent, you know.' The vizier drew himself up stiffly. 'Oh, yes. But they wouldn't accept me at your University. They said I was mentally unstable, can you believe that?'

'No,' said Rincewind, truthfully. Most of the wizards at Unseen had always seemed to him to be several bricks short of a shilling. Abrim seemed pretty normal wizard material.

Abrim gave him an encouraging smile.

Rincewind looked sideways at the hat. It said nothing. He looked back at the vizier. If the laughter had been weird, the smile made it sound as normal as birdsong. It looked as though the vizier had learned it from diagrams.

'Wild horses wouldn't get me to help you in any way,' he said.

'Ah,' said the vizier. 'A challenge.' He beckoned to the nearest guard.

'Do we have any wild horses in the stables?'

'Some fairly angry ones, master.'

'Infuriate four of them and take them to the turnwise courtyard. And, oh, bring several lengths of chain.'

'Right away, master.'

'Um. Look,' said Rincewind.

'Yes?' said Abrim.

'Well, if you put it like that . . .'

'You wish to make a point?'

'It's the Archchancellor's hat, if you must know,' said Rincewind. 'The symbol of wizardry.'

'Powerful?'

Rincewind shivered. 'Very,' he said.

'Why is it called the Archchancellor's hat?'

'The Archchancellor is the most senior wizard, you see. The leader. But, look—'

Abrim picked up the hat and turned it around and around in his hands.

'It is, you might say, the symbol of office?'

'Absolutely, but look, if you put it on, I'd better warn you—'

Shut up.

Abrim leapt back, the hat dropping to the floor.

The wizard knows nothing. Send him away. We must negotiate.

The vizier stared down at the glittering octarines around the hat.

'I *negotiate*? With an item of apparel?'

I have much to offer, on the right head.

Rincewind was appalled. It has already been indicated that he had the kind of instinct for danger usually found only in certain small rodents, and it was currently battering on the side of his skull in an attempt to run away and hide somewhere.

'Don't listen!' he shouted.

Put me on, said the hat beguilingly, in an ancient voice that sounded as though the speaker had a mouthful of felt.

If there really was a school for viziers, Abrim had come top of the class.

'We'll talk first,' he said. He nodded at the guards, and pointed to Rincewind.

'Take him away and throw him in the spider tank,' he said.

'No, not spiders, on top of everything else!' moaned Rincewind.

The captain of the guard stepped forward and knuckled his forehead respectfully.

'Run out of spiders, master,' he said.

'Oh.' The vizier looked momentarily blank. 'In that case, lock him in the tiger cage.'

The guard hesitated, trying to ignore the sudden outburst of whimpering beside him. 'The tiger's been ill, master. Backwards and forwards all night.'

'Then throw this snivelling coward down the shaft of eternal fire!'

A couple of the guards exchanged glances over the head of Rincewind, who had sunk to his knees.

'Ah. We'll need a bit of notice of that, master—'

'—to get it going again, like.'

The vizier's fist came down hard on the table. The captain of the guard brightened up horribly.

'There's the snake pit, master,' he said. The other guards nodded. There was always the snake pit.

Four heads turned towards Rincewind, who stood up and brushed the sand off his knees.

'How do you feel about snakes?' said one of the guards.

'Snakes? I don't like snakes much—'

'The snake pit,' said Abrim.

'Right. The snake pit,' agreed the guards.

'—I mean, *some* snakes are okay—' Rincewind continued, as two guards grabbed him by the elbows.

In fact there was only one very cautious snake, which remained obstinately curled up in a corner of the shadowy pit watching Rincewind suspiciously, possibly because he reminded it of a mongoose.

'Hi,' it said, eventually. 'Are you a wizard?'

As a line of snake dialogue this was a considerable improvement on the normal string of esses, but Rincewind was sufficiently despondent not to waste time wondering and simply replied, 'It's on my hat, can't you read?'

'In seventeen languages, actually. I taught myself.'

'Really?'

'I sent off for courses. But I try not to read, of course. It's not in character.'

'I suppose it wouldn't be.' It was certainly the most cultured snake voice that Rincewind had ever heard.

'It's the same with the voice, I'm afraid,' the snake added. 'I shouldn't really be talking to you now. Not like this, anyway. I suppose I could grunt a bit. I rather think I should be trying to kill you, in fact.'

'I have curious and unusual powers,' said Rincewind. Fair enough, he thought, an almost total inability to master any form of magic is pretty unusual for a wizard and anyway, it doesn't matter about lying to a snake.

'Gosh. Well, I expect you won't be in here long, then.'

'Hmm?'

'I expect you'll be levitating out of here like a shot, any minute.'

Rincewind looked up at the fifteen-foot-deep walls of the snake pit, and rubbed his bruises.

'I might,' he said cautiously.

'In that case, you wouldn't mind taking me with you, would you?'

'Eh?'

'It's a lot to ask, I know, but this pit is, well, it's the pits.'

'Take you? But you're a snake, it's *your* pit. The idea is that you stay here and people come to you. I mean, I know about these things.'

A shadow behind the snake unfolded itself and stood up.

'That's a pretty unpleasant thing to say about anyone,' it said.

The figure stepped forward, into the pool of light.

It was a young man, taller than Rincewind. That is to say, Rincewind was sitting down, but the boy would have been taller than him even if he was standing up.

To say that he was lean would be to miss a perfect opportunity to use the word 'emaciated'. He looked as though toast racks and deckchairs had figured in his ancestry, and the reason it was so obvious was his clothes.

Rincewind looked again.

He had been right the first time.

The lank-haired figure in front of him was wearing the practically traditional garb for barbarian heroes – a few studded leather thongs, big furry boots, a little leather holdall and goosepimples. There was nothing unusual about that, you'd see a score of similarly-dressed adventurers in any street of Ankh-Morpork, except that you'd never see another one wearing—

The young man followed his gaze, looked down, and shrugged.

'I can't help it,' he said. 'I promised my mother.'

'*Woolly underwear?*'

Strange things were happening in Al Khali that night. There was a certain silveriness rolling in from the sea, which baffled the city's astronomers, but that wasn't the strangest thing. There were little flashes of raw magic discharging off sharp edges, like static electricity, but that wasn't the strangest thing.

The strangest thing walked into a tavern on the edge of the city, where the everlasting wind blew the smell of the desert through every unglazed window, and sat down in the middle of the floor.

The occupants watched it for some time, sipping their coffee laced with desert *orakh*. This drink, made from cacti sap and scorpion venom, is one of the most virulent alcoholic beverages in the universe, but the desert nomads don't drink it for its intoxicating effects. They use it because they need something to mitigate the effect of Klatchian coffee.

Not because you could use the coffee to waterproof roofs. Not because it went through the untrained stomach lining like a hot ball bearing through runny butter. What it did was worse.

It made you knurd.[*]

The sons of the desert glanced suspiciously into their thimble-sized coffee cups, and wondered whether they had overdone the orakh. Were they all seeing the same thing? Would it be foolish to pass a remark? These are the sort of things you need to worry about if you want to retain any credibility as a steely-eyed son of the deep desert. Pointing a shaking finger and saying, 'Hey, look, a box just walked in here on hundreds of little legs, isn't that extraordinary!' would show a terrible and possibly fatal lack of machismo.

The drinkers tried not to catch one another's eye, even when the Luggage slid up to the row of orakh jars against the far wall. The Luggage had a way of standing still that was somehow even more terrible than watching it move about.

Finally one of them said, 'I think it wants a drink.'

There was a long silence, and then one of the others said, with the precision of a chess Grand Master making a killing move, 'What does?'

The rest of the drinkers gazed impassively into their glasses.

There was no sound for a while other than the plop-plopping of a gecko's footsteps across the sweating ceiling.

The first drinker said, 'The demon that's just moved up behind you is what I was referring to, O brother of the sands.'

The current holder of the All-Wadi Imperturbability Championship smiled glassily until he felt a tugging on his robe. The smile stayed where it was but the rest of his face didn't seem to want to be associated with it.

The Luggage was feeling crossed in love and was doing what any sensible person would do in these circumstances, which was get drunk. It had no money and no way of asking for what it wanted, but the Luggage somehow never had much difficulty in making itself understood.

The tavern keeper spent a very long lonely night filling a saucer with orakh, before the Luggage rather unsteadily walked out through one of the walls.

The desert was silent. It wasn't normally silent. It was normally

---

[*] In a truly magical universe everything has its opposite. For example, there's anti-light. That's not the same as darkness, because darkness is merely the absence of light. Anti-light is what you get if you pass through darkness and *out the other side*. On the same basis, a state of knurdeness isn't like sobriety. By comparison, sobriety is like having a bath in cotton wool. Knurdness strips away all illusion, all the comforting pink fog in which people normally spend their lives, and lets them see and think clearly for the first time ever. Then, after they've screamed a bit, they make sure they never get knurd again.

alive with the chirruping of crickets, the buzz of mosquitoes, the hiss and whisper of hunting wings skimming across the cooling sands. But tonight it was silent with the thick, busy silence of dozens of nomads folding their tents and getting the hell out of it.

'I promised my mother,' said the boy. 'I get these colds, you see.'

'Perhaps you should try wearing, well, a bit more clothing?'

'Oh, I couldn't do that. You've got to wear all this leather stuff.'

'I wouldn't call it *all*,' said Rincewind. 'There's not enough of it to call it *all*. Why have you got to wear it?'

'So people know I'm a barbarian hero, of course.'

Rincewind leaned his back against the fetid walls of the snake pit and stared at the boy. He looked at two eyes like boiled grapes, a shock of ginger hair, and a face that was a battleground between its native freckles and the dreadful invading forces of acne.

Rincewind rather enjoyed times like this. They convinced him that he wasn't mad because, if he *was* mad, that left no word at all to describe some of the people he met.

'Barbarian hero,' he murmured.

'It's all right, isn't it? All this leather stuff was very expensive.'

'Yes, but, look – what's your name, lad?'

'Nijel—'

'You see, Nijel—'

'Nijel the Destroyer,' Nijel added.

'You see, Nijel—'

'—the Destroyer—'

'All right, the Destroyer—' said Rincewind desperately.

'—son of Harebut the Provision Merchant—'

'What?'

'You've got to be the son of someone,' Nijel explained. 'It says it here somewhere—' He half-turned and fumbled inside a grubby fur bag, eventually bringing out a thin, torn and grubby book.

'There's a bit in here about selecting your name,' he muttered.

'How come you ended up in this pit, then?'

'I was intending to steal from Creosote's treasury, but I had an asthma attack,' said Nijel, still fumbling through the crackling pages.

Rincewind looked down at the snake, which was still trying to keep out of everyone's way. It had a good thing going in the pit, and knew trouble when it saw it. It wasn't about to cause any aggro for anyone. It stared right back up at Rincewind and shrugged, which is pretty clever for a reptile with no shoulders.

'How long have you been a barbarian hero?'

'I'm just getting started. I've always wanted to be one, you see, and I thought maybe I could pick it up as I went along.' Nijel peered short-sightedly at Rincewind. 'That's all right, isn't it?'

'It's a desperate sort of life, by all accounts,' Rincewind volunteered.

'Have you thought what it might be like selling groceries for the next fifty years?' Nijel muttered darkly.

Rincewind thought.

'Is lettuce involved?' he said.

'Oh yes,' said Nijel, shoving the mysterious book back in his bag. Then he started to pay close attention to the pit walls.

Rincewind sighed. He liked lettuce. It was so incredibly boring. He had spent years in search of boredom, but had never achieved it. Just when he thought he had it in his grasp his life would suddenly become full of near-terminal interest. The thought that someone could voluntarily give up the prospect of being bored for fifty years made him feel quite weak. With fifty years ahead of him, he thought, he could elevate tedium to the status of an art form. There would be no end to the things he wouldn't do.

'Do you know any lamp-wick jokes?' he said, settling himself comfortably on the sand.

'I don't think so,' said Nijel politely, tapping a slab.

'I know hundreds. They are very droll. For example, do you know how many trolls it takes to change a lamp-wick?'

'This slab moves,' said Nijel. 'Look, it's a sort of door. Give me a hand.'

He pushed enthusiastically, his biceps standing out on his arms like peas on a pencil.

'I expect it's some sort of secret passage,' he added. 'Come on, use a bit of magic, will you? It's stuck.'

'Don't you want to hear the rest of the joke?' said Rincewind, in a pained voice. It was warm and dry down here, with no immediate danger, not counting the snake, which was trying to look inconspicuous. Some people were never satisfied.

'I think not right at the moment,' said Nijel. 'I think I would prefer a bit of magical assistance.'

'I'm not very good at it,' said Rincewind. 'Never got the hang of it, see, it's more than just pointing a finger at it and saying "Kazam—"'

There was a sound like a thick bolt of octarine lightning zapping into a heavy rock slab and smashing it into a thousand bits of spitting, white-hot shrapnel, and no wonder.

After a while Nijel slowly got to his feet, beating out the small fires in his vest.

'Yes,' he said, in the voice of one determined not to lose his self-control. 'Well. Very good. We'll just let it cool down a bit, shall we? And then we, then we, we might as well be going.'

He cleared his throat a bit.

'Nnh,' said Rincewind. He was staring fixedly at the end of his finger, holding it out at arm's length in a manner that suggested he was very sorry he hadn't got longer arms.

Nijel peered into the smouldering hole.

'It seems to open into some kind of room,' he said.

'Nnh.'

'After you,' said Nijel. He gave Rincewind a gentle push.

The wizard staggered forward, bumped his head on the rock and didn't appear to notice, and then rebounded into the hole.

Nijel patted the wall, and his brow wrinkled. 'Can you feel something?' he said. 'Should the stone be trembling?'

'Nnh.'

'Are you all right?'

'Nnh.'

Nijel put his ear to the stones. 'There's a very strange noise,' he said. 'A sort of humming.' A bit of dust shook itself free from the mortar over his head and floated down.

Then a couple of much heavier rocks danced free from the walls of the pits and thudded into the sand.

Rincewind had already staggered off down the tunnel, making little shocked noises and completely ignoring the stones that were missing him by inches and, in some cases, hitting him by kilograms.

If he had been in any state to notice it, he would have known what was happening. The air had a greasy feel and smelled like burning tin. Faint rainbows filmed every point and edge. A magical charge was building up somewhere very close to them, and it was a big one, and it was trying to earth itself.

A handy wizard, even one as incapable as Rincewind, stood out like a copper lighthouse.

Nijel blundered out of the rumbling, broiling dust and bumped into him standing, surrounded by an octarine corona, in another cave.

Rincewind looked terrible. Creosote would have probably noted his flashing eyes and floating hair.

He looked like someone who had just eaten a handful of pineal glands and washed them down with a pint of adrenochrome. He looked so high you could bounce intercontinental TV off him.

Every single hair stood out from his head, giving off little sparks. Even his skin gave the impression that it was trying to get away from him. His eyes appeared to be spinning horizontally; when he opened his mouth, peppermint sparks flashed from his teeth. Where he had trodden, stone melted or grew ears or turned into something small and scaly and purple and flew away.

'I say,' said Nijel, 'are you all right?'

'Nnh,' said Rincewind, and the syllable turned into a large doughnut.

'You don't *look* all right,' said Nijel with what might be called, in the circumstances, unusual perspicacity.

'Nnh.'

'Why not try getting us out of here?' Nijel added, and wisely flung himself flat on the floor.

Rincewind nodded like a puppet and pointed his loaded digit at the ceiling, which melted like ice under a blowlamp.

Still the rumbling went on, sending its disquieting harmonics dancing through the palace. It is a well-known factoid that there are frequencies that can cause panic, and frequencies that can cause embarrassing incontinence, but the shaking rock was resonating at the frequency that causes reality to melt and run out at the corners.

Nijel regarded the dripping ceiling and cautiously tasted it.

'Lime custard,' he said, and added, 'I suppose there's no chance of stairs, is there?'

More fire burst from Rincewind's ravaged fingers, coalescing into an almost perfect escalator, except that possibly no other moving staircase in the universe was floored with alligator skin.

Nijel grabbed the gently spinning wizard and leapt aboard.

Fortunately they had reached the top before the magic vanished, very suddenly.

Sprouting out of the centre of the palace, shattering rooftops like a mushroom bursting through an ancient pavement, was a white tower taller than any other building in Al Khali.

Huge double doors had opened at its base and out of them, striding along as though they owned the place, were dozens of wizards. Rincewind thought he could recognise a few faces, faces which he'd seen before bumbling vaguely in lecture theatres or peering amiably at the world in the University grounds. They weren't faces built for evil. They didn't have a fang between them.

But there was some common denominator among their expressions that could terrify a thoughtful person.

Nijel was pulled back behind a handy wall. He found himself looking into Rincewind's worried eyes.

'Hey, that's magic!'

'I know,' said Rincewind, 'It's not right!' Nijel peered up at the sparkling tower.

'But—'

'It *feels* wrong,' said Rincewind. 'Don't ask me why.'

Half a dozen of the Seriph's guards erupted from an arched doorway and plunged towards the wizards, their headlong rush made all the more sinister by their ghastly battle silences. For a moment their swords flashed in the sunlight, and then a couple of the wizards turned, extended their hands and—

Nijel looked away.

'Urgh,' he said.

A few curved swords dropped on to the cobbles.

'I think we should very quietly go away,' said Rincewind.

'But didn't you see what they just turned them into?'

'Dead people,' said Rincewind. 'I know. I don't want to think about it.'

Nijel thought he'd never stop thinking about it, especially around 3am on windy nights. The point about being killed by magic was that it was so much more *inventive* than, say, steel; there were all sorts of interesting new ways to die, and he couldn't put out of his mind the shapes he'd seen, just for an instant, before the wash of octarine fire had mercifully engulfed them.

'I didn't think wizards were like that,' he said, as they hurried down a passageway. 'I thought they were more, well, more silly than sinister. Sort of figures of fun.'

'Laugh that one off, then,' muttered Rincewind. 'But they just killed them, without even—'

'I wish you wouldn't go on about it. I saw it as well.'

Nijel drew back. His eyes narrowed.

'You're a wizard, too,' he said accusingly.

'Not that kind I'm not,' said Rincewind shortly.

'What kind are you, then?'

'The non-killing kind.'

'It was the way they looked at them as if it just didn't matter—' said Nijel, shaking his head. 'That was the worst bit.'

'Yes.'

Rincewind dropped the single syllable heavily in front of Nijel's train of thought, like a tree trunk. The boy shuddered, but at least he shut up. Rincewind actually began to feel sorry for him, which was very unusual – he normally felt he needed all his pity for himself.

'Is that the first time you've seen someone killed?' he said.

'Yes.'

'Exactly how long have you been a barbarian hero?'

'Er. What year is this?'

Rincewind peered around a corner, but such people as were around and vertical were far too busy panicking to bother about them.

'Out on the road, then?' he said quietly. 'Lost track of time? I know how it is. This is the Year of the Hyena.'

'Oh. In that case, about—' Nijel's lips moved soundlessly – 'about three days. Look,' he added quickly, 'how can people kill like that? Without even thinking about it?'

'I don't know,' said Rincewind, in a tone of voice that suggested he *was* thinking about it.

'I mean, even when the vizier had me thrown in the snake pit, at least he seemed to be taking an interest.'

'That's good. Everyone should have an interest.'

'I mean, he even laughed!'

'Ah. A sense of humour, too.'

Rincewind felt that he could see his future with the same crystal clarity that a man falling off a cliff sees the ground, and for much the same reason. So when Nijel said: 'They just pointed their fingers without so much as—', Rincewind snapped: 'Just shut up, will you? How do you think I feel about it? *I'm* a wizard, too!'

'Yes, well, *you'll* be all right then,' muttered Nijel.

It wasn't a heavy blow, because even in a rage Rincewind still had muscles like tapioca, but it caught the side of Nijel's head and knocked him down more by the weight of surprise than its intrinsic energy.

'Yes, I'm a wizard all right,' Rincewind hissed. 'A wizard who isn't much good at magic! I've managed to survive up till now by not being important enough to die! And when all wizards are hated and feared, exactly how long do you think I'll last?'

'That's ridiculous!'

Rincewind couldn't have been more taken aback if Nijel had struck him.

'What?'

'Idiot! All you have to do is stop wearing that silly robe and get rid of that daft hat and no one will even know you're a wizard!'

Rincewind's mouth opened and shut a few times as he gave a very lifelike impression of a goldfish trying to grasp the concept of tap-dancing.

'Stop wearing the robe?' he said.

'Sure. All those tatty sequins and things, it's a total give-away,' said Nijel, struggling to his feet.

'Get rid of the hat?'

'You've got to admit that going around with "wizzard" written on it is a bit of a heavy hint.'

Rincewind gave him a worried grin.

'Sorry,' he said, 'I don't quite follow you—'

'Just get rid of them. It's easy enough, isn't it? Just drop them somewhere and then you could be a, a, well, whatever. Something that isn't a wizard.'

There was a pause, broken only by the distant sounds of fighting.

'Er,' said Rincewind, and shook his head. 'You've lost me there . . .'

'Good grief, it's perfectly simple to understand!'

' . . . not sure I quite catch your drift . . .' murmured Rincewind, his face ghastly with sweat.

'You can just *stop being a wizard*.'

Rincewind's lips moved soundlessly as he replayed every word, one at a time, then all at once.

'What?' he said, and then he said, 'Oh.'

'Got it? Want to try it one more time?'

Rincewind nodded gloomily.

'I don't think you understand. A wizard isn't what you *do*, it's what you *are*. If I wasn't a wizard, I wouldn't be *anything*.' He took off his hat and twiddled nervously with the loose star on its point, causing a few more cheap sequins to part company.

'I mean, it's got wizard written on my hat,' he said. 'It's very important—'

He stopped and stared at the hat.

'Hat,' he said vaguely, aware of some importunate memory pressing its nose up against the windows of his mind.

'It's a *good* hat,' said Nijel, who felt that something was expected of him.

'Hat,' said Rincewind again, and then added, 'the hat! We've got to get the hat!'

'You've got the hat,' Nijel pointed out.

'Not this hat, the other hat. And Conina!'

He took a few random steps along a passageway, and then sidled back.

'Where do you suppose they are?' he said.

'Who?'

'There's a magic hat I've got to find. And a girl.'

'Why?'

'It might be rather difficult to explain. I think there might be screaming involved somewhere.'

Nijel didn't have much of a jaw but, such as it was, he stuck it out.

'There's a girl needs rescuing?' he said grimly.

Rincewind hesitated. 'Someone will probably need rescuing,' he admitted. 'It might possibly be her. Or at least in her vicinity.'

'Why didn't you say so? This is more like it, this is what I was expecting. This is what heroism is all about. Let's go!'

There was another crash, and the sound of people yelling.

'Where?' said Rincewind.

'Anywhere!'

Heroes usually have an ability to rush madly around crumbling palaces they hardly know, save everyone and get out just before the whole place blows up or sinks into the swamp. In fact Nijel and Rincewind visited the kitchens, assorted throne rooms, the stables (twice) and what seemed to Rincewind like several miles of corridor. Occasionally groups of black-clad guards would scurry past them, without so much as a second glance.

'This is ridiculous,' said Nijel. 'Why don't we ask someone? Are you all right?'

Rincewind leaned against a pillar decorated with embarrassing sculpture and wheezed.

'You could grab a guard and torture the information out of him,' he said, gulping air. Nijel gave him an odd look.

'Wait here,' he said, and wandered off until he found a servant industriously ransacking a cupboard.

'Excuse me,' he said, 'which way to the harem?'

'Turn left three doors down,' said the man, without looking around.

'Right.'

He wandered back again and told Rincewind.

'Yes, but did you torture him?'

'No.'

'That wasn't very barbaric of you, was it?'

'Well, I'm working up to it,' said Nijel. 'I mean, I didn't say "thank you".'

Thirty seconds later they pushed aside a heavy bead curtain and entered the seraglio of the Seriph of Al Khali.

114

There were gorgeous songbirds in cages of gold filigree. There were tinkling fountains. There were pots of rare orchids through which humming-birds skimmed like tiny, brilliant jewels. There were about twenty young women wearing enough clothes for, say, about half a dozen, huddled together in a silent crowd.

Rincewind had eyes for none of this. That is not to say that the sight of several dozen square yards of hip and thigh in every shade from pink to midnight black didn't start certain tides flowing deep in the crevasses of his libido, but they were swamped by the considerably bigger flood of panic at the sight of four guards turning towards him with scimitars in their hands and the light of murder in their eyes.

Without hesitation, Rincewind took a step backwards.

'Over to you, friend,' he said.

'Right!'

Nijel drew his sword and held it out in front of him, his arms trembling at the effort.

There were a few seconds of total silence as everyone waited to see what would happen next. And then Nijel uttered the battle cry that Rincewind would never quite forget to the end of his life.

'Erm,' he said, 'excuse me . . .'

'It seems a shame,' said a small wizard.

The others didn't speak. It *was* a shame, and there wasn't a man among them who couldn't hear the hot whine of guilt all down their backbones. But, as so often happens by that strange alchemy of the soul, the guilt made them arrogant and reckless.

'Just shut up, will you?' said the temporary leader. He was called Benado Sconner, but there is something in the air tonight that suggests that it is not worth committing his name to memory. The air is dark and heavy and full of ghosts.

The Unseen University isn't empty, there just aren't any people there.

But of course the six wizards sent to burn down the Library aren't afraid of ghosts, because they're so charged with magic that they practically buzz as they walk, they're wearing robes more splendid than any Archchancellor has worn, their pointy hats are more pointed than any hats have hitherto been, and the reason they're standing so close together is entirely coincidental.

'It's awfully dark in here,' said the smallest of the wizards.

'It's midnight,' said Sconner sharply, 'and the only dangerous things in here are us. Isn't that right, boys?'

There was a chorus of vague murmurs. They were all in awe of Sconner, who was rumoured to do positive-thinking exercises.

'And we're not scared of a few old books, are we, lads?' He glowered at the smallest wizard. 'You're not, are you?' he added sharply.

'Me? Oh. No. Of course not. They're just paper, like *he* said,' said the wizard quickly.

'Well, then.'

'There's ninety thousand of them, mind,' said another wizard.

'I always heard there was no end to 'em,' said another. 'It's all down to the dimensions, I heard, like what we see is only the tip of the whatever, you know, the thing that is mostly underwater—'

'Hippopotamus?'

'Alligator?'

'Ocean?'

'Look, just shut up, all of you!' shouted Sconner. He hesitated. The darkness seemed to suck at the sound of his voice. It packed the air like feathers.

He pulled himself together a bit.

'Right then,' he said, and turned towards the forbidding doors of the Library.

He raised his hands, made a few complicated gestures in which his fingers, in some eye-watering way, appeared to pass through each other, and shattered the doors into sawdust.

The waves of silence poured back again, strangling the sound of falling woodchips.

There was no doubt that the doors were smashed. Four forlorn hinges hung trembling from the frame, and a litter of broken benches and shelves lay in the wreckage. Even Sconner was a little surprised.

'There,' he said. 'It's as easy as that. You see? Nothing happened to me. Right?'

There was a shuffling of curly-toed boots. The darkness beyond the doorway was limned with the indistinct, eye-aching glow of thaumaturgic radiation as possibility particles exceeded the speed of reality in a strong magical field.

'Now then,' said Sconner, brightly, 'who would like the honour of setting the fire?'

Ten silent seconds later he said, 'In that case I will do it myself. Honestly, I might as well be talking to the wall.'

He strode through the doorway and hurried across the floor to the little patch of starlight that lanced down from the glass dome high above the centre of the Library (although, of course, there has always been considerable debate about the precise geography of the place; heavy concentrations of magic distort time and space, and it is possible that the Library doesn't even have an edge, never mind a centre).

He stretched out his arms.

'There. See? Absolutely nothing has happened. Now come on in.'

The other wizards did so, with great reluctance and a tendency to duck as they passed through the ravished arch.

'Okay,' said Sconner, with some satisfaction. 'Now, has everyone got their matches as instructed? Magical fire won't work, not on these books, so I want everyone to—'

'Something moved up there,' said the smallest wizard.

Sconner blinked.

'What?'

'Something moved up by the dome,' said the wizard, adding by way of explanation, 'I saw it.'

Sconner squinted upwards into the bewildering shadows, and decided to exert a bit of authority.

'Nonsense,' he said briskly. He pulled out a bundle of foul-smelling yellow matches, and said, 'Now, I want you all to pile—'

'I did see it, you know,' said the small wizard, sulkily.

'All right, what did you see?'

'Well, I'm not exactly—'

'You don't know, do you?' snapped Sconner.

'I saw *someth*—'

'You don't know!' repeated Sconner, 'You're just seeing shadows, just trying to undermine my authority, isn't that it?' Sconner hesitated, and his eyes glazed momentarily. 'I am calm,' he intoned, 'I am totally in control. I will not let—'

'It *was*—'

'Listen, shortarse, you can just jolly well shut up, all right?'

One of the other wizards, who had been staring upwards to conceal his embarrassment, gave a strangled little cough.

'Er, Sconner—'

'And that goes for you too!' Sconner pulled himself to his full, bristling height and flourished the matches.

'As *I* was saying,' he said, 'I want you to light the matches and – I suppose I'll have to show you how to light matches, for the benefit of shortarse there – and *I'm not out of the window, you know.* Good grief. Look at me. You take a match—'

He lit a match, the darkness blossomed into a ball of sulphurous white light, and the Librarian dropped on him like the descent of Man.

117

They all knew the Librarian, in the same definite but diffused way that people know walls and floors and all the other minor but necessary scenery on the stage of life. If they recalled him at all, it was as a sort of gentle mobile sigh, sitting under his desk repairing books, or knuckling his way among the shelves in search of secret smokers. Any wizard unwise enough to hazard a clandestine rollup wouldn't know anything about it until a soft leathery hand reached up and removed the offending home-made, but the Librarian never made a fuss, he just looked extremely hurt and sorrowful about the whole sad business and then ate it.

Whereas what was now attempting with considerable effort to unscrew Sconner's head by the ears was a screaming nightmare with its lips curled back to reveal long yellow fangs.

The terrified wizards turned to run and found themselves bumping into bookshelves that had unaccountably blocked the aisles. The smallest wizard yelped and rolled under a table laden with atlases, and lay with his hands over his ears to block out the dreadful sounds as the remaining wizards tried to escape.

Eventually there was nothing but silence, but it was that particularly massive silence created by something moving very stealthily, as it might be, in search of something else. The smallest wizard ate the tip of his hat out of sheer terror.

The silent mover grabbed him by the leg and pulled him gently but firmly out into the open, where he gibbered a bit with his eyes shut and then, when ghastly teeth failed to meet in his throat, ventured a quick glance.

The Librarian picked him up by the scruff of his neck and dangled him reflectively a foot off the ground, just out of reach of a small and elderly wire-haired terrier who was trying to remember how to bite people's ankles.

'Er—' said the wizard, and was then thrown in an almost flat trajectory through the broken doorway, where his fall was broken by the floor.

After a while a shadow next to him said, 'Well, that's it, then. Anyone seen that daft bastard Sconner?'

And a shadow on the other side of him said, 'I think my neck's broken.'

'Who's that?'

'*That daft bastard*,' said the shadow, nastily.

'Oh. Sorry, Sconner.'

Sconner stood up, his whole body now outlined in magical aura. He was trembling with rage as he raised his hands.

'I'll show that wretched throwback to respect his evolutionary superiors—' he snarled.

'Get him, lads!'

And Sconner was borne to the flagstones again under the weight of all five wizards.

'Sorry, but—'

'—you know that if you use—'

'—magic near the Library, with all the magic that's in there—'

'—get one thing wrong and it's a critical Mass and then—'

'BANG! Goodnight, world!'

Sconner growled. The wizards sitting on him decided that getting up was not the wisest thing they could do at this point.

Eventually he said, 'Right. You're right. Thank you. It was wrong of me to lose my temper like that. Clouded my judgment. Essential to be dispassionate. You're absolutely right. Thank you. Get off.'

They risked it. Sconner stood up.

'That monkey,' he said, 'has eaten its last banana. Fetch—'

'Er. Ape, Sconner,' said the smallest wizard, unable to stop himself. 'It's an ape, you see. Not a monkey . . .'

He wilted under the stare.

'Who cares? Ape, monkey, what's the difference?' said Sconner. 'What's the difference, Mr Zoologist?'

'I don't know, Sconner,' said the wizard meekly. 'I think it's a class thing.'

'Shut up.'

'Yes, Sconner.'

'You ghastly little man,' said Sconner.

He turned and added, in a voice as level as a sawblade: 'I am perfectly controlled. My mind is as cool as a bald mammoth. My intellect is absolutely in charge. Which one of you sat on my head? No, I must not get angry. I am *not* angry. I am thinking positively. My faculties are fully engaged – do any of you wish to argue?'

'No, Sconner,' they chorused.

'Then get me a dozen barrels of oil and all the kindling you can find! That ape's gonna *fry*!'

From high in the Library roof, home of owls and bats and other things, there was a clink of chain and the sound of glass being broken as respectfully as possible.

'They don't look very worried,' said Nijel, slightly affronted.

'How can I put this?' said Rincewind. 'When they come to write the list of Great Battle Cries of the World, "Erm, excuse me" won't be one of them.'

He stepped to one side. 'I'm not with him,' he said earnestly to a grinning guard. 'I just met him, somewhere. In a pit.' He gave a little laugh. 'This sort of thing happens to me all the time,' he said.

The guards stared through him.

'Erm,' he said.

'Okay,' he said.

He sidled back to Nijel.

'Are you any good with that sword?'

Without taking his eyes off the guards, Nijel fumbled in his pack and handed Rincewind the book.

'I've read the whole of chapter three,' he said. 'It's got illustrations.'

Rincewind turned over the crumpled pages. The book had been used so hard you could have shuffled it, but what was probably once the front cover showed a rather poor woodcut of a muscular man. He had arms like two bags full of footballs, and he was standing knee-deep in languorous women and slaughtered victims with a smug expression on his face.

About him was the legend: *Inne Juste 7 Dayes I wille make You a Barbearian Hero!* Below it, in slightly smaller type, was the name: *Cohen the Barbarean.* Rincewind rather doubted it. He had met Cohen and, while he could read after a fashion, the old boy had never really mastered the pen and still signed his name with an 'X', which he usually spelled wrong. On the other hand, he gravitated rapidly to anything with money in it.

Rincewind looked again at the illustration, and then at Nijel.

'Seven days?'

'Well, I'm a slow reader.'

'Ah,' said Rincewind.

'And I didn't bother with chapter six, because I promised my mother I'd stick with just the looting and pillaging, until I find the right girl.'

'And this book teaches you how to be a hero?'

'Oh, yes. It's very good.' Nijel gave him a worried glance. 'That's all right, isn't it? It cost a lot of money.'

'Well, er. I suppose you'd better get on with it, then.'

Nijel squared his, for want of a better word, shoulders, and waved his sword again.

'You four had better just jolly well watch out,' he said, 'or . . . hold on a moment.' He took the book from Rincewind and riffled through the pages until he found what he was looking for, and continued, 'Yes, or "the chill winds of fate will blow through your bleached skeletons/ the legions of Hell will drown your living soul in acid". There. How d'you like them . . . excuse me a moment . . . apples?'

There was a metallic chord as four men drew their swords in perfect harmony.

Nijel's sword became a blur. It made a complicated figure eight in the air in front of him, spun over his arm, flicked from hand to hand behind his back, seemed to orbit his chest twice, and leapt like a salmon.

One or two of the harem ladies broke into spontaneous applause. Even the guards looked impressed.

'That's a Triple Orcthrust with Extra Flip,' said Nijel proudly. 'I broke a lot of mirrors learning that. Look, they're stopping.'

'They've never seen anything like it, I imagine,' said Rincewind weakly, judging the distance to the doorway.

'I should think not.'

'Especially the last bit, where it stuck in the ceiling.'

Nijel looked upwards.

'Funny,' he said, 'it always did that at home, too. I wonder what I'm doing wrong.'

'Search me.'

'Gosh, I'm sorry,' said Nijel, as the guards seemed to realise that the entertainment was over and closed in for the kill.

'Don't blame yourself—' said Rincewind, as Nijel reached up and tried unsuccessfully to free the blade.

'Thank you.'

'—I'll do it for you.'

Rincewind considered his next step. In fact, he considered several steps. But the door was too far away and anyway, by the sound of it, things were not a lot healthier out there.

There was only one thing for it. He'd have to try magic.

He raised his hand and two of the men fell over. He raised his other hand and the other two fell over.

Just as he was beginning to wonder about this, Conina stepped daintily over the prone bodies, idly rubbing the sides of her hands.

'I thought you'd never turn up,' she said. 'Who's your friend?'

As has already been indicated, the Luggage seldom shows any sign of emotion, or at least any emotion less extreme than blind rage and hatred, and therefore it is hard to gauge its feelings when it woke up, a few miles outside Al Khali, on its lid in a dried-up wadi with its legs in the air.

Even a few minutes after dawn the air was like the breath of a furnace. After a certain amount of rocking the Luggage managed to get most of its feet pointing the right way, and stood doing a complicated slow-motion jig to keep as few of them on the burning sand as possible.

It wasn't lost. It always knew exactly where it was. It was always *here*.

It was just that everywhere else seemed to have been temporarily mislaid.

After some deliberation the Luggage turned and walked, very slowly, into a boulder.

It backed away and sat down, rather puzzled. It felt as though it had been stuffed with hot feathers, and it was dimly aware of the benefits of shade and a nice cool drink.

After a few false starts it walked to the top of a nearby sand dune, which gave it an unrivalled view of hundreds of other dunes.

Deep in its heartwood the Luggage was troubled. It had been spurned. It had been told to go *away*. It had been rejected. It had also drunk enough orakh to poison a small country.

If there is one thing a travel accessory needs more than anything else, it is someone to belong to. The Luggage set off unsteadily across the scorching sand, full of hope.

'I don't think we've got time for introductions,' said Rincewind, as a distant part of the palace collapsed with a thump that vibrated the floor. 'It's time we were—'

He realised he was talking to himself.

Nijel let go of the sword.

Conina stepped forward.

'Oh, no,' said Rincewind, but it was far too late. The world had suddenly separated into two parts – the bit which contained Nijel and Conina, and the bit which contained everything else. The air between them crackled. Probably, in their half, a distant orchestra was playing, bluebirds were tweeting, little pink clouds were barrelling through the sky, and all the other things that happen at times like this. When that sort of thing is going on, mere collapsing palaces in the next world don't stand a chance.

'Look, perhaps we can just get the introductions over with,' said Rincewind desperately. 'Nijel—'

'—the Destroyer—' said Nijel dreamily.

'All right, Nijel the Destroyer,' said Rincewind, and added, 'Son of Harebut the—'

'Mighty,' said Nijel. Rincewind gaped a bit, and then shrugged.

'Well, whoever,' he conceded. 'Anyway, this is Conina. Which is rather a coincidence, because you'll be interested to know that her father was mmph.'

Conina, without turning her gaze, had extended a hand and held Rincewind's face in a gentle grip which, with only a slight increase in finger pressure, could have turned his head into a bowling ball.

'Although I could be mistaken,' he added, when she took her hand away. 'Who knows? Who cares? What does it matter?'

They didn't take any notice.

'I'll just go and see if I can find the hat, shall I?' he said.

'Good idea,' murmured Conina.

'I expect I shall get murdered, but I don't mind,' said Rincewind.

'Jolly good,' said Nijel.

'I don't expect anyone will even notice I'm gone,' said Rincewind.

'Fine, fine,' said Conina.

'I shall be chopped into small pieces, I expect,' said Rincewind, walking toward the door at the speed of a dying snail.

Conina blinked.

'What hat?' she said, and then, 'Oh, that hat.'

'I suppose there's no possible chance that you two might be of some assistance?' Rincewind ventured.

Somewhere inside Conina and Nijel's private world the bluebirds went to roost, the little pink clouds drifted away and the orchestra packed up and sneaked off to do a private gig at a nightclub somewhere. A bit of reality reasserted itself.

Conina dragged her admiring gaze away from Nijel's rapt face and turned it on to Rincewind, where it grew slightly cooler.

She sidled across the floor and grabbed the wizard by the arm.

'Look,' she said, 'you won't tell him who I *really* am, will you? Only boys get funny ideas and – well, anyway, if you do I will personally break all your—'

'I'll be far too busy,' said Rincewind, 'what with you helping me get the hat and everything. Not that I can imagine what you see in him,' he added, haughtily.

'He's nice. I don't seem to meet many nice people.'

'Yes, well—'

'He's looking at us!'

'So what? You're not frightened of him, are you?'

'Suppose he talks to me!'

Rincewind looked blank. Not for the first time in his life, he felt that there were whole areas of human experience that had passed him by, if areas could pass by people. Maybe *he* had passed *them* by. He shrugged.

'Why did you let them take you off to the harem without a fight?' he said.

'I've always wanted to know what went on in one.'

There was a pause. 'Well?' said Rincewind.

'Well, we all sat round, and then after a bit the Seriph came in, and then he asked me over and said that since I was new it would be my turn, and then, you'll never guess what he wanted me to do. The girls said it's the only thing he's interested in.'

'Er.'

'Are you all right?'

'Fine, fine,' Rincewind muttered.

'Your face has gone all shiny.'

'No, I'm fine, fine.'

'He asked me to tell him a story.'

'What about?' said Rincewind suspiciously.

'The other girls said he prefers something with rabbits in it.'

'Ah. Rabbits.'

'Small fluffy white ones. But the only stories I know are the ones father taught me when I was little, and I don't think they're really suitable.'

'Not many rabbits?'

'Lots of arms and legs being chopped off,' said Conina, and sighed. 'That's why you mustn't tell him about me, you see? I'm just not cut out for a normal life.'

'Telling stories in a harem isn't bloody normal,' said Rincewind. 'It'll never catch on.'

'He's looking at us again!' Conina grabbed Rincewind's arm.

He shook her off. 'Oh, good grief,' he said, and hurried across the room to Nijel, who grabbed his other arm.

'You haven't been telling her about me, have you?' he demanded. 'I'll never live it down if you've told her that I'm only just learning how—'

'Nonono. She just wants you to help us. It's a sort of quest.'

Nijel's eyes gleamed.

'You mean a geas?' he said.

124

'Pardon?'

'It's in the book. To be a proper hero it says you've got to labour under a geas.'

Rincewind's forehead wrinkled. 'Is it a sort of bird?'

'I think it's more a sort of obligation, or something,' said Nijel, but without much certainty.

'Sounds more like a kind of bird to me,' said Rincewind, 'I'm sure I read it in a bestiary once. Large. Couldn't fly. Big pink legs, it had.' His face went blank as his ears digested what they had just heard his lips say.

Five seconds later they were out of the room, leaving behind four prone guards and the harem ladies themselves, who settled down for a bit of story-telling.

The desert rimwards of Al Khali is bisected by the river Tsort, famed in myth and lies, which insinuates its way through the brown landscapes like a long damp descriptive passage punctuated with sandbanks. And every sandbank is covered with sunbaked logs, and most of the logs are the kind of logs that have teeth, and most of the logs opened one lazy eye at the distant sounds of splashing from upstream, and suddenly most of the logs had legs. A dozen scaly bodies slipped into the turbid waters, which rolled over them again. The dark waters were unruffled, except for a few inconsequential V-shaped ripples.

The Luggage paddled gently down the stream. The water was making it feel a little better. It spun gently in the weak current, the focus of several mysterious little swirls that sped across the surface of the water.

The ripples converged.

The Luggage jerked. Its lid flew open. It shot under the surface with a brief, despairing creak.

The chocolate-coloured waters of the Tsort rolled back again. They were getting good at it.

And the tower of sourcery loomed over Al Khali like a vast and beautiful fungus, the kind that appear in books with little skull-and-crossbones symbols beside them.

The Seriph's guard had fought back, but there were now quite a lot of bewildered frogs and newts around the base of the tower, and they were the fortunate ones. They still had arms and legs, of a sort, and most of their essential organs were still on the inside. The city was under the rule of sourcery . . . martial lore.

Some of the buildings nearest the base of the tower were already turning into the bright white marble that the wizards obviously preferred.

The trio stared out through a hole in the palace walls.

'Very impressive,' said Conina critically. 'Your wizards are more powerful than I thought.'

'Not *my* wizards,' said Rincewind. 'I don't know whose wizards they are. I don't like it. All the wizards *I* knew couldn't stick one brick on another.'

'I don't like the idea of wizards ruling everybody,' said Nijel. 'Of course, as a hero I am philosophically against the whole idea of wizardry in any case. The time will come when,' his eyes glazed slightly, as if he was trying to remember something he'd seen somewhere, 'the time will come when all wizardry has gone from the face of the world and the sons of, of – anyway, we can all be a bit more practical about things,' he added lamely.

'Read it in a book, did you?' said Rincewind sourly. 'Any geas in it?'

'He's got a point,' said Conina. 'I've nothing against wizards, but it's not as if they do much good. They're just a bit of decoration, really. Up to now.'

Rincewind pulled off his hat. It was battered, stained and covered with rock dust, bits of it had been sheared off, the point was dented and the star was shedding sequins like pollen, but the word 'Wizzard' was still just readable under the grime.

'See this?' he demanded, red in the face. 'Do you see it? Do you? What does it tell you?'

'That you can't spell?' said Nijel.

'What? No! It says I'm a wizard, that's what! Twenty years behind the staff, and proud of it! I've done my time, I have! I've pas – I've sat dozens of exams! If all the spells I've read were piled on top of one another, they'd . . . it'd . . . you'd have a lot of spells!'

'Yes, but—' Conina began.

'*Yes?*'

'You're not actually very good at them, are you?'

Rincewind glared at her. He tried to think of what to say next, and a small receptor area opened in his mind at the same time as an inspiration particle, its path bent and skewed by a trillion random events, screamed down through the atmosphere and burst silently just at the right spot.

'Talent just defines what you do,' he said. 'It doesn't define what you are. Deep down, I mean. When you know what you are, you can do anything.'

He thought a bit more and added, 'That's what makes sourcerers so powerful. The important thing is to know what you really are.'

There was a pause full of philosophy.

'Rincewind?' said Conina, kindly.

'Hmm?' said Rincewind, who was still wondering how the words got into his head.

'You really are an idiot. Do you know that?'

'*You will all stand very still.*'

Abrim the vizier stepped out of a ruined archway. He was wearing the Archchancellor's hat.

The desert fried under the flame of the sun. Nothing moved except the shimmering air, hot as a stolen volcano, dry as a skull.

A basilisk lay panting in the baking shade of a rock, dribbling corrosive yellow slime. For the last five minutes its ears had been detecting the faint thump of hundreds of little legs moving unsteadily over the dunes, which seemed to indicate that dinner was on the way.

It blinked its legendary eyes and uncoiled twenty feet of hungry body, winding out and on to the sand like fluid death.

The Luggage staggered to a halt and raised its lid threateningly. The basilisk hissed, but a little uncertainly, because it had never seen a walking box before, and certainly never one with lots of alligator teeth stuck in its lid. There were also scraps of leathery hide adhering to it, as though it had been involved in a fight in a handbag factory, and in a way that the basilisk wouldn't have been able to describe even if it could talk, it appeared to be glaring.

Right, the reptile thought, if that's the way you want to play it.

It turned on the Luggage a stare like a diamond drill, a stare that nipped in via the staree's eyeballs and flayed the brain from the inside, a stare that tore the frail net curtains on the windows of the soul, a stare that—

The basilisk realised something was very wrong. An entirely new and unwelcome sensation started to arise just behind its saucer-shaped eyes. It started small, like the little itch in those few square inches of back that no amount of writhing will allow you to scratch, and grew until it became a second, red-hot, internal sun.

The basilisk was feeling a terrible, overpowering and irresistible urge to blink . . .

It did something incredibly unwise.

It blinked.

'He's talking through his hat,' said Rincewind.

'Eh?' said Nijel, who was beginning to realise that the world of the barbarian hero wasn't the clean, simple place he had imagined in the days when the most exciting thing he had ever done was stack parsnips.

'The hat's talking through him, you mean,' said Conina, and she backed away too, as one tends to do in the presence of horror.

'Eh?'

'*I will not harm you. You have been of some service,*' said Abrim, stepping forwards with his hands out. '*But you are right. He thought he could gain power through wearing me. Of course, it is the other way around. An astonishingly devious and clever mind.*'

'So you tried his head on for size?' said Rincewind. He shuddered. *He'd* worn the hat. Obviously he didn't have the right kind of mind. Abrim did have the right kind of mind, and now his eyes were grey and colourless, his skin was pale and he walked as though his body was hanging down from his head.

Nijel had pulled out his book and was riffling feverishly through the pages.

'What on earth are you doing?' said Conina, not taking her eyes off the ghastly figure.

'I'm looking up the Index of Wandering Monsters,' said Nijel. 'Do you think it's an Undead? They're awfully difficult to kill, you need garlic and—'

'You won't find this in there,' said Rincewind slowly. 'It's – it's a vampire hat.'

'Of course, it might be a Zombie,' said Nijel, running his finger down a page. 'It says here you need black pepper and sea salt, but—'

'You're supposed to fight the bloody things, not eat them,' said Conina.

'*This is a mind I can use,*' said the hat. '*Now I can fight back. I shall rally wizardry. There is room for only one magic in this world, and I embody it. Sourcery beware!*'

'Oh, no,' said Rincewind under his breath.

'*Wizardry has learned a lot in the last twenty centuries. This upstart can be beaten. You three will follow me.*'

It wasn't a request. It wasn't even an order. It was a sort of forecast. The voice of the hat went straight to the hindbrain without bothering to deal with the consciousness, and Rincewind's legs started to move of their own accord.

The other two also jerked forward, walking with the awkward doll-like jerking that suggested that they, too, were on invisible strings.

'Why the oh, no?' said Conina, 'I mean, "Oh, no" on general principles I can understand, but was there any particular reason?'

'If we get a chance we must run,' said Rincewind.

'Did you have anywhere in mind?'

'It probably won't matter. We're doomed anyway.'

'Why?' said Nijel.

'Well,' said Rincewind, 'have you ever heard of the Mage Wars?'

There were a lot of things on the Disc that owed their origin to the Mage Wars. Sapient pearwood was one of them.

The original tree was probably perfectly normal and spent its days drinking groundwater and eating sunshine in a state of blessed unawareness, and then the magic wars broke around it and pitch-forked its genes into a state of acute perspicacity.

It also left it ingrained, as it were, with a bad temper. But sapient pearwood got off lightly.

Once, when the level of background magic on the Disc was young and high and found every opportunity to burst on the world, wizards were all as powerful as sourcerers and built their towers on every hilltop. And if there was one thing a really powerful wizard can't stand, it is another wizard. His instinctive approach to diplomacy is to hex 'em till they glow, then curse them in the dark.

That could only mean one thing. All right, two things. Three things.

All-out. Thaumaturgical. War.

And there were of course no alliances, no sides, no deals, no mercy, no cease. The skies twisted, the seas boiled. The scream and whizz of fireballs turned the night into day, but that was all right because the ensuing clouds of black smoke turned the day into night. The landscape rose and fell like a honeymoon duvet, and the very fabric of space itself was tied in multidimensional knots and bashed on a flat stone down by the river of Time. For example, a popular spell at the time was Pelepel's Temporal Compressor, which on one occasion resulted in a race of giant reptiles being created, evolving, spreading, flourishing and then being destroyed in the space of about five minutes, leaving only its bones in the earth to mislead forthcoming generations completely. Trees swam, fishes walked, mountains strolled down to the shops for a packet of cigarettes, and the mutability of existence was such that the first thing any cautious person would do when they woke up in the mornings was count their arms and legs.

That was, in fact, the problem. All the wizards were pretty evenly matched and in any case lived in high towers well protected with spells, which meant that most magical weapons rebounded and landed on the common people who were trying to scratch an honest living from what was, temporarily, the soil, and lead ordinary, decent (but rather short) lives.

But still the fighting raged, battering the very structure of the universe of order, weakening the walls of reality and threatening to topple the whole rickety edifice of time and space into the darkness of the Dungeon Dimensions . . .

One story said that the gods stepped in, but the gods don't usually take a hand in human affairs unless it amuses them. Another one – and this was the one that the wizards themselves told, and wrote down in their books – was that the wizards themselves got together and settled their differences amicably for the good of mankind. And this was generally accepted as the true account, despite being as internally likely as a lead lifebelt.

The truth isn't easily pinned to a page. In the bathtub of history the truth is harder to hold than the soap, and much more difficult to find . . .

'What happened, then?' said Conina.

'It doesn't matter,' said Rincewind, mournfully. 'It's going to start all over again. I can feel it. I've got this instinct. There's too much magic flowing into the world. There's going to be a horrible war. It's all going to happen. The Disc is too old to take it this time. Everything's been worn too thin. Doom, darkness and destruction bear down on us. The Apocralypse is nigh.'

'Death walks abroad,' added Nijel helpfully.

'What?' snapped Rincewind, angry at being interrupted.

'I said, Death walks abroad,' said Nijel.

'Abroad I don't mind,' said Rincewind. 'They're all foreigners. It's Death walking around here I'm not looking forward to.'

'It's only a metaphor,' said Conina.

'That's all you know. I've met him.'

'What did he look like?' said Nijel.

'Put it like this—'

'Yes?'

'He didn't need a hairdresser.'

Now the sun was a blowlamp nailed to the sky, and the only difference between the sand and red-hot ash was the colour.

The Luggage plodded erratically across the burning dunes. There were a few traces of yellow slime rapidly drying on its lid.

The lonely little oblong was watched, from atop of a stone pinnacle the shape and temperature of a firebrick, by a chimera.* The chimera was an extremely rare species, and this particular one wasn't about to do anything to help matters.

It judged its moment carefully, kicked away with its talons, folded its leathery wings and plummeted down towards its victim.

The chimera's technique was to swoop low over the prey, lightly boiling it with its fiery breath, and then turn and rend its dinner with its teeth. It managed the fire part but then, at the point where experience told the creature it should be facing a stricken and terrified victim, found itself on the ground in the path of a scorched and furious Luggage.

The only thing incandescent about the Luggage was its rage. It had spent several hours with a headache, during which it seemed the whole world had tried to attack it. It had had enough.

When it had stamped the unfortunate chimera into a greasy puddle on the sand it paused for a moment, apparently considering its future. It was becoming clear that not belonging to anyone was a lot harder than it had thought. It had vague, comforting recollections of service and a wardrobe to call its own.

It turned around very slowly, pausing frequently to open its lid. It might have been sniffing the air, if it had a nose. At last it made up its mind, if it had a mind.

The hat and its wearer also strode purposefully across the rubble that had been the legendary Rhoxie to the foot of the tower of sourcery, their unwilling entourage straggling along behind them.

There were doors at the foot of the tower. Unlike those of Unseen

*For a description of the chimera we shall turn to Broomfog's famous bestiary *Anima Unnaturale*: 'It have thee legges of an mermade, the hair of an tortoise, the teeth of an fowel, and the winges of an snake. Of course, I have only my worde for it, the beast having the breathe of an furnace and the temperament of an rubber balloon in a hurricane.'

University, which were usually propped wide open, they were tightly shut. They seemed to glow.

'*You three are privileged to be here,*' said the hat through Abrim's slack mouth. '*This is the moment when wizardry stops running,*' he glanced witheringly at Rincewind, '*and starts fighting back. You will remember it for the rest of your lives.*'

'What, until lunchtime?' said Rincewind weakly.

'*Watch closely,*' said Abrim. He extended his hands.

'If we get a chance,' whispered Rincewind to Nijel, 'we run, right?'

'Where to?'

'From,' said Rincewind, 'the important word is *from*.'

'I don't trust this man,' said Nijel. 'I try not to judge from first impressions, but I definitely think he's up to no good.'

'He had you thrown in a snake pit!'

'Perhaps I should have taken the hint.'

The vizier started to mutter. Even Rincewind, whose few talents included a gift for languages, didn't recognise it, but it sounded the kind of language designed specifically for muttering, the words curling out like scythes at ankle height, dark and red and merciless. They made complicated swirls in the air, and then drifted gently towards the doors of the tower.

Where they touched the white marble it turned black and crumbled.

As the remains drifted to the ground a wizard stepped through and looked Abrim up and down.

Rincewind was used to the dressy ways of wizards, but this one was really impressive, his robe so padded and crenellated and buttressed in fantastic folds and creases that it had probably been designed by an architect. The matching hat looked like a wedding cake that had collided intimately with a Christmas tree.

The actual face, peering through the small gap between the baroque collar and the filigreed fringe of the brim, was a bit of a disappointment. At some time in the past it had thought its appearance would be improved by a thin, scruffy moustache. It had been wrong.

'That was our bloody door!' it said. 'You're really going to regret this!'

Abrim folded his arms.

This seemed to infuriate the other wizard. He flung up his arms, untangled his hands from the lace on his sleeves, and sent a flare screaming across the gap.

It struck Abrim in the chest and rebounded in a gout of incandescence, but when the blue after-images allowed Rincewind to see he saw Abrim, unharmed.

His opponent frantically patted out the last of the little fires in his own clothing and looked up with murder in his eyes.

'You don't seem to understand,' he rasped. 'It's sourcery you're dealing with now. You can't fight sourcery.'

'*I can use sourcery,*' said Abrim.

The wizard snarled and lofted a fireball, which burst harmlessly inches from Abrim's dreadful grin.

A look of acute puzzlement passed across the other one's face. He tried again, sending lines of blue-hot magic lancing straight from infinity towards Abrim's heart. Abrim waved them away.

'*Your choice is simple,*' he said. '*You can join me, or you can die.*'

It was at this point that Rincewind became aware of a regular scraping sound close to his ear. It had an unpleasant metallic ring.

He half-turned, and felt the familiar and very uncomfortable prickly feeling of Time slowing down around him.

Death paused in the act of running a whetstone along the edge of his scythe and gave him a nod of acknowledgement, as between one professional and another.

He put a bony digit to his lips, or rather, to the place where his lips would have been if he'd had lips.

All wizards can see Death, but they don't necessarily want to.

There was a popping in Rincewind's ears and the spectre vanished.

Abrim and the rival wizard were surrounded by a corona of randomised magic, and it was evidently having no effect on Abrim. Rincewind drifted back into the land of the living just in time to see the man reach out and grab the wizard by his tasteless collar.

'*You cannot defeat me,*' he said in the hat's voice. '*I have had two thousand years of harnessing power to my own ends. I can draw my power from your power. Yield to me or you won't even have time to regret it.*'

The wizard struggled and, unfortunately, let pride win over caution.

'Never!' he said.

'*Die,*' suggested Abrim.

Rincewind had seen many strange things in his life, most of them with extreme reluctance, but he had never seen anyone actually killed by magic.

Wizards didn't kill ordinary people because a) they seldom

noticed them and b) it wasn't considered sporting and c) besides, who'd do all the cooking and growing food and things. And killing a brother wizard with magic was well-nigh impossible on account of the layers of protective spells that any cautious wizard maintained about his person at all times.* The first thing a young wizard learns at Unseen University – apart from where his peg is, and which way to the lavatory – is that he must protect himself at all times.

Some people think this is paranoia, but it isn't. Paranoids only think everyone is out to get them. Wizards *know* it.

The little wizard was wearing the psychic equivalent of three feet of tempered steel and it was being melted like butter under a blowlamp. It streamed away, vanished.

If there are words to describe what happened to the wizard next then they're imprisoned inside a wild thesaurus in the Unseen University Library. Perhaps it's best left to the imagination, except that anyone able to imagine the kind of shape that Rincewind saw writhing painfully for a few seconds before it mercifully vanished must be a candidate for the famous white canvas blazer with the optional long sleeves.

'*So perish all enemies,*' said Abrim.

He turned his face up to the heights of the tower.

'*I challenge,*' he said. '*And those who will not face me must follow me, according to the Lore.*'

There was a long, thick pause caused by a lot of people listening very hard. Eventually, from the top of the tower, a voice called out uncertainly, 'Whereabouts in the Lore?'

'*I embody the Lore.*'

There was a distant whispering and then the same voice called out, 'The Lore is dead. Sourcery is above the Lo—'

The sentence ended in a scream because Abrim raised his left hand and sent a thin beam of green light in the precise direction of the speaker.

It was at about this moment that Rincewind realised that he could move his limbs himself. The hat had temporarily lost interest in them. He glanced sideways at Conina. In instant, unspoken agreement they each grasped one of Nijel's arms and turned and ran, and didn't stop until they'd put several walls between them and the tower. Rincewind ran expecting something to hit him in the back of the neck. Possibly the world.

---

*Of course, wizards often killed one another by ordinary, non-magical means, but this was perfectly allowable and death by assassination was considered natural causes for a wizard.

All three landed in the rubble and lay there panting.

'You needn't have done that,' muttered Nijel. 'I was just getting ready to really give him a seeing-to. How can I ever—'

There was an explosion behind them and shafts of multicoloured fire screamed overhead, striking sparks off the masonry. Then there was a sound like an enormous cork being pulled out of a small bottle, and a peal of laughter that, somehow, wasn't very amusing. The ground shook.

'What's going on?' said Conina.

'Magical war,' said Rincewind.

'Is that good?'

'No.'

'But surely you want wizardry to triumph?' said Nijel.

Rincewind shrugged, and ducked as something unseen and big whirred overhead making a noise like a partridge.

'I've never seen wizards fight,' said Nijel. He started to scramble up the rubble and screamed as Conina grabbed him by the leg.

'I don't think that would be a good idea,' she said. 'Rincewind?'

The wizard shook his head gloomily, and picked up a pebble. He tossed it up above the ruined wall, where it turned into a small blue teapot. It smashed when it hit the ground.

'The spells react with one another,' he said. 'There's no telling what they'll do.'

'But we're safe behind this wall?' said Conina.

Rincewind brightened a bit. 'Are we?' he said.

'I was asking you.'

'Oh. No. I shouldn't think so. It's just ordinary stone. The right spell and . . . phooey.'

'Phooey?'

'Right.'

'Shall we run away again?'

'It's worth a try.'

They made it to another upright wall a few seconds before a randomly spitting ball of yellow fire landed where they had been lying and turned the ground into something awful. The whole area around the tower was a tornado of sparkling air.

'We need a plan,' said Nijel.

'We could try running again,' said Rincewind.

'That doesn't solve anything!'

'Solves most things,' said Rincewind.

'How far do we have to go to be safe?' said Conina.

Rincewind risked a look around the wall.

'Interesting philosophical question,' he said. 'I've been a long way, and I've never been safe.'

Conina sighed and stared at a pile of rubble nearby. She stared at it again. There was something odd there, and she couldn't quite put her finger on it.

'I could rush at them,' said Nijel, vaguely. He stared yearningly at Conina's back.

'Wouldn't work,' said Rincewind. 'Nothing works against magic. Except stronger magic. And then the only thing that beats stronger magic is even stronger magic. And next thing you know . . .'

'Phooey?' suggested Nijel.

'It happened before,' said Rincewind. 'Went on for thousands of years until not a—'

'Do you know what's odd about that heap of stone?' said Conina.

Rincewind glanced at it. He screwed up his eyes.

'What, apart from the legs?' he said.

It took several minutes to dig the Seriph out. He was still clutching a wine bottle, which was almost empty, and blinked at them all in vague recognition.

'Powerful,' he said, and then after some effort added, 'stuff, this vintage. Felt,' he continued, 'as though the place fell on me.'

'It did,' said Rincewind.

'Ah. That would be it, then.' Creosote focused on Conina, after several attempts, and rocked backwards. 'My word,' he said, 'the young lady again. Very impressive.'

'I say—' Nijel began.

'Your hair,' said the Seriph, rocking slowly forward again, 'is like, is like a flock of goats that graze upon the side of Mount Gebra.'

'Look here—'

'Your breasts are like, like,' the Seriph swayed sideways a little, and gave a brief, sorrowful glance at the empty bottle, 'are like the jewelled melons in the fabled gardens of dawn.'

Conina's eyes widened. 'They are?' she said.

'No,' said the Seriph, 'doubt about it. I know jewelled melons when I see them. As the white does in the meadows of the water margin are your thighs, which—'

'Erm, excuse me—' said Nijel, clearing his throat with malice aforethought.

Creosote swayed in his direction.

'Hmm?' he said.

'Where I come from,' said Nijel stonily, 'we don't talk to ladies like that.'

136

Conina sighed as Nijel shuffled protectively in front of her. It was, she reflected, absolutely true.

'In fact,' he went on, sticking out his jaw as far as possible, which still made it appear like a dimple, 'I've a jolly good mind—'

'Open to debate,' said Rincewind, stepping forward. 'Er, sir, sire, we need to get out. I suppose you wouldn't know the way?'

'Thousands of rooms,' said the Seriph, 'in here, you know. Not been out in years.' He hiccuped. 'Decades. Ians. Never been out, in fact.' His face glazed over in the act of composition. 'The bird of Time has but, um, a little way to walk and lo! the bird is on its feet . . .'

'It's a geas,' muttered Rincewind.

Creosote swayed at him. 'Abrim does all the ruling, you see. Terrible hard work.'

'He's not,' said Rincewind, 'making a very good job of it just at present.'

'And we'd sort of like to get away,' said Conina, who was still turning over the phrase about the goats.

'And I've got this geas,' said Nijel, glaring at Rincewind.

Creosote patted him on the arm.

'That's nice,' he said. 'Everyone should have a pet.'

'So if you happen to know if you own any stables or anything . . .' prompted Rincewind.

'Hundreds,' said Creosote. 'I own some of the finest, most . . . finest horses in the world.' His brow wrinkled. 'So they tell me.'

'But you wouldn't happen to know where they are?'

'Not as such,' the Seriph admitted. A random spray of magic turned the nearby wall into arsenic meringue.

'I think we might have been better off in the snake pit,' said Rincewind, turning away.

Creosote took another sorrowful glance at his empty wine bottle.

'I know where there's a magic carpet,' he said.

'No,' said Rincewind, raising his hands protectively. 'Absolutely not. Don't even—'

'It belonged to my grandfather—'

'A real magic carpet?' said Nijel.

'Listen,' said Rincewind urgently. 'I get vertigo just listening to tall stories.'

'Oh, quite,' the Seriph burped gently, 'genuine. Very pretty pattern.' He squinted at the bottle again, and sighed. 'It was a lovely blue colour,' he added.

'And you wouldn't happen to know where it is?' said Conina

slowly, in the manner of one creeping up very carefully to a wild animal that might take fright at any moment.

'In the treasury. I know the way *there*. I'm extremely rich, you know. Or so they tell me.' He lowered his voice and tried to wink at Conina, eventually managing it with both eyes. 'We could sit on it,' he said, breaking into a sweat. 'And you could tell me a story . . .'

Rincewind tried to scream through gritted teeth. His ankles were already beginning to sweat.

'I'm not going to ride on a magic carpet!' he hissed. 'I'm afraid of grounds!'

'You mean heights,' said Conina. 'And stop being silly.'

'I know what I mean! It's the grounds that kill you!'

The battle of Al Khali was a hammer-headed cloud, in whose roiling depths weird shapes could be heard and strange sounds were seen. Occasional misses seared across the city. Where they landed things were . . . *different*.

For example, a large part of the *soak* had turned into an impenetrable forest of giant yellow mushrooms. No-one knew what effect this had on its inhabitants, although possibly they hadn't noticed.

The temple of Offler the Crocodile God, patron deity of the city, was now a rather ugly sugary thing constructed in five dimensions. But this was no problem because it was being eaten by a herd of giant ants.

On the other hand, not many people were left to appreciate this statement against uncontrolled civic alteration, because most of them were running for their lives. They fled across the fertile fields in a steady stream. Some had taken to boats, but this method of escape had ceased when most of the harbour area turned into a swamp in which, for no obvious reason, a couple of small pink elephants were building a nest.

Down below the panic on the roads the Luggage paddled slowly up one of the reed-lined drainage ditches. A little way ahead of it a moving wave of small alligators, rats and snapping turtles was pouring out of the water and scrambling frantically up the bank, propelled by some vague but absolutely accurate animal instinct.

The Luggage's lid was set in an expression of grim determination. It didn't want much out of the world, except for the total extinction of every other lifeform, but what it needed more than anything else now was its owner.

*

138

It was easy to see that the room was a treasury by its incredible emptiness. Doors hung off hooks. Barred alcoves had been smashed in. Lots of smashed chests lay around, and this gave Rincewind a pang of guilt and he wondered, for about two seconds, where the Luggage had got to.

There was a respectful silence, as there always is when large sums of money have just passed away. Nijel wandered off and prodded some of the chests in a forlorn search for secret drawers, as per the instructions in Chapter Eleven.

Conina reached down and picked up a small copper coin.

'How horrible,' said Rincewind eventually. 'A treasury with no treasure in it.'

The Seriph stood and beamed.

'Not to worry,' he said.

'But all your money has been stolen!' said Conina.

'The servants, I expect,' said Creosote. 'Very disloyal of them.'

Rincewind gave him an odd look. 'Doesn't it worry you?'

'Not much. I never really spent anything. I've often wondered what being poor was like.'

'You're going to get a huge opportunity to find out.'

'Will I need training?'

'It comes naturally,' said Rincewind. 'You pick it up as you go along.' There was a distant explosion and part of the ceiling turned to jelly.

'Erm, excuse me,' said Nijel, 'this carpet . . .'

'Yes,' said Conina, 'the carpet.'

Creosote gave them a benevolent, slightly tipsy smile.

'Ah, yes. The carpet. Push the nose of the statue behind you, peach-buttocked jewel of the desert dawn.'

Conina, blushing, performed this act of minor sacrilege on a large green statue of Offler the Crocodile God.

Nothing happened. Secret compartments assiduously failed to open.

'Um. Try the left hand.'

She gave it an experimental twist. Creosote scratched his head.

'Maybe it was the right hand . . .'

'I should try and remember, if I were you,' said Conina sharply, when that didn't work either. 'There aren't many bits left that I'd care to pull.'

'What's that thing there?' said Rincewind.

'You're really going to hear about it if it isn't the tail,' said Conina, and gave it a kick.

There was a distant metallic groaning noise, like a saucepan in pain. The statue shuddered. It was followed by a few heavy clonks somewhere inside the wall, and Offler the Crocodile God grated ponderously aside. There was a tunnel behind him.

'My grandfather had this built for our more interesting treasures,' said Creosote. 'He was very—' he groped for a word – 'ingenious.'

'If you think I'm setting foot in there—' Rincewind began.

'Stand aside,' said Nijel, loftily. 'I will go first.'

'There could be traps—' said Conina doubtfully. She shot the Seriph a glance.

'Oh, probably, O gazelle of Heaven,' he said. 'I haven't been in there since I was six. There were some slabs you shouldn't tread on, I think.'

'Don't worry about that,' said Nijel, peering into the gloom of the tunnel. 'I shouldn't think there's a booby trap that *I* couldn't spot.'

'Had a lot of experience at this sort of thing, have you?' said Rincewind sourly.

'Well, I know Chapter Fourteen off by heart. It had illustrations,' said Nijel, and ducked into the shadows.

They waited for several minutes in what would have been a horrified hush if it wasn't for the muffled grunts and occasional thumping noises from the tunnel. Eventually Nijel's voice echoed back down to them from a distance.

'There's absolutely nothing,' he said. 'I've tried everything. It's as steady as a rock. Everything must have seized up, or something.'

Rincewind and Conina exchanged glances.

'He doesn't know the first thing about traps,' she said. 'When I was five, my father made me walk all the way down a passage that he'd rigged up, just to teach me—'

'He got through, didn't he?' said Rincewind.

There was a noise like a damp finger dragged across glass, but amplified a billion times, and the floor shook.

'Anyway, we haven't got a lot of choice,' he added, and ducked into the tunnel. The others followed him. Many people who had got to know Rincewind had come to treat him as a sort of two-legged miner's canary[*] and tended to assume that if Rincewind was still upright and not actually running then some hope remained.

'This is fun,' said Creosote. 'Me, robbing my own treasury. If I catch myself I can have myself flung into the snake pit.'

[*] All right. But you've got the general idea.

'But you could throw yourself on your mercy,' said Conina, running a paranoid eye over the dusty stonework.

'Oh, no. I think I would have to teach me a lesson, as an example to myself.'

There was a little click above them. A small slab slid aside and a rusty metal hook descended slowly and jerkily. Another bar creaked out of the wall and tapped Rincewind on the shoulder. As he swung around, the first hook hung a yellowing notice on his back and retracted into the roof.

'What'd it do? What'd it do?' screamed Rincewind, trying to read his own shoulderblades.

'It says, *Kick Me*,' said Conina.

A section of wall slid up beside the petrified wizard. A large boot on the end of a complicated series of metal joints gave a half-hearted wobble and then the whole thing snapped at the knee.

The three of them looked at it in silence. Then Conina said, 'We're dealing here with a warped brain, I can tell.'

Rincewind gingerly unhooked the sign and let it drop. Conina pushed past him and stalked along the passage with an air of angry caution, and when a metal hand extended itself on a spring and waggled in a friendly fashion she didn't shake it but instead traced its moulting wiring to a couple of corroded electrodes in a big glass jar.

'Your grandad was a man with a sense of humour?' she said.

'Oh, yes. Always liked a chuckle,' said Creosote.

'Oh, good,' said Conina. She prodded gingerly at a flagstone which, to Rincewind, looked no different to any of its fellows. With a sad little springy noise a moulting feather duster wobbled out of the wall at armpit height.

'I think I would have quite liked to meet the old Seriph,' she said, through gritted teeth, 'although not to shake him by the hand. You'd better give me a leg up here, wizard.'

'Pardon?'

Conina pointed irritably to a half-open stone doorway just ahead of them.

'I want to look up there,' she said. 'You just put your hands together for me to stand on, right? How do you manage to be so useless?'

'Being useful always gets me into trouble,' muttered Rincewind, trying to ignore the warm flesh brushing against his nose.

He could hear her rooting around above the door.

'I thought so,' she said.

'What is it? Fiendishly sharp spears poised to drop?'

'No.'

'Spiked grill ready to skewer—?'

'It's a bucket,' said Conina flatly, giving it a push.

'What, of scalding, poisonous—?'

'Whitewash. Just a lot of old, dried-up whitewash.' Conina jumped down.

'That's grandfather for you,' said Creosote. 'Never a dull moment.'

'Well, I've just about had enough,' Conina said firmly, and pointed to the far end of the tunnel. 'Come on, you two.'

They were about three feet from the far end when Rincewind felt a movement in the air above him. Conina struck him in the small of the back, shoving him forward into the room beyond. He rolled when he hit the floor, and something nicked his foot at the same time as a loud thump deafened him.

The entire roof, a huge block of stone four feet thick, had dropped into the tunnel.

Rincewind crawled forward through the dust clouds and, with a trembling finger, traced the lettering on the side of the slab.

'*Laugh This One Off*,' he said.

He sat back.

'That's grandad,' said Creosote happily, 'always a—'

He intercepted Conina's gaze, which had the force of a lead pipe, and wisely shut up.

Nijel emerged from the clouds, coughing.

'I say, what happened?' he said. 'Is everyone all right? It didn't do that when I went through.'

Rincewind sought for a reply, and couldn't find anything better than, 'Didn't it?'

Light filtered into the deep room from tiny barred windows up near the roof. There was no way out except by walking through the several hundred tons of stone that blocked the tunnel or, to put it in another way, which was the way Rincewind put it, they were undoubtedly trapped. He relaxed a bit.

At least there was no mistaking the magic carpet. It lay rolled up on a raised slab in the middle of the room. Next to it was a small, sleek oil lamp and – Rincewind craned to see – a small gold ring. He groaned. A faint octarine corona hung over all three items, indicating that they were magical.

When Conina unrolled the carpet a number of small objects tumbled on to the floor, including a brass herring, a wooden ear, a few large square sequins and a lead box with a preserved soap bubble in it.

'What on earth are they?' said Nijel.

'Well,' said Rincewind, 'before they tried to eat that carpet, they were probably moths.'

'Gosh.'

'That's what you people never understand,' said Rincewind, wearily. 'You think magic is just something you can pick up and use, like a, a—'

'Parsnip?' said Nijel.

'Wine bottle?' said the Seriph.

'Something like that,' said Rincewind cautiously, but rallied somewhat and went on, 'But the truth is, is—'

'Not like that?'

'More like a wine bottle?' said the Seriph hopefully.

'Magic *uses* people,' said Rincewind hurriedly. 'It affects you as much as you affect it, sort of thing. You can't mess around with magical things without it affecting you. I just thought I'd better warn you.'

'Like a wine bottle,' said Creosote, 'that—'

'—*drinks you back*,' said Rincewind. 'So you can put down that lamp and ring for a start, and for goodness' sake don't rub anything.'

'My grandfather built up the family fortunes with them,' said Creosote wistfully. 'His wicked uncle locked him in a cave, you know. He had to set himself up with what came to hand. He had nothing in the whole world but a magic carpet, a magic lamp, a magic ring and a grotto-ful of assorted jewels.'

'Came up the hard way, did he?' said Rincewind.

Conina spread the carpet on the floor. It had a complex pattern of golden dragons on a blue background. They were extremely complicated dragons, with long beards, ears and wings, and they seemed to be frozen in motion, caught in the transition from one state to another, suggesting that the loom which wove them had rather more dimensions than the usual three, but the worst thing about it was that if you looked at it long enough the pattern became blue dragons on a gold background, and a terrible feeling stole over you that if you kept on trying to see both types of dragon at once your brains would trickle out of your ears.

Rincewind tore his gaze away with some difficulty as another distant explosion rocked the building.

'How does it work?' he said.

Creosote shrugged. 'I've never used it,' he said. 'I suppose you just say "up" and "down" and things like that.'

'How about "fly through the wall"?' said Rincewind.

All three of them looked up at the high, dark and, above all, solid walls of the room.

'We could try sitting on it and saying "rise",' Nijel volunteered. 'And then, before we hit the roof, we could say, well, "stop".' He considered this for a bit, and then added, 'If that's the word.'

'Or, "drop",' said Rincewind, 'or "descend", "dive", "fall", "sink". Or "plunge".'

' "Plummet",' suggested Conina gloomily.

'Of course,' said Nijel, 'with all this wild magic floating around, you could try using some of it.'

'Ah—' said Rincewind, and, 'Well—'

'You've got "wizzard" written on your hat,' said Creosote.

'Anyone can write things on their hat,' said Conina. 'You don't want to believe everything you read.'

'Now hold on a minute,' said Rincewind hotly.

They held on a minute.

They held on for a further seventeen seconds.

'Look, it's a lot harder than you think,' he said.

'What did I tell you?' said Conina. 'Come on, let's dig the mortar out with our fingernails.'

Rincewind waved her into silence, removed his hat, pointedly blew the dust off the star, put the hat on again, adjusted the brim, rolled up his sleeves, flexed his fingers and panicked.

In default of anything better to do, he leaned against the stone.

It was vibrating. It wasn't that it was being shaken; it felt that the throbbing was coming from inside the wall.

It was very much the same sort of trembling he had felt back at the University, just before the sourcerer arrived. The stone was definitely very unhappy about something.

He sidled along the wall and put his ear to the next stone, which was a smaller, wedge-shaped stone cut to fit an angle of the wall, not a big, distinguished stone, but a bantam stone, patiently doing its bit for the greater good of the wall as a whole. It was also shaking.

'Shh!' said Conina.

'I can't hear anything,' said Nijel loudly. Nijel was one of those people who, if you say 'don't look now', would immediately swivel his head like an owl on a turntable. These are the same people who, when you point out, say, an unusual crocus just beside them, turn around aimlessly and put their foot down with a sad little squashy noise. If they were lost in a trackless desert you could find them by putting down, somewhere on the sand, something small and fragile like a valuable old mug that had been in your family for generations, and then hurrying back as soon as you heard the crash.

Anyway.

'That's the point! What happened to the war?'

A little cascade of mortar poured down from the ceiling on to Rincewind's hat.

'Something's acting on the stones,' he said quietly. 'They're trying to break free.'

'We're right underneath quite a lot of them,' observed Creosote.

There was a grinding noise above them and a shaft of daylight lanced down. To Rincewind's surprise it wasn't accompanied by sudden death from crushing. There was another silicon creak, and the hole grew. The stones were falling out, and they were falling *up*.

'I think,' he said, 'that the carpet might be worth a try at this point.'

The wall beside him shook itself like a dog and drifted apart, its masonry giving Rincewind several severe blows as it soared away.

The four of them landed on the blue and gold carpet in a storm of flying rock.

'We've got to get out of here,' said Nijel, keeping up his reputation for acute observation.

'Hang on,' said Rincewind. 'I'll say—'

'You won't,' snapped Conina, kneeling beside him. '*I'll* say. I don't trust you.'

'But you've—'

'Shut up,' said Conina. She patted the carpet.

'Carpet – rise,' she commanded.

There was a pause.

'Up.'

'Perhaps it doesn't understand the language,' said Nijel.

'Lift. Levitate. Fly.'

'Or it could be, say, sensitive to one particular voice—'

'Shut. Up.'

'You tried up,' said Nijel. 'Try ascend.'

'Or soar,' said Creosote. Several tons of flagstone swooped past an inch from his head.

'If it was going to answer to them it would have done, wouldn't it?' said Conina. The air around her was thick with dust as the flying stones ground together. She thumped the carpet.

'Take off, you blasted mat! Arrgh!'

A piece of cornice clipped her shoulder. She rubbed the bruise irritably, and turned to Rincewind, who was sitting with his knees under his chin and his hat pulled down over his head.

'Why doesn't it work?' she said.

'You're not saying the right words,' he said.

'It doesn't understand the language?'

'Language hasn't got anything to do with it. You've neglected something fundamental.'

'Well?'

'Well what?' sniffed Rincewind.

'Look, this isn't the time to stand on your dignity!'

'You keep on trying, don't you mind me.'

'Make it fly!'

Rincewind pulled his hat further over his ears.

'Please?' said Conina.

The hat rose a bit.

'We'd all be terribly bucked,' said Nijel.

'Hear hear,' said Creosote.

The hat rose some more. 'You're quite sure?' said Rincewind.

'Yes!'

Rincewind cleared his throat.

'Down,' he commanded.

The carpet rose from the ground and hovered expectantly a few feet over the dust.

'How did—' Conina began, but Nijel interrupted her.

'Wizards are privy to arcane knowledge, that's probably what it is,' he said. 'Probably the carpet's got a geas on it to do the opposite of anything that's said. Can you make it go up further?'

'Yes, but I'm not going to,' said Rincewind. The carpet drifted slowly forward and, as happens so often at times like this, a rolling slab of masonry bounced right across the spot where it had lain.

A moment later they were out in the open air, the storm of stone behind them.

The palace was pulling itself to pieces, and the pieces were funnelling up into the air like a volcanic eruption in reverse. The sourcerous tower had completely disappeared, but the stones were dancing towards the spot where it had stood and . . .

'They're building another tower!' said Nijel.

'Out of my palace, too,' said Creosote.

'The hat's won,' said Rincewind. 'That's why it's building its own tower. It's a sort of reaction. Wizards always used to build a tower around themselves, like those . . . what do you call those things you find at the bottom of rivers?'

'Frogs.'

'Stones.'

'Unsuccessful gangsters.'

'Caddis flies is what I meant,' said Rincewind. 'When a wizard set out to fight, the first thing he always did was build a tower.'

'It's very big,' said Nijel.

Rincewind nodded glumly.

'Where are we going?' said Conina.

Rincewind shrugged.

'Away,' he said.

The outer palace wall drifted just below them. As they passed over it began to shake, and small bricks began to loop towards the storm of flying rock that buzzed around the new tower.

Eventually Conina said, 'All right. How did you get the carpet to fly? Does it really do the opposite of what you command?'

'No. I just paid attention to certain fundamental details of laminar and spatial arrangements.'

'You've lost me there,' she admitted.

'You want it in non-wizard talk?'

'Yes.'

'You put it on the floor upside down,' said Rincewind.

Conina sat very still for a while. Then she said, 'I must say this is very comfortable. It's the first time I've ever flown on a carpet.'

'It's the first time I've ever flown one,' said Rincewind vaguely.

'You do it very well,' she said.

'Thank you.'

'You said you were frightened of heights.'

'Terrified.'

'You don't show it.'

'I'm not thinking about it.'

Rincewind turned and looked at the tower behind them. It had grown quite a lot in the last minute, blossoming at the top into a complexity of turrets and battlements. A swarm of tiles was hovering over it, individual tiles swooping down and clinking into place like ceramic bees on a bombing run. It was impossibly high – the stones at the bottom would have been crushed if it wasn't for the magic that crackled through them.

Well, that was just about *it* as far as organised wizardry was concerned. Two thousand years of peaceful magic had gone down the drain, the towers were going up again, and with all this new raw magic floating around something was going to get very seriously hurt. Probably the universe. Too much magic could wrap time and space around itself, and that wasn't good news for the kind of person who had grown used to things like effects following things like causes.

And, of course, it would be impossible to explain things to his companions. They didn't seem to grasp ideas properly; more particularly, they didn't seem able to get the hang of doom. They suffered from the terrible delusion that something could be done. They seemed prepared to make the world the way they wanted it or die in the attempt, and the trouble with dying in the attempt was that you died in the attempt.

The whole point about the old University organisation was that it kept a sort of peace between wizards who got along with one another about as easily as cats in a sack, and now the gloves were off anyone who tried to interfere was going to end up severely scratched. This wasn't the old, gentle, rather silly magic that the Disc was used to; this was magic war, white-hot and searing.

Rincewind wasn't very good at precognition; in fact he could barely see into the present. But he knew with weary certainty that at some point in the very near future, like thirty seconds or so, someone would say: 'Surely there's something we could do?'

The desert passed below them, lit by the low rays of the setting sun.

'There don't seem to be many stars,' said Nijel. 'Perhaps they're scared to come out.'

Rincewind looked up. There was a silver haze high in the air.

'It's raw magic settling out of the atmosphere,' he said. 'It's saturated.'

Twenty-seven, twenty-eight, twen—

'Surely there's—' Conina began.

'There isn't,' said Rincewind flatly, but with just the faintest twinge of satisfaction. 'The wizards will fight each other until there's one victor. There isn't anything anyone else can do.'

'I could do with a drink,' said Creosote. 'I suppose we couldn't stop somewhere where I could buy an inn?'

'What with?' said Nijel. 'You're poor, remember?'

'Poor I don't mind,' said the Seriph. 'It's sobriety that is giving me diffiiculties.'

Conina prodded Rincewind gently in the ribs.

'Are you steering this thing?' she said.

'No.'

'Then where is it going?'

Nijel peered downwards.

'By the look of it,' he said, 'it's going hubwards. Towards the Circle Sea.'

'*Someone* must be guiding it.'

Hallo, said a friendly voice in Rincewind's head.

You're not my conscience again, are you? thought Rincewind. I'm feeling really bad.

Well, I'm sorry, Rincewind thought, but none of this is my fault. I'm just a victim of circuses. I don't see why I should take the blame.

Yes, but you could do something about it.

Like what?

You could destroy the sourcerer. All this would collapse then.

I wouldn't stand a chance.

Then at least you could die in the attempt. That might be preferable to letting magical war break out.

'Look, just shut up, will you?' said Rincewind.

'What?' said Conina.

'Um?' said Rincewind, vaguely. He looked down blankly at the blue and gold pattern underneath him, and added, 'You're flying this, aren't you? Through me! That's sneaky!'

'What are you talking about?'

'Oh. Sorry. Talking to myself.'

'I think,' said Conina, 'that we'd better land.'

They glided down towards a crescent of beach where the desert reached the sea. In normal light it would have been blinding white with a sand made up of billions of tiny shell fragments, but at this time of day it was blood-red and primordial. Ranks of driftwood, carved by the waves and bleached by the sun, were piled up on the tideline like the bones of ancient fish or the biggest floral art accessory counter in the universe. Nothing stirred, apart from the waves. There were a few rocks around, but they were firebrick hot and home to no mollusc or seaweed.

Even the sea looked arid. If any proto-amphibian emerged on to a beach like this, it would have given up there and then, gone back into the water and told all its relatives to forget the legs, it wasn't worth it. The air felt as though it had been cooked in a sock.

Even so, Nijel insisted that they light a fire.

'It's more friendly,' he said. 'Besides, there could be monsters.'

Conina looked at the oily wavelets, rolling up the beach in what appeared to be a half-hearted attempt to get out of the sea.

'In that?' she said.

'You never can tell.'

Rincewind mooched along the waterline, distractedly picking up stones and throwing them in the sea. One or two were thrown back.

After a while Conina got a fire going, and the bone-dry, salt-saturated wood sent blue and green flames roaring up under a fountain of sparks. The wizard went and sat in the dancing shadows, his back against a pile of whitened wood, wrapped in a cloud of such impenetrable gloom that even Creosote stopped complaining of thirst and shut up.

Conina woke up after midnight. There was a crescent moon on the horizon and a thin, chilly mist covered the sand. Creosote was snoring on his back. Nijel, who was theoretically on guard, was sound asleep.

Conina lay perfectly still, every sense seeking out the thing that had awoken her.

Finally she heard it again. It was a tiny, diffident clinking noise, barely audible above the muted slurp of the sea.

She got up, or rather, she slid into the vertical as bonelessly as a jellyfish, and flicked Nijel's sword out of his unresisting hand. Then she sidled through the mist without causing so much as an extra swirl.

The fire sank down further into its bed of ash. After a while Conina came back, and shook the other two awake.

'Warrizit?'

'I think you ought to see this,' she hissed. 'I think it could be important.'

'I just shut my eyes for a second—' Nijel protested.

'Never mind about that. Come on.'

Creosote squinted around the impromptu campsite.

'Where's the wizard fellow?'

'You'll see. And don't make a noise. It could be dangerous.'

They stumbled after her, knee-deep in vapour, towards the sea.

Eventually Nijel said, 'Why dangerous—'

'Shh! Did you hear it?'

Nijel listened.

'Like a sort of ringing noise?'

'Watch . . .'

Rincewind walked jerkily up the beach, carrying a large round rock in both hands. He walked past them without a word, his eyes staring straight ahead.

They followed him along the cold beach until he reached a bare area between the dunes, where he stopped and, still moving with all the grace of a clothes horse, dropped the rock. It made a clinking noise.

There was a wide circle of other stones. Very few of them had actually stayed on top of another one.

The three of them crouched down and watched him.

'Is he asleep?' said Creosote.

Conina nodded.

'What's he trying to do?'

'I think he's trying to build a tower.'

Rincewind lurched back into the ring of stones and, with great care, placed another rock on empty air. It fell down.

'He's not very good at it, is he,' said Nijel.

'It is very sad,' said Creosote.

'Maybe we ought to wake him up,' said Conina. 'Only I heard that if you wake up sleepwalkers their legs fall off, or something. What do you think?'

'Could be risky, with wizards,' said Nijel.

They tried to make themselves comfortable on the chilly sand.

'It's rather pathetic, isn't it?' said Creosote. 'It's not as if he's really a proper wizard.'

Conina and Nijel tried to avoid one another's gaze. Finally the boy coughed, and said, 'I'm not exactly a barbarian hero, you know. You may have noticed.'

They watched the toiling figure of Rincewind for a while, and then Conina said, 'If it comes to that, I think I lack a certain something when it comes to hairdressing.'

They both stared fixedly at the sleepwalker, busy with their own thoughts and red with mutual embarrassment.

Creosote cleared his throat.

'If it makes anyone feel any better,' he said, 'I sometimes perceive that my poetry leaves a lot to be desired.'

Rincewind carefully tried to balance a large rock on a small pebble. It fell off, but he appeared to be happy with the result.

'Speaking as a poet,' said Conina carefully, 'what would you say about this situation?'

Creosote shifted uneasily. 'Funny old thing, life,' he said.

'Pretty apt.'

Nijel lay back and looked up at the hazy stars. Then he sat bolt upright.

'Did you see that?' he demanded.

'What?'

'It was a sort of flash, a kind of—'

The hubward horizon exploded into a silent flower of colour, which expanded rapidly through all the hues of the conventional spectrum before flashing into brilliant octarine. It etched itself on their eyeballs before fading away.

After a while there was a distant rumble.

'Some sort of magical weapon,' said Conina, blinking. A gust of warm wind picked up the mist and streamed it past them.

'Blow this,' said Nijel, getting to his feet. 'I'm going to wake him up, even if it means we end up carrying him.'

He reached out for Rincewind's shoulder just as something went past very high overhead, making a noise like a flock of geese on nitrous oxide. It disappeared into the desert behind them. Then there was a sound that would have set false teeth on edge, a flash of green light, and a thump.

'I'll wake him up,' said Conina. 'You get the carpet.'

She clambered over the ring of rocks and took the sleeping wizard gently by the arm, and this would have been a textbook way of waking a somnambulist if Rincewind hadn't dropped the rock he was carrying on his foot.

He opened his eyes.

'Where am I?' he said.

'On the beach. You've been . . . er . . . dreaming.'

Rincewind blinked at the mist, the sky, the circle of stones, Conina, the circle of stones again, and finally back at the sky.

'What's been happening?' he said.

'Some sort of magical fireworks.'

'Oh. It's started, then.'

He lurched unsteadily out of the circle, in a way that suggested to Conina that perhaps he wasn't quite awake yet, and staggered back towards the remains of the fire. He walked a few steps and then appeared to remember something.

He looked down at his foot, and said, 'Ow.'

He'd almost reached the fire when the blast from the last spell reached them. It had been aimed at the tower in Al Khali, which was twenty miles away, and by now the wavefront was extremely diffuse. It was hardly affecting the nature of things as it surged over the dunes with a faint sucking noise; the fire burned red and green for a second, one of Nijel's sandals turned into a small and irritated badger, and a pigeon flew out of the Seriph's turban.

Then it was past and boiling out over the sea.

'What was *that*?' said Nijel. He kicked the badger, who was sniffing at his foot.

'Hmm?' said Rincewind.

'*That!*'

'Oh, that,' said Rincewind. 'Just the backwash of a spell. They probably hit the tower in Al Khali.'

'It must have been pretty big to affect us here.'

'It probably was.'

'Hey, that was my palace,' said Creosote weakly. 'I mean, I know it was a lot, but it was all I had.'

'Sorry.'

'But there were people in the city!'

'They're probably all right,' said Rincewind.

'Good.'

'Whatever they are.'

'What?'

Conina grabbed his arm. 'Don't shout at him,' she said. 'He's not himself.'

'Ah,' said Creosote dourly, 'an improvement.'

'I say, that's a bit unfair,' Nijel protested. 'I mean, he got me out of the snake pit and, well, he knows a lot—'

'Yes, wizards are good at getting you out of the sort of trouble that only wizards can get you into,' said Creosote. 'Then they expect you to thank them.'

'Oh, I think—'

'It's got to be said,' said Creosote, waving his hands irritably. He was briefly illuminated by the passage of another spell across the tormented sky.

'Look at that!' he snapped. 'Oh, he *means* well. They all mean well. They probably all think the Disc would be a better place if they were in charge. Take it from me, there's nothing more terrible than someone out to do the world a favour. Wizards! When all's said and done, what good are they? I mean, can you name me something worthwhile any wizard's done?'

'I think that's a bit cruel,' said Conina, but with an edge in her voice that suggested that she could be open to persuasion on the subject.

'Well, they make me sick,' muttered Creosote, who was feeling acutely sober and didn't like it much.

'I think we'll all feel better if we try to get a bit more sleep,' said Nijel diplomatically. 'Things always look better by daylight. Nearly always, anyway.'

'My mouth feels all horrible, too,' muttered Creosote, determined to cling on to the remnant of his anger.

Conina turned back to the fire, and became aware of a gap in the scenery. It was Rincewind-shaped.

'He's gone!'

In fact Rincewind was already half a mile out over the dark sea, squatting on the carpet like an angry buddha, his mind a soup of rage, humiliation and fury, with a side order of outrage.

He hadn't wanted much, ever. He'd stuck with wizardry even though he wasn't any good at it, he'd always done his best, and now the whole world was conspiring against him. Well, he'd show them. Precisely who 'they' were and what they were going to be shown was merely a matter of detail.

He reached up and touched his hat for reassurance, even as it lost its last few sequins in the slipstream.

The Luggage was having problems of its own.

The area around the tower of Al Khali, under the relentless magical bombardment, was already drifting beyond that reality horizon where time, space and matter lose their separate identities and start wearing one another's clothes. It was quite impossible to describe.

Here is what it looked like.

It looked like a piano sounds shortly after being dropped down a well. It tasted yellow, and felt Paisley. It smelled like a total eclipse of the moon. Of course, nearer to the tower it got *really* weird.

Expecting anything unprotected to survive in that would be like expecting snow on a supernova. Fortunately the Luggage didn't know this, and slid through the maelstrom with raw magic crystallising on its lid and hinges. It was in a foul mood but, again, there was nothing very unusual about this, except that the crackling fury earthing itself spectacularly all over the Luggage in a multi-coloured corona gave it the appearance of an early and very angry amphibian crawling out of a burning swamp.

It was hot and stuffy inside the tower. There were no internal floors, just a series of walkways around the walls. They were lined with wizards, and the central space was a column of octarine light that creaked loudly as they poured their power into it. At its base stood Abrim, the octarine gems on the hat blazing so brightly that they looked more like holes cut through into a different universe where, in defiance of probability, they had come out inside a sun.

The vizier stood with his hands out, fingers splayed, eyes shut, mouth a thin line of concentration, balancing the forces. Usually a wizard could control power only to the extent of his own physical capability, but Abrim was learning fast.

You made yourself the pinch in the hourglass, the fulcrum on the balance, the roll around the sausage.

Do it right and you *were* the power, it was part of you and you were capable of—

Has it been pointed out that his feet were several inches off the ground? His feet were several inches off the ground.

Abrim was pulling together the potency for a spell that would soar away into the sky and beset the Ankh tower with a thousand screaming demons when there came a thunderous knock at the door.

There is a mantra to be said on these occasions. It doesn't matter if the door is a tent flap, a scrap of hide on a wind-blown yurt, three inches of solid oak with great iron nails in or a rectangle of chipboard with mahogany veneer, a small light over it made of horrible bits of coloured glass and a bellpush that plays a choice of twenty popular melodies that no music lover would want to listen to even after five years' sensory deprivation.

One wizard turned to another and duly said: 'I wonder who that can be at this time of night?'

There was another series of thumps on the woodwork.

'There can't be anyone alive out there,' said the other wizard, and he said it nervously, because if you ruled out the possibility of it being anyone alive that always left the suspicion that perhaps it was someone dead.

This time the banging rattled the hinges.

'One of us had better go out,' said the first wizard.

'Good man.'

'Ah. Oh. Right.'

He set off slowly down the short, arched passage.

'I'll just go and see who it is, then?' he said.

'First class.'

It was a strange figure that made its hesitant way to the door. Ordinary robes weren't sufficient protection in the high-energy field inside the tower, and over his brocade and velvet the wizard wore a thick, padded overall stuffed with rowan shavings and embroidered with industrial-grade sigils. He'd affixed a smoked glass visor to his pointy hat and his gauntlets, which were extremely big, suggested that he was a wicket keeper in a game of cricket played at supersonic speeds. The actinic flashes and pulsations from the great work in the main hall cast harsh shadows around him as he fumbled for the bolts.

He pulled down the visor and opened the door a fraction.

'We don't want any—' he began, and ought to have chosen his words better, because they were his epitaph.

It was some time before his colleague noticed his continued absence, and wandered down the passage to find him. The door had been thrown wide open, the thaumatic inferno outside roaring against the web of spells that held it in check. In fact the door hadn't been pushed *completely* back; he pulled it aside to see why, and gave a little whimper.

There was a noise behind him. He turned around.

'Wha—' he began, which is a pretty poor syllable on which to end a life.

High over the Circle Sea Rincewind was feeling a bit of an idiot.

This happens to everyone sooner or later.

For example, in a tavern someone jogs your elbow and you turn around quickly and give a mouthful of abuse to, you become slowly aware, the belt buckle of a man who, it turns out, was probably hewn rather than born.

Or a little car runs into the back of yours and you rush out to show a bunch of fives to the driver who, it becomes apparent as he goes on unfolding more body like some horrible conjuring trick, must have been sitting on the back seat.

Or you might be leading your mutinous colleagues to the captain's cabin and you hammer on the door and he sticks his great head out with a cutlass in either hand and you say 'We're taking over the ship, you scum, and the lads are right with me!' and he says 'What lads?' and you suddenly feel a great emptiness behind you and you say 'Um . . .'

In other words, it's the familiar hot sinking feeling experienced by everyone who has let the waves of their own anger throw them far up on the beach of retribution, leaving them, in the poetic language of the everyday, up shit creek.

Rincewind was still angry and humiliated and so forth, but these emotions had died down a bit and something of his normal character had reasserted itself. It was not very pleased to find itself on a few threads of blue and gold wool high above the phosphorescent waves.

He'd been heading for Ankh-Morpork. He tried to remember why.

Of course, it was where it had all started. Perhaps it was the presence of the University, which was so heavy with magic it lay like a cannonball on the incontinence blanket of the Universe, stretching reality very thin. Ankh was where things started, and finished.

It was also his home, such as it was, and it called to him.

It has already been indicated that Rincewind appeared to have a certain amount of rodent in his ancestry, and in times of stress he felt an overpowering urge to make a run for his burrow.

He let the carpet drift for a while on the air currents while dawn, which Creosote would probably have referred to as pink-fingered, made a ring of fire around the edge of the Disc. It spread its lazy light over a world that was subtly different.

Rincewind blinked. There was a weird light. No, now he came to think about it, not weird but wyrd, which was much weirder. It was like looking at the world through a heat haze, but a haze that had a sort of life of its own. It danced and stretched, and gave more than a hint that it wasn't just an optical illusion but that it was reality itself that was being tensed and distended, like a rubber balloon trying to contain too much gas.

The wavering was greatest in the direction of Ankh-Morpork, where flashes and fountains of tortured air indicated that the struggle hadn't abated. A similar column hung over Al Khali, and then Rincewind realised that it wasn't the only one.

Wasn't that a tower over in Quirm, where the Circle Sea opened on to the great Rim Ocean? And there were others.

It had all gone critical. Wizardry was breaking up. Goodbye to the University, the levels, the Orders; deep in his heart, every wizard knew that the natural unit of wizardry was one wizard. The towers would multiply and fight until there was one tower left, and then the wizards would fight until there was one wizard.

By then, he'd probably fight himself.

The whole edifice that operated as the balance wheel of magic was falling to bits. Rincewind resented that, deeply. He'd never been any good at magic, but that wasn't the point. He knew where he fitted. It was right at the bottom, but at least he fitted. He could look up and see the whole delicate machine ticking away, gently, browsing off the natural magic generated by the turning of the Disc.

All he had was nothing, but that was something, and now it had been taken away.

Rincewind turned the carpet until it was facing the distant gleam that was Ankh-Morpork, which was a brilliant speck in the early morning light, and a part of his mind that wasn't doing anything else wondered why it was so bright. There also seemed to be a full moon, and even Rincewind, whose grasp of natural philosophy was pretty vague, was sure there had been one of those only the other day.

Well, it didn't matter. He'd had enough. He wasn't going to try to understand anything any more. He was going home. Except that wizards can never go home.

This is one of the ancient and deeply meaningful sayings about wizards and it says something about most of them that they have never been able to work out what it means. Wizards aren't allowed to have wives but they are allowed to have parents, and many of them go back to the old home town for Hogswatchnight or Soul Cake Thursday, for a bit of a sing-song and the heart-warming sight of all their boyhood bullies hurriedly avoiding them in the street.

It's rather like the other saying they've never been able to understand, which is that you can't cross the same river twice. Experiments with a long-legged wizard and a small river say you can cross the same river thirty, thirty-five times a minute.

Wizards don't like philosophy very much. As far as they are concerned, one hand clapping makes a noise like 'cl'.

In this particular case, though, Rincewind couldn't go home because it actually wasn't there any more. There was a city straddling the river Ankh, but it wasn't one he'd ever seen before; it was white and clean and didn't smell like a privy full of dead herrings.

He landed in what had once been the Plaza of Broken Moons, and also in a state of some shock. There were *fountains*. There had been fountains before, of course, but they had oozed rather than played and they had looked like thin soup. There were milky flagstones underfoot, with little glittery bits in. And, although the sun was sitting on the horizon like half a breakfast grapefruit, there was hardly anyone around. Normally Ankh was permanently crowded, the actual shade of the sky being a mere background detail.

Smoke drifted over the city in long greasy coils from the crown of boiling air above the University. It was the only movement, apart from the fountains.

Rincewind had always been rather proud of the fact that he always felt alone, even in the teeming city, but it was even worse being alone when he was by himself.

He rolled up the carpet and slung it over one shoulder and padded through the haunted streets towards the University.

The gates hung open to the wind. Most of the buildings looked half ruined by misses and ricochets. The tower of sourcery, far too high to be real, seemed to be unscathed. Not so the old Tower of

Art. Half the magic aimed at the tower next door seemed to have rebounded on it. Parts of it had melted and started to run; some parts glowed, some parts had crystallised, a few parts seemed to have twisted partly out of the normal three dimensions. It made you feel sorry even for stone that it should have to undergo such treatment. In fact nearly everything had happened to the tower except actual collapse. It looked so beaten that possibly even gravity had given up on it.

Rincewind sighed, and padded around the base of the tower towards the Library.

Towards where the Library had been.

There was the arch of the doorway, and most of the walls were still standing, but a lot of the roof had fallen in and everything was blackened by soot.

Rincewind stood and stared for a long time.

Then he dropped the carpet and ran, stumbling and sliding through the rubble that half-blocked the doorway. The stones were still warm underfoot. Here and there the wreckage of a bookcase still smouldered.

Anyone watching would have seen Rincewind dart backwards and forwards across the simmering heaps, scrabbling desperately among them, throwing aside charred furniture, pulling aside lumps of fallen roof with less than superhuman strength.

They would have seen him pause once or twice to get his breath back, then dive in again, cutting his hands on shards of half-molten glass from the dome of the roof. They would have noticed that he seemed to be sobbing.

Eventually his questing fingers touched something warm and soft.

The frantic wizard heaved a charred roof beam aside, scrabbled through a drift of fallen tiles and peered down.

There, half squashed by the beam and baked brown by the fire, was a large bunch of overripe, squashy bananas.

He picked one up, very carefully, and sat and watched it for some time until the end fell off.

Then he ate it.

'We shouldn't have let him go like that,' said Conina.

'How could we have stopped him, oh beauteous doe-eyed eaglet?'

'But he may do something stupid!'

'I should think that is very likely,' said Creosote primly.

'While we do something clever and sit on a baking beach with nothing to eat or drink, is that it?'

'You could tell me a story,' said Creosote, trembling slightly.

'Shut up.'

The Seriph ran his tongue over his lips.

'I suppose a quick anecdote is out of the question?' he croaked.

Conina sighed. 'There's more to life than narrative, you know.'

'Sorry. I lost control a little, there.'

Now that the sun was well up the crushed-shell beach glowed like a salt flat. The sea didn't look any better by daylight. It moved like thin oil.

Away on either side the beach stretched in long, excruciatingly flat curves, supporting nothing but a few clumps of withered dune grass which lived off the moisture in the spray. There was no sign of any shade.

'The way I see it,' said Conina, 'this is a beach, and that means sooner or later we'll come to a river, so all we have to do is keep walking in one direction.'

'And yet, delightful snow on the slopes of Mount Eritor, we do not know which one.'

Nijel sighed, and reached into his bag.

'Erm,' he said, 'excuse me. Would this be any good? I stole it. Sorry.'

He held out the lamp that had been in the treasury.

'It's magic, isn't it?' he said hopefully. 'I've heard about them, isn't it worth a try?'

Creosote shook his head.

'But you said your grandfather used it to make his fortune!' said Conina.

'*A* lamp,' said the Seriph, 'he used *a* lamp. Not this lamp. No, the real lamp was a battered old thing, and one day this wicked pedlar came round offering new lamps for old and my great-grandmother gave it to him for this one. The family kept it in the vault as a sort of memorial to her. A truly stupid woman. It doesn't work, of course.'

'You tried it?'

'No, but he wouldn't have given it away if it was any good, would he?'

'Give it a rub,' said Conina. 'It can't do any harm.'

'I wouldn't,' warned Creosote.

Nijel held the lamp gingerly. It had a strangely sleek look, as if someone had set out to make a lamp that could go fast.

He rubbed it.

The effects were curiously unimpressive. There was a half-hearted pop and a puff of wispy smoke near Nijel's feet. A line appeared in the beach several feet away from the smoke. It spread quickly to outline a square of sand, which vanished.

A figure barrelled out of the beach, jerked to a stop, and groaned.

It was wearing a turban, an expensive tan, a small gold medallion, shiny shorts and advanced running shoes with curly toes.

It said, 'I want to get this absolutely straight. Where am I?'

Conina recovered first.

'It's a beach,' she said.

'Yah,' said the genie. 'What I mean was, which lamp? What world?'

'Don't you know?'

The creature took the lamp out of Nijel's unresisting grasp.

'Oh, this old thing,' he said. 'I'm on time share. Two weeks every August but, of course, usually one can never get away.'

'Got a lot of lamps, have you?' said Nijel.

'I am somewhat over-committed on lamps,' the genie agreed. 'In fact I am thinking of diversifying into rings. Rings are looking big at the moment. There's a lot of movement in rings. Sorry, people; what can I do you for?' The last phrase was turned in that special voice which people use for humorous self-parody, in the mistaken hope that it will make them sound less like a prat.

'We—' Conina began.

'I want a drink,' snapped Creosote. 'And you are *supposed* to say that my wish is your command.'

'Oh, absolutely no-one says that sort of thing any more,' said the genie, and produced a glass out of nowhere. He treated Creosote to a brilliant smile lasting a small percentage of one second.

'We want you to take us across the sea to Ankh-Morpork,' said Conina firmly.

The genie looked blank. Then he pulled a very thick book[*] from the empty air and consulted it.

'It sounds a really neat concept,' he said eventually. 'Let's do lunch next Tuesday, okay?'

'Do what?'

---

[*] It was a Fullomyth, an invaluable aid for all whose business is with the arcane and hermetic. It contained lists of things that didn't exist and, in a very significant way, weren't important. Some of its pages could only be read after midnight, or by strange and improbable illuminations. There were descriptions of underground constellations and wines as yet unfermented. For the really up-to-the-epoch occultist, who could afford the version bound in spider skin, there was even an insert showing the London Underground with the three stations they never dare show on the public maps.

'I'm a little energetic right now.'

'*You're a little*—?' Conina began.

'Great,' said the genie, sincerely, and glanced at his wrist. 'Hey, is that the time?' He vanished.

The three of them looked at the lamp in thoughtful silence, and then Nijel said, 'Whatever happened to, you know, the fat guys with the baggy trousers and I Hear And Obey O Master?'

Creosote snarled. He'd just drunk his drink. It had turned out to be water with bubbles in it and a taste like warm flatirons.

'I'm bloody well not standing for it,' snarled Conina. She snatched the lamp from his hand and rubbed it as if she was sorry she wasn't holding a handful of emery cloth.

The genie reappeared at a different spot, which still managed to be several feet away from the weak explosion and obligatory cloud of smoke.

He was now holding something curved and shiny to his ear, and listening intently. He looked hurriedly at Conina's angry face and contrived to suggest, by waggling his eyebrows and waving his free hand urgently, that he was currently and inconveniently tied up by irksome matters which, regretfully, prevented him giving her his full attention as of now but, as soon as he had disentangled himself from this importunate person, she could rest assured that her wish, which was certainly a wish of tone and brilliance, would be his command.

'I shall smash the lamp,' she said quietly.

The genie flashed her a smile and spoke hastily into the thing he was cradling between his chin and his shoulder.

'Fine,' he said. 'Great. It's a slice, believe me. Have your people call my people. Stay beyond, okay? Bye.' He lowered the instrument. 'Bastard,' he said vaguely.

'I really shall smash the lamp,' said Conina.

'Which lamp is this?' said the genie hurriedly.

'How many have you got?' said Nijel. 'I always thought genies had just the one.'

The genie explained wearily that in fact he had several lamps. There was a small but well-appointed lamp where he lived during the week, another rather unique lamp in the country, a carefully restored peasant rushlight in an unspoilt wine-growing district near Quirm, and just recently a set of derelict lamps in the docks area of Ankh-Morpork that had great potential, once the smart crowd got there, to become the occult equivalent of a suite of offices and a wine bar.

162

They listened in awe, like fish who had inadvertently swum into a lecture on how to fly.

'Who are your people the other people have got to call?' said Nijel, who was impressed, although he didn't know why or by what.

'Actually, I don't have any people yet,' said the genie, and gave a grimace that was definitely upwardly-mobile at the corners. 'But I will.'

'Everyone shut up,' said Conina firmly, 'and *you*, take us to Ankh-Morpork.'

'I should, if I were you,' said Creosote. 'When the young lady's mouth looks like a letter box, it's best to do what she says.'

The genie hesitated.

'I'm not very deep on transport,' he said.

'Learn,' said Conina. She was tossing the lamp from hand to hand.

'Teleportation is a major headache,' said the genie, looking desperate. 'Why don't we do lun—'

'Right, that's it,' said Conina. 'Now I just need a couple of big flat rocks—'

'Okay, okay. Just hold hands, will you? I'll give it my best shot, but this could be one big mistake—'

The astro-philosophers of Krull once succeeded in proving conclusively that all places are one place and that the distance between them is an illusion, and this news was an embarrassment to all thinking philosophers because it did not explain, among other things, signposts. After years of wrangling the whole thing was then turned over to Ly Tin Wheedle, arguably the Disc's greatest philosopher*, who after some thought proclaimed that although it was indeed true that all places were one place, that place was *very large*.

And so psychic order was restored. Distance is, however, an entirely subjective phenomenon and creatures of magic can adjust it to suit themselves.

They are not necessarily very good at it.

Rincewind sat dejectedly in the blackened ruins of the Library, trying to put his finger on what was wrong with them.

Well, everything, for a start. It was unthinkable that the Library should be burned. It was the largest accumulation of magic on the Disc. It underpinned wizardry. Every spell ever used was written down in it somewhere. Burning them was, was, was . . .

---

*He always argued that he was.

There weren't any ashes. Plenty of wood ashes, lots of chains, lots of blackened stone, lots of mess. But thousands of books don't burn easily. They would leave bits of cover and piles of feathery ash. And there wasn't any.

Rincewind stirred the rubble with his toe.

There was only the one door into the Library. Then there were the cellars – he could see the stairs down to them, choked with garbage – but you couldn't hide all the books down there. You couldn't teleport them out either, they would be resistant to such magic; anyone who tried something like that would end up wearing his brains outside his hat.

There was an explosion overhead. A ring of orange fire formed about halfway up the tower of sourcery, ascended quickly and soared off towards Quirm.

Rincewind slid around on his makeshift seat and stared up at the Tower of Art. He got the distinct impression that it was looking back at him. It was totally without windows, but for a moment he thought he saw a movement up among the crumbling turrets.

He wondered how old the tower really was. Older than the University, certainly. Older than the city, which had formed about it like scree around a mountain. Maybe older than geography. There had been a time when the continents were different, Rincewind understood, and then they'd sort of shuffled more comfortably together like puppies in a basket. Perhaps the tower had been washed up on the waves of rock, from somewhere else. Maybe it had been there before the Disc itself, but Rincewind didn't like to consider that, because it raised uncomfortable questions about who built it and what for.

He examined his conscience.

It said: I'm out of options. Please yourself.

Rincewind stood up and brushed the dust and ash off his robe, removing quite a lot of the moulting red plush as well. He removed his hat, made a preoccupied attempt at straightening the point, and replaced it on his head.

Then he walked unsteadily towards the Tower of Art.

There was a very old and quite small door at the base. He wasn't at all surprised when it opened as he approached.

'Strange place,' said Nijel. 'Funny curve to the walls.'

'Where are we?' said Conina.

'And is there any alcohol?' said Creosote. 'Probably not,' he added.

164

'And why is it rocking?' said Conina. 'I've never been anywhere with metal walls before.' She sniffed. 'Can you smell oil?' she added, suspiciously.

The genie reappeared, although this time without the smoke and erratic trapdoor effects. It was noticeable that he tried to keep as far away from Conina as politely possible.

'Everyone okay?' he said.

'Is this Ankh?' she said. 'Only when we wanted to go there, we rather hoped you'd put us somewhere with a door.'

'You're on your way,' said the genie.

'In what?'

Something about the way in which the spirit hesitated caused Nijel's mind to leap a tall conclusion from a standing start. He looked down at the lamp in his hands.

He gave it an experimental jerk. The floor shook.

'Oh, no,' he said. 'It's physically impossible.'

'We're in the *lamp*?' said Conina.

The room trembled again as Nijel tried to look down the spout.

'Don't worry about it,' said the genie. 'In fact, don't think about it if possible.'

He explained – although 'explained' is probably too positive a word, and in this case really means failed to explain but at some length – that it was perfectly possible to travel across the world in a small lamp being carried by one of the party, the lamp itself moving because it was being carried by one of the people inside it, because of a) the fractal nature of reality, which meant that everything could be thought of as being inside everything else and b) creative public relations. The trick relied on the laws of physics failing to spot the flaw until the journey was complete.

'In the circumstances it is best not to think about it, yuh?' said the genie.

'Like not thinking about pink rhinoceroses,' said Nijel, and gave an embarrassed laugh as they stared at him.

'It was a sort of game we had,' he said. 'You had to avoid thinking of pink rhinoceroses.' He coughed. 'I didn't say it was a particularly good game.'

He squinted down the spout again.

'No,' said Conina, 'not very.'

'Uh,' said the genie, 'Would anyone like coffee? Some sounds? A quick game of Significant Quest?*

---

*Very popular among gods, demi-gods, daemons and other supernatural creatures, who feel at home with questions like 'What is It all About?' and 'Where will It all End?'

165

'Drink?' said Creosote.

'White wine?'

'Foul muck.'

The genie looked shocked.

'Red is bad for—' it began.

'—but any port in a storm,' said Creosote hurriedly. 'Or sauterne, even. But no umbrella in it.' It dawned on the Seriph that this wasn't the way to talk to the genie. He pulled himself together a bit. 'No umbrella, by the Five Moons of Nasreem. Or bits of fruit salad or olives or curly straws or ornamental monkeys, I command thee by the Seventeen Siderites of Sarudin—'

'I'm not an umbrella person,' said the genie sulkily.

'It's pretty sparse in here,' said Conina, 'Why don't you furnish it?'

'What I don't understand,' said Nijel, 'is, if we're all in the lamp I'm holding, then the me in the lamp is holding a smaller lamp and in *that* lamp—'

The genie waved his hands urgently.

'Don't talk about it!' he commanded. 'Please!'

Nijel's honest brow wrinkled. 'Yes, but,' he said, 'is there a lot of me, or what?'

'It's all cyclic, but stop drawing attention to it, yuh? . . . Oh, shit.'

There was the subtle, unpleasant sound of the universe suddenly catching on.

It was dark in the tower, a solid core of antique darkness that had been there since the dawn of time and resented the intrusion of the upstart daylight that nipped in around Rincewind.

He felt the air move as the door shut behind him and the dark poured back, filling up the space where the light had been so neatly that you couldn't have seen the join even if the light had still been there.

The interior of the tower smelled of antiquity, with a slight suspicion of raven droppings.

It took a great deal of courage to stand there in that dark. Rincewind didn't have that much, but stood there anyway.

Something started to snuffle around his feet, and Rincewind stood very still. The only reason he didn't move was for fear of treading on something worse.

Then a hand like an old leather glove touched his, very gently, and a voice said: 'Oook.'

Rincewind looked up.

The dark yielded, just once, to a vivid flash of light. And Rincewind saw.

The whole tower was lined with books. They were squeezed on every step of the rotting spiral staircase that wound up inside. They were piled up on the floor, although something about the way in which they were piled suggested that the word 'huddled' would be more appropriate. They had lodged – all right, they had perched – on every crumbling ledge.

They were observing him, in some covert way that had nothing to do with the normal six senses. Books are pretty good at conveying meaning, not necessarily their own personal meanings of course, and Rincewind grasped the fact that they were trying to tell him something.

There was another flash. He realised that it was magic from the sourcerer's tower, reflected down from the distant hole that led on to the roof.

At least it enabled him to identify Wuffles, who was wheezing at his right foot. That was a bit of a relief. Now if he could just put a name to the soft, repetitive slithering noise near his left ear . . .

There was a further obliging flash, which found him looking directly into the little yellow eyes of the Patrician, who was clawing patiently at the side of his glass jar. It was a gentle, mindless scrabbling, as if the little lizard wasn't particularly trying to get out but was just vaguely interested in seeing how long it would take to wear the glass away.

Rincewind looked down at the pear-shaped bulk of the Librarian.

'There's thousands of them,' he whispered, his voice being sucked away and silenced by the massed ranks of books. 'How did you get them all in here?'

'Oook oook.'

'They what?'

'Oook,' repeated the Librarian, making vigorous flapping motions with his bald elbows.

'Fly?'

'Oook.'

'Can they do that?'

'Oook,' nodded the Librarian.

'That must have been pretty impressive. I'd like to see that one day.'

'Oook.'

Not every book had made it. Most of the important grimoires had got out, but a seven-volume herbal had lost its index to the flames and many a trilogy was mourning for its lost volume. Quite a few books had scorch marks on their bindings; some had lost their covers, and trailed their stitching unpleasantly on the floor.

A match flared, and pages rippled uneasily around the walls. But it was only the Librarian, who lit a candle and shambled across the floor at the base of a menacing shadow big enough to climb skyscrapers. He had set up a rough table against one wall and it was covered with arcane tools, pots of rare adhesives and a bookbinder's vice which was already holding a stricken folio. A few weak lines of magic fire crawled across it.

The ape pushed the candlestick into Rincewind's hand, picked up a scalpel and a pair of tweezers, and bent low over the trembling book. Rincewind went pale.

'Um,' he said, 'er, do you mind if I go away? I faint at the sight of glue.'

The Librarian shook his head and jerked a preoccupied thumb towards a tray of tools.

'Oook,' he commanded. Rincewind nodded miserably, and obediently handed him a pair of long-nosed scissors. The wizard winced as a couple of damaged pages were snipped free and dropped to the floor.

'What are you doing to it?' he managed.

'Oook.'

'An appendectomy? Oh.'

The ape jerked his thumb again, without looking up. Rincewind fished a needle and thread out of the ranks on the tray and handed them over. There was silence broken only by the scritching sound of thread being pulled through paper until the Librarian straightened up and said:

'Oook.'

Rincewind pulled out his handkerchief and mopped the ape's brow.

'Oook.'

'Don't mention it. Is it – going to be all right?'

The Librarian nodded. There was also a general, almost inaudible sigh of relief from the tier of books above them.

Rincewind sat down. The books were frightened. In fact they were terrified. The presence of the sourcerer made their spines creep, and the pressure of their attention closed in around him like a vice.

'All right,' he mumbled, 'but what can I do about it?'

'Oook.' The Librarian gave Rincewind a look that would have been exactly like a quizzical look over the top of a pair of half-moon spectacles, if he had been wearing any, and reached for another broken book.

'I mean, you know I'm no good at magic.'

'Oook.'

'The sourcery that's about now, it's terrible stuff. I mean, it's the original stuff, from right back in the dawn of time. Or around breakfast, at any rate.'

'Oook.'

'It'll destroy everything eventually, won't it?'

'Oook.'

'It's about time someone put a stop to this sourcery, right?'

'Oook.'

'Only it can't be me, you see. When I came here I thought I could do something, but that tower! It's so big! It must be proof against all magic! If really powerful wizards won't do anything about it, how can I?'

'Oook,' agreed the Librarian, sewing a ruptured spine.

'So, you see, I think someone else can save the world this time. I'm no good at it.'

The ape nodded, reached across and lifted Rincewind's hat from his head.

'Hey!'

The Librarian ignored him, picked up a pair of shears.

'Look, that's my hat, if you don't mind *don't you dare do that to my*—'

He leapt across the floor and was rewarded with a thump across the side of the head, which would have astonished him if he'd had time to think about it; the Librarian might shuffle around the place like a good-natured wobbly balloon, but underneath that oversized skin was a framework of superbly-cantilevered bone and muscle that could drive a fistful of calloused knuckles through a thick oak plank. Running into the Librarian's arm was like hitting a hairy iron bar.

Wuffles started to bounce up and down, yelping with excitement.

Rincewind screamed a hoarse, untranslatable yell of fury, bounced off the wall, snatched up a fallen rock as a crude club, kicked forward and stopped dead.

The Librarian was crouched in the centre of the floor with the shears touching – but not yet cutting – the hat.

And he was grinning at Rincewind.

They stood like a frozen tableau for some seconds. Then the ape dropped the shears, flicked several imaginary flecks of dust off the hat, straightened the point, and placed it on Rincewind's head.

A few shocked moments after this Rincewind realised that he was holding up, at arm's length, a very large and extremely heavy rock. He managed to force it away on one side before it recovered from the shock and remembered to fall on him.

'I see,' he said, sinking back against the wall and rubbing his elbows. 'And all that's supposed to tell me something, is it? A moral lesson, let Rincewind confront his true self, let him work out what he's really prepared to fight for. Eh? Well, it was a very cheap trick. And I've news for you. If you think it worked—' he snatched the hat brim – 'if you think it worked. If you think I've. You've got another thought. Listen, it's. If you think.'

His voice stuttered into silence. Then he shrugged.

'All right. But when you get down to it, what can I actually *do*?'

The Librarian replied with an expansive gesture that indicated, as clearly as if he had said 'oook', that Rincewind was a wizard with a hat, a library of magical books and a tower. This could be regarded as everything a magical practitioner could need. An ape, a small terrier with halitosis and a lizard in a jar were optional extras.

Rincewind felt a slight pressure on his foot. Wuffles, who was extremely slow on the uptake, had fastened his toothless gums on the toe of Rincewind's boot and was giving it a vicious suck.

He picked the little dog up by the scruff of its neck and the bristly stub that, for the want of a better word, it called its tail, and gently lifted it sideways.

'Okay,' he said. 'You'd better tell me what's been happening here.'

From the Carrack Mountains, overlooking the vast cold Sto Plain in the middle of which Ankh-Morpork sprawled like a bag of dropped groceries, the view was particularly impressive. Mishits and ricochets from the magical battle were expanding outwards and upwards, in a bowl-shaped cloud of curdled air at the heart of which strange lights flashed and sparkled.

The roads leading away from it were packed with refugees, and every inn and wayside tavern was crowded out. Or nearly every one.

No-one seemed to want to stop at the rather pleasant little pub nestling among trees just off the road to Quirm. It wasn't that they were frightened to go inside, it was just that, for the moment, they weren't being allowed to notice it.

There was a disturbance in the air about half a mile away and three figures dropped out of nowhere into a thicket of lavender.

They lay supine in the sunshine among the broken, fragrant branches, until their sanity came back. Then Creosote said, 'Where are we, do you suppose?'

'It smells like someone's underwear drawer,' said Conina.

'Not mine,' said Nijel, firmly.

He eased himself up gently and added, 'Has anyone seen the lamp?'

'Forget it. It's probably been sold to build a wine-bar,' said Conina.

Nijel scrabbled around among the lavender stems until his hands found something small and metallic.

'Got it!' he declared.

'Don't rub it!' said the other two, in harmony. They were too late anyway, but that didn't much matter, because all that happened when Nijel gave it a cautious buff was the appearance of some small smoking red letters in mid-air.

'"Hi",' Nijel read aloud. '"Do not put down the lamp, because your custom is important to us. Please leave a wish after the tone and, very shortly, it will be our command. In the meantime, have a nice eternity."' He added, 'You know, I think he's a bit over-committed.'

Conina said nothing. She was staring out across the plains to the broiling storm of magic. Occasionally some of it would detach and soar away to some distant tower. She shivered, despite the growing heat of the day.

'We ought to get down there as soon as possible,' she said.

'It's very important.'

'Why?' said Creosote. One glass of wine hadn't really restored him to his former easygoing nature.

Conina opened her mouth, and – quite unusually for her – shut it again. There was no way to explain that every gene in her body was dragging her onwards, telling her that she should get involved; visions of swords and spiky balls on chains kept invading the hair-dressing salons of her consciousness.

Nijel, on the other hand, felt no such pounding. All he had to drive him onwards was imagination, but he did have enough of that to float a medium-sized war galley. He looked towards the city with what would have been, but for his lack of chin, an expression of set-jawed determination.

Creosote realised that he was outnumbered.

'Do they have any drink down there?' he said.

'Lots,' said Nijel.

'That might do for a start,' the Seriph conceded. 'All right, lead on, O peach-breasted daughter of—'

'And no poetry.'

They untangled themselves from the thicket and walked down the hillside until they reached the road which, before very long, went past the aforementioned tavern or, as Creosote persisted in calling it, caravanserai.

They hesitated about going in. It didn't seem to welcome visitors. But Conina, who by breeding and upbringing tended to skulk around the back of buildings, found four horses tethered in the yard.

They considered them carefully.

'It would be stealing,' said Nijel, slowly.

Conina opened her mouth to agree and the words 'Why not?' slid past her lips. She shrugged.

'Perhaps we should leave some money—' Nijel suggested.

'Don't look at me,' said Creosote.

'—or maybe write a note and leave it under the bridle. Or something. Don't you think?'

By way of answer Conina vaulted up on to the largest horse, which by the look of it belonged to a soldier. Weaponry was slung all over it.

Creosote hoisted himself uneasily on to the second horse, a rather skittish bay, and sighed.

'She's got that letter-box look,' he said. 'I should do what she says.'

Nijel regarded the other two horses suspiciously. One of them was very large and extremely white, not the off-white which was all that most horses could manage, but a translucent, ivory white tone which Nijel felt an unconscious urge to describe as 'shroud'. It also gave him a distinct impression that it was more intelligent than he was.

He selected the other one. It was a bit thin, but docile, and he managed to get on after only two tries.

They set off.

The sound of their hoofbeats barely penetrated the gloom inside the tavern. The innkeeper moved like someone in a dream. He knew he had customers, he'd even spoken to them, he could even see them sitting round a table by the fire, but if asked to describe *who* he'd talked to and *what* he had seen he'd have been at a loss.

This is because the human brain is remarkably good at shutting out things it doesn't want to know. His could currently have shielded a bank vault.

And the drinks! Most of them he'd never heard of, but strange bottles kept appearing on the shelves above the beer barrels. The trouble was that whenever he tried to think about it, his thoughts just slid away . . .

The figures around the table looked up from their cards.

One of them raised a hand. It's stuck on the end of his arm and it's got five fingers, the innkeeper's mind said. It must be a hand.

One thing the innkeeper's brain couldn't shut out was the sound of the voices. This one sounded as though someone was hitting a rock with a roll of sheet lead.

BAR PERSON.

The innkeeper groaned faintly. The thermic lances of horror were melting their way steadily through the steel door of his mind.

LET ME SEE, NOW. THAT'S A – WHAT WAS IT AGAIN?

'A Bloody Mary.' *This* voice made a simple drinks order sound like the opening of hostilities.

OH, YES. AND—

'Mine was a small egg nog,' said Pestilence.

AN EGG NOG.

'With a cherry in it.'

GOOD, lied the heavy voice. AND THAT'LL BE A SMALL PORT WINE FOR ME AND, the speaker glanced across the table at the fourth member of the quartet and sighed, YOU'D BETTER BRING ANOTHER BOWL OF PEANUTS.

About three hundred yards down the road the horse thieves were trying to come to terms with a new experience.

'Certainly a smooth ride,' Nijel managed eventually.

'And a lovely – a lovely view,' said Creosote, his voice lost in the slipstream.

'But I wonder,' said Nijel, 'if we have done exactly the right thing.'

'We're moving, aren't we?' demanded Conina. 'Don't be petty.'

'It's just that, well, looking at cumulus clouds from *above* is—'

'Shut up.'

'Sorry.'

'Anyway, they're stratus. Strato-cumulus at most.'

'Right,' said Nijel miserably.

'Does it make any difference?' said Creosote, who was lying flat on his horse's neck with his eyes shut.

'About a thousand feet.'

'Oh.'

'Could be seven hundred and fifty,' conceded Conina.

'Ah.'

The tower of sourcery trembled. Coloured smoke rolled through its vaulted rooms and shining corridors. In the big room at the very tip, where the air was thick and greasy and tasted of burning tin, many wizards had passed out with the sheer mental effort of the battle. But enough remained. They sat in a wide circle, locked in concentration.

It was just possible to see the shimmering in the air as the raw sourcery swirled out of the staff in Coin's hand and into the centre of the octogram.

Outlandish shapes appeared for a brief instant and vanished. The very fabric of reality was being put through the wringer in there.

Carding shuddered, and turned away in case he saw anything he really couldn't ignore.

The surviving senior wizards had a simulacrum of the Disc hovering in front of them. As Carding looked at it again the little red glow over the city of Quirm flared and went out.

The air creaked.

'There goes Quirm,' murmured Carding.

'That just leaves Al Khali,' said one of the others.

'There's some clever power there.'

Carding nodded glumly. He'd quite liked Quirm, which was a – had been a pleasant little city overlooking the Rim Ocean.

He dimly recalled being taken there, once, when he was small. For a moment he gazed sadly into the past. It had wild geraniums, he recalled, filling the sloping cobbled streets with their musky fragrance.

'Growing out of the walls,' he said out loud. 'Pink. They were pink.'

The other wizards looked at him oddly. One or two, of a particularly paranoid frame of mind even for wizards, glanced suspiciously at the walls.

'Are you all right?' said one of them.

'Um?' said Carding, 'Oh. Yes, Sorry. Miles away.'

He turned back to look at Coin, who was sitting off to one side of the circle with the staff across his knees. The boy appeared to be asleep. Perhaps he was. But Carding knew in the tormented pit of his soul that the staff didn't sleep. It was watching him, testing his mind.

It knew. It even knew about the pink geraniums.

'I never wanted it to be like this,' he said softly. 'All we really wanted was a bit of respect.'

'Are you *sure* you're all right?'

Carding nodded vaguely. As his colleagues resumed their concentration he glanced sideways at them.

Somehow, all his old friends had gone. Well, not friends. A wizard never had friends, at least not friends who were wizards. It needed a different word. Ah yes, that was it. *Enemies*. But a very decent class of enemies. Gentlemen. The cream of their profession. Not like these people, for all that they seemed to have risen in the craft since the sourcerer had arrived.

Other things besides the cream floated to the top, he reflected sourly.

He turned his attention to Al Khali, probing with his mind, knowing that the wizards there were almost certainly doing the same, seeking constantly for a point of weakness.

He thought: am I a point of weakness? Spelter tried to tell me something. It was about the staff. A man should lean on his staff, not the other way around . . . it's steering him, leading him . . . I wish I'd listened to Spelter . . . this is wrong, I'm a point of weakness . . .

He tried again, riding the surges of power, letting them carry his mind into the enemy tower. Even Abrim was making use of sourcery, and Carding let himself modulate the wave, insinuating himself past the defences erected against him.

The image of the interior of the Al Khali tower appeared, focused . . .

. . . *the Luggage trundled along the glowing corridors. It was exceedingly angry now. It had been awoken from hibernation, it had been scorned, it had been briefly attacked by a variety of mythological and now extinct lifeforms, it had a headache and now, as it entered the Great Hall, it detected the hat. The horrible hat, the cause of everything it was currently suffering. It advanced purposefully . . .*

Carding, testing the resistance of Abrim's mind, felt the man's attention waver. For a moment he saw through the enemy's eyes, saw the squat oblong cantering across the stone. For a moment Abrim attempted to shift his concentration and then, no more able to help himself than is a cat when it sees something small and squeaky run across the floor, Carding struck.

Not much. It didn't need much. Abrim's mind was attempting to balance and channel huge forces, and it needed hardly any pressure to topple it from its position.

Abrim extended his hands to blast the Luggage, gave the merest beginnings of a scream, and imploded.

The wizards around him thought they saw him grow impossibly small in a fraction of a second and vanish, leaving a black after-image . . .

The more intelligent of them started to run . . .

And the magic he had been controlling surged back out and flooded free in one great, randomised burst that blew the hat to bits, took out the entire lower levels of the tower and quite a large part of what remained of the city.

So many wizards in Ankh had been concentrating on the hall that the sympathetic resonance blew them across the room. Carding ended up on his back, his hat over his eyes.

They hauled him out and dusted him off and carried him to Coin and the staff, amid cheers – although some of the older wizards forbore to cheer. But he didn't seem to pay any attention.

He stared sightlessly down at the boy, and then slowly raised his hands to his ears.

'Can't you hear them?' he said.

The wizards fell silent. Carding still had power, and the tone of his voice would have quelled a thunderstorm.

Coin's eyes glowed.

'I hear nothing,' he said.

Carding turned to the rest of the wizards.

'Can't *you* hear them?'

They shook their heads. One of them said, 'Hear what, brother?'

Carding smiled, and it was a wide, mad smile. Even Coin took a step backwards.

'You'll hear them soon enough,' he said. 'You've made a beacon. You'll all hear them. But you won't hear them for long.' He pushed aside the younger wizards who were holding his arms and advanced on Coin.

'You're pouring sourcery into the world and other things are coming with it,' he said. 'Others have given them a pathway but you've given them an *avenue!*'

He sprang forward and snatched the black staff out of Coin's hands and swung it up in the air to smash it against the wall.

Carding went rigid as the staff struck back. Then his skin began to blister . . .

176

Most of the wizards managed to turn their heads away. A few – and there are always a few like that – watched in obscene fascination.

Coin watched, too. His eyes widened in wonder. One hand went to his mouth. He tried to back away. He couldn't.

'*They're* cumulus.'

'Marvellous,' said Nijel weakly.

WEIGHT DOESN'T COME INTO IT. MY STEED HAS CARRIED ARMIES. MY STEED HAS CARRIED CITIES. YEA, HE HATH CARRIED ALL THINGS IN THEIR DUE TIME, said Death. BUT HE'S NOT GOING TO CARRY YOU THREE.

'Why not?'

IT'S A MATTER OF THE LOOK OF THE THING.

'It's going to look pretty good, then, isn't it,' said War testily, 'the One Horseman and Three Pedestrians of the Apocralypse.'

'*Perhaps you could ask them to wait for us?*' said Pestilence, his voice sounding like something dripping out of the bottom of a coffin.

I HAVE THINGS TO ATTEND TO, said Death. He made a little clicking noise with his teeth. I'M SURE YOU'LL MANAGE. YOU NORMALLY DO.

War watched the retreating horse.

'Sometimes he really gets on my nerves. Why is he always so keen to have the last word?' he said.

'*Force of habit, I suppose.*'

They turned back to the tavern. Neither spoke for some time, and then War said, 'Where's Famine?'

'*Went to find the kitchen.*'

'Oh.' War scuffed one armoured foot in the dust, and thought about the distance to Ankh. It was a very hot afternoon. The Apocralypse could jolly well wait.

'One for the road?' he suggested.

'*Should we?*' said Pestilence, doubtfully. '*I thought we were expected. I mean, I wouldn't like to disappoint people.*'

'We've got time for a quick one, I'm sure,' War insisted. 'Pub clocks are never right. We've got bags of time. All the time in the world.'

*

Carding slumped forward and thudded on the shining white floor. The staff rolled out of his hands and upended itself.

Coin prodded the limp body with his foot.

'I did warn him,' he said. 'I told him what would happen if he touched it again. What did he mean, *them*?'

There was an outbreak of coughing and a considerable inspection of fingernails.

'What did he mean?' Coin demanded.

Ovin Hakardly, lecturer in Lore, once again found that the wizards around him were parting like morning mist. Without moving he appeared to have stepped forward. His eyes swivelled backwards and forwards like trapped animals.

'Er,' he said. He waved his thin hands vaguely. 'The world, you see, that is, the reality in which we live, in fact, it can be thought of as, in a manner of speaking, a rubber sheet.' He hesitated, aware that the sentence was not going to appear in anyone's book of quotable quotes.

'In that,' he added hurriedly, 'it is distorted, uh, *distended* by the presence of magic in any degree and, if I may make a point here, too much magical potentiality, if foregathered in one spot, forces our reality, um, downwards, although of course one should not take the term literally (because in no sense do I seek to suggest a physical dimension) and it has been postulated that a sufficient exercise of magic can, shall we say, um, break through the actuality at its lowest point and offer, perhaps, a pathway to the inhabitants or, if I may use a more correct term, *denizens* of the lower plane (which is called by the loose-tongued the Dungeon Dimensions) who, because perhaps of the difference in energy levels, are naturally attracted to the brightness of this world. Our world.'

There was the typical long pause which usually followed Hakardly's speeches, while everybody mentally inserted commas and stitched the fractured clauses together.

Coin's lips moved silently for a while. 'Do you mean magic attracts these creatures?' he said eventually.

His voice was quite different now. It lacked its former edge. The staff hung in the air above the prone body of Carding, rotating slowly. The eyes of every wizard in the place were on it.

'So it appears,' said Hakardly. 'Students of such things say their presence is heralded by a coarse susurration.'

Coin looked uncertain.

'They buzz,' said one of the other wizards helpfully. The boy knelt down and peered closely at Carding.

'He's very still,' he said curiously. 'Is anything bad happening to him?'

'It may be,' said Hakardly, guardedly. 'He's dead.'

'I wish he wasn't.'

'It is a view, I suspect, which he shares.'

'But I can help him,' said Coin. He held out his hands and the staff glided into them. If it had a face, it would have smirked.

When he spoke next his voice once again had the cold distant tones of someone speaking in a steel room.

'If failure had no penalty success would not be a prize,' he said.

'Sorry?' said Hakardly. 'You've lost me there.'

Coin turned on his heel and strode back to his chair.

'We can fear nothing,' he said, and it sounded more like a command. 'What of these Dungeon Dimensions? If they should trouble us, away with them! A true wizard will fear nothing! Nothing!'

He jerked to his feet again and strode to the simulacrum of the world. The image was perfect in every detail, down to a ghost of Great A'Tuin paddling slowly through the interstellar deeps a few inches above the floor.

Coin waved his hand through it disdainfully.

'Ours is a world of magic,' he said. 'And what can be found in it that can stand against us?'

Hakardly thought that something was expected of him.

'Absolutely no-one,' he said. 'Except for the gods, of course.'

There was dead silence.

'The gods?' said Coin quietly.

'Well, yes. Certainly. We don't challenge the gods. They do their job, we do ours. No sense in—'

'Who rules the Disc? Wizards or gods?'

Hakardly thought quickly.

'Oh, wizards. Of course. But, as it were, *under* the gods.'

When one accidentally puts one boot in a swamp it is quite unpleasant. But not as unpleasant as pushing down with the other boot and hearing that, too, disappear with a soft sucking noise. Hakardly pressed on.

'You see, wizardry is more—'

'Are we not more powerful than the gods, then?' said Coin.

Some of the wizards at the back of the crowd began to shuffle their feet.

'Well. Yes and no,' said Hakardly, up to his knees in it now.

The truth was that wizards tended to be somewhat nervous about the gods. The beings who dwelt on Cori Celesti had never made their feelings plain on the subject of ceremonial magic, which after all had a certain godness about it, and wizards tended to avoid the whole subject. The trouble with gods was that if they didn't like something they didn't just drop hints, so common sense suggested that it was unwise to put the gods in a position where they had to decide.

'There seems to be some uncertainty?' said Coin.

'If I may counsel—' Hakardly began.

Coin waved a hand. The walls vanished. The wizards stood at the top of the tower of sourcery, and as one man their eyes turned to the distant pinnacle of Cori Celesti, home of the gods.

'When you've beaten everyone else, there's only the gods left to fight,' said Coin. 'Have any of you seen the gods?'

There was a chorus of hesitant denials.

'I will show them to you.'

'You've got room for another one in there, old son,' said War.

Pestilence swayed unsteadily. *'I'm sure we should be getting along,'* he muttered, without much conviction.

'Oh, go on.'

'Just a half, then. And then we really must be going.'

War slapped him on the back, and glared at Famine.

'And we'd better have another fifteen bags of peanuts,' he added.

'Oook,' the Librarian concluded.

'Oh,' said Rincewind. 'It's the staff that's the problem, then.'

'Oook.'

'Hasn't anyone tried to take it away from him?'

'Oook.'

'What happened to them, then?'

'Eeek.'

Rincewind groaned.

The Librarian had put his candle out because the presence of the naked flame was unsettling the books, but now that Rincewind had grown accustomed to the dark, he realised it wasn't dark at all. The soft octarine glow from the books filled the inside of the tower with something that, while it wasn't exactly light, was a blackness you could see by. Now and again the ruffle of stiff pages floated down from the gloom.

'So, basically, there's no way our magic could defeat him, isn't that right?'

The Librarian oooked disconsolate agreement and continued to spin around gently on his bottom.

'Pretty pointless, then. It may have struck you that I am not exactly gifted in the magical department? I mean, any duel is going to go on the lines of "Hallo, I'm Rincewind" closely followed by bazaam!'

'Oook.'

'Basically, what you're saying is that I'm on my own.'

'Oook.'

'Thanks.'

By their own faint glow Rincewind regarded the books that had stacked themselves around the inner walls of the ancient tower.

He sighed, and marched briskly to the door, but slowed down noticeably as he reached it.

'I'll be off, then,' he said.

'Oook.'

'To face who knows what dreadful perils,' Rincewind added. 'To lay down my life in the service of mankind—'

'Eeek.'

'All right, bipeds—'

'Woof.'

'—and quadrupeds, all right.' He glanced at the Patrician's jamjar, a beaten man.

'And lizards,' he added. 'Can I go now?'

A gale was howling down out of a clear sky as Rincewind toiled towards the tower of sourcery. Its high white doors were shut so tightly it was barely possible to see their outline in the milky surface of the stone.

He hammered on it for a bit, but nothing much happened. The doors seemed to absorb the sound.

'Fine thing,' he muttered to himself, and remembered the carpet. It was lying where he had left it, which was another sign that Ankh had changed. In the thieving days before the sourcerer nothing stayed for long where you left it. Nothing printable, anyway.

He rolled it out on the cobbles so that the golden dragons writhed against the blue ground, unless of course the blue dragons were flying against a golden sky.

He sat down.

He stood up.

He sat down again and hitched up his robe and, with some effort, unrolled one of his socks. Then he replaced his boot and wandered around for a bit until he found, among the rubble, a half-brick. He inserted the half-brick into the sock and gave the sock a few thoughtful swings.

Rincewind had grown up in Morpork. What a Morpork citizen liked to have on his side in a fight was odds of about twenty to one, but failing that a sockful of half-brick and a dark alley to lurk in was generally considered a better bet than any two magic swords you cared to name.

He sat down again.

'Up,' he commanded.

The carpet did not respond. Rincewind peered at the pattern, then lifted a corner of the carpet and tried to make out if the underside was any better.

'All right,' he conceded, 'down. Very, very carefully. Down.'

'Sheep,' slurred War. 'It was sheep.' His helmeted head hit the bar with a clang. He raised it again. 'Sheep.'

'Nonono,' said Famine, raising a thin finger unsteadily. 'Some other domess . . . dummist . . . tame animal. Like pig. Heifer. Kitten? Like that. Not sheep.'

'*Bees*,' said Pestilence, and slid gently out of his seat.

'O-kay,' said War, ignoring him, 'right. Once again, then. From the top.' He rapped the side of his glass for the note.

'We are poor little . . . unidentified domesticated animals . . . that have lost our way . . .' he quavered.

'*Baabaabaa*,' muttered Pestilence, from the floor.

War shook his head. 'It isn't the same, you know,' he said. 'Not without him. He used to come in beautifully on the bass.'

'*Baabaabaa*,' Pestilence repeated.

'Oh, shut up,' said War, and reached uncertainly for a bottle.

The gale buffeted the top of the tower, a hot, unpleasant wind that whispered with strange voices and rubbed the skin like fine sandpaper.

In the centre of it Coin stood with the staff over his head. As dust filled the air the wizards saw the lines of magic force pouring from it.

They curved up to form a vast bubble that expanded until it must have been larger than the city. And shapes appeared in it. They were shifting and indistinct, wavering horribly like visions in a distorting mirror, no more substantial than smoke rings or pictures in the clouds, but they were dreadfully familiar.

There, for a moment, was the fanged snout of Offler. There, clear for an instant in the writhing storm, was Blind Io, chief of the gods, with his orbiting eyes.

Coin muttered soundlessly and the bubble began to contract. It bulged and jerked obscenely as the things inside it fought to get out, but they could not stop the contraction.

Now it was bigger than the University grounds.

Now it was taller than the tower.

Now it was twice the height of a man, and smoke grey.

Now it was an iridescent pearl, the size of . . . well, the size of a large pearl.

The gale had gone, replaced by a heavy, silent calm. The very air groaned with the strain. Most of the wizards were flat on the floor, pressed there by the unleashed forces that thickened the air and deadened sound like a universe of feathers, but every one of them could hear his own heart beating loud enough to smash the tower.

'Look at me,' Coin commanded.

They turned their eyes upwards. There was no way they could disobey.

He held the glistening thing in one hand. The other held the staff, which had smoke pouring from its ends.

'The gods,' he said. 'Imprisoned in a thought. And perhaps they were never more than a dream.'

His voice become older, deeper. 'Wizards of Unseen University,' it said, 'have I not given you absolute dominion?'

Behind him the carpet rose slowly over the side of the tower, with Rincewind trying hard to keep his balance. His eyes were wide with the sort of terror that comes naturally to anyone standing on a few threads and several hundred feet of empty air.

He lurched off the hovering thing and on to the tower, swinging the loaded sock around his head in wide, dangerous sweeps.

Coin saw him reflected in the astonished stares of the assembled wizards. He turned carefully and watched the wizard stagger erratically towards him.

'Who are you?' he said.

'I have come,' said Rincewind thickly, 'to challenge the sourcerer. Which one is he?'

He surveyed the prostrate wizardry, hefting the half-brick in one hand.

Hakardly risked a glance upwards and made frantic eyebrow movements at Rincewind who, even at the best of times, wasn't much good at interpreting non-verbal communication. This wasn't the best of times.

'With a sock?' said Coin. 'What good is a sock?'

The arm holding the staff rose. Coin looked down at it in mild astonishment.

'No, stop,' he said. 'I want to talk to this man.' He stared at Rincewind, who was swaying back and forth under the influence of sleeplessness, horror and the after-effects of an adrenaline overdose.

'Is it magical?' he said, curiously. 'Perhaps it is the sock of an Archchancellor? A sock of force?'

Rincewind focused on it.

'I don't think so,' he said. 'I think I bought it in a shop or something. Um. I've got another one somewhere.'

'But in the end it has something heavy?'

'Um. Yes,' said Rincewind. He added, 'It's a half-brick.'

'But it has great power.'

'Er. You can hold things up with it. If you had another one, you'd have a brick.' Rincewind spoke slowly. He was assimilating the situation by a kind of awful osmosis, and watching the staff turn ominously in the boy's hand.

'So. It is a brick of ordinariness, within a sock. The whole becoming a weapon.'

'Um. Yes.'

'How does it work?'

'Um. You swing it, and then you. Hit something with it. Or sometimes the back of your hand, sometimes.'

'And then perhaps it destroys a whole city?' said Coin.

Rincewind stared into Coin's golden eyes, and then at his sock. He had pulled it on and off several times a year for years. It had darns he'd grown to know and lo – well, know. Some of them had whole families of darns of their own. There were a number of descriptions that could be applied to the sock, but slayer-of-cities wasn't among them.

'Not really,' he said at last. 'It sort of kills people but leaves buildings standing.'

Rincewind's mind was operating at the speed of continental drift. Parts of it were telling him that he was confronting the sourcerer, but they were in direct conflict with other parts. Rincewind had heard quite a lot about the power of the sourcerer, the staff of the sourcerer, the wickedness of the sourcerer and so on. The only thing no-one had mentioned was the age of the sourcerer.

He glanced towards the staff.

'And what does *that* do?' he said slowly.

And the staff said, *You must kill this man.*

The wizards, who had been cautiously struggling upright, flung themselves flat again.

The voice of the hat had been bad enough, but the voice of the staff was metallic and precise; it didn't sound as though it was offering advice but simply stating the way the future had to be. It sounded quite impossible to ignore.

Coin half-raised his arm, and hesitated.

'Why?' he said.

You do not disobey me.

'You don't have to,' said Rincewind hurriedly. 'It's only a thing.'

'I do not see why I should hurt him,' said Coin. 'He looks so harmless. Like an angry rabbit.'

He defies us.

'Not me,' said Rincewind, thrusting the arm with the sock behind his back and trying to ignore the bit about the rabbit.

'Why should I do everything you tell me?' said Coin to the staff. 'I always do everything you tell me, and it doesn't help people at all.'

People must fear you. Have I taught you nothing?

'But he looks so funny. He's got a sock,' said Coin.

He screamed, and his arm jerked oddly. Rincewind's hair stood on end.

You will do as you are commanded.

'I won't!'

You know what happens to boys who are bad.

There was a crackle and a smell of scorched flesh. Coin dropped to his knees.

'Here, hang on a minute—' Rincewind began.

Coin opened his eyes. They were gold still, but flecked with brown.

Rincewind swung his sock around in a wide humming arc that connected with the staff halfway along its length. There was a brief explosion of brick dust and burnt wool and the staff spun out of the boy's hand. Wizards scattered as it tumbled end over end across the floor.

It reached the parapet, bounced upwards and shot over the edge.

But, instead of falling, it steadied itself in the air, spun in its own length and sped back again trailing octarine sparks and making a noise like a buzzsaw.

Rincewind pushed the stunned boy behind him, threw away the ravaged sock and whipped his hat off, flailing wildly as the staff bored towards him. It caught him on the side of the head, delivering a shock that almost welded his teeth together and toppled him like a thin and ragged tree.

The staff turned again in mid-air, glowing red-hot now, and swept back for another and quite definitely final run.

Rincewind struggled up on his elbows and watched in horrified fascination as it swooped through the chilly air which, for some reason he didn't understand, seemed to be full of snowflakes.

And became tinged with purple, blotched with blue. Time slowed and ground to a halt like an underwound phonograph.

Rincewind looked up at the tall black figure that had appeared a few feet away.

It was, of course, Death.

He turned his glowing eyesockets towards Rincewind and said, in a voice like the collapse of undersea chasms, GOOD AFTERNOON.

He turned away as if he had completed all necessary business for the time being, stared at the horizon for a while, and started to tap one foot idly. It sounded like a bagful of maracas.

'Er,' said Rincewind.

Death appeared to remember him. I'M SORRY? he said politely.

'I always wondered how it was going to be,' said Rincewind.

Death took an hourglass out from the mysterious folds of his ebon robes and peered at it.

DID YOU? he said, vaguely.

'I suppose I can't complain,' said Rincewind virtuously. 'I've had a good life. Well, quite good.' He hesitated. 'Well, not all that good. I suppose most people would call it pretty awful.' He considered it further. '*I* would,' he added, half to himself.

WHAT ARE YOU TALKING ABOUT, MAN?

Rincewind was nonplussed. 'Don't you make an appearance when a wizard is about to die?'

OF COURSE. AND I MUST SAY YOU PEOPLE ARE GIVING ME A BUSY DAY.

'How do you manage to be in so many places at the same time?'

GOOD ORGANISATION.

Time returned. The staff, which had been hanging in the air a few feet away from Rincewind, started to scream forward again.

And there was a metallic thud as Coin caught it one-handedly in mid-flight.

The staff uttered a noise like a thousand fingernails dragging across glass. It thrashed wildly up and down, flailing at the arm that held it, and bloomed into evil green flame along its entire length.

So. At the last, you fail me.

Coin groaned but held on as the metal under his fingertips went red, then white.

He thrust the arm out in front of him, and the force streaming from the staff roared past him and drew sparks from his hair and whipped his robe up into weird and unpleasant shapes. He screamed and whirled the staff round and smashed it on the parapet, leaving a long bubbling line in the stone.

Then he threw it away. It clattered against the stones and rolled to a halt, wizards scattering out of its path.

Coin sagged to his knees, shaking.

'I don't like killing people,' he said. 'I'm sure it can't be right.'

'Hold on to that thought,' said Rincewind fervently.

'What happens to people after they're dead?' said Coin.

Rincewind glanced up at Death.

'I think this one's for you,' he said.

HE CANNOT SEE OR HEAR ME, said Death, UNTIL HE WANTS TO.

There was a little clinking noise. The staff was rolling back towards Coin, who looked down at it in horror.

Pick me up.

'You don't have to,' said Rincewind again.

You cannot resist me. You cannot defeat yourself, said the staff.

Coin reached out very slowly, and picked it up.

Rincewind glanced at his sock. It was a stub of burnt wool, its brief career as a weapon of war having sent it beyond the help of any darning needle.

Now kill him.

Rincewind held his breath. The watching wizards held their breath. Even Death, who had nothing to hold but his scythe, held it tensely.

'No,' said Coin.

You know what happens to boys who are bad.

Rincewind saw the sourcerer's face go pale.

The staff's voice changed. Now it wheedled.

Without me, who would there be to tell you what to do?

'That is true,' said Coin slowly.

187

See what you have achieved.

Coin stared slowly around at the frightened faces.

'I am seeing,' he said.

I taught you everything I know.

'I am thinking,' said Coin, 'that you do not know enough.'

Ingrate! Who gave you your destiny?

'You did,' said the boy. He raised his head.

'I realise that I was wrong,' he added, quietly.

Good—

'I did not throw you far enough!'

Coin got to his feet in one movement and swung the staff over his head. He stood still as a statue, his hand lost in a ball of light that was the colour of molten copper. It turned green, ascended through shades of blue, hovered in the violet and then seared into pure octarine.

Rincewind shaded his eyes against the glare and saw Coin's hand, still whole, still gripping tight, with beads of molten metal glittering between his fingers.

He slithered away, and bumped into Hakardly. The old wizard was standing like a statue, with his mouth open.

'What'll happen?' said Rincewind.

'He'll never beat it,' said Hakardly hoarsely. 'It's his. It's as strong as him. He's got the power, but *it* knows how to channel it.'

'You mean they'll cancel each other out?'

'Hopefully.'

The battle was hidden in its own infernal glow. Then the floor began to tremble.

'They're drawing on everything magical,' said Hakardly. 'We'd better leave the tower.'

'Why?'

'I imagine it will vanish soon enough.'

And, indeed, the white flagstones around the glow looked as though they were unravelling and disappearing into it.

Rincewind hesitated.

'Aren't we going to help him?' he said.

Hakardly stared at him, and then at the iridescent tableau. His mouth opened and shut once or twice.

'I'm sorry,' he said.

'Yes, but just a bit of help on his side, you've seen what that *thing* is like—'

'I'm sorry.'

'He helped *you*.' Rincewind turned on the other wizards, who

188

were scurrying away. 'All of you. He gave you what you wanted, didn't he?'

'We may never forgive him,' said Hakardly.

Rincewind groaned.

'What will be left when it's all over?' he said. 'What will be left?'

Hakardly looked down.

'I'm sorry,' he repeated.

The octarine light had grown brighter and was beginning to turn black around the edge. It wasn't the black that is merely the opposite of light, though; it was the grainy, shifting blackness that glows beyond the glare and has no business in any decent reality. And it buzzed.

Rincewind did a little dance of uncertainty as his feet, legs, instincts and incredibly well-developed sense of self-preservation overloaded his nervous system to the point where, just as it was on the point of fusing, his conscience finally got its way.

He leapt into the fire and reached the staff.

The wizards fled. Several of them levitated down from the tower.

They were a lot more perspicacious than those that used the stairs because, about thirty seconds later, the tower vanished.

The snow continued to fall around a column of blackness, which buzzed.

And the surviving wizards who dared to look back saw, tumbling slowly down the sky, a small object trailing flames behind it. It crashed into the cobbles, where it smouldered for a bit before the thickening snow put it out.

Pretty soon it became just a small mound.

A little while later a squat figure swung itself across the courtyard on its knuckles, scrabbled in the snow, and hauled the thing out.

It was, or rather it had been, a hat. Life had not been kind to it. A large part of the wide brim had been burned off, the point was entirely gone, and the tarnished silver letters were almost unreadable. Some of them had been torn off in any case. Those that were left spelled out: WIZD.

The Librarian turned around slowly. He was entirely alone, except for the towering column of burning blackness and the steadily falling flakes.

The ravaged campus was empty. There were a few other pointy hats that had been trampled by terrified feet, and no other sign that people had been there.

All the wizards were wazards.

*

'War?'

'Wazzat?'

'Wasn't there,' Pestilence groped for his glass, 'something?'

'Wazzat?'

'We ought to be . . . there's something we ought to be doing,' said Famine.

'S'right. Got an appointment.'

'The—' Pestilence gazed reflectively into his drink. 'Thingy.'

They stared gloomily at the bar counter. The innkeeper had long ago fled. There were several bottles still unopened.

'Okra,' said Famine, eventually. 'That was it.'

'Nah.'

'The Apos . . . the Apostrophe,' said War, vaguely.

They shook their heads. There was a lengthy pause.

'What does "apocrustic" mean?' said Pestilence, gazing intently into some inner world.

'Astringent,' said War, 'I think.'

'It's not that, then?'

'Shouldn't think so,' said Famine, glumly.

There was another long, embarrassed silence.

'Better have "nother drink," said War, pulling himself together.

'S'right.'

About fifty miles away and several thousand feet up, Conina at last managed to control her stolen horse and brought it to a gentle trot on the empty air, displaying some of the most determined nonchalance the Disc had ever seen.

'Snow?' she said.

Clouds were roaring soundlessly from the direction of the Hub. They were fat and heavy and shouldn't be moving so fast. Blizzards trailed beneath them, covering the landscape like a sheet.

It didn't look like the kind of snow that whispers down gently in the pit of the night and in the morning turns the landscape into a glittering wonderland of uncommon and ethereal beauty. It looked like the kind of snow that intends to make the world as bloody cold as possible.

'Bit late in the year,' said Nijel. He glanced downwards, and then immediately closed his eyes.

Creosote watched in delighted astonishment. 'Is that how it happens?' he said. 'I've only heard about it in stories. I thought it sprouted out of the ground somehow. Bit like mushrooms, I thought.'

'Those clouds aren't right,' said Conina.

'Do you mind if we go down now?' said Nijel weakly.

'Somehow it didn't look so bad when we were moving.'

Conina ignored this. 'Try the lamp,' she commanded. 'I want to know about this.'

Nijel fumbled in his pack and produced the lamp. The voice of the genie sounded rather tinny and far off, and said: 'If you would care to relax a little . . . trying to connect you.' There then followed some tinkly little music, the kind that perhaps a Swiss chalet would make if you could play it, before a trapdoor outlined itself in the air and the genie himself appeared. He looked around him, and then at them.

'Oh, wow,' he said.

'Something's happening to the weather,' said Conina.

'Why?'

'You mean you don't know?' said the genie.

'We're asking you, aren't we?'

'Well, I'm no judge, but it rather looks like the Apocralypse, yuh?'

'*What?*'

The genie shrugged. 'The gods have vanished, okay?' he said. 'And, according to, you know, legend, that means—'

'The Ice Giants,' said Nijel, in a horrified whisper.

'Speak up,' said Creosote.

'The Ice Giants,' Nijel repeated loudly, with a trace of irritation. 'The gods keep them imprisoned, see. At the Hub. But at the end of the world they'll break free at last, and ride out on their dreadful glaciers and regain their ancient domination, crushing out the flames of civilisation until the world lies naked and frozen under the terrible cold stars until Time itself freezes over. Or something like that, apparently.'

'But it isn't *time* for the Apocralypse,' said Conina desperately. 'I mean, a dreadful ruler has to arise, there must be a terrible war, the four dreadful horsemen have to ride, and then the Dungeon Dimensions will break into the world—' She stopped, her face nearly as white as the snow.

'Being buried under a thousand-foot ice sheet sounds awfully like it, anyway,' said the genie. He reached forward and snatched his lamp out of Nijel's hands.

'Mucho apologies,' he said, 'but it's time to liquidise my assets in this reality. See you around. Or something.' He vanished up to the waist, and then with a faint last cry of 'Shame about lunch', disappeared entirely.

The three riders peered through the veils of driving snow towards the Hub.

'It may be my imagination,' said Creosote, 'but can either of you hear a sort of creaking and groaning?'

'Shut up,' said Conina distractedly.

Creosote leaned over and patted her hand.

'Cheer up,' he said, 'it's not the end of the world.' He thought about this statement for a bit, and then added, 'Sorry. Just a figure of speech.'

'What are we going to *do*?' she wailed.

Nijel drew himself up.

'I think,' he said, 'that we should go and explain.'

They turned towards him with the kind of expression normally reserved for messiahs or extreme idiots.

'Yes,' he said, with a shade more confidence. 'We should explain.'

'Explain to the Ice Giants?' said Conina.

'Yes.'

'Sorry,' said Conina, 'have I got this right? You think we should go and find the terrifying Ice Giants and sort of tell them that there are a lot of warm people out here who would rather they didn't sweep across the world crushing everyone under mountains of ice, and could they sort of reconsider things? Is that what you think we should do?'

'Yes. That's right. You've got it exactly.'

Conina and Creosote exchanged glances. Nijel remained sitting proudly in the saddle, a faint smile on his face.

'Is your geese giving you trouble?' said the Seriph.

'Geas,' said Nijel calmly. 'It's not giving me trouble, it's just that I must do something brave before I die.'

'That's it, though,' said Creosote. 'That's the whole rather sad point. You'll do something brave, and then you'll die.'

'What alternative have we got?' said Nijel.

They considered this.

'I don't think I'm much good at explaining,' said Conina, in a small voice.

'I am,' said Nijel, firmly. 'I'm always having to explain.'

The scattered particles of what had been Rincewind's mind pulled themselves together and drifted up through the layers of dark unconsciousness like a three-day corpse rising to the surface.

It probed its most recent memories, in much the same way that one might scratch a fresh scab.

He could recall something about a staff, and a pain so intense that it appeared to insert a chisel between every cell in his body and hammer on it repeatedly.

He remembered the staff fleeing, dragging him after it. And then there had been that dreadful bit where Death had appeared and reached *past* him, and the staff had twisted and become suddenly alive and Death had said, IPSLORE THE RED, I HAVE YOU NOW.

And now there was this.

By the feel of it Rincewind was lying on sand. It was very cold.

He took the risk of seeing something horrible and opened his eyes.

The first thing he saw was his left arm and, surprisingly, his hand. It was its normal grubby self. He had expected to see a stump.

It seemed to be night-time. The beach, or whatever it was, stretched on towards a line of distant low mountains, under a night sky frosted with a million white stars.

A little closer to him there was a rough line in the silvery sand. He lifted his head slightly and saw the scatter of molten droplets. They were octiron, a metal so intrinsically magical that no forge on the Disc could even warm it up.

'Oh,' he said. 'We won, then.'

He flopped down again.

After a while his right hand came up automatically and patted the top of his head. Then it patted the sides of his head. Then it began to grope, with increasing urgency, in the sand around him.

Eventually it must have communicated its concern to the rest of Rincewind, because he pulled himself upright and said, 'Oh, bugger.'

There seemed to be no hat anywhere. But he could see a small white shape lying very still in the sand a little way away and, further off—

A column of daylight.

It hummed and swayed in the air, a three-dimensional hole into somewhere else. Occasional flurries of snow blew out of it. He could see skewed images in the light, that might be buildings or landscapes warped by the weird curvature. But he couldn't see them very clearly, because of the tall, brooding shadows that surrounded it.

The human mind is an astonishing thing. It can operate on several levels at once. And, in fact, while Rincewind had been wasting his intellect in groaning and looking for his hat, an inner part of his brain had been observing, assessing, analysing and comparing.

Now it crept up to his cerebellum, tapped it on the shoulder, thrust a message into its hand and ran for it.

The message ran something like this: I hope I find me well. The last trial of magic has been too much for the tortured fabric of reality. It has opened a hole. I am in the Dungeon Dimensions. And the things in front of me are . . . the Things. It has been nice knowing me.

The particular thing nearest Rincewind was at least twenty feet high. It looked like a dead horse that had been dug up after three months and then introduced to a range of new experiences, at least one of which had included an octopus.

It hadn't noticed Rincewind. It was too busy concentrating on the light.

Rincewind crawled back to the still body of Coin and nudged it gently.

'Are you alive?' he said. 'If you're not, I'd prefer it if you didn't answer.'

Coin rolled over and stared up at him with puzzled eyes. After a while he said, 'I remember—'

'Best not to,' said Rincewind.

The boy's hand groped vaguely in the sand beside him.

'It isn't here any more,' said Rincewind, quietly. The hand stopped its searching.

Rincewind helped Coin to sit up. He looked blankly at the cold silver sand, then at the sky, then at the distant Things, and then at Rincewind.

'I don't know what to do,' he said.

'No harm in that. I've never known what to do,' said Rincewind with hollow cheerfulness. 'Been completely at a loss my whole life.' He hesitated. 'I think it's called being human, or something.'

'But I've *always* known what to do!'

Rincewind opened his mouth to say that he'd seen some of it, but changed his mind. Instead he said, 'Chin up. Look on the bright side. It could be worse.'

Coin took another look around.

'In what respect, exactly?' he said, his voice a shade more normal.

'Um.'

'What is this place?'

'It's a sort of other dimension. The magic broke though and we went with it, I think.'

'And those things?'

They regarded the Things.

'I think they're Things. They're trying to get back through the hole,' said Rincewind. 'It isn't easy. Energy levels, or something. I remember we had a lecture on them once. Er.'

Coin nodded, and reached out a thin pale hand towards Rincewind's forehead.

'Do you mind—?' he began.

Rincewind shuddered at the touch. 'Mind what?' he said.

—if I have a look in your head?

'Aargh.'

It's rather a mess in here. No wonder you can't find things.

'Ergh.'

You ought to have a clear out.

'Oogh.'

'Ah.'

Rincewind felt the presence retreat. Coin frowned.

'We can't let them get through,' he announced. 'They have horrible powers. They're trying to will the hole bigger, and they can do it. They've been waiting to break into our world for—' he frowned – '*ians?*'

'Aeons,' said Rincewind.

Coin opened his other hand, which had been tightly clenched, and showed Rincewind the small grey pearl.

'Do you know what this is?' he said.

'No. What is it?'

'I – can't remember. But we should put it back.'

'Okay. Just use sourcery. Blow them to bits and let's go home.'

'No. They live on magic. It'd only make them worse. I can't use magic.'

'Are you sure?' said Rincewind.

'I'm afraid your memory was very clear on the subject.'

'Then what shall we do?'

'I don't *know!*'

Rincewind thought about this and then, with an air of finality, started to take off his last sock.

'No half-bricks,' he said, to no-one in particular. 'Have to use sand.'

'You're going to attack them with a sockful of sand?'

'No. I'm going to run away from them. The sockful of sand is for when they follow.'

People were returning to Al Khali, where the ruined tower was a smoking heap of stones. A few brave souls turned their attention to the wreckage, on the basis that there might be survivors who could be rescued or looted or both.

And, among the rubble, the following conversation might have been heard:

'There's something moving under here!'

'Under that? By the two beards of Imtal, you are mishearing. It must weigh a ton.'

'Over here, brothers!'

And then sounds of much heaving would have been heard, and then:

'It's a box!'

'It could be treasure, do you think?'

'It's growing legs, by the Seven Moons of Nasreem!'

'*Five* moons—'

'Where'd it go? Where'd it go?'

'Never mind about that, it's not important. Let's get this straight, according to the legend it was *five* moons—'

In Klatch they take their mythology seriously. It's only real life they don't believe.

The three horsepersons sensed the change as they descended through the heavy snowclouds at the Hub end of the Sto Plain. There was a sharp scent in the air.

'Can't you smell it?' said Nijel, 'I remember it when I was a boy, when you lay in bed on that first morning in winter, and you could sort of taste it in the air and—'

The clouds parted below them and there, filling the high plains country from end to end, were the herds of the Ice Giants.

They stretched for miles in every direction, and the thunder of their stampede filled the air.

The bull glaciers were in the lead, bellowing their vast creaky calls and throwing up great sheets of earth as they ploughed relentlessly forward. Behind them pressed the great mass of cows and their calves, skimming over land already ground down to the bedrock by the leaders.

They bore as much resemblance to the familiar glaciers the world thought it knew as a lion dozing in the shade bears to three hundred pounds of wickedly co-ordinated muscle bounding towards you with its mouth open.

'. . . and . . . and . . . when you went to the window,' Nijel's mouth, lacking any further input from his brain, ran down.

Moving, jostling ice packed the plain, roaring forward under a great cloud of clammy steam. The ground shook as the leaders passed below, and it was obvious to the onlookers that whoever was going to stop this would need more than a couple of pounds of rock salt and a shovel.

'Go on, then,' said Conina, 'explain. I think you'd better shout.'

Nijel looked distractedly at the herd.

'I think I can see some figures,' said Creosote helpfully. 'Look, on top of the leading . . . things.'

Nijel peered through the snow. There were indeed beings moving around on the backs of the glaciers. They were human, or humanoid, or at least humanish. They didn't look very big.

That turned out to be because the glaciers themselves were very big, and Nijel wasn't very good at perspective. As the horses flew lower over the leading glacier, a huge bull heavily crevassed and scarred by moraine, it became apparent that one reason why the Ice Giants were known as the Ice Giants was because they were, well, giants.

The other was that they were made of ice.

A figure the size of a large house was crouched at the crest of the bull, urging it to greater efforts by means of a spike on a long pole. It was craggy, in fact it was more nearly faceted, and glinted green and blue in the light; there was a thin band of silver in its snowy locks, and its eyes were tiny and black and deep set, like lumps of coal.*

There was a splintering crash ahead as the leading glaciers smacked into a forest. Birds rattled up in panic. Snow and splinters rained down around Nijel as he galloped on the air alongside the giant.

He cleared his throat.

'Erm,' he said, 'excuse me?'

Ahead of the boiling surf of earth, snow and smashed timber a herd of caribou was running in blind panic, their rear hooves a few feet from the tumbling mess.

---

* Although this was the only way in which they resembled the idols built, in response to ancient and unacknowledged memories, by children in snowy weather; it was extremely unlikely that this Ice Giant would be a small mound of grubby ice with a carrot in it by the morning.

Nijel tried again.

'I say?' he shouted.

The giant's head turned towards him.

'Vot you vant?' it said. 'Go avay, hot person.'

'Sorry, but is this really necessary?'

The giant looked at him in frozen astonishment. It turned around slowly and regarded the rest of the herd, which seemed to stretch all the way to the Hub. It looked at Nijel again.

'Yarss,' it said, 'I tink so. Othervise, why ve do it?'

'Only there's a lot of people out there who would prefer you not to, you see,' said Nijel, desperately. A rock spire loomed briefly ahead of the glacier, rocked for a second and then vanished.

He added, 'Also children and small furry animals.'

'They vill suffer in the cause of progress. Now is the time ve reclaim the vorld,' rumbled the giant. 'Whole vorld of ice. According to inevitability of history and triumph of thermodynamics.'

'Yes, but you don't have to,' said Nijel.

'Ve *vant* to,' said the giant. 'The gods are gone, ve throw off shackles of outmoded superstition.'

'Freezing the whole world solid doesn't sound very progressive to me,' said Nijel.

'Ve like it.'

'Yes, yes,' said Nijel, in the maniacally glazed tones of one who is trying to see all sides of the issue and is certain that a solution will be found if people of goodwill will only sit around a table and discuss things rationally like sensible human beings. 'But is this the right time? Is the world ready for the triumph of ice?'

'It bloody vell better be,' said the giant, and swung his glacier prod at Nijel. It missed the horse but caught him full in the chest, lifting him clean out of the saddle and flicking him on to the glacier itself. He spun, spreadeagled, down its freezing flanks, was carried some way by the boil of debris, and rolled into the slush of ice and mud between the speeding walls.

He staggered to his feet, and peered hopelessly into the freezing fog. Another glacier bore down directly on him.

So did Conina. She leaned over as her horse swept down out of the fog, caught Nijel by his leather barbarian harness, and swung him up in front of her.

As they rose again he wheezed, 'Cold-hearted bastard. I really thought I was getting somewhere for a moment there. You just can't talk to some people.'

The herd breasted another hill, scraping off quite a lot of it, and the Sto Plain, studded with cities, lay helpless before it.

Rincewind sidled towards the nearest Thing, holding Coin with one hand and swinging the loaded sock in the other.

'No magic, right?' he said.

'Yes,' said the boy.

'Whatever happens, you mustn't use magic?'

'That's it. Not here. They haven't got much power here, if you don't use magic. Once they break through, though . . .'

His voice trailed away.

'Pretty awful,' Rincewind nodded.

'Terrible,' said Coin.

Rincewind sighed. He wished he still had his hat. He'd just have to do without it.

'All right,' he said. 'When I shout, you make a run for the light. Do you understand? No looking back or anything. No matter what happens.'

'No matter what?' said Coin uncertainly.

'No matter what.' Rincewind gave a brave little smile. 'Especially no matter what you hear.'

He was vaguely cheered to see Coin's mouth become an 'O' of terror.

'And then,' he continued, 'when you get back to the other side—'

'What shall I do?'

Rincewind hesitated. 'I don't know,' he said. 'Anything you can. As much magic as you like. Anything. Just stop them. And . . . um . . .'

'Yes?'

Rincewind gazed up at the Thing, which was still staring into the light.

'If it . . . you know . . . if anyone gets out of this, you know, and everything is all right after all, sort of thing, I'd like you to sort of tell people I sort of stayed here. Perhaps they could sort of write it down somewhere. I mean, I wouldn't want a statue or anything,' he added virtuously.

After a while he added, 'I think you ought to blow your nose.'

Coin did so, on the hem of his robe, and then shook Rincewind's hand solemnly.

'If ever you . . .' he began, 'that is, you're the first . . . it's been a great . . . you see, I never really . . .' His voice trailed off, and then he said, 'I just wanted you to know that.'

'There was something else I was trying to say,' said Rincewind, letting go of the hand. He looked blank for a moment, and then added, 'Oh, yes. It's vital to remember who you really are. It's very important. It isn't a good idea to rely on other people or things to do it for you, you see. They always get it wrong.'

'I'll try and remember,' said Coin.

'It's very important,' Rincewind repeated, almost to himself. 'And now I think you'd better run.'

Rincewind crept closer to the Thing. This particular one had chicken legs, but most of the rest of it was mercifully hidden in what looked like folded wings.

It was, he thought, time for a few last words. What he said now was likely to be very important. Perhaps they would be words that would be remembered, and handed down, and maybe even carved deeply in slabs of granite.

Words without too many curly letters in, therefore.

'I really wish I wasn't here,' he muttered.

He hefted the sock, whirled it once or twice, and smashed the Thing on what he hoped was its kneecap.

It gave a shrill buzz, spun wildly with its wings creaking open, lunged vaguely at Rincewind with its vulture head and got another sockful of sand on the upswing.

Rincewind looked around desperately as the Thing staggered back, and saw Coin still standing where he had left him. To his horror he saw the boy begin to walk towards him, hands raised instinctively to fire the magic which, here, would doom both of them.

'Run away, you idiot!' he screamed, as the Thing began to gather itself for a counter-attack. From out of nowhere he found the words, 'You know what happens to boys who are bad!'

Coin went pale, turned and ran towards the light. He moved as though through treacle, fighting against the entropy slope. The distorted image of the world turned inside out hovered a few feet away, then inches, wavering uncertainly . . .

A tentacle curled around his leg, tumbling him forward.

He flung his hands out as he fell, and one of them touched snow. It was immediately grabbed by something else that felt like a warm, soft leather glove, but under the gentle touch was a grip as tough as tempered steel and it tugged him forward, also dragging whatever it was that had caught him.

Light and grainy dark flicked around him and suddenly he was sliding over cobbles slicked with ice.

The Librarian let go his hold and stood over Coin with a length of heavy wooden beam in his hand. For a moment the ape reared against the darkness, the shoulder, elbow and wrist of his right arm unfolding in a poem of applied leverage, and in a movement as unstoppable as the dawn of intelligence brought it down very heavily. There was a squashy noise and an offended screech, and the burning pressure on Coin's leg vanished.

The dark column wavered. There were squeals and thumps coming from it, distorted by distance.

Coin struggled to his feet and started to run back into the dark, but this time the Librarian's arm blocked his path.

'We can't just leave him in there!'

The ape shrugged.

There was another crackle from the dark, and then a moment of almost complete silence.

But only almost complete. Both of them thought they heard, a long way off but very distinct, the sound of running feet fading into the distance.

They found an echo in the outside world. The ape glanced around, and then pushed Coin hurriedly to one side as something squat and battered and with hundreds of little legs barrelled across the stricken courtyard and, without so much as pausing in its stride, leapt into the disappearing darkness, which flickered for one last time and vanished.

There was a sudden flurry of snow across the air where it had been.

Coin wrenched free of the Librarian's grip and ran into the circle, which was already turning white. His feet scuffed up a sprinkle of fine sand.

'He didn't come out!' he said.

'Oook,' said the Librarian, in a philosophic manner.

'I thought he'd come out. You know, just at the last minute.'

'Oook?'

Coin looked closely at the cobbles, as if by mere concentration he could change what he saw. 'Is he dead?'

'Oook,' observed the Librarian, contriving to imply that Rincewind was in a region where even things like time and space were a bit iffy, and that it was probably not very useful to speculate as to his exact state at this point in time, if indeed he was at any point in time at all, and that, all in all, he might even turn up tomorrow or, for that matter, yesterday, and finally that if there was any chance at all of surviving then Rincewind almost certainly would.

'Oh,' said Coin.

He watched the Librarian shuffle around and head back for the Tower of Art, and a desperate loneliness overcame him.

'I say!' he yelled.

'Oook?'

'What should I do now?'

'Oook?'

Coin waved vaguely at the desolation.

'You know, perhaps I could do something about all this,' he said in a voice tilting on the edge of terror. 'Do you think that would be a good idea? I mean, I could help people. I'm sure you'd like to be human again, wouldn't you?'

The Librarian's everlasting smile hoisted itself a little further up his face, just enough to reveal his teeth.

'Okay, perhaps not,' said Coin hurriedly, 'but there's other things I could do, isn't there?'

The Librarian gazed at him for some time, then dropped his eyes to the boy's hand. Coin gave a guilty start, and opened his fingers.

The ape caught the little silver ball neatly before it hit the ground and held it up to one eye. He sniffed it, shook it gently, and listened to it for a while.

Then he wound up his arm and flung it away as hard as possible.

'What—' Coin began, and landed full length in the snow when the Librarian pushed him over and dived on top of him.

The ball curved over at the top of its arc and tumbled down, its perfect path interrupted suddenly by the ground. There was a sound like a harp string breaking, a brief babble of incomprehensible voices, a rush of hot wind, and the gods of the Disc were free.

They were *very* angry.

'There is nothing we can do, is there?' said Creosote.

'No,' said Conina.

'The ice is going to win, isn't it?' said Creosote.

'Yes,' said Conina.

'No,' said Nijel.

He was trembling with rage, or possibly with cold, and was nearly as pale as the glaciers that rumbled past below them.

Conina sighed. 'Well, just how do you think—' she began.

'Take me down somewhere a few minutes ahead of them,' said Nijel.

'I really don't see how that would help.'

'I wasn't asking your opinion,' said Nijel, quietly. 'Just do it. Put me down a little way ahead of them so I've got a while to get sorted out.'

'Get what sorted out?'

Nijel didn't answer.

'I *said*,' said Conina, 'get what—'

'Shut up!'

'I don't see why—'

'Look,' said Nijel, with the patience that lies just short of axe-murdering. 'The ice is going to cover the whole world, right? Everyone's going to die, okay? Except us for a little while, I suppose, until these horses want their, their, their oats or the lavatory or whatever, which isn't much use to us except maybe Creosote will just about have time to write a sonnet or something about how cold it is all of a sudden, and the whole of human history is about to be scraped up and in these circumstances I would like very much to make it completely clear that I am not about to be argued with, is that absolutely understood?'

He paused for breath, trembling like a harpstring.

Conina hesitated. Her mouth opened and shut a few times, as though she was considering arguing, and then she thought better of it.

They found a small clearing in a pine forest a mile or two ahead of the herd, although the sound of it was clearly audible and there was a line of steam above the trees and the ground was dancing like a drumtop.

Nijel strolled to the middle of the clearing and made a few practice swings with his sword. The others watched him thoughtfully.

'If you don't mind,' whispered Creosote to Conina, 'I'll be off. It's at times like this that sobriety loses its attractions and I'm sure the end of the world will look a lot better through the bottom of a glass, if it's all the same to you. Do you believe in Paradise, o peach-cheeked blossom?'

'Not as such, no.'

'Oh,' said Creosote. 'Well, in that case we probably won't be seeing each other again.' He sighed. 'What a waste. All this just because of a geas. Um. Of course, if by some unthinkable chance—'

'Goodbye,' said Conina.

Creosote nodded miserably, wheeled the horse and disappeared over the treetops.

Snow was shaking down from the branches around the clearing. The thunder of the approaching glaciers filled the air.

Nijel started when she tapped him on the shoulder, and dropped his sword.

'What are you doing here?' he snapped, fumbling desperately in the snow.

'Look, I'm not prying or anything,' said Conina meekly, 'but what exactly do you have in mind?'

She could see a rolling heap of bulldozed snow and soil bearing down on them through the forest, the mind-numbing sound of the leading glaciers now overlaid with the rhythmic snapping of tree trunks. And, advancing implacably above the treeline, so high that the eye mistook them at first for sky, the blue-green prows.

'Nothing,' said Nijel, 'nothing at all. We've just got to resist them, that's all there is to it. That's what we're here for.'

'But it won't make any difference,' she said.

'It will to me. If we're going to die anyway, I'd rather die like this. Heroically.'

'Is it heroic to die like this?' said Conina.

'*I* think it is,' he said, 'and when it comes to dying, there's only one opinion that matters.'

'Oh.'

A couple of deer blundered into the clearing, ignored the humans in their blind panic, and rocketed away.

'You don't have to stay,' said Nijel. 'I've got this geas, you see.'

Conina looked at the backs of her hands.

'I think I should,' she said, and added, 'You know, I thought maybe, you know, if we could just get to know one another better—'

'Mr and Mrs Harebut, was that what you had in mind?' he said bluntly.

Her eyes widened. 'Well—' she began.

'Which one did you intend to be?' he said.

The leading glacier smashed into the clearing just behind its bow wave, its top lost in a cloud of its own creation.

At exactly the same time the trees opposite it bent low as a hot wind blew from the Rim. It was loaded with voices – petulant, bickering voices – and tore into the clouds like a hot iron into water.

Conina and Nijel threw themselves down into snow which turned to warm slush under them. Something like a thunderstorm crashed overhead, filled with shouting and what they at first thought were screams although, thinking about them later, they seemed more like very angry arguments. It went on for a long time, and then began to fade in the direction of the Hub.

Warm water flooded down the front of Nijel's vest. He lifted himself cautiously, and then nudged Conina.

Together they scrambled through the slush and mud to the top of the slope, climbed through a logjam of smashed timber and boulders, and stared at the scene.

The glaciers were retreating, under a cloud stuffed with lightning. Behind them the landscape was a network of lakes and pools.

'Did we do that?' said Conina.

'It would be nice to think so, wouldn't it?' said Nijel.

'Yes, but *did*—' she began.

'Probably not. Who knows? Let's just find a horse,' he said.

'The Apogee,' said War, 'or something. I'm pretty sure.'

They had staggered out of the inn and were sitting on a bench in the afternoon sunshine. Even War had been persuaded to take off some of his armour.

'Dunno,' said Famine, 'Don't think so.'

Pestilence shut his crusted eyes and leaned back against the warm stones.

'*I think,*' he said, '*it was something about the end of the world.*'

War sat and thoughtfully scratched his chin. He hiccuped.

'What, the whole world?' he said.

'*I reckon.*'

War gave this some further consideration. 'I reckon we're well out of it, then,' he said.

People were returning to Ankh-Morpork, which was no longer a city of empty marble but was once again its old self, sprawling as randomly and colourfully as a pool of vomit outside the all-night takeaway of History.

And the University had been rebuilt, or had rebuilt itself, or in some strange way had never been unbuilt, every strand of ivy, every rotting casement, was back in place. The sourcerer had offered to replace everything as good as new, all wood sparkling, all stone unstained, but the Librarian had been very firm on the subject. He wanted everything replaced as good as old.

The wizards came creeping back with the dawn, in ones or twos, scuttling for their old rooms, trying to avoid one another's gaze, trying to remember a recent past that was already becoming unreal and dream-like.

Conina and Nijel arrived around breakfast time and, out of kindness, found a livery stable for War's horse.* It was Conina who insisted that they look for Rincewind at the University, and who, therefore, first saw the books.

They were flying out of the Tower of Art, spiralling around the University buildings and swooping through the door of the reincarnated Library. One or two of the more impudent grimoires were chasing sparrows, or hovering hawk-like over the quad.

The Librarian was leaning against the doorway, watching his charges with a benevolent eye. He waggled his eyebrows at Conina, the nearest he ever got to a conventional greeting.

'Is Rincewind here?' she said.

'Oook.'

'Sorry?'

The ape didn't answer but took them both by the hand and, walking between them like a sack between two poles, led them across the cobbles to the tower.

There were a few candles alight inside, and they saw Coin seated on a stool. The Librarian bowed them into his presence like an ancient retainer in the oldest family of all, and withdrew.

Coin nodded at them. 'He knows when people don't understand him,' he said. 'Remarkable, isn't he?'

'Who are you?' said Conina.

'Coin,' said Coin.

'Are you a student here?'

'I'm learning quite a lot, I think.'

Nijel was wandering around the walls, giving them the occasional prod. There had to be some good reason why they didn't fall down, but if there was it didn't lie in the realms of civil engineering.

'Are you looking for Rincewind?' said Coin.

Conina frowned. 'How did you guess that?'

'He told me some people would come looking for him.'

Conina relaxed. 'Sorry,' she said, 'we've had a bit of a trying time. I thought perhaps it was magic, or something. He's all right, isn't he? I mean, what's been happening? Did he fight the sorcerer?'

'Oh, yes. And he won. It was very . . . interesting. I saw it all. But then he had to go,' said Coin, as though reciting.

'What, just like that?' said Nijel.

'Yes.'

---

* Which wisely decided not to fly again, was never claimed, and lived out the rest of its days as the carriage horse of an elderly lady. What War did about this is unrecorded; it is pretty certain that he got another one.

'I don't believe it,' said Conina. She was beginning to crouch, her knuckles whitening.

'It is true,' said Coin. 'Everything I say is true. It has to be.'

'I want to—' Conina began, and Coin stood up, extended a hand and said, 'Stop.'

She froze. Nijel stiffened in mid-frown.

'You will leave,' said Coin, in a pleasant, level voice, 'and you will ask no more questions. You will be totally satisfied. You have all your answers. You will live happily ever after. You will forget hearing these words. You will go now.'

They turned slowly and woodenly, like puppets, and trooped to the door. The Librarian opened it for them, ushered them through, and shut it behind them.

Then he stared at Coin, who sagged back on to the stool.

'All right, all right,' said the boy, 'but it was only a little magic. I had to. You said yourself people had to forget.'

'Oook?'

'I can't help it! It's too easy to change things!' He clutched his head. 'I've only got to *think* of something! I can't stay, everything I touch goes wrong, it's like trying to sleep on a heap of eggs! This world is too thin! *Please tell me what to do!*'

The Librarian spun around on his bottom a few times, a sure sign of deep thought.

Exactly what he said is not recorded, but Coin smiled, nodded, shook the Librarian's hand, and opened his own hands and drew them up and around him and stepped into another world. It had a lake in, and some distant mountains, and a few pheasants watching him suspiciously from under the trees. It was the magic all sourcerers learned, eventually.

Sourcerers never become part of the world. They merely wear it for a while.

He looked back, halfway across the turf, and waved at the Librarian. The ape gave him an encouraging nod.

And then the bubble shrank inside itself, and the last sourcerer vanished from this world and into a world of his own.

Although it has nothing much to do with the story, it is an interesting fact that, about five hundred miles away, a small flock, or rather in this case a herd, of birds were picking their way cautiously through the trees. They had heads like a flamingo, bodies like a turkey, and legs like a Sumo wrestler; they walked in a jerky, bobbing fashion, as though their heads were attached to their feet by elastic bands. They belonged to a species unique even among Disc fauna, in that their prime means of defence was to cause a predator to laugh so much that they could run away before it recovered.

Rincewind would have been vaguely satisfied to know that they were geas.

Custom was slow in the Mended Drum. The troll chained to the doorpost sat in the shade and reflectively picked someone out of his teeth.

Creosote was singing softly to himself. He had discovered beer and wasn't having to pay for it, because the coinage of compliments – rarely employed by the swains of Ankh – was having an astonishing effect on the landlord's daughter. She was a large, good-natured girl, with a figure that was the colour and, not to put too fine a point on it, the same shape as unbaked bread. She was intrigued. No-one had ever referred to her breasts as jewelled melons before.

'Absolutely,' said the Seriph, sliding peacefully off his bench, 'no doubt about it.' Either the big yellow sort or the small green ones with huge warty veins, he told himself virtuously.

'And what was that about my hair?' she said encouragingly, hauling him back and refilling his glass.

'Oh.' The Seriph's brow wrinkled. 'Like a goat of flocks that grazes on the slopes of Mount Wossname, and no mistake. And as for your ears,' he added quickly, 'no pink-hued shells that grace the sea-kissed sands of—'

'Exactly *how* like a flock of goats?' she said.

The Seriph hesitated. He'd always considered it one of his best lines. Now it was meeting Ankh-Morpork's famous literal-mindedness head-on for the first time. Strangely enough, he felt rather impressed.

'I mean, in size, shape or smell?' she went on.

'I think,' said the Seriph, 'that perhaps the phrase I had in mind was exactly *not* like a flog of gits.'

'Ah?' The girl pulled the flagon toward her.

'And I think perhaps I would like another drink,' he said indistinctly, 'and then – and then—' He looked sideways at the girl, and took the plunge. 'Are you much of a raconteur?'

'What?'

He licked his suddenly dry lips. 'I mean, do you know many stories?' he croaked.

'Oh, yes. Lots.'

'Lots?' whispered Creosote. Most of his concubines only knew the same old one or two.

'Hundreds. Why, do you want to hear one?'

'What, now?'

'If you like. It's not very busy in here.'

Perhaps I did die, Creosote thought. Perhaps this is Paradise. He took her hand. 'You know,' he said, 'it's ages since I've had a good narrative. But I wouldn't want you to do anything you don't want to.'

She patted his arm. What a nice old gentleman, she thought. Compared to some we get in here.

'There's one my granny used to tell me. I know it backwards,' she said.

Creosote sipped his beer and watched the wall in a warm glow. Hundreds, he thought. And she knows some of them *backwards*.

She cleared her throat, and said, in a sing-song voice that made Creosote's pulse fuse, 'There was a man and he had eight sons—'

The Patrician sat by his window, writing. His mind was full of fluff as far as the last week or two was concerned, and he didn't like that much.

A servant had lit a lamp to dispel the twilight, and a few early evening moths were orbiting it. The Patrician watched them carefully. For some reason he felt very uneasy in the presence of glass but that, as he stared fixedly at the insects, wasn't what bothered him most.

What bothered him was that he was fighting a terrible urge to catch them with his tongue.

And Wuffles lay on his back at his master's feet, and barked in his dreams.

Lights were going on all over the city, but the last few strands of sunset illuminated the gargoyles as they helped one another up the long climb to the roof.

The Librarian watched them from the open door, while giving himself a philosophic scratch. Then he turned and shut out the night.

It was warm in the Library. It was *always* warm in the Library, because the scatter of magic that produced the glow also gently cooked the air.

The Librarian looked at his charges approvingly, made his last rounds of the slumbering shelves, and then dragged his blanket underneath his desk, ate a goodnight banana, and fell asleep.

Silence gradually reclaimed the Library. Silence drifted around the remains of a hat, heavily battered and frayed and charred around the edges, that had been placed with some ceremony in a niche in the wall. No matter how far a wizard goes, he will always come back for his hat.

Silence filled the University in the same way that air fills a hole. Night spread across the Disc like plum jam, or possibly blackberry preserve.

But there would be a morning. There would always be another morning.

Eric

~~FAUST~~

13 Midden Lane,
Pseudopolis,
Sto Plains,
The Discworld,
On top of Great
A'tuin,
The Univers,
Space.
nr. More Space.

The bees of Death are big and black, they buzz low and sombre, they keep their honey in combs of wax as white as altar candles. The honey is black as night, thick as sin and sweet as treacle.

It is well known that eight colours make up white. But there are also eight colours of blackness, for those that have the seeing of them, and the hives of Death are among the black grass in the black orchard under the black-blossomed, ancient boughs of trees that will, eventually, produce apples that . . . put it like this . . . probably won't be red.

The grass was short now. The scythe that had done the work leaned against the gnarled bole of a pear tree. Now Death was inspecting his bees, gently lifting the combs in his skeletal fingers.

A few bees buzzed around him. Like all beekeepers, Death wore a veil. It wasn't that he had anything to sting, but sometimes a bee would get inside his skull and buzz around and give him a headache.

As he held a comb up to the grey light of his little world between the realities there was the faintest of tremors. A hum went up from the hive, a leaf floated down. A wisp of wind blew for a moment through the orchard, and that was the most uncanny thing, because the air in the land of Death is always warm and still.

Death fancied that he heard, very briefly, the sound of running feet and a voice saying, no, a voice thinking *oshitoshitoshit, I'm gonna die I'm gonna die I'm gonna DIE!*

Death is almost the oldest creature in the universe, with habits and modes of thought that mortal man cannot begin to understand, but because he was also a good beekeeper he carefully replaced the comb in its rack and put the lid on the hive before reacting.

He strode back through the dark garden to his cottage, removed the veil, carefully dislodged a few bees who had got lost in the depths of his cranium, and retired to his study.

As he sat down at his desk there was another rush of wind, which rattled the hour-glasses on the shelves and made the big pendulum clock in the hall pause ever so briefly in its interminable task of slicing time into manageable bits.

Death sighed, and focused his gaze.

There is nowhere Death will not go, no matter how distant and dangerous. In fact the more dangerous it is, the more likely he is to be there already.

Now he stared through the mists of time and space.

Oh, he said. It's him.

It was a hot afternoon in late summer in Ankh-Morpork, normally the most thriving, bustling and above all the most crowded city on the Disc. Now the spears of the sun had achieved what innumerable invaders, several civil wars and the curfew law had never achieved. It had pacified the place.

Dogs lay panting in the scalding shade. The river Ankh, which never what you might call sparkled, oozed between its banks as if the heat had sucked all the spirit out of it. The streets were empty, oven-brick hot.

No enemies had ever taken Ankh-Morpork. Well, *technically* they had, quite often; the city welcomed free-spending barbarian invaders, but somehow the puzzled raiders always found, after a few days, that they didn't own their own horses any more, and within a couple of months they were just another minority group with its own graffiti and food shops.

But the heat had besieged the city and triumphed over the walls. It lay over the trembling streets like a shroud. Under the blowlamp of the sun assassins were too tired to kill. It turned thieves honest. In the ivy-covered fastness of Unseen University, premier college of wizardry, the inmates dozed with their pointy hats over their faces. Even bluebottles were too exhausted to bang against windowpanes. The city siesta'd, awaiting the sunset and the brief, hot, velvet surcease of the night.

Only the Librarian was cool. He was also swinging and hanging out.

This was because he'd rigged up a few ropes and rings in one of the sub-basements of the Unseen University library – the one where they kept the, um, erotic* books. In vats of crushed ice. And he was dreamily dangling in the chilly vapour above them.

All books of magic have a life of their own. Some of the really energetic ones can't simply be chained to the bookshelves; they have to be nailed shut or kept between steel plates. Or, in the case of

---

*Just erotic. Nothing kinky. It's the difference between using a feather and using a chicken.

the volumes on tantric sex magic for the serious connoisseur, kept under very cold water to stop them bursting into flames and scorching their severely plain covers.

The Librarian swung gently back and forth above the seething vats, dozing peacefully.

Then the footsteps came out of nowhere, raced across the floor with a noise that scraped the raw surface of the soul, and disappeared through the wall. There was a faint, distant scream that sounded like *ogodsogodsogods, this is IT, I'm gonna DIE.*

The Librarian woke up, lost his grip, and flopped into the few inches of tepid water that was all that stood between *The Joy of Tantric Sex with Illustrations for the Advanced Student*, by A Lady, and spontaneous combustion.

And it would have gone badly for him if the Librarian had been a human being. Fortunately, he was currently an orang-utan. With so much raw magic sloshing around in the Library it would be surprising if accidents did not happen sometimes, and one particularly impressive one had turned him into an ape. Not many people get the chance to leave the human race while still alive, and he'd strenuously resisted all efforts since to turn him back. Since he was the only librarian in the universe who could pick up books with his feet the University hadn't pressed the point.

It also meant that his idea of desirable female companionship now looked something like a sack of butter thrown through a roll of old inner tubes, and so he was lucky to get away with only mild burns, a headache, and some rather ambivalent feelings about cucumbers, which wore off by teatime.

In the Library above, the grimoires creaked and rustled their pages in astonishment as the invisible runner passed straight through the bookshelves and disappeared, or rather, disappeared even more . . .

Ankh-Morpork gradually awoke from its slumber. Something invisible and yelling at the top of its voice was passing through every part of the city, dragging in its wake a trail of destruction. Wherever it went, things changed.

A fortune-teller in the Street of Cunning Artificers heard the footsteps run across her bedroom floor and found her crystal ball had turned into a little glass sphere with a cottage in it, plus snowflakes.

In a quiet corner of the Mended Drum tavern, where the adventuresses Herrena the Henna-Haired Harridan, Red Scharron and Diome, Witch of the Night, were meeting for some girl talk and a game of canasta, all the drinks turned into small yellow elephants.

'It's them wizards up at the University,' said the barman, hastily replacing the glasses. 'It oughtn't to be allowed.'

Midnight dropped off the clock.

The Council of Wizardry rubbed their eyes and stared blearily at one another. They felt it oughtn't to be allowed too, especially since they weren't the ones that were allowing it.

Finally the new Archchancellor, Ezrolith Churn, suppressed a yawn, sat up straight in his chair, and tried to look suitably magisterial. He knew he wasn't really Archchancellor material. He hadn't really wanted the job. He was ninety-eight, and had achieved this worthwhile age by carefully not being any trouble or threat to anyone. He had hoped to spend his twilight years completing his seven-volume treatise on *Some Little Known Aspects of Kuian Rain-making Rituals*, which were an ideal subject for academic study in his opinion since the rituals only ever worked in Ku, and that particular continent had slipped into the ocean several thousand years ago.* The trouble was that in recent years the lifespan of Archchancellors seemed to be a bit on the short side, and the natural ambition of all wizards for the job had given way to a curious, self-effacing politeness. He'd come down one morning to find everyone calling him 'sir'. It had taken him days to find out why.

His head ached. He felt it was several weeks past his bedtime. But he had to say something.

'Gentlemen—' he began.

'Oook.'

'Sorry, *and* mo—'

'*Oook.*'

'I mean apes, of course—'

'Oook.'

The Archchancellor opened and shut his mouth in silence for a while, trying to re-route his train of thought. The Librarian was, ex officio, a member of the college council. No-one had been able to find any rule about orang-utans being barred, although they had surreptitiously looked very hard for one.

---

*It took thirty years to subside. The inhabitants spent a lot of the time wading. It went down in history as the multiverse's most embarrassing continental catastrophe.

'It's a haunting,' he ventured. 'Some sort of a ghost, maybe. A bell, book and candle job.'

The Bursar sighed. 'We tried that, Archchancellor.'

The Archchancellor leaned towards him.

'Eh?' he said.

'I *said*, we tried that, Archchancellor,' said the Bursar loudly, directing his voice at the old man's ear. 'After dinner, you remember? We used Humptemper's *Names of the Ants* and rang Old Tom.'*

'Did we, indeed. Worked, did it?'

'No, Archchancellor.'

'Eh?'

'Anyway, we've never had any trouble with ghosts before,' said the Senior Tutor. 'Wizards just don't haunt places.'

The Archchancellor groped for a crumb of comfort.

'Perhaps it's just something natural,' he said. 'Possibly the rumblings of an underground spring. Earth movements, perhaps. Something in the drains. They can make very funny noises, you know, when the wind is in the right direction.'

He sat back and beamed.

The rest of the council exchanged glances.

'The drains don't sound like hurrying feet, Archchancellor,' said the Bursar wearily.

'Unless someone left a tap running,' said the Senior Tutor.

The Bursar scowled at him. He'd been in the tub when the invisible screaming thing had hurtled through his room. It was not an experience he wanted to repeat.

The Archchancellor nodded at him.

'That's settled, then,' he said, and fell asleep.

The Bursar watched him in silence. Then he pulled the old man's hat off and tucked it gently under his head.

'Well?' he said wearily. 'Has anyone got any suggestions?'

The Librarian put his hand up.

'Oook,' he said.

'Yes, well done, good boy,' said the Bursar, breezily. 'Anyone else?'

The orang-utan glared at him as the other wizards shook their heads.

---

* Old Tom was the single cracked bronze bell in the University bell tower. The clapper dropped out shortly after it was cast, but the bell still tolled out some tremendously sonorous silences every hour.

'It's a tremor in the texture of reality,' said the Senior Tutor. 'That's what it is.'

'What should we do about it, then?'

'Search me. Unless we tried the old—'

'Oh, no,' said the Bursar. 'Don't say it. Please. It's far too dangerous—'

His words were chopped off by a scream that began at the far end of the room and dopplered along the table, accompanied by the sound of many running feet. The wizards ducked in a scatter of overturned chairs.

The candle flames were drawn into long thin tongues of octarine light before being snuffed out.

Then there was silence, the special kind that you get after a really unpleasant noise.

And the Bursar said, 'All right. I give in. We *will* try the Rite of AshkEnte.'

It is the most serious ritual eight wizards can undertake. It summons Death, who naturally knows everything that is going on everywhere.

And of course it's done with reluctance, because senior wizards are generally very old and would prefer not to do anything to draw Death's attention in their direction.

It took place in the midnight in the University's Great Hall, in a welter of incense, candlesticks, runic inscriptions and magic circles, none of which was strictly necessary but which made the wizards feel better. Magic flared, the chants were chanted, the invocations were truly invoked.

The wizards stared into the magic octogram, which remained empty. After a while the circle of robed figures began to mutter amongst themselves.

'We must have done something wrong.'

'Oook.'

'Maybe He is out.'

'Or busy . . .'

'Do you think we could give up and go back to bed?'

WHO ARE WE WAITING FOR, EXACTLY?

The Bursar turned slowly to the figure beside him. You could always tell a wizard's robe; it was bedecked with sequins, sigils, fur and lace, and there was usually a considerable amount of wizard inside it. This robe, however, was very black. The material looked as though it had been chosen for its hard-wearing qualities. So did its owner. He looked as though if he wrote a diet book, it would be a bestseller.

Death was watching the octogram with an expression of polite interest.

'Er,' said the Bursar. 'The fact is, in fact, that, er, you should be on the *inside*.'

I'M SO SORRY.

Death stalked in a dignified way into the centre of the room and watched the Bursar expectantly.

I HOPE WE ARE NOT GOING TO HAVE ANY OF THIS 'FOUL FIEND' BUSINESS AGAIN, he said.

'I trust we are not interrupting any important enterprise?' said the Bursar politely.

ALL MY WORK IS IMPORTANT, said Death.

'Naturally,' said the Bursar.

TO SOMEBODY.

'Er. Er. The reason, o fou— sir, that we have called you here, is for the reason—'

IT IS RINCEWIND.

'What?'

THE REASON YOU SUMMONED ME. THE ANSWER IS: IT IS RINCEWIND.

'But we haven't asked you the question yet!'

NEVERTHELESS. THE ANSWER IS: IT IS RINCEWIND.

'Look, what we want to know *is*, what's causing this outbreak of . . . oh.'

Death pointedly picked invisible particles off the edge of his scythe.

The Archchancellor cupped a gnarled hand over his ear.

'What'd he say? Who's the fella with the stick?'

'It's Death, Archchancellor,' said the Bursar patiently.

'Eh?'

'It's Death, sir. *You* know.'

'Tell him we don't want any,' said the old wizard, waving his stick.

The Bursar sighed. 'We summoned him, Archchancellor.'

'Is it? What'd we go and do that for? Bloody silly thing to do.'

The Bursar gave Death an embarrassed grin. He was on the point of asking him to excuse the Archchancellor on account of his age, but realised that this would in the circumstances be a complete waste of breath.

'Are we talking about the wizard Rincewind? The one with the—' the Bursar gave a shudder – 'horrible Luggage on legs? But he got blown up when there was all that business with the sourcerer, didn't he?'*

INTO THE DUNGEON DIMENSIONS. AND NOW HE IS TRYING TO GET BACK HOME.

'Can he do that?'

THERE WOULD NEED TO BE AN UNUSUAL CONJUNCTION OF CIRCUMSTANCES. REALITY WOULD NEED TO BE WEAKENED IN CERTAIN UNEXPECTED WAYS.

'That isn't likely to happen, is it?' said the Bursar anxiously. People who have it on record that they were visiting their aunt for two months are always nervous about people turning up who may have mistakenly thought that they weren't, and owing to some trick of the light might have believed they had seen them doing things that they couldn't have been doing owing to being at their aunt's.

IT WOULD BE A MILLION TO ONE CHANCE, said Death. EXACTLY A MILLION TO ONE CHANCE.

'Oh,' said the Bursar, intensely relieved. 'Oh dear. What a shame.' He brightened up considerably. 'Of course, there's all the noise. But, unfortunately, I expect he won't survive for long.'

THIS COULD BE THE CASE, said Death blandly. I AM SURE, THOUGH, THAT YOU WOULD NOT WISH ME TO MAKE A PRACTICE OF ISSUING DEFINITIVE STATEMENTS IN THIS FIELD.

'No! No, of course not,' said the Bursar hurriedly. 'Right. Well, many thanks. Poor chap. What a great pity. Still, can't be helped. Perhaps we should be philosophical about these things.'

PERHAPS YOU SHOULD.

'And we had better not keep you,' the Bursar added politely.

THANK YOU.

---

* The Bursar was referring obliquely to the difficult occasion when the University very nearly caused the end of the world, and would in fact have done so had it not been for a chain of events involving Rincewind, a magic carpet and a half-brick in a sock. (See *Sourcery*.) The whole affair was very embarrassing to wizards, as it always is to people who find out afterwards that they were on the wrong side all along*, and it was remarkable how many of the University's senior staff were now adamant that at the time they had been off sick, visiting their aunt, or doing research with the door locked while humming loudly and had had no idea of what was going outside. There had been some desultory talk about putting up a statue to Rincewind but, by the curious alchemy that tends to apply in these sensitive issues, this quickly became a plaque, then a note on the Roll of Honour, and finally a motion of censure for being improperly dressed.

* ie, the one that lost.

'Goodbye.'

BE SEEING YOU.

In fact the noise stopped just before breakfast. The Librarian was the only one unhappy about it. Rincewind had been his assistant and his friend, and was a good man when it came to peeling a banana. He had also been uniquely good at running away from things. He was not, the Librarian considered, the type to be easily caught.

There had probably been an unusual conjunction of circumstances.

That was a far more likely explanation.

There *had* been an unusual conjunction of circumstances.

By exactly a million to one chance there had been someone watching, studying, looking for the right tools for a special job.

And here was Rincewind.

It was almost too easy.

So Rincewind opened his eyes. There was a ceiling above him; if it was the floor, then he was in trouble.

So far, so good.

He cautiously felt the surface he was lying on. It was grainy, woody in fact, with the odd nail-hole. A *human* sort of surface.

His ears picked up the crackle of a fire and a bubbling noise, source unknown.

His nose, feeling that it was being left out of things, hastened to report a whiff of brimstone.

Right. So where did that leave him? Lying on a rough wooden floor in a firelit room with something that bubbled and gave off sulphurous smells. In his unreal, dreamy state he felt quite pleased at this process of deduction.

What else?

Oh, yes.

He opened his mouth and screamed and screamed and screamed. This made him feel slightly better.

He lay there a bit longer. Through the tumbled heap of his memories came the recollections of mornings in bed when he was a little boy, desperately subdividing the passing time into smaller and smaller units to put off the terrible moment of getting up and having to face all the problems of life such as, in this case, who he was, where he was, and why he was.

'*What* are you?' said a voice on the edge of his consciousness.

'I was coming to that,' muttered Rincewind.

The room oscillated into focus as he pushed himself up on his elbows.

'I warn you,' said the voice, which seemed to be coming from a table,' I am protected by many powerful amulets.'

'Jolly good,' said Rincewind. 'I wish I was.'

Details began to distil out of the blur. It was a long, low room, one end of which was entirely occupied by an enormous fireplace. A bench all down one wall contained a selection of glassware apparently created by a drunken glassblower with hiccups, and inside its byzantine coils coloured liquids seethed and bubbled. A skeleton hung from a hook in a relaxed fashion. On a perch beside it someone had nailed a stuffed bird. Whatever sins it had committed in life, it hadn't deserved what the taxidermist had done to it.

Rincewind's gaze then swept across the floor. It was obvious that it was the only sweeping the floor had had for some time. Only around him had space been cleared among the debris of broken glass and overturned retorts for—

A magic circle.

It looked an extremely thorough job. Whoever had chalked it was clearly very aware that its purpose was to divide the universe into two bits, the inside and the outside.

Rincewind was, of course, inside.

'Ah,' he said, feeling a familiar and almost comforting sense of helpless dread sweep over him.

'I adjure and conjure thee against all aggressive acts, o demon of the pit,' said the voice from, Rincewind now realised, *behind* the table.

'Fine, fine,' said Rincewind quickly. 'That's all right by me. Er. It isn't possible that there has been the *teeniest* little mistake here, could there?'

'Avaunt!'

'Right!' said Rincewind. He looked around him desperately. 'How?'

'Don't you think you can lure me to my doom with thy lying tongue, o fiend of Shamharoth,' said the table. 'I am learned in the ways of demons. Obey my every command or I will return thee unto the boiling hell from which you came. Thou came, sorry. Thou came'st, in fact. And I really mean it.'

The figure stepped out. It was quite short, and most of it was hidden by a variety of charms, amulets and talismans which, even if not effective against magic, would probably have protected it against a tolerably determined sword thrust. It wore glasses and had a hat with long sidepieces that gave it the air of a short-sighted spaniel.

It held a sword in one shaking hand. It was so heavily etched with sigils that it was beginning to bend.

'Boiling hell, did you say?' said Rincewind weakly.

'Absolutely. Where the screams of anguish and the tortured torments—'

'Yes, yes, you've made your point,' said Rincewind. 'Only, you see, the thing is, in fact, that I am not a demon. So if you would just let me out?'

'I am not fooled by thy outer garb, demon,' said the figure. In a more normal voice it added, 'Anyway, demons always lie. Well-known fact.'

'It is?' said Rincewind, clutching at this straw. 'In that case, then— I *am* a demon.'

'Aha! Condemned out of your own mouth!'

'Look, I don't have to put up with this,' said Rincewind. 'I don't know who you are or what's happening, but I'm going to have a drink, all right?'

He went to walk out of the circle, and went rigid with shock as sparks crackled up from the runic inscriptions and earthed themselves all over his body.

'Thou mays'nt – thou maysn't – thou mays'n't—' The conjurer of demons gave up. 'Look, you can't step over the circle until I release you, right? I mean, I don't want to be unpleasant, it's just that if I let you out of the circle you will be able to resume your true shape, and a pretty awful shape it is too, I expect. Avaunt!' he added, feeling that he wasn't keeping up the tone.

'All right. I'm avaunting. I'm avaunting,' said Rincewind, rubbing his elbow. 'But I'm still not a demon.'

'How come you answered the conjuration, then? I suppose you just happened to be passing through the paranatural dimensions, eh?'

'Something like that, I think. It's all a bit blurred.'

'Pull the other one, it has got bells on.' The conjurer leaned his sword against a lectern on which a heavy book, dripping book-marks, lay open. Then he did a mad little jig on the floor.

'It's worked!' he said. 'Heheh!' He caught sight of Rincewind's horrified gaze and pulled himself together. He gave an embarrassed cough, and stepped up to the lectern.

'I really am not—' Rincewind began.

'I had this list here somewhere,' said the figure. 'Let's see, now. Oh, yes. I command you – thee, I mean – to, ah, grant me three wishes. Yes. I want mastery of the kingdoms of the world, I want to meet the most beautiful woman who has ever lived, *and* I want to live for ever.' He gave Rincewind an encouraging look.

'All that?' said Rincewind.

'Yes.'

'Oh, no problem,' said Rincewind sarcastically. 'And then I get the rest of the day off, right?'

'And I want a chest full of gold, too. Just to be going on with.'

'I can see you've got it all thought out.'

'Yes. Avaunt!'

'Right, right. Only—' Rincewind thought hurriedly, he's quite mad, but mad with a sword in his hands, the only chance I've got is to argue him out of it on his own terms, '—only d'you see, I'm not a very superior kind of demon and I'm afraid those sort of errands are a bit out of my league, sorry. You can avaunt as much as you like, but they're just beyond me.'

The little figure peered over the top of its glasses.

'I see,' he said testily. 'What could you manage then, do you think?'

'Well, er—' said Rincewind, 'I suppose I could go down to the shops and get you a packet of mints, or something.'

There was a pause.

'You really can't do all those things?'

'Sorry. Look, I'll tell you what. You just release me, and I'll be sure to pass the word around when I get back to—' Rincewind hesitated. Where the hell *did* demons live, anyway? 'Demon City,' he said, hopefully.

'You mean Pandemonium?' said his captor suspiciously.

'Yes, that's right. That's what I meant. I'll tell everyone, next time you're in the real world be sure and look up – what's your name?'

'Thursley. Eric Thursley.'

'Right.'

'Demonologist. Midden Lane, Pseudopolis. Next door to the tannery,' said Thursley hopefully.

'Right you are. Don't you worry about it. Now, if you'll just let me out—'

Thursley's face fell.

'You're sure you really can't do it?' he said, and Rincewind couldn't help noticing the edge of pleading in his voice. 'Even a small chest of gold would do. And, I mean, it needn't be the most beautiful woman in the whole of history. Second most beautiful would do. Or third. You pick any one out of, you know, the top one hundr— thousand. Whatever you've got in stock, sort of thing.' By the end of the sentence his voice twanged with longing.

Rincewind wanted to say: Look, what you should do is stop all this messing around with chemicals in dark rooms and have a shave, a haircut, a bath, make that *two* baths, buy yourself a new wardrobe and get out of an evening and then – but he'd have to be honest, because even washed, shaved and soaked in body splash Thursley wasn't going to win any prizes – and then you could have your face slapped by any woman of your choice.

I mean, it wouldn't be much, but it would be body contact.

'Sorry,' he said again.

Thursley sighed. 'The kettle's on,' he said. 'Would you like a cup of tea?'

Rincewind stepped forward into a crackle of psychic energy.

'Ah,' said Thursley uncertainly, as the wizard sucked at his fingers, 'I'll tell you what. I'll put you under a conjuration of duress.'

'There's no need, I assure you.'

'No, it's best this way. It means you can move around. I had it all ready anyway, in case you could go and fetch, you know, *her.*'

'Fine,' said Rincewind. As the demonologist mumbled words from the book he thought: Feet. Door. Stairs. What a great combination.

It occurred to him that there was something about the demonologist that wasn't quite usual, but he couldn't put his finger on it. He *looked* pretty much like the demonologists Rincewind had known back in Ankh-Morpork, who were all bent and chemical-stained and had eyes with pupils like pinheads from all the chemical fumes. This one would have fitted in easily. It was just that there was something odd.

'To be honest,' said Thursley, industriously mopping away part of the circle, 'you're my first demon. It's never worked before. What is your name?'

'Rincewind.'

Thursley thought about this. 'It doesn't ring a bell,' he said. 'There's a Riinjswin in the *Demonologie*. And a Winswin. But they've got more wings than you. You can step out now. I must say that's a first-class materialisation. No-one would think you were a fiend, to look at you. Most demons, when they want to look

225

human, materialise in the shape of nobles, kings and princes. This moth-eaten-wizard look is very clever. You could've almost fooled me. It's a shame you can't do any of those things.'

'I can't see why you'd want to live for ever,' said Rincewind, privately determining that the words 'moth-eaten' would be paid for, if ever he got the opportunity. 'Being *young* again, I can understand that.'

'Huh. Being young's not much fun,' said Thursley, and then clapped his hand over his mouth.

Rincewind leaned forward.

About fifty years. *That* was what was missing.

'That's a false beard!' he said. 'How old are you?'

'Eighty-seven!' squeaked Thursley.

'I can see the hooks over your ears!'

'Seventy-eight, honest! Avaunt!'

'You're a little boy!'

Eric pulled himself up haughtily. 'I'm not!' he snapped. 'I'm nearly fourteen!'

'Ah-*ha*!'

The boy waved the sword at Rincewind. 'It doesn't matter, anyway!' he shouted. 'Demonologists can be any age, you're still my demon and you have to do as I say!'

'*Eric!*' came a voice from somewhere below them.

Eric's face went white.

'Yes, mother?' he shouted, his eyes fixed on Rincewind. His mouth shaped the words: don't say anything, *please*.

'What's all that noise up there?'

'Nothing, mother!'

'Come down and wash your hands, dear, your breakfast's ready!'

'Yes, mother.' He looked sheepishly at Rincewind. 'That's my mother,' he said.

'She's got a good pair of lungs, hasn't she,' said Rincewind.

'I'd, I'd better go, then,' said Eric. 'You'll have to stay up here, of course.'

It dawned on him that he was losing a certain amount of credibility at this point. He waved the sword again.

'Avaunt!' he said. 'I command you not to leave this room!'

'Right. Sure,' said Rincewind, eyeing the windows.

'Promise? Otherwise you'll be sent back to the Pit.'

'Oh, I don't want that,' said Rincewind. 'Off you trot. Don't worry about me.'

'I'm going to leave the sword and stuff here,' said Eric, removing

226

most of his accoutrements to reveal a slim, dark-haired young man whose face would be a lot better when his acne cleared up. 'If you touch them, terrible things will befall.'

'Wouldn't dream of it,' said Rincewind.

When he was left alone he wandered over to the lectern and looked at the book. The title, in impressively flickering red letters, was *Mallificarum Sumpta Diabolicite Occularis Singularum*, the Book of Ultimate Control. He knew about it. There was a copy in the Library somewhere, although wizards never bothered with it.

This might seem odd, because if there is one thing a wizard would trade his grandmother for, it is power. But it wasn't all *that* strange, because any wizard bright enough to survive for five minutes was also bright enough to realise that if there was any power in demonology, then it lay with the demons. Using it for your own purposes would be like trying to beat mice to death with a rattlesnake.

Even wizards thought demonologists were odd; they tended to be surreptitious, pale men who got up to complicated things in darkened rooms and had damp, weak handshakes. It wasn't like good clean magic. No self-respecting wizard would have any truck with the demonic regions, whose inhabitants were as big a collection of ding-dongs as you'd find outside a large belfry.

He inspected the skeleton closely, just in case. It didn't seem inclined to make a contribution to the situation.

'It belonged to his wossname, grandfather,' said a cracked voice behind him.

'Bit of an unusual bequest,' said Rincewind.

'Oh, not *personally*. He got it in a shop somewhere. It's one of them wossname, articulate wossnames.'

'It's not saying much right now,' said Rincewind, and then went very quiet and thoughtful.

'Er,' he said, without moving his head, 'what, precisely, am I talking to?'

'I'm a wossname. Tip of my tongue. Begins with a P.'

Rincewind turned around slowly.

'You're a parrot?' he said.

'That's it.'

Rincewind stared at the thing on the perch. It had one eye that glittered like a ruby. Most of the rest of it was pink and purple skin, studded with the fag-ends of feathers, so that the net effect was of an oven-ready hairbrush. It jiggled arthritically on its perch and then slowly lost its balance, until it was hanging upside down.

227

'I thought you were stuffed,' said Rincewind.

'Up yours, wizard.'

Rincewind ignored it and crept over to the window. It was small, but gave out on to a gently sloping roof. And out there was real life, real sky, real buildings. He reached out to open the shutters—

A crackling current coursed up his arm and earthed itself in his cerebellum.

He sat on the floor, sucking his fingers.

'He *tole* you,' said the parrot, swinging backwards and forwards upside down. 'But you wouldn't wossname. He's got you by the wossnames.'

'But it should only work on demons!'

'Ah,' said the parrot, achieving enough momentum to swing upright again, whereupon it steadied itself with the stubby remains of what had once been wings. 'It's all according, isn't it. If you come in through the door marked "Wossnames" that means you get treated as a wossname, right? Demon, I mean. Subject to all the rules and wossnames. Tough one for you.'

'But *you* know I'm a wizard, don't you!'

The parrot gave a squawk. 'I've seen 'em, mate. The real McWossname. Some of the ones we've had in here, they'd make you choke on your millet. Great scaly fiery wossnames. Took weeks to get the soot off the walls,' it added, in an approving tone of voice. 'That was in his granddad's day, of course. The kid hasn't been any good at it. Up to now. Bright lad. I blame the wossnames, parents. New money, you know. Wine business. Spoil him rotten, let him play with his wossname's old stuff, "Oh, he's *such* an intelligent lad, nose always in a book",' the parrot mimicked. 'They never give him any of the things a sensitive growing wossname really needs, if you was to ask me.'

'What, you mean love and guidance?' said Rincewind.

'I was thinking of a bloody good wossname, thrashing,' said the parrot.

Rincewind clutched at his aching head. If this was what demons usually had to go through, no wonder they were always so annoyed.

'Polly want a biscuit,' said the parrot vaguely, in much the same way as a human would say 'Er' or 'As I was saying', and went on, 'His granddad was keen on it. That and his pigeons.'

'Pigeons,' said Rincewind.

'Not that he was particularly successful. It was all a bit trial and wossname.'

'I thought you said great big scaly—'

'Oh, *yes*. But that wasn't what he was after. He was trying to conjure up a succubus.' It should be impossible to leer when all you've got is a beak, but the parrot managed it. 'That's a female demon what comes in the night and makes mad passionate wossn—'

'I've heard of them,' said Rincewind. 'Bloody dangerous things.'

The parrot put its head on one side. 'It never worked. All he ever got was a neuralger.'

'What's that?'

'It's a demon that comes and has a headache at you.'

Demons have existed on the Discworld for at least as long as the gods, who in many ways they closely resemble. The difference is basically the same as that between terrorists and freedom fighters.

Most of the demons occupy a spacious dimension close to reality, traditionally decorated in shades of flame and maintained at roasting point. This isn't actually necessary, but if there is one thing that your average demon is, it is a traditionalist.

In the centre of the inferno, rising majestically from a lake of lava substitute and with unparalleled views of the Eight Circles, lies the city of Pandemonium.* At the moment, it was living up to its name.

Astfgl, the new King of the Demons, was furious. Not simply because the air-conditioning had broken down again, not because he felt surrounded by idiots and plotters on every side, and not even because no-one could pronounce his name properly yet, but also because he had just been given bad news. The demon who had been chosen by lottery to deliver it cowered in front of his throne with its tail between its legs. It was immortally afraid that something wonderful was soon going to happen to it.†

'It did *what*?' said Astfgl.

* Demons and their Hell are quite different from the Dungeon Dimensions, those endless parallel wastelands outside space and time. The sad, mad Things in the Dungeon Dimensions have no understanding of the world but simply crave light and shape and try to warm themselves by the fires of reality, clustering around it with about the same effect – if they ever broke through – as an ocean trying to warm itself around a candle. Whereas demons belong to the same space-time wossname, more or less, as humans, and have a deep and abiding interest in humanity's day-to-day affairs. Interestingly enough, the gods of the Disc have never bothered much about judging the souls of the dead, and so people only go to hell if that's where they believe, in their deepest heart, that they deserve to go. Which they won't do if they don't know about it. This explains why it is important to shoot missionaries on sight.

† Demons have a distorted sense of values.

'It, er, it opened, o lord. The circle in Pseudopolis.'

'Ah. The clever boy. We have great hopes of him.'

'Er. Then it closed again, lord.' The demon shut its eyes.

'And who went through?'

'Er.' The demon looked around at its colleagues, clustered at the far end of the mile-long throne room.

'I said, and who went through?'

'In point of fact, o lord—'

'Yes?'

'We don't know. Someone.'

'I gave orders, did I not, that when the boy succeeded the Duke Vassenego was to materialise unto him, and offer him forbidden pleasures and dark delights to bend him to Our will?'

The King growled. The problem with being evil, he'd been forced to admit, was that demons were not great innovatory thinkers and really needed the spice of human ingenuity. And he'd really been looking forward to Eric Thursley, whose brand of super-intelligent gormlessness was a rare delight. Hell needed horribly-bright, self-centred people like Eric. They were much better at being nasty than demons could ever manage.

'Indeed, lord,' said the demon, 'And the duke has been awaiting the summons there for years, shunning all other temptations, steadfastly and patiently studying the world of men—'

'So *where was he*?'

'Er. Call of supernature, lord,' the demon gabbled. 'Hadn't turned his back for two minutes when—'

'And *someone* went through?'

'We're trying to find out—'

Lord Astfgl's patience, which in any case had the tensile strength of putty, snapped at this point. That just about summed it up. He had the kind of subjects who used the words 'find out' when they meant 'ascertain'. Damnation was too good for them.

'Get out,' he whispered. 'And I shall see to it that you get a commendation for this—'

'O master, I plead—'

'Get out!'

The King stamped along the glowing corridors to his private apartments.

His predecessors had favoured shaggy hind legs and hoofs. Lord Astfgl had rejected all that sort of thing out of hand. He held that no-one would ever get taken seriously by those stuck-up bastards in Dunmanifestin when their rear end kept ruminating all the time, and so he favoured a red silk cloak, crimson tights, a cowl with two rather sophisticated little horns on it, and a trident. The end kept dropping off the trident but, he felt, it was the sort of get-up in which a demon king could be taken seriously . . .

In the coolness of his chambers – oh, by all the gods or, rather, not by all the gods, it had taken him *ages* to get them up to some sort of civilised standard, his predecessors had been quite content just to lounge around and tempt people, they had never heard of executive stress – he gently lifted the cover off the Mirror of Souls and watched it flicker into life.

Its cool black surface was surrounded by an ornate frame, from which curls of greasy smoke constantly unfolded and drifted.

Your wish, master? it said.

'Show me the events around the Pseudopolis gate over the last hour,' said the King, and settled down to watch.

After a while he went and looked up the name 'Rincewind' in the filing cabinet he had recently had installed, in place of the distressingly-bound old ledgers that had been there; the system still needed ironing out, though, because the bewildered demons filed everything under P for People.

Then he sat watching the flickering pictures and absentmindedly played with the stuff on his desk, to soothe his nerves.

He had any amount of desk things: notepads with magnets for paperclips, handy devices for holding pens and those tiny jotters that always came in handy, incredibly funny statuettes with slogans like 'You're the Boss!', and little chromium balls and spirals operated by a sort of ersatz and short-lived perpetual motion. No-one looking at that desk could have any doubt that they were, in cold fact, truly damned.

'I *see*,' said Lord Astfgl, setting a selection of shiny balls swinging with one tap of a talon.

He couldn't remember any demon called Rincewind. On the other hand, there were *millions* of the wretched things, swarming all over the place with no sense of order, and he hadn't yet had time to carry out a proper census and retire the unnecessary ones. This one seemed to have fewer appendages and more vowels in its name than most. But it *had* to be a demon.

Vassenego was a proud old fool, one of the elder demons who smiled and despised him and not-quite-obeyed him, just because the King'd worked hard over the millennia to get from humble beginnings to where he was today. He wouldn't put it past the old devil to do this on purpose, just to spite him.

Well, he'd have to see about that later. Send him a memo or something. Too late to do anything about it now. He'd have to take a personal interest. Eric Thursley was too good a prospect to pass up. Getting Eric Thursley would really annoy the gods.

Gods! How he hated the gods! He hated the gods even more than he hated the old guard like Vassenego, even more than he hated humans. He'd thrown a little soirée last week, he'd put a lot of thought into it, he wanted to show that he was prepared to let bygones be bygones, work with them for a new, better and more efficient universe. He'd called it a 'Getting to Know You!' party. There'd been sausages on sticks and everything, he'd done his best to make it nice.

They hadn't even bothered to answer the invitations. And he'd made a special point of putting RSVP on them.

'Demon?'

Eric peered around the door.

'What shape are you?' he said.

'Pretty poor shape,' said Rincewind.

'I've brought you some food. You do eat, do you?'

Rincewind tried some. It was a bowl of cereal, nuts, and dried fruit. He didn't have any quarrel with any of that. It was just that somewhere in the preparation something had apparently done to these innocent ingredients what it takes a million gravities to do to a neutron star. If you died of eating this sort of thing they wouldn't have to bury you, they would just need to drop you somewhere where the ground was soft.

He managed to swallow it. It wasn't difficult. The trick would have been preventing it from heading downwards.

'Lovely,' he choked. The parrot did a splendid impersonation of someone being sick.

'I've decided to let you go,' said Eric. 'It's pretty pointless keeping you, isn't it.'

'Absolutely.'

'You haven't any powers at all?'

'Sorry. Dead failure.'

'You don't *look* too demonic, come to think about it,' said Eric.

'They never do. You can't trust them wossnames,' chortled the parrot. It lost its balance again. 'Polly want a biscuit,' it said, upside down.

Rincewind spun around. 'You stay out of this, beaky!'

There was a sound behind them, like the universe clearing its throat. The chalk marks of the magic circle grew terribly bright for a moment, became fiery lines against the scuffed planks, and something dropped out of the empty air and landed heavily on the floor.

It was a large, metal-bound chest. It had fallen on its curved lid. After a while it started to rock violently, and then it extended hundreds of little pink legs and with considerable effort flipped itself over.

Finally it shuffled around until it was watching the pair of them. It was all the more disconcerting because it was staring without having any eyes to do it with.

Eric moved first. He grasped the home-made magic sword, which flapped wildly.

'You *are* a demon!' he said. 'I nearly believed you when you said you weren't!'

'Wheee!' said the parrot.

'It's just my Luggage,' said Rincewind desperately. 'It's a sort of . . . well, it goes everywhere with me, there's nothing demonic about it . . . er.' He hesitated. 'Not much, anyway,' he finished lamely.

'Avaunt!'

'Oh, not again.'

The boy looked at the open book. 'My commands earlier resume,' he said firmly. 'The most beautiful woman who has ever lived, mastery of all the kingdoms of the world, and to live for ever. Get on with it.'

Rincewind stood frozen.

'Well, go on,' said Eric. 'You're supposed to disappear in a puff of smoke.'

'Listen, do you think I can just snap my fingers—'

Rincewind snapped his fingers.

There was a puff of smoke.

Rincewind gave his fingers a long shocked stare, as one might regard a gun that has been hanging on the wall for decades and has suddenly gone off and perforated the cat.

'They've hardly ever done that before,' he said.

He looked down.

'Aargh,' he said, and closed his eyes.

It was a better world in the darkness behind his eyelids. If he tapped his foot he could persuade himself that he could *feel* the floor, he could know that he was really standing in the room, and that the urgent signals from all his other senses, which were telling him that he was suspended in the air some thousand miles or so above the Disc, were just a bad dream he'd wake up from. He hastily cancelled that thought. If he was asleep he'd prefer to stay that way. You could *fly* in dreams. If he woke up, it was a long way to fall.

Perhaps I have died and I really am a demon, he thought.

It was an interesting point.

He opened his eyes again.

'*Wow!*' said Eric, his eyes gleaming. 'Can I have *all* of it?'

The boy was standing in the same position as he had been in the room. So was the Luggage. So, to Rincewind's annoyance, was the parrot. It was perching in mid-air, looking speculatively at the cosmic panorama below.

The Disc might almost have been designed to be seen from space; it hadn't, Rincewind was damn sure, been designed to be lived on. But he had to admit that it was impressive.

The sun was about to rise on the far rim and made a line of fire that glittered around half the circumference. A long slow dawn was just beginning its sweep across the dark, massive landscape.

Below, harshly lit in the arid vacuum of space, Great A'Tuin the world turtle toiled under the weight of Creation. On his – or her, the matter had never really been resolved – carapace the four giant elephants strained to support the Disc itself.

There might have been more efficient ways to build a world. You might start with a ball of molten iron and then coat it with successive layers of rock, like an old-fashioned gobstopper. And you'd have a very efficient planet, but it wouldn't look so nice. Besides, things would drop off the bottom.

'Pretty good,' said the parrot. 'Polly want a continent.'

'It's so *big*,' breathed Eric.

'Yes,' said Rincewind flatly.

He felt that something more was expected of him.

'Don't break it,' he added.

He had a nagging doubt about all this. If he was for the sake of argument a demon, and so many things had happened to him recently he was prepared to concede that he might have died and not noticed it in the confusion*, then he still didn't quite see how the world was his to give away. He was pretty sure that it had owners who felt the same way.

Also, he was sure that a demon had to get something in writing.

'I think you have to sign for it,' he said. 'In blood.'

'Whose?' said Eric.

'Yours, I think,' said Rincewind. 'Or bird blood will do, at a pinch.' He glared meaningfully at the parrot, which growled at him.

'Aren't I allowed to try it out first?'

'What?'

'Well, supposing it doesn't work? I'm not signing for it until I've seen it work.'

Rincewind stared at the boy. Then he looked down at the broad panorama of the kingdoms of the world. I wonder if I was like him at his age? he thought. I wonder how I survived?

'It's the world,' he said patiently. 'Of course it will bloody well work. I mean, *look* at it. Hurricanes, continental drift, rainfall cycle – it's all there. All ticking over like a bloody watch. It'll last you a lifetime, a world like that. Used carefully.'

Eric gave the world a critical examination. He wore the expression of someone who knows that all the best gifts in life seem to require the psychic equivalent of two U2 batteries and the shops won't be open until after the holidays.

'There's got to be tribute,' he said flatly.

'You what?'

'The kings of the world,' said Eric. 'They've got to pay me tribute.'

'You've really been studying this, haven't you,' said Rincewind sarcastically. 'Just tribute? You don't fancy the moon while we're up here? This week's special offer, one free satellite with every world dominated?'

'Are there any useful minerals?'

'*What!*'

Eric gave a sigh of long-suffering patience.

'Minerals,' he said. 'Ores. You know.'

Rincewind coloured. 'I don't think a lad your age should be thinking of—'

'I mean metal and things. It's no use to me if it's just a load of rock.'

Rincewind looked down. The Discworld's tiny moonlet was just

---

*Rincewind had been told that death was just like going into another room. The difference is, when you shout, 'Where's my clean socks?', no-one answers.

rising over the far edge, and shed a pale radiance across the jigsaw pattern of land and sea.

'Oh, I don't know. It looks quite nice,' he volunteered. 'Look, it's dark now. Perhaps everyone can pay you tribute in the morning?'

'I want some tribute *now*.'

'I thought you might.'

Rincewind gave his fingers a careful examination. It wasn't as if he'd ever been particularly good at snapping them.

He gave it another try.

When he opened his eyes again he was standing up to his ankles in mud.

Pre-eminent amongst Rincewind's talents was his skill in running away, which over the years he had elevated to the status of a genuinely pure science; it didn't matter if you were fleeing from or to, so long as you were fleeing. It was flight alone that counted. I run, therefore I am; more correctly, I run, therefore with any luck I'll still *be*.

But he was also skilled in languages and in practical geography. He could shout 'help!' in fourteen languages and scream for mercy in a further twelve. He had passed through many of the countries on the Disc, some of them at high speed, and during the long, lovely, *boring* hours when he'd worked in the Library he'd whiled away the time by reading up on all the exotic and faraway places he'd never visited. He remembered that at the time he'd sighed with relief that he'd never have to visit them.

And, now, here he was.

Jungle surrounded him. It wasn't nice, interesting, open jungle, such as leopard-skin-clad heroes might swing through, but serious, real jungle, jungle that towered up like solid slabs of greenness, thorned and barbed, jungle in which every representative of the vegetable kingdom had really rolled up its bark and got down to the strenuous business of outgrowing all competitors. The soil was hardly soil at all, but dead plants on the way to composthood; water dripped from leaf to leaf, insects whined in the humid, spore-laden air, and there was the terrible breathless silence made by the motors of photosynthesis running flat out. Any yodelling hero who tried to swing through that lot might just as well take his chances with a bean-slicer.

'How do you *do* that?' said Eric.

'It's probably a knack,' said Rincewind.

Eric subjected the wonders of Nature to a cursory and disdainful glance.

'This doesn't look like a kingdom,' he complained. 'You said we could go to a kingdom. Do you call this a kingdom?'

'This is probably the rain forests of Klatch,' said Rincewind. 'They're stuffed full of lost kingdoms.'

'You mean mysterious ancient races of Amazonian princesses who subject all male prisoners to strange and exhausting progenitative rites?' said Eric, his glasses beginning to fog.

'Haha,' said Rincewind stonily. 'What an imagination the child has.'

'Wossname, wossname, wossname!' shrieked the parrot.

'I've read about them,' said Eric, peering into the greenery. 'Of course, I own those kingdoms as well.' He stared at some private inner vision. 'Gosh,' he said, hungrily.

'I should concentrate on the tribute if I was you,' said Rincewind, setting off down what was possibly a path.

The brightly-coloured blooms on a tree nearby turned to watch him go.

In the jungles of central Klatch there are, indeed, lost kingdoms of mysterious Amazonian princesses who capture male explorers for specifically masculine duties. These are indeed rigorous and exhausting and the luckless victims do not last long.*

There are also hidden plateaux where the reptilian monsters of a bygone epoch romp and play, as well as elephants' graveyards, lost diamond mines, and strange ruins decorated with hieroglyphs the very sight of which can freeze the most valiant heart. On any reasonable map of the area there's barely room for the trees.

The few explorers who have returned have passed on a number of handy hints to those who follow after, such as: 1) avoid if possible any hanging-down creepers with beady eyes and a forked tongue at one end; 2) don't pick up any orange-and-black-striped creepers that are apparently lying across the path, twitching, because there is often a tiger on the other end; and 3) don't go.

If I'm a demon, Rincewind thought hazily, why is everything stinging me and trying to trip me up? I mean, surely I can only be harmed by a wooden dagger through my heart? Or do I mean garlic?

Eventually the jungle opened out into a very wide, cleared area that stretched all the way to a distant blue range of volcanoes. The land fell away below them to a patchwork of lakes and swampy fields, here and there punctuated by great stepped pyramids, each

---

*This is because wiring plugs, putting up shelves, sorting out the funny noise in attics and mowing lawns can eventually reduce even the strongest constitution.

one crowned with a thin plume of smoke curling into the dawn air. The jungle track opened out into a narrow, but paved, road.

'Where's this, demon?' said Eric.

'It looks like one of the Tezuman kingdoms,' said Rincewind. 'They're ruled over by the Great Muzuma, I think.'

'She's an Amazonian princess, is she?'

'Strangely enough, no. You'd be astonished how many kingdoms aren't ruled by Amazonian princesses, Eric.'

'It looks pretty primitive, anyway. A bit Stone Age.'

'The Tezuman priests have a sophisticated calendar and an advanced horology,' quoted Rincewind.

'Ah,' said Eric, 'Good.'

'No,' said Rincewind patiently. 'It means time measurement.'

'Oh.'

'You'd approve of them. They're superb mathematicians, apparently.'

'Huh,' said Eric, blinking solemnly. 'Shouldn't think they've got a lot to count in a backward civilisation like this.'

Rincewind eyed the chariots that were heading rapidly towards them.

'I think they usually count victims,' he said.

The Tezuman Empire in the jungle valleys of central Klatch is known for its organic market gardens, its exquisite craftsmanship in obsidian, feathers and jade, and its mass human sacrifices in honour of Quezovercoatl, the Feathered Boa, god of mass human sacrifices. As they said, you always knew where you stood with Quezovercoatl. It was generally with a lot of people on top of a great stepped pyramid with someone in an elegant feathered headdress chipping an exquisite obsidian knife for your very own personal use.

The Tezumen are renowned on the continent for being the most suicidally gloomy, irritable and pessimistic people you could ever hope to meet, for reasons that may soon be made clear. It was true about the time measurement as well. The Tezumen had realised long ago that everything was steadily getting worse and, having a terrible literal-mindedness, had developed a complex system to keep track of how much worse each succeeding day was.

Contrary to general belief, the Tezumen *did* invent the wheel. They just had radically different ideas about what you used it for.

*

It was the first chariot Rincewind had ever seen that was pulled by llamas. That wasn't what was odd about it. What was odd about it was that it was being carried by people, two holding each side of the axle and running after the animals, their sandalled feet flapping on the flagstones.

'Do you think it's got the tribute in it?' said Eric.

All the leading chariot seemed to contain, apart from the driver, was a squat, basically cube-shaped man wearing a puma-skin outfit and a feather headdress.

The runners panted to a halt, and Rincewind saw that each man wore what would probably be described as a primitive sword, made by affixing shards of obsidian into a wooden club. They looked to him no less deadly than sophisticated, extremely civilised swords. In fact, they looked worse.

'Well?' said Eric.

'Well what?' said Rincewind.

'Tell him to give me my tribute.'

The fat man got down ponderously, marched over to Eric and, to Rincewind's extreme surprise, grovelled.

Rincewind felt something claw its way up his back and on to his shoulder, where a voice like a sheet of metal being torn in half said, 'That's better. Very wossname, comfy. If you try and knock me off, demon, you can wossname your ear goodbye. What a turn up for the scrolls, eh? They seemed to be expecting him.'

'Why do you keep saying wossname?' said Rincewind.

'Limited wossname. Doodah. Thingy. You know. It's got words in it,' said the parrot.

'Dictionary?' said Rincewind. The passengers in the other chariots had got out and were also grovelling to Eric, who was beaming like an idiot.

The parrot considered this.

'Yeah, probably,' it said. 'I've got to wing it to you,' it went on. 'I thought you were a bit of a wossname at the start, but you seem to be delivering the wossname.'

'Demon?' said Eric, airily.

'Yes?'

'What are they saying? Can't you speak their language?'

'Er, no,' said Rincewind. 'I can read it, though,' he called out, as Eric turned away. 'If you could just sort of make signs for them to write it down . . .'

*

It was around noon. In the jungle behind Rincewind creatures whooped and gibbered. Mosquitoes the size of humming-birds whined around his head.

'Of course,' he said, for the tenth time, 'They've never really got round to inventing paper.'

The stonemason stood back, handed the latest blunted obsidian chisel to his assistant, and gave Rincewind an expectant look.

Rincewind stood back and examined the rock critically.

'It's very good,' he said. 'I mean, it's a very good likeness. You've got his hairstyle and everything. Of course, he's not as, er, *square* as that normally but, yes, very good. And here's the chariot and there's the step-pyramids. Yes. Well, it looks as though they want you to go to the city with them,' he said to Eric.

'Tell them yes,' said Eric firmly.

Rincewind turned to the headman.

'Yes,' he said.

'¿[*Hunched-figure-in-triple-feathered-headdress-over-three-dots*]?'

Rincewind sighed. Without saying a word, the stonemason put a fresh stone chisel into his unresisting fingers and manhandled a new slab of granite into position.

One of the problems of being a Tezuman, apart from having a god like Quezovercoatl, is that if you unexpectedly need to order an extra pint of milk tomorrow you probably should have started writing the note for the milkman last month. Tezumen are the only people who beat themselves to death with their own suicide notes.

It was late afternoon by the time the chariot trotted into the slab city around the largest pyramid, between lines of cheering Tezumen.

'This is more like it,' said Eric, graciously acknowledging the cheers. 'They're very pleased to see us.'

'Yes,' said Rincewind, gloomily. 'I wonder why?'

'Well, because I'm the new ruler, of course.'

'Hmm.' Rincewind glanced sidelong at the parrot, who had been unnaturally silent for some time and was now cowering up against his ear like an elderly spinster in a strip club. It was having serious thoughts about the exquisite feather headdresses.

'Wossname bastards,' it croaked. 'Any wossname lays a hand on me and that wossname is minus one finger, I'm telling you.'

'There's something not right about this,' said Rincewind.

'What's that?' said the parrot.

'Everything.'

'I'm telling you, one feather out of place—'

Rincewind wasn't used to people being pleased to see him. It was unnatural, and boded no good. These people were not only cheering, they were throwing flowers and hats. The hats were made out of stone, but the thought was there.

Rincewind thought they were rather odd hats. They didn't have crowns. They were, in fact, mere discs with holes in the middle.

The procession trotted up the wide avenues of the city to a cluster of buildings at the foot of the pyramid, where another group of civic dignitaries was waiting for them.

They were wearing lots of jewellery. It was all basically the same. There are quite a lot of uses to which you can put a stone disc with a hole in the middle, and the Tezumen had explored all but one of them.

More important, though, were the boxes and boxes of treasure stacked in front of them. They were stuffed with jewels.

Eric's eyes widened.

'The tribute!' he said.

Rincewind gave up. It really was working. He didn't know how, he didn't know why, but at last it was all going Right. The setting sun glinted off a dozen fortunes. Of *course*, it belonged to Eric, presumably, but maybe there was enough for him, too . . .

'Naturally,' he said weakly. 'What else did you expect?'

And there was feasting, and long speeches that Rincewind couldn't understand but which were punctuated with cheers and nods and bows in Eric's direction. And there were long recitals of Tezuman music, which sounds like someone clearing a particularly difficult nostril.

Rincewind left Eric sitting proudly enthroned in the firelight and wandered disconsolately across to the pyramid.

'I was enjoying the wossname,' said the parrot reproachfully.

'I can't settle down,' said Rincewind. 'I'm sorry, but this sort of thing has never happened to me before. All the jewels and things. Everything going as expected. It's not right.'

He looked up the monstrous face of the steep pyramid, red and flickering in the firelight. Every huge block was carved with a bas-relief of Tezumen doing terribly inventive things to their enemies.

It suggested that the Tezumen, whatever sterling qualities they possessed, were not traditionally inclined to welcome perfect strangers and heap them with jewels. The overall effect of the great heap of carvings was very artistic – it was just the details that were horrible.

While working his way along the wall he came to a huge door, which artistically portrayed a group of prisoners apparently being given a complete medical check-up.*

It opened into a short, torch-lit tunnel. Rincewind took a few steps along it, telling himself he could always hurry out again, and came out into a lofty space which occupied most of the inside of the pyramid.

There were more torches all around the walls, which illuminated everything quite well.

That wasn't really welcome because what they mainly illuminated was a giant-sized statue of Quezovercoatl, the Feathered Boa.

If you had to be in a room with that statue, you'd prefer it to be pitch dark.

Or, then again, perhaps not. A better option would be to put the thing in a darkened room while you had insomnia a thousand miles away, trying to forget what it looked like.

It's just a statue, Rincewind told himself. It's not real. They've just used their imagination, that's all.

'What the wossname is it?' said the parrot.

'It's their god.'

'Get away?'

'No, really. It's Quezovercoatl. Half man, half chicken, half jaguar, half serpent, half scorpion and half mad.'

The parrot's beak moved as it worked this out.

'That makes a wossname total of three homicidal maniacs,' it said.

'About right, yes,' said the statue.

'*On the other hand*,' said Rincewind instantly, 'I do think it's frightfully important for people to have the right to worship in their own special way, and now I think we'll just be going, so just—'

'Please don't leave me here,' said the statue. 'Please take me with you.'

'Could be tricky, could be tricky,' Rincewind said hurriedly, backing away. 'It's not me, you understand, it's just that where I come from everyone has this racial prejudice thing against thirty-

---

* From a distance it did, anyway. Close to, no.

foot-high people with fangs and talons and necklaces of skulls all over them. I just think you'll have trouble fitting in.'

The parrot tweaked his ear. 'It's coming from *behind* the statue, you stupid wossname,' it croaked.

It turned out to be coming from a hole in the floor. A pale face peered short-sightedly up at Rincewind from the depths of a pit. It was an elderly, good-natured face with a faintly worried expression.

'Hallo?' said Rincewind.

'You don't know what it means to hear a friendly voice again,' said the face, breaking into a grin. 'If you could just sort of help me up . . .?'

'Sorry?' said Rincewind. 'You're a prisoner, are you?'

'Alas, this is so.'

'I don't know that I ought to go around rescuing prisoners just like that,' said Rincewind. 'I mean, you might have done *anything*.'

'I am entirely innocent of all crimes, I assure you.'

'Ah, well, so you say,' said Rincewind gravely. 'But if the Tezumen have judged—'

'Wossname, wossname, *wossname*!' shrieked the parrot in his ear as it bounced up and down on his shoulder. 'Haven't you got the faintest? Where've you been? He's a prisoner! A prisoner in a temple! You've got to rescue prisoners in temples! That's what they're bloody there for!'

'No it isn't,' snapped Rincewind. 'That's all you know! He's probably here to be sacrificed! Isn't that right?' He looked at the prisoner for confirmation.

The face nodded. 'Indeed, you are correct. Flayed alive, in fact.'

'There!' said Rincewind to the parrot. 'See? You think you know everything! He's here to be flayed alive.'

'Every inch of skin removed to the accompaniment of exquisite pain,' added the prisoner, helpfully.

Rincewind paused. He thought he knew the meaning of the word 'exquisite', and it didn't seem to belong anywhere near 'pain'.

'What, every bit?' he said.

'This is apparently the case.'

'Gosh. What was it you did?'

The prisoner sighed. 'You'd never believe me . . .' he said.

The Demon King let the mirror darken and drummed his fingers on his desk for a moment. Then he picked up a speaking tube and blew into it.

Eventually a distant voice said: 'Yes, guv?'

'Yes *sir*!' snapped the King.

The distant voice muttered something. 'Yes, SIR?' it added.

'Do we have a Quezovercoatl working here?'

'I'll see, guv.' The voice faded, came back. 'Yes, guv.'

'Is he a Duke, Earl, Count or Baron?' said the King.

'No, guv.'

'Well, what is he?'

There was a long silence at the other end.

'Well?' said the King.

'He's no-one much, guv.'

The King glared at the tube for some time. You try, he thought. You make proper plans, you try to get organised, you try to *help* people, and this is what you get.

'*Send him to see me*,' he said.

Outside, the music rose to a crescendo and stopped. The fires crackled. From the distant jungles a thousand glowing eyes watched the proceedings.

The high priest stood up and made a speech. Eric beamed like a pumpkin. A long line of Tezumen brought baskets of jewels which they scattered before him.

Then the high priest made a second speech. This one seemed to end on a question.

'Fine,' said Eric. 'Jolly good. Keep it up.' He scratched his ear and ventured, 'You can all have a half holiday.'

The high priest repeated the question again, in a slightly impatient tone of voice.

'I'm the one, yes,' said Eric, just in case they were unclear. 'You've got it exactly right.'

The high priest spoke again. This time there was no slightly about it.

'Let's just run through this again, shall we?' said the Demon King. He leaned back in his throne.

'You happened to find the Tezumen one day and decided, I think I recall your words correctly, that they were "a bunch of Stone-Age no-hopers sitting around in a swamp being no trouble to anyone", am I right? Whereupon you entered the mind of one of their high priests – I believe at that time they worshipped a small stick – drove

him insane and inspired the tribes to unite, terrorise their neigh-
bours and bring forth upon the continent a new nation dedicated to
the proposition that all men should be taken to the top of ceremonial pyramids and be chopped up with stone knives.' The King
pulled his notes towards him. 'Oh yes, some of them were also to be
flayed alive,' he added.

Quezovercoatl shuffled his feet.

'Whereupon,' said the King, 'they immediately engaged in a
prolonged war with just about everyone else, bringing death and
destruction to thousands of moderately blameless people, ekcetra,
ekcetra. *Now, look, this sort of thing has got to stop.*'

Quezovercoatl swayed back a bit.

'It was only, you know, a hobby,' said the imp. 'I thought, you
know, it was the right thing, sort of thing. Death and destruction
and that.'

'You did, did you?' said the King. 'Thousands of more-or-less
innocent people dying? Straight out of our hands,' he snapped his
fingers, 'just like that. Straight off to their happy hunting ground or
whatever. That's the trouble with you people. You don't think of
the Big Picture. I mean, look at the Tezumen. Gloomy, unimaginative, obsessive . . . by now they could have invented a whole
bureaucracy and taxation system that could have turned the minds
of the continent to slag. Instead of which, they're just a bunch of
second-rate axe-murderers. What a waste.'

Quezovercoatl squirmed.

The King swivelled the throne back and forth a bit.

'Now, I want you to go straight back down there and tell them
you're sorry,' he said.

'Pardon?'

'Tell them you've changed your mind. Tell them that what you
really wanted them to do was strive day and night to improve the
lot of their fellow men. It'll be a winner.'

'What?' said Quezovercoatl, looking extremely shifty. 'You want
me to manifest myself?'

'They've seen you already, haven't they? I saw the statue, it's very
lifelike.'

'Well, *yes.* I've appeared in dreams and that,' said the demon
uncertainly.

'Right, then. Get on with it.'

Quezovercoatl was clearly unhappy about something.

'Er,' he said. 'You want me to actually materialise, sort of thing? I
mean, actually sort of turn up on the spot?'

'Yes!'
'Oh.'

The prisoner dusted himself down and extended a wrinkled hand to Rincewind.

'Many thanks. Ponce da Quirm,' he said.

'Pardon?'

'It's my name.'

'Oh.'

'It's a proud old name,' said da Quirm, searching Rincewind's eyes for any traces of mockery.

'Fine,' said Rincewind blankly.

'We were searching for the Fountain of Youth,' da Quirm went on.

Rincewind looked him up and down.

'Any luck?' he said politely.

'Not significantly, no.'

Rincewind peered back down into the pit.

'You said *we*,' he said. 'Where's everyone else?'

'They got religion.'

Rincewind looked up at the statue of Quezovercoatl. It took no imagination whatsoever to imagine what kind.

'I think,' he said carefully, 'that we had better go.'

'Too true,' said the old man. 'And quickly, too. Before the Ruler of the World turns up.'

Rincewind went cold. It starts, he thought. I knew it was all going to turn out badly, and this is where it starts. I must have an instinct for these things.

'How do you know about that?' he said.

'Oh, they've got this prophecy. Well, not a prophecy, really, it's more the entire history of the world, start to finish. It's written all over this pyramid,' said da Quirm, cheerfully. 'My word, I wouldn't like to be the Ruler when he arrives. They've got *plans*.'

Eric stood up.

'Now just you listen to me,' he said. 'I'm not going to stand for this sort of thing. I'm your ruler, you know . . .'

Rincewind stared at the blocks nearest the statue. It had taken the Tezumen two storeys, twenty years and ten thousand tons of granite to explain what they intended to do to the Ruler of the World, but the result was, well, graphic. He would be left in no doubt that they were annoyed. He might even go so far as to deduce that they were quite vexed.

'But why do they give him all these jewels to start with?' he said, pointing.

'Well, he *is* the Ruler,' said da Quirm. 'He's entitled to some respect, I suppose.'

Rincewind nodded. There was a sort of justice in it. If you were a tribe who lived in a swamp in the middle of a damp forest, didn't have any metal, had been saddled with a god like Quezovercoatl, and then found someone who said he was in charge of the whole affair, you probably *would* want to spend some time explaining to him how incredibly disappointed you were. The Tezumen had never seen any reason to be subtle in dealing with deities.

It was a very good likeness of Eric.

His eye followed the story on to the next wall.

This block showed a very good likeness of Rincewind. He had a parrot on his shoulder.

'Hang on,' he said. 'That's me!'

'You should see what they're doing to you on the next block,' said the parrot smugly. 'It'll turn your wossname.'

Rincewind looked at the block. His wossname revolved.

'We'll just leave very quietly,' he said firmly. 'I mean, we won't stop to thank them for the meal. We can always send them a letter later. You know, so's not to be impolite.'

'Just a moment,' said da Quirm, as Rincewind dragged at his arm, 'I haven't had a chance to read all the blocks yet. I want to see how the world's going to end—'

'How it's going to end for everyone else I don't know,' said Rincewind grimly, dragging him down the tunnel. 'I know how it's going to end for *me*.'

He stepped out into the dawn light, which was fine. Where he went wrong was stepping into a semi-circle of Tezumen. They had spears. They had exquisitely chipped obsidian spearheads, which, like their swords, were nowhere near as sophisticated as ordinary, coarse, inferior steel weapons. Was it better to know that you were going to be skewered by delicate examples of genuine ethnic origin rather than nasty forge-made items hammered out by people not in contact with the cycles of nature?

Probably not, Rincewind decided.

*

'I always say,' said da Quirm, 'that there is a good side to every-thing.'

Rincewind, trussed to the next slab, turned his head with difficulty.

'Where is it at the moment, precisely?' he said.

Da Quirm squinted down across the swamps and the forest roof.

'Well. It's a first-class view from up here, to begin with.'

'Oh, good,' said Rincewind. 'You know, I never would have looked at it like that. You're absolutely right. It's the kind of view you'll remember for the rest of your life, I expect. I mean, it's not as if it will be any great feat of recollection.'

'There's no need to be sarcastic. I was only passing a remark.'

'I want my mum,' said Eric, from the middle slab.

'Chin up, lad,' said da Quirm. 'At least you're being sacrificed for something worthwhile. *I* just suggested they tried using the wheels upright, so they'd roll. I'm afraid they're not very responsive to new ideas around here. Still, *nil desperandum*. Where there's life there's hope.'

Rincewind growled. If there was one thing he couldn't stand, it was people who were fearless in the face of death. It seemed to strike at something absolutely fundamental in him.

'In fact,' said da Quirm, 'I think—' He rolled from side to side experimentally, tugging at the vines which were holding him down. 'Yes, I think when they did these ropes up – yes, definitely, they—'

'What? What?' said Rincewind.

'Yes, definitely,' said da Quirm. 'I'm absolutely sure about it. They did them up very tightly and professionally. Not an inch of give in them anywhere.'

'Thank you,' said Rincewind.

The flat top of the truncated pyramid was in fact quite large, with plenty of room for statues, priests, slabs, gutters, knife-chipping production lines and all the other things the Tezumen needed for the bulk disposal of religion. In front of Rincewind several priests were busily chanting a long list of complaints about swamps, mosquitoes, lack of metal ore, volcanoes, the weather, the way obsidian never kept its edge, the trouble with having a god like Quezovercoatl, the way wheels never worked properly however often you laid them flat and pushed them, and so on.

The prayers of most religions generally praise and thank the gods involved, either out of general piety or in the hope that he or she will take the hint and start acting responsibly. The Tezumen, having taken a long hard look around their world and decided bluntly that things were just about as bad as they were ever going to get, had perfected the art of the plain-chant winge.

'Won't be long now,' said the parrot, from its perch atop a statue of one of the Tezumen's lesser gods.

It had got there by a complicated sequence of events that had involved a lot of squawking, a cloud of feathers and three Tezuman priests with badly swollen thumbs.

'The high priest is just performing a wossname in honour of Quezovercoatl,' it went on, conversationally. 'You've drawn quite a crowd.'

'I suppose you wouldn't kind of hop down here and bite through these ropes, would you?' said Rincewind.

'Not a chance.'

'Thought so.'

'Sun's coming up soon,' the parrot continued. Rincewind felt that it sounded unnecessarily cheerful.

'I'm going to complain about this, demon,' moaned Eric. 'You wait till my mother finds out. My parents have got influence, you know.'

'Oh, good,' said Rincewind weakly. 'Why don't you tell the high priest that if he cuts your heart out she'll be right down to the school tomorrow to complain.'

The Tezuman priests bowed towards the sun, and all eyes in the crowd below turned to the jungle.

Where something was happening. There was the sound of crackling undergrowth. Tropical birds erupted through the trees, shrieking.

Rincewind, of course, could not see this.

'You never should have wanted to be ruler of the world,' he said. 'I mean, what did you expect? You can't expect people to be happy about seeing you. No-one ever is when the landlord turns up.'

'But they're going to kill me!'

'It's just their way of saying that, metaphorically, they're fed up with waiting for you to repaint the place and see to the drains.'

The whole jungle was in uproar now. Animals exploded out of the bushes as if running from a fire. A few heavy thumps indicated that trees were falling over.

At last a frantic jaguar crashed through the undergrowth and loped down the causeway. The Luggage was a few feet behind it.

It was covered with creepers, leaves and the feathers of various rare jungle fowls, some of which were now even rarer. The jaguar could have avoided it by zigging or zagging to either side, but sheer idiot terror prevented it. It made the mistake of turning its head to see what was behind.

This was the last mistake it ever made.

'You know that box of yours?' said the parrot.

'What about it?' said Rincewind.

'It's heading this way.'

The priests peered down at the running figure far below. The Luggage had a straightforward way of dealing with things between it and its intended destination: it ignored them.

It was at this moment, against all his instincts, in great trepidation and, most unfortunately of all, in deep ignorance of what was happening, that Quezovercoatl himself chose to materialise on top of the pyramid.

Several of the priests noticed him. The knives fell from their fingers.

'Er,' squeaked the demon.

Other priests turned around.

'Right. Now, I want you all to pay attention,' squeaked Quezovercoatl, cupping his tiny hands around his main mouth in an effort to be heard.

This was very embarrassing. He'd enjoyed being the Tezuman god, he'd been really impressed by their single-minded devotion to duty, he'd been very gratified by the incredible lifelike statue in the pyramid, and it really hurt to have to reveal that, in one important particular, it was incorrect.

He was six inches high.

'Now then,' he began, 'this is very important—'

Unfortunately, no-one ever found out why. At that moment the Luggage breasted the top of the pyramid, its legs whirring like propellers, and landed squarely on the slabs.

There was a brief, flat squeak.

It was a funny old world, said da Quirm. You had to laugh, really. If you didn't, you'd go mad, wouldn't you? One minute strapped to a slab and about to undergo exquisite torture, the next being given breakfast, a change of clothes, a hot tub and a free lift out of the kingdom. It made you believe there was a god. Of course, the Tezumen *knew* there was a god, and that he was currently a small and distressing greasy patch on top of the pyramid. Which left them with a bit of a problem.

The Luggage squatted in the city's main plaza. The entire priesthood was sitting around it and watching it carefully, in case it did anything amusing or religious.

'Are you going to leave it behind?' said Eric.

'It's not as simple as that,' said Rincewind. 'It generally catches up. Let's just go away quickly.'

'But we'll take the tribute, won't we?'

'I think that could be an amazingly bad idea,' said Rincewind. 'Let's just quietly go, while they're in a good temper. The novelty will wear off soon, I expect.'

'And I've got to get on with my search for the Fountain of Youth,' said da Quirm.

'Oh yes,' said Rincewind.

'I've devoted my whole life to it, you know,' said the old man proudly.

Rincewind looked him up and down. 'Really?' he said.

'Oh, yes. Exclusively. Ever since I was a boy.'

Rincewind's expression was one of acute puzzlement.

'In that case,' he began, in the manner of one talking to a child, 'wouldn't it have been better . . . you know, more sensible . . . if you'd just got on with . . .'

'What?' said da Quirm.

'Oh, never mind,' said Rincewind. 'I'll tell you what, though,' he added, 'I think, in order to prevent you getting, you know, *bored*, we should present you with this wonderful talking parrot.' He made a swift grab, while keeping his thumbs firmly out of harm's way. 'It's a jungle fowl,' he said. 'Cruel to subject it to city life, isn't it?'

'I was born in a cage, you raving wossname!' screamed the parrot. Rincewind faced it, nose to beak.

'It's that or fricassee time,' he said. The parrot opened its beak to bite his nose, saw his expression, and thought better of it.

'Polly want a biscuit,' it managed, adding, *sotto voce*, 'wossnamewossnamewossname.'

'A dear little bird of my very own,' said da Quirm. 'I shall look after it.'

'*wossnamewossname*.'

They reached the jungle. A few minutes later the Luggage trotted after them.

It was noon in the kingdom of Tezuma.

From inside the main pyramid came the sounds of a very large statue being dismantled.

The priests sat around thoughtfully. Occasionally one of them stood up and made a short speech.

It was clear that points were being made. For example, how the economics of the kingdom depended on a buoyant obsidian knife industry, how the enslaved neighbouring kingdoms had come to rely on the smack of firm government, and incidentally on the hack, slash and disembowelling of firm government as well, and on the terrible fate that awaited any people who didn't have gods. Godless people might get up to *anything*, they might turn against the fine old traditions of thrift and non-self-sacrifice that had made the kingdom what it was today, they might start wondering why, if they didn't have a god, they needed all these priests, *anything*.

The point was well put by Mazuma, the high priest, when he said: '[*Squashed-figure-with-broken-nose, jaguar claw, three feathers, stylised spiny anteater*].'

After a while a vote was taken.

By nightfall, the kingdom's leading stonemasons were at work on a new statue.

It was basically oblong, with lots of legs.

The Demon King drummed his fingers on his desk. It wasn't that he was unhappy about the fate of Quezovercoatl, who would now have to spend several centuries in one of the nether hells while he grew a new corporeal body. Serve him right, the ghastly little imp. Nor was it the broad trend of events on the pyramid. After all, the whole point of the wish business was to see to it that what the client got was exactly what he asked for and exactly what he didn't really want.

It was just that he didn't feel in control of things.

Which was of course ridiculous. If the best came to the best he could always materialise and sort things out personally. But he liked people to believe that all the bad things happening to them were just fate and destiny. It was one of the few things that cheered him up.

He turned back to the mirror. After a while he had to adjust the temporal control.

One minute the breathless, humid jungles of Klatch, the next . . .

'I thought we were going to go back to my room,' Eric complained.

'I thought that, too,' said Rincewind, shouting to be heard over the rumbling.

'Snap your fingers again, demon.'

'Not on your life! There's plenty of places worse than this!'

'But it's all hot and dark.'

Rincewind had to concede that. It was also shaking and noisy. When his eyes grew used to the blackness he could make out a few spots of light here and there, whose dim radiance suggested that they were inside something like a boat. There was a definite feel of carpentry about everything, and a powerful smell of wood shavings and glue. If it was a boat, then it was having an awfully painful launching down a slipway greased with rocks.

A jolt slung him heavily against a bulkhead.

'I must say,' complained Eric, 'if this is where the most beautiful woman in the world lives I don't think much of her choice of boodwah. You'd think she'd put a few cushions or something around the place.'

'Boodwah?' said Rincewind.

'She's bound to have one,' said Eric smugly. 'I've read about 'em. She reclines on it.'

'Tell me,' said Rincewind, 'have you ever felt the need to have a cold bath and a brisk run around the playing fields?'

'Never.'

'It could be worth a try.'

The rumbling stopped abruptly.

There was a distant clanging noise, such as might be made by a pair of great big gates being shut. Rincewind thought he heard some voices fading into the distance, and a chuckle. It wasn't a particularly pleasant chuckle, it was more of a snigger, and it boded no good for someone. Rincewind had a pretty good idea who.

He'd stopped wondering how he'd come to be here, wherever it was. Malign forces, that was probably it. At least nothing particularly dreadful was happening to him right now. Probably it was only a matter of time.

He groped around a bit until his fingers encountered what turned out to be, following an inspection by the light of the nearest knothole, a rope ladder. Further probing at one end of the hull, or whatever it was, brought him in contact with a small, round hatchway. It was bolted on the inside.

He crawled back to Eric.

'There's a door,' he whispered.

'Where does it go?'

'It stays where it is, I think,' said Rincewind.

'Find out where it leads to, demon!'

'Could be a bad idea,' said Rincewind cautiously.

'Get on with it!'

Rincewind crawled gloomily to the hatch and grasped the bolt.

The hatch creaked open.

Down below – quite a long way below – there were damp cobblestones, across which a breeze was driving a few shreds of morning mist. With a little sigh, Rincewind unrolled the ladder.

Two minutes later they were standing in the gloom of what appeared to be a large plaza. A few buildings showed through the mist.

'Where are we?' said Eric.

'Search me.'

'You don't *know*?'

'Not a clue,' said Rincewind.

Eric glared at the mist-shrouded architecture. 'Fat chance of finding the most beautiful woman in the world in a dump like this,' he said.

It occurred to Rincewind to see what they had just climbed out of. He looked up.

Above them – a long way above them – and supported on four massive legs, which ran down to a huge wheeled platform, there was undoubtedly a huge wooden horse. More correctly, the rear of a huge wooden horse.

The builder could have put the exit hatch in a more dignified place, but for humorous reasons of his own had apparently decided not to.

'Er,' said Rincewind.

Someone coughed.

He looked down.

The evaporating mists now revealed a broad circle of armed men, many of them grinning and all of them carrying mass-produced, soulless but above all *sharp* long spears.

'Ah,' said Rincewind.

He looked back up at the hatchway. It said it all, really.

'The only thing I don't understand,' said the captain of the guard, 'is: why two of you? We were expecting maybe a hundred.'

He leaned back on his stool, his great plumed helmet in his lap, a pleased smile on his face.

'Honestly, you Ephebians!' he said. 'Talk about laugh! You must think we was born yesterday! All night nothing but sawing and hammering, the next thing there's a damn great wooden horse outside the gates, so I think, that's funny, a bloody great wooden horse with *airholes*. That's the kind of little detail I notice, see. *Airholes*. So I muster all the lads and we nips out extra early and drag it in the gates, as per expectations, and then we bides quiet, like, around it, waiting to see what it coughs up. In a manner of speaking. *Now*,' he pushed his unshaven face close to Rincewind, 'you've got a choice, see? Top seat or bottom seat, it's up to you. I just have to put the word in. You play discus with me and I'll play discus with you.'*

'What seat?' said Rincewind, reeling from the gusts of garlic.

'It's the war triremes,' said the sergeant cheerfully. 'Three seats, see, one above the other? *Tri*-remes. You get chained to the oars for years, see, and it's all according whether you're in the top seat, up in the fresh air and that, or the bottom seat where' – he grinned – 'you're not. So it's down to you, lads. Be co-operative and all you'll need to worry about will be the seagulls. *Now*. Why only the two of you?'

He leaned back again.

'Excuse me,' said Eric, 'is that Tsort, by any chance?'

'You wouldn't be trying to make fun of me, would you now, boy? Only there's such a thing as quinquiremes, see? You wouldn't like that at *all*.'

'No, *sir*,' said Eric. 'If you please, sir, I'm just a little lad led astray by bad companionship.'

'Oh, *thank* you,' said Rincewind bitterly. 'You just accidentally drew a lot of occult circles, did you, and—'

'Sarge! Sarge!' A soldier burst into the guardroom. The sergeant looked up.

'There's another of 'em, sarge! Right outside the gates this time!'

The sergeant grinned triumphantly at Rincewind.

'Oh, that's it, is it?' he said. 'You were just the advance party, come to open the gates or whatever. *Right*. We'll just go and sort your friends out, and we'll be right back.' He indicated the captives. 'You stay here. If they move, do something horrible to them.'

Rincewind and Eric were left alone with the guard.

'You know what you've done, don't you,' said Eric. 'You've only taken us all the way back to the Tsortean Wars! Thousands of years!

* Ball games were unknown in the Discworld at this time.

255

We did it at school, the wooden horse, everything! How the beautiful Elenor was kidnapped from the Ephebians – or maybe it was by the Ephebians – and there was this siege to get her back and everything.' He paused. 'Hey, that means I'm going to meet *her*.' He paused again. 'Wow!' he said.

Rincewind looked around the room. It didn't *look* ancient, but then it wouldn't, because it wasn't, yet. Everywhere in time was now, once you were there, or then. He tried to remember what little he knew of classical history, but it was just a confusion of battles, one-eyed giants and women launching thousands of ships with their faces.

'Don't you see?' hissed Eric, his glasses aglow. 'They must have brought the horse in before the soldiers had hidden in it! We know what's going to happen! We could make a fortune!'

'How, exactly?'

'Well . . .' The boy hesitated. 'We could bet on horses, sort of thing.'

'Great idea,' said Rincewind.

'Yes, and—'

'All we've got to do is escape, then find out if they have horse races here, and then really try hard to remember the names of the horses that won races in Tsort thousands of years ago.'

They went back to looking glumly at the floor. That was the thing about time travel. You were never ready for it. About the only thing he could hope for, Rincewind decided, was finding da Quirm's Fountain of Youth and managing to stay alive for a few thousand years so he'd be ready to kill his own grandfather, which was the only aspect of time travel that had ever remotely appealed to him. He had always felt that his ancestors had it coming to them.

Funny thing, though. He could remember the famous wooden horse, which had been used to trick a way into the fortified city. He didn't remember anything about there being two of them. There was something inevitable about the next thought that turned up.

'Excuse me,' he said to the guard. 'This, er, this second wooden thing outside the gate . . . it's probably not a horse, I expect?'

'Well, of course you'd know that, wouldn't you?' said the guard. 'You're spies.'

'I bet it's more oblong and sort of smaller?' said Rincewind, his face a picture of innocent enquiry.

'You bet. Pretty unimaginative bastards, aren't you?'

'I *see*.' Rincewind folded his hands on his lap.

'Try to escape,' said the guard. 'Go on, just try it. You try it and see what happens.'

'I expect your colleagues will be bringing it into the city,' Rincewind went on.

'They might do,' the guard conceded.

Eric began to giggle.

It had begun to dawn on the guard that there was a lot of shouting going on in the distance. Someone tried to blow a bugle, but the notes gurgled into silence after a few bars.

'Bit of a fight going on out there, by the sound of it,' said Rincewind. 'People winning their spurs, doing heroic deeds of valour, being noticed by superior officers, that sort of thing. And here's you hanging around in here with us.'

'I've got to stick to my post,' said the guard.

'Exactly the right attitude,' said Rincewind. 'Never mind about everyone else out there fighting valiantly to defend their city and womenfolk against the foe. You stop in here and guard us. That's the spirit. They'll probably put up a statue to you in the city square, if there's one left. "He did his duty," they'll write on it.'

The soldier appeared to think about this, and while he was doing so there was a terrible splintering creak from the direction of the main gates.

'Look,' he said desperately, 'if I just pop out for a moment . . .'

'Don't you worry about us,' said Rincewind encouragingly. 'It's not even as if we're armed.'

'Right,' said the soldier. 'Thanks.'

He gave Rincewind a worried smile and hurried off in the direction of the noise. Eric looked at Rincewind with something like admiration.

'That was actually quite amazing,' he said.

'Going to go a long way, that lad,' said Rincewind. 'A sound military thinker if ever I saw one. Come on. Let's run away.'

'Where to?'

Rincewind sighed. He'd tried to make his basic philosophy clear time and again, and people never got the message.

'Don't you worry about to,' he said. 'In my experience that always takes care of itself. The important word is *away*.'

The captain raised his head cautiously over the barricade, and snarled.

'It's just a little box, sergeant,' he snapped. 'It's not even as if it could hold one or two men.'

'Beg pardon, sir,' said the sergeant, and his face was the face of a man whose world has changed a lot in a few short minutes. 'It holds at least four, sir. Corporal Disuse and his squad, sir. I sent them out to open it, sir.'

'Are you drunk, sergeant?'

'Not yet, sir,' said the sergeant, with feeling.

'Little boxes don't eat people, sergeant.'

'After that it got angry, sir. You can see what it did to the gates.'

The captain peered over the broken timbers again.

'I suppose it grew legs and walked over there, did it?' he said sarcastically.

The sergeant broke into a relieved grin. At last they seemed to be on the same wavelength.

'Got it in one, sir,' he said. 'Legs. Hundreds of the little bleeders, sir.'

The captain glared at him. The sergeant put on the poker face which has been handed down from NCO to NCO ever since one protoamphibian told another, lower-ranking protoamphibian to muster a squad of newts and Take That Beach. The captain was eighteen and fresh from the academy, where he had passed with flying colours in such subjects as Classical Tactics, Valedictory Odes and Military Grammar. The sergeant was fifty-five, and instead of an education he had spent about forty years attacking or being attacked by harpies, humans, cyclopses, furies and horrible things on legs. He felt put upon.

'Well, I'm going to have a look at it, sergeant—'

'—not a good plan, sir, if I may—'

'—and after I've had a look at it, sergeant, there is going to be trouble.'

The sergeant threw him a salute. 'Right you are, sir,' he predicted.

The captain snorted and climbed over the barricade towards the box which sat, silent and unmoving, in its circle of devastation. The sergeant, meanwhile, slid into a sitting position behind the stoutest timber he could find and, with great determination, pulled his helmet down hard over his ears.

Rincewind crept through the streets of the city, with Eric tagging along behind.

'Are we going to find Elenor?' the boy said.

'No,' said Rincewind firmly. 'What we're going to do is, we're going to find another way out. And we're going to go out through it.'

'That's not fair!'

'She's thousands of years older than you! I mean, attraction of the mature woman, all *right*, but it'd never work out.'

'I demand that you take me to her,' wailed Eric. 'Avaunt!'

Rincewind stopped so sharply that Eric walked into him.

'Listen,' he said. 'We're in the middle of the most famously fatuous war there has ever been, any minute now thousands of warriors will be locked in mortal combat, and you want me to go and find this over-rated female and say, my friend wants to know if you'll go out with him. Well, I won't.' Rincewind stalked up to another gateway in the city wall; it was smaller than the main one, didn't have any guards, and had a wicket gate in it. Rincewind slid back the bolts.

'This isn't anything to do with us,' he said. 'We haven't even been born yet, we're not old enough to fight, it isn't our business and we're not going to do anything more to upset the course of history, all right?'

He opened the door, which saved the entire Ephebian army a bit of effort. They were just about to knock.

All day long the noise of battle raged. This was chronicled by later historians, who went on at length about beautiful women being kidnapped, fleets being assembled, wooden animals being constructed, heroes fighting one another, and completely failed to mention the part played by Rincewind, Eric and the Luggage. The Ephebians did notice, however, how enthusiastically the Tsortean soldiery ran towards them . . . not so much keen to get into battle as very anxious to get away from something else.

The historians also failed to note another interesting fact about ancient Klatchian warfare, which was that it was still at that stage quite primitive and just between soldiers and hadn't yet been thrown open to the general public. Basically, everyone knew that one side or the other would win, a few unlucky generals would get their heads chopped off, large sums of money would be paid in tribute to the winners, everyone would go home for the harvest and that bloody woman would have to make up her mind whose side she was on, the hussy.

So Tsortean street life went on more or less as normal, with the citizens stepping around the occasional knots of fighting men or trying to sell them kebabs. Several of the more enterprising ones began dismantling the wooden horse for souvenirs.

Rincewind didn't attempt to understand it. He sat down at a street café and watched a spirited battle take place between market stalls, so that amid the cries of 'Ripe olives!' there were the screams of the wounded and shouts of 'Mind your backs *please*, mêlée coming through.'

The hard part was watching the soldiers apologise when they bumped into customers. The even harder part was getting the café owner to accept a coin bearing the head of someone whose great-great-great-grandfather wasn't born yet. Fortunately, Rincewind was able to persuade the man that the future was another country.

'And a lemonade for the boy,' he added.

'My parents let me drink wine,' said Eric. 'I'm allowed one glass.'

'I bet you are,' said Rincewind.

The owner industriously swabbed the tabletop, spreading its coating of dregs and spilt retsina into a thin varnish.

'Up for the fight, are you?' he said.

'In a manner of speaking,' said Rincewind guardedly.

'I shouldn't wander around too much,' said the owner. 'They do say a civilian let the Ephebians in – *not that I've got anything against Ephebians, a fine body of men*,' he added hurriedly, as a knot of soldiery jogged past. 'A stranger, they say. That's cheating, using civilians. There's people out looking for him so's they can explain.' He made a chopping motion with his hand.

Rincewind stared at the hand as though hypnotised.

Eric opened his mouth. Eric screeched and clutched at his shins.

'Have they got a description?' Rincewind said.

'Don't think so.'

'Well, best of luck to them,' said Rincewind, rather more cheerfully.

'What's up with the lad?'

'Cramp.'

When the man had gone back behind his counter Eric hissed, 'You didn't have to go and kick me!'

'You're quite right. It was an entirely voluntary act on my part.'

A heavy hand dropped on to Rincewind's shoulder. He looked around and up into the face of an Ephebian centurion. A soldier beside him said: 'That's the one, sarge. I'd bet a year's salt.'

'Who'd of thought it?' said the sergeant. He gave Rincewind an evil grin. 'Up we come, chummy. The chief would like a word with you.'

*

Some talk of Alexander and some of Hercules, of Hector and Lysander and such great names as these. In fact, throughout the history of the multiverse people have said nice things about every cauliflower-eared sword-swinger, at least in their vicinity, on the basis that it is a lot safer that way. It's funny how the people have always respected the kind of commander who comes up with strategies like 'I want fifty thousand of you chappies to rush at the enemy', whereas the more thoughtful commanders who say things like 'Why don't we build a damn great wooden horse and then nip in at the back gate while they're all round the thing waiting for us to come out' are considered only one step above common oiks and not the kind of person you'd lend money to.

This is because most of the first type of commander are brave men, whereas cowards make far better strategists.

Rincewind was dragged before the Ephebian leaders, who had set up a command post in the city's main square so that they could oversee the storming of the central citadel, which loomed over the city on its vertiginous hill. They were not too close, however, because the defenders were dropping rocks.

They were discussing strategy when Rincewind arrived. The consensus seemed to be that if really large numbers of men were sent to storm the mountain, then enough might survive the rocks to take the citadel. This is essentially the basis of all military thinking.

Several of the more impressively dressed chieftains glanced up when Rincewind and Eric approached, gave them a look which suggested that maggots were more interesting, and turned away again. The only person who seemed pleased to see them—

—didn't look like a soldier at all. He had the armour, which was tarnished, and he had the helmet, which looked as though its plume had been used as a paintbrush, but he was skinny and had all the military bearing of a weasel. There was something vaguely familiar about his face, though. Rincewind thought it looked quite handsome.

'Pleased to see them' was only a comparative description. He was the only one who acknowledged their existence.

He was lounging in a chair and feeding the Luggage with sandwiches.

'Oh, hallo,' he said gloomily. 'It's you.'

It was amazing how much information can be crammed into a couple of words. To achieve the same effect the man could have said: It's been a long night, I'm having to organise everything from wooden horse building to the laundry rota, these idiots are about as much help as a rubber hammer, I never wanted to be here anyway and, on top of all this, there's you. Hallo, you.

He indicated the Luggage, which opened its lid expectantly.

'This yours?' he said.

'Sort of,' said Rincewind guardedly. 'I can't afford to pay for anything it's done, mind you.'

'Funny little thing, isn't it?' said the soldier. 'We found it herding fifty Tsorteans into a corner. Why was it doing that, do you think?'

Rincewind thought quickly. 'It has this amazing ability to know when people are thinking about harming me,' he said. He glared at the Luggage as one might glare at a sly, evil-tempered and generally reprehensible family pet who, after years of biting visitors, has rolled over on its scabby back and played at Lovable Puppy to impress the bailiffs.

'Yes?' said the man, without much surprise. 'Magic, is it?'

'Yes.'

'Something in the wood, is it?'

'Yes.'

'Good job we didn't build the sodding horse out of it, then.'

'Yes.'

'Got into it by magic, did you?'

'Yes.'

'Thought so.' He threw another sandwich at the Luggage. 'Where you from?'

Rincewind decided to come clean. 'The future,' he said. This didn't have the expected effect. The man just nodded.

'Oh,' he said, and then he said, 'Did we win?'

'Yes.'

'Oh. I suppose you can't remember the results of any horse races?' said the man, without much hope.

'No.'

'I thought you probably wouldn't. Why did you open the gate for us?'

It occurred to Rincewind that saying it was because he had always been a firm admirer of the Ephebian political position would not, strangely enough, be the right thing to do. He decided to try the truth again. It was a novel approach and worth experimenting with.

'I was looking for a way out,' he said.

'To run away.'

'Yes.'

'Good man. Only sensible thing, in the circumstances.' He

262

noticed Eric, who was staring at the other captains clustered around their table and deep in argument.

'You, lad,' he said. 'Want to be a soldier when you grow up?'

'No, sir.'

The man brightened a bit.

'That's the stuff,' he said.

'I want to be a eunuch, sir,' Eric added.

Rincewind's head turned as though it was being dragged.

'*Why?*' he said, and then came up with the obvious answer at the same time as Eric: 'Because you get to work in a harem all day long,' they chorused slowly.

The captain coughed.

'You're not this boy's teacher, are you?' he said.

'No.'

'Do you think anyone has explained to him—?'

'No.'

'Perhaps it would be a good idea if I got one of the centurions to have a word? You'd be amazed at the grasp of language those chaps have got.'

'Do him the power of good, I expect,' said Rincewind.

The soldier picked up his helmet, sighed, nodded at the sergeant and smoothed out the creases in his cloak. It was a grubby cloak.

'I think I'm expected to tell you off, or something,' he said.

'What for?'

'Spoiling the war, apparently.'

'*Spoiling the war?*'

The soldier sighed. 'Come on. Let's go for a stroll. Sergeant – you and a couple of lads, please.'

A stone whistled down from the fort high above them, and shattered.

'They can hold out for bloody weeks, up there,' said the soldier gloomily, as they walked away with the Luggage padding patiently behind them. 'I'm Lavaeolus. Who're you?'

'He's my demon,' said Eric.

Lavaeolus raised an eyebrow, the closest he ever came to expressing surprise at anything.

'Is he? I suppose it takes all sorts. Any good at getting in places, is he?'

'He's more the getting-out kind,' said Eric.

'Right,' said Lavaeolus. He stopped beside a building and walked up and down a bit with his hands in his pockets, tapping on the flagstones with the toe of his sandal.

'Just here, I think, sergeant,' he said, after a while.

'Right you are, sir.'

'Look at that lot, will you?' said Lavaeolus, while the sergeant and his men started to lever up the stones. 'That bunch around the table. Brave lads, I'll grant you, but look at them. Too busy posing for triumphant statues and making sure the historians spell their names right. Bloody *years* we've been laying siege to this place. More *military*, they said. You know, they actually enjoy it? I mean, when all's said and done, who cares? Let's just get it over with and go home, that's what I say.'

'Found it, sir,' said the sergeant.

'Right.' Lavaeolus didn't look round. '*O-kay.*' He rubbed his hands together. 'Let's sort this out, and then we can get an early night. Would you care to accompany me? Your pet might be useful.'

'What are we going to do?' said Rincewind suspiciously.

'We're just going to meet some people.'

'Is it dangerous?'

A stone smashed through the roof of a building nearby.

'No, not really,' said Lavaeolus. 'Compared to staying out here, I mean. And if the rest of them try to storm the place, you know, in a proper military way—'

The hole led into a tunnel. The tunnel, after winding a bit, led to stairs. Lavaeolus mooched along it, occasionally kicking bits of fallen masonry as if he had a personal grudge against them.

'Er,' said Rincewind, 'where does this lead?'

'Oh, it's just a secret passageway into the centre of the citadel.'

'You know, I thought it would be something like that,' said Rincewind. 'I've got an instinct for it, you know. And I expect all the really top Tsorteans will be up there, will they?'

'I hope so,' said Lavaeolus, trudging up the steps.

'With lots of guards?'

'Dozens, I imagine.'

'Highly trained, too?'

Lavaeolus nodded. 'The best.'

'And this is where we're going,' said Rincewind, determined to explore the full horror of the plan as one probes the site of a rotting tooth.

'That's right.'

'All six of us.'

'And your box, of course.'

'Oh, yes,' said Rincewind, making a face in the darkness.

The sergeant tapped him gently on the shoulder and leaned forward.

'Don't you worry about the captain, sir,' he said. 'He's got the finest military brain on the continent.'

'How do you know? Has anyone ever *seen* it?' said Rincewind.

'You see, sir, what it is, he likes to get it over with without anyone getting hurt, sir, especially him. That's why he dreams up things like the horse, sir. And bribing people and that. We got into civvies last night and come in and got drunk in a pub with one of the palace cleaners, see, and found out about this tunnel.'

'Yes, but secret passages!' said Rincewind. 'There'll be guards and everything at the other end!'

'No, sir. They use it to store the cleaning things, sir.'

There was a clang in the darkness ahead of them. Lavaeolus had tripped over a mop.

'Sergeant?'

'Sir?'

'Just open the door, will you?'

Eric was tugging at Rincewind's robe.

'What?' said Rincewind testily.

'You know who Lavaeolus *is*, don't you?' whispered Eric.

'Well—'

'He's *Lavaeolus*!'

'Get away?'

'Don't you know the Classics?'

'That isn't one of these horse races we're supposed to remember, is it?'

Eric rolled his eyes. 'Lavaeolus was responsible for the fall of Tsort, on account of being so cunning,' he said. 'And then afterwards it took him ten years to get home and he had all sorts of adventures with temptresses and sirens and sensual witches.'

'Well, I can see why you've been studying him. Ten years, eh? Where did he live?'

'About two hundred miles away,' said Eric earnestly.

'Kept getting lost, did he?'

'And when he got home he fought his wife's suitors and everything, and his dear old dog recognised him and died.'

'Oh, dear.'

'It was the carrying his slippers in its mouth for fifteen years that killed it off.'

'Shame.'

'And you know what, demon? All this *hasn't happened yet*. We could save him all that trouble!'

Rincewind thought about this. 'We could tell him to get a better navigator, for a start,' he said.

There was a creak. The soldiers had got the door open.

'Everyone fall in, or whatever the bloody stupid command is,' said Lavaeolus. 'The magic box to the front, please. No killing anyone unless it's really necessary. Try not to damage things. Right. Forward.'

The door led into a column-lined corridor. There was the distant murmur of voices.

The troop crept towards the sound until it reached a heavy curtain. Lavaeolus took a deep breath, pushed it aside and stepped forward and launched into a prepared speech.

'Now, I want to make myself *absolutely* clear,' he said. 'I don't want there to be any unpleasantness of any kind, or any shouting for guards and so forth. Or indeed any shouting at all. We will just take the young lady and go home, which is where anyone of any sense ought to be. Otherwise I shall really have to put everyone to the sword, and I hate having to do things like that.'

The audience to this statement did not appear to be impressed. This was because it was a small child on a potty.

Lavaeolus changed mental gear and went on smoothly: 'On the other hand, if you don't tell me where everyone is, I shall ask the sergeant here to give you a really hard smack.'

The child took its thumb out of its mouth. 'Mummy is seeing to Cassie,' it said. 'Are you Mr Beekle?'

'I don't think so,' said Lavaeolus.

'Mr Beekle is a silly.' The child withdrew its thumb and, with the air of one concluding some exhaustive research, added: 'Mr Beekle is a poo.'

'Sergeant?'

'Sir?'

'Guard this child.'

'Yessir. Corporal?'

'Sarge?'

'Take care of the kid.'

'Yes, sarge. Private Archeios?'

'Yes, corp,' said the soldier, his voice gloomy with prescience.

'See to the sprog.'

Private Archeios looked around. There were only Rincewind and Eric left and, while it was true that a civilian was in every respect the lowest possible rank there was, coming somewhere after the regimental donkey, the expressions on their faces suggested that they weren't about to take any orders.

Lavaeolus wandered across the room and listened at another curtain.

'We could tell him all kinds of stuff about his future,' hissed Eric. 'He had – I mean, he *will* have – all kinds of things happen to him. Shipwrecks and magic and all his crew turned into animals and stuff like that.'

'Yes. We could say "Walk home",' said Rincewind.

The curtain swished aside.

There was a woman there – plump, good-looking in a slightly faded way, wearing a black dress and the beginnings of a moustache. A number of children of varying sizes were trying to hide behind her. Rincewind counted at least seven of them.

'Who's that?' said Eric.

'Ahem,' said Rincewind. 'I rather think it's Elenor of Tsort.'

'Don't be silly,' whispered Eric. 'She looks like my mum. Elenor was much younger and was all—' His voice gave out and he made several wavy motions with his hand, indicative of the shape of a woman who would probably be unable to keep her balance.

Rincewind tried not to catch the sergeant's eye.

'Yes,' he said, going a bit red. 'Well, you see. Er. You're absolutely right, but well, it's been a long siege, hasn't it, what with one thing and another.'

'I don't see what that's got to do with it,' said Eric sternly. 'The Classics never said anything about children. They said she spent all her time mooning around the towers of Tsort and pining for her lost love.'

'Well, yes, I expect she did pine a *bit*,' said Rincewind. 'Only, you know, you can only pine so much, and it must have been a bit chilly up on those towers.'

'You can catch your death, mooning,' nodded the sergeant.

Lavaeolus watched the woman thoughtfully. Then he bowed.

'I expect you know why we're here, my lady?' he said.

'If you touch any of the children I shall scream,' said Elenor flatly.

Once again Lavaeolus showed that along with his guerrilla abilities was a marked reluctance to waste a prepared speech once he had it all sorted out in his head.

'Fair maiden,' he began. 'We have faced many dangers in order to rescue you and take you back to your loved . . .' His voice faltered. ' . . . ones. Er. This has all gone terribly wrong, hasn't it?'

'I can't help it,' said Elenor. 'The siege seemed to go on for such a long time and King Mausoleum was very kind and I never liked it much in Ephebe anyway—'

'Where is everyone now? The Tsorteans, I mean. Apart from you.'

'They're all out on the battlements throwing rocks, if you must know.'

Lavaeolus flung up his hands in desperation.

'Couldn't you, you know, have slipped us a note or something? Or invited us to one of the christenings?'

'You all seemed to be enjoying yourselves so much,' she said.

Lavaeolus turned and shrugged gloomily. 'All right,' he said. 'Fine. QED. No problem. I *wanted* to leave home and spend ten years sitting in a swamp with a bunch of meat-headed morons. It wasn't as if I had anything important to do back home, just a little kingdom to rule, that sort of thing. O-*kay*. Well, then. We might as well be off. I'm sure I don't know how I shall break it to everyone,' he said bitterly, 'they were having such fun. They'll probably have a bloody great banquet and laugh about it and get drunk, it'd be their style.'

He looked at Rincewind and Eric.

'You might as well tell me what happens next,' he said. 'I'm sure you know.'

'Um,' said Rincewind.

'The city burns down,' said Eric. 'Especially the topless towers. I didn't get to see them,' he added sulkily.

'Who did it? Their lot or our lot?' said Lavaeolus.

'Your lot, I think,' said Eric.

Lavaeolus sighed. 'Sounds like them,' he said. He turned to Elenor. 'Our lot – that is, my lot – are going to burn down the city,' he said. 'It sounds very heroic. It's just the kind of thing they go for. It might be a good idea to come with us. Bring the kids. Make it a day out for all the family, why don't you?'

Eric pulled Rincewind's ear towards his mouth.

'This is a joke, isn't it?' he said. 'She's not really the fair Elenor, you're just having me on?'

'It's always the same with these hot-blooded types,' said Rincewind. 'They definitely go downhill at thirty-five.'

'It's the pasta that does it,' said the sergeant.

'But I read where she was the most beautiful—'

'Ah, well,' said the sergeant. 'If you're going to go around *reading*—'

'The thing is,' said Rincewind quickly, 'it's what they call dramatic necessity. No-one's going to be interested in a war fought over a, a quite pleasant lady, moderately attractive in a good light. Are they?'

Eric was nearly in tears.

'But it said her face launched a thousand ships—'

'That's what you call metaphor,' said Rincewind.

'Lying,' the sergeant explained, kindly.

'Anyway, you shouldn't believe everything you read in the Classics,' Rincewind added. 'They never check their facts. They're just out to sell legends.'

Lavaeolus, meanwhile, was deep in argument with Elenor.

'All right, all right,' he said. 'Stay here if you like. Why should I care? Come on, you lot. We're going. What are you doing, Private Archeios?'

'I'm being a horse, sir,' explained the soldier.

'He's Mr Poo,' said the child, who was wearing Private Archeios' helmet.

'Well, when you've finished being a horse, find us an oil lamp. I caught my knees a right wallop in that tunnel.'

Flames roared over Tsort. The entire hubward sky was red.

Rincewind and Eric watched from a rock down by the beach.

'They're not topless towers, anyway,' said Eric after a while. 'I can see the tops.'

'I think they meant toppleless towers,' Rincewind hazarded, as another one collapsed, red-hot, into the ruins of the city. 'And that was wrong, too.'

They watched in silence for a while longer, and then Eric said, 'Funny, that. The way you tripped over the Luggage and dropped the lamp and everything.'

'Yes,' said Rincewind shortly.

'Makes you think history is always going to find a way to work itself out.'

'Yes.'

'Good, though, the way your Luggage rescued everyone.'

'Yes.'

'Funny to see all those kids riding on its back.'

'Yes.'

'Everyone seems quite pleased about it.'

The opposing armies were, at any rate. No-one was bothering to ask the civilians, whose views on warfare were never very reliable. Among the soldiery, at least among the soldiery of a certain rank, there was a lot of back-slapping and telling of anecdotes, jovial exchanging of shields and a general consensus that, what with fires

269

and sieges and armadas and wooden horses and everything, it had been a jolly good war. The sound of singing echoed across the wine-dark sea.

'Hark at them,' said Lavaeolus, emerging from the gloom around the beached Ephebian ships. 'It'll be fifteen choruses of "The Ball of Philodelphus" next, you mark my words. Lot of idiots with their brains in their jockstraps.'

He sat down on the rock. 'Bastards,' he said, with feeling.

'Do you think Elenor will be able to explain it all to her boyfriend?' said Eric.

'I imagine so,' said Lavaeolus. 'They usually can.'

'She did get married. And she's got lots of children,' said Eric.

Lavaeolus shrugged. 'A moment's wild passion,' he said. He gave Rincewind a sharp look.

'Hey, you, demon,' he said. 'I'd like a quiet word, if I may.'

He led Rincewind towards the boats, pacing heavily across the damp sand as if there was a lot weighing on his mind.

'I'm going home tonight, on the tide,' he said. 'No sense in hanging about here, what with the war being over and everything.'

'Good idea.'

'If there's one thing I hate, it's sea voyages,' said Lavaeolus. He gave the nearest boat a kick. 'It's all idiots striding around and shouting, you know? Pull this, lower that, avast the other. And I get seasick, too.'

'It's heights with me,' said Rincewind, sympathetically.

Lavaeolus kicked the boat again, obviously wrestling with some big emotional problem.

'The thing *is*,' he said, wretchedly. 'You wouldn't happen to know if I get home all right, would you?'

'What?'

'It's only a few hundred miles, it shouldn't take too long, should it?' said Lavaeolus, radiating anxiety like a lighthouse.

'Oh.' Rincewind looked at the man's face. Ten years, he thought. And all kinds of weird stuff with winged wossnames and sea-monsters. On the other hand, would it do him any good to know?

'You get home okay,' he said. 'You're well-known for it, in fact. There's whole legends about you going home.'

'Phew.' Lavaeolus leaned against a hull, took off his helmet and wiped his forehead. 'That's a load off my mind, I'll tell you. I was afraid the gods might have a grudge against me.'

Rincewind said nothing.

'They get a bit angry if you go around thinking up ideas like wooden horses and tunnels,' said Lavaeolus. 'They're traditionalists, you know. They prefer people just to hack at one another. I thought, you see, that if I could show people how to get what they wanted more easily they'd stop being so bloody stupid.'

From further along the shoreline came the sound of male voices raised in song:

'—vestal virgins, Came down from Heliodeliphilodelphiboschromenos, And when the ball was over, There were—'

'It never works,' said Rincewind.

'It's got to be worth a try, though. Hasn't it?'

'Oh, yes.'

Lavaeolus slapped him on the back. 'Cheer up,' he said. 'Things can only get better.'

They walked out into the dark breakers where Lavaeolus' ship was riding at anchor, and Rincewind watched him swim out and climb aboard. After a while the oars were shipped, or unshipped, or whatever they called it when they were stuck through the holes in the sides, and the boat moved slowly out into the bay.

A few voices floated back over the surf.

'Point the pointed end that way, sergeant.'

'Aye aye, sir!'

'And don't *shout*. Did I tell you to shout? Why do you all have to shout? Now I'm going downstairs for a lie down.'

Rincewind trudged back up the beach. 'The trouble is,' he said, 'is that things *never* get better, they just stay the same, only more so. But he's going to have enough to worry about.'

Behind him, Eric blew his nose.

'That was the saddest thing I've ever heard,' he said.

From further along the beach the Ephebian and Tsortean armies were still in full voice around their convivial campfires.

'—the village harpy she was there—'

'Come on,' said Rincewind. 'Let's go home.'

'You know the funny thing about his name?' said Eric, as they strolled along the sand.

'No. What do you mean?'

'Lavaeolus means "Rinser of winds".'

Rincewind looked at him.

'He's my ancestor?' he said.

'Who knows?' said Eric.

'Oh. Gosh.' Rincewind thought about this. 'Well, I wish I'd told him to avoid getting married. Or visiting Ankh-Morpork.'

'It probably isn't even built yet . . .'
Rincewind tried snapping his fingers.
This time it worked.

Astfgl sat back. He wondered what *did* happen to Lavaeolus.

Gods and demons, being creatures outside of time, don't move in it like bubbles in the stream. Everything happens at the same time for them. This should mean that they know everything that is going to happen because, in a sense, it already has. The reason they don't is that reality is a big place with a lot of interesting things going on, and keeping track of all of them is like trying to use a very big video recorder with no freeze button or tape counter. It's usually easier just to wait and see.

One day he'd have to go and look.

Right here and now, insofar as the words can be employed about an area outside of space and time, matters were not progressing well. Eric seemed marginally more likeable, which wasn't acceptable. He also appeared to have changed the course of history, although this is impossible since the only thing you can do to the course of history is facilitate it.

What was needed was something climactic. Something really soul-destroying.

The Demon King realised he was twirling his moustaches.

The trouble with snapping your fingers is that you never knew what it would lead to . . .

Everything around Rincewind was black. It wasn't simply an absence of colour. It was a darkness that flatly denied any possibility that colour might ever have existed.

His feet weren't touching anything, and he appeared to be floating. There was something else missing. He couldn't quite put his finger on it.

'Are you there, Eric?' he ventured.

A clear voice nearby said: 'Yes. Are you there, demon?'

'Ye – ess.'

'Where are we? Are we falling?'

'I don't think so,' said Rincewind, speaking from experience. 'There's no rushing wind. You get a rushing wind when you're falling. Also your past life flashes before your eyes, and I haven't seen anything I recognise yet.'

'Rincewind?'

'Yes?'

'When I open my mouth no sounds come out.'

'Don't be—' Rincewind hesitated. He wasn't making any sound either. He knew what he was saying, it just wasn't reaching the outside world. But he could hear Eric. Perhaps the words just gave up on his ears and went straight to his brain.

'It's probably some kind of magic, or something,' he said. 'There's no air. That's why there's no sound. All the little bits of air sort of knock together, like marbles. That's how you get sound, you know.'

'Is it? Gosh.'

'So we're surrounded by absolutely nothing,' said Rincewind. 'Total nothing.' He hesitated. 'There's a word for it,' he said. 'It's what you get when there's nothing left and everything's been used up.'

'Yes. I think it's called the bill,' said Eric.

Rincewind gave this some thought. It sounded about right. 'Okay,' he said. 'The bill. That's where we are. Floating in absolute bill. Total, complete, rock-hard bill.'

Astfgl was going frantic now. He had spells that could find anyone anywhere, anywhen, and they weren't *anywhere*. One minute he was watching them on the beach, the next . . . nothing.

That left only two other places.

Fortunately he chose the wrong one first.

'Even some stars would be nice,' said Eric.

'There's something very odd about all this,' said Rincewind. 'I mean, do you feel cold?'

'No.'

'Well, do you feel warm?'

'No. I don't feel anything much, really.'

'No hot, no cold, no light, no heat, no air,' said Rincewind. 'Just bill. How long have we been here?'

'Don't know. Seems like ages, but . . .'

'Aha. I'm not sure there's any time, either. Not what you'd call proper time. Just the kind of time people make up as they go along.'

'*Well, I didn't expect to see anyone else here,*' said a voice by Rincewind's ear.

It was a slightly put-upon voice, a voice made for complaining in, but at least there was no hint of menace. Rincewind let himself float around.

A little rat-faced man was sitting cross-legged, watching him with vague suspicion. He had a pencil behind one ear.

'Ah. Hallo,' said Rincewind. 'And where is here, exactly?'

'Nowhere. S'whole point, innit?'

'Nowhere at all?'

'Not yet.'

'All right,' said Eric. 'When is it going to be somewhere?'

'Hard to say,' said the little man. 'Looking at the pair of you, and taking one thing with another, metabolic rates and that, I'd say that this place is due to become somewhere in, well, give or take a bit, in about five hundred seconds.' He began to unwrap the pack in his lap. 'Fancy a sandwich while we're waiting?'

'What? Would I—' At this point Rincewind's stomach, aware that if his brain was allowed to make the running it was in danger of losing the initiative, cut in and prompted him to say, 'What sort?'

'Search me. What sort would you like it to be?'

'Sorry?'

'Don't mess about. Just say what sort you'd like it to be.'

'Oh?' Rincewind stared at him. 'Well, if you've got egg and cress—'

'Let there be egg and cress, sort of thing,' said the little man. He reached into the package, and proffered a white triangle to Rincewind.

'Gosh,' said Rincewind. 'What a coincidence.'

'It should be starting any minute now,' said the little man. 'Over – not that they've got any proper directions sorted out yet, of course, not them – there.'

'All I can see is darkness,' said Eric.

'No you can't,' said the little man, triumphantly. 'You're just seeing what there is before the darkness has been installed, sort of thing.' He gave the not-yet-darkness a dirty look. 'Come *on*,' he said. 'Why are we waiting, why-eye are we waiting?'

'Waiting for what?' said Rincewind.

'Everything.'

'Everything what?' said Rincewind.

'Everything. Not everything what. Everything, sort of thing.'

Astfgl peered around through the swirling gas clouds. At least he was in the right place. The whole point about the end of the universe was that you couldn't go past it accidentally.

274

The last few embers winked out. Time and space collided silently, and collapsed.

Astfgl coughed. It can get so very lonely, when you're twenty million light-years from home.

'Anyone there?' he said.

YES.

The voice was right by his ear. Even demon kings can shiver.

'Apart from you, I mean,' he said. 'Have you seen anybody?'

YES.

'Who?'

EVERYONE.

Astfgl sighed. 'I mean anyone *recently*.'

IT'S BEEN VERY QUIET, said Death.

'Damn.'

WERE YOU EXPECTING SOMEONE ELSE?

'I thought there might be someone called Rincewind, but—' Astfgl began.

Death's eyesockets flared red. THE WIZARD? he said.

'No, he's a dem—' Astfgl stopped. For what would have been several seconds, had time still existed, he floated in a state of horrible suspicion.

'A *human*?' he growled.

IT IS STRETCHING THE TERM A LITTLE, BUT YOU ARE BROADLY CORRECT.

'Well, I'll be damned!' Astfgl said.

I BELIEVE YOU ALREADY ARE.

The Demon King extended a shaking hand. His mounting fury was over-riding his sense of style; his red silk gloves ripped as the talons unfolded.

And then, because it's never a good idea to get on the wrong side of anyone with a scythe, Astfgl said, 'Sorry you've been troubled,' and vanished. Only when he judged himself out of Death's extremely acute hearing did he scream his rage.

Nothingness uncoiled its interminable length through the draughty spaces at the end of time.

Death waited. After a while his skeletal fingers began to drum on the handle of his scythe.

Darkness lapped around him. There wasn't even any infinity any more.

He attempted to whistle a few snatches of unpopular songs between his teeth, but the sound was simply sucked into nothingness.

Forever was over. All the sands had fallen. The great race between entropy and energy had been run, and the favourite had been the winner after all.

Perhaps he ought to sharpen the blade again?

No.

Not much point, really.

Great roils of absolutely nothing stretched into what would have been called the distance, if there had been a space-time reference frame to give words like 'distance' any sensible meaning any more.

There didn't seem to be much to *do*.

PERHAPS IT'S TIME TO CALL IT A DAY, he thought.

Death turned to go but, just as he did so, he heard the faintest of noises. It was to sound what one photon is to light, so weak and feeble that it would have passed entirely unheard in the din of an operating universe.

It was a tiny piece of matter, popping into existence.

Death stalked over to the point of arrival and watched carefully.

It was a paperclip.*

Well, it was a start.

There was another pop, which left a small white shirt-button spinning gently in the vacuum.

Death relaxed a little. Of course, it was going to take some time. There was going to be an interlude before all this got complicated enough to produce gas clouds, galaxies, planets and continents, let alone tiny corkscrew-shaped things wiggling around in slimy pools and wondering whether evolution was worth all the bother of growing fins and legs and things. But it indicated the start of an unstoppable trend.

All he had to do was be patient, and he was good at that. Pretty soon there'd be living creatures, developing like mad, running and laughing in the new sunlight. Growing tired. Growing old.

---

* Many people think it should have been a hydrogen molecule, but this is against the observed facts. Everyone who has found a hitherto unknown egg-whisk jamming an innocent kitchen drawer knows that raw matter is continually flowing into the universe in fairly developed forms, popping into existence normally in ashtrays, vases and glove compartments. It chooses its shape to allay suspicion, and common manifestations are paperclips, the pins out of shirt packaging, the little keys for central heating radiators, marbles, bits of crayon, mysterious sections of herb-chopping devices and old Kate Bush albums. Why matter does this is unclear, but it is evident that matter has Plans.

It is also apparent that creators sometimes favour the Big Bang method of universe construction, and at other times use the more gentle methods of Continuous Creation. This follows studies by cosmotherapists which have revealed that the violence of the Big Bang can give a universe serious psychological problems when it gets older.

Death sat back. He could wait.

Whenever they needed him, he'd be there.

The Universe came into being.

Any created-again cosmogonist will tell you that all the interesting stuff happened in the first couple of minutes, when nothingness bunched together to form space and time and lots of really tiny black holes appeared and so on. After that, they say, it became just a matter of, well, matter. It was basically all over bar the microwave radiation.

Seen from close by, though, it had a certain gaudy attraction.

The little man sniffed.

'Too showy,' he said. 'You don't need all that noise. It could just as easily have been a Big Hiss, or a bit of music.'

'Could it?' said Rincewind.

'Yeah, and it looked pretty iffy around the two picosecond mark. Definitely a bit of ropey filling-in. But that's how it goes these days. No craftsmanship. When I was a lad it took *days* to make a universe. You could take a bit of pride in it. Now they just throw it together and it's back on the lorry and away. And, you know what?'

'No?' said Rincewind weakly.

'They pinches stuff off the site. They finds someone nearby who wants to expand their universe a bit, next thing you know they've had it away with a bunch of firmament and flogged it for an extension somewhere.'

Rincewind stared at him.

'Who *are* you?'

The man took the pencil from behind his ear and looked reflectively at the space around Rincewind. 'I makes things,' he said.

'What sort of things?'

'What sort of things would you like?'

'You're the *Creator*?'

The little man looked very embarrassed. 'Not the. Not *the*. Just *a*. I don't contract for the big stuff, the stars, the gas giants, the pulsars and so on. I just specialise in what you might call the bespoke trade.' He gave them a look of defiant pride. 'I do all my own trees, you know,' he confided. 'Craftsmanship. Takes years to learn how to make a tree. Even the conifers.'

'Oh,' said Rincewind.

'I don't get someone in to finish them off. No sub-contracting, that's my motto. The buggers always keep you hanging about while

277

they're installing stars or something for someone else.' The little man sighed. 'You know, people think it must all be very easy, creating. They think you just have to move on the face of the waters and wave your hands a bit. It's not like that at all.'

'It isn't?'

The little man scratched his nose again. 'You soon run out of ideas for snowflakes, for example.'

'Oh.'

'You start thinking it'd be a doddle to sneak in a few identical ones.'

'You do?'

'You thinks to yourself, 'There's a billion trillion squillion of them, no-one's going to notice'. But that's where professionalism comes in, sort of thing.'

'It does?'

'*Some* people' – and here the creator looked sharply at the unformed matter still streaming past – 'think it's enough to install a few basic physical formulas and then take the money and run. A billion years later you got leaks all over the sky, black holes the size of your head, and when you pray up to complain there's just a girl on the counter who says she don't know where the boss is. I think people appreciate the *personal* touch, don't you?'

'Ah,' said Rincewind. 'So . . . when people get struck by lightning . . . er . . . it's not just because of all that stuff about electrical discharges and high points and everything . . . er . . . you actually *mean* it?'

'Oh, not me. I don't run the things. It's a big enough job just building 'em, you can't expect me to operate them as well. There's a load of other universes, you know,' he added, a slight note of accusation in his voice. 'Got a list of jobs as long as your arm.'

He reached underneath him and produced a large, leatherbound book, which he had apparently been sitting on. It opened with a creak.

Rincewind felt a tugging at his robe.

'Look,' said Eric. 'This isn't really . . . *Him*, is it?'

'He says it is,' said Rincewind.

'What are we doing here?'

'I don't know.'

The creator glared at him. 'A little quiet there, please,' he said.

'But listen,' hissed Eric, 'if he really is the creator of the world, that sandwich is a religious relic!'

'Gosh,' said Rincewind weakly. He hadn't eaten for ages. He

wondered what the penalty was for eating a venerated object. It was probably severe.

'You could put it in a temple somewhere and millions of people would come to look at it.'

Rincewind cautiously levered up the top slice of bread.

'It's got no mayonnaise in it,' he said. 'Will that still count?'

The creator cleared his throat, and began to read aloud.

Astfgl surfed across the entropy slope, an angry red spark against the swirls of interspace. He was so angry now that the last vestiges of self-control were slipping away; his jaunty cap with its stylish hornlets had become a mere wisp of crimson dangling from the tip of one of the great coiled ramshorns that framed his skull.

With a rather sensuous ripping noise the red silk across his back tore open and his wings unfolded.

They are conventionally represented as leathery, but leather wouldn't survive more than a few seconds in that environment. Besides, it doesn't fold up very well.

These wings were made of magnetism and shaped space, and spread out until they were a faint curtain against the incandescent firmament and they beat as slowly and inexorably as the rise of civilisations.

They still *looked* batlike, but that was just for the sake of tradition.

Somewhere around the 29th millennium he was overtaken, quite without noticing, by something small and oblong and probably even angrier than he was.

Eight spells go to make up the world. Rincewind knew that well enough. He knew that the book which contained them was the Octavo, because it still existed in the library of Unseen University – currently inside a welded iron box at the bottom of a specially-dug shaft, where its magical radiations could be kept under control.

Rincewind had wondered how it had all started. He'd imagined a sort of explosion in reverse, with interstellar gases roaring together to form Great A'Tuin, or at least a roll of thunder or something.

Instead there was a faint, musical twang, and where the Discworld hadn't been, there the Discworld was, as if it had been hiding somewhere the whole time.

He also realised that the feeling of falling he had so recently learned to live with was one he was probably going to die with, too. As the world appeared beneath him it brought this aeon's special offer – gravity, available in a choice of strengths from your nearest massive planetary body.

He said, as so often happens on these occasions, 'Aargh.'

The creator, still sitting serenely in mid-air, appeared beside him as he plummeted.

'Nice clouds, don't you think? Done a good job on the clouds,' he said.

'Aargh,' Rincewind repeated.

'Something the matter?'

'Aargh.'

'That's humans for you,' said the creator. 'Always rushing off somewhere.' He leaned closer. 'It's not up to me, of course, but I've often wondered what it is that goes through your heads.'

'It's going to be my feet in a minute!' screamed Rincewind.

Eric, falling alongside him, tugged at his ankle. 'That's not the way to talk to the creator of the universe!' he shouted. 'Just tell him to do something, make the ground soft or something!'

'Oh, I dunno if I could do that,' said the creator. 'It's causality regulations. I'd have the Inspector down on me like a ton of, a ton of, a ton of weight,' he added. 'I could probably knock you up a really spongy bog. Or quicksand's very popular at the moment. I could do you a complete quicksand with marsh and swamp *en suite*, no problem.'

'!' said Rincewind.

'You're going to have to speak up a bit, I'm sorry. Wait a moment.'

There was another harmonious twanging noise.

When Rincewind opened his eyes he was standing on a beach. So was Eric. The creator floated nearby.

There was no rushing wind. He hadn't got so much as a bruise.

'I just wedged a thingy in the velocities and positions,' said the creator, noticing his expression. 'Now: what was it you were saying?'

'I rather wanted to stop plunging to my death,' said Rincewind.

'Oh. Good. Glad that's sorted out, then.' The creator looked around distractedly. 'You haven't seen my book around, have you? I thought I had it in my hand when I started.' He sighed. 'Lose me own head next. I done a whole world once and completely left out the fingles. Not one of the buggers. Couldn't get 'em at the time, told myself I could nip back when they were in stock, completely forgot. Imagine that. No-one spotted it, of course, because obviously they just evolved there and they didn't know there ought to *be* fingles, but it was definitely causing them deep, you know, psychological problems. Deep down inside they could tell there was something missing, sort of thing.'

The creator pulled himself together.

'Anyway, I can't hang about all day,' he said. 'Like I said, I've got a lot of jobs on.'

'Lots?' said Eric. 'I thought there was only one.'

'Oh, no. There's masses of them,' said the creator, beginning to fade away. 'That's quantum mechanics for you, see. You don't do it once and have done. No, they keep on branching off. Multiple choice they call it, it's like painting the – painting the – painting something very big that you have to keep on painting, sort of thing. It's all very well saying you just have to change one little detail, but which one, that's the real bugger. Well, nice to have met you. If you need any extra work, you know, an extra moon or something—'

'Hey!'

The creator reappeared, his eyebrows raised in polite surprise.

'What happens now?' said Rincewind.

'Now? Well, I imagine there'll be some gods along soon. They don't wait long to move in, you know. Like flies around a – flies around a – like flies. They tend to be a bit high-spirited to start with, but they soon settle down. I suppose they take care of all the people, ekcetra.' The creator leaned forward. 'I've never been good at doing people. Never seem to get the arms and legs right.' He vanished.

They waited.

'I think he's really gone this time,' said Eric, after a while. 'What a nice man.'

'You certainly understand a lot more about why the world is like it is after talking to him,' said Rincewind.

'What're quantum mechanics?'

'I don't know. People who repair quantums, I suppose.'

Rincewind looked at the egg and cress sandwich, still in his hand. There was still no mayonnaise in it, and the bread was soggy, but it would be thousands of years before there was another one. There had to be the dawn of agriculture, the domestication of animals, the evolution of the breadknife from its primitive flint ancestry, the development of dairy technology – and, if there was any desire to make a proper job of it, the cultivation of olive trees, pepper plants, salt pans, vinegar fermentation processes and the techniques of elementary food chemistry – before the world would see another one like it. It was unique, a little white triangle full of anachronisms, lost and all alone in an unfriendly world.

He bit it anyway. It wasn't very nice.

'What I don't understand,' said Eric, 'is why we are here.'

'I take it that isn't a philosophical question,' said Rincewind, 'I take it you mean: why are we here at the dawn of creation on this beach which has hardly been used?'

'Yes. That's what I meant.'

Rincewind sat down on a rock and sighed. 'I think it's pretty obvious, isn't it?' he said. 'You wanted to live forever.'

'I didn't say anything about travelling in time,' said Eric. 'I was very clear about it so there'd be no tricks.'

'There isn't a trick. The wish is trying to be helpful. I mean, it's pretty obvious when you think about it. "Forever" means the entire span of space and time. Forever. For Ever. See?'

'You mean you have to sort of start at Square One?'

'Precisely.'

'But that's no good! It's going to be years before there's anyone else around!'

'Centuries,' corrected Rincewind gloomily. 'Millennia. lains. And then there's going to be all kinds of wars and monsters and stuff. Most of history is pretty appalling, when you look hard at it. Or even not very hard.'

'But what I meant was, I just wanted to go on living for ever *from now*,' said Eric frantically. 'I mean, from *then*. I mean, *look* at this place. No girls. No people. Nothing to do on Saturday nights . . .'

'It won't even have any Saturday nights for thousands of years,' said Rincewind. 'Just nights.'

'You must take me back at once,' said Eric. 'I order it. Avaunt!'

'You say that one more time and I will give you a thick ear,' said Rincewind.

'But all you have to do is snap your fingers!'

'It won't work. You've had your three wishes. Sorry.'

'What shall I do?'

'Well, if you see anything crawl out of the sea and try to breathe, you could try telling it not to bother.'

'You think this is funny, don't you?'

'It is rather amusing, since you mention it,' said Rincewind, his face expressionless.

'The joke's going to be wearing pretty thin over the years, then,' said Eric.

'What?'

'Well, you're not going to go anywhere, are you? You'll have to stay with me.'

'Nonsense, I'll—' Rincewind looked around desperately. I'll what? he thought.

The waves rolled peacefully up the beach, not very strongly at the moment because they were still feeling their way. The first high tide was coming in, cautiously. There was no tideline, no streaky line of old seaweed and shells to give it some idea of what was expected of it. The air had the clean, fresh smell of air that has yet to know the effusions of a forest floor or the ins and outs of a ruminant's digestive system.

Rincewind had grown up in Ankh-Morpork. He liked air that had been around a bit, had got to know people, had been lived in.

'We've got to get back,' he said urgently.

'That's what I've been saying,' said Eric, with strained patience.

Rincewind took another bite of the sandwich. He'd looked death in the face many times, or more precisely Death had looked him in the back of his rapidly-retreating head many times, and suddenly the prospect of living forever didn't appeal. There were of course great questions he might learn the answer to, such as how life evolved and all the rest of it, but looked at as a way of spending all your spare time for the next infinity it wasn't a patch on a quiet evening strolling through the streets of Ankh.

Still, he'd acquired an ancestor. That was something. Not everyone had an ancestor. What would his ancestor have done in a situation like this?

He wouldn't have been here.

Well, yes, of course, but apart from that, he would have – he would have used his fine military mind to consider the tools available, that's what he would have done.

He had: item, one half-eaten egg and cress sandwich. No help there. He threw it away.

He had: item, himself. He drew a tick in the sand. He wasn't certain what use he could be, but he could come back to that later.

He had: item, Eric. Thirteen-year-old demonologist and acne attack ground zero.

That seemed to be about it.

He stared at the clean, fresh sand for a while, doodling in it.

Then he said, quietly: 'Eric. Come here a moment . . .'

The waves were a lot stronger now. They had really got the hang of the tide thing, and were venturing a little ebb and flow.

Astfgl materialised in a puff of blue smoke.

'Aha!' he said, but this fell rather flat because there was no-one to hear it.

He looked down. There were footprints in the sand. Hundreds of them. They ran backwards and forwards, as if something had been frantically searching, and then vanished.

He leaned nearer. It was hard to make out, what with all the footprints and the effects of the wind and the tide, but just on the edge of the encroaching surf were the unmistakable signs of a magic circle.

Astfgl said a swearword that fused the sand around him into glass, and vanished.

The tide got on with things. Further down the beach the last surge poured into a hollow in the rocks, and the new sun beamed down on the soaking remains of a half-eaten egg and cress sandwich. Tidal action turned it over. Thousands of bacteria suddenly found themselves in the midst of a taste explosion, and started to breed like mad.

If only there had been some mayonnaise, life might have turned out a whole lot different. More piquant, and perhaps with a little extra cream in it.

Travelling by magic always had major drawbacks. There was the feeling that your stomach was lagging behind. And your mind filled up with terror because the destination was always a little uncertain. It wasn't that you could come out anywhere. 'Anywhere' represented a very restricted range of choices compared to the kind of places magic could transport you to. The actual travelling was easy. It was achieving a destination which would, for example, allow you to survive in all four dimensions at once that took the real effort.

In fact the scope for error was so huge it seemed something of an anti-climax to emerge in a fairly ordinary, sandy-floored cavern.

It contained, on the far wall, a door.

There was no doubt it was a forbidding door. It looked as though its designer had studied all the cell doors he could find and had then gone away and produced a version for, as it were, full visual orchestra. It was more of a portal. Some ancient and probably fearful warning was etched over its crumbling arch, but it was destined to remain unread because over it someone else had pasted a bright red-and-white notice which read: 'You Don't Have To Be "Damned" To Work Here, But It Helps!!!'

Rincewind squinted up at the notice.

'Of course I can read it,' he said. 'I just don't happen to believe it.'

'Multiple exclamation marks,' he went on, shaking his head, 'are a sure sign of a diseased mind.'

He looked behind him. The glowing outlines of Eric's magic circle faded and winked out.

'I'm not being picky, you understand,' he said. 'It's just that I thought you said you could get us back to Ankh. This isn't Ankh. I can tell by the little details, like the flickering red shadows and the distant screaming. In Ankh the screaming is usually much closer,' he added.

'I think I did very well to get it to work at all,' said Eric, bridling. 'You're not supposed to be able to run magic circles in reverse. In theory it means you stay in the circle and reality moves around you. I think I did very well. You see,' he added, his voice suddenly vibrating with enthusiasm, 'if you rewrite the source codex and, this is the difficult bit, you route it through a high-level—'

'Yes, yes, very clever, what will you people think up next,' said Rincewind. 'The only thing is, we're, I think it's quite possible that we're in Hell.'

'Oh?'

Eric's lack of reaction made Rincewind curious.

'You know,' he added. 'The place with all the demons in it?'

'Oh?'

'Not a good place to be, it's generally felt,' said Rincewind.

'You think we might be able to explain?'

Rincewind thought about this. He wasn't, when you got right down to it, quite sure what it was that demons did to you. But he *did* know what humans did to you, and after a lifetime in Ankh-Morpork this place could turn out to be an improvement. Warmer, at any rate.

He looked at the door-knocker. It was black and horrible, but that didn't matter because it was also tied up so that it couldn't be used. Beside it, with all the signs of being installed recently by someone who didn't know what they were doing and didn't want to do it, was a button set into the splintered woodwork. Rincewind gave it an experimental prod.

The sound it produced might once have been a popular tune, possibly even one written by a skilled composer to whom had been vouchsafed, for a brief ecstatic moment, the music of the spheres. Now, however, it just went bing-BONG-ding-DONG.

And it would be a lazy use of language to say that the thing that answered the door was a nightmare. Nightmares are usually rather daft things and it's very hard to explain to a listener what was so dreadful about your socks coming alive or giant carrots jumping out of the hedgerows. This thing was the kind of terrifying thing that could only be created by someone sitting down and thinking horrible thoughts very clearly. It had more tentacles than legs, but fewer arms than heads.

It also had a badge.

The badge said: 'My name is Urglefloggah, Spawn of the Pit and Loathly Guardian of the Dread Portal: How May I Help You?'

It was not very happy about this.

'Yes?' it rasped.

Rincewind was still reading the badge.

'How *may* you help us?' he said, aghast.

Urglefloggah, who bore a certain resemblance to the late Quezovercoatl, ground some of its teeth.

' "Hi . . . there",' it intoned, in the manner of one who has had the script patiently explained to him by someone with a red-hot branding iron. ' "My name is Urglefloggah, Spawn of the Pit, and I am your host for today . . . May I be the first to welcome you to our luxuriously-appointed—" '

'Hang on a moment,' said Rincewind.

' "—chosen for your convenience—",' Urglefloggah rumbled.

'There's something not right here,' said Rincewind.

' "—full regard for the wishes of YOU, the consumer—",' the demon continued stoically.

'Excuse me,' said Rincewind.

' "—as pleasurable as possible",' said Urglefloggah. It made a noise like a sigh of relief, from somewhere deep in its mandibles. Now it appeared to be listening for the first time. 'Yes? What?' it said.

'Where are we?' said Rincewind.

Various mouths beamed. 'Quail, mortals!'

'What? We're in a bird?'

'Grovel and cower, mortals!' the demon corrected itself, 'for you are condemned to everlast—' It paused, and gave a little whimper.

'There will be a period of corrective therapy,' it corrected itself again, spitting out each word, 'which we hope to make as instructive and enjoyable as possible, with due regard to all the rights of YOU, the customer.'

It eyed Rincewind with several eyes. 'Dreadful, isn't it?' it said, in a more normal voice. 'Don't blame me. If it was up to me it would be the old burning thingys up the whatsit, toot sweet.'

286

'This is Hell, isn't it,' said Eric. 'I've seen pictures.'

'You're right there,' said the demon mournfully. It sat down, or at least folded itself in some complicated way. 'Personal service, that's what it used to be. People used to feel that we were taking an interest, that they weren't just numbers but, well, victims. We had a tradition of service. Fat lot *he* cares. But what am I telling you *my* troubles for? It's not as if you haven't got plenty of your own, what with being dead and being here. You're not musicians, are you?'

'Actually we're not even dea—' Rincewind began. The demon ignored him, but got up and began to plod ponderously down the dank corridor, beckoning them to follow.

'You'd really hate it here if you was musicians. Hate it more, I mean. The walls play music all day long, well, he *calls* it music, I've got nothing against a good tune, mark you, something to scream along with, but this isn't it, I mean, I heard where we're supposed to have all the *best* tunes, so why've we got all this stuff that sounds like someone turned on the piano and then walked away and left it?'

'In point of fact—'

'And then there's the potted plants. Don't get me wrong, I like to see a bit of green around the place. Only some of the lads says these plants aren't real but what I say is, they must be, no-one in their right mind would *make* a plant that looks like dark green leather and smells like a dead sloth. *He* says it gives the place a friendly and open aspect. Friendly and open aspect! I've seen keen gardeners break down and cry. I'm telling you, they said it made everything we did to them afterwards seem like an improvement.'

'Dead is not what we—' said Rincewind, trying to hammer the words into a gap in the thing's endless monotone, but he was too late.

'The coffee machine, now, the coffee machine's a good one, I'll grant you. We only used to drown people in lakes of cat's pee, we didn't make them buy it by the cup.'

'We're not dead!' Eric shouted.

Urglefloggah came to a quivering halt.

'Of course you're dead,' it said. 'Else you wouldn't be here. Can't imagine live people coming here. They wouldn't last five minutes.' It opened several of its mouths, showing a choice of fangs. 'Hur hur,' it added. 'If I was to catch any live people down here—'

Not for nothing had Rincewind survived for years in the paranoid complexities of Unseen University. He felt almost at home. His reflexes operated with incredible precision.

'You mean you weren't told?' he said.

It was hard to see if Urglefloggah's expression changed, if only because it was hard to know what part of it *was* expression, but it definitely projected a familiar air of sudden and resentful uncertainty.

'Told what?' it said.

Rincewind looked at Eric. 'You'd think they'd tell people, wouldn't you?'

'Tell them wh – *argarg*,' said Eric, clutching his ankle.

'That's modern management for you,' said Rincewind, his face radiating angry concern. 'They go ahead and make all these changes, all these new arrangements, and do they consult the very people who form the backbone—'

'—exoskeleton—' corrected the demon.

'—or other calcareous or chitinous structure, of the organisation?' Rincewind finished smoothly. He waited expectantly for what he knew would have to come.

'Not them,' said Urglefloggah. 'Too busy sticking up notices, they are.'

'I think that's pretty disgusting,' said Rincewind.

'D'you know,' said Urglefloggah, 'they wouldn't let me on the Club 18,000–30,000 holiday? Said I was too old. Said I would spoil the fun.'

'What's the netherworld coming to?' said Rincewind sympathetically.

'They never come down here, you know,' said the demon, sagging a bit. 'They never tell me anything. Oh yes, very important, only keeping the bloody gate, most important, I don't think!'

'Look,' said Rincewind. 'You wouldn't like me to have a word, would you?'

'Down here all hours, seeing 'em in—'

'Perhaps if we spoke to someone?' said Rincewind.

The demon sniffed, from several noses at once.

'Would you?' it said.

'Be happy to,' said Rincewind.

Urglefloggah brightened a little, but not too much, just in case. 'Can't do any harm, can it?' it said.

Rincewind steeled himself and patted the thing on what he fervently hoped was its back.

'Don't you worry about it,' he said.

'That's very kind of you.'

Rincewind looked across the shuddering heap at Eric.

'We'd better go,' he said. 'So we're not late for our appointment.' He made frantic signals over the demon's head.

Eric grinned. 'Yeah, right, appointment,' he said. They walked up the wide passage.

Eric started to giggle hysterically.

'This is where we run, right?' he said.

'This is where we walk,' said Rincewind. 'Just walk. The important thing is to act nonchalant. The important thing is to get the timing right.'

He looked at Eric.

Eric looked at him.

Behind them, Urglefloggah made a kind of I've-just-worked-it-out noise.

'About now?' said Eric.

'About now I think would do it, yes.'

They ran.

Hell wasn't what Rincewind had been led to expect, although there were signs of what it might once have been – a few clinkers in a corner, a bad scorch mark on the ceiling. It was hot, though, with the kind of heat that you get by boiling air inside an oven for years—

Hell, it has been suggested, is other people.

This has always come as a bit of a surprise to many working demons, who had always thought that hell was sticking sharp things into people and pushing them into lakes of blood and so on.

This is because demons, like most people, have failed to distinguish between the body and the soul.

The fact was that, as droves of demon kings had noticed, there was a limit to what you could do to a soul with, e.g., red-hot tweezers, because even fairly evil and corrupt souls were bright enough to realise that since they didn't have the concomitant body and nerve endings attached to them there was no real reason, other than force of habit, why they should suffer excruciating agony. So they didn't. Demons went on doing it anyway, because numb and mindless stupidity is part of what being a demon is all about, but since no-one was suffering they didn't enjoy it much either and the whole thing was pointless. Centuries and centuries of pointlessness.

Astfgl had adopted, without realising what he was doing, a radically new approach.

Demons can move interdimensionally, and so he'd found the basic ingredients for a very worthwhile lake of blood equivalent, as it were, for the soul. Learn from humans, he'd told the demon lords. Learn from humans. It's amazing what you can learn from humans.

You take, for example, a certain type of hotel. It is probably an English version of an American hotel, but operated with that peculiarly English genius for taking something American and subtracting from it its one worthwhile aspect, so that you end up with slow fast food, West Country and Western music and, well, this hotel.

It's early closing day. The bar is really just a pastel-pink panelled table with a silly ice bucket on it, set in one corner, and it won't be open for hours yet. And then you add rain, and let the one channel available on the only TV be, perhaps, Welsh Channel Four, showing its usual mobius Eisteddfod from Pant-y-gyrdl. And there is only one book in this hotel, left behind by a previous victim. It is one of those where the name of the author is on the front in raised gold letters much bigger than the title, and it probably has a rose and a bullet on there too. Half the pages are missing.

And the only cinema in the town is showing something with subtitles and French umbrellas in it.

And then you stop time, but not experience, so that it seems as though the very fluff in the carpet is gradually rising up to fill the brain and your mouth starts to taste like an old denture.

And you make it last for ever and ever. That's even longer than from now until opening time.

And then you distil it.

Of course the Discworld lacks a number of the items listed above, but boredom is universal and Astfgl had achieved in Hell a particularly high brand of boredom which is like the boredom you get which a) is costing you money, and b) is taking place *while you should be having a nice time.*

The caverns that opened before Rincewind were full of mist and tasteful room dividers. Now and again screams of ennui rose from between the pot plants, but mainly there was the terrible numbing silence of the human brain being reduced to cream cheese from the inside out.

'I don't understand,' said Eric. 'Where are the furnaces? Where are the flames? Where,' he added, hopefully, 'are the succubi?'

Rincewind peered at the nearest exhibit.

A disconsolate demon, whose badge proclaimed it to be Azaremoth, the Stench of Dog Breath, and moreover hoped that the reader would have a nice day, was sitting on the edge of a shallow pit wherein lay a rock on which a man was chained and spreadeagled.

A very tired-looking bird was perched beside him. Rincewind thought that Eric's parrot had it bad, but this bird had definitely been through the mangle of Life. It looked as though it had been plucked first and then had its feathers stuck back on.

Curiosity overcame Rincewind's usual cowardice.

'What's going on?' he said. 'What's happening to him?'

The demon stopped kicking his heels on the edge of the pit. It didn't occur to it to question Rincewind's presence. It assumed that he wouldn't be here unless he had a right to be. The alternative was unbelievable.

'I don't know what he *done*,' it said, 'but when I first come here his punishment was to be chained to that rock and every day an eagle would come down and peck his liver out. Bit of an old favourite, that one.'

'It doesn't look as though it's attacking him now,' said Rincewind.

'Nah. That's all changed. *Now* it flies down every day and tells him about its hernia operation. Now it's effective, I'll grant you,' said the demon sadly, 'but it's not what *I'd* call torture.'

Rincewind turned away, but not before catching a glimpse of the look of terminal agony on the victim's face. It was terrible.

There was worse, however. In the next pit several chained and groaning people were being shown a series of paintings. A demon in front of them was reading from a script.

'—this is when we were in the Fifth Circle, only you can't see where we stayed, it was just off to the left there, and *this* is that funny couple we met, you'd never believe it, they lived on the Icy Plains of Doom just next door to—'

Eric looked at Rincewind.

'It's showing them pictures of itself on holiday?' he said.

They both shrugged and walked away, shaking their heads.

Then there was a small hill. At the bottom of the hill there was a round rock. Beside the rock sat a manacled man, his despairing head buried in his hands. A squat green demon stood beside him, almost buckling under the weight of an enormous book.

'I've heard of *this* one,' said Eric. 'Man who went and defied the gods or something. Got to keep pushing that rock up the hill even though it rolls back all the time—'

The demon looked up.

'But first,' it trilled, 'he must listen to the Unhealthy and Unsafely Regulations governing the Lifting and Moving of Large Objects.'

*

Volume 93 of the Commentaries, in fact. The Regulations themselves comprised a further 1,440 volumes. Part I, that is.

Rincewind had always liked boredom, treasuring it if only because of its rarity value. It had always seemed to him that the only times in his life when he wasn't being chased, imprisoned or hit were when he was being dropped from things, and while falling a long way always had a certain sameness about it, it did not really count as 'boring'. The only time he could look back on with a certain amount of fondness was his brief spell as assistant Librarian at Unseen University, when there wasn't much to do except read books, make sure the Librarian's banana supply wasn't interrupted and, rarely, help him with a particularly recalcitrant grimoire.

Now he realised what made boredom so attractive. It was the knowledge that worse things, dangerously exciting things, were going on just around the corner and that you were well out of them. For boredom to be enjoyable there had to be something to compare it with.

Whereas this was just boredom on top of more boredom, winding in on itself until it became a great crushing sledgehammer which paralysed all thought and experience and pounded eternity into something like flannel.

'This is dreadful,' he said.

The chained man raised a haggard face. 'You're telling me?' he said. 'I used to *like* pushing the ball up the hill. You could stop for a chat, you could see what was going on, you could try various holds and everything. I was a bit of a tourist attraction, people used to point me out. I wouldn't say it was *fun*, but it gave you a purpose in the afterlife.'

'And I used to help him,' said the demon, its voice raw with sullen indignation. 'Give you a bit of a hand, sometimes, didn't I? Pass on a bit of gossip and that. Sort of encourage him when it rolled back and that. I'd say things like "whoops, there goes the bleeder again," and he'd say "Bugger it". We had some times, dint we? Great times.' It blew its nose.

Rincewind coughed.

''Sgetting too much,' said the demon. 'We used to be happy in the old days. It wasn't as if it used to hurt anyone much and, well, we was all in it together.'

'That's it,' said the chained man. 'You knew if you kept your nose clean you'd stand a chance of getting out one day. You know, once a week now I have to stop this for craft lessons?'

'That must be nice,' said Rincewind uncertainly.

The man's eyes narrowed. *'Basketwork?'* he said.

'I been here eighteen millennia, demon and imp,' grumbled the demon. 'I learned my trade, I did. Eighteen thousand bloody years behind the pitchfork, and now this. Reading a—'

A sonic boom echoed the length of Hell.

'Oi oi,' said the demon. 'He's back. He sounds angry, too. We'd better get our heads down.' And indeed, all over the circles of Hades, demons and damned were groaning in unison and getting back to their private hells.

The chained man broke into a sweat.

'Look, Vizzimuth,' he said, 'couldn't we just sort of miss out one or two paragraphs—'

'It's my *job*,' said the demon wretchedly. 'You know He checks up, it's more than my job's worth—' He broke off, gave Rincewind a sad grimace, and patted the sobbing figure with a gentle talon.

'Tell you what,' he said kindly, 'I'll skip some of the sub-clauses.'

Rincewind took Eric by an unresisting shoulder.

'We'd better get along,' he said quietly.

'This is really horrible,' said Eric, as they walked away. 'It gives evil a bad name.'

'Um,' said Rincewind. He didn't like the sound of Him being back and Him being angry. Whenever something important enough to deserve capital letters was angry in the vicinity of Rincewind, it was usually angry with him.

'If you know such a lot about this place,' he said, 'perhaps you can remember how to get out?'

Eric scratched his head. 'It helps if one of you is a girl,' he said. 'According to Ephebian mythology, there's a girl who comes down here every winter.'

'To keep warm?'

'I think the story says she actually *creates* the winter, sort of.'

'I've known women like that,' said Rincewind, nodding wisely.

'Or it helps if you've got a lyre, I think.'

'Ah. We could be on firmer ground here,' said Rincewind. He thought for a bit and then said, 'Er. My dog . . . my dog has six legs.'

'The kind you play,' said Eric patiently.

'Oh.'

'And, and, and when you *do* leave, if you look back . . . I think pomegranates come into it somewhere, or, or, or you turn into a piece of wood.'

'I never look back,' said Rincewind firmly. 'One of the first rules of running away is, never look back.'

There was a roar behind them.

'Especially when you hear loud noises,' Rincewind went on. 'When it comes to cowardice, that's what sorts out the men from the sheep. You run straight away.' He grabbed the skirts of his robe.

And they ran and ran, until a familiar voice said: 'Ho there, dear lads. Hop up. It's amazing how you meet old friends down here.'

And another voice said, 'Wossname? Wossname?'

'Where are they!'

The sub-lords of Hell trembled. This was going to be dreadful. It might even result in a memo.

'They can't have escaped,' rasped Astfgl. 'They're here some- where. Why can you not *find* them? Am I surrounded by incompe- tents as well as fools?'

'My lord—'

The demon princes turned.

The speaker was Duke Vassenego, one of the oldest demons. How old, no-one knew. But if he didn't actually invent original sin, at least he made one of the first copies. In terms of sheer enterprise and deviousness of mind he might even have passed for human and, in fact, generally took the form of an old, rather sad lawyer with an eagle somewhere in his ancestry.

And every demonic mind thought: poor old Vassenego, he's done it this time. This won't be just a memo, this will be a policy statement, c.c.'d to all departments and a copy for files.

Astfgl turned slowly, as though mounted on a turntable. He was back in his preferred form now but had pulled himself together, as it were, on a higher level of emotion. The mere thought of living humans in his domain made him twang with fury like a violin string. You couldn't trust them. They were unreliable. The last human allowed down here alive had given the place a terribly bad Press. Above all, they made him feel inferior.

Now the full wattage of his anger focused on the old demon.

'You had a point to make?' he said.

'I was merely going to say, lord, that we have made an extensive search of all eight circles and I am really certain—'

'Silence! Don't think I don't know what's going on,' growled Astfgl, circling the drawn figure. 'I've seen you – and *you*, and *you*'—his trident pointed at some of the other old lords—'plotting in corners, encouraging rebellion! *I* rule here, is that not so? And I will be obeyed!'

Vassenego was pale. His patrician nostrils flared like jet intakes. Everything about him said: you pompous little creature, of course we encourage rebellion, we're demons! And I was maddening the minds of princes when you were encouraging cats to leave dead mice under the bed, you small-minded, paper-worshipping nincompoop! Everything about him said this except for his voice, which said, calmly, 'No-one is denying this, sire.'

'Then search again! And the demon who let them in is to be taken to the lowest pit and disassembled, is that clear?'

Vassenego's eyebrows rose. 'Old Urglefloggah, sire? He was foolish, certainly, but he is a loyal—'

'Are you by any chance endeavouring to contradict me?'

Vassenego hesitated. Dreadful as he privately held the King to be, demons are strong believers in precedence and hierarchy. There were too many young demons pressing below them for the senior lords to openly demonstrate the ways of regicide and coup, no matter what the provocation. Vassenego had plans of his own. No sense in spoiling things now.

'No, sire,' he said. 'But that will mean, sire, that the dread portal is no longer—'

'*Do it!*'

The Luggage arrived at the dread portal.

There was no way to describe how angry you can get running nearly twice the length of the space-time continuum, and the Luggage had been pretty annoyed to start with.

It looked at the hinges. It looked at the locks. It backed away a bit and appeared to read the new sign over the portal.

Possibly this made it angrier, although with the Luggage there wasn't any reliable way of telling because it spent all its time beyond, in a manner of speaking, the hostility event horizon.

The doors of Hell were ancient. It wasn't just time and heat that had baked their wood to something like black granite. They'd picked up fear and dull evil. They were more than mere things to fill a hole in the wall. They were bright enough to be dimly aware of what their future was likely to hold.

They watched the Luggage shuffle back across the sand, flex its legs and crouch down.

The lock clicked. The bolts dragged themselves back hurriedly.

The great bars jerked from their sockets. The doors flung themselves back against the wall.

The Luggage untensed. It straightened. It stepped forward. It almost strutted. It passed between the straining hinges and, when it was nearly through, turned and gave the nearest door a damn good kick.

There was a great treadmill. It didn't power anything, and had particularly creaky bearings. It was one of Astfgl's more inspired ideas, and had no use whatsoever except to show several hundred people that if they had thought their lives had been pretty pointless, they hadn't seen anything yet.

'We can't stay here for ever,' said Rincewind. 'We need to do things. Like *eat*.'

'That's one of the tremendous advantages of being a damned soul,' said Ponce da Quirm. 'All the old bodily cares fade away. Of course, you get a completely *new* set of cares, but I have always found it advisable to look for the silver lining.'

'Wossname!' said the parrot, who was sitting on his shoulder.

'Fancy that,' said Rincewind. 'I never knew animals could go to Hell. Although I can quite see why they made an exception in this case.'

'Up yours, wizard!'

'Why don't they look for us here, that's what I don't understand?' said Eric.

'Shut up and keep walking,' said Rincewind. 'They're stupid, that's why. They can't imagine that we would be doing something like this.'

'Yes, they're right there. *I* can't imagine that we are doing something like this, either,' said Eric.

Rincewind treadled for a bit, watching a crowd of frantically searching demons hurry past.

'So you didn't find the Fountain of Youth, then,' he said, feeling that he should make some conversation.

'Oh, but I did,' said da Quirm earnestly. 'A clear spring, deep in the jungle. It was very impressive. I had a good long drink, too. Or draught, which I think is the more appropriate word.'

'And—?' said Rincewind.

'It definitely worked. Yes. For a while there I could definitely feel myself getting younger.'

'But—' Rincewind waved a vague hand to take in da Quirm, the treadmill, the towering circles of the Pit.

'Ah,' said the old man. 'Of course, that's the really annoying bit. I'd read so much about the Fountain, and you'd have thought someone in all those books would have mentioned the really vital thing about the water, wouldn't you?'

'Which was—?'

'*Boil it first*. Says it all, doesn't it? Terrible shame, really.'

The Luggage trotted down the great spiral road that linked the circles of the Pit. Even if conditions had been normal it probably would not have attracted much attention. If anything, it was rather less astonishing than most of the denizens.

'This is really boring,' said Eric.

'That's the point,' said Rincewind.

'We shouldn't be lurking here, we should be trying to find a way out!'

'Well, yes, but there isn't one.'

'There is, in fact,' said a voice behind Rincewind. It was the voice of someone who had seen it all and hadn't liked any of it very much.

'Lavaeolus?' said Rincewind. His ancestor was right behind them.

'"You'll get home all right,"' said Lavaeolus bitterly. 'Your very words. Huh. Ten years of one damn thing after another. You might have told a chap.'

'Er,' said Eric. 'We didn't want to upset the course of history.'

'You didn't want to upset the course of history,' said Lavaeolus slowly. He stared down at the woodwork of the treadmill. 'Oh. Good. That makes it all all right. I feel a lot better for knowing that. Speaking as the course of history, I'd like to say thank you very much.'

'Excuse me,' said Rincewind.

'Yes?'

'You said there's another way out?'

'Oh, yes. A back way.'

'Where *is* it?'

Lavaeolus stopped treadling for a moment and pointed across the misty hollow.

'See that arch over there?'

Rincewind peered into the distance.

'Just about,' he said. 'Is that it?'

'Yes. A long steep climb. Don't know where it comes out, though.'

'How did you find out about it?'

Lavaeolus shrugged. 'I asked a demon,' he said. 'There's always an easier way of doing everything, you know.'

'It'd take forever to get there,' said Eric. 'It's right on the other side, we'd never make it.'

Rincewind nodded, and glumly continued the endless walk. After a few minutes he said: 'Has it struck you we seem to be going faster?'

Eric turned around.

The Luggage had stepped aboard and was trying to catch up with them.

Astfgl stood in front of his mirror.

'Show me what they can see,' he commanded.

Yes, master.

Astfgl inspected the whirring image for a moment.

'Tell me what this means,' he said.

I'm just a mirror, master. What do I know?

Astfgl growled. 'And I'm Lord of Hades,' he said, gesturing with his trident. 'And I'm prepared to risk another seven years' bad luck.'

The mirror considered the available options.

I might be able to hear some creaking, lord, it ventured.

'And?'

I smell smoke.

'No smoke. I specifically banned all open fires. A very old-fashioned concept. It gave the place a bad name.'

Nevertheless, master.

'Show me . . . Hades.'

The mirror gave of its best. The King was just in time to see the treadwheel, its bearings glowing red hot, crash down from its mountings and roll, as deceptively slowly as an avalanche, across the country of the damned.

Rincewind hung from the pushbar, watching the rungs whirr past at a speed that would have burned the soles off his sandals if he'd been foolish enough to let his feet down. The dead, however, were taking it all with the cheerful aplomb of those who know that the worst has already happened to them. Cries of 'Pass the candyfloss,' drifted down. He heard Lavaeolus commending the wheel's splendid traction and explaining to da Quirm how, if you have a vehicle which put down its road in front of it, just like the Luggage was in fact doing, and then you covered it with armour, then wars would be less bloody, over in half the time and everyone could spend even longer going home.

The Luggage made no comment at all. It could see its master hanging a few feet away, and just kept going. It may have occurred to it that the journey was taking some time, but that was Time's problem. And so, flinging out the occasional screaming soul, bumping and gyrating and crushing the occasional luckless demon, the wheel bowled on.

It smashed against the opposite cliff.

Lord Vassenego smiled.

'Now,' he said, 'it is time.'

The other senior demons looked a bit shifty. They were, of course, steeped in evil, and Astfgl was definitely Not One Of Us and the most revolting little oik ever to oil his way into the post . . .

But . . . well, *this* . . . perhaps there were some things that were *too* . . .

'"Learn from the ways of humans",' mimicked Vassenego. 'He bade *me* learn from humans. Me! The impudence! The arrogance! But I watched, oh, yes. I learned. I *planned*.'

The look on his face was unspeakable. Even the lords of the nethermost circles, who gloried in villainy, had to turn their heads.

Duke Drazometh the Putrid raised a hesitant talon.

'But if he even suspects,' he said, 'I mean, he has a foul temper on him. Those memos—' He shuddered.

'But what are we doing?' Vassenego spread his hands in a gesture of innocence. 'Where is the harm in it? Brothers, I ask you: where is the harm?'

His fingers curled. The knuckles shone white under the thin, blue-veined skin as he surveyed the doubting faces.

'Or would you rather receive another statement of policy?' he said.

Expressions twitched as the lords made up their minds like a row of dominoes falling over. There were some things on which even they were united. No more policy statements, no more consultative documents, no more morale-boosting messages to all staff. This was Hell, but you had to draw the line somewhere.

Earl Beezlemoth rubbed one of his three noses. 'And humans somewhere thought this up all by themselves?' he said. 'We didn't give them any, you know, hints?'

Vassenego shook his head.

'All their own work,' he said proudly, like a fond schoolmaster who has just seen a star pupil graduate summa cum laude.

The earl stared into infinity. 'I thought *we* were supposed to be the ghastly ones,' he said, his voice filled with awe.

The old lord nodded. He'd waited a long time for this. While others had talked of red-hot revolution he'd just stared out into the world of men, and watched, and marvelled.

This Rincewind character had been extremely useful. He'd managed to keep the King totally occupied. He'd been worth all the effort. The damn-fool human still thought it was his fingers doing the business! Three wishes, indeed!

And thus it was, when Rincewind pulled himself free of the wreckage of the wheel, he found Astfgl, King of Demons, Lord of Hell, Master of the Pit, standing over him.

Astfgl had passed through the earlier stage of fury and was now in that calm lagoon of rage where the voice is steady, the manner is measured and polite, and only a faint trace of spittle at the corner of the mouth betrays the inner inferno.

Eric crawled out from under a broken spar and looked up.

'Oh dear,' he said.

The Demon King twirled the trident. Suddenly, it didn't look comical any more. It looked like a heavy metal stick with three horrible spikes on the end.

Astfgl smiled, and looked around. 'No,' he said, apparently to himself. 'Not here. It is not public enough. Come!'

A hand grasped each of them by the shoulder. They could no more resist it than a couple of non-identical snowflakes could resist a flamethrower. There was a moment's disorientation, and Rincewind found himself in the largest room in the universe.

It was the great hall. You could have built moon rockets in it. The kings of Hell might have heard of words like 'subtlety' and 'discretion', but they had also heard that if you had it you should flaunt it and reasoned that, if you didn't have it, you should flaunt it even more, and what they didn't have was good taste. Astfgl had done what he could but even he had been unable to add much to the basic bad design, the clashing colours, and the terrible wallpaper. He'd put in a few coffee tables and a bullfight poster, but they were more or less lost in the overall chaos, and the new antimacassar on the back of the Throne of Dread only served to highlight some of its more annoying bas-reliefs.

The two humans sprawled on the floor.

'And now—' said Astfgl.

But his voice was lost in a sudden cheering.

He looked up.

Demons of every size and shape filled almost all the hall, piling up the walls and even hanging from the ceiling. A demonic band struck up a choice of chords on a variety of instruments. A banner, slung from one side of the hall to the other, read: Hale To Ther Cheve.

Astfgl's brows knitted in instant paranoia as Vassenego, trailed by the other lords, bore down on him. The old demon's face was split in a totally guileless grin, and the King nearly panicked and hit it with the trident before Vassenego reached out and slapped him on the back.

'Well done!' he cried.

'What?'

'Oh, very well done!'

Astfgl looked down at Rincewind.

'Oh,' he said. 'Yes. Well.' He coughed. 'It was nothing,' he said, straightening up, 'I knew you people weren't getting anywhere so I just—'

'Not *these*,' sneered Vassenego. 'Such trivial things. No, sire. I was referring to your elevation.'

'Elevation?' said Astfgl.

'Your *promotion*, sire!'

A great cheer went up from the younger demons, who would cheer anything.

'Promotion? But, but I *am* the King—' Astfgl protested weakly. He could feel his grasp on events beginning to slip.

'Pfooie!' said Vassenego expansively.

'Pfooie?'

'Indeed, sire. King? *King?* Sire, I speak for us all when I say that is no title for a demon such as you, sire, a demon whose grasp of organisational matters and priorities, whose insight into the proper functions of our being, whose – if I may say so – sheer intellectual capabilities have taken us to new and greater depths, sire!'

Despite himself, Astfgl preened. 'Well, you know—' he began.

'And yet we find, despite your position, that you interest yourself in the tiniest details of our work,' said Vassenego, looking down his nose at Rincewind. 'Such dedication! Such devotion!'

Astfgl swelled. 'Of course, I've always felt—'

Rincewind pulled himself up on his elbows, and thought: look out, behind you . . .

'And so,' said Vassenego, beaming like a coastful of lighthouses, 'the Council met and has decided, and may I add, sire, has decided unanimously, to create an entirely new award in honour of your outstanding achievements!'

'The importance of proper paperwork has – what award?' said Astfgl, the minnows of suspicion suddenly darting across the oceans of self-esteem.

'The position, sire, of Supreme Life President of Hell!'

The band struck up again.

'With your own office – much bigger than the pokey thing you have had to suffer all these years, sire. Or rather, Mr President!'

The band had a go at another chord.

The demons waited.

'Will there be . . . potted plants?' said Astfgl, slowly.

'Hosts! Plantations! *Jungles!*'

Astfgl appeared to be lit by a gentle, inner glow.

'And carpets? I mean, wall to wall—?'

'The walls have had to be moved apart especially to accommodate them all, sire. And thick pile, sire? Whole tribes of pygmies are wondering why the light stays on at night, sire!'

The bewildered King allowed himself to have an expansive arm thrown across his shoulder and was gently led, all thoughts of vengeance forgotten, through the cheering crowds.

'I've always fancied one of those special things for making coffee,' he murmured, as the last vestiges of self-control were eroded.

'A positive manufactory has been installed, sire! And a speaking tube, sire, for you to communicate your instructions to your underlings. And the very latest in diaries, two aeons to a page, and a thing for—'

'Coloured marker pens. I've always held that—'

'Complete rainbows, sire,' Vassenego boomed. 'And let us go there without delay, sire, for I suspect that with your normal keen insight you cannot wait to get to grips with the mighty tasks ahead of you, sire.'

'Certainly, certainly! Time they were done, indeed—' An expression of vague perplexity passed across Astfgl's flushed face. 'These mighty tasks . . .'

'Nothing less than a complete, full, authoritative, searching and in-depth analysis of our role, function, priorities and goals, sire!'

Vassenego stood back.

The demon lords held their breath.

Astfgl frowned. The universe appeared to slow down. The stars halted momentarily in their courses.

'With forward planning?' he said, at last.

'A top priority, sire, which you have instantly pinpointed with your normal incisiveness,' said Vassenego quickly.

The demon lords breathed again.

Astfgl's chest expanded several inches. 'I shall need special staff, of course, in order to formulate—'

'Formulate! The very thing!' said Vassenego, who was perhaps getting just a bit carried away. Astfgl gave him a faintly suspicious glance, but at that moment the band struck up again.

The last words that Rincewind heard, as the King was led out of the hall, were: 'And in order to analyse information, I shall need—'

And then he was gone.

The rest of the demons, aware that the entertainment seemed to be over for the day, started to mill around and drift out of the great doors. It was beginning to dawn on the brightest of them that the fires would soon be roaring again.

No-one seemed to be taking any notice of the two humans. Rincewind tugged at Eric's robe.

'*This* is where we run, right?' said Eric.

'Where we *walk*,' said Rincewind firmly. 'Nonchalantly, calmly, and, er—'

'Fast?'

'You pick things up quickly, don't you?'

It is essential that the proper use of three wishes should bring happiness to the greatest available number of people, and this is what in fact had happened.

The Tezumen were happy. When no amount of worshipping caused the Luggage to come back and trample their enemies they poisoned all their priests and tried enlightened atheism instead, which still meant they could kill as many people as they liked but didn't have to get up so early to do it.

The people of Tsort and Ephebe were happy – at least, the ones who write and feature in the dramas of history were happy, which is all that mattered. Now their long war was over and they could get on with the proper concern of civilised nations, which is to prepare for the next one.

The people of Hell were happy, or at least happier than hitherto.

The flames were flickering brightly again, the same old familiar tortures were being inflicted on ethereal bodies quite incapable of feeling them, and the damned had been given that insight which makes hardship so easy to bear – the absolute and certain knowledge that things could be worse.

The demon lords were happy:

They stood around the magic mirror, enjoying a celebratory drink. Occasionally one of them would risk slapping Vassenego on the back.

'Shall we let them go, sire?' said a duke, peering at the climbing figures in the mirror's dark image.

'Oh, I think so,' said Vassenego airily. 'It's always a good thing to let a few tales spread, you know. *Pour encouragy le – poor encoura –* to make everyone sit up and damn well take notice. And they have been useful, after their fashion.' He looked into the depths of his drink, exulting quietly.

And yet, and yet, in the depths of his curly mind he thought he could hear the tiny voice that would grow louder over the years, the voice that haunts all demon kings, everywhere: look out, behind you . . .

It is hard to say whether the Luggage was happy or not. It had viciously attacked fourteen demons so far, and had three of them cornered in their own pit of boiling oil. Soon it would have to follow its master, but it didn't have to rush.

One of the demons made a frantic grab for the bank. The Luggage stamped heavily on its fingers.

The creator of universes was happy. He'd just inserted one seven-sided snowflake into a blizzard as an experiment, and no-one had noticed. Tomorrow he was half-inclined to try small, delicately-crystallised letters of the alphabet. Alphabet Snow. It could be a winner.

Rincewind and Eric were happy:

'I can see blue sky!' said Eric. 'Where do you think we'll come out?' he added. 'And when?'

'Anywhere,' said Rincewind. 'Anytime.'

He looked down at the broad steps they were climbing. They were something of a novelty; each one was built out of large stone letters. The one he was just stepping on to, for example, read: I Meant It For The Best.

The next one was: I Thought You'd Like It.

Eric was standing on: For the Sake of the Children.

'Weird, isn't it?' he said. 'Why do it like this?'

'I think they're meant to be good intentions,' said Rincewind. This was a road to Hell, and demons were, after all, traditionalists.

And, while they are of course irredeemably evil, they are not always bad. And so Rincewind stepped off We Are Equal Opportunity Employers and through a wall, which healed up behind him, and into the world.

It could, he had to admit, have been a lot worse.

President Astfgl, sitting in a pool of light in his huge, dark office, blew into the speaking tube again.

'Hallo?' he said. 'Hallo?'

There didn't seem to be anyone answering.

Strange.

He picked up one of his coloured pens, and looked around at the stack of work behind him. All those records, to be analysed, considered, assessed and evaluated, and then suitable management directives to be arrived at, and an in-depth policy document to be drafted and then, after due consideration, redrafted again . . .

He tried the tube once more.

'Hallo? Hallo?'

No-one there. Still, not to worry, lots to do. His time was far too important to waste.

He sank his feet into his thick, warm carpet.

He looked proudly at his potted plants.

He tapped a complicated assembly of chromed wire and balls, which began to swing and click executively.

He unscrewed the top of his pen with a firm, decisive hand.

He wrote: What business are we in???

He thought for a bit, and then carefully wrote, underneath: We are in the damnation business!!!

And this, too, was happiness. Of a sort.

INTERESTING
TIMES

There is a curse.

They say:
May You Live in Interesting Times

This is where the gods play games with the lives of men, on a board which is *at one and the same time* a simple playing area and the whole world.

And Fate always wins.

Fate always wins. Most of the gods throw dice but Fate plays chess, and you don't find out until too late that he's been using two queens all along.

Fate wins. At least, so it is claimed. Whatever happens, they say afterwards, it must have been Fate.[*]

Gods can take any form, but the one aspect of themselves they cannot change is their eyes, which show their nature. The eyes of Fate are hardly eyes at all – just dark holes into an infinity speckled with what may be stars or, there again, may be other things.

He blinked them, smiled at his fellow players in the smug way winners do just before they become winners, and said:

'I accuse the High Priest of the Green Robe in the library with the double-handed axe.'

And he won.

He beamed at them.

'No one likesh a poor winner,' grumbled Offler the Crocodile God, through his fangs.

'It seems that I am favouring myself today,' said Fate. 'Anyone fancy something else?'

The gods shrugged.

'Mad Kings?' said Fate pleasantly. 'Star-Crossed Lovers?'

'I think we've lost the rules for that one,' said Blind Io, chief of the gods.

'Or Tempest-Wrecked Mariners?'

'You always win,' said Io.

'Floods and Droughts?' said Fate. 'That's an easy one.'

---

[*] People are always a little confused about this, as they are in the case of miracles. When someone is saved from certain death by a strange concatenation of circumstances, they say that's a miracle. But of course if someone is *killed* by a freak chain of events – the oil spilled just *there*, the safety fence broken just *there* – that must *also* be a miracle. Just because it's not nice doesn't mean it's not miraculous.

A shadow fell across the gaming table. The gods looked up.

'Ah,' said Fate.

'Let a game begin,' said the Lady.

There was always an argument about whether the newcomer was a goddess at all. Certainly no one ever got anywhere by worshipping her, and she tended to turn up only where she was least expected, such as now. And people who trusted in her seldom survived. Any temples built to her would surely be struck by lightning. Better to juggle axes on a tightrope than say her name. Just call her the waitress in the Last Chance saloon.

She was generally referred to as the Lady, and her eyes were green; not as the eyes of humans are green, but emerald green from edge to edge. It was said to be her favourite colour.

'Ah,' said Fate again. 'And what game will it be?'

She sat down opposite him. The watching gods looked sidelong at one another. This looked interesting. These two were ancient enemies.

'How about . . .' she paused, ' . . . Mighty Empires?'

'Oh, I *hate* that one,' said Offler, breaking the sudden silence. 'Everyone dief at the end.'

'Yes,' said Fate, 'I believe they do.' He nodded at the Lady, and in much the same voice as professional gamblers say 'Aces high?' said, 'The Fall of Great Houses? Destinies of Nations Hanging by a Thread?'

'Certainly,' she said.

'Oh, *good*.' Fate waved a hand across the board. The Discworld appeared.

'And where shall we play?' he said.

'The Counterweight Continent,' said the Lady. 'Where five noble families have fought one another for centuries.'

'Really? Which families are these?' said Io. He had little involvement with individual humans. He generally looked after thunder and lightning, so from his point of view the only purpose of humanity was to get wet or, in occasional cases, charred.

'The Hongs, the Sungs, the Tangs, the McSweeneys and the Fangs.'

'Them? I didn't know they were noble,' said Io.

'They're all very rich and have had millions of people butchered or tortured to death merely for reasons of expediency and pride,' said the Lady.

The watching gods nodded solemnly. That was certainly noble behaviour. That was exactly what they would have done.

'*McFweeneyf?*' said Offler.

'Very old established family,' said Fate.

'Oh.'

'And they wrestle one another for the Empire,' said Fate. 'Very good. Which will you be?'

The Lady looked at the history stretched out in front of them.

'The Hongs are the most powerful. Even as we speak, they have taken yet more cities,' she said. 'I see they are fated to win.'

'So, no doubt, you'll pick a weaker family.'

Fate waved his hand again. The playing pieces appeared, and started to move around the board as if they had a life of their own, which was of course the case.

'But,' he said, 'we shall play without dice. I don't trust you with dice. You throw them where I can't see them. We will play with steel, and tactics, and politics, and war.'

The Lady nodded.

Fate looked across at his opponent.

'And your move?' he said.

She smiled. 'I've already made it.'

He looked down. 'But I don't see your pieces on the board.'

'They're not on the board yet,' she said.

She opened her hand.

There was something black and yellow on her palm. She blew on it, and it unfolded its wings.

It was a butterfly.

Fate always wins . . .

At least, when people stick to the rules.

According to the philosopher Ly Tin Wheedle, chaos is found in greatest abundance wherever order is being sought. It always defeats order, because it is better organized.

This is the butterfly of the storms.

See the wings, slightly more ragged than those of the common fritillary. In reality, thanks to the fractal nature of the universe, this means that those ragged edges are infinite – in the same way that the edge of any rugged coastline, when measured to the ultimate microscopic level, is infinitely long – or, if not infinite, then at least so close to it that Infinity can be seen on a clear day.

And therefore, if their edges are infinitely long, the wings must logically be infinitely big.

They may *look* about the right size for a butterfly's wings, but that's only because human beings have always preferred common sense to logic.

The Quantum Weather Butterfly (*Papilio tempestae*) is an undistinguished yellow colour, although the mandelbrot patterns on the wings are of considerable interest. Its outstanding feature is its ability to create weather.

This presumably began as a survival trait, since even an extremely hungry bird would find itself inconvenienced by a nasty localized tornado.* From there it possibly became a secondary sexual characteristic, like the plumage of birds or the throat sacs of certain frogs. Look at *me*, the male says, flapping his wings lazily in the canopy of the rain forest. I may be an undistinguished yellow colour but in a fortnight's time, a thousand miles away, Freak Gales Cause Road Chaos.

This is the butterfly of the storms.

It flaps its wings . . .

This is the Discworld, which goes through space on the back of a giant turtle.

Most worlds do, at some time in their perception. It's a cosmological view the human brain seems pre-programmed to take.

On veldt and plain, in cloud jungle and silent red desert, in swamp and reed marsh, in fact in any place where something goes 'plop' off a floating log as you approach, variations on the following take place at a crucial early point in the development of the tribal mythology . . .

'You see dat?'

'What?'

'It just went plop off dat log.'

'Yeah? Well?'

'I reckon . . . I reckon . . . like, I *reckon* der world is carried on der back of one of dem.'

A moment of silence while this astrophysical hypothesis is considered, and then . . .

'The whole world?'

'Of course, when I say one of dem, I mean a *big* one of dem.'

'It'd have to be, yeah.'

'Like . . . really big.'

---

* Usually about six inches across.

314

"'S funny, but . . . I see what you mean.'

'Makes sense, right?'

'Makes sense, yeah. Thing is . . .'

'What?'

'I just hope it never goes plop.'

But this *is* the Discworld, which has not only the turtle but also the four giant elephants on which the wide, slowly turning wheel of the world revolves.[*]

There is the Circle Sea, approximately halfway between the Hub and the Rim. Around it are those countries which, according to History, constitute the civilized world, i.e., a world that can support historians: Ephebe, Tsort, Omnia, Klatch and the sprawling city state of Ankh-Morpork.

This is a story that starts somewhere else, where a man is lying on a raft in a blue lagoon under a sunny sky. His head is resting on his arms. He is happy – in his case, a mental state so rare as to be almost unprecedented. He is whistling an amiable little tune, and dangling his feet in the crystal clear water.

They're pink feet with ten toes that look like little piggy-wiggies.

From the point of view of a shark, skimming over the reef, they look like lunch, dinner and tea.

It was, as always, a matter of protocol. Of discretion. Of careful etiquette. Of, ultimately, alcohol. Or at least the illusion of alcohol.

Lord Vetinari, as supreme ruler of Ankh-Morpork, could in theory summon the Archchancellor of Unseen University to his presence and, indeed, have him executed if he failed to obey.

On the other hand Mustrum Ridcully, as head of the college of wizards, had made it clear in polite but firm ways that *he* could turn *him* into a small amphibian and, indeed, start jumping around the room on a pogo stick.

Alcohol bridged the diplomatic gap nicely. Sometimes Lord Vetinari invited the Archchancellor to the palace for a convivial drink. And of course the Archchancellor went, because it would be *bad manners* not to. And everyone understood the position, and everyone was on their best behaviour, and thus civil unrest and slime on the carpet were averted.

[*] People wonder how this works, since a terrestrial elephant would be unlikely to bear a revolving load for any length of time without some serious friction burns. But you may as well ask why the axle of a planet doesn't squeak, or where love goes, or what sound yellow makes.

315

It was a beautiful afternoon. Lord Vetinari was sitting in the palace gardens, watching the butterflies with an expression of mild annoyance. He found something very slightly offensive about the way they just fluttered around enjoying themselves in an unprofitable way.

He looked up.

'Ah, Archchancellor,' he said. 'So good to see you. Do sit down. I trust you are well?'

'Yes indeed,' said Mustrum Ridcully. 'And yourself? You are in good health?'

'Never better. The weather, I see, has turned out nice again.'

'I thought yesterday was particularly fine, certainly.'

'Tomorrow, I am told, could well be even better.'

'We could certainly do with a fine spell.'

'Yes, indeed.'

'Yes.'

'Ah . . .'

'Certainly.'

They watched the butterflies. A butler brought long, cool drinks.

'What is it they actually do with the flowers?' said Lord Vetinari.

'What?'

The Patrician shrugged. 'Never mind. It was not at all important. But – since you are here, Archchancellor, having dropped by on your way to something infinitely more important, I am sure, most kind – I wonder if you could tell me: who is the Great Wizard?'

Ridcully considered this.

'The Dean, possibly,' he said. 'He must be all of twenty stone.'

'Somehow I feel that is not perhaps the right answer,' said Lord Vetinari. 'I suspect from context that "great" means superior.'

'Not the Dean, then,' said Ridcully.

Lord Vetinari tried to recollect the faculty of Unseen University. The mental picture that emerged was of a small range of foothills in pointy hats.

'The context does not, I feel, suggest the Dean,' he said.

'Er . . . what context would this be?' said Ridcully.

The Patrician picked up his walking stick.

'Come this way,' he said. 'I suppose you had better see for yourself. It is very vexing.'

Ridcully looked around with interest as he followed Lord Vetinari. He did not often have a chance to see the gardens, which had been written up in the 'How Not To Do It' section of gardening manuals everywhere.

They had been laid out, and a truer phrase was never used, by the renowned or at least notorious landscape gardener and all round inventor 'Bloody Stupid' Johnson, whose absent-mindedness and blindness to elementary mathematics made every step a walk with danger. His genius . . . well, as far as Ridcully understood it, his genius was exactly the opposite of whatever kind of genius it was that built earthworks that tapped the secret yet beneficent forces of the leylines.

No one was quite certain what forces Bloody Stupid's designs tapped, but the chiming sundial frequently exploded, the crazy paving had committed suicide and the cast iron garden furniture was known to have melted on three occasions.

The Patrician led the way through a gate and into something like a dovecot. A creaking wooden stairway led around the inside. A few of Ankh-Morpork's indestructible feral pigeons muttered and sniggered in the shadows.

'What's this?' said Ridcully, as the stairs groaned under him.

The Patrician took a key out of his pocket. 'I have always understood that Mr Johnson originally planned this to be a beehive,' he said. 'However, in the absence of bees ten feet long we have found . . . other uses.'

He unlocked a door to a wide, square room with a big unglazed window in each wall. Each rectangle was surrounded by a wooden arrangement to which was affixed a bell on a spring. It was apparent that anything large enough, entering by one of the windows, would cause the bell to ring.

In the centre of the room, standing on a table, was the largest bird Ridcully had ever seen. It turned and fixed him with a beady yellow eye.

The Patrician reached into a pocket and took out a jar of anchovies. 'This one caught us rather unexpectedly,' he said. 'It must be almost ten years since a message last arrived. We used to keep a few fresh mackerel on ice.'

'Isn't that a Pointless Albatross?' said Ridcully.

'Indeed,' said Lord Vetinari. 'And a highly trained one. It will return this evening. Six thousand miles on one jar of anchovies and a bottle of fish paste my clerk Drumknott found in the kitchens. Amazing.'

'I'm sorry?' said Ridcully. 'Return to where?'

Lord Vetinari turned to face him.

'*Not*, let me make it clear, to the Counterweight Continent,' he said. 'This is *not* one of those birds the Agatean Empire uses for its

317

message services. It is a well-known fact that we have no contact with that mysterious land. And this bird is *not* the first to arrive here for many years, and it did *not* bring a strange and puzzling message. Do I make myself clear?'

'No.'

'Good.'

'This is not an albatross?'

The Patrician smiled. 'Ah, I can see you're getting the hang of it.'

Mustrum Ridcully, though possessed of a large and efficient brain, was not at home with duplicity. He looked at the long vicious beak.

'Looks like a bloody albatross to me,' he said. 'And you just said it was. I said, isn't that a—'

The Patrician waved a hand irritably. 'Leaving aside our ornitho-logical studies,' he said, 'the point is that this bird had, in its message pouch, the following piece of paper—'

'You mean did *not* have the following piece of paper?' said Ridcully, struggling for a grip.

'Ah, yes. Of course, that is what I mean. And this isn't it. Observe.'

He handed a single small sheet to the Archchancellor.

'Looks like paintin',' said Ridcully.

'Those are Agatean pictograms,' said the Patrician.

'You mean they're *not* Agatean pictograms?'

'Yes, yes, certainly,' sighed the Patrician, 'I can see you are well alongside the essential business of diplomacy. Now . . . your views, please.'

'Looks like slosh, slosh, slosh, slosh, Wizzard,' said Ridcully.

'And from that you deduce . . . ?'

'He took Art because he wasn't any good at spelling? I mean, who wrote it? Painted it, I mean?'

'I don't know. The Grand Viziers used to send the occasional message, but I gather there has been some turmoil in recent years. It is unsigned, you notice. However, I cannot ignore it.'

'Wizzard, wizzard,' said Ridcully, thoughtfully.

'The pictograms mean "Send Us Instantly The Great",' said Lord Vetinari.

' . . . wizzard . . .' said Ridcully to himself, tapping the paper.

The Patrician tossed an anchovy to the albatross, which swal-lowed it greedily.

'The Empire has a million men under arms,' he said. 'Happily, it suits the rulers to pretend that everywhere outside the Empire is a valueless howling waste peopled only by vampires and ghosts. They usually have no interest whatsoever in our affairs. This is fortunate for us, because they are both cunning, rich and powerful. Frankly, I had hoped they had forgotten about us altogether. And now this. I was hoping to be able to dispatch the wretched person and forget about it.'

' . . . wizzard . . .' said Ridcully.

'Perhaps you would like a holiday?' said the Patrician, a hint of hope in his voice.

'Me? No. Can't abide foreign food,' said Ridcully quickly. He repeated, half to himself, 'Wizzard . . .'

'The word seems to fascinate you,' said Lord Vetinari.

'Seen it spelled like that before,' said Ridcully. 'Can't remember where.'

'I'm sure you *will* remember. And will be in a position to send the Great Wizard, however he is spelled, to the Empire by teatime.'

Ridcully's jaw dropped.

'Six thousand miles? By magic? Do you know how hard that is?'

'I cherish my ignorance on the subject,' said Lord Vetinari.

'Besides,' Ridcully went on, 'they're, well . . . foreign over there. I thought they had enough wizards of their own.'

'I really couldn't say.'

'We don't know why they want this wizard?'

'No. But I'm sure there is someone you could spare. There seems to be such a lot of you down there.'

'I mean, it could be for some terrible foreign purpose,' said Ridcully. For some reason the face of the Dean waddled across his mind, and he brightened up. 'They might be happy with *a* great wizard, do you think?' he mused.

'I leave that entirely to you. But by tonight I would like to be able to send back a message saying that the Great Wizzard is duly on his way. And then we can forget about it.'

'Of course, it would be very hard to bring the chap back,' said Ridcully. He thought of the Dean again. 'Practically impossible,' he added, in an inappropriately happy way. 'I expect we'd try for months and months without succeeding. I expect we'd attempt everything with no luck. Damn it.'

'I can see you are agog to rise to this challenge,' said the Patrician. 'Let me not detain you from rushing back to the University and putting measures in hand.'

'But . . . "wizzard" . . .' Ridcully murmured. 'Rings a faint bell, that. Think I've seen it before, somewhere.'

*

The shark didn't think much. Sharks don't. Their thought processes can largely be represented by '='. You see it = you eat it.

But, as it arrowed through the waters of the lagoon, its tiny brain began to receive little packages of selachian existential dread that could only be called doubts.

It knew it was the biggest shark around. All the challengers had fled, or run up against good old '='. Yet its body told it that something was coming up fast behind it.

It turned gracefully, and the first thing it saw was *hundreds* of legs and *thousands* of toes, a whole pork pie factory of piggy-wiggies.

Many things went on at Unseen University and, regrettably, teaching had to be one of them. The faculty had long ago confronted this fact and had perfected various devices for avoiding it. But this was perfectly all right because, to be fair, so had the students.

The system worked quite well and, as happens in such cases, had taken on the status of a tradition. Lectures clearly took place, because they were down there on the timetable in black and white. The fact that no one attended was an irrelevant detail. It was occasionally maintained that this meant that the lectures did not in fact happen at all, but no one ever attended them to find out if this was true. Anyway, it was argued (by the Reader in Woolly Thinking[*]) that lectures had taken place *in essence*, so that was all right, too.

And therefore education at the University mostly worked by the age-old method of putting a lot of young people in the vicinity of a lot of books and hoping that something would pass from one to the other, while the actual young people put themselves in the vicinity of inns and taverns for exactly the same reason.

It was the middle of the afternoon. The Chair of Indefinite Studies was giving a lecture in room 3B and therefore his presence asleep in front of the fire in the Uncommon Room was a technicality upon which no diplomatic man would comment.

Ridcully kicked him on the shins.

'Ow!'

'Sorry to interrupt, Chair,' said Ridcully, in a very perfunctory way. 'Gods help me, I need the Council of Wizards. Where is everybody?'

[*] Which is like Fuzzy Logic, only less so.

The Chair of Indefinite Studies rubbed his leg. 'I know the Lecturer in Recent Runes is giving a lecture in 3B,'* he said. 'But I don't know where he *is*. You know, that really hurt—'

'Round everyone up. My study. Ten minutes,' said Ridcully. He was a great believer in this approach. A less direct Archchancellor would have wandered around looking for everyone. His policy was to find one person and make their life difficult until everything happened the way he wanted it to.†

Nothing in nature had that many feet. True, some things had that many *legs* – damp, wriggling things that live under rocks – but those weren't legs with feet, they were just legs that ended without ceremony.

Something brighter than the shark might have been wary.

But '=' swung treacherously into play and shot it forward.

That was its first mistake.

In these circumstances, one mistake = oblivion.

Ridcully was waiting impatiently when, one by one, the senior wizards filed in from serious lecturing in room 3B. Senior wizards needed a lot of lecturing in order to digest their food.

'Everyone here?' he said. 'Right. Sit down. Listen carefully. Now . . . Vetinari hasn't had an albatross. It hasn't come all the way from the Counterweight Continent, and there isn't a strange message that we've got to obey, apparently. Follow me so far?'

The senior wizards exchanged glances.

'I think we may be a shade unclear on the detail,' said the Dean.

'I was using diplomatic language.'

'Could you, perhaps, try to be a little more indiscreet?'

'We've got to send a wizard to the Counterweight Continent,' said Ridcully. 'And we've got to do it by teatime. Someone's asked for a Great Wizard and it seems we've got to send one. Only they spell it Wizzard—'

'Oook?'

'Yes, Librarian?'

Unseen University's Librarian, who had been dozing with his head on the table, was suddenly sitting bolt upright. Then he

---

* All *virtual* lectures took place in room 3B, a room not locatable on any floor plan of the University and also, it was considered, infinite in size.
† A policy adopted by almost all managers and several notable gods.

pushed back his chair and, arms waving wildly for balance, left the room at a bow-legged run.

'Probably remembered an overdue book,' said the Dean. He lowered his voice. 'Am I alone in thinking, by the way, that it doesn't add to the status of this University to have an ape on the faculty?'

'Yes,' said Ridcully flatly. 'You are. We've got the only librarian who can rip off your arm with his leg. People respect that. Only the other day the head of the Thieves' Guild was asking me if we could turn *their* librarian into an ape and, besides, he's the only one of you buggers who stays awake more'n an hour a day. Anyway—'

'Well, I find it embarrassing,' said the Dean. 'Also, he's not a proper orang-utan. I've been reading a book. It says a dominant male should have huge cheek pads. Has he got huge cheek pads? I don't think so. And—'

'Shut up, Dean,' said Ridcully, 'or I won't let you go to the Counterweight Continent.'

'I don't see what raising a perfectly valid— What?'

'They're asking for the Great Wizzard,' said Ridcully. 'And I immediately thought of you.' As the only man I know who can sit on two chairs at the same time, he added silently.

'The Empire?' squeaked the Dean. 'Me? But they hate foreigners!'

'So do you. You should get on famously.'

'It's six thousand miles!' said the Dean, trying a new tack. 'Everyone knows you can't get that far by magic.'

'Er. As a matter of fact you can, I think,' said a voice from the other end of the table.

They all looked at Ponder Stibbons, the youngest and most depressingly keen member of the faculty. He was holding a complicated mechanism of sliding wooden bars and peering at the other wizards over the top of it.

'Er. Shouldn't be too much of a problem,' he added. 'People used to think it was, but I'm pretty sure it's all a matter of energy absorption and attention to relative velocities.'

The statement was followed with the kind of mystified and suspicious silence that generally succeeded one of his remarks.

'Relative velocities,' said Ridcully.

'Yes, Archchancellor.' Ponder looked down at his prototype slide rule and waited. He *knew* that Ridcully would feel it necessary to add a comment at this point in order to demonstrate that he'd grasped something.

'My mother could move like lightning when—'

'I mean how fast things are going when compared to other things,' Ponder said quickly, but not quite quickly enough. 'We should be able to work it out quite easily. Er. On Hex.'

'Oh, no,' said the Lecturer in Recent Runes, pushing his chair back. 'Not that. That's meddling with things you don't understand.'

'Well, we *are* wizards,' said Ridcully. 'We're supposed to meddle with things we don't understand. If we hung around waitin' till we understood things we'd never get anything done.'

'Look, I don't mind summoning some demon and asking it,' said the Lecturer in Recent Runes. 'That's normal. But building some mechanical contrivance to do your thinking for you, that's . . . against Nature. Besides,' he added in slightly less foreboding tones, 'last time you did a big problem on it the wretched thing broke and we had ants all over the place.'

'We've sorted that out,' said Ponder. 'We—'

'I must admit there was a ram's skull in the middle of it last time I looked,' said Ridcully.

'We had to add that to do occult transformations,' said Ponder, 'but—'

'And cogwheels and springs,' the Archchancellor went on.

'Well, the ants aren't very good at differential analysis, so—'

'And that strange wobbly thing with the cuckoo?'

'The unreal time clock,' said Ponder. 'Yes, we think that's essential for working out—'

'Anyway, it's all quite immaterial, because I certainly have no intention of going anywhere,' said the Dean. 'Send a student, if you must. We've got a lot of spare ones.'

'Good so be would you if, duff plum of helping second A,' said the Bursar.

The table fell silent.

'Anyone understand that?' said Ridcully.

The Bursar was not technically insane. He had passed through the rapids of insanity some time previously, and was now sculling around in some peaceful pool on the other side. He was often quite coherent, although not by normal human standards.

'Um, he's going through yesterday again,' said the Senior Wrangler. 'Backwards, this time.'

'We should send the Bursar,' said the Dean firmly.

'Certainly not! You probably can't get dried frog pills there—'

'Oook!'

The Librarian re-entered the study at a bandy-legged run, waving something in the air.

323

It was red, or at least had at some time been red. It might well once have been a pointy hat, but the point had crumpled and most of the brim was burned away. A word had been embroidered on it in sequins. Many had been burned off, but:

WIZZARD

. . . could just be made out as pale letters on the scorched cloth.

'I *knew* I'd seen it before,' said Ridcully. 'On a shelf in the Library, right?'

'Oook.'

The Archchancellor inspected the remnant.

'Wizzard?' he said. 'What kind of sad, hopeless person needs to write WIZZARD on their hat?'

A few bubbles broke the surface of the sea, causing the raft to rock a little. After a while, a couple of pieces of shark skin floated up.

Rincewind sighed and put down his fishing rod. The rest of the shark would be dragged ashore later, he knew it. He couldn't imagine why. It wasn't as if they were good eating. They tasted like old boots soaked in urine.

He picked up a makeshift oar and set out for the beach.

It wasn't a bad little island. Storms seemed to pass it by. So did ships. But there were coconuts, and breadfruit, and some sort of wild fig. Even his experiments in alcohol had been quite successful, although he hadn't been able to walk properly for two days. The lagoon provided prawns and shrimps and oysters and crabs and lobsters, and in the deep green water out beyond the reef big silver fish fought each other for the privilege of biting a piece of bent wire on the end of a bit of string. After six months on the island, in fact, there was only one thing Rincewind lacked. He'd never really thought about it before. Now he thought about it – or, more correctly, *them* – all the time.

It was odd. He'd hardly ever thought about them in Ankh-Morpork, because they were there if ever he wanted them. Now they weren't, and he *craved*.

His raft bumped the white sand at about the same moment as a large canoe rounded the reef and entered the lagoon.

Ridcully was sitting at his desk now, surrounded by his senior wizards. They were trying to tell him things, despite the known danger of trying to tell Ridcully things, which was that he picked up the facts he liked and let the others take a running jump.

'So,' he said, '*not* a kind of cheese.'

'*No*, Archchancellor,' said the Chair of Indefinite Studies. 'Rincewind is a kind of wizard.'

'Was,' said the Lecturer in Recent Runes.

'Not a cheese,' said Ridcully, unwilling to let go of a fact.

'No.'

'Sounds a sort of name you'd associate with cheese. I mean, a pound of Mature Rincewind, it rolls off the tongue . . .'

'*Godsdammit*, Rincewind is not a cheese!' shouted the Dean, his temper briefly cracking. 'Rincewind is not a yoghurt or any kind of sour milk derivative! Rincewind is a bloody nuisance! A complete and utter disgrace to wizardry! A fool! A failure! Anyway, he hasn't been seen here since that . . . unpleasantness with the Sourcerer, years ago.'

'Really?' said Ridcully, with a certain kind of nasty politeness. 'A lot of wizards behaved very badly then, I understand.'

'Yes indeed,' said the Lecturer in Recent Runes, scowling at the Dean, who bridled.

'I don't know anything about that, Runes. I wasn't Dean at the time.'

'No, but you were very senior.'

'Perhaps, but it just so happens that at the time I was visiting my aunt, for your information.'

'They nearly blew up the whole city!'

'She lives in Quirm.'

'*And* Quirm was heavily involved, as I recall.'

'—*near* Quirm. *Near* Quirm. Not all that near, actually. Quite a way along the coast—'

'Hah!'

'Anyway, *you* seem to be very well informed, eh, Runes?' said the Dean.

'I – What? – I – was studying hard at the time. Hardly knew what was going on—'

'Half the University was blown down!' The Dean remembered himself and added, 'That is, so I heard. Later. After getting back from my aunt's.'

'Yes, but I've got a very thick door—'

'And I happen to *know* the Senior Wrangler was here, because—'

'—with that heavy green baize stuff you can hardly hear any—'

'Nap my for time it's think I.'

'Will you all shut up right now this minute!'

Ridcully glared at his faculty with the clear, innocent glare of someone who was blessed at birth with no imagination whatsoever, and who had genuinely been hundreds of miles away during the University's recent embarrassing history.

'Right,' he said, when they had quietened down. 'This Rincewind. Bit of an idiot, yes? You talk, Dean. Everyone else will shut up.'

The Dean looked uncertain.

'Well, er . . . I mean, it makes no sense, Archchancellor. He couldn't even do proper magic. What good would he be to anyone? Besides . . . where Rincewind went' – he lowered his voice – *'trouble followed behind.'*

Ridcully noticed that the wizards drew a little closer together.

'Sounds all right to me,' he said. 'Best place for trouble, behind. You certainly don't want it in front.'

'You don't understand, Archchancellor,' said the Dean. 'It followed behind on hundreds of little legs.'

The Archchancellor's smile stayed where it was while the rest of his face went solid behind it.

'You been on the Bursar's pills, Dean?'

'I assure you, Mustrum—'

'Then don't talk rubbish.'

'Very *well*, Archchancellor. But you do realise, don't you, that it might take years to find him?'

'Er,' said Ponder, 'if we can work out his thaumic signature, I think Hex could probably do it in a day . . .'

The Dean glared.

'That's not magic!' he snapped. 'That's just . . . engineering!'

Rincewind trudged through the shallows and used a sharp rock to hack the top off a coconut that had been cooling in a convenient shady rock pool. He put it to his lips.

A shadow fell across him.

It said, 'Er, hello?'

It was possible, if you kept on talking at the Archchancellor for long enough, that some facts might squeeze through.

'So what you're *tellin'* me,' said Ridcully, eventually, 'is that this Rincewind fella has been chased by just about every army in the world, has been bounced around life like a pea on a drum, and probably is the one wizard who knows anything about the Agatean Empire on account of once being friends with,' he glanced at his notes, ' "a strange little man in glasses" who came from there and gave him this funny thing with the legs you all keep alluding to. And he can speak the lingo. Am I right so far?'

'Exactly, Archchancellor. Call me an idiot if you like,' said the Dean, 'but why would anyone want him?'

Ridcully looked down at his notes again. '*You've* decided to go, then?' he said.

'No, of course not—'

'What I don't think you've spotted here, Dean,' he said, breaking into a determinedly cheery grin, 'is what I might call the common denominator. Chap stays alive. Talented. Find him. And bring him here. Wherever he is. Poor chap could be facing something *dreadful.*'

The coconut stayed where it was, but Rincewind's eyes swivelled madly from side to side.

Three figures stepped into his line of vision. They were obviously female. They were *abundantly* female. They were not wearing a great deal of clothing and seemed to be altogether too fresh-from-the-hairdressers for people who have just been paddling a large war canoe, but this is often the case with beautiful Amazonian warriors.

A thin trickle of coconut milk began to dribble off the end of Rincewind's beard.

The leading woman brushed aside her long blonde hair and gave him a bright smile.

'I know this sounds a little unlikely,' she said, 'but I and my sisters here represent a hitherto undiscovered tribe whose menfolk were recently destroyed in a deadly but short-lived and highly specific plague. Now we have been searching these islands for a man to enable us to carry on our line.'

'*How much do you think he weighs?*'

Rincewind's eyebrows raised. The woman looked down shyly.

'You may be wondering why we are all blonde and white-skinned when everyone else in the islands around here is dark,' she said. 'It just seems to be one of those genetic things.'

'*About 120, 125 pounds. Put another pound or two of junk on the heap. Er. Can you detect . . . you know . . . IT?*'

'*This is all going to go wrong, Mr Stibbons, I just know it.*'

'*He's only six hundred miles away and we know where we are,*' and he's on the right half of the Disc. Anyway, I've worked this out on Hex so nothing can possibly go wrong.'

'Yes, but can anyone see . . . that . . . you know . . . with the . . . feet?'

Rincewind's eyebrows waggled. A sort of choking noise came from his throat.

''Can't see . . . it. Will you lot stop huffing on my crystal ball?'

'And, of course, if you were to come with us we could promise you . . . earthly and sensual pleasures such as those of which you may have dreamed . . .'

'All right. On the count of three—'

The coconut dropped away. Rincewind swallowed. There was a hungry, dreamy look in his eyes.

'Can I have them mashed?' he said.

'NOW!'

First there was the sensation of pressure. The world opened up in front of Rincewind and sucked him into it.

Then it stretched out thin and went *twang*.

Cloud rushed past him, blurred by speed. When he dared open his eyes again it was to see, far ahead of him, a tiny black dot.

It got bigger.

It resolved itself into a tight cloud of objects. There were a couple of heavy saucepans, a large brass candlestick, a few bricks, a chair and a large brass blancmange mould in the shape of a castle.

They hit him one after the other, the blancmange mould making a humorous clang as it bounced off his head, and then whirled away behind him.

The next thing ahead of him was an octagon. A chalked one.

He hit it.

Ridcully stared down.

'A shade less than 125 pounds, I fancy,' he said. 'All the same . . . well done, gentlemen.'

The dishevelled scarecrow in the centre of the circle staggered to its feet and beat out one or two small fires in its clothing. Then it looked around blearily and said, 'Hehehe?'

'He could be a little disorientated,' the Archchancellor went on. 'More than six hundred miles in two seconds, after all. Don't give him a nasty shock.'

'Like sleepwalkers, you mean?' said the Senior Wrangler.

'What do you mean, sleepwalkers?'

'If you wake sleepwalkers, their legs drop off. So my grandmother used to aver.'

'And are we *sure* it's Rincewind?' said the Dean.

'Of *course* it's Rincewind,' said the Senior Wrangler. 'We spent *hours* looking for him.'

'It could be some dangerous occult creature,' said the Dean stubbornly.

'With that hat?'

It was a pointy hat. In a way. A kind of cargo-cult pointy hat, made out of split bamboo and coconut leaves, in the hope of attracting passing wizardliness. Picked out on it, in seashells held in place with grass, was the word WIZZARD.

Its wearer gazed right through the wizards and, as if driven by some sudden recollection of purpose, lurched abruptly out of the octagon and headed towards the door of the hall.

The wizards followed cautiously.

'I'm not sure I believe her. How many times did she see it happen?'

'I don't know. She never said.'

'The Bursar sleepwalks most nights, you know.'

'Does he? Tempting . . .'

Rincewind, if that was the creature's name, headed out into Sator Square.

It was crowded. The air shimmered over the braziers of chestnut sellers and hot potato merchants and echoed with the traditional street cries of Old Ankh-Morpork.*

The figure sidled up to a skinny man in a huge overcoat who was frying something over a little oil-heater in a wide tray around his neck.

The possibly-Rincewind grabbed the edge of the tray.

'Got . . . any . . . potatoes?' it growled.

'Potatoes? No, squire. Got some sausages inna bun.'

The possibly-Rincewind froze. And then it burst into tears.

'Sausage inna b*uuunnnnn*!' it bawled. 'Dear old sausage inna inna inna b*uuunnn*! Gimme saussaaage inna b*uunnnnn*!'

It grabbed three off the tray and tried to eat them all at once.

'Good grief!' said Ridcully.

---

* Such as 'Ouch!', 'Aargh!', 'Give me back my money, you scoundrel!' and 'You call these chestnuts? I call them little balls of charcoal, that's what I call them!'

The figure half ran, half capered away, fragments of bun and pork-product debris cascading from its unkempt beard.

'I've never seen anyone eat three of Throat Dibbler's sausages inna bun and look so happy,' said the Senior Wrangler.

'*I've* never seen someone eat three of Throat Dibbler's sausages inna bun and look so upright,' said the Dean.

'I've never seen anyone eat anything of Dibbler's and get away without paying,' said the Lecturer in Recent Runes.

The figure spun happily around the square, tears streaming down its face. The gyrations took it past an alley mouth, whereupon a smaller figure stepped out behind it and with some difficulty hit it on the back of the head.

The sausage-eater fell to his knees, saying, to the world in general, 'Ow!'

'Nonononononono!'

A rather older man stepped out and removed the cosh from the young man's hesitant hands, while the victim knelt and moaned.

'I think you ought to apologize to the poor gentleman,' said the older man. 'I don't know, what's he going to think? I mean, look at him, he made it so easy for you and what does he get? I mean, what did you think you were doing?'

'Mumblemumble, Mr Boggis,' said the boy, looking at his feet.

'What was that again? Speak up!'

'Overarm Belter, Mr Boggis.'

'*That* was an Overarm Belter? You call that an Overarm Belter? That was an Overarm Belter, was it? *This* – excuse me, sir, we'll just have you up on your feet for a moment, sorry about this – *this* is an Overarm Belter—'

'Ow!' shouted the victim and then, to the surprise of all concerned, he added: 'Hahahaha!'

'What *you* did was – sorry to impose again, sir, this won't take a minute – what you did was *this*—'

'Ow! Hahahaha!'

'Now, you lot, you saw that? Come on, gather round . . .'

Half a dozen other youths slouched out of the alleyway and formed a ragged audience around Mr Boggis, the luckless student and the victim, who was staggering in a circle and making little 'oomph oomph' sounds but still, for some reason, apparently enjoying himself immensely.

'Now,' said Mr Boggis, with the air of an old skilled craftsman imparting his professional expertise to an ungrateful posterity, 'when inconveniencing a customer from your basic alley entrance, the correct procedure is— Oh, hello, Mr Ridcully, didn't see you there.'

The Archchancellor gave him a friendly nod.

'Don't mind us, Mr Boggis. Thieves' Guild training, is it?'

Boggis rolled his eyes.

'Dunno what they teaches 'em at school,' he said. 'It's jus' nothing but reading and writing all the time. When I was a lad school was where you learned somethin' *useful*. Right – you, Wilkins, stop that giggling, you have a go, excuse us just another moment, sir—'

'Ow!'

'*Nonononono!* My old granny could do better than that! Now *look*, you steps up trimly, places one hand on his shoulder here, for control . . . go on, you do it . . . and then smartly—'

'Ow!'

'All right, can anyone tell me what he was doing wrong?'

The figure crawled away unnoticed, except by the wizards, while Mr Boggis was demonstrating the finer points of head percussion on Wilkins.

It staggered to his feet and plunged on along the road, still moving like one hypnotized.

'He's crying,' said the Dean.

'Not surprising,' said the Archchancellor. 'But why's he grinnin' at the same time?'

'Curiouser and curiouser,' said the Senior Wrangler.

Bruised and possibly poisoned, the figure headed back for the University, the wizards still trailing behind.

'*You must mean "curious and more curious", surely? And even then it doesn't make much sense—*'

It entered the gates but, this time, hurried jerkily through the main hall and into the Library.

The Librarian was waiting, holding – with something of a smirk on his face, and an orang-utan can really smirk – the battered hat.

'Amazin',' said Ridcully. 'It's true! A wizard *will* always come back for his hat!'

The figure grabbed the hat, evicted some spiders, threw away the sad affair made of leaves and put the hat on his head.

Rincewind blinked at the puzzled faculty. A light came on behind his eyes for the first time, as if up to now he'd merely been operating by reflex action.

'Er. What have I just eaten?'

'Er. Three of Mr Dibbler's finest sausages,' said Ridcully. 'Well, when I say finest, I mean "most typical", don'tcheknow.'

'I see. And who just hit me?'

'Thieves' Guild apprentices out trainin'.'

Rincewind blinked. 'This is Ankh-Morpork, isn't it?'

'Yes.'

'I thought so.' Rincewind blinked, slowly. 'Well,' he said, just as he fell forward, 'I'm back.'

Lord Hong was flying a kite. It was something he did perfectly.

Lord Hong did everything perfectly. His watercolours were perfect. His poetry was perfect. When he folded paper, every crease was perfect. Imaginative, original, and definitely perfect. Lord Hong had long ago ceased pursuing perfection because he already had it nailed up in a dungeon somewhere.

Lord Hong was twenty-six, and thin, and handsome. He wore very small, very circular steel-rimmed spectacles. When asked to describe him, people often used the word 'smooth' or even 'lacquered'.* And he had risen to the leadership of one of the most influential families in the Empire by relentless application, total focusing of his mental powers, and six well-executed deaths. The last one had been that of his father, who'd died happy in the knowledge that his son was maintaining an old family tradition. The senior families venerated their ancestors, and saw no harm in prematurely adding to their number.

And now his kite, the black kite with the two big eyes, plunged out of the sky. He'd calculated the angle, needless to say, perfectly. Its string, coated with glue and ground glass, sawed through those of his fellow contestants and sent their kites tumbling.

There was genteel applause from the bystanders. People generally found it advisable to applaud Lord Hong.

He handed the string to a servant, nodded curtly at the fellow flyers, and strode towards his tent.

Once inside, he sat down and looked at his visitor. 'Well?' he said.

'We sent the message,' said the visitor. 'No one saw us.'

'On the contrary,' said Lord Hong. 'Twenty people saw you. Do you know how hard it is for a guard to look straight ahead and see nothing when people are creeping around making a noise like an army and whispering to one another to be quiet? Frankly, your

---

* And often the phrase 'a bastard you don't want to cross, and I didn't say that'.

332

people do not seem to possess that revolutionary spark. What is the matter with your hand?'

'The albatross bit it.'

Lord Hong smiled. It occurred to him that it might have mistaken his visitor for an anchovy, and with some justification. There was the same fishy look about the eyes.

'I don't understand, o lord,' said the visitor, whose name was Two Fire Herb.

'Good.'

'But they believe in the Great Wizzard and you *want* him to come here?'

'Oh, certainly. I have my . . . people in' – he tried the alien syllables – 'Ankh-More-Pork. The one so foolishly called the Great Wizzard *does* exist. But, I might tell you, he is renowned for being incompetent, cowardly and spineless. Quite proverbially so. So I think the Red Army should have their leader, don't you? It will . . . raise their morale.'

He smiled again. 'This is politics,' he said.

'Ah.'

'Now go.'

Lord Hong picked up a book as his visitor left. But it was hardly a real book; pieces of paper had simply been fastened together with string, and the text was handwritten.

He'd read it many times before. It still amused him, mainly because the author had managed to be wrong about so many things.

Now, every time he finished a page, he ripped it out and, while reading the next page, carefully folded the paper into the shape of a chrysanthemum.

'Great Wizard,' he said, aloud. 'Oh, indeed. Very great.'

Rincewind awoke. There were clean sheets and no one was saying 'Go through his pockets,' so he chalked that up as a promising beginning.

He kept his eyes shut, just in case there was anyone around who, once he was seen to be awake, would make life complicated for him.

Elderly male voices were arguing.

'You're all missin' the point. He survives. You keep on tellin' me he's had all these adventures and he's *still* alive.'

'What do you mean? He's got scars all over him!'

'My point exactly, Dean. Most of 'em on his back, too. He leaves trouble behind. Someone Up There smiles on him.'

Rincewind winced. He had always been aware that Someone Up There was doing *something* on him. He'd never considered it was smiling.

'He's not even a proper wizard! He never got more than two per cent in his exams!'

'I think he's awake,' said someone.

Rincewind gave in, and opened his eyes. A variety of bearded, overly pink faces looked down upon him.

'How're you feeling, old chap?' said one, extending a hand. 'Name's Ridcully. Archchancellor. How're you feeling?'

'It's all going to go wrong,' said Rincewind flatly.

'What d'you mean, old fellow?'

'I just know it. It's all going to go wrong. Something dreadful's going to happen. I thought it was too good to last.'

'You see?' said the Dean. 'Hundreds of little legs. I *told* you. Would you listen?'

Rincewind sat up. 'Don't start being nice to me,' he said. 'Don't start offering me grapes. No one ever wants me for something *nice*.' A confused memory of his very recent past floated across his mind and he experienced a brief moment of regret that potatoes, while uppermost in his mind at that point, had not been similarly positioned in the mind of the young lady. No one dressed like that, he was coming to realize, could be thinking of any kind of root vegetable.

He sighed. 'All right, what happens now?'

'How do you feel?'

Rincewind shook his head. 'It's no good,' he said. 'I hate it when people are nice to me. It means something bad is going to happen. Do you mind shouting?'

Ridcully had had enough. 'Get out of that bed you horrible little man and follow me this minute or it will go very hard for you!'

'Ah, that's better. I feel *right* at home now. *Now* we're cooking with charcoal,' said Rincewind, glumly. He swung his legs off the bed and stood up carefully.

Ridcully stopped halfway to the door, where the other wizards had lined up.

'Runes?'

'Yes, Archchancellor?' said the Lecturer in Recent Runes, his voice oozing innocence.

'What is that you've got behind your back?'

'Sorry, Archchancellor?' said the Lecturer in Recent Runes.

'Looks like some kind of tool,' said Ridcully.

'Oh, *this*,' said the Lecturer in Recent Runes, as if he'd only just at that moment noticed the eight-pound lump hammer he'd been holding. 'My word . . . it's a *hammer*, isn't it? My word. A hammer. I suppose I must just have . . . picked it up somewhere. You know. To keep the place tidy.'

'And I can't help noticing,' said Ridcully, 'that the Dean seems to be tryin' to conceal a battle-axe about his person.'

There was a musical twang from the rear of the Chair of Indefinite Studies.

'And that sounded like a saw to me,' said Ridcully. 'Is there anyone here not concealin' some kind of implement? Right. Would anyone care to explain what the hell you think you're doin'?'

'Hah, you don't know what it was like,' muttered the Dean, not meeting the Archchancellor's eye. 'A man daren't turn his back for five minutes in those days. You'd hear the patter of those damn feet and—'

Ridcully ignored him. He put an arm around Rincewind's bony shoulders and led the way towards the Great Hall.

'Well, now, Rincewind,' he said. 'They tell me you're no good at magic.'

'That's right.'

'Never passed any exams or anything?'

'None, I'm afraid.'

'But everyone calls you Rincewind the wizard.'

Rincewind looked at his feet. 'Well, I kind of worked here as sort of deputy Librarian—'

'—an ape's number two—' said the Dean.

'—and, you know, did odd jobs and things and kind of, you know, helped out—'

'*I say, did anyone notice that? An ape's number two? Rather clever, I thought.*'

'But you have never, in fact, actually been *entitled* to call yourself a wizard?' said Ridcully.

'Not technically, I suppose . . .'

'I *see*. That *is* a problem.'

'I've got this hat with the word "Wizzard" on it,' said Rincewind hopefully.

'Not a great help, I'm afraid. Hmm. This presents us with a bit of a difficulty, I'm afraid. Let me see . . . How long can you hold your breath?'

'*I* don't know. A couple of minutes. Is that important?'

'It is in the context of being nailed upside down to one of the supports of the Brass Bridge for two high tides and then being beheaded which, I'm afraid, is the statutory punishment for impersonating a wizard. I looked it up. No one was more sorry than me, I can tell you. But the Lore is the Lore.'

'Oh, no!'

'Sorry. No alternative. Otherwise we'd be knee-deep in people in pointy hats they'd no right to. It's a terrible shame. Can't do a thing. Wish I could. Hands tied. The statutes say you can only be a wizard by passing through the University in the normal way or by performing some great service of benefit to magic, and I'm afraid that—'

'Couldn't you just send me back to my island? I *liked* it there. It was dull!'

Ridcully shook his head sadly.

'No can do, I'm afraid. The offence has been committed over a period of many years. And since you haven't passed any exams or performed,' Ridcully raised his voice slightly, '*any service of great benefit to magic*, I'm afraid I shall have to instruct the bledlows* to fetch some rope and—'

'Er. I think I may have saved the world a couple of times,' said Rincewind. 'Does that help?'

'Did anyone from the University see you do it?'

'No, I don't think so.'

Ridcully shook his head. 'Probably doesn't count, then. It's a shame, because *if you had performed any service of great benefit to magic* then I'd be happy to let you keep that hat and, of course, something to wear it on.'

Rincewind looked crestfallen. Ridcully sighed, and had one last try.

'So,' he said, 'since it seems that you haven't actually passed your exams OR PERFORMED A SERVICE OF GREAT BENEFIT TO MAGIC, then—'

'I suppose . . . I could try to perform some great service?' said Rincewind, with the expression of one who knows that the light at the end of the tunnel is an oncoming train.

'Really? Hmm? Well, that's definitely a thought,' said Ridcully.

'What sort of services are they?'

'Oh, typically you'd be expected to, for the sake of example, go on a quest, or find the answer to some very ancient and important question— *What the hell is that thing with all the legs?*'

---

*The UU college porters. Renowned among the entire faculty for the hardness of their skulls, their obtuseness in the face of reasonable explanation, and their deeply held conviction that the whole place would collapse without them.

Rincewind didn't even bother to look round. The expression on Ridcully's face, as it stared over his shoulder, was quite familiar.

'Ah,' he said, 'I think I know that one.'

Magic isn't like maths. Like the Discworld itself, it follows common sense rather than logic. And nor is it like cookery. A cake's a cake. Mix the ingredients up right and cook them at the right temperature and a cake happens. No casserole requires moonbeams. No soufflé ever demanded to be mixed by a virgin.

Nevertheless, those afflicted with an enquiring turn of mind have often wondered whether there are *rules* of magic. There are more than five hundred known spells to secure the love of another person, and they range from messing around with fern seed at midnight to doing something rather unpleasant with a rhino horn at an unspecified time, but probably not just after a meal. Was it possible (the enquiring minds enquired) that an analysis of all these spells might reveal some small powerful common denominator, some meta-spell, some simple little equation which would achieve the required end far more simply, and incidentally come as a great relief to all rhinos?

To answer such questions Hex had been built, although Ponder Stibbons was a bit uneasy about the word 'built' in this context. He and a few keen students had put it together, certainly, but . . . well . . . sometimes he thought bits of it, strange though this sounded, *just turned up.*

For example, he was pretty sure no one had designed the Phase of the Moon Generator, but there it was, clearly a part of the whole thing. They *had* built the Unreal Time Clock, although no one seemed to have a very clear idea how it worked.

What he suspected they were dealing with was a specialized case of formative causation, always a risk in a place like Unseen University, where reality was stretched so thin and therefore blown by so many strange breezes. If that was so, then they weren't exactly designing something. They were just putting physical clothes on an idea that was already there, a shadow of something that had been waiting to exist.

He'd explained at length to the Faculty that Hex didn't *think.* It was obvious that it couldn't think. Part of it was clockwork. A lot of it was a giant ant farm (the interface, where the ants rode up and down on a little paternoster that turned a significant cogwheel was a little masterpiece, he thought) and the intricately controlled rushing of the ants through their maze of glass tubing was the most important part of the whole thing.

But a lot of it had just . . . accumulated, like the aquarium and wind chimes which now seemed to be essential. A mouse had built a nest in the middle of it all and had been allowed to become a fixture, since the thing stopped working when they took it out. Nothing in that assemblage could possibly think, except in fairly limited ways about cheese or sugar. Nevertheless . . . in the middle of the night, when Hex was working hard, and the tubes rustled with the toiling ants, and things suddenly went 'clonk' for no obvious reason, and the aquarium had been lowered on its davits so that the operator would have something to watch during the long hours . . . nevertheless, *then* a man might begin to speculate about what a brain was and what thought was and whether things that weren't alive could think and whether a brain was just a more complicated version of Hex (or, around 4 a.m., when bits of the clockwork reversed direction suddenly and the mice squeaked, a *less* complicated version of Hex) and wonder if the whole produced something not apparently inherent in the parts.

In short, Ponder was just a little bit worried.

He sat down at the keyboard. It was almost as big as the rest of Hex, to allow for the necessary levers and armatures. The various keys allowed little boards with holes in them to drop briefly into slots, forcing the ants into new paths.

It took him some time to compose the problem, but at last he braced one foot on the structure and tugged on the Enter lever.

The ants scurried on new paths. The clockwork started to move. A small mechanism which Ponder would be prepared to swear had not been there yesterday, but which looked like a device for measuring wind speed, began to spin.

After several minutes a number of blocks with occult symbols on them dropped into the output hopper.

'Thank you,' said Ponder, and then felt extremely silly for saying so.

There was a tension to the thing, a feeling of mute straining and striving towards some distant and incomprehensible goal. As a wizard, it was something that Ponder had only before encountered in acorns: a tiny soundless voice which said, yes, I am but a small, green, simple object - but I dream about forests.

Only the other day Adrian Turnipseed had typed in 'Why?' to see what happened. Some of the students had forecast that Hex would

338

go mad trying to work it out; Ponder had expected Hex to produce the message ?????, which it did with depressing frequency.

Instead, after some unusual activity among the ants, it had laboriously produced: 'Because.'

With everyone else watching from behind a hastily overturned desk, Turnipseed had volunteered: 'Why anything?'

The reply had finally turned up: 'Because Everything. ????? Eternal Domain Error. +++++ Redo From Start +++++.'

No one knew who Redo From Start was, or why he was sending messages. But there were no more funny questions. No one wanted to risk getting answers.

It was shortly afterwards that the thing like a broken umbrella with herrings on it appeared just behind the thing like a beachball that went 'parp' every fourteen minutes.

Of course, books of magic developed a certain . . . *personality*, derived from all that power in their pages. That's why it was unwise to go into the Library without a stick. And now Ponder had helped build an engine for studying magic. Wizards had always known that the act of observation changed the thing that was observed, and sometimes forgot that it also changed the observer too.

He was beginning to suspect that Hex was redesigning itself.

And he'd just said 'Thank you'. To a thing that looked like it had been made by a glassblower with hiccups.

He looked at the spell it had produced, hastily wrote it down and hurried out.

Hex clicked to itself in the now empty room. The thing that went 'parp' went parp. The Unreal Time Clock ticked sideways.

There was a rattle in the output slot.

'Dont mention it. ++?????++ Out of Cheese Error. Redo From Start.'

It was five minutes later.

'Fascinatin',' said Ridcully. 'Sapient pearwood, eh?' He knelt down in an effort to see underneath.

The Luggage backed away. It was used to terror, horror, fear and panic. It had seldom encountered interest before.

The Archchancellor stood up and brushed himself off.

'Ah,' he said, as a dwarfish figure approached. 'Here's the gardener with the stepladder. The Dean's in the chandelier, Modo.'

'I'm quite happy up here, I assure you,' said a voice from the ceiling regions. 'Perhaps someone would be kind enough to pass me up my tea?'

'And I was amazed the Senior Wrangler could ever *fit* in the sideboard,' said Ridcully. 'It's amazin' how a man can fold himself up.'

'I was just – just inspecting the silverware,' said a voice from the depths of a drawer.

The Luggage opened its lid. Several wizards jumped back hurriedly.

Ridcully examined the shark teeth stuck here and there in the woodwork.

'Kills sharks, you say?' he said.

'Oh, yes,' said Rincewind. 'Sometimes it drags them ashore and jumps up and down on them.'

Ridcully was impressed. Sapient pearwood was very rare in the countries between the Ramtops and the Circle Sea. There were probably no living trees left. A few wizards were lucky enough to have inherited staffs made out of it.

Economy of emotion was one of Ridcully's strong points. He had been impressed. He had been fascinated. He'd even, when the thing had landed in the middle of the wizards and caused the Dean's remarkable feat of vertical acceleration, been slightly aghast. But he hadn't been frightened, because he didn't have the imagination.

'My goodness,' said a wizard.

The Archchancellor looked up.

'Yes, Bursar?'

'It's this book the Dean loaned me, Mustrum. It's about apes.'

'Really.'

'It's most fascinating,' said the Bursar, who was on the median part of his mental cycle and therefore vaguely on the right planet even if insulated from it by five miles of mental cotton wool. 'It's true what he said. It says here that an adult male orang-utan doesn't grow the large flamboyant cheek pads unless he's the dominant male.'

'And that's fascinating, is it?'

'Well, yes, because he hasn't got 'em. I wonder why? He certainly dominates the Library, I should think.'

'Ah, yes,' said the Senior Wrangler, 'but he knows he's a wizard, too. So it's not as though he dominates the whole University.'

One by one, as the thought sank in, they grinned at the Archchancellor.

'Don't you look at my cheeks like that!' said Ridcully. 'I don't dominate anybody!'

340

'I was only—'

'So you can all shut up or there will be big trouble!'

'You should read it,' said the Bursar, still happily living in the valley of the dried frogs. 'It's amazing what you can learn.'

'What? Like . . . how to show your bottom to people?' said the Dean, from on high.

'No, Dean. That's baboons,' said the Senior Wrangler.

'I beg your pardon, I think you'll find it's gibbons,' said the Chair of Indefinite Studies.

'No, gibbons are the ones that hoot. It's baboons if you want to see bottoms.'

'Well, he's never shown *me* one,' said the Archchancellor.

'Hah, well, he wouldn't, would he?' said a voice from the chandelier. 'Not with you being dominant male and everything.'

'Two Chairs, you come down here this minute!'

'I seem to be entangled, Mustrum. A candle is giving me some difficulty.'

'Hah!'

Rincewind shook his head and wandered away. There had certainly been some changes around the place since he had been there and, if it came to it, he didn't know how long ago that had been . . .

He'd never *asked* for an exciting life. What he really liked, what he sought on every occasion, was boredom. The trouble was that boredom tended to explode in your face. Just when he thought he'd found it he'd be suddenly involved in what he supposed other people – thoughtless, feckless people – would call an adventure. And he'd be forced to visit many strange lands and meet exotic and colourful people, although not for very long because usually he'd be running. He'd seen the creation of the universe, although not from a good seat, and had visited Hell and the afterlife. He'd been captured, imprisoned, rescued, lost and marooned. Sometimes it had all happened on the same day.

Adventure! People talked about the idea as if it was something worthwhile, rather than a mess of bad food, no sleep and strange people inexplicably trying to stick pointed objects in bits of you.

The *root* problem, Rincewind had come to believe, was that he suffered from pre-emptive karma. If it even *looked* as though something nice was going to happen to him in the near future, something bad would happen right now. And it went on happening to him right through the part where the good stuff should be happening, so that he never actually experienced it. It was as if he always got the indigestion *before* the meal and felt so dreadful that he never actually managed to eat anything.

Somewhere in the world, he reasoned, there was someone who was on the other end of the see-saw, a kind of mirror Rincewind whose life was a succession of wonderful events. He hoped to meet him one day, preferably while holding some sort of weapon.

Now people were babbling about sending him to the Counterweight Continent. He'd heard that life was dull there. And Rincewind really craved dullness.

He'd really liked that island. He'd *enjoyed* Coconut Surprise. You cracked it open and, hey, there was coconut inside. That was the kind of surprise he liked.

He pushed open a door.

The place inside *had* been his room. It was a mess. There was a large and battered wardrobe, and that was about the end of it as far as proper furniture was concerned unless you wanted to broaden the term to include a wicker chair with no bottom and three legs and a mattress so full of the life that inhabits mattresses that it occasionally moved sluggishly around the floor, bumping into things. The rest of the room was a litter of objects dragged in from the street – old crates, bits of planking, sacks . . .

Rincewind felt a lump in his throat. They'd left his room just as it was.

He opened the wardrobe and rummaged through the moth-haunted darkness within, until his questing hand located—

—an ear—

—which was attached to a dwarf.

'Ow!'

'What,' said Rincewind, 'are you doing in my wardrobe?'

'Wardrobe? Er . . . Er . . . Isn't this the Magic Kingdom of Scrumptiousness?' said the dwarf, trying not to look guilty.

'No, and these shoes you're holding aren't the Golden Jewels of the Queen of the Fairies,' said Rincewind, snatching them out of the thief's hands. 'And *this* isn't the Wand of Invisibility and *these* aren't Giant Grumblenose's Wonderful Socks but *this* is my boot—'

'Ow!'

'And stay out!'

The dwarf ran for the door and paused, but only briefly, to shout: 'I've got a Thieves' Guild card! And you shouldn't hit dwarfs! That's speciesism!'

'Good,' said Rincewind, retrieving items of clothing.

He found another robe and put it on. Here and there moths had worked their lacemaking skills and most of the red colour had faded to shades of orange and brown, but to his relief it was a proper wizard's robe. It's hard to be an impressive magic-user with bare knees.

Gentle footsteps pattered to a halt behind him. He turned.

'Open.'

The Luggage obediently cracked its lid. In theory it should have been full of shark; in fact it was half full of coconuts. Rincewind turfed them out on to the floor and put the rest of the clothes inside.

'Shut.'

The lid slammed.

'Now go down to the kitchen and get some potatoes.'

The chest did a complicated, many-legged about-turn and trotted away. Rincewind followed it out and headed towards the Archchancellor's study. Behind him he could hear the wizards still arguing.

He'd become familiar with the study through long years at Unseen. Generally he was there to answer quite difficult questions, like 'How can *anyone* get a negative mark in Basic Firemaking?' He'd spent a lot of time staring at the fixtures while people harangued him.

There had been changes here, too. Gone were the alembics and bubbling flagons that were the traditional props of wizardry; Ridcully's study was dominated by a full-size snooker table, on which he'd piled papers until there was no room for any more and no sign of green felt. Ridcully assumed that anything people had time to write down couldn't be important.

The stuffed heads of a number of surprised animals stared down at him. From the antlers of one stag hung a pair of corroded boots Ridcully had won as a Rowing Brown for the University in his youth.*

There was a large model of the Discworld on four wooden elephants in a corner of the room. Rincewind was familiar with it. Every student was . . .

The Counterweight Continent was a blob. It was a *shaped* blob; a not very inviting comma shape. Sailors had brought back news of it. They'd said that at one point it broke into a pattern of large islands, stretching around the Disc to the even more mysterious island of

---

*Except during extreme flood conditions it is extremely difficult to make much progress on the Ankh, and the University rowing teams compete by running over the surface of the river. This is generally quite safe provided they don't stand in one place for very long and, of course, it eats the soles off their boots.

Bhangbhangduc and the completely mythical continent known only on the charts as 'XXXX'.

Not that many sailors went near the Counterweight Continent. The Agatean Empire was known to ignore a very small amount of smuggling; presumably Ankh-Morpork had some things it wanted. But there was nothing official; a boat might come back loaded with silk and rare wood and, these days, a few wild-eyed refugees, or it might come back with its captain riveted upside down to the mast, or it might not come back.

Rincewind had been very nearly everywhere, but the Counterweight Continent was an unknown land, or *terror incognita*. He couldn't imagine why they'd want any kind of wizard.

Rincewind sighed. He knew what he should do now.

He shouldn't even wait for the return of the Luggage from its argosy to the kitchens, from which the sound of yelling and something being repeatedly hit with a large brass preserving pan suggested it was going about his business.

He should just gather up what he could carry and get the hell out of here. He—

'Ah, Rincewind,' said the Archchancellor, who had an amazingly silent walk for such a large man. 'Keen to leave, I see.'

'Yes, indeed,' said Rincewind. 'Oh, yes. Very much so.'

The Red Army met in secret session. They opened their meeting by singing revolutionary songs and, since disobedience to authority did not come easily to the Agatean character, these had titles like 'Steady Progress And Limited Disobedience While Retaining Well-Formulated Good Manners'.

Then it was time for the news.

'The Great Wizard *will* come. We sent the message, at great personal risk.'

'How will we know when he arrives?'

'If he's the Great Wizard, we'll hear about it. And then—'

'Gently Push Over The Forces Of Repression!' they chorused.

Two Fire Herb looked at the rest of the cadre. 'Exactly,' he said. 'And then, comrades, we must strike at the very heart of the rottenness. We must storm the Winter Palace!'

There was silence from the cadre. Then someone said, 'Excuse me, Two Fire Herb, but it is June.'

'Then we can storm the Summer Palace!'

*

A similar session, although without singing and with rather older participants, was taking place in Unseen University, although one member of the College Council had refused to come down from the chandelier. This was of some considerable annoyance to the Librarian, who usually occupied it.

'All right, if you don't trust my calculations, then what are the alternatives?' said Ponder Stibbons hotly.

'Boat?' said the Chair of Indefinite Studies.

'They sink,' said Rincewind.

'It'd get you there in no time at all,' said the Senior Wrangler. 'We're wizards, after all. We could give you your own bag of wind.'

'Ah. Forward the Dean,' said Ridcully, pleasantly.

'I heard that,' said a voice from above.

'Overland,' said the Lecturer in Recent Runes. 'Up around the Hub? It's ice practically all the way.'

'No,' said Rincewind.

'But you don't sink on ice.'

'No. You tip up and *then* you sink and *then* the ice hits you on the head. Also killer whales. And great big seals vif teece ike iff.'

'This is off the wall, I know,' said the Bursar, brightly.

'What is?' said the Lecturer in Recent Runes.

'A hook for hanging pictures on.'

There was a brief embarrassed silence.

'Good lord, is it that time already?' said the Archchancellor, taking out his watch. 'Ah, so it is. The bottle's in your left-hand pocket, old chap. Take three.'

'No, magic is the only way,' said Ponder Stibbons. 'It worked when we brought him here, didn't it?'

'Oh, yes,' said Rincewind. 'Just send me thousands of miles with my pants on fire and you don't even know where I'll land? Oh, yes, that's ideal, that is.'

'Good,' said Ridcully, a man impervious to sarcasm. 'It's a big continent; we can't possibly miss it even with Mr Stibbons' precise calculations.'

'Supposing I end up crushed in the middle of a mountain?' said Rincewind.

'Can't. The rock'll be brought back here when we do the spell,' said Ponder, who hadn't liked the crack about his maths.

'So I'll still be in the middle of a mountain but in a me-shaped hole,' said Rincewind. 'Oh, good. Instant fossil.'

'Don't *worry*,' said Ridcully. 'It's just a matter of . . . thingummy, you know, all that stuff about three right angles making a triangle . . .'

'Is it possible you're talking about geometry?' said Rincewind, eyeing the door.

'That kind of thing, yes. And you'll have your amazing Luggage item. Why, it'll practically be a holiday. It'll be easy. They probably just want to . . . to . . . ask you something, or something. And I hear you've got a talent for languages, so no problem there.[*] You'll probably be away for a couple of hours at the most. Why do you keep sayin' "hah"[†] under your breath?'

'Was I?'

'And everyone will be so grateful if you come back.'

Rincewind looked around – and, in one case, up – at the Council.

'How *will* I get back?' he said.

'Same way you went. We'll find you and bring you out. With surgical precision.'

Rincewind groaned. He knew what surgical precision meant in Ankh-Morpork. It meant 'to within an inch or two, accompanied by a lot of screaming, and then they pour hot tar on you just where your leg was'.

But . . . if you put aside for the moment the certainty that something would definitely go horribly wrong, it looked foolproof. The trouble was that wizards were such ingenious fools.

'And then I can have my old job back?'

'Certainly.'

'And officially call myself a wizard?'

'Of course. With any kind of spelling.'

'And never have to go anywhere again as long as I live?'

'Fine. We'll actually ban you leaving the premises, if you like.'

'And a new hat?'

'What?'

'A new hat. This one's practically had it.'

'Two new hats.'

'Sequins?'

'Of course. And those, you know, like glass chandelier things?

---

[*] This at least was true. Rincewind could scream for mercy in nineteen languages, and just scream in another forty-four.

[†] This is important. Inexperienced travellers might think that 'Aargh!' is universal, but in Betrobi it means 'highly enjoyable' and in Howondaland it means, variously, 'I would like to eat your foot', 'Your wife is a big hippo' and 'Hello, Thinks Mr Purple Cat.' One particular tribe has a fearsome reputation for cruelty merely because prisoners appear, to them, to be shouting 'Quick! Extra boiling oil!'

Lots of those all round the brim. As many as you like. And we'll spell Wizzzard with three Zs.'

Rincewind sighed. 'Oh, all right. I'll do it.'

Ponder's genius found itself rather cramped when it came to explaining things to people. And this was the case now, as the wizards forgathered to kick some serious magic.

'Yes, but you see, Archchancellor, he's being sent to the opposite side of the Disc, you see—'

Ridcully sighed. 'It's *spinnin'* isn't it,' he said. 'We're all going the same way. It stands to reason. If people're going the other way just because they're on the Counterweight Continent we'd crash into them once a year. I mean twice.'

'Yes, yes, they're *spinning* the same way, of course, but the direction of motion is entirely opposite. I mean,' said Ponder, lapsing into logic, 'you have to think about vectors, you, you have to ask yourself: what direction would they go in if the Disc wasn't here?'

The wizards stared at him.

'Down,' said Ridcully.

'No, no, *no*, Archchancellor,' said Ponder. 'They wouldn't go down because there'd be nothing to pull them down, they—'

'You don't need anything to *pull* you down. Down's where you go if there's nothing to keep you up.'

'They'd keep on going in the same direction!' shouted Ponder.

'Right. Round and round,' said Ridcully. He rubbed his hands together. 'You've got to maintain a grip if you want to be a wizard, lad. How're we doing, Runes?'

'I . . . I can make out something,' said the Lecturer in Recent Runes, squinting into the crystal ball. 'There's a *lot* of interference . . .'

The wizards gathered round. White specks filled the crystal. There *were* vague shapes just visible in the mush. Some of them could be human.

'Very peaceful place, the Agatean Empire,' said Ridcully. 'Very tranquil. Very cultured. They set great store in politeness.'

'Well, yes,' said the Lecturer in Recent Runes, 'I heard it was because people who *aren't* tranquil and quiet get serious bits cut off, don't they? I heard the Empire has a tyrannical and repressive government!'

'What form of government is that?' said Ponder Stibbons.

'A tautology,' said the Dean, from above.

'How serious are these bits?' said Rincewind. They ignored him.

'I heard that gold's very common there.' said the Dean. 'Lying around like dirt, they say. Rincewind could bring back a sackful.'

'I'd rather bring back all my bits,' said Rincewind.

After all, he thought, I'm only the one who's going to end up in the middle of it all. So please don't anyone bother to listen to me.

'Can't you stop it blurring like that?' said the Archchancellor.

'I'm sorry, Archchancellor—'

'These bits . . . big bits or small bits?' said Rincewind, unheard.

'Just find us an open space with something about the right size and weight.'

'It's very hard to—'

'Very serious bits? Are we in arms and legs territory here?'

'They say it's very boring there. Their biggest curse is "May you live in interesting times", apparently.'

'There's a thing . . . it's very blurry. Looks like a wheelbarrow or something. Quite small, I think.'

'—or toes, ears, that kind of thing?'

'Good, let's get started,' said Ridcully.

'Er, I think it'll help if he's a bit heavier than the thing we move here,' said Ponder. 'He won't arrive at any speed, then. I think—'

'Yes, yes, thank you very much, Mister Stibbons, now get in the circle and let us see that staff crackle, there's a good chap.'

'Fingernails? Hair?'

Rincewind tugged at the robe of Ponder Stibbons, who seemed slightly more sensible than the others.

'Er. What's my next move here?' he said.

'Um. About six thousand miles, I hope,' said Ponder Stibbons.

'But . . . I mean . . . Have you got any advice?'

Ponder wondered how to put things. He thought: I've done my best with Hex, but the actual business will be undertaken by a bunch of wizards whose idea of experimental procedure is to throw it and then sit down and argue about where it's going to land. We want to change your position with that of something six thousand miles away which, whatever the Archchancellor says, is heading through space in a quite different direction. The key is *precision*. It's no good using any old travelling spell. It'd come apart halfway, and so would you. I'm pretty sure that we'll get you there in one or, at worst, two pieces. But we've no way of knowing the weight of the thing we change you with. If it's pretty much the same weight as you, then it might just all work out provided you don't mind jogging on the spot when you land. But if it's a *lot* heavier than you, then my suspicion is that you'll appear over there travelling at the sort of speed normally only experienced by sleep-walkers in clifftop villages in a very terminal way.

'Er,' he said. 'Be afraid. Be very afraid.'

'Oh, *that*,' said Rincewind. 'No problem there. I'm good at that.'

'We're going to try to put you in the centre of the continent, where Hunghung is believed to be,' said Ponder.

'The capital city?'

'Yes. Er.' Ponder felt guilty. 'Look, whatever happens I'm sure you'll get there alive, which is more than would happen if it'd just been left to them. And I'm *pretty* sure you'll end up on the right continent.'

'Oh, good.'

'Come *along*, Mr Stibbons. We're all agog to hear how you wish us to do this,' said Ridcully.

'Ah, er, yes. Right. Now, you, Mr Rincewind, if you will go and stand in the centre of the octagon . . . thank you. Um. You see, gentlemen, what has always been the problem with teleporting over large distances is Heisenberg's Uncertainty Principle,* since the object teleported, that's from *tele*, "I see", and *porte*, "to go", the whole meaning "I see it's gone", er, the object teleported, er, no matter how large, is reduced to a thaumic particle and is therefore the subject of an eventually fatal dichotomy: it can either know what it is or where it is going, but not both. Er, the tension this creates in the morphic field eventually causes it to disintegrate, leaving the subject as a randomly shaped object, er, smeared across up to eleven dimensions. But I'm sure you all know this.'

There was a snore from the Chair of Indefinite Studies, who was suddenly giving a lecture in room 3B.

Rincewind was grinning. At least, his mouth had gaped open and his teeth were showing.

'Er, excuse me,' he said. 'I don't remember anyone saying anything about being sm—'

'Of course,' said Ponder, 'the subject would not, er, actually experience this—'

'Oh.'

'—as far as we know—'

'What?'

---

* Named after the wizard Sangrit Heisenberg and not after the more famous Heisenberg who is renowned for inventing what is *possibly* the finest lager in the world.

'—although it is theoretically possible for the psyche to remain present—'

'Eh?'

'—to briefly witness the explosive discorporation.'

'Hey?'

'Now, we're all familiar with the use of the spell as a fulcrum, er, so that one does not actually move *one* object but simply exchanges the position of two objects of similar mass. It is my aim tonight, er, to demonstrate that by imparting exactly the right amount of spin and the maximum velocity to the object—'

'Me?'

'—from the very first moment, it is virtually certain—'

'Virtually?'

'—to hold together for distances of up to, er, six thousand miles—'

'*Up to?*'

'—give or take ten per cent—'

'*Give or take?*'

'So if you'd – excuse me, Dean, I'd be obliged if you'd stop dripping wax – if you'd all take up the positions I've marked on the floor . . .'

Rincewind looked longingly towards the door. It was no distance at all for the experienced coward. He could just trot out of here and they could . . . they could . . . What could they do? They could just take his hat away and stop him ever coming back to the University. Now he came to think about it, they probably wouldn't be bothered about the nailing bit if he was too much bother to find.

And that was the problem. He wouldn't be dead, but then neither would he be a wizard. And, he thought, as the wizards shuffled into position and screwed down the knobs on the end of their staffs, not being able to think of himself as a wizard *was* being dead.

The spell began.

Rincewind the shoemaker? Rincewind the beggar? Rincewind the thief? Just about everything apart from Rincewind the corpse demanded training or aptitudes that he didn't have.

He was no good at anything else. Wizardry was the only refuge. Well, actually he was no good at wizardry either, but at least he was *definitively* no good at it. He'd always felt he had a right to exist as a wizard in the same way that you couldn't do proper maths without the number 0, which wasn't a number at all but, if it went away, would leave a lot of larger numbers looking bloody stupid. It was a vaguely noble thought that had kept him warm during those occasional 3 a.m. awakenings when he had evaluated his life and found it weighed a little less than a puff of warm hydrogen. And he probably *had* saved the world a few times, but it had generally happened accidentally, while he was trying to do something else. So you almost certainly didn't actually get any karmic points for that. It probably only counted if you started out by thinking in a loud way 'By criminy, it's jolly well time to save the world, and no two ways about it!' instead of 'Oh shit, this time I'm *really* going to die.'

The spell continued.

It didn't seem to be going very well.

'Come on, you chaps,' said Ridcully. 'Put some backbone into it!'

'Are you sure . . . it's . . . just something small?' said the Dean, who'd broken into a sweat.

'Looks like a . . . wheelbarrow . . .' muttered the Lecturer in Recent Runes.

The knob on the end of Ridcully's staff began to smoke.

'Will you look at the magic I'm using!' he said. 'What's goin' on, Mr Stibbons?'

'Er. Of course, size isn't the same as mass . . .'

And then, in the same way that it can take considerable effort to push at a sticking door and no effort at all to fall full length into the room beyond, the spell caught.

Ponder hoped, afterwards, that what he saw was an optical illusion. Certainly no one normally was suddenly stretched to about twelve feet tall and then snapped back into shape so fast that their boots ended up under their chin.

There was a brief cry of 'Oooooohhhhshhhhhh—' which ended abruptly, and this was probably just as well.

The first thing that struck Rincewind when he appeared on the Counter-weight Continent was a cold sensation.

The next things, in order of the direction of travel, were: a surprised man with a sword, another man with a sword, a third man who'd dropped *his* sword and was trying to run away, two other men who were less alert and didn't even see him, a small tree, about fifty yards of stunted undergrowth, a snowdrift, a bigger snowdrift, a few rocks, and one more and quite final snowdrift.

Ridcully looked at Ponder Stibbons.

'Well, he's gone,' he said. 'But aren't we supposed to get something back?'

'I'm not sure the transit time is instantaneous,' said Ponder.

'You've got to allow for zooming-through-the-occult-dimensions time?'

'Something like that. According to Hex, we might have to wait several—'

Something appeared in the octagon with a 'pop', exactly where Rincewind had been, and rolled a few inches.

It did, at least, have four small wheels such as might carry a cart. But these weren't workmanlike wheels; these were mere discs such as may be put on something heavy for those rare occasions it needs to be moved.

Above the wheels things became rather more interesting.

There was a large round cylinder, like a barrel on its side. A considerable amount of effort had been put into its construction; large amounts of brass had gone into making it look like a very large, fat dog with its mouth open. A minor feature was a length of string, which was smoking and hissing because it was on fire.

It didn't do anything dangerous. It just sat there, while the smouldering string slowly got shorter.

The wizards gathered round.

'Looks pretty heavy,' said the Lecturer in Recent Runes.

'A statue of a dog with a big mouth,' said the Chair of Indefinite Studies. 'That's rather dull.'

'Bit of a lap-dog, too,' said Ridcully.

'Lot of work gone into it,' said the Dean. 'Can't imagine why any-one'd want to set fire to it.'

Ridcully poked his head into the wide tube.

'Some kind of big round ball in here,' he said, his voice echoing a little. 'Someone pass me a staff or something. I'll see if I can wiggle it out.'

Ponder was staring at the fizzing string.

'Er,' he said, 'I . . . er . . . think we should all just step away from it, Archchancellor. Er. We should all just step back, yes, step back a little way. Er.'

'Hah, yes, really? So much for research,' said Ridcully. 'You don't mind messing around with cogwheels and ants but when it comes to really trying to find out how things work and—'

'Getting your hands dirty,' said the Lecturer in Recent Runes.

'Yes, getting your hands dirty, you come over all shy.'

'It's not that, Archchancellor,' said Ponder. 'But I believe it may be dangerous.'

352

'I think I'm working it loose,' said Ridcully, poking in the depths of the tube. 'Come on, you fellows, tip the thing up a bit . . .'

Ponder took a few more steps back. 'Er, I really don't think—' he began.

'Don't think, eh? Call yourself a wizard and you don't think? Blast! I've got my staff wedged now! That's what comes of listening to you when I should have been paying attention, Mr Stibbons.'

Ponder heard a scuffling behind him. The Librarian, with an animal's instinct for danger and a human's instinct for trouble, had upturned a table and was peering over the top of it with a small cauldron on his head, the handle under one of his chins like a strap.

'Archchancellor, I really *do* think—'

'Oh, you think, do you? Did anyone tell you it's your job to think? Ow! It's got my fingers now, thanks to you!'

It needed all Ponder's courage to say, 'I think . . . it might perhaps be some kind of firework, sir.'

The wizards turned their attention to the fizzling string.

'What . . . coloured lights, stars, that sort of thing?' said Ridcully.

'Possibly, sir.'

'Must be planning a hell of a display. Apparently they're very keen on firecrackers, over in the Empire.' Ridcully spoke in the tone of voice of a man over whom the thought is slowly stealing that he just might have done something very silly.

'Would you like me to extinguish the string, sir?' said Ponder.

'Yes, dear boy, why not? Good idea. Good thinking, that man.'

Ponder stepped forward and pinched the string.

'I do hope we haven't ruined something,' he said.

Rincewind opened his eyes.

This was *not* cool sheets. It was white, and it was cold, but it lacked basic sheetness. It made up for this by having vast amounts of snowosity.

And a groove. A *long* groove.

Let's see now . . . He could remember the sensation of movement. And he vaguely remembered something small but incredibly *heavy*-looking roaring past in the opposite direction. And then he was here, moving so fast that his feet left this . . .

. . . groove. Yes, groove, he thought, in the easy-going way of the mildly concussed. With people lying around it groaning.

But they looked like people who, once they'd stopped crawling around groaning, were going to draw the swords they had about their persons and pay detailed attention to serious bits.

He stood up, a little shakily. There didn't seem to be anywhere to run to. There was just this wide, snowy waste with a border of mountains.

The soldiers were definitely looking a lot more conscious. Rincewind sighed. A few hours ago he'd been sitting on a warm beach with young women about to offer him potatoes,[*] and here he was on a windswept, chilly plain with some large men about to offer him violence.

The soles of his shoes, he noticed, were steaming.

And then someone said, 'Hey! Are you . . . you're not, are you . . . are you . . . whatsyername . . . Rincewind, isn't it?'

Rincewind turned.

There was a very old man behind him. Despite the bitter wind he was wearing nothing except a leather loincloth and a grubby beard so long that the loincloth wasn't really necessary, at least from the point of view of decency. His legs were blue from the cold and his nose was red from the wind, giving him overall quite a patriotic look if you were from the right country. He had a patch over one eye but rather more notable than that were his teeth. They glittered.

'Don't stand there gawping like a big gawper! Get these damn things off me!'

There were heavy shackles around his ankles and wrists; a chain led to a group of more or less similarly clad men who were huddling in a crowd and watching Rincewind in terror.

'Heh! They think you're some kind of demon,' cackled the old man. 'But I knows a wizard when I sees one! That bastard over there's got the keys. Go and give him a good kicking.'

Rincewind took a few hesitant steps towards a recumbent guard and snatched at his belt. 'Right,' said the old man, 'now chuck 'em over here. And then get out of the way.'

'Why?'

''Cos you don't want to get blood all over you.'

'But you haven't got a weapon and there's one of you and they've got big swords and there's five of them!'

'I know,' said the old man, wrapping the chain around one of his fists in a businesslike manner. 'It's unfair, but I can't wait around all day.'

He grinned.

---

[*] There was still a certain amount of confusion on this point.

Gems glittered in the morning light. Every tooth in the man's head was a diamond. And Rincewind knew of only one man who had the nerve to wear troll teeth.

'Here? Cohen the Barbarian?'

'Ssh! Ingconitar! Now get out of the way, I said.' The teeth flashed at the guards, who were now vertical. 'Come on, boys. There's five of you, after all. An' I'm an old man. Mumble, mumble, oo me leg, ekcetra . . .'

To their credit, the guards hesitated. It was probably not, to judge from their faces, because there's something reprehensible about five large, heavily be-weaponed men attacking a frail old man. It might have been because there's something odd about a frail old man who keeps on grinning in the face of obvious oblivion.

'Oh, come *on*,' said Cohen. The men edged closer, each waiting for one of the others to make the first move.

Cohen took a few steps forward, waving his arms wearily. 'Oh, *no*,' he said. 'It makes me ashamed, honestly it does. This is *not* how you attack someone, all milling around like a lot of millers; when you attack someone the important thing to remember is the element of . . . *surprise—*'

Ten seconds later he turned to Rincewind.

'All right, Mister Wizard. You can open your eyes now.'

One guard was upside down in a tree, one was a pair of feet sticking out of a snowdrift, two were slumped against rocks, and one was . . . generally around the place. Here and there. Certainly hanging out.

Cohen sucked his wrist thoughtfully.

'I reckon that last one came within an inch of getting me,' he said. 'I must be getting old.'

'Why are you h—' Rincewind paused. One packet of curiosity over-took the first one. 'How old *are* you, exactly?'

'Is this still the Century of the Fruitbat?'

'Yes.'

'Oh, I dunno. Ninety? Could be ninety. Maybe ninety-five?' Cohen fished the keys out of the snow and ambled over to the group of men, who were cowering even more. He unlocked the first set of manacles and handed the shocked prisoner the keys.

'Bugger off, the lot of you,' he said, not unkindly. 'And don't get caught again.'

He strolled back to Rincewind.

'What brings you into this dump, then?'

'Well—'

'Interestin',' said Cohen, and that was that. 'But can't stay chatting all day, got work to do. You coming, or what?'

'What?'

'Please yourself.' Cohen tied the chain around his waist as a make-shift belt and wedged a couple of swords in it.

'Incidentally,' he said, 'what did you do with the Barking Dog?'

'What dog?'

'I expect it doesn't matter.'

Rincewind scuttled after the retreating figure. It wasn't that he felt safe when Cohen the Barbarian was around. *No one* was safe when Cohen the Barbarian was around. Something seemed to have gone wrong with the ageing process there. Cohen had always been a barbarian hero because barbaric heroing was all he knew how to do. And while he got old he seemed to get harder, like oak.

But he was a known figure, and therefore comforting. He just wasn't in the right place.

'No future in it, back around the Ramtops,' said Cohen, as they trudged through the snow. 'Fences and farms, fences and farms *everywhere*. You kill a dragon these days, people *complain*. You know what? You know what happened?'

'No. What happened?'

'Man came up to me, said my teeth were offensive to trolls. What about that, eh?'

'Well, they *are* made of—'

'I said they never complained to *me*.'

'Er, did you ever give them a cha—'

'I said, I see a troll up in the mountains with a necklace o' human skulls, I say good luck to him. Silicon Anti-Defamation League, my bottom. It's the same all over. So I thought I'd try my luck the other side of the icecap.'

'Isn't it dangerous, going around the Hub?' said Rincewind.

'Used to be,' said Cohen, grinning horribly.

'Until you left, you mean?'

''S right. You still got that box on legs?'

'On and off. It hangs around. You know.'

Cohen chuckled.

'I'll get the bloody lid off that thing one day, mark my words. Ah. Horses.'

There were five, looking depressed in a small depression.

Rincewind looked back at the freed prisoners, who seemed to be milling around aimlessly.

'We're not taking all five horses, are we?' he said.

356

'Sure. We might need 'em.'

'But . . . one for me, one for you . . . What's the rest for?'

'Lunch, dinner and breakfast?'

'It's a little . . . unfair, isn't it? Those people look a bit . . . bewildered.'

Cohen sneered the sneer of a man who has never been truly imprisoned even when he's been locked up.

'I freed 'em,' he said. 'First time they've ever been free. Comes as a bit of a shock, I expect. They're waiting for someone to tell 'em what to do next.'

'Er . . .'

'I could tell 'em to starve to death, if you like.'

'Er . . .'

'Oh, all *right*. You lot! Formee uppee right now toot sweet chop chop!'

The small crowd hurried over to Cohen and stood expectantly behind his horse.

'I tell you, I don't regret it. This is the land of opportunity,' said Cohen, urging the horse into a trot. The embarrassed free men jogged behind. 'Know what? Swords are banned. No one except the army, the nobles and the Imperial Guard are allowed to own weapons. Couldn't believe it! Gods' own truth, though. Swords are outlawed, so only outlaws have swords. And *that*,' said Cohen, giving the landscape another glittering grin, 'suits me fine.'

'But . . . you were in chains . . .' Rincewind ventured.

'Glad you reminded me,' said Cohen. 'Yeah. We'll find the rest of the lads, then I'd better try and find who did it and talk to them about that.'

The tone of his voice suggested very clearly that all they were likely to say would be, 'Highly enjoyable! Your wife is a big hippo!'

'Lads?'

'No future in one-man barbarianing,' said Cohen. 'Got myself a . . . Well, you'll see.'

Rincewind turned to look at the trailing party, and at the snow, and at Cohen.

'Er. Do you know where Hunghung is?'

'Yeah. It's the boss city. We're on our way. Sort of. It's under siege right now.'

'Siege? You mean like . . . lots of armies outside, everyone inside eating rats, that sort of thing?'

'Yeah, but this is the Counterweight Continent, see, so it's a polite siege. Well, I call it a siege . . . The old Emperor's dying, so the big families are all waiting to move in. That's how it goes in these parts. There's five different top nobs and they're all watching one another, and no one's going to be the first to move. You've got to think sideways to understand anything in this place.'

'Cohen?'

'Yes, lad?'

'What the hell's going on?'

Lord Hong was watching the tea ceremony. It took three hours, but you couldn't hurry a good cuppa.

He was also playing chess, against himself. It was the only way he could find an opponent of his calibre but, currently, things were stalemated because both sides were adopting a defensive strategy which was, admittedly, brilliant.

Lord Hong sometimes wished he could have an enemy as clever as himself. Or, because Lord Hong was indeed very clever, he sometimes wished for an enemy *almost* as clever as himself, one perhaps given to flights of strategic genius with nevertheless the occasional fatal flaw. As it was, people were so *stupid*. They seldom thought more than a dozen moves ahead.

Assassination was meat and drink to the Hunghung court; in fact, meat and drink were often the means. It was a game that everyone played. It was just another kind of move. It was not considered good manners to assassinate the Emperor, of course. The correct move was to put the Emperor in a position where you had control. But moves at this level were very dangerous; happy as the warlords were to squabble amongst themselves, they could be relied upon to unite against any who looked in danger of rising above the herd. And Lord Hong had risen like bread, by making everyone else believe that, while *they* were the obvious candidate for the Emperorship, Lord Hong would be better than any of the alternatives.

It amused him to know that they thought he was plotting for the Imperial pearl . . .

He glanced up from the board and caught the eye of the young woman who was busy at the tea table. She blushed and looked away.

The door slid back. One of his men entered, on his knees.

'Yes?' said Lord Hong.

'Er . . . O lord . . .'

Lord Hong sighed. People seldom began like this when the news was good.

'What happened?' he said.

'The one they call the Great Wizard arrived, o lord. Up in the mountains. Riding on a dragon of wind. Or so they say,' the messenger added quickly, aware of Lord Hong's views about superstition.

'Good. But? I assume there is a but.'

'Er . . . one of the Barking Dogs has been lost. The new batch? That you commanded should be tested? We don't quite . . . that is to say . . . we think Captain Three High Trees was ambushed, perhaps . . . our information is somewhat confused . . . the, um, the informant says the Great Wizard magicked it away . . .' The messenger crouched lower.

Lord Hong merely sighed again. Magic. It had fallen out of favour in the Empire, except for the most mundane purposes. It was *uncultured*. It put power in the hands of people who couldn't write a decent poem to save their lives, and sometimes hadn't.

He believed in coincidence a lot more than he did in magic.

'This is most vexing,' said Lord Hong.

He stood up and took his sword off the rack. It was long and curved and had been made by the finest sword-maker in the Empire, who was Lord Hong. He'd heard it took twenty years to learn the art, so he had stretched himself a little. It had taken him three weeks. People never *concentrated*, that was their trouble . . .

The messenger grovelled.

'The officer concerned has been executed?' he said.

The messenger tried to scrabble through the floor and decided to let truth stand in for honesty.

'Yes!' he piped.

Lord Hong swung. There was a hiss like the fall of silk, a thump and clatter as of a coconut hitting the ground, and the tinkle of crockery.

The messenger opened his eyes. He concentrated on his neck region, fearful that the slightest movement might leave him a good deal shorter. There were dire stories about Lord Hong's swords.

'Oh, do get up,' said Lord Hong. He wiped the blade carefully and replaced the sword. Then he reached across and pulled a small black bottle from the robe of the tea girl.

Uncorked, it produced a few drops that hissed when they hit the floor.

'Really,' said Lord Hong. 'I wonder why people bother.' He looked up. 'Lord Tang or Lord McSweeney has probably stolen the Dog to vex me. Did the Wizard escape?'

'So it seems, o lord.'

'Good. See that harm almost comes to him. And send me another tea girl. One with a head.'

There was this to be said about Cohen. If there was no reason for him to kill you, such as you having any large amount of treasure or being between him and somewhere he wanted to get to, then he was good company. Rincewind had met him a few times before, generally while running away from something.

Cohen didn't bother overmuch with questions. As far as Cohen was concerned, people appeared, people disappeared. After a five-year gap he'd just say, 'Oh, it's you.' He never added, 'And how are you?' You were alive, you were upright, and beyond that he didn't give a damn.

It was a lot warmer beyond the mountains. To Rincewind's relief a spare horse didn't have to be eaten because a leopardly sort of creature dropped off a tree branch and tried to disembowel Cohen.

It had a rather strong flavour.

Rincewind *had* eaten horse. Over the years he'd nerved himself to eat anything that couldn't actually wriggle off his fork. But he was feeling shaken enough without eating something you could call Dobbin.

'How did they catch you?' he said, when they were riding again.

'I was busy.'

'Cohen the Barbarian? Too busy to *fight*?'

'I didn't want to upset the young lady. Couldn't help meself. Went down to a village to pick up some news, one thing led to another, next thing a load of soldiers were all over the place like cheap armour, and I can't fight that well with my arms shackled behind my back. Real nasty bugger in charge, face I won't forget in a hurry. Half a dozen of us were rounded up, made to push the Barking Dog thing all the way out here, then we were chained to that tree and someone lit the bit of string and they all legged it behind a snowdrift. Except you came along and vanished it.'

'I didn't vanish it. Not exactly, anyway.'

Cohen leaned across towards Rincewind. 'I reckon I know what it was,' he said, and sat back looking pleased with himself.

'Yes?'

'I reckon it was some kind of firework. They're very big on fireworks here.'

'You mean the sort of things where you light the blue touch paper and stick it up your nose?'*

'They use 'em to drive evil spirits away. There's a lot of evil spirits, see. Because of all the slaughtering.'

'Slaughtering?'

Rincewind had always understood that the Agatean Empire was a peaceful place. It was civilized. They *invented* things. In fact, he recalled, he'd been instrumental in introducing a few of their devices to Ankh-Morpork. Simple, innocent things, like clocks worked by demons, and boxes that painted pictures, and extra glass eyes you could wear over the top of your own eyes to help you see better, even if it did mean you made a spectacle of yourself.

It was supposed to be *dull*.

'Oh, yeah. Slaughtering,' said Cohen. 'Like, supposing the population is being a bit behind with its taxes. You pick some city where people are being troublesome and kill everyone and set fire to it and pull down the walls and plough up the ashes. That way you get rid of the trouble and all the other cities are suddenly really well behaved and polite and all your back taxes turn up in a big rush, which is handy for governments, I understand. Then if they ever give trouble you just have to say "Remember Nangnang?" or whatever, and they say "Where's Nangnang?" and you say, "My point exactly." '

'Good grief! If that sort of thing was tried back home—'

'Ah, but this place has been going a long time. People think that's how a country is supposed to run. They do what they're told. The people here are treated like slaves.'

Cohen scowled. 'Now, I've got nothing against slaves, you know, as slaves. Owned a few in my time. *Been* a slave once or twice. But where there's slaves, what'll you expect to find?'

Rincewind thought about this. 'Whips?' he said at last.

'Yeah. Got it in one. Whips. There's something *honest* about slaves and whips. Well . . . they ain't got whips here. They got something worse than whips.'

'What?' said Rincewind, looking slightly panicky.

'You'll find out.'

Rincewind found himself looking around at the half-dozen other prisoners, who had trailed after them and were watching in awe

---

*KIDS! Only very silly wizards with bad sinus trouble do this. *Sensible* people go off to a roped-off enclosure where they can watch a heavily protected man, in the middle distance, light (with the aid of a very long pole) something that goes 'fsst'. And then they can shout 'Hooray'.

from a distance. He'd given them a bit of leopard, which they'd looked at initially as if it was poison and then eaten as if it was food.

'They're still following us,' he said.

'Yeah, well . . . you did give 'em meat,' cackled Cohen, starting to roll a post-prandial cigarette. 'Shouldn't have done that. Should've let 'em have the whiskers and the claws and you'd've been *amazed* at what they'd cook up. You know their big dish down on the coast?'

'No.'

'Pig's ear soup. Now, what's that tell you about a place, eh?'

Rincewind shrugged. 'Very provident people?'

'Some other bugger pinches the pig.'

He turned in the saddle. The group of ex-prisoners shrank back.

'Now, see here,' he said. 'I *told* you. You're free. Understand?'

One of the braver men spoke up. 'Yes, master.'

'I ain't your master. You're *free*. You can go wherever you like, excepting if you follow me I'll kill the lot of you. And now – go away!'

'Where, master?'

'Anywhere! Somewhere not here!'

The men gave one another some worried looks and then the whole group, as one man, turned and trotted away along the path.

'Probably go straight back to their village,' he said, rolling his eyes. 'Worse than whips, I tell you.'

He waved a scrawny hand at the landscape as they rode on.

'Strange bloody country,' he said. 'Did you know there's a wall all round the Empire?'

'That's to keep . . . barbarian invaders . . . out . . .'

'Oh, yes, very defensive,' said Cohen sarcastically. 'Like, oh my goodness, there's a twenty-foot wall, dear me, I suppose we'd just better ride off back over a thousand miles of steppe and not, e.g., take a look at the ladder possibilities inherent in that pine wood over there. Nah. It's to keep the people in. And rules? They've got rules for everything. No one even goes to the privy without a piece of paper.'

'Well, as a matter of fact I myself—'

'A piece of paper saying they can go, is what I meant. Can't leave your village without a chit. Can't get married without a chit. Can't even have a sh— Ah, we're here.'

'Yes, indeed,' said Rincewind.

Cohen glared at him. 'How did you know?' he demanded.

Rincewind tried to think. It had been a long day. In fact it had, because of the thaumic equivalent of jetlag, been several hours

362

longer than most other days he'd experienced and had contained two lunch-times, neither of which had contained anything worth eating.

'Er . . . I thought you were making a general philosophical point,' he hazarded. 'Er. Like, "We'd better make the best of it"?'

'I meant we're here at my hideout,' said Cohen. Rincewind stared around them. There were scrubby bushes, a few rocks, and a sheer cliff face.

'I can't see anything,' he said.

'Yep. That's how you can tell it's mine.'

The Art of War was the ultimate basis of diplomacy in the Empire.

Clearly war had to exist. It was a cornerstone of the processes of government. It was the way the Empire got its leaders. The competitive examination system was how it got its bureaucrats and public officials, and warfare was for its leaders, perhaps, only a different kind of competitive examination. Admittedly, if you lost you probably weren't allowed to re-sit next year.

But there had to be rules. Otherwise it was just a barbaric scuffle.

So, hundreds of years ago, the Art of War had been formulated. It was a book of rules. Some were very specific: there was to be no fighting within the Forbidden City, the person of the Emperor was sacrosanct . . . and some were more general guidelines for the good and civilised conduct of warfare. There were the rules of position, of tactics, of the enforcement of discipline, of the correct organization of supply lines. The Art laid down the optimum course to take in every conceivable eventuality. It meant that warfare in the Empire had become far more *sensible*, and generally consisted of short periods of activity followed by long periods of people trying to find things in the index.

No one remembered the author. Some said it was One Tzu Sung, some claimed it was Three Sun Sung. Possibly it was even some unsung genius who had penned, or rather painted, the very first principle: Know the enemy, and know yourself.

Lord Hong felt that he knew himself very well, and seldom had trouble knowing his enemies. And he made a point of keeping his enemies alive and healthy.

Take the Lords Sung, Fang, Tang and McSweeney. He cherished them. He cherished their *adequacy*. They had adequate military brains, which was to say that they had memorised the Five Rules and Nine Principles of the Art of War. They wrote adequate poetry, and were cunning enough to counter such coups as were attempted in their own ranks. They occasionally sent against him assassins who were sufficiently competent to keep Lord Hong interested and observant and entertained.

He even admired their adequate treachery. No one could fail to realise that Lord Hong would be the next Emperor, but when it came to it they would nevertheless contest the throne. At least, officially. In fact, each warlord had privately pledged his personal support to Lord Hong, being adequately bright to know what was likely to happen if he didn't. There would still have to be a battle, of course, for custom's sake. But Lord Hong had a place in his heart for any leader who would sell his own men.

Know your enemy. Lord Hong had decided to find a worthwhile one. So Lord Hong had seen to it that he got books and news from Ankh-Morpork. There were ways. He had his spies. At the moment Ankh-Morpork didn't know it was the enemy, and that was the best kind of enemy to have.

And he had been amazed, and then intrigued, and finally lost in admiration for what he saw . . .

I should have been born there, he thought as he watched the other members of the Serene Council. Oh, for a game of chess with someone like Lord Vetinari. No doubt he would carefully watch the board for three hours before he even made his first move . . .

Lord Hong turned to the Serene Council's minutes eunuch.

'Can we get on?' he said.

The man licked his brush nervously. 'Nearly finished, o lord,' he said.

Lord Hong sighed.

Damn calligraphy! There would be changes! A written language of seven thousand letters and it took all day to write a thirteen-syllable poem about a white pony trotting through wild hyacinths. And that was fine and beautiful, he had to concede, and no one did it better than Lord Hong. But Ankh-Morpork had an alphabet of twenty-six unexpressive, ugly, crude letters, suitable only for peasants and artisans . . . and had produced poems and plays that left white-hot trails across the soul. And you could also use it to write the bloody minutes of a five-minute meeting in less than a day.

'How far have you got?' he said.

The eunuch coughed politely.

' "How softly the bloom of the apric—" ' he began.

'Yes, yes, yes,' said Lord Hong. 'Could we on this occasion dispense with the poetic framework, please.'

'Uh. "The minutes of the last meeting were duly signed." '

'Is that all?'

'Uh . . . you see, I have to finish painting the petals on—'

'I wish this council to be concluded by this evening. Go away.'

The eunuch looked anxiously around the table, grabbed his scrolls and brushes and scuttled out.

'Good,' said Lord Hong. He nodded at the other warlords. He saved a special friendly nod for Lord Tang. Lord Hong had prodded the thought with some intrigued interest, but it really did seem that Lord Tang was a man of honour. It was a rather cowed and crabbed honour, but it was definitely in there somewhere, and would have to be dealt with.

'It would be better in any case, my lords, if we spoke in private,' he said. 'On the matter of the rebels. Disturbing intelligence has reached me of their activities.'

Lord McSweeney nodded. 'I have seen to it that thirty rebels in Sum Dim have been executed,' he said. 'As an example.'

As an example of the mindlessness of Lord McSweeney, thought Lord Hong. To his certain knowledge, and none had better knowledge than he, there had not even been a cadre of the Red Army in Sum Dim. But, almost certainly, there was one now. It was really too easy.

The other warlords also made small but proud speeches about their efforts to turn barely noticeable unrest into bloody revolution, although they hadn't managed to see it like that.

They were nervous, under the bravado, like sheepdogs who'd had a glimpse of a world where the sheep did not run.

Lord Hong cherished the nervousness. He intended to use it, by and by. He smiled and smiled.

Finally he said: 'However, my lords, despite your sterling efforts the situation remains grave. I have information that a very senior wizard from Ankh-Morpork has arrived to assist the rebels here in Hunghung, and that there is a plot to overthrow the good organization of the celestial world and assassinate the Emperor, may he live for ten thousand years. I must naturally assume that the foreign devils are behind this.'

'I know nothing of this!' snapped Lord Tang.

'My dear Lord Tang, I was not suggesting that you should,' said Lord Hong.

'I meant—' Lord Tang began.

'Your devotion to the Emperor is unquestioned,' Lord Hong continued, as smoothly as a knife through warm butter. 'It is true that there is almost certainly someone highly placed assisting these people, but not one shred of evidence points to you.'

'I should hope not!'

'Indeed.'

The Lords Fang and McSweeney moved very slightly away from Lord Tang.

'How can we have let this happen?' said Lord Fang. 'Certainly it is true that people, foolish deranged people, have sometimes ventured out beyond the Wall. But to let one come *back*—'

'I am afraid the Grand Vizier at the time was a man of changeable humours,' said Lord Hong. 'He thought it would be interesting to see what intelligence was brought back.'

'Intelligence?' said Lord Fang. 'This city of Ank . . . More . . . Pork is an abomination! Mere anarchy! There appear to be no nobles of consequence and the society is that of a termite nest! It would be better for us, my lords, if it was wiped from the face of the world!'

'Your incisive comments are duly noted, Lord Fang,' said Lord Hong, while part of him rolled on the floor laughing. 'In any event,' he went on, 'I shall see that extra guards are posted in the Emperor's chambers. However all this trouble began, we must see that it ends here.'

He watched them watching him. They think I want to rule the Empire, he thought. So they're all – except for Lord Tang, rebel fellow traveller as he will undoubtedly prove to be – working out how this will be to their advantage . . .

He dismissed them, and retired to his chambers.

It was a fact that the ghosts and devils who lived beyond the Wall had no grasp of culture and certainly no concept of books, and being in possession of such a patently impossible object was punishable by eventual death. And confiscation.

Lord Hong had built up quite a library. He had even acquired maps.

And more than maps. There was a box he kept locked, in the room with the full-length mirror . . .

Not now. Later on . . .

Ankh-Morpork! Even the name sounded rich.

All he needed was a year. The dreadful scourge of the rebellion would allow him to wield the kind of powers that even the maddest Emperor had not dreamed of. And then it would be unthinkable not to build a vengeful fleet to wreak terror on the foreign devils. Thank you, Lord Fang. Your point is duly noted.

As if it mattered who was Emperor! The Empire was possibly a bonus, to be acquired later, perhaps, in passing. Let him just have Ankh-Morpork, with its busy dwarfs and its grasp, above all, of machinery. Look at the Barking Dogs. Half the time they blew up. They were inaccurate. The principle was sound but the execution was terrible, especially when they blew up.

It had come as a revelation to Lord Hong when he looked at the problem the Ankh-Morpork way and realised that it might just possibly be better to give the job of Auspicious Dog-maker to some peasant with a fair idea about metal and explosive earths than to some clerk who'd got the highest marks in an examination to find the best poem about iron. In Ankh-Morpork people *did* things.

Let him just walk down Broadway as owner, and eat the pies of the famous Mr Dibbler. Let him play one game of chess against Lord Vetinari. Of course, it would mean leaving the man one arm.

He was shaking with excitement. Not later . . . now. His fingers reached for the secret key on its chain around his neck.

It was barely a track. Rabbits would have walked right past it. And you'd have sworn there was a sheer, passless rock wall until you found the gap.

Once you *did* find it, it was hardly worth the bother. It led to a long gully with a few natural caves in it, and a bit of grass, and a spring.

And, as it turned out, Cohen's gang. Except that he called it a horde. They were sitting in the sun, complaining about how it wasn't as warm as it used to be.

'I'm back then, lads,' said Cohen.

'Been away, have you?'

'Whut? Whut's he say?'

'He said HE'S BACK.'

'Black what?'

Cohen beamed at Rincewind. 'I brought 'em with me,' he said. 'Like I said, no future in going it alone these days.'

'Er,' said Rincewind, after surveying the little scene, 'are any of these men under eighty years old?'

'Stand up, Boy Willie,' said Cohen.

A dehydrated man only marginally less wrinkled than the others got to his feet. It was his feet that were particularly noticeable. He wore boots with extremely thick soles.

'So's me feet touch the ground,' he said.

'Don't they . . . er . . . touch the ground in ordinary boots?'

'Nope. Orthopaedic problem, see. Like . . . you know how a lot of people've got one leg shorter than the other? Funny thing, with me it's—'

'Don't tell me,' said Rincewind. 'Sometimes I get these amazing flashes . . . *Both* legs are shorter than the other, right?'

'Amazing. O' course, I can see you're a wizard,' said Boy Willie. 'You'd know about this sort of thing.'

Rincewind gave the next member of the Horde a bright mad smile. It was almost certainly a human being, because wizened little monkeys didn't usually go around in a wheelchair while wearing a helmet with horns on it. It grimaced at Rincewind.

'This is—'

'Whut? Whut?'

'Mad Hamish,' said Cohen.

'Whut? Whozee?'

'I bet that wheelchair *terrifies* them,' said Rincewind. 'Especially the blades.'

'We had the devil of a job getting it over the wall,' Cohen conceded. 'But you'd be amazed at his turn of speed.'

'Whut?'

'And this is Truckle the Uncivil.'

'Sod off, wizard.'

Rincewind beamed at Exhibit B. 'Those walking sticks . . . Fascinating! Very impressive the way you've got LOVE and HATE written on them.'

Cohen smiled proprietorially.

'Truckle used to be reckoned one of the biggest badasses in the world,' he said.

'Really? Him?'

'But it's amazing what you can do with a herbal suppository.'

'Up yours, mister,' said Truckle.

Rincewind blinked. 'Er. Can I have a word, Cohen?'

He drew the ancient barbarian aside.

'I don't want to seem to be making trouble here,' he said, 'but it doesn't strike you, does it, that these men are a bit, well, past their sell-by date? A little, not to put too fine a point on it, old?'

'Whut? Whutzeesayin'?'

'He says IT'S COLD.'

'Whut?'

'What're you saying? There's nearly five hundred years of con-centrated barbarian hero experience in 'em,' said Cohen.

'Five hundred years' experience in a fighting unit is good,' said

Rincewind. 'It's *good*. But it should be spread over more than one person. I mean, what are you expecting them to do? Fall over on people?'

'Nothin' wrong with 'em,' said Cohen, indicating a frail man who was staring intently at a large block of teak. 'Look at ole Caleb the Ripper over there. See? Killed more'n four hundred men with his bare hands. Eighty-five now and but for the dust he's marvellous.'

'What the hell is he *doing*?'

'Ah, see, they're into bare-handed combat here. Very big thing, unarmed combat, on account of most people not being allowed weapons. So Caleb reckons he's on to a good thing. See that big lump of teak? It's amazin'. He just gives this bloodcurdlin' shout and—'

'Cohen, they're all *very old men*.'

'They're the cream!'

Rincewind sighed.

'Cohen, they're the cheese. Why've you brought them all the way here?'

'Gonna help me steal something,' said Cohen.

'What? A jewel or something?'

''S something,' said Cohen, sulkily. ''S in Hunghung.'

'Really? My word,' said Rincewind. 'And there's a lot of people in Hunghung, I expect?'

'About half a million,' said Cohen.

'Lots of guards, no doubt?'

'About forty thousand, I heard. About three-quarters of a million if you count all the armies.'

'Right,' said Rincewind. 'So, with these half-dozen old men—'

'The Silver Horde,' said Cohen, with a touch of pride.

'What? Pardon?'

'That's their name. Got to have a name in the horde business. The Silver Horde.'

Rincewind turned around. Several of the Horde had fallen asleep.

'The Silver Horde,' he said. 'Right. Matches the colour of their hair. Those that have *got* hair. So . . . with this . . . Silver Horde you're going to rush the city, kill all the guards and steal all the treasure?'

Cohen nodded. 'Yeah . . . something like that. Of course, we won't have to kill *all* the guards . . .'

'Oh, no?'

'It'd take too long.'

'Yes, and of course you'll want to leave something to do tomorrow.'

'I mean they'll be busy, what with the revolution and everything.'

'A revolution too? My word.'

'They say it's a time of portents,' said Cohen. 'They—'

'I'm surprised they've got time to worry about the state of their camping equipment,' said Rincewind.

'You'd be well advised to stay along o' us,' said Ghenghiz Cohen. 'You'll be safer with us.'

'Oh, I'm not sure about that,' said Rincewind, grinning horribly. 'I'm not sure about that at all.'

By myself, he thought, only *ordinary* horrible things can happen to me.

Cohen shrugged, and then stared around the clearing until his gaze lighted on a slight figure who was sitting a little apart from the rest, reading a book.

'Look at him,' he said, benevolently, like a man pointing out a dog doing a good trick. 'Always got his nose in a book.' He raised his voice. 'Teach? Come and show this wizard the way to Hunghung.'

He turned back to Rincewind. 'Teach'll tell you anything you want to know, 'cos he knows everything. I'll leave you with him. I've got to go and have a talk with Old Vincent.' He waved a hand dismissively. 'Not that there's anything wrong with him, at all,' he said defiantly. 'It's just that his memory's bad. We had a bit of trouble on the way over. I keep telling him, it's rape the *women* and set fire to the *houses*.'

'Rape?' said Rincewind. 'That's not very—'

'He's eighty-seven,' said Cohen. 'Don't go and spoil an old man's dreams.'

Teach turned out to be a tall, stick-like man with an amiably absent-minded expression and a fringe of white hair so that, when viewed from above, he would appear to be a daisy. He certainly did not appear to be a bloodthirsty brigand, even though he was wearing a chain-mail vest slightly too big for him and a huge scabbard strapped across his back, which contained no sword but held a variety of scrolls and brushes. His chain-mail shirt had a breast pocket with three different coloured pens in a leather pocket protector.

'Ronald Saveloy,' he said, shaking Rincewind's hand. 'The gentlemen do rather assume considerable knowledge on my part. Let me see . . . You want to go to Hunghung, yes?'

Rincewind had been thinking about this.

'I want to know the *way* to Hunghung,' he said guardedly.

'Yes. Well. At this time of year I'd head towards the setting sun until I left the mountains and reached the alluvial plain where you'll see evidence of drumlins and some quite fine examples of obviously erratic boulders. It's about ten miles.'

Rincewind stared at him. A brigand's directions were usually more on the lines of 'keep straight on past the burning city and turn right when you've passed all the citizens hanging up by their ears'.

'Those drumlins sound dangerous,' he said.

'They're just a type of post-glacial hill,' said Mr Saveloy.

'What about these erratic boulders? They sound like the kind of thing that'd pounce on—'

'Just boulders dropped a long way from home by a glacier,' said Mr Saveloy. 'Nothing to worry about. The landscape is not hostile.'

Rincewind didn't believe him. He'd had the ground hit him very hard many times.

'However,' said Mr Saveloy, 'Hunghung is a little dangerous at the moment.'

'No, really?' said Rincewind wearily.

'It's not *exactly* a siege. Everyone's waiting for the Emperor to die. These are what they call here' – he smiled – 'interesting times.'

'I *hate* interesting times.'

The other Horders had wandered off, fallen asleep again or were complaining to one another about their feet. The voice of Cohen could be heard somewhere in the distance: 'Look, *this* is a match, and *this* is—'

'You know, you sound a very educated man for a barbarian,' said Rincewind.

'Oh, dear me, I didn't start out a barbarian. I used to be a school teacher. That's why they call me Teach.'

'What did you teach?'

'Geography. And I was very interested in Auriental[*] studies. But I decided to give it up and make a living by the sword.'

'After being a teacher all your life?'

'It did mean a change of perspective, yes.'

'But . . . well . . . surely . . . the privation, the terrible hazards, the daily risk of death . . .'

Mr Saveloy brightened up. 'Oh, you've *been* a teacher, have you?'

Rincewind looked around when someone shouted. He turned, to see two of the Horde arguing nose to nose.

[*] The Ankh-Morpork name for the Counterweight Continent and its nearby islands. It means 'place where the gold comes from'.

Mr Saveloy sighed.

'I'm trying to teach them chess,' he said. 'It's vital to the understanding of the Auriental mind. But I am afraid they have no concept of taking turns at moving, and their idea of an opening gambit is for the King and all the pawns to rush up the board together and set fire to the opposing rooks.'

Rincewind leaned closer.

'Look, I mean . . . *Ghenghiz* Cohen?' he said. 'Has he gone off his head? I mean . . . just killing half a dozen geriatric priests and nicking some paste gems, *yes*. Attacking forty thousand guards all by himself is certain death!'

'Oh, he won't be by himself,' said Mr Saveloy.

Rincewind blinked. There was something about Cohen. People caught optimism off him as though it was the common cold.

'Oh, yes. Of course. Sorry. I'd forgotten that. Seven against forty thousand? I shouldn't think you'll have any problems. I'll just be going. Fairly quickly, I think.'

'We have a plan. It's a sort of—' Mr Saveloy hesitated. His eyes unfocused slightly. 'You know? Thing. Bees do it. Wasps, too. Also some jellyfish, I believe . . . Had the word only a moment ago . . . er. It's going to be the biggest one ever, I think.'

Rincewind gave him another blank stare. 'I'm sure I saw a spare horse,' he said.

'Let me give you this,' said Mr Saveloy. 'Then perhaps you'll understand. It's what it's all about, really . . .'

He handed Rincewind a small bundle of papers fastened together by a loop of string through one corner.

Rincewind, shoving it hastily into his pocket, noticed only the title on the first page.

It said:

WHAT I DID ON MY HOLIDAYS

The choices seemed very clear to Rincewind. There was the city of Hunghung, under siege, apparently throbbing with revolution and danger, and there was everywhere else.

Therefore it was important to know where Hunghung was so that he didn't blunder into it by accident. He paid a lot of attention to Mr Saveloy's instructions, and then rode the other way.

He could get a ship somewhere. Of course, the wizards would be surprised to see him back, but he could always say there'd been no one in.

The hills gave way to scrubland which in turn led down to an apparently endless damp plain which contained, in the misty distance, a river so winding that half the time it must have been flowing backwards.

The land was a chequerboard of cultivation. Rincewind liked the countryside in theory, providing it wasn't rising up to meet him and was for preference happening on the far side of a city wall, but this was hardly countryside. It was more like one big, hedgeless farm. Occasional huge rocks, looking dangerously erratic, rose out of the fields.

Sometimes he'd see people hard at work in the distance. As far as he could tell, their chief activity was moving mud around.

Occasionally he'd see a man standing ankle deep in a flooded field holding a water buffalo on the end of a length of string. The buffalo grazed and occasionally moved its bowels. The man held the string. It seemed to be his entire goal and occupation in life.

There were a few other people on the road. Usually they were pushing wheelbarrows loaded with water buffalo dung or, possibly, mud. They didn't pay any attention to Rincewind. In fact they made a *point* of not paying attention; they scurried past staring intently at the scenes of mud dynamics or bovine bowel movement happening in the fields.

Rincewind would be the first to admit that he was a slow thinker.* But he'd been around long enough to spot the signs. These people weren't paying him any attention because they didn't *see* people on horseback.

They were probably descended from people who learned that if you look too hard at anyone on horseback you receive a sharp stinging sensation such as might be obtained by a stick around the ear. Not looking up at people on horseback had become hereditary. People who stared at people on horseback in what was considered to be a funny way never survived long enough to breed.

He decided to try an experiment. The next wheelbarrow that trundled past was carrying not mud but people, about half a dozen of them, on seats either side of the huge central wheel. The method of propulsion was secondarily by a small sail erected to catch the wind but primarily by that pre-eminent source of motive power in a peasant community, someone's great-grandfather, or at least some-one who looked like someone's great-grandfather.

Cohen had said, 'There's men here who can push a wheelbarrow

---

*In fact, he'd be about the seventy-third to admit it.

for thirty miles on a bowl of millet with a bit of scum in it. What does that tell you? It tells *me* someone's porking all the beef.'

Rincewind decided to explore the social dynamics and also try out the language. It had been years since he'd last used it, but he had to admit that Ridcully had been right. He did have a gift for languages. Agatean was a language of few basic syllables. It was really all in the tone, inflection and context. Otherwise, the word for military leader was also the word for long-tailed marmot, male sexual organ and ancient chicken coop.

'Hey there, you!' he shouted. 'Er . . . to bend bamboo? An expression of disapproval? Er . . . I mean . . . Stop!'

The barrow slewed to a halt. No one looked at him. They looked past him, or around him, or towards his feet.

Eventually the wheelbarrow-pusher, in the manner of a man who knows he's in for it no matter what he does, mumbled, 'Your honour commands?'

Rincewind felt very sorry, later, for what he said next.

He said, 'Just give me all your food and . . . unwilling dogs, will you?'

They watched him impassively.

'Damn. I mean . . . arranged beetles? . . . variety of waterfall? . . . Oh, yes . . . *money*.'

There was a general fumbling and shifting among the passengers. Then the wheelbarrow-pusher sidled towards Rincewind, head down, and held up his hat. It contained some rice, some dried fish, a highly dangerous-looking egg. And about a pound of gold, in big round coins.

Rincewind stared at the gold.

Gold was as common as copper on the Counterweight Continent. That was one of the few things everyone knew about the place. There was no *point* in Cohen trying any kind of big robbery. There was a limit to what anyone could carry. He might as well rob one peasant village and live like a king for the rest of his life. It wouldn't be as if he'd need that much . . .

The 'later' suddenly caught up with him, and he did indeed feel quite ashamed. These people had hardly anything, apart from loads of gold.

'Er. Thanks. Thank you. Yes. Just checking. Yes. You can all have it back now. I'll . . . er . . . keep . . . the elderly grandmother . . . to run sideways . . . oh, damn . . . *fish*.'

Rincewind had always been on the bottom of the social heap. It didn't matter what size heap it was. The top got higher or lower, but the bottom was always in the same place. But at least it was an Ankh-Morpork heap.

No one bowed to anyone in Ankh-Morpork. And anyone who tried what he'd just tried in Ankh-Morpork would, by now, be scrabbling in the gutter for his teeth and whimpering about the pain in his groin and his horse would already have been repainted twice and sold to a man who'd be swearing he'd owned it for years.

He felt oddly proud of the fact.

Something strange welled up from the sludgy depths of his soul. It was, to his amazement, a generous impulse.

He slid off the horse and held out the reins. A horse was useful, but he was used to doing without one. Besides, over a short distance a man could run faster than a horse, and this was a fact very dear to Rincewind's heart.

'Here,' he said. 'You can have it. For the fish.'

The wheelbarrow-pusher screamed, grabbed the handles of his conveyance and hurtled desperately away. Several people were thrown off, took one almost-look at Rincewind, also screamed, and ran after him.

Worse than whips, Cohen had said. They've got something here worse than whips. They don't *need* whips any more. Rincewind hoped he'd never find out what it was, if it had done this to people.

He rode on through an endless panorama of fields. There weren't even any patches of roadside scrub, or taverns. Away among the fields were shapes that might be small towns or villages, but no apparent paths to them, possibly because paths used up valuable agricultural mud.

Finally he sat down on a rock that presumably not even the peasants' most concerted efforts had been able to move, and reached into his pocket for his shameful dried fish lunch.

His hand touched the bundle of papers Mr Saveloy had given him. He pulled them out, and got crumbs on them.

This is what it's all about, the barbarian teacher had said. He hadn't explained what 'it' was.

WHAT I DID ON MY HOLIDAYS, said the title. It was in bad handwriting or, rather, bad painting – the Agateans wrote with paintbrushes, assembling little word pictures out of handy components. One picture wasn't just worth a thousand words, it *was* a thousand words.

Rincewind wasn't much good at reading the language. There were very few Agatean books even in the Unseen University Library. And this one looked as though whoever had written it had been trying to make sense of something unfamiliar.

He turned over a couple of pages. It was a story about a Great City, containing magnificent things – 'beer strong like an ox', it said, and 'pies containing many many parts of pig'. Everyone in the city seemed to be wise, kind, strong or all three, especially some character called the Great Wizard who seemed to feature largely in the text.

And there were mystifying little comments, as in, 'I saw a man tread upon the toes of a City Guard who said to him "Your wife is a big hippo!" to which the man responded "Place it where the sun does not shed daylight, enormous person", upon which the Guard [this bit was in red ink and the handwriting was shaky, as if the writer was quite excited] *did not remove the man's head according to ancient custom.*' The statement was followed by a pictogram of a dog passing water, which was for some obscure reason the Agatean equivalent of an exclamation mark. There were five of these.

Rincewind flicked through the pages. They were filled with the same dull stuff, sentences stating the blindingly obvious but often followed by several incontinent dogs. Such as: 'The innkeeper said the City had demanded tax but he did not intend to pay, and when I asked if he was not afraid he vouchsafed: "[Complicated pictogram] them all except one and he can [complicated pictogram] himself" [urinating dog, urinating dog]. He went on to say, "The [pictogram indicating Supreme Ruler] is a [another pictogram which, after some thought and holding up the picture at various angles, Rincewind decided meant 'a horse's bottom'] and you can tell him I said so", *at which point* a Guard in the tavern *did not disembowel him* [urinating dog, urinating dog] but said, "Tell him from me also" [urinating dog, urinating dog, urinating dog, urinating dog, urinating dog].'

What was so odd about that? People talked like that in Ankh-Morpork all the time, or at least expressed those sentiments. Apart from the dog.

Mind you, a country that'd wipe out a whole city to teach the other cities a lesson was a mad place. Perhaps this was a book of jokes and he just hadn't seen the point. Perhaps comedians here got big laughs with lines like: 'I say, I say, I say, I met a man on the way to the theatre and *he didn't chop my legs off*, urinating dog, urinating dog—'

He had been aware of the jingle of harness on the road, but hadn't paid it any attention. He hadn't even looked up at the sound of someone approaching. By the time he did think of looking up it was too late, because someone had their boot on his neck.

'Oh, urinating dog,' he said, before passing out.

There was a puff of air and the Luggage appeared, dropping heavily into a snowdrift.

There was a meat cleaver sticking into its lid.

It remained motionless for some time and then, its legs moving in a complicated little dance, it turned around 360 degrees.

The Luggage did not think. It had nothing to think with. Whatever processes went on inside it probably had more to do with the way a tree reacts to sun and rain and sudden storms, but speeded up very fast.

After a while it seemed to get its bearings and ambled off across the melting snow.

The Luggage did not feel, either. It had nothing to feel with. But it reacted, in the same way that a tree reacts to the changing of the seasons.

Its pace quickened.

It was close to home.

Rincewind had to concede that the shouting man was right. Not, that is, about Rincewind's father being the diseased liver of a type of mountain panda and his mother being a bucket of turtle slime; Rincewind had no personal experience of either parent but felt that they were probably at least vaguely humanoid, if only briefly. But on the subject of appearing to own a stolen horse he had Rincewind bang to rights and, also, a foot on his neck. A foot on the neck is nine points of the law.

He felt hands rummaging in his pockets.

Another person – Rincewind was not able to see much beyond a few inches of alluvial soil, but from context it appeared to be an unsympathetic person – joined in the shouting.

Rincewind was hauled upright.

The guards were pretty much like guards as Rincewind had experienced them everywhere. They had exactly the amount of intellect required to hit people and drag them off to the scorpion pit. They were league champions at shouting at people a few inches from their face.

The effect was made surreal by the fact that the guards

377

themselves had no faces, or at least no faces they could call their own. Their ornate, black-enamelled helmets had huge moustachioed visages painted on them, leaving only the owner's mouth uncovered so that he could, for example, call Rincewind's grandfather a box of inferior goldfish droppings.

What I Did On My Holidays was waved in front of his face.

'Bag of rotted fish!'

'I don't know what it means,' said Rincewind. 'Someone just gave it to—'

'Feet of extreme rotted milk!'

'Could you perhaps not shout quite so loud? I think my eardrum has just exploded.'

The guard subsided, possibly only because he had run out of breath. Rincewind had a moment to look at the scenery.

There were two carts on the road. One of them seemed to be a cage on wheels; he made out faces watching him in terror. The other was an ornate palanquin carried by eight peasants; rich curtains covered the sides but he could see where they had been twitched aside so that someone within could look at him.

The guards were aware of this. It seemed to make them awkward.

'If I could just expl—'

'Silence, mouth of—' The guard hesitated.

'You've used turtle, goldfish and what you probably meant to be cheese,' said Rincewind.

'Mouth of chicken gizzards!'

A long thin hand emerged from the curtains and beckoned, just once.

Rincewind was hustled forward. The hand had the longest fingernails he'd ever seen on something that didn't purr.

'Kowtow!'

'Sorry?' said Rincewind.

'*Kowtow!*'

Swords were produced.

'I don't know what you mean!' Rincewind wailed.

'Kowtow, please,' whispered a voice by his ear. It was not a particularly friendly voice but compared to all the other voices it was positively affectionate. It sounded as though it belonged to quite a young man. And it was speaking very good Morporkian.

'*How?*'

'You don't know *that*? Kneel down, press your forehead on the ground. That's if you want to be able to wear a hat again.'

Rincewind hesitated. He was a free-born Morporkian, and on the list of things a citizen didn't do was bow down to any, not to put too fine a point on it, *foreigner*.

On the other hand, right at the *top* of the list of things a citizen didn't do was get their head chopped off.

'That's better. That's good. How did you know you ought to tremble?'

'Oh, I thought up that bit myself.'

The hand beckoned with a finger.

A guard slapped Rincewind in the face with the mud-encrusted *What I Did . . .* Rincewind clutched it guiltily as the guard scurried towards his master's digit.

'Voice?' said Rincewind.

'Yes?'

'What happens if I claim immunity because I'm a foreigner?'

'There's a special thing they do with a wire-mesh waistcoat and a cheesegrater.'

'Oh.'

'And there are torturers in Hunghung who can keep a man alive for years.'

'I suppose you're not talking about healthy early morning runs and a high-fibre diet?'

'No. So keep quiet and with any luck you'll be sent to be a slave in the palace.'

'Luck is my middle name,' said Rincewind, indistinctly. 'Mind you, my first name is Bad.'

'Remember to gibber and grovel.'

'I'll do my very best.'

The white hand emerged bearing a scrap of paper. The guard took it, turned towards Rincewind and cleared his throat.

'Harken to the wisdom and justice of District Commissioner Kee, ball of swamp emanations! Not him, I mean you!'

He cleared his throat again and peered closer at the paper in the manner of one who learned to read by saying the name of each letter very carefully to himself.

' "The white pony runs through the . . . the . . ." '

The guard turned and held a whispered conversation with the curtains, and turned back again.

> ' " . . . chrysanthemum . . . mumum blossoms,
> The cold wind stirs the
> Apricot trees. Send him to
> The palace to slave

379

Until all appendages drop
Off." '

Several of the other guards applauded.

'Look up and clap,' said the Voice.

'I'm afraid my appendages will drop off.'

'It's a *big* cheesegrater.'

'Encore! Wow! Superb! That bit about the chrysanthemumums?
Wonderful!'

'Good. Listen. You're from Bes Pelargic. You've got the right
accent, damned if I know why. It's a seaport and people there are a
little strange. You were robbed by bandits and escaped on one of
their horses. That's why you haven't got your papers. You need
pieces of paper for everything here, including being anybody. And
pretend you don't know me.'

'I *don't* know you.'

'Good. Long Live The Changing Things To A More Equitable
State While Retaining Due Respect For The Traditions Of Our
Forebears And Of Course Not Harming The August Personage Of
The Emperor Endeavour!'

'Good. Yes. What?'

A guard kicked Rincewind in the region of the kidneys. This
suggested, in the universal language of the boot, that he should get
up.

He managed to get up on one knee, and saw the Luggage.

It wasn't his, and there were three of them.

The Luggage trotted to the crest of a low hill and stopped so fast that
it left a lot of little grooves in the dirt.

In addition to not having any equipment with which to think or
feel, the Luggage also had no means of seeing. The manner in which
it perceived events was a complete mystery.

It perceived the other Luggages.

The three of them stood patiently in a line behind the palanquin.
They were big. They were black.

The Luggage's legs disappeared inside its body.

After a while it very cautiously opened its lid, just a fraction.

Of the three things that most people know about the horse, the third is that, over a short distance, it can't run as fast as a man. As Rincewind had learned to his advantage, it has more legs to sort out.

There are additional advantages if a) the people on horseback aren't expecting you to run and b) you happen to be, very conveniently, in an athletic starting position.

Rincewind rose like a boomerang curry from a sensitive stomach.

There was a lot of shouting but the comforting thing, the important thing, was that it was all behind him. It would soon try to catch him up but that was a problem for the future. He could also consider where he was running to as well, but an experienced coward never bothered with the *to* when the *from* held such fascination.

A less practised runner would have risked a glance behind, but Rincewind instinctively knew all about wind drag and the tendency of inconvenient rocks to position themselves under the unwary foot. Besides, why look behind? He was already running as fast as he could. Nothing he could see would make him run any faster.

There was a large shapeless village ahead, a construction apparently of mud and dung. In the fields in front of it a dozen peasants looked up from their toil at the accelerating wizard.

Perhaps it was Rincewind's imagination, but as he passed them he could have sworn that he heard the cry:

'Necessarily Extended Duration To The Red Army! Regrettable Decease Without Undue Suffering To The Forces Of Oppression!'

Rincewind dived through the huts as the soldiers charged at the peasants.

Cohen had been right. There seemed to be a revolution. But the Empire had been in unchanged existence for thousands of years, courtesy and a respect for protocol were part of its very fabric, and by the sound of it the revolutionaries had yet to master the art of impolite slogans.

Rincewind preferred running to hiding. Hiding was all very well, but if you were found then you were stuck. But the village was the only cover for miles around, and some of the soldiers had horses. A man might be faster than a horse over a short distance, but over this panorama of flat, open fields a horse had a running man bang to rights.

So he ducked into a building at random and pushed aside the first door he came to.

It had, pasted on it, the words: Examination. Silence!

Forty expectant and slightly worried faces looked up at him from their writing stools. They weren't children, but full-grown adults.

There was a lectern at the end of the room and, on it, a pile of papers sealed with string and wax.

Rincewind felt the atmosphere was familiar. He'd breathed it before, even if it had been a world away. It was full of those cold sweaty odours created by the sudden realization that it was probably too late to do that revision you'd kept on putting off. Rincewind had faced many horrors in his time, but none held quite the same place in the lexicon of dread as those few seconds after someone said, 'Turn over your papers *now*.'

The candidates were watching him.

There was shouting somewhere outside.

He hurried up to the lectern, tore at the string and distributed the papers as fast as he could. Then he dived back to the safety of the lectern, removed his hat, and was bent low when the door opened slowly.

'Go away!' he screamed. 'Examination in progress!'

The unseen figure behind the door murmured something to someone else. The door was closed again.

The candidates were still staring at him.

'Er. Very well. Turn over your papers.'

There was a rustle, a few moments of that dreadful silence, and then much activity with brushes.

Competitive examinations. Oh, yes. That was another thing people knew about the Empire. They were the only way to get any kind of public post and the security that brought. People had said that this must be a very good system, because it opened up opportunities for people of merit.

Rincewind picked up a spare paper and read it.

It was headed: Examination for the post of Assistant Night-Soil Operative for the District of W'ung.

He read question one. It required candidates to write a sixteen-line poem on evening mist over the reed beds.

Question two seemed to be about the use of metaphor in some book Rincewind had never heard of.

Then there was a question about music . . .

Rincewind turned the paper over a couple of times. There didn't seem to be any mention, anywhere, of words like 'compost' or 'bucket' or 'wheelbarrow'. But presumably all this produced a better class of person than the Ankh-Morpork system, which asked just one question: 'Got your own shovel, have you?'

The shouting outside seemed to have died away; Rincewind risked poking his head out of the door. There was a commotion near the road but it no longer seemed Rincewind-orientated.

He ran for it.

The students got on with their examination. One of the more enterprising, however, rolled up his trouser leg and copied down a poem about mist he'd composed, at great effort, some time previously. After a while you got to know what kind of questions the examiners asked.

Rincewind trotted onwards, trying to keep to ditches wherever these weren't knee deep in sucking mud. It wasn't a landscape built for concealment. The Agateans grew crops on any piece of ground the seeds wouldn't roll off. Apart from the occasional rocky outcrop there was a distinct lack of places in which to lurk.

No one paid him much attention once he'd left the village far behind. The occasional water buffalo operative would turn to watch him until he was out of sight, but displayed no special curiosity; it was merely that Rincewind was marginally more interesting than watching a water buffalo defecate.

He kept the road just in sight and, by evening, reached a crossroads.

There was an inn.

Rincewind hadn't eaten since the leopard. The inn meant food, but food meant money. He was hungry, and he had no money.

He chided himself for this kind of negative thinking. That was not the right approach. What he should do was go in and order a large, nourishing meal. Then instead of being hungry with no money he'd be well fed with no money, a net gain on his current position. Of course, the world was likely to raise some objections, but in Rincewind's experience there were few problems that couldn't be solved with a scream and a good ten yards' start. And, of course, he would just have had a strengthening meal.

Besides, he liked Hunghungese food. A few refugees had opened restaurants in Ankh-Morpork and Rincewind considered himself something of an expert on the dishes.*

The one huge room was thick with smoke and, insofar as this could be determined through the swirls and coils, quite busy. A couple of old men were sitting in front of a complicated pile of ivory tiles, playing *Shibo Yangcong-san*. He wasn't sure what they were smoking but, by the looks on their faces, they were happy they'd chosen it.

Rincewind made his way to the fireplace, where a skinny man was tending a cauldron.

_____

* Such as Dish of Glistening Brown Stuff, Dish of Glistening Crunchy Orange Stuff, and Dish of Soft White Lumps.

383

He gave him a cheery smile. 'Good morning! Can I partake of your famous delicacy "Meal A for two People with extra Prawn Cracker"?'

'Never heard of it.'

'Um. Then . . . could I see a painful ear . . . a croak of a frog . . . a menu?'

'What's a menu, friend?'

Rincewind nodded. He knew what it meant when a stranger called you 'friend' like that. No one who called someone else 'friend' was feeling very kindly disposed.

'What is there to eat, I meant.'

'Noodles, boiled cabbage and pork whiskers.'

'Is that *all*?'

'Pork whiskers don't grow on trees, san.'

'I've been seeing water buffalo all day,' Rincewind said. 'Don't you people ever eat beef?'

The ladle splashed into the cauldron. Somewhere behind him a *shibo* tile dropped on to the floor. The back of Rincewind's head prickled under the stares.

'We don't serve rebels in this place,' said the landlord loudly.

Probably too meaty, Rincewind thought. But it seemed to him that the words had been addressed to the world in general rather than to him.

'Glad to hear it,' he said, 'because—'

'Yes indeed,' said the landlord, a little louder. 'No rebels welcome here.'

'That's fine by me, because—'

'If I knew of any rebels I would be certain to alert the authorities,' the landlord bellowed.

'I'm not a rebel, I'm just hungry,' said Rincewind. 'I'd, er, like a bowlful, please.'

A bowl was filled. Rainbow patterns shimmered on its oily surface.

'That'll be half a *rhinu*,' said the landlord.

'You mean you want me to pay before I eat it?' said Rincewind.

'You might not want to afterwards, friend.'

A *rhinu* was more gold than Rincewind had ever owned. He patted his pockets theatrically.

'In fact, it seems that—' he began. There was a small thump beside him. *What I Did On My Holidays* had fallen on to the floor.

'Yes, thank you, that will do nicely,' said the landlord to the room at large. He pushed the bowl into Rincewind's hand and, in one movement, scooped up the booklet and crammed it back into the wizard's pocket.

'Go and sit down in the corner!' he hissed. 'And you'll be told what to do!'

'But I'm sure I *know* what to do. Dip spoon in bowl, raise spoon to mouth—'

'Sit down!'

Rincewind found the darkest corner and sat down. People were still watching him.

To avoid the group gaze he pulled out *What I Did* and opened it at random, in an effort to find out why it had a magical effect on the landlord.

' . . . sold me a bun containing what was called a [complicated pictogram] made *entirely of the inside of pigs* [urinating dog]' he read. 'And such as these could be bought for small coin at any time, and so replete were the citizens that hardly any bought these [complicated pictogram] from the stall of [complicated pictogram, but it seemed to involve a razor]-san.'

Sausages filled with pig parts, thought Rincewind. Well, perhaps they *might* be amazing if, up until then, a bowl of dishwater with something congealing on the top of it had been your idea of a hearty meal.

Hah! Mister What-I-Did-On-My-Holidays should try coming to Ankh-Morpork next time, and see how much he liked one of old . . . Dibbler's sausages . . . full of genuine . . . pig product . . .

The spoon splashed into the bowl.

Rincewind turned the pages hurriedly.

' . . . peaceful streets, along which I walked, were quite free of crime and brigandage . . .'

'Of course they were, you four-eyed little git!' shouted Rincewind. 'That was because it was all happening to me!'

' . . . a city where all men are free . . .'

'Free? *Free?* Well, yes, free to starve, get robbed by the Thieves' Guild . . .' said Rincewind to the book.

He fumbled through to another page.

' . . . my companion was the Great Wizard [complicated pictogram, but now that Rincewind studied it he realized with a plummeting heart it had a few lines that looked like the Agatean for 'wind'], the most prominent and powerful wizard in the entire country . . .'

'I never said that! I—' Rincewind stopped. Memory treacherously dredged up a few phrases, such as *Oh, the Archchancellor listens to everything I say* and *That place would just fall down without me around*. But that was just the sort of thing you said after a few beers, surely no one would be so gullible as to write . . .

A picture focused itself in Rincewind's memory. It was of a happy, smiling little man with huge spectacles and a trusting, innocent approach to life which brought terror and destruction everywhere he wandered. Twoflower had been quite unable to believe that the world was a bad place and that was largely because, to him, it wasn't. It saved it all up for Rincewind.

Rincewind's life had been quite uneventful before he'd met Twoflower. Since then, as far as he could remember, it had contained events in huge amounts.

And the little man had gone back home, hadn't he? To Bes Pelargic – the Empire's only proper seaport.

Surely no one would be so gullible as to write this sort of thing?

Surely no one apart from one person would be so gullible.

Rincewind was not politically minded but there were some things he could work out not because they were to do with politics but because they had a lot to do with human nature. Nasty images moved into place like bad scenery.

The Empire had a wall around it. If you lived in the Empire then you learned how to make soup out of pig squeals and swallow spit because that's how it was done, and you were bullied by soldiers all the time because that was how the world worked.

But if someone wrote a cheerful little book about . . .

. . . what I did on my holidays . . .

. . . in a place where the world worked quite differently . . .

. . . then however fossilized the society there would always be *some* people who asked themselves dangerous questions like 'Where's the pork?'

Rincewind stared glumly at the wall. Peasants of the Empire, Rebel! You have nothing to lose but your heads and hands and feet and there's this thing they do with a wire waistcoat and a cheese-grater . . .

He turned the book over. There was no author's name. There was simply a little message: Increased Luck! Make Copies! Extended Duration And Happiness To The Endeavour!

Ankh-Morpork had had the occasional rebellion, too, over the years. But no one went around *organizing* things. They just grabbed themselves a weapon and took to the streets. No one bothered with a formal battlecry, relying instead on the well-tried 'There 'e goes! Get 'im! Got 'im? Now *kick* 'im inna fork!'

The point was . . . whatever *caused* that sort of thing wasn't usually the *reason* for it. When Mad Lord Snapcase had been hung up by his figgin* it hadn't *really* been because he'd made poor old Spooner Boggis eat his own nose, it had been because years of inventive nastiness had piled on one another until the grievances reached—

There was a terrible scream from the far side of the room. Rincewind was half out of his seat before he noticed the little stage, and the actors.

A trio of musicians had squatted down on the floor. The inn's customers turned to watch.

It was, in a way, quite enjoyable. Rincewind didn't quite follow the plot, but it went something like: man gets girl, man loses girl to other man, man cuts couple in half, man falls on own sword, all come up front for a bow to what might be the Agatean equivalent of 'Happy Days Are Here Again'. It was a little hard to make out the fine detail because the actors shouted 'Hoorrrrrraa!' a lot and spent much of their time talking to the audience and their masks all looked the same to Rincewind. The musicians were in a world of their own or, by the sound of it, three different worlds.

'Fortune cookie?'

'Huh?'

Rincewind re-emerged from the thickets of thespianism to see the landlord beside him.

A dish of vaguely bivalvular biscuits was thrust under his nose.

'Fortune cookie?'

Rincewind reached out. Just as his fingers were about to close on one, the plate was jerked sideways an inch or two, bringing another under his hand.

Oh, well. He took it.

The thing was – his thoughts resumed, as the play screamed on – at least in Ankh-Morpork you *could* lay your hands on real weapons.

Poor devils. It took more than well-turned slogans and a lot of enthusiasm to run a good rebellion. You needed well-trained fighters and, above all, a good leader. He hoped they found one when he was well away.

---

* According to the history books. However, in common with every other young student, Rincewind had hopefully looked up 'figgin' in the dictionary and found it was 'a small bun with currants in it'. This meant that either the language had changed a little over the years, or that there really was some horrifying aspect to suspending a man alongside a teacake.

He unrolled the fortune and read it idly, oblivious to the landlord walking around behind him.

Instead of the usual 'You have just enjoyed an inferior meal' it was quite a complicated pictogram.

Rincewind's fingers traced the brush strokes.

'"Many . . . many . . . apologies . . ." What kind—'

The musician with the cymbals clashed them together sharply.

The wooden cosh bounced off Rincewind's head.

The old men playing *shibo* nodded happily to themselves and turned back to their game.

It was a fine morning. The hideout echoed to the sounds of the Silver Horde getting up, groaning, adjusting various home-made surgical supports, complaining that they couldn't find their spectacles, and mistakenly gumming one another's dentures.

Cohen sat with his feet in a bath of warm water, enjoying the sunshine.

'Teach?'

The former geography teacher concentrated on a map he was making.

'Yes, Ghenghiz?'

'What's Mad Hamish going on about?'

'He says the bread's stale and he can't find his teeth.'

'Tell him if things go right for us he can have a dozen young women just to chew his bread for him,' said Cohen.

'That is not very hygienic, Ghenghiz,' said Mr Saveloy, without bothering to look up. 'Remember, I explained about hygiene.'

Cohen didn't bother to answer. He was thinking: six old men. And you can't really count Teach, he's a thinker, not a fighter . . .

Self-doubt was not something regularly entertained within the Cohen cranium. When you're trying to carry a struggling temple maiden and a sack of looted temple goods in one hand and fight off half a dozen angry priests with the other there is little time for reflection. Natural selection saw to it that professional heroes who at a crucial moment tended to ask themselves questions like 'What is my purpose in life?' very quickly lacked both.

But: six old men . . . and the Empire had almost a million men under arms.

When you looked at the odds in the cold light of dawn, or even this rather pleasant warm light of dawn, they made you stop and do the arithmetic of death. If the Plan went wrong . . .

Cohen bit his lip thoughtfully. If the Plan went wrong, it'd take *weeks* to kill all of them. Maybe he should have let old Thog the Butcher come along too, even though he had to stop fighting every ten minutes to go to the lavatory.

Oh, well. He was committed now, so he might as well make the best of it.

Cohen's father had taken him to a mountain top, when he was no more than a lad, and explained to him the hero's creed and told him that there was no greater joy than to die in battle.

Cohen had seen the flaw in this straight away, and a lifetime's experience had reinforced his belief that in fact a greater joy was to kill the *other* bugger in battle and end up sitting on a heap of gold higher than your horse. It was an observation that had served him well.

He stood up and stretched in the sunshine.

'It's a lovely morning, lads,' he said. 'I feel like a million dollars. Don't you?'

There was a murmur of reluctant agreement.

'Good,' said Cohen. 'Let's go and get some.'

The Great Wall completely surrounds the Agatean Empire. The word is *completely*.

It is usually about twenty feet high and sheer on its inner side. It is built along beaches and across howling deserts and even on the lip of sheer cliffs where the possibility of attack from outside is remote. On subject islands like Bhangbhangduc and Tingling there are similar walls, all metaphorically the same wall, and that seems strange to those of an unthinking military disposition who do not realise what its function really is.

It is more than just a wall, it is a marker. On one side is the Empire, which in the Agatean language is a word identical with 'universe'. On the other side is – nothing. After all, the universe is everything there is.

Oh, there may *appear* to be things, like sea, islands, other continents and so on. They may even appear solid, it may be possible to conquer them, walk on them . . . but they are not *ultimately* real. The Agatean word for foreigner is the same as the word for ghost, and only one brush stroke away from the word for victim.

The walls are sheer in order to discourage those boring people who persist in believing that there might be anything interesting on the other side. Amazingly enough there are people who simply won't take the hint, even after thousands of years. The ones near the coast build rafts and head out across lonely seas to lands that are a fable. The ones inland resort to man-carrying kites and chairs propelled by fireworks. Many of them die in the attempt, of course. Most of the others are soon caught, and made to live in interesting times.

But some did make it to the great melting pot called Ankh-Morpork. They arrived with no money – sailors charged what the market would bear, which was everything – but they had a mad gleam in their eye and they opened shops and restaurants and worked twenty-four hours a day. People called this the Ankh-Morpork Dream (of making piles of cash in a place where your death was unlikely to be a matter of public policy). And it was dreamed all the stronger by people who didn't sleep.

Rincewind sometimes thought that his life was punctuated by awakenings. They were not always rude ones. Sometimes they were merely impolite. A very few – one or two, perhaps – had been quite nice, especially on the island. The sun had come up in its humdrum fashion, the waves had washed the beach in quite a boring way, and on several occasions he'd managed to erupt from unconsciousness without his habitual small scream.

This one wasn't just rude. It was downright insolent. He was being bumped about and someone had tied his hands together. It was dark, a fact occasioned by the sack over his head.

Rincewind did some calculation, and reached a conclusion.

'This is the seventeenth worst day of my life so far,' he thought.

Being knocked unconscious in pubs was quite commonplace. If it happened in Ankh-Morpork then you'd likely as not wake up lying on the Ankh with all your money gone or, if a ship was due out on a long and unpopular voyage, chained up in some scupper somewhere with no option for the next two years but to plough the ocean wave.* But generally the knocker wanted to keep you alive. The Thieves' Guild were punctilious about that. As they said: 'Hit a man too hard and you can only rob him once; hit him just hard enough and you can rob him every week.'

If he was in what felt like a cart then someone had some purpose in keeping him alive.

He wished he hadn't thought of that.

---

* A dismal prospect, especially when the horses keep sinking.

Someone pulled the sack off. A terrifying visage stared down at him.

'"I would like to eat your foot!"' said Rincewind.

'Don't worry. I am a friend.'

The mask was lifted away. There was a young woman behind it – round faced, snub nosed and quite different from any other citizen Rincewind had met hitherto. That was, he realised, because she was looking straight at him. Her clothes, if not her face, had last been seen on the stage.

'Don't cry out,' she said.

'Why? What are you going to do?'

'We would have welcomed you properly but there was no time.' She sat down among the bundles in the back of the swaying cart and regarded him critically.

'Four Big Sandal said you arrived on a dragon and slaughtered a regiment of soldiers,' she said.

'I did?'

'And then you worked magic on a venerable old man and he became a great fighter.'

'He did?'

'And you gave him whole meat, even though Four Big Sandal is only of the *pung* class.'

'I did?'

'And you have your hat.'

'Yes, yes, got my hat.'

'And yet,' said the girl, 'you don't *look* like a Great Wizard.'

'Ah. Well, the fact is—'

The girl looked as fragile as a flower. But she had just pulled out, from somewhere in the folds of her costume, a small but perfectly serviceable knife.

Rincewind had picked up an instinct for this sort of thing. This was probably not the time to deny Great Wizardry.

'The fact is . . .' he repeated, 'that . . . how do I know I can trust you?'

The girl looked indignant. 'Do you not have amazing wizardly powers?'

'Oh, yes. Yes! Certainly! But—'

'Say something in wizard language!'

'Er. *Stercus, stercus, stercus, moriturus sum,*' said Rincewind, his eye on the knife.

'"O excrement, I am about to die?"'

'It's . . . er . . . a special mantra I say to raise the magical fluxes.'

The girl subsided a little.

'But it takes it out of you, wizarding,' said Rincewind. 'Flying on dragons, magically turning old men into warriors . . . I can only do so much of that sort of thing before it's time for a rest. Right now I'm very weak on account of the *tremendous* amounts of magic I've just used, you see.'

She looked at him with doubt still in her eyes.

'All the peasants believe in the imminent arrival of the Great Wizard,' she said. 'But, in the words of the great philosopher Ly Tin Wheedle, "When many expect a mighty stallion they will find hooves on an ant."'

She gave him another calculating look.

'When you were on the road,' she said, 'you grovelled in front of District Commissioner Kee. You could have blasted him with terrible fire.'

'Biding my time, spying out the land, not wanting to break my cover,' Rincewind gabbled. 'Er. No good revealing myself straight away, is there?'

'You are maintaining a disguise?'

'Yes.'

'It is a very good one.'

'Thank you, because—'

'Only a great wizard would dare to look like such a pathetic piece of humanity.'

'Thank you. Er . . . how *did* you know I was on the road?'

'They would have killed you there and then if I had not told you what to do.'

'You were the *guard*?'

'We had to catch up with you quickly. It was sheer luck you were seen by Four Big Sandal.'

'We?'

She ignored the question. 'They are only provincial soldiers. I would not have got away with it in Hunghung. But I can play many roles.' She put away the knife, but Rincewind had a feeling that he hadn't talked her into believing him, only into not killing him.

He groped for a straw.

'I've got a magic box on legs,' he said, with a touch of pride. 'It follows me around. It seems to have got itself mislaid right now, but it's quite an amazing thing.'

The girl gave him a wooden look. Then she reached down with a delicate hand and hauled him upright.

'Is it,' she said, 'something like this?'

She twitched aside the curtains at the rear of the cart.

Two boxes were trundling along in the dust. They were more battered and cheaper looking than the Luggage, but recognizably the same general species, if you could apply the word to travel accessories.

'Er. Yes.'

She let go. Rincewind's head hit the floor.

'Listen to me,' she said. 'A lot of bad things are happening. I don't believe in great wizards, but other people do, and sometimes people need something to believe in. And if these other people die because we've got a wizard who is not so very great, then he will be a very unlucky wizard indeed. You may be the Great Wizard. If you are not, then I suggest you study very hard to be great. Do I make myself clear?'

'Er. Yes.'

Rincewind had been faced with death on numerous occasions. Often there was armour and swords involved. This occasion just involved a pretty girl and a knife, but somehow managed to be among the worst. She sat back.

'We are a travelling theatre,' she said. 'It is convenient. Noh actors are allowed to move around.'

'Aren't they?' said Rincewind.

'You do not understand. We *are* Noh actors.'

'Oh, you weren't too bad.'

'Great Wizard, "Noh" is a non-realist symbolic form of theatre employing archaic language, stylized gestures and an accompaniment of flutes and drums. Your pretence of stupidity is masterly. So much so that I could even believe that you are no actor.'

'Excuse me, what is your name?' Rincewind said.

'Pretty Butterfly.'

'Er. Yes?'

She glared at him and slipped away towards the front of the cart.

It rumbled on. Rincewind lay with his head in a sack smelling of onions and methodically cursed things. He cursed women with knives, and history generally, and the entire faculty of Unseen University, and his absent Luggage, and the population of the Agatean Empire. But right now, at the top of the list, was whoever had designed this cart. By the feel of it, whoever had thought that rough, splintery wood was the right surface for a floor was also the person who thought 'triangular' was a nice shape for a wheel.

*

The Luggage lurked in a ditch, watched without much interest by a man holding a water buffalo on the end of a piece of string.

It was feeling ashamed, and baffled, and lost. It was lost because everywhere around it was . . . familiar. The light, the smells, the feel of the soil . . . But it didn't feel *owned*.

It was made of wood. Wood is sensitive to these things.

One of its many feet idly traced an outline in the mud. It was a random, wretched pattern familiar to anyone who's had to stand in front of the class and be scolded.

Finally, it reached something that was probably as close as timber can get to a decision.

It had been given away. It had spent many years trailing through strange lands, meeting exotic creatures and jumping up and down on them. Now it was back in the country where it had once been a tree. Therefore, it was free.

It was not the most logical chain of thought, but pretty good when all you've got to think with are knotholes.

And there was something it very much wanted to do.

'*When* you're ready, Teach?'

'Sorry, Ghenghiz. I'm just finishing . . .'

Cohen sighed. The Horde were taking advantage of the rest to sit in the shade of a tree and tell one another lies about their exploits, while Mr Saveloy stood on top of a boulder squinting through some kind of home-made device and doodling on his maps.

Bits of paper ruled the world now, Cohen told himself. It certainly ruled this part of it. And Teach . . . well, Teach ruled bits of paper. He might not be traditional barbarian hero material, despite his deeply held belief that all headmasters should be riveted to a cowshed door, but the man was *amazing* with bits of paper.

And he could speak Agatean. Well, speak it better than Cohen, who'd picked it up in a rough and ready way. He said he'd learned it out of some old book. He said it was amazing how much interesting stuff was in old books.

Cohen struggled up alongside him.

'What exactly you plannin', Teach?' he said.

Mr Saveloy squinted at Hunghung, just visible on the dusty horizon.

'Do you see that hill behind the city?' he said. 'The huge round mound?'

'Looks like my dad's burial mound to me,' said Cohen.

'No, it must be a natural formation. It's far too big. There's some kind of pagoda on top, I see. Interesting. Perhaps, later, I shall take a closer look.'

Cohen peered at the big round hill. It was a big round hill. It wasn't threatening him and it didn't look valuable. End of saga as far as he was concerned. There were more pressing matters.

'People appear to be entering and leaving the outer city,' Mr Saveloy continued. 'The siege is more a threat than a reality. So getting inside should not be a problem. Of course, getting into the Forbidden City itself will be a lot more difficult.'

'How about if we kill everyone?' said Cohen.

'A good idea, but impractical,' said Mr Saveloy. 'And liable to cause comment. No, my current methodology is predicated on the fact that Hunghung is some considerable way from the river yet has almost a million inhabitants.'

'Predicated, yeah,' said Cohen.

'And the local geography is quite wrong for artesian wells.'

'Yeah, 's what I thought . . .'

'And yet there is no visible aqueduct, you notice.'

'No aqueduct, right,' said Cohen. 'Prob'ly flown to the Rim for the summer. Some birds do that.'

'Which rather leads me to doubt the saying that not even a mouse can get into the Forbidden City,' said Mr Saveloy, with just a trace of smugness. 'I suspect a mouse could get into the Forbidden City *if it could hold its breath.*'

'Or ride on one of them invisible ducks,' said Cohen.

'Indeed.'

The cart stopped. The sack came off. Instead of the cheese-grater Rincewind was secretly expecting, the view consisted of a couple of young, concerned faces. One of them was female, but Rincewind was relieved to see that she wasn't Pretty Butterfly. This one looked younger, and made Rincewind think a little of potatoes.*

'How you are?' she said, in fractured but recognizable Morporkian. 'We are very sorry. All better now? We speak you in language of celestial city of Ankh-More-Pork. Language of freedom and progress. Language of One Man, One Vote!'

'Yes,' said Rincewind. A vision of Ankh-Morpork's Patrician

---

*When you're on a desert island, your appetites can become a bit confused.

floated across his memory. One man, one vote. Yes. 'I've met him. He's definitely got the vote. But—'

'Extra Luck To The People's Endeavour!' said the boy. 'Advance Judiciously!' He looked as though he'd been built with bricks.

'Excuse me,' said Rincewind, 'but why did you . . . a paper lantern for ceremonial purposes . . . bale of cotton . . . *rescue* me? Uh, that is, when I say rescue, I suppose I mean: why did you hit me on the head, tie me up, and bring me to wherever this is? Because the worst that could have happened to me in the inn was a ding around the ear for not paying for lunch—'

'The worst that *would* have happened was an agonizing death over several years,' said the voice of Butterfly. She appeared around the cart and smiled grimly at Rincewind. Her hands were tucked demurely in her kimono, presumably to hide the knives.

'Oh. Hello,' he said.

'Great Wizard,' said Butterfly, bowing. 'I you already know, but these two are Lotus Blossom and Three Yoked Oxen, other members of our cadre. We had to bring you here like this. There are spies everywhere.'

'Timely Demise To All Enemies!' said the boy, beaming.

'Good, yes, right,' said Rincewind. 'All enemies, yes.'

The cart was in a courtyard. The general noise level on the other side of the very high walls suggested a large city. Nasty certainty crystallised.

'And you've brought me to Hunghung, haven't you?' he said.

Lotus Blossom's eyes widened.

'Then it are *true*,' she said, in Rincewind's own language. 'You *are* the Great Wizard!'

'Oh, you'd be amazed at the things I can foresee,' said Rincewind despondently.

'You two, go and stable the horses,' said Butterfly, not taking her eyes off Rincewind. When they'd hurried away, with several backward glances, she walked up to him.

'They believe,' she said. 'Personally, I have my doubts. But Ly Tin Wheedle says an ass may do the work of an ox in a time of no horses. One of his less convincing aphorisms, I've always thought.'

'Thank you. What is a cadre?'

'Have you heard of the Red Army?'

'No. Well . . . I heard someone shout something . . .'

'According to legend, an unknown person known only as the Great Wizard led the first Red Army to an impossible victory. Of course, that was thousands of years ago. But the people believe that he – that is, *you* – will return to do it again. So . . . there should be a Red Army ready and waiting.'

'Well, of course, a man can get a little stiff after several thousand years—'

Her face was suddenly level with his own.

'*Personally* I suspect there has been a misunderstanding,' she hissed. 'But now you're here you'll be a Great Wizard. If I have to prod you every step of the way!'

The other two returned. Butterfly went from snarling tiger to demure doe in an instant.

'And now you must come and *meet* the Red Army,' she said.

'Won't they be a little smelly—' Rincewind began, and stopped when he saw her expression.

'The original Red Army was clearly only a legend,' she said, in fast and faultless Ankh-Morporkian. 'But legends have their uses. You'd better know the legend . . . Great Wizard. When One Sun Mirror was fighting all the armies of the world the Great Wizard came to his aid and the earth itself rose up and fought for the new Empire. And lightning was involved. The army was made from the earth but in some way driven by the lightning. Now, lightning may kill but I suspect it lacks discipline. And earth cannot fight. But no doubt our army of the earth and sky was nothing more nor less than an uprising of the peasants themselves. Well, now we have a new army, and a name that fires the imagination. And a Great Wizard. I don't believe in legends. But I believe that other people believe.'

The younger girl, who had been trying to follow this, stepped forward and gripped his arm.

'You come seeing Red Army *now*,' she said.

'Forward Motion With Masses!' said the boy, taking Rincewind's other arm.

'Does he always talk like that?' said Rincewind, as he was propelled gently towards a door.

'Three Yoked Oxen does not study,' said the girl.

'Extra Success Attend Our Leaders!'

'"Tuppence A Bucket, Well Stamped Down!"' said Rincewind encouragingly.

'Much Ownership Of Means Of Production!'

'"How's Your Granny Off For Soap?"'

Three Yoked Oxen beamed.

Butterfly opened the door. That left Rincewind outside with the other two.

'Very useful slogans,' he said, moving sideways just a little. 'But I would draw your attention to the famous saying of the Great Wizard Rincewind.'

'Indeed, I am all ear,' said Lotus Blossom politely.

'Rincewind, he say . . . Goodbyeeeeeeeee—'

His sandals skidded on the cobbles but he was already travelling fast when he hit the doors, which turned out to be made of bamboo and smashed apart easily.

There was a street market on the other side. That was something Rincewind remembered later about Hunghung; as soon as there was a space, any kind of space, even the space created by the passage of a cart or a mule, people flowed into it, usually arguing with one another at the tops of their voices over the price of a duck which was being held upside down and quacking.

His foot went through a wicker cage containing several chickens, but he pressed on, scattering people and produce. In an Ankh-Morpork street market something like this would have caused some comment, but since everyone around him already seemed to be screaming into other people's faces Rincewind was merely a momentary and unremarked nuisance as he half ran, half limped with one squawking foot past the stalls.

Behind him, the people flowed back. There may have been some cries of pursuit, but they were lost in the hubbub.

He didn't stop until he found an overlooked alcove between a stall selling songbirds and another purveying something that bubbled in bowls. His foot crowed.

He smashed it against cobbles until the cage broke; the cockerel, maddened by the heady air of freedom, pecked him on the knee and fluttered away.

There were no sounds of pursuit. However, a battalion of trolls in tin boots would have had trouble making themselves heard above a normal Hunghung street market.

He let himself get his breath back.

Well, he was his own man again. So much for the Red Army. Admittedly he was in the capital city, where he didn't want to be, and it was only a matter of time before something else unpleasant happened to him, but it wasn't actually happening at the moment. Let him find his bearings and five minutes' start and they could watch his dust. Or mud. There was a lot of both, here.

So . . . this was Hunghung . . .

There didn't seem to be streets in the sense Rincewind understood the term. Alleys opened on to alleys, all of them narrow and made narrower by the stalls that lined them. There was a large animal population in the marketplace. Most of the stalls had their share of caged chickens, ducks in sacks and strange wriggling things in bowls. From one stall a tortoise on top of a struggling heap of other tortoises under a sign saying: *3r. each, good for Ying* gave Rincewind a slow, 'You think you've got troubles?' look.

But it was hard to tell where the stalls ended and the buildings began in any case. Dried-up things hanging on a string might be merchandise or someone's washing or quite possibly next week's dinner.

The Hunghungese were an outdoor kind of people; from the look of it, they conducted most of their lives on the street and at the top of their voice.

Progress was made by viciously elbowing and shoving people until they got out of the way. Standing still and saying, 'Er, excuse me' was a recipe for immobility.

The crowds did part, though, at the banging of a gong and a succession of loud 'pops'. A group of people in white robes danced past, throwing fireworks around and banging on gongs, saucepans and odd bits of metal. The din contrived to be louder than the street noise, but only by very great effort.

Rincewind had been getting the occasional puzzled glance from people who stopped screaming long enough to notice him. Perhaps it was time to act like a native.

He turned to the nearest person and screamed, 'Pretty good, eh?'

The person, a little old lady in a straw hat, stared at him in distaste.

'It's Mr Whu's funeral,' she snapped, and walked off.

There were a couple of soldiers nearby. If this had been Ankh-Morpork, then they'd have been sharing a cigarette and trying not to see anything that might upset them. But these had an alert look.

Rincewind backed into another alley. An untutored visitor could clearly find himself in big trouble here.

This alley was quieter and, at the far end, opened into something much wider and empty looking. On the basis that people also meant trouble, Rincewind headed in that direction.

Here, at last, was an open space. It was very open indeed. It was a paved square, big enough to hold a couple of armies. It had cherry trees growing along the verges. And, given the heaving mob every-where else, a surprising absence of anyone . . .

'You!'

. . . apart from the soldiers.

They appeared abruptly from behind every tree and statue.

Rincewind tried to back away, but that proved unfortunate since there was a guard behind him.

A terrifying armoured mask confronted him.

'Peasant! Do you not know this is the Imperial Square?'

'Was that a capital S on Square, please?' said Rincewind.

'You do not ask questions!'

'Ah. I'll take that as a "yes". So it's important, then. Sorry. I'll just sort of go away, then . . .'

'You stay!'

But what struck Rincewind as amazingly odd was that none of them actually took hold of him. And then he realized that this must be because they hardly ever needed to. People did what they were told.

There's something worse than whips in the Empire, Cohen had said.

At this point, he realized, he should be on his knees. He crouched down, hands placed lightly in front of him.

'I wonder,' he said brightly, rising into the starting position, 'if this is the time to draw your attention to a famous saying?'

Cohen was familiar with city gates. He'd broken down a number in his time, by battering ram, siege gun and on one occasion with his head.

But the gates of Hunghung were pretty damn good gates. They weren't like the gates of Ankh-Morpork, which were usually wide open to attract the spending customer and whose concession to defence was the sign 'Thank You For Not Attacking Our City. Bonum Diem'. *These* things were big and made of metal and there was a guardhouse and a squad of unhelpful men in black armour.

'Teach?'

'Yes, Cohen?'

'Why're we doing this? I thought we were going to use the invisible duck the mice use.'

Mr Saveloy waggled a finger.

'That's for the Forbidden City itself. I hope we'll find that inside. Now, remember your lessons,' he said. 'It's important that you all learn how to behave in cities.'

'I *know* how to bloody well behave in cities,' said Truckle the Uncivil. 'Pillage, ravish, loot, set fire to the damn place on your way out. Just like towns only it takes longer.'

'That's all very well if you're just passing through,' said Mr Saveloy, 'but what if you want to come back next day?'

'It ain't bloody well there next day, mister.'

'Gentlemen! Bear with me. You will have to learn the ways of civilization!'

People couldn't just walk through. There was a line. And the guards gathered rather offensively around each cowering visitor to examine their papers.

And then it was Cohen's turn.

'Papers, old man?'

Cohen nodded happily, and handed the guard captain a piece of paper on which was written, in Mr Saveloy's best handwriting:

WE ARE WANDERING MADMEN WHO
HAVE NO PAPERS. SORRY.

The guard's gaze lifted from the paper and met Cohen's cheerful grin.

'Indeed,' he said nastily. 'Can't you speak, grandfather?'

Cohen, still grinning, looked questioningly at Mr Saveloy. They hadn't rehearsed this part.

'Foolish dummy,' said the guard.

Mr Saveloy looked outraged.

'I thought you were supposed to show special consideration for the insane!' he said.

'You cannot be insane without papers to say you're insane,' said the guard.

'Oh, I'm fed up with this,' said Cohen. 'I *said* it wouldn't work if we came across a thick guard.'

'Insolent peasant!'

'I'm not as insolent as my friends here,' said Cohen.

The Horde nodded.

'That's us, flatfoot.'

'Bum to you.'

'Whut?'

'Extremely foolish soldier.'

'Whut?'

The captain was taken aback. Deeply ingrained in the Agatean psyche was the habit of obedience. But even stronger was a veneration of one's ancestors and a respect for the elderly, and the captain had never seen anyone so elderly while still vertical. They

401

practically *were* ancestors. The one in the wheelchair certainly smelled like one.

'Take them to the guardhouse!' he shouted.

The Horde let themselves be manhandled, and did it quite well. Mr Saveloy had spent hours training them in this, since he knew he was dealing with men whose response to a tap on the shoulder was to turn around and hack off someone's arm.

It was crowded in the guardhouse, with the Horde and the guards and with Mad Hamish's wheelchair. One of the guards looked down at Hamish, glowering under his blanket.

'What do you have there, grandfather?'

A sword came up through the cloth and stabbed the guard in the thigh.

'Whut? Whut? Whutzeesay?'

'He said, "Aargh!", Hamish,' said Cohen, a knife appearing in his hand. With one movement his skinny arms had the captain in a lock, the knife at his throat.

'Whut?'

'He said, "Aargh!"'

'Whut? I ain't even married!'

Cohen put a little more pressure on the captain's neck.

'Now then, friend,' he said. 'You can have it the easy way, see, or the hard way. It's up to you.'

'Blood-sucking pig! You call this the easy way?'

'Well, *I* ain't sweatin'.'

'May you live in interesting times! I would rather die than betray my Emperor!'

'Fair enough.'

It took the captain only a fraction of a second to realise that Cohen, being a man of his word, assumed that other people were too. He might, if he had time, have reflected that the purpose of civilization is to make violence the final resort, while to a barbarian it is the first, preferred, only and above all most enjoyable option. But by then it was too late. He slumped forward.

'I *always* lives in interestin' times,' said Cohen, in the satisfied voice of someone who did a lot to keep them interesting.

He pointed his knife at the other guards. Mr Saveloy's mouth was wide open in horror.

'By rights I should be cleanin' this,' said Cohen. 'But I ain't goin' to bother if it's only goin' to get dirty again. Now, *person'ly*, I'd as soon kill you as look at you but Teach here says I've got to stop doin' that and become respectable.'

One of the guards looked sideways at his fellows and then fell on his knees.

'What is your wish, o master?' he said.

'Ah, officer material,' said Cohen. 'What's your name, lad?'

'Nine Orange Trees, master.'

Cohen looked at Mr Saveloy.

'What do I do now?'

'Take them prisoner, *please*.'

'How do I do that?'

'Well . . . I suppose you tie them up, that sort of thing.'

'Ah. And then cut their throats?'

'No! No. You see, once you've got them at your mercy, you're not allowed to kill them.'

The Silver Horde, to a man, stared at the ex-teacher.

'I'm afraid that's civilization for you,' he added.

'But you said the sods haven't got any bloody weapons!' said Truckle.

'Yes,' said Mr Saveloy, shuddering a little. 'That's why you're not allowed to kill them.'

'Are you mad? Got mad papers, have you?'

Cohen scratched his stubbly chin. The remainder of the guard watched him in trepidation. They were used to cruel and unusual punishment, but they were unaccustomed to argument first.

'You haven't had a lot of military experience, have you, Teach?' he said.

'Apart from Form Four? Not a lot. But I'm afraid this is the way it has to be done. I'm sorry. You did say you wanted me—'

'Well, *I* vote we just cuts their throats right now,' said Boy Willie. 'I can't be having with this prisoner business either. I mean, who's gonna feed them?'

'I'm afraid you have to.'

'Who, me? Not likely! I vote we make them eat their own eyeballs. Hands up all in favour.'

There was a chorus of assent from the Horde and, among the raised hands, Cohen noticed one belonging to Nine Orange Trees.

'What you voting for, lad?' he said.

'Please, sir, I would like to go to the lavatory.'

'You listen to me, you lot,' said Cohen. 'This slaughtering and butchering business isn't how you do it these days, right? That's what Mr Saveloy says and he knows how to spell words like "marmalade" which is more than you do. Now, we know why we're here, and we'd better start as we mean to go on.'

'Yeah, but you just killed that guard,' said Truckle.

'I'm breaking myself in,' said Cohen. 'You've got to creep up on civilization a bit at a time.'

'I still say we should cut their heads off. That's what I did to the Mad Demon-Sucking Priests of Ee!'

The kneeling guard had cautiously raised his hand again.

'Please, master?'

'Yes, lad?'

'You could lock us up in that cell over there. Then we wouldn't be any trouble to anyone.'

'Good thinking,' said Cohen. 'Good lad. The boy keeps his head in a crisis. Lock 'em up.'

Thirty seconds later the Horde had limped off, into the city.

The guards sat in the cramped, hot cell.

Eventually one said, 'What were they?'

'I think they might have been ancestors.'

'I thought you had to be dead to be an ancestor.'

'The one in the wheelchair *looked* dead. Right up to the point where he stabbed Four White Fox.'

'Should we shout for help?'

'They might hear us.'

'Yes, but if we don't get let out we'll be stuck in here. And the walls are very thick and the door is very strong.'

'Good.'

Rincewind stopped running in some alley somewhere. He hadn't bothered to see if they'd followed him. It was true – here, with one mighty bound, you *could* be free. Provided you realized it was one of your options.

Freedom did, of course, include man's age-old right to starve to death. It seemed a long time since his last proper meal.

The voice erupted further down the alley, as if on cue.

'Rice cakes! Rice cakes! Get chore nice rice cakes! Tea! Hundred-Year-Old Eggs! Eggs! Get them while they're nice and vintage! Get chore – Yeah, what is it?'

An elderly man had approached the salesman.

'Dibhala-san! This egg you sold me—'

'What about it, venerable squire?'

'Would you care to smell it?'

The street vendor took a sniff.

'Ah, yes, lovely,' he said.

404

'Lovely? *Lovely?* This egg,' said the customer, 'this egg is practically fresh!'

'Hundred years old if it's a day, shogun,' said the vendor happily.

'Look at the colour of that shell, nice and black—'

'It rubs off!'

Rincewind listened. There was, he thought, probably something in the idea that there were only a few people in the world. There were lots of *bodies*, but only a few people. That's why you kept running into the same ones. There was probably some mould somewhere.

'You saying my produce is fresh? May I disembowel myself honourably! Look, I'll tell you what I'll do—'

Yes, there seemed to be something familiar and magical about that trader. Someone had come to complain about a fresh egg, and yet within a couple of minutes he'd somehow been talked into forgetting this and purchasing two rice cakes and something strange wrapped in leaves.

The rice cakes looked nice. Well . . . nicer than the other things.

Rincewind sidled over. The trader was idly jigging from one foot to the other and whistling under his breath, but he stopped and gave Rincewind a big, honest, friendly grin.

'Nice ancient egg, shogun?'

The bowl in the middle of the tray was full of gold coins. Rincewind's heart sank. The price of one of Mr Dibhala's foul eggs would have bought a street in Ankh-Morpork.

'I suppose you don't give . . . credit?' he suggested.

Dibhala gave him a Look.

'I'll pretend I never heard that, shogun,' he said.

'Tell me,' said Rincewind. 'Do you know if you have any relatives overseas?'

This got him another look – a sideways one, full of sudden appraisal.

'What? There's nothing but evil blood-sucking ghosts beyond the seas. Everyone knows that, shogun. I'm surprised you don't.'

'Ghosts?' said Rincewind.

'Trying to get here, do us harm,' said Disembowel-Meself-Honourably. 'Maybe even steal our merchandise. Give 'em a dose of the old firecracker, that's what *I* say. They don't like a good loud bang, ghosts.'

He gave Rincewind another look, even longer and more calculating.

'Where you from, shogun?' he asked, and his voice suddenly had the little barbed edge of suspicion.

405

'Bes Pelargic,' said Rincewind quickly. 'That explains my strange accent and mannerisms that might otherwise lead people to think I was some sort of foreigner,' he added.

'Oh, Bes Pelargic,' said Disembowel-Meself-Honourably. 'Well, in that case, I expect you know my old friend Five Tongs who lives in the Street of Heavens, yes?'

Rincewind was ready for this old trick.

'No,' he said. 'Never heard of him, never heard of the street.'

Disembowel-Meself-Honourably Dibhala grinned happily. 'If I yell "foreign devil" loud enough you won't get three steps,' he said in conversational tones. 'The guards will drag you off to the Forbidden City where there's this special thing they do with—'

'I've heard about it,' said Rincewind.

'Five Tongs has been the district commissioner for three years and the Street of Heavens is the main street,' said Disembowel-Meself-Honourably. 'I've always wanted to meet a blood-sucking foreign ghost. Have a rice cake.'

Rincewind's gaze darted this way and that. But strangely enough the situation didn't seem dangerous, or at least inevitably dangerous. It seemed that danger was negotiable.

'Supposing I was to admit I *was* from behind the Wall?' he said, keeping his voice as low as possible.

Dibhala nodded. One hand reached into his robe and, in a quick movement, revealed and then concealed the corner of something which Rincewind was not entirely surprised to see was entitled WHAT I DID . . .

'Some people say that beyond the Wall there's nothing but deserts and burning wastes and evil ghosts and terrible monsters,' said Dibhala, 'but *I* say, what about the merchandizing opportunities? A man with the right contacts . . . Know what I mean, shogun? He could go a *long* way in the land of blood-sucking ghosts.'

Rincewind nodded. He didn't like to point out that if you turned up in Ankh-Morpork with a handful of gold then about three hundred people would turn up with a handful of steel.

'The way I see it, what with all this uncertainty about the Emperor and talk of rebels and that – Long Live His Excellency The Son Of Heaven, of course – there might just be a nitch for the open-minded trader, am I right?'

'Nitch?'

'Nitch. Like . . . we've got this stuff' – he leaned closer – 'comes out of a caterpillar's [unidentified pictogram]. 'S called . . . *silk*. It's—'

'Yes, I know. We get it from Klatch,' said Rincewind.

'Or, well, there's this bush, see, you dry the leaves, but then you put it in hot water and you drin—'

'Tea, yes,' said Rincewind. 'That comes from Howondaland.'

D. M. H. Dibhala looked taken aback.

'Well . . . we've got this powder, you put it in tubes—'

'Fireworks? Got fireworks.'

'How about this really fine china, it's so—'

'In Ankh-Morpork we've got dwarfs that can make china you can read a book through,' said Rincewind. 'Even if it's got tiny footnotes in it.'

Dibhala frowned.

'Sounds like you are very clever blood-sucking ghosts,' he said, backing away. 'Maybe it's true and you *are* dangerous.'

'Us? Don't worry about us,' said Rincewind. 'We hardly ever kill foreigners in Ankh-Morpork. It makes it so hard to sell them things afterwards.'

'What've we got that you want, though? Go on, have a rice cake. On the pagoda. Wanna try some pork balls? Onna chopstick?'

Rincewind selected a cake. He didn't like to ask about the other stuff.

'You've got gold,' he said.

'Oh, *gold*. It's too soft to do much with,' said Dibhala. 'It's all right for pipes and putting on roofs, though.'

'Oh . . . I daresay people in Ankh-Morpork could find a use for some,' said Rincewind. His gaze returned to the coins in Dibhala's tray.

A land where gold was as cheap as lead . . .

'What's that?' he said, pointing to a crumpled rectangle half covered with coins.

D. M. H. Dibhala looked down. 'It's this thing we have here,' he said, speaking slowly. 'Of course, it's probably all new to you. It's called mon-ey. It's a way of carrying around your—'

'I meant the bit of paper,' said Rincewind.

'So did I,' said Dibhala. 'That's a ten-*rhinu* note.'

'What does that mean?' said Rincewind.

'Means what it says,' said Dibhala. 'Means it's worth ten of these.' He held up a gold coin about the size of a rice cake.

'Why'd you want to buy a piece of paper?' said Rincewind.

'You don't buy it, it's for buying things *with*,' said Dibhala.

Rincewind looked blank.

'You go to a mark-et stall,' said Dibhala, getting back into the slow-voice-for-the-hard-of-thinking, 'and you say, "Good morn-ing, but-cher, how much for those dog noses?" and he says, "Three *rhinu*, shogun," and *you* say, "I've only got a pony, okay?" (look, there's an etch-ing of a pony on it, see, that's what you get on ten-*rhinu* notes) and he gives you the dog noses and seven coins in what we call "change". Now, if you had a monkey, that's fifty *rhinu*, he'd say "Got anything smal-ler?" and—'

'But it's only a bit of paper!' Rincewind wailed.

'It may be a bit of paper to you but it's ten rice cakes to me,' said Dibhala. 'What do you foreign blood-suckers use? Big stones with holes in them?'

Rincewind stared at the paper money.

There were dozens of papermills in Ankh-Morpork, and some of the craftsmen in the Engravers' Guild could engrave their name and address on a pinhead.

He suddenly felt immensely proud of his countrymen. They might be venal and greedy, but by heaven they were *good* at it and they never assumed that there wasn't any more to learn.

'I think you'll find,' he said, 'that there's a lot of buildings in Ankh-Morpork that need new roofs.'

'Really?' said Dibhala.

'Oh, yes. The rain's just pouring in.'

'And people can pay? Only I heard—'

Rincewind looked at the paper money again. He shook his head. Worth more than gold . . .

'They'll pay with notes at least as good as that,' he said. 'Probably even better. I'll put in a good word for you. And now,' he added hurriedly, 'which way is out?'

Dibhala scratched his head.

'Could be a bit tricky,' he said. 'There's armies outside. You look a bit foreign with that hat. Could be tricky—'

There was a commotion further along the alley or, rather, a general increase in the commotion. The crowd parted in that hurried way common to unarmed crowds in the presence of weaponry, and a group of guards hurried towards Disembowel-Meself-Honourably.

He stepped back and gave them the friendly grin of one happy to sell at a discount to anyone with a knife.

A limp figure was being dragged between two of the guards. As it went past it raised a slightly bloodstained head and said, 'Extended Duration to the—' before a gloved fist smacked across its mouth.

And then the guards were heading down the street. The crowd flowed back.

'Tch, tch,' said D. M. H. 'Seems to be – Hello? Where'd you go?'

Rincewind reappeared from around a corner. D. M. H. looked impressed. There had actually been a small thunderclap when Rincewind moved.

'See they got another of 'em,' he said. 'Putting up wall posters again, I expect.'

'Another one of who?' said Rincewind.

'Red Army. Huh!'

'Oh.'

'I don't pay much attention,' said D. M. H. 'They say some old legend's going to come true about emperors and stuff. Can't see it myself.'

'He didn't look very legendary,' said Rincewind.

'Ach, some people will believe anything.'

'What'll happen to him?'

'Difficult to say, with the Emperor about to die. Hands and feet cut off, probably.'

'What? Why?'

''Cos he's young. That's leniency. A bit older and it's his head on a spike over one of the gates.'

'That's punishment for putting up a *poster*?'

'Stops 'em doing it again, see,' said D. M. H.

Rincewind backed away.

'Thank you,' he said, and hurried off.

'Oh, no,' he said, pushing his way through the crowds. 'I'm *not* getting mixed up in people's heads getting chopped off—'

And then someone hit him again. But politely.

As he sank to his knees, and then to his chin, he wondered what had happened to the good old-fashioned 'Hey, you!'

The Silver Horde wandered through the alleys of Hunghung.

'I don't call *this* bloody well sweeping through a city, slaughtering every bugger,' muttered Truckle. 'When I was riding with Bruce the Hoon, we *never* walked in through a front gate like a bunch of soppy mother—'

'Mr Uncivil,' said Mr Saveloy hurriedly, 'I wonder if this might be a good time to refer you to that list I drew up for you?'

'What bloody list?' said Truckle, sticking out his jaw belligerently.

'The list of acceptable *civilized* words, yes?' He turned to the others. 'Remember I was telling you about civ-il-ized be-hav-iour. Civilized behaviour is vital to our long-term strategy.'

'What's a long-term strategy?' said Caleb the Ripper.

'It's what we're going to do later,' said Cohen.

'And what's that, then?'

'It's the Plan,' said Cohen.

'Well, I'll be f—' Truckle began.

'The list, Mr Uncivil, only the words on the *list*,' snapped Mr Saveloy. 'Listen, I bow to your expertise when it comes to crossing wildernesses, but this is civilization and you must use the right words. Please?'

'Better do what he says, Truckle,' said Cohen.

With bad grace, Truckle fished a grubby piece of paper out of his pocket and unfolded it.

' "Dang"?' he said. 'Wassat mean? And what's this "darn" and "heck"?'

'They are . . . *civilized* swearwords,' said Mr Saveloy.

'Well, you can take 'em and—'

'Ah?' said Mr Saveloy, raising a cautionary finger.

'You can shove them up—'

'Ah?'

'You can—'

'Ah?'

Truckle shut his eyes and clenched his fists.

'Dang it all to heck!' he shouted.

'Good,' said Mr Saveloy. 'That's much better.'

He turned to Cohen, who was grinning happily at Truckle's discomfort.

'Cohen,' he said, 'there's an apple stall over there. Do you fancy an apple?'

'Yeah, might do,' Cohen conceded, in the cautious manner of someone giving a conjuror his watch while remaining aware that the man is grinning and holding a hammer.

'Right. Now, then, cla— I mean, gentlemen. Ghenghiz wants an apple. There's a stall over there selling fruit and nuts. What does he do?' Mr Saveloy looked hopefully at his charges. 'Anyone? Yes?'

'Easy. You kill that little' – there was a rustle of unfolding paper again – '*chap* behind the stall, then—'

'No, Mr Uncivil. Anyone else?'

'Whut?'

'You set fire to—'

'No, Mr Vincent. Anyone else . . .?'

'You rape—'

'No, no, Mr Ripper,' said Mr Saveloy. 'We take out some muh – muh—?' He looked at them expectantly.

'—money—' chorused the Horde.

'—and we . . . What do we do? Now, we've gone through this hundreds of times. We . . .'

This was the difficult bit. The Horde's lined faces creased and puckered still further as they tried to force their minds out of the chasms of habit.

'Gi . . .?' said Cohen hesitantly. Mr Saveloy gave him a big smile and a nod of encouragement.

'Give? . . . it . . . to . . .' Cohen's lips tensed around the word ' . . . him?'

'Yes! Well done. In *exchange* for the apple. We'll talk about making change and saying "thank you" later on, when you're ready for it. Now then, Cohen, here's the coin. Off you go.'

Cohen wiped his forehead. He was beginning to sweat.

'How about if I just cut him up a bit—'

'No! This is *civilization*.'

Cohen nodded uncomfortably. He threw back his shoulders and walked over to the stall, where the apple merchant, who had been eyeing the group suspiciously, nodded at him.

Cohen's eyes glazed and his lips moved silently, as if he were rehearsing a script. Then he said:

'Ho, fat merchant, give me all your . . . one apple . . . and I will give you . . . this coin . . .'

He looked around. Mr Saveloy had his thumb up.

'You want an apple, is that it?' said the apple merchant.

'Yes!'

The apple merchant selected one. Cohen's sword had been hidden in the wheelchair again but the merchant, in response to some buried acknowledgement, made sure it was a *good* apple. Then he took the coin. This proved a little difficult, since his customer seemed loath to let go of it.

'Come on, hand it over, venerable one,' he said.

Seven crowded seconds passed.

Then, when they were safely around the corner, Mr Saveloy said, 'Now, everyone: who can tell me what Ghenghiz did wrong?'

'Didn't say please?'

'Whut?'

'No.'

'Didn't say thank you?'

'Whut?'

'No.'

'Hit the man over the head with a melon and thumped him into the strawberries and kicked him in the nuts and set fire to his stall and stole all the money?'

'Whut?'

'Correct!' Mr Saveloy sighed. 'Ghenghiz, you were doing *so* well up to then.'

'He didn't ort to have called me what he did!'

'But "venerable" means old and wise, Ghenghiz.'

'Oh. Does it?'

'Yes.'

'We-ell . . . I did leave him the money for the apple.'

'Yes, but, you see, I do believe you took all his other money.'

'But I *paid* for the apple,' said Cohen, rather testily.

Mr Saveloy sighed. 'Ghenghiz, I do rather get the impression that several thousand years of the patient development of fiscal propriety have somewhat passed you by.'

'Come again?'

'It is possible sometimes for money to legitimately belong to other people,' said Mr Saveloy patiently.

The Horde paused to wrap their minds around this, too. It was, of course, something they knew to be true in theory. Merchants always had money. But it seemed wrong to think of it as *belonging* to them; it *belonged* to whoever took it off them. Merchants didn't actually *own* it, they were just looking after it until it was needed.

'Now, there is an elderly lady over there selling ducks,' said Mr Saveloy. 'I think the next stage – Mr Willie, I am not over there, I am sure whatever you are looking at is very interesting, but please pay attention – is to practise our grasp of social intercourse.'

'Hur, hur, hur,' said Caleb the Ripper.

'I mean, Mr Ripper, that you should go and enquire how much it would be for a duck,' said Mr Saveloy.

'Hur, hur, hur – What?'

'And you are not to rip all her clothes off. That's not civilized.'

Caleb scratched his head. Flakes fell out.

'Well, what else am I supposed to do?'

'Er . . . engage her in conversation.'

'Eh? What's there to talk about with a woman?'

Mr Saveloy hesitated again. To some extent this was unknown territory to him as well. His experience with women at his last school had been limited to an occasional chat with the house-keeper, and on one occasion the matron had let him put his hand on her knee. He had been forty before he found out that oral sex didn't mean talking about it. Women had always been to him strange and distant and wonderful creatures rather than, as the Horde to a man believed, something to do. He was struggling a little.

'The weather?' he hazarded. His memory threw in vague recollections of the staple conversation of the maiden aunt who had brought him up. 'Her health? The trouble with young people today?'

'And then I rip her clothes off?'

'Possibly. Eventually. If she wants you to. I might draw your attention to the discussion we had the other day about taking regular baths' – or even *a* bath, he added to himself – 'and attention to fingernails and hair and changing your clothes more often.'

'This is leather,' said Caleb. 'You don't have to change it, it don't rot for *years*.'

Once again Mr Saveloy readjusted his sights. He'd thought that Civilization could be overlaid on the Horde like a veneer. He had been mistaken.

But the funny thing – he mused, as the Horde watched Caleb's painful attempts at conversation with a representative of half the world's humanity – was that although they were as far away as possible from the kind of people he normally mixed with in staff-rooms, or possibly because they were as far away as possible from the kind of people he normally mixed with in staffrooms, he actually *liked* them. Every one of them saw a book as either a lavatorial accessory or a set of portable firelighters and thought that hygiene was a greeting. Yet they were honest (from their specialized point of view) and decent (from their specialized point of view) and saw the world as hugely simple. They stole from rich merchants and temples and kings. They didn't steal from poor people; this was not because there was anything virtuous about poor people, it was simply because poor people had no money.

And although they didn't set out to give the money *away* to the poor, that was nevertheless what they did (if you accepted that the poor consisted of innkeepers, ladies of negotiable virtue, pickpockets, gamblers and general hangers-on), because although they would go to great lengths to steal money they then had as much control over it as a man trying to herd cats. It was there to be spent and lost. So they kept the money in circulation, always a praiseworthy thing in any society.

They never worried about what other people thought. Mr Saveloy, who'd spent his whole life worrying about what other people thought and had been passed over for promotion and generally treated as a piece of furniture as a result, found this strangely attractive. And they never agonized about anything, or wondered if they were doing the right thing. And they enjoyed themselves immensely. They had a kind of honour. He *liked* the Horde. They weren't his kind of people.

Caleb returned, looking unusually thoughtful.

'Congratulations, Mr Ripper!' said Mr Saveloy, a great believer in positive reinforcement. 'She still appears to be fully clothed.'

'Yeah, what'd she say?' said Boy Willie.

'She smiled at me,' said Caleb. He scratched his crusty beard uneasily. 'A bit, anyway,' he added.

'Good,' said Mr Saveloy.

'She, er . . . she said she'd . . . she wouldn't mind seein' me . . . later . . .'

'Well done!'

'Er . . . Teach? What's a *shave*?'

Saveloy explained.

Caleb listened carefully, grimacing occasionally. He turned round occasionally to look at the duck seller, who gave him a little wave.

'Cor,' he said. 'Er. I dunno . . .' He looked around again. 'Never seen a woman who wasn't running away before.'

'Oh, women are like deer,' said Cohen loftily. 'You can't just charge in, you gotta stalk 'em—'

'Hur, hur, h— Sorry,' said Caleb, catching Mr Saveloy's stern eye.

'I think perhaps we should end the lesson here,' said Mr Saveloy. 'We don't want to get you *too* civilized, do we . . .? I suggest we take a stroll around the Forbidden City, yes?'

They'd all seen it. It dominated the centre of Hunghung. Its walls were forty feet high.

'There's a lot of soldiers guarding the gates,' said Cohen.

'So they should. A great treasure lies within,' said Mr Saveloy. He didn't raise his eyes, though. He seemed to be staring intently at the ground, as though searching for something he'd lost.

'Why don't we just rush up and kill the guards?' Caleb demanded. He was still feeling a bit shaken.

'Whut?'

'Don't be daft,' said Cohen. 'It'd take all day. Anyway,' he added, feeling a little proud despite himself, 'Teach here is goin' to get us in on an invisible duck, ain't that so, Teach?'

Mr Saveloy stopped.

'Ah. Eureka,' he said.

'That's Ephebian, that is,' Cohen told the Horde. 'It means "Give me a towel."'

'Oh yeah,' said Caleb, who had been surreptitiously trying to untangle the knots in his beard. 'And when were you ever in Ephebe?'

'Went bounty hunting there once.'

'Who for?'

'You, I think.'

'Hah! Did you find me?'

'Dunno. Nod your head and see if it falls off.'

'Ah. Gentlemen . . . behold . . .'

Mr Saveloy's orthopaedic sandal was prodding an ornamental metal square in the ground.

'Behold what?' said Truckle.

'Whut?'

'We should look for more of these,' said Mr Saveloy. 'But I think we have it. All we need to do now is wait until dark.'

There was an argument going on. All Rincewind could make out were the voices; another sack had been tied over his head, while he himself was tied to a pillar.

'Does he even *look* like a Great Wizard?'

'That's what it says on his hat in the language of ghosts—'

'So you say!'

'What about the testimony of Four Big Sandal, then?'

'He was overtaxed. He could have imagined it!'

'I did not! He came out of thin air, flying like a dragon! He knocked over five soldiers. And Three Maximum Luck saw it also. And the others. And then he freed an ancient man and turned him into a mighty fighting warrior!'

'And he can speak our language, just as it says in the book.'

'All right. Supposing he *is* the Great Wizard? Then we should kill him now!'

In the darkness of his sack, Rincewind shook his head furiously.

'Why?'

'He will be on the side of the Emperor.'

'But the legend says the Great Wizard led the Red Army!'

'Yes, for Emperor One Sun Mirror. It crushed the people!'

'No, it crushed all the bandit chiefs! Then it built the Empire!'

'So? The Empire is so great? Untimely Demise To The Forces Of Oppression!'

'But *now* the Red Army is on the side of the people! Maximum Advancement With The Great Wizard!'

'The Great Wizard is the Enemy of the People!'

'I saw him, I tell you! A legion of soldiers collapsed with the wind of his passage!'

The wind of his passage was beginning to worry Rincewind as well. It always tended to when he was frightened.

'If he is such a great wizard, why is he still tied up? Why has he not made his bonds disappear in puffs of green smoke?'

'Perhaps he is saving his magic for some even mightier deeds. He wouldn't do firecracker tricks for earthworms.'

'Hah!'

'And he had the Book! He was looking for us! It is his destiny to lead the Red Army!'

Shake, shake, shake.

'We can lead ourselves!'

Nod, nod, nod.

'We don't need any suspicious Great Wizards from illusionary places!'

Nod, nod, nod.

'So we should kill him now!'

Nod, no – *Shakeshakeshake.*

'Hah! He laughs at you with scorn! He waits to make your head explode with snakes of fire!'

Shake, shake, shake.

'You do know that while we're arguing Three Yoked Oxen is being tortured?'

'The People's Army is more than just individuals, Lotus Blossom!'

In the foetid sack Rincewind grimaced. He was already beginning to take a dislike to the first speaker, as one naturally does with people urging that you be put to death without delay. But when that sort of person started talking about things being more important than people, you knew you were in big trouble.

'I'm sure the Great Wizard could rescue Three Yoked Oxen,' said a voice by his ear. It was Butterfly.

'Yes, he could easily rescue Three Yoked Oxen!' said Lotus Blossom.

'Hah! You say? He could get into the Forbidden City? Impossible! It's certain death!'

Nod, nod, nod.

416

'Not to the Great Wizard,' said the voice of Butterfly.

'*Shut up!*' hissed Rincewind.

'*Would you like to know how big the meat cleaver is that Two Fire Herb is holding in his hand?*' whispered Butterfly.

'*No!*'

'*It's very big.*'

'*He said that going into the Forbidden City is certain death!*'

'*No. It's only probable death. I assure you, if you run away from me again that is* certain *death.*'

The sack was pulled away.

The face immediately in front of him was that of Lotus Blossom, and a man could see a lot worse things with his daylight than her face, which made him think of cream and masses of butter and just the right amount of salt.[*]

One of the things he might see, for example, was the face of Two Fire Herb. This was not a nice face. It was podgy and had tiny little pupils in its eyes, and looked like a living example of the fact that although the people could be oppressed by kings and emperors and mandarins, the job could often be done just as well by the man next door.

'Great Wizard? Hah!' Two Fire Herb said now.

'He can do it!' said Lotus Blossom (and cream cheese, thought Rincewind, and maybe coleslaw on the side). 'He *is* the Great Wizard come back to us! Did he not guide the Master through the lands of ghosts and blood-sucking vampires?'

'Oh, I wouldn't say—' Rincewind began.

'Such a great wizard allowed you to bring him here in a sack?' said Two Fire Herb, sneering. 'Let us see him do some conjuring . . .'

'A truly *great* wizard would not stoop to doing party tricks!' said Lotus Blossom.

'That's right,' said Rincewind. 'Not stoop.'

'Shame on Herb to suggest such a thing!'

'Shame,' Rincewind agreed.

'Besides, he will need all of his power to enter the Forbidden City,' said Butterfly. Rincewind found himself hating the sound of her voice.

'Forbidden City,' he murmured.

'Everyone knows there are terrible snares and traps and many, many guards.'

---

[*] Much later, Rincewind had to have therapy for this. It involved a pretty woman, a huge plate of potatoes and a big stick with a nail in it.

417

'Snares, traps . . .'

'Why, if his magic should fail him because he did tricks for Herb, he would find himself in the deepest dungeon, dying by inches.'

'Inches . . . er . . . which particular inch—'

'So much shame to Two Fire Herb!'

Rincewind gave her a sickly grin.

'Actually,' he said, 'I'm not *that* great. I'm a *bit* great,' he added quickly, as Butterfly began to frown, 'but not *very* great—'

'The writings of the Master say that you defeated many powerful enchanters and resolutely succeeded in dangerous situations.'

Rincewind nodded glumly. It was more or less true. But most of the time he hadn't intended to. Whereas the Forbidden City had looked . . . well . . . forbidden. It didn't look inviting. It didn't look as though it sold postcards. The only souvenir they were likely to give you would be, perhaps, your teeth. In a bag.

'Er . . . I expect this Oxen lad is in some deep dungeon, yes?'

'The deepest,' said Two Fire Herb.

'And . . . you've never seen anyone again? Who's been taken prisoner, I mean.'

'We have seen *bits* of them,' said Lotus Blossom.

'Usually their heads,' said Two Fire Herb. 'On spikes over the gates.'

'But not Three Yoked Oxen,' said Lotus Blossom firmly. 'The Great Wizard has spoken!'

'Actually, I'm not sure I actually said—'

'You have spoken,' said Butterfly firmly.

As Rincewind got accustomed to the gloom he realized that he was in some storeroom or cellar; the noise of the city came, rather muffled, from grilles near the ceiling. It was half full of barrels and bundles, and every one of them was a perch for someone. The room was crowded. The people were watching him with expressions of rapt attention, but that wasn't the only thing they had in common.

Rincewind turned right around.

'Who are all these children?' he said.

'This,' said Lotus Blossom, 'is the Hunghung cadre of the Red Army.'

Two Fire Herb snorted.

'Why did you tell him that?' he said. 'Now we may have to kill him.'

'But they're all so young!'

'They may be underprivileged in years,' said Two Fire Herb, 'but they are ancient in courage and honour.'

'And experienced in fighting?' said Rincewind hotly. 'The guards I've seen do not look like nice people. I mean, do you even have any weapons?'

'We will wrest the weapons we need from our enemies!' said Two Fire Herb. A cheer went up.

'Really? How do you actually make them let go?' said Rincewind. He pointed to a very small girl, who leaned away from his digit as though it were loaded. She looked about seven and was holding a toy rabbit.

'What's your name?'

'One Favourite Pearl, Great Wizard!'

'And what do you do in the Red Army?'

'I have earned a medal for putting up of wall posters, Great Wizard!'

'What . . . like "Slightly Bad Things Please Happen To Our Enemies"? That sort of thing?'

'Er . . .' said the girl, looking imploringly at Butterfly.

'Rebellion is not easy for us,' said the older girl. 'We don't have . . . experience.'

'Well, I'm here to tell you that you don't do it by singing songs and putting up posters and fighting bare-handed,' said Rincewind. 'Not when you're up against real people with real weapons. You . . .' His voice trailed away as he realized that a hundred pairs of eyes were watching him intently, and two hundred ears were carefully listening.

He played back his own words in the echo chamber of his head.

He'd said, 'I'm here to tell you . . .'

He spread out his hands and waved them frantically.

' . . . that is, it's not up to me to tell you anything,' he said.

'That is *correct*,' said Two Fire Herb. 'We will overcome because history is on our side.'

'We will overcome because the Great Wizard is on our side,' said Butterfly sharply.

'I'll tell you this!' shouted Rincewind. 'I'd rather trust me than history! Oh, shit, did I just say that?'

'So you *will* help Three Yoked Oxen,' said Butterfly.

'Please!' said Lotus Blossom.

Rincewind looked at her, and the tears in the corners of her eyes, and the bunch of awed teenagers who really thought that you could beat an army by singing rousing songs.

There was only one thing he could do, if he really thought about it.

He could play along for now and then get the hell out of it at the very first opportunity. Butterfly's anger was bad, but a spike was a spike. Of course, he'd feel a bit of a heel for a while, but that was the point. He'd feel a heel, but he wouldn't feel a spike.

The world had too many heroes and didn't need another one. Whereas the world had only one Rincewind and he owed it to the world to keep this one alive for as long as possible.

There was an inn. There was a courtyard. There was a corral, for the Luggages.

There were large travelling trunks, big enough to carry the needs of an entire household for a fortnight. There were merchant's sample cases, mere square boxes on crude legs. There were sleek overnight bags.

They shuffled aimlessly in their pen. Occasionally there was the rattle of a handle or the creak of a hinge, and once or twice the snap of a lid and the bonk-bonk-bonk of boxes trying to get out of the way.

Three of them were big and covered with studded leather. They looked the kind of travelling accessories that hang around outside cheap hotels and make suggestive remarks to handbags.

The object of their attention was a rather smaller trunk with an inlaid lid and dainty feet. It had already backed into a corner as far as it could go.

A large spiked lid creaked open a couple of times as the largest of the boxes edged closer.

The smaller box had retreated so far its back legs were trying to climb the corral fence.

There was the sound of running feet on the other side of the courtyard wall. They got closer, and then stopped abruptly.

Then there was a twang such as would be made by an object landing on the taut roof of a cart.

For a moment, against the rising moon, there was the shape of something somersaulting slowly through the evening air.

It landed heavily in front of the three big chests, bounced upright and charged.

Eventually various travellers spilled out into the night but by then items of clothing were strewn and trampled around the courtyard. Three black chests, battered and scarred, were discovered on the roof, each one scrabbling on the tiles and butting the others

420

in an effort to be the highest. Others had panicked and broken down the wall and headed out across the country.

Eventually, all but one of them were found.

The Horde were feeling quite proud of themselves when they sat down for dinner. They acted, Mr Saveloy thought, rather like boys who'd just got their first pair of long trousers.

Which they had done. Each man had one baggy pair of same, plus a long grey robe.

'We've been *shopping*,' said Caleb proudly. 'Paying for things with *money*. We're dressed up like civilized people.'

'Yes indeed,' said Mr Saveloy indulgently. He was hoping that they could all get through this without the Horde finding out what *kind* of civilized people they were dressed up as. As it was, the beards were a problem. The kind of people who wore these kind of clothes in the Forbidden City didn't usually have beards. They were proverbial for not having them. Actually, they were more properly proverbial for not having other things but, as a sort of consequence of this lack, also for not having beards.

Cohen shifted. 'Itchy,' he said. 'This is pants, is it? Never worn 'em before. Same with shirts. What good's a shirt that's not chain mail?'

'We did very well, though,' said Caleb. He had even had a shave, obliging the barber, for the first time in his experience, to use a chisel. He kept rubbing his naked, baby-pink chin.

'Yeah, we're really civilized,' said Vincent.

'Except for the bit where you set fire to that shopkeeper,' said Boy Willie.

'Nah, I only set fire to him a bit.'

'Whut?'

'Teach?'

'Yes, Cohen?'

'Why did you tell that firework merchant that everyone you knew had died suddenly?'

Mr Saveloy's foot tapped gently against the large parcel under the table, alongside a nice new cauldron.

'So he wouldn't get suspicious about what I was buying,' he said.

'Five thousand firecrackers?'

'Whut?'

'Well,' said Mr Saveloy. 'Did I ever tell you that after I taught geography in the Assassins' Guild and the Plumbers' Guild I did it for a few terms in the Alchemists' Guild?'

'Alchemists? Loonies, the lot of them,' said Truckle.

'But they're keen on geography,' said Mr Saveloy. 'I suppose they need to know where they've landed. Eat up, gentlemen. It may be a long night.'

'What is this stuff?' said Truckle, spearing something with his chopstick.

'Er. Chow,' said Mr Saveloy.

'Yes, but what *is* it?'

'Chow. A kind of . . . er . . . dog.'

The Horde looked at him.

'There's nothing *wrong* with it,' he said hurriedly, with the sincerity of a man who had ordered bamboo shoots and bean curd for himself. 'I've eaten everything else,' said Truckle, 'but I ain't eating dog. I had a dog once. Rover.'

'Yeah,' said Cohen. 'The one with the spiked collar? The one who used to eat people?'

'Say what you like, he was a friend to me,' said Truckle, pushing the meat to one side.

'Rabid death to everyone else. I'll eat yours. Order him some chicken, Teach.'

'Et a man once,' mumbled Mad Hamish. 'In a siege, it were.'

'You ate someone?' said Mr Saveloy, beckoning to the waiter.

'Just a leg.'

'That's terrible!'

'Not with mustard.'

Just when I think I know them, Mr Saveloy mused . . .

He reached for his wine glass. The Horde reached for their glasses too, while watching him carefully.

'A toast, gentlemen,' he said. 'And remember what I said about not quaffing. Quaffing just gets your ears wet. Just sip. To Civilization!'

The Horde joined in with their own toasts.

' "Pcharn'kov!" '*

' "Lie down on the floor and no one gets hurt!" '

' "May you live in interesting pants!" '

' "What's the magic word? Gimme!" '

' "Death to most tyrants!" '

'Whut?'

*

* 'Your feet shall be cut off and be buried several yards from your body so your ghost won't walk.'

422

'The walls of the Forbidden City are forty feet high,' said Butterfly. 'And the gates are made of brass. There are hundreds of guards. But of course we have the Great Wizard.'

'Who?'

'You.'

'Sorry, I was forgetting.'

'Yes,' said Butterfly, giving Rincewind a long, appraising look. Rincewind remembered tutors giving him a look like that when he'd got high marks in some test by simply guessing at the answers.

He looked down hurriedly at the charcoal scrawls Lotus Blossom had made.

Cohen'd know what to do, he thought. *He'd* just slaughter his way through. It'd never cross his mind to be afraid or worried. He's the kind of man you need at a time like this.

'No doubt you have magic spells that can blow down the walls,' said Lotus Blossom.

Rincewind wondered what they would do to him when it turned out that he couldn't. Not a lot, he thought, if I'm already running. Of course they could curse his memory and call him names, but he was used to that. Sticks and stones may break my bones, he thought. He was vaguely aware that there was a second half to the saying, but he'd never bothered because the first half always occupied all his attention.

Even the Luggage had left him. That was a minor bright spot, but he missed that patter of little feet . . .

'Before we start,' he said, 'I think you ought to sing a revolutionary song.'

The cadre liked the idea. Under cover of their chanting he sidled over to Butterfly, who gave him a knowing smile.

'You know I can't do it!'

'The Master said you were very resourceful.'

'I can't magic a hole in a wall!'

'I'm sure you'll think of something. And . . . Great Wizard?'

'Yes, what?'

'Favourite Pearl, the child with the toy rabbit . . .'

'Yes?'

'The cadre is all she has. The same goes for many of the others. When the warlords fight, lots of people die. Parents. Do you understand? I was one of the first to read *What I Did On My Holidays*, Great Wizard, and what *I* saw in there was a foolish man who for some reason is always lucky. Great Wizard . . . I hope for everyone's sake you have a great deal of luck. Especially for yours.'

*

423

Fountains tinkled in the courts of the Sun Emperor. Peacocks made their call, which sounds like a sound made by something that shouldn't look as beautiful as that. Ornamental trees cast their shade as only they knew how – ornamentally.

The gardens occupied the heart of the city and it was possible to hear the noises from outside, although these were muted because of the straw spread daily on the nearest streets and also because any sound considered too loud would earn its originator a very brief stay in prison.

Of the gardens, the most aesthetically pleasing was the one laid out by the first Emperor, One Sun Mirror. It consisted entirely of gravel and stones, but artfully raked and laid out as it might be by a mountain torrent with a refined artistic sense. It was here that One Sun Mirror, in whose reign the Empire had been unified and the Great Wall built, came to refresh his soul and dwell upon the essential unity of all things, while drinking wine out of the skull of some enemy or possibly a gardener who had been too clumsy with his rake.

At the moment the garden was occupied by Two Little Wang, the Master of Protocol, who came there because he felt it was good for his nerves.

Perhaps it was the number two, he'd always told himself. It was an unlucky birth number. Being called Little Wang was merely a lack-of-courtesy detail, a sort of minor seagull dropping after the great heap of buffalo excrement that Heaven had pasted into his very horoscope. Although he had to admit that he hadn't made things any better by allowing himself to become Master of Protocol.

It had seemed such a good idea at the time. He'd risen gently through the Agatean civil service by mastering those arts essential to the practice of good government and administration (such as calligraphy, origami, flower arranging and the Five Wonderful Forms of poetry). He'd dutifully got on with the tasks assigned to him and noticed only vaguely that there didn't seem to be quite as many high-ranking members of the civil service as there used to be, and then one day a lot of senior mandarins – most of them a lot more senior than he was, it occurred to him later – had rushed up to him while he was trying to find a rhyme for 'orange blossom' and congratulated him on being the new Master.

That had been three months ago.

And of the things that had occurred to him in those intervening three months the most shameful was this: he had come to believe that the Sun Emperor was not, in fact, the Lord of Heaven, the Pillar of the Sky and the Great River of Blessings, but an evil-minded madman whose death had been too long delayed.

It was an awful thought. It was like hating motherhood and raw fish, or objecting to sunlight. Most people develop their social conscience when young, during that brief period between leaving school and deciding that injustice isn't necessarily all bad, and it was something of a shock to suddenly find one at the age of sixty.

It wasn't that he was against the Golden Rules. It made sense that a man prone to thieving should have his hands cut off. It prevented him from thieving again and thus tarnishing his soul. A peasant who could not pay his taxes *should* be executed, in order to prevent him falling into the temptations of slothfulness and public disorder. And since the Empire was created by Heaven as the only true world of human beings, all else outside being a land of ghosts, it was certainly in order to execute those who questioned this state of affairs.

But he felt that it wasn't right to laugh happily while doing so. It wasn't *pleasant* that these things should happen, it was merely necessary.

From somewhere in the distance came the screams. The Emperor was playing chess again. He preferred to use live pieces.

Two Little Wang felt heavy with knowledge. There had been better times. He knew that now. Things hadn't always been the way they were. Emperors didn't use to be cruel clowns, around whom it was as safe as mudbanks in the crocodile season. There hadn't always been a civil war every time an Emperor died. Warlords hadn't run the country. People had rights as well as duties.

And then one day the succession had been called into question and there was a war and since then it'd never seemed to go right.

Soon, with any luck, the Emperor would die. No doubt a special Hell was being made ready. And there'd be the usual battle, and then there'd be a new Emperor, and if he was very lucky Two Little Wang would be beheaded, which was what tended to happen to people who had risen to high office under a previous incumbent. But that was quite reasonable by modern standards, since it was possible these days to be beheaded for interrupting the Emperor's thoughts or standing in the wrong place.

At which point, Two Little Wang heard ghosts.

They seemed to be right under his feet.

425

They were talking in a strange language, so to Two Little Wang the speech was merely sounds, which went as follows:

'Where the hell are we?'

'Somewhere under the palace, I'm sure. Look for another manhole in the ceiling . . .'

'Whut?'

'I'm fed up with pushing this damn wheelchair!'

'It's me for a hot footbath after this, I'm telling you.'

'You call this a way to enter a city? You call this a way to enter a city? Waist deep in water? We didn't enter a . . . wretched . . . city like this when I rode with Bruce the Hoon! You enter a . . . lovemaking . . . city by overrunning it with a thousand horsemen, that's how you take a city—!'

'Yeah, but there ain't room for 'em in this pipe.'

The sounds had a hollow, booming quality to them. With a kind of fascinated puzzlement Two Little Wang followed them, walking across the manicured gravel in an unthinking way that would have earned him an immediate tongue-extraction from its original lover of peace and tranquillity.

'Can we please hurry? I'd like us to be out of here when the cauldron goes off and I didn't really have much time to experiment with the fuses.'

'I still don't understand about the cauldron, Teach.'

'I hope all those firecrackers will blow a hole in the wall.'

'Right! So why ain't we there? Why are we in this pipe?'

'Because all the guards will rush to see what the bang was.'

'Right! So we should be there!'

'No! We should be here, Cohen. The word is decoy. It's . . . more civilized this way.'

Two Little Wang pressed his ear to the ground.

'What's the penalty for entering the Forbidden City again. Teach?'

'I believe it's a punishment similar to hanging, drawing and quartering. So, you see, it would be a good idea if—'

There was a very faint splashing.

'How're you drawn, then?'

'I think your innards are cut out and shown to you.'

'What for?'

'I don't really know. To see if you recognize them, I suppose.'

'What . . . like, "Yep, that's my kidneys, yep, that's my breakfast"?'

'How're you quartered? Is that, like, they give you somewhere to stay?'

426

'I think not, from context.'

For a while there was no sound but the splash of six pairs of feet and the *squeak-squeak* of what sounded like a wheel.

'Well, how're you hung?'

'Excuse me?'

'Hur, hur, hur . . . sorry, sorry.'

Two Little Wang tripped over a two-hundred-year-old bonsai tree and hit his head on a rock chosen for its fundamental serenity. When he came round, a few seconds later, the voices had gone. If there had ever been any.

Ghosts. There were a lot of ghosts around these days. Two Little Wang wished he had a few firecrackers to scatter around.

Being Master of Protocol was even worse than trying to find a rhyme for 'orange blossom'.

Flares lit the alleys of Hunghung. With the Red Army chattering behind him, Rincewind wandered up to the wall of the Forbidden City.

No one knew better than Rincewind that he was totally incapable of proper magic. He'd only ever done it by accident.

So he could be sure that if he waved a hand and said some magic words the wall would in all probability become just a little bit less full of holes than it was now.

It was a shame to disappoint Lotus Blossom, with her body that reminded Rincewind of a plate of crinkle-cut chips, but it was about time she learned that you couldn't rely on wizards.

And then he could be out of here. What could Butterfly do to him if he tried and failed? And, much to his surprise, he found himself hoping that, on the way out, he could poke Herb in the eye. He was amazed the others couldn't spot him for what he was.

This area of wall was between gates. The life of Hunghung lapped against it like a muddy sea; there were stalls and booths every-where. Rincewind had thought Ankh-Morpork citizens lived out on the streets, but they were agoraphobes compared to the Hunghungese. Funerals (with associated firecrackers) and wedding parties and religious ceremonies went on alongside, and inter-mingled with, the normal market activities such as free-form live-stock slaughter and world-class arguing.

Herb pointed to a clear area of wall stacked with timber.

'Just about there, Great Wizard,' he sneered. 'Do not exert yourself unduly. A small hole should be sufficient.'

'But there's hundreds of people around!'

'Is that a problem to such a great wizard? Perhaps you can't do it with people watching?'

'I have no doubt that the Great Wizard will astonish us,' said Butterfly.

'When the people see the power of the Great Wizard they will speak of it for ever!' said Lotus Blossom.

'Probably,' muttered Rincewind.

The cadre stopped talking, although it was only possible to notice this by watching their closed mouths. The hole left by their silence was soon filled by the babble of the market.

Rincewind rolled up his sleeves.

He wasn't even certain about a spell for blowing things up . . .

He waved a hand vaguely.

'I should stand well back, everyone,' said Herb, grinning unpleasantly.

'Quanti canicula illa in fenestre?' said Rincewind. 'Er . . .'

He stared desperately at the wall and, with that heightened perception that comes to those on the edge of terror, noticed a cauldron half hidden in the timber. There seemed to be a little glowing string attached to it.

'Er,' he said, 'there seems to be—'

'Having problems?' said Herb, nastily.

Rincewind squared his shoulders.

'—' he said.

There was a sound like a marshmallow gently landing on a plate, and everything in front of him went white.

Then the white turned red, streaked with black, and the terrible noise clapped its hands across his ears.

A crescent-shaped piece of something glowing scythed the top off his hat and embedded itself in the nearest house, which caught fire.

There was a strong smell of burning eyebrows.

When the debris settled Rincewind saw quite a large hole in the wall. Around its edge the brickwork, now a red-hot ceramic, started to cool with a noise like *glinka-glinka*.

He looked down at his soot-blackened hands.

'Gosh,' he said.

And then he said, 'All *right*!'

And then he turned and began to say, 'How about that, then?' but his voice faded when it became apparent that everyone was lying flat on the ground.

A duck watched him suspiciously from its cage. Owing to the

slight protection afforded by the bars, its feathers were patterned alternately natural and crispy.

He'd always *wanted* to do magic like that. He'd always been able to visualize it perfectly. He'd just never been able to do it . . .

A number of guards appeared in the gap. One, whose ferocity of helmet suggested that he was an officer, glared at the charred hole and then at Rincewind.

'Did you do this?' he demanded.

'Stand back!' shouted Rincewind, drunk with power. 'I'm the Great Wizard, I am! You see this finger? Don't make me use it!'

The officer nodded to a couple of his men.

'Get him.'

Rincewind took a step back.

'I warn you! Anyone lays a hand on me, he'll be eating flies and hopping for the rest of his life!'

The guards advanced with the determination of those who were prepared to risk the uncertainty of magic against the definite prospect of punishment for disobeying orders.

'Stand back! This could go off! All right, then, since you force—'

He waved his hand. He snapped his fingers a few times.

'Er—'

The guards, after checking that they were still the same shape, each grabbed an arm.

'It may be delayed action,' he ventured, as they gripped harder.

'Alternatively, would you be interested in hearing a famous quotation?' he said. His feet were lifted off the ground. 'Or perhaps not?'

Rincewind, running absent-mindedly in mid-air, was brought in front of the officer.

'On your knees, rebel!' said the officer.

'I'd like to, but—'

'I saw what you did to Captain Four White Fox!'

'What? Who's he?'

'Take . . . him . . . to . . . the . . . Emperor.'

As he was dragged off Rincewind saw, for one brief moment, the guards closing on the Red Army, swords flashing . . .

A metal plate shuddered for a moment, and then dropped on the floor.

'Careful!'

'I ain't used to being careful! Bruce the Hoon wasn't care—'

429

'Shut up about Bruce the Hoon!'

'Well, dang you too!'

'Whut?'

'Anyone out there?'

Cohen stuck his head out of the pipe. The room was dark, damp and full of pipes and runnels. Water went off in every direction to feed fountains and cisterns.

'No,' he said, in a disappointed voice.

'Very well. Everyone out of the pipe.'

There was some echoey swearing and the scrape of metal as Hamish's wheelchair was manoeuvred into the long, low cellar.

Mr Saveloy lit a match as the Horde spread out and examined their surroundings.

'Congratulations, gentlemen,' he said. 'I believe we are in the palace.'

'Yeah,' said Truckle. 'We've conquered a f— a *lovemaking* pipe. What good is that?'

'We could rape it,' said Caleb hopefully.

'Hey, this wheel thing turns . . .'

'What's a lovemaking pipe?'

'What does this lever do?'

'Whut?'

'How about we find a door, rush out, and kill everyone?'

Mr Saveloy closed his eyes. There was something familiar about this situation, and now he realized what it was. He'd once taken an entire class on a school trip to the city armoury. His right leg still hurt him on wet days.

'No, no, *no!*' he said. 'What good would that do? Boy Willie, please don't pull that lever.'

'Well, *I'd* feel better, for one,' said Cohen. 'Ain't killed anyone all day except a guard, and they hardly count.'

'Remember that we're here for theft, not murder,' said Mr Saveloy. 'Now, please, out of all that wet leather and into your nice new clothes.'

'I don't like this part,' said Cohen, pulling on a shirt. 'I like people to know who I was.'

'Yeah,' said Boy Willie. 'Without our leather and mail people'll just think we're a load of old men.'

'Exactly,' said Mr Saveloy. 'That is part of the subterfuge.'

'Is that like tactics?' said Cohen.

'Yes.'

'All right, but *I* don't like it,' said Old Vincent. 'S'posing we win?

430

What kind of song will the minstrels sing about people who invaded through a pipe?'

'An echoey one,' said Boy Willie.

'They won't sing anything like that,' said Cohen firmly. 'You pay a minstrel enough, he'll sing whatever you want.'

A flight of damp steps led to a door. Mr Saveloy was already at the top, listening.

'That's right,' said Caleb. 'They say that whoever pays the piper calls the tune.'

'But, gentlemen,' said Mr Saveloy, his eyes bright, 'whoever holds a knife to the piper's throat writes the symphony.'

The assassin moved slowly through Lord Hong's chambers.

He was one of the best in Hunghung's small but very select guild, and he certainly was not a rebel. He disliked rebels. They were invariably poor people, and therefore unlikely to be customers.

His mode of movement was unusual and cautious. It avoided the floor; Lord Hong was known to tune his floorboards. It made considerable use of furniture and decorative screens, and occasionally of the ceiling as well.

And the assassin was very good at it. When a messenger entered the room through a distant door he froze for an instant, and then moved in perfect rhythm towards his quarry, letting the newcomer's clumsy footsteps mask his own.

Lord Hong was making another sword. The folding of the metal and all the tedious yet essential bouts of heating and hammering were, he found, conducive to clear thinking. Too much pure cerebration was bad for the mind. Lord Hong liked to use his hands sometimes.

He plunged the sword back into the furnace and pumped the bellows a few times.

'Yes?' he said. The messenger looked up from his prone position near the floor.

'Good news, o lord. We have captured the Red Army!'

'Well, that *is* good news,' said Lord Hong, watching the blade carefully for the change of colour. 'Including the one they call the Great Wizard?'

'Indeed! But he is not that great, o lord!' said the messenger.

His cheerfulness faded when Lord Hong raised an eyebrow.

'Really? On the contrary, I suspect him of being in possession of huge and dangerous powers.'

'Yes, o lord! I did not mean—'

'See that they are all locked up. And send a message to Captain Five Hong Man to undertake the orders I gave him today.'

'Yes, o lord!'

'And now, stand up!'

The messenger stood up, trembling. Lord Hong pulled on a thick glove and reached for the sword handle. The furnace roared.

'Chin up, man!'

'My lord!'

'Now open your eyes wide!'

There was no need for that order. Lord Hong peered into the mask of terror, noted the flicker of movement, nodded, and then in one almost balletic movement pulled the spitting blade from the furnace, turned, thrust . . .

There was a very brief scream, and a rather longer hiss.

Lord Hong let the assassin sag. Then he tugged the sword free and inspected the steaming blade.

'Hmm,' he said. 'Interesting . . .'

He caught sight of the messenger.

'Are you still here?'

'No, my lord!'

'See to it.'

Lord Hong turned the sword so that the light caught it, and examined the edge.

'And, er, shall I send some servants to clear away the, er, body?'

'What?' said Lord Hong, lost in thought.

'The body, Lord Hong?'

'What body? Oh. Yes. See to it.'

The walls were beautifully decorated. Even Rincewind noticed this, though they went past in a blur. Some had marvellous birds painted on them, or mountain scenes, or sprays of foliage, every leaf and bud done in exquisite detail with just a couple of brush strokes.

Ceramic lions reared on marble pedestals. Vases bigger than Rincewind lined the corridors.

Lacquered doors opened ahead of the guards. Rincewind was briefly aware of huge, ornate and empty rooms stretching away on either side.

Finally they passed through yet another set of doors and he was flung down on a wooden floor.

In these circumstances, he always found, it was best not to look up.

Eventually an officious voice said, 'What do you have to say for yourself, miserable louse?'

'Well, I—'

'Silence!'

Ah. So it was going to be *that* kind of interview.

A different voice, a cracked, breathless and elderly voice, said, 'Where is the Grand . . . Vizier?'

'He has retired to his rooms, O Great One. He said he had a headache.'

'Summon him at . . . once.'

'Certainly, O Great One.'

Rincewind, his nose pressed firmly to the floor, made some further assumptions. Grand Vizier was always a bad sign; it generally meant that people were going to suggest wild horses and red-hot chains. And when people were called things like 'O Great One', it was pretty certain that there was no appeal.

'This is a . . . rebel, is it?' The sentence was wheezed rather than spoken.

'Indeed, O Great One.'

'I think I would like a clo . . . ser look.'

There was a general murmur, suggesting that a number of people had been greatly surprised, and then the sound of furniture being moved.

Rincewind thought he saw a blanket on the edge of his vision. Someone was wheeling a bed across the floor . . .

'Make it . . . stand up.' The gurgle in the pause was like the last bathwater going down the plughole. It sucked as wetly as an outgoing wave.

Once again a foot kicked Rincewind in the kidneys, making its usual explicit request in the Esperanto of brutality. He got up.

It *was* a bed, and quite the biggest Rincewind had ever seen. In it, swathed in brocades and almost lost in pillows, was an old man. Rincewind had never seen anyone look so ill. The face was pale, with a greenish pallor; veins showed up under the skin of his hands like worms in a jar.

The Emperor had all the qualifications for a corpse except, as it were, the most vital one.

'So . . . this is the new Great Wizard of . . . whom we have read so much, is . . . it?' he said.

433

When he spoke, people waited expectantly for the final gurgle in mid-sentence.

'Well, I—' Rincewind began.

'Silence!' screamed a chamberlain.

Rincewind shrugged.

He hadn't known what to expect of an Emperor, but the mental picture had room for a big fat man with lots of rings. Talking to this one was a hair's breadth from necromancy.

'Can you show us some more . . . magic, Great Wizard?'

Rincewind glanced at the chamberlain.

'W—'

'Silence!'

The Emperor waved a hand vaguely, gurgled with the effort, and gave Rincewind another enquiring look. Rincewind decided to chance things.

'I've got a good one,' he said. 'It's a vanishing trick.'

'Can you . . . do it now?'

'Only if everyone opens all the doors and turns their back.'

The Emperor's expression did not change. The court fell silent. Then there was a sound like a number of small rabbits being choked to death.

The Emperor was laughing. Once this was established, everyone else laughed too. No one can get a laugh like a man who can have you put to death more easily than he goes to the lavatory.

'What *shall* we do with . . . you?' he said. 'Where *is* the . . . Grand . . . Vizier?'

The crowd parted.

Rincewind risked a sideways squint. Once you were in the hands of a Grand Vizier, you were dead. Grand Viziers were *always* scheming megalomaniacs. It was probably in the job description: 'Are you a devious, plotting, unreliable madman? Ah, good, then you can be my most trusted minister.'

'Ah, Lord . . . Hong,' said the Emperor.

'Mercy?' suggested Rincewind.

'Silence!' screamed the chamberlain.

'Tell me, Lord . . . Hong,' said the ancient Emperor. 'What would be the punishment for a . . . foreigner . . . entering the Forbidden City?'

'Removal of all limbs, ears and eyes, and then allowed to go free,' said Lord Hong.

Rincewind raised his hand.

'First offence?' he said.

434

'Silence!'

'We find, generally, that there is no second offence,' said Lord
Hong.

'What is this person?'

'I like him,' said the Emperor. 'I think I shall . . . keep him. He
makes me . . . laugh.'

Rincewind opened his mouth.

'Silence!' screamed the chamberlain, perhaps unwisely in view of
current thinking.

'Er . . . could you stop him shouting "Silence!" every time I try to
speak?' Rincewind ventured.

'Certainly . . . Great Wizard,' said the Emperor. He nodded at
some guards. 'Take the chamberlain . . . away and cut his . . . lips
off.'

'Great One, I—!'

'And his ears . . . also.'

The wretched man was dragged away. A pair of lacquered doors
slammed shut. There was a round of applause from the courtiers.

'Would you . . . like to watch him eat . . . them?' said the
Emperor grinning happily. 'It's tre . . . mendous fun.'

'Ahahaha,' said Rincewind.

'A good decision, lord,' said Lord Hong. He turned his head
towards Rincewind.

To the wizard's immense surprise, and some horror too, he
winked.

'O Great One . . .' said a plump courtier, dropping to his knees,
bouncing slightly, and then nervously approaching the Emperor, 'I
wonder if perhaps it is entirely wise to be so merciful to this foreign
dev—'

The Emperor looked down. Rincewind would have sworn that
dust fell off him.

There was a gentle movement among the crowd. Without anyone
apparently doing anything so gross as activating their feet, there
was nevertheless a widening space around the kneeling man.

Then the Emperor smiled.

'Your concern is well . . . received,' he said. The courtier risked a
relieved grin. The Emperor added, 'However, your presumption is
not. Kill him slowly . . . over several . . . days.'

'Aaargh!'

'Yes in . . . deed! Lots of boiling . . . oil!'

'An excellent idea, o lord,' said Lord Hong.

The Emperor turned back to Rincewind.

'I am sure the . . . Great Wizard is my friend,' he suctioned.

'Ahahaha,' said Rincewind.

He'd been in this approximate position before, gods knew. But he'd always been facing someone – well, usually someone who looked like Lord Hong, not a near-corpse who was clearly so far round the bend he couldn't poke sanity with a long pole.

'We shall have *such* . . . fun,' said the Emperor. 'I read . . . all about you.'

'Ahahaha,' said Rincewind.

The Emperor waved a hand at the court again.

'Now I will retire,' he said. There was a general movement and much ostensible yawning. Clearly no one stayed up later than the Emperor.

'Emperor,' said Lord Hong wearily, 'what will you have us do with this Great Wizard of yours?'

The old man gave Rincewind the look a present gets around the time the batteries have run out.

'Put him in the special . . . dungeon,' he said. 'For . . . now.'

'Yes, Emperor,' said Lord Hong. He nodded at a couple of guards.

Rincewind managed a quick look back as he was dragged from the room. The Emperor was lying back in his movable bed, quite oblivious to him.

'Is he mad or what?' he said.

'Silence!'

Rincewind looked up at the guard who'd said that.

'A mouth like that could get a man into big trouble around here,' he muttered.

Lord Hong always found himself depressed by the general state of humanity. It often seemed to him to be flawed. There was no *concentration*. Take the Red Army. If *he* had been a rebel the Emperor would have been assassinated months ago and the country would now be aflame, except for those bits too damp to burn. But these? Despite his best efforts, their idea of revolutionary activity was a surreptitious wall poster saying something like 'Unpleasantness To Oppressors When Convenient!'

They had tried to set fire to guardhouses. That was good. That was proper revolutionary activity, except for the bit where they tried to make an appointment first. It had taken Lord Hong some considerable effort to see that the Red Army appeared to achieve any victories at all.

Well, he'd given them the Great Wizard they so sincerely believed in. They had no excuse now. And by the look of him, the wretch was as craven and talentless as Lord Hong had hoped. Any army led by him would either flee or be slaughtered, leaving the way open for the counter-revolution.

The counter-revolution would *not* be inefficient. Lord Hong would see to that.

But things had to be done one step at a time. There were enemies everywhere. Suspicious enemies. The path of the ambitious man was a nightingale floor. One wrong step and it would sing out. It was a shame the Great Wizard would turn out to be so good at locks. Lord Tang's men were guarding the prison block tonight. Of course, if the Red Army were to escape, no blame at all could possibly attach to Lord Tang . . .

Lord Hong risked a little chuckle to himself as he strode back to his suite. Proof, that was the thing. There must never be proof. But that wouldn't matter very long. There was nothing like a fearsomely huge war to unite people, and the fact that the Great Wizard – that is, the leader of the terrible rebel army – was an evil foreign troublemaker was just the spark to light the firecracker.

And then . . . Ankh-Morpork [urinating dog].

Hunghung was old. The culture was based on custom, the alimentary tract of the common water buffalo, and base treachery. Lord Hong was in favour of all three, but they did not add up to world domination, and Lord Hong was particularly in favour of that, provided it was achieved by Lord Hong.

If I was the traditional type of Grand Vizier, he thought as he sat down before his tea table, I'd cackle with laughter at this point.

He smiled to himself, instead.

Time for the box again? No. Some things were all the better for the anticipation.

Mad Hamish's wheelchair caused a few heads to turn, but no actual comment. Undue curiosity was not a survival trait in Hunghung. They just got on with their work, which appeared to be the endless carrying of stacks of paper along the corridors.

Cohen looked down at what was in his hand. Over the decades he'd fought with many weapons – swords, of course, and bows and spears and clubs and . . . well, now he came to think of it, just about anything.

Except this . . .

'I *still* don't like it,' said Truckle. 'Why're we carrying pieces of paper?'

'Because no one looks at you in a place like this if you're carrying a piece of paper,' said Mr Saveloy.

'Why?'

'Whut?'

'It's – a kind of magic.'

'I'd feel happier if it was a weapon.'

'As a matter of fact, it can be the greatest weapon there is.'

'I know, I've just cut myself on my bit,' said Boy Willie, sucking his finger.

'Whut?'

'Look at it like this, gentlemen,' said Mr Saveloy. 'Here we are, actually *inside* the Forbidden City, and no one is dead!'

'Yes. That's what we're . . . *danging* . . . complaining about,' said Truckle.

Mr Saveloy sighed. There was something in the way Truckle used words. It didn't matter what he actually said, what you heard was in some strange way the word he actually *meant*. He could turn the air blue just by saying 'socks'.

The door slammed shut behind Rincewind, and there was the sound of a bolt shooting into place.

The Empire's jails were pretty much like the ones at home. When you want to incarcerate such an ingenious creature as the common human being, you tend to rely on the good old-fashioned iron bar and large amounts of stone. It looked as though this well-tried pattern had been established here for a very long time.

Well, he'd definitely scored a hit with the Emperor. For some reason this did not reassure him. The man gave Rincewind the distinct impression of being the kind of person who is at least as dangerous to his friends as to his enemies.

He remembered Noodle Jackson, back in the days when he was a very young student. Everyone wanted to be friends with Noodle but somehow, if you were in his gang, you found yourself being trodden on or chased by the Watch or being hit in fights you didn't start, while Noodle was somewhere on the edge of things, laughing.

Besides, the Emperor wasn't simply at Death's door but well inside the hallway, admiring the carpet and commenting on the hatstand. And you didn't have to be a political genius to know that when someone like that died, scores were being settled before he'd even got cold. Anyone he'd publicly called a friend would have a life expectancy more normally associated with things that hover over trout streams at sunset.

Rincewind moved aside a skull and sat down. There was the possibility of rescue, he supposed, but the Red Army would be hard put to it to rescue a rubber duck from drowning. Anyway, that'd put him back in the clutches of Butterfly, who terrified him almost as much as the Emperor.

He had to believe that the gods didn't intend for Rincewind, after all his adventures, to rot in a dungeon.

No, he added bitterly, they probably had something much more inventive in mind.

What light reached the dungeon came from a very small grille and had a second-hand look. The rest of the furnishing was a pile of what had possibly once been straw. There was—

—a gentle tapping at the wall.

Once, twice, three times.

Rincewind picked up the skull and returned the signal.

One tap came back.

He repeated it.

Then there were two.

He tapped twice.

Well, this was familiar. Communication without meaning . . . it was just like being back at Unseen University.

'Fine,' he said, his voice echoing in the cell. 'Fine. Très prisoner. But what are we *saying*?'

There was a gentle scraping noise and one of the blocks in the wall very gently slid out of the wall, dropping on to Rincewind's foot.

'Aargh!'

'What big hippo?' said a muffled voice.

'What?'

'Sorry?'

'What?'

'You wanted to know about the tapping code? It's how we communicate between cells, you see. One tap means—'

'Excuse me, but aren't we communicating now?'

'Yes, but not formally. Prisoners are not . . . allowed . . . to talk . . .' The voice slowed down, as if the speaker had suddenly remembered something important.

'Ah, yes,' said Rincewind. 'I was forgetting. This is . . . Hung-hung. Everyone . . . obeys . . . the rules . . .'

439

Rincewind's voice died away too.

On either side of the wall there was a long, thoughtful silence.

'*Rincewind?*'

'*Twoflower?*'

'What are *you* doing here?' said Rincewind.

'Rotting in a dungeon!'

'Me too!'

'Good grief! How long has it been?' said the muffled voice of Twoflower.

'What? How long has what been?'

'But *you* . . . why are . . .'

'You wrote that damn book!'

'I just thought it would be interesting for people!'

'Interesting? *Interesting?*'

'I thought people would find it an interesting account of a foreign culture. I never meant it to cause trouble.'

Rincewind leaned against his side of the wall. No, of course, Twoflower never wanted to cause any trouble. Some people never did. Probably the last sound heard before the Universe folded up like a paper hat would be someone saying, 'What happens if I do this?'

'It must have been Fate that brought you here,' said Twoflower.

'Yes, it's the sort of thing he likes to do,' said Rincewind.

'You remember the good times we had?'

'Did we? I must have had my eyes shut.'

'The adventures!'

'Oh, *them*. You mean hanging from high places, that sort of thing . . .?'

'Rincewind?'

'Yes? What?'

'I feel a lot happier about things now *you're* here.'

'That's amazing.'

Rincewind enjoyed the comfort of the wall. It was just rock. He felt he could rely on it.

'Everyone seems to have a copy of your book,' he said. 'It's a revolutionary document. And I do mean *copy*. It looks as though they make their own copy and pass it on.'

'Yes, it's called *samizdat*.'

'What does that mean?'

'It means each one must be the same as the one before. Oh, dear. I thought it would just be entertainment. I didn't think people would take it seriously. I do hope it's not causing too much bother.'

'Well, your revolutionaries are still at the slogan-and-poster stage, but I shouldn't think that'll count for much if they're caught.'

'Oh, dear.'

'How come you're still alive?'

'I don't know. I think they may have forgotten about me. That tends to happen, you know. It's the paperwork. Someone makes the wrong stroke with the brush or forgets to copy a line. I believe it happens a lot.'

'You mean that there's people in prison and no one can remember why?'

'Oh, yes.'

'Then why don't they set them free?'

'I suppose it is felt that they must have done something. All in all, I'm afraid our government does leave something to be desired.'

'Like a new government.'

'Oh, dear. You could get locked up for saying things like that.'

People slept, but the Forbidden City never slept. Torches flickered all night in the great Bureaux as the ceaseless business of Empire went on.

This largely involved, as Mr Saveloy had said, moving paper.

Six Beneficent Winds was Deputy District Administrator for the Langtang district, and good at a job which he rather enjoyed. He was not a wicked man.

True, he had the same sense of humour as a chicken casserole. True, he played the accordion for amusement, and disliked cats intensely, and had a habit of dabbing his upper lip with his napkin after his tea ceremony in a way that had made Mrs Beneficent Winds commit murder in her mind on a regular basis over the years. And he kept his money in a small leather shovel purse, and counted it out very thoroughly whenever he made a purchase, especially if there was a queue behind him.

But on the other hand, he was kind to animals and made small but regular contributions to charity. He frequently gave moderate sums to beggars in the street, although he made a note of this in the little notebook he always carried to remind him to visit them in his official capacity later on.

And he never took away from people more money than they actually had.

He was also, unusually for men employed in the Forbidden City after dark, not a eunuch. Guards were not eunuchs, of course, and people had got around this by classifying them officially as furniture. And it had been found that tax officials also needed every faculty at their disposal to combat the wiles of the average peasant, who had this regrettable tendency to avoid paying taxes.

There were much nastier people in the building than Six Beneficent Winds and it was therefore just his inauspicious luck that his paper and bamboo door slid aside to reveal seven strange-looking old eunuchs, one of them in a wheeled contrivance.

They didn't even bow, let alone fall on their knees. And he not only had an official red hat but it had a white button on it!

His brush dropped from his hands when the men wandered into his office as if they owned it. One of them started poking holes in the wall and speaking gibberish.

'Hey, the walls are just made of paper! Hey, look, if you lick your finger it goes right through! See?'

'I will call for the guards and have you all flogged!' shouted Six Beneficent Winds, his temper moderated slightly by the extreme age of the visitors.

'What did he say?'

'He said he'd call for the guards.'

'Ooo, yes. Please let him call for the guards!'

'No, we don't want that yet. Act normally.'

'You mean cut his throat?'

'I meant a more normal kind of normally.'

'It's what I call normal.'

One of the old men faced the speechless official and gave him a big grin.

'Excuse us, your supreme . . . *oh dear, what's the word?* . . . pushcart sail? . . . immense rock? . . . *ah, yes* . . . venerableness, but we seem to be a little lost.'

A couple of the old men shuffled around behind Six Beneficent Winds and started to read, or at least try to read, what he'd been working on. A sheet of paper was snatched from his hand.

'What's this say, Teach?'

'Let me see . . . "The first wind of autumn shakes the lotus flower. Seven Lucky Logs to pay one pig and three [*looks like a four-armed man waving a flag*] of rice on pain of having his [*rather a stylized thing here, can't quite make it out*] struck with many blows. By order of Six Beneficent Winds, Collector of Revenues, Langtang."'

There was a subtle change among the old men. Now they were all grinning, but not in a way that gave him any comfort. One of them, with teeth like diamonds, leaned towards him and said, in bad Agatean:

'You are a tax collector, Mr Knob on Your Hat?'

Six Beneficent Winds wondered if he'd be able to summon the guard. There was something terrible about these old men. They weren't venerable at all. They were horribly menacing and, although he couldn't see any obvious weapons, he knew for a cold frozen fact that he wouldn't be able to get out more than the first syllable before he'd be killed. Besides, his throat had gone dry and his pants had gone wet.

'Nothing wrong with being a tax collector . . .' he croaked.

'We never said that,' said Diamond Teeth. 'We always like to meet tax collectors.'

'Some of our most favouritest people, tax collectors,' said another old man.

'Saves a lot of trouble,' said Diamond Teeth.

'Yeah,' said a third old man. 'Like, it means you don't have to go from house to house killin' everyone for their valuables, you just wait and kill the—'

'Gentlemen, can I have a word?'

The speaker was the slightly goat-faced one that didn't seem quite so unpleasant as the others. The terrible men clustered around him and Six Beneficent Winds heard the strange syllables of a coarse foreign tongue:

'What? But he's a tax collector! That's what they're for!'

'Whut?'

'A firm tax base is the foundation of sound governance, gentlemen. Please trust me.'

'I understood all of that up to "A firm tax".'

'Nevertheless, no useful purpose will be served by killing this hard-working tax gatherer.'

'He'd be dead. I call that useful.'

There was some more of the same. Six Beneficent Winds jumped when the group broke up and the goat-faced man gave him a smile.

'My humble friends are overawed by your . . . variety of plum . . . small knife for cutting seaweed . . . presence, noble sir,' he said, his every word slandered by Truckle's vigorous gesticulations behind his back.

'How about if we just cut a bit off?'

'Whut?'

'How did you get in here?' said Six Beneficent Winds. 'There are many strong guards.'

443

'I *knew* we missed something,' said Diamond Teeth.

'We would like you to show us around the Forbidden City,' said Goat Face. 'My name is . . . Mr Stuffed Tube, I think you would call it. Yes. Stuffed Tube, I'm pretty sure—'

Six Beneficent Winds glanced hopefully towards the door.

'—and we are here to learn more about your wonderful . . . mountain . . . variety of bamboo . . . sound of running water at evening . . . *drat* . . . civilization.'

Behind him, Truckle was energetically demonstrating to the rest of the Horde what he and Bruce the Hoon's Skeletal Riders once did to a tax gatherer. The sweeping arm movements in particular occupied Six Beneficent Winds' attention. He couldn't understand the words but, somehow, you didn't need to.

'*Why are you talking to him like that?*'

'*Ghenghiz, I'm lost. There are no maps of the Forbidden City. We need a guide.*'

Goat Face turned back to the taxman. 'Perhaps you would like to come with us?' he said.

Out, thought Six Beneficent Winds. Yes! There may be guards out there!

'Just a minute,' said Diamond Teeth, as he nodded. 'Pick up your paintbrush and write down what I say.'

A minute later, they'd gone. All that remained in the taxman's office was an amended piece of paper, which read as follows:

'Roses are red, violets are blue. Seven Lucky Logs to be given one pig and all the rice he can carry, because he is now One Lucky Peasant. By order of Six Beneficent Winds, Collector of Revenues, Langtang. Help. Help. If anyone reads this I am being held prisoner by an evil eunuch. Help.'

Rincewind and Twoflower lay in their separate cells and talked about the good old days. At least, Twoflower talked about the good old days. Rincewind worked at a crack in the stone with a piece of straw, it being all he had to hand. It would take several thousand years to make any kind of impression, but that was no reason to give up.

'Do we get fed in here?' he said, interrupting the flow of reminiscence.

'Oh, sometimes. But it's not like the marvellous food in Ankh-Morpork.'

'Really,' murmured Rincewind, scratching away. A tiny piece of mortar seemed ready to move.

'I'll always remember the taste of Mr Dibbler's sausages.'

'People do.'

'A once-in-a-lifetime experience.'

'Frequently.'

The straw broke.

'Damn and blast!' Rincewind sat back. 'What's so important about the Red Army?' he said. 'I mean, they're just a bunch of kids. Just a nuisance!'

'Yes, I'm afraid things got rather confused,' said Twoflower.

'Um. Have you ever heard of the theory that History goes in cycles?'

'I saw a drawing in one of Leonard of Quirm's notebooks—' Rincewind began, trying again with another straw.

'No, I mean . . . like a . . . wheel, spinning. If you stand in the same place it all comes round again?'

'Oh, *that*. Blast!'

'Well, a lot of people believe it here. They think History starts again every three thousand years.'

'Could be,' said Rincewind, who was looking for another straw and wasn't really listening. Then the words sank in. 'Three thousand years? That's a bit short, isn't it? The whole thing? Stars and oceans and intelligent life evolving from arts graduates, that sort of thing?'

'Oh, no. That's just . . . stuff. *Proper* history started with the founding of the Empire by One Sun Mirror. The first Emperor. And his servant, the Great Wizard. Just a legend, really. It's the sort of thing peasants believe. They look at something like the Great Wall and say, that's such a marvellous thing it must have been built by magic . . . And the Red Army . . . what it *probably* was was just a well-organised body of trained fighting men. The first real army, you see. All there was before was just undisciplined mobs. That's what it must have been. Not magical at all. The Great Wizard couldn't really have *made* . . . What the peasants believe is silly . . .'

'Why, what do they believe?'

'They say the Great Wizard made the earth come alive. When all the armies on the continent faced One Sun Mirror the Great Wizard . . . flew a kite.'

'Sounds sensible to me,' said Rincewind. 'When there's war around take the day off, that's my motto.'

'No, you don't understand. This was a special kite. It trapped the lightning in the sky and the Great Wizard stored it in bottles and

445

then took the mud itself and . . . baked it with the lightning, and made it into an army.'

'Never heard of any spells for that.'

'And they have funny ideas about reincarnation, too . . .'

Rincewind conceded that they probably would. It probably whiled away those long water-buffaloid hours: hey, after I die I hope I come back as . . . a man holding a water buffalo, but facing a different way.

'Er . . . no,' said Twoflower. 'They don't think you come *back* at all. Er . . . I'm not using the right words, am I? . . . Bit corroded on this language . . . I mean *pre*incarnation. It's like reincarnation backwards. They think you're born before you die.'

'Oh, really?' said Rincewind, scratching at the stones. 'Amazing! Born before you die? Life before death? People will get really excited when they hear about that.'

'That's not exactly . . . er. It's all tied in with ancestors. You should always venerate ancestors because you might be them one day, and . . . Are you listening?'

The little piece of mortar fell away. Not bad for ten minutes' work, thought Rincewind. Come the next Ice Age, we're out of here . . .

It dawned on him that he was working on the wall that led to Twoflower's cell. Taking several thousand years to break into an adjoining cell could well be thought a waste of time.

He started on a different wall. Scratch . . . scratch . . .

There was a terrible scream.

Scratchscratchscratch—

'Sounds like the Emperor has woken up,' said Twoflower's voice from the hole in the wall.

'That's kind of an early morning torture, is it?' said Rincewind. He started to hammer at the huge blocks with a piece of shattered stone.

'It's not really his fault. He just doesn't understand about people.'

'Is that so?'

'You know how common kids go through a stage of pulling the wings off flies?'

'*I* never did,' said Rincewind. 'You can't trust flies. They may look small but they can turn nasty.'

'Kids generally, I mean.'

'Yes? Well?'

'*He* is an Emperor. No one ever dared tell him it was wrong. It's just a matter of, you know, scaling up. All the five families fight among themselves for the crown. He killed his nephew to become Emperor. No one has ever told him that it's not right to keep killing people for fun. At least, no one who has ever managed to get to the end of the first sentence. And the Hongs and the Fangs and the Tangs and the Sungs and the McSweeneys have been killing one another for thousands of years. It's all part of the royal succession.'

'McSweeneys?'

'Very old-established family.'

Rincewind nodded gloomily. It was probably like breeding horses. If you have a system where treacherous murderers tend to win, you end up breeding *really* treacherous murderers. You end up with a situation where it's dangerous to lean over a cradle . . .

There was another scream.

Rincewind started kicking at the stones.

A key turned in the lock.

'Oh,' said Twoflower.

But the door didn't open.

Finally Rincewind walked over and tried the big iron ring.

The door swung outwards, but not too far because the recumbent body of a guard makes an unusual but efficient doorstop.

There was a whole ring of keys hanging from the one in the door . . .

An inexperienced prisoner would simply have run for it. But Rincewind was a post-graduate student in the art of staying alive, and knew that in circumstances like these much the best thing to do was let out every single prisoner, pat each one hurriedly on the back and say, 'Quick! They're coming for you!' and then go and sit somewhere nice and quiet until the pursuit has disappeared in the distance.

He opened the door to Twoflower's cell first.

The little man was skinnier and grubbier than he remembered, and had a wispy beard, but in one very significant way he had the feature that Rincewind remembered so well – the big, beaming, *trusting* smile that suggested that anything bad currently happening to him was just some sort of laughable mistake and would be bound to be sorted out by reasonable people.

'Rincewind! It *is* you! I certainly never thought I'd see *you* again!' he said.

'Yes, I thought something on those lines,' said Rincewind.

Twoflower looked past Rincewind at the fallen guard.

'Is he dead?' he said, speaking of a man with a sword half buried in his back.

447

'Extremely likely.'

'Did *you* do that?'

'I was *inside* the cell!'

'Amazing! Good trick!'

Despite several years of exposure to the facts of the matter, Rincewind remembered, Twoflower had never really wanted to grasp the fact that his companion had the magical abilities of the common house fly. It was useless to try to dissuade him. It just meant that modesty was added to the list of non-existent virtues.

He tried some of the keys in other cell doors. Various raggedy people emerged, blinking in the slightly better light. One of them, turning his body slightly in order to get it through the door, was Three Yoked Oxen. From the look of him he'd been beaten up, but this might just have been someone's attempt to attract his attention.

'This is Rincewind,' said Twoflower proudly. 'The Great Wizard. Did you know he killed the guard from inside the cell?'

They politely inspected the corpse.

'I didn't, really,' said Rincewind.

'And he's modest, too!'

'Long Life To The People's Endeavour!' said Three Yoked Oxen through rather swollen lips.

' "Mine's A Pint!" ' said Rincewind. 'Here's bigfella keys belong door, you go lettee people outee chopchop.'

One of the freed prisoners limped to the end of the passage.

'There's a dead guard here,' he said.

'It wasn't me,' said Rincewind plaintively. 'I mean, perhaps I *wished* they were dead, but—'

People edged away. You didn't want to be too close to anyone who could wish like that.

If this had been Ankh-Morpork someone would have said, 'Oh, yeah, sure, he magically stabbed them in the back?' But that was because people in Ankh-Morpork knew Rincewind, and they knew that if a wizard really wanted you dead you'd have no back left to stab.

Three Yoked Oxen had been able to master the technical business of opening doors. More swung open . . .

'Lotus Blossom?' said Rincewind.

She clung to Oxen's arm and smiled at Rincewind. Other members of the cadre trooped out behind her.

Then, to Rincewind's amazement, she looked at Twoflower, screamed, and threw her arms around his neck.

'Extended Continuation To Filial Affection!' chanted Three Yoked Oxen.

'"Close Cover Before Striking!"' said Rincewind. 'Er. What exactly is happening?'

A very small Red soldier tugged at his robe.

'He is her daddy,' it said.

'You never said you had children!'

'I'm sure I did. Often,' said Twoflower, disentangling himself. 'Anyway . . . it is allowed.'

'You're *married*?'

'I was, yes. I'm sure I must have said.'

'We were probably running away from something at the time. So there's a Mrs Twoflower, is there?'

'There was for a while,' said Twoflower, and for a moment an expression almost of anger distorted his preternaturally benign countenance. 'Not, alas, any more.'

Rincewind looked away, because that was better than looking at Twoflower's face.

Butterfly had also emerged. She stood just outside the cell door, with her hands clasped in front of her, looking down demurely at her feet.

Twoflower rushed over to her.

'Butterfly!'

Rincewind looked down at the rabbit clutcher.

'She another daughter, Pearl?'

'Yeth.'

The little man came towards Rincewind, dragging the girls.

'Have you met my daughters?' he said. 'This is Rincewind, who—'

'We have had the pleasure,' said Butterfly, gravely.

'How did you all get here?' said Rincewind.

'We fought as hard as we could,' said Butterfly. 'But there were simply too many of them.'

'I hope you didn't try to grab their weapons,' said Rincewind, as sarcastically as he dared.

Butterfly glared at him.

'Sorry,' said Rincewind.

'Herb says it is the system that is to blame,' said Lotus Blossom.

'I bet he's got a better system all worked out.' Rincewind looked at the throng of prisoners. 'They usually have. Where is he, by the way?'

The girls looked around.

'I don't see him here,' said Lotus Blossom. 'But I think that when the guards attacked us he laid down his life for the cause.'

'Why?'

'Because that's what he said we should do. I am ashamed that I did not. But they seemed to want to capture us, not kill us.'

'I did not see him,' said Butterfly. She and Rincewind exchanged a glance. 'I think perhaps . . . he was not there.'

'You mean he had been caught already?' said Lotus Blossom.

Butterfly looked at Rincewind again. It occurred to him that whereas Lotus Blossom had inherited a Twoflower view of the world, Butterfly *must* have taken after her mother. She thought more like Rincewind, i.e., the worst of everyone.

'Perhaps,' she said.

'Make Considerable Sacrifice For The Common Good,' said Three Yoked Oxen.

' "There's One Born Every Minute," ' said Rincewind, absently.

Butterfly seemed to get a grip on herself.

'However,' she said, 'we must make the most of this opportunity.'

Rincewind, who had been heading for the stairs, froze.

'Exactly what do you mean?' he said.

'Don't you see? We are at large in the Forbidden City!'

'Not me!' said Rincewind. 'I've never been at large. I've always been at hunched.'

'The enemy brought us in here and now we are free—'

'Thanks to the Great Wizard,' said Lotus Blossom.

'—and we must seize the day!'

She picked up a sword from a stricken guard and waved it dramatically.

'We must storm the palace, just as Herb suggested!'

'There's only thirty of you!' said Rincewind. 'You're not a storm! You're a shower!'

'There are hardly any guards within the city itself,' said Butterfly. 'If we can overcome those around the Emperor's apartments—'

'You'll be killed!' said Rincewind.

She turned on him. 'Then at least we shall have died for something!'

'Cleanse The State With The Blood Of Martyrs,' rumbled Three Yoked Oxen.

Rincewind spun around and waved a finger under Three Yoked Oxen's nose, which was as high as he could reach.

'I'll bloody well thump you if you trot out something like that one

450

more time!' he shouted, and then grimaced at the realization that he had just threatened a man three times heavier than he was.

'Listen to me, will you?' he said, settling down a little. 'I know about people who talk about suffering for the common good. It's never bloody them! When you hear a man shouting "Forward, brave comrades!" you'll see he's the one behind the bloody big rock and wearing the only really arrow-proof helmet! Understand?'

He stopped. The cadre were looking at him as if he was mad. He stared at their young, keen faces, and felt very, very old.

'But there are causes worth dying for,' said Butterfly.

'No, there aren't! Because you've only got one life but you can pick up another five causes on any street corner!'

'Good grief, how can you *live* with a philosophy like that?'

Rincewind took a deep breath.

'Continuously!'

Six Beneficent Winds had thought it was a pretty good plan. The horrible old men were lost in the Forbidden City. Although they had a wiry look, rather like natural bonsai trees that had managed to flourish on a wind-swept cliff, they were nevertheless *very* old and not at all heavily armed.

So he led them in the direction of the gymnasium.

And when they were inside he screamed for help at the top of his voice. To his amazement, they didn't turn and run.

'Can we kill him *now*?' said Truckle.

A couple of dozen muscular men had stopped pounding logs of wood and piles of bricks and were regarding them suspiciously.

'Got any ideas?' said Cohen to Mr Saveloy.

'Oh, dear. They're so very *tough* looking, aren't they?'

'You can't think of anything civilized?'

'No. It's over to you, I'm afraid.'

'Hah! Hah! I bin *waiting* for this,' said Caleb, pushing forward. 'Bin practising every day, 'n I? With my big lump o' teak.'

'These are ninjas,' said Six Beneficent Winds proudly, as a couple of the men wandered towards the door and pulled it shut. 'The finest fighters in the world! Yield now!'

'That's interesting,' said Cohen. 'Here, you, in the black pyjamas . . . Just got out of bed, have you? Who's the best out of all of you?'

One of the men stared fixedly at Cohen and thrust out a hand at the nearest wall. It left a dent.

Then he nodded at the tax gatherer. 'What are these old fools you've brought us?'

'I think they're barbarian invaders,' said the taxman.

'How'd you – How'd he know that?' said Boy Willie. 'We're wearin' itchy trousers and eatin' with forks and *everythin'*—'

The leading ninja sneered. 'Heroic eunuchs?' he said. 'Old men?'

'Who're you calling a eunuch?' Cohen demanded.

'Can I just show him what I've been practising with my lump o' teak?' said Caleb, hopping arthritically from one foot to the other.

The ninja eyed the slab of timber.

'You could not make a dent on that, old man,' he said.

'You watch,' said Caleb. He held out the wood at arm's length. Then he raised his other hand, grunting a little as it got past shoulder height.

'You watching this hand? You watching this hand?' he demanded.

'I am watching,' said the ninja, trying not to laugh.

'Good,' said Caleb. He kicked the man squarely in the groin and then, as he doubled up, hit him over the head with the teak. ''Cos you should've been watchin' this foot.'

And that would have been all there was to it if there had only been one ninja. But there was a clatter of rice flails and an unsheathing of long, curved swords.

The Horde drew closer together. Hamish pushed back his rug to reveal their armoury, although the collection of notched blades looked positively homely compared with the shiny toys ranged against them.

'Teach, why don't you take Mr Taxman over to the corner out of harm's way?' said Ghenghiz.

'This is madness!' said Six Beneficent Winds. 'They're the finest fighters in the world and you're just old men! Give in now and I'll see if I can get you a rebate!'

'Calm down, calm down,' said Mr Saveloy. 'No one's going to get hurt. Metaphorically, at least.'

Ghenghiz Cohen waved his sword a few times.

'Okay, you lads,' he said. 'Give us your best ninje.'

Six Beneficent Winds looked on in horror as the Horde squared up.

'But it will be terrible slaughter!' he said.

'I'm afraid so,' said Mr Saveloy. He fished in his pockets for a bag of peppermints.

'Who are these mad old men? What do they *do*?'

'Barbarian heroing, generally,' said Mr Saveloy. 'Rescuing princesses, robbing temples, fighting monsters, exploring ancient and
terror-filled ruins . . . that sort of thing.'

'But they look old enough to be dead! Why do they do it?'

Saveloy shrugged. 'That's all they've ever done.'

A ninja somersaulted down the room, screaming, a sword in
either hand; Cohen waited in an attitude rather similar to that of a
baseball batter.

'I wonder,' said Mr Saveloy, 'if you have ever heard of the term
"evolution"?'

The two met. The air blurred.

'Or "survival of the fittest"?' said Mr Saveloy.

The scream continued, but rather more urgently.

'I didn't even see his sword move!' whispered Six Beneficent
Winds.

'Yes. People often don't,' said Mr Saveloy.

'But . . . they're so old!'

'Indeed,' said the teacher, raising his voice above the screams,
'and of course this is true. They are very *old* barbarian heroes.'

The taxman stared.

'Would you like a peppermint?' said Mr Saveloy, as Hamish's
wheelchair thundered past in pursuit of a man with a broken sword
and a pressing desire to stay alive. 'You may find it helps, if you are
around the Horde for any length of time.'

The aroma from the proffered paper bag hit Six Beneficent Winds
like a flamethrower.

'How can you smell anything after eating those?'

'You can't,' said Mr Saveloy happily.

The taxman continued to stare. The fighting was a fast and
furious affair but, somehow, only on one side. The Horde fought
like you'd expect old men to fight – slowly, and with care. All the
activity was on the part of the ninjas, but no matter how well flung
the throwing star or speedy the kick, the target was always, without
any obvious effort, not there.

'Since we have this moment to chat,' said Mr Saveloy, as some-
thing with a lot of blades hit the wall just above the taxman's head,
'I wonder: could you tell me about the big hill just outside the city?
It is quite a remarkable feature.'

'What?' said Six Beneficent Winds distractedly.

'The big hill.'

'You want to know about *that*? *Now*?'

'Geography is a little hobby of mine.'

Someone's ear hit Six Beneficent Winds on the ear.

'Er. What? We call it the Big Hill . . . Hey, look at what he's doing with his—'

'It seems remarkably regular. Is it a natural feature?'

'What? Eh? Oh . . . I don't know, they say it turned up thousands of years ago. During a terrible storm. When the first Emperor died. He . . . he's going to be killed! He's going to be killed! He's going to be – How did he do that?'

Six Beneficent Winds suddenly remembered, as a child, playing *Shibo Yangcong-san* with his grandfather. The old man always won. No matter how carefully he'd assembled his strategy, he'd find Grandfather would place a tile quite innocently right in the crucial place just before he could make his big move. The ancestor had spent his whole life playing *shibo*. The fight was just like that.

'Oh, my,' he said.

'That's right,' said Mr Saveloy. 'They've had a lifetime's experience of not dying. They've become very good at it.'

'But . . . why here? Why come here?'

'We're going to undertake a robbery,' said Mr Saveloy.

Six Beneficent Winds nodded sagely. The wealth of the Forbidden City was legendary. Probably even blood-sucking ghosts had heard of it.

'The Talking Vase of Emperor P'gi Su?' he said.

'No.'

'The Jade Head of Sung Ts'uit Li?'

'No. Wrong track entirely, I'm afraid.'

'Not the secret of how silk is made?'

'Good grief. Silkworms' bottoms. Everyone knows that. No. Something rather more precious than that.'

Despite himself, Six Beneficent Winds was impressed. Apart from anything else, only seven ninjas were still standing and Cohen was fencing with one of them while rolling a cigarette in the other hand.

And Mr Saveloy could see *it* dawning in the fat man's eyes.

The same thing had happened to him.

Cohen came into people's lives like a rogue planet into a peaceful solar system, and you felt yourself being dragged along simply because nothing like that would ever happen to you again.

He himself had been peacefully hunting for fossils during the school holidays when he had, more or less, stumbled into the camp of those particular fossils called the Horde. They'd been quite friendly, because he had neither weapons nor money. And they'd

454

taken to him, because he knew things they didn't. And that had been it.

He'd decided there and then. It must have been something in the air. His past life had suddenly unrolled behind him and he couldn't remember a single day of it that had been any fun. And it had dawned on him that he could join the Horde or go back to school and, pretty soon, a limp handshake, a round of applause and his pension.

It was something about Cohen. Maybe it was what they called charisma. It overpowered even his normal smell of a goat that had just eaten curried asparagus. He did everything wrong. He cursed people and used what Mr Saveloy considered very offensive language to foreigners. He shouted terms that would have earned anyone else a free slit throat from a variety of interesting ethnic weapons – and he got away with it, partly because it was clear that there was no actual malice there but mainly because he was, well, Cohen, a sort of basic natural force on legs.

It worked on everything. When he wasn't actually fighting them, he got on a lot better with trolls than did people who merely thought that trolls had rights just like everyone else. Even the Horde, bloody-minded individualists to a man, fell for it.

But Mr Saveloy had also seen the aimlessness in their lives and, one night, he'd brought the conversation round to the opportunities offered in the Aurient . . .

There was a light in Six Beneficent Winds' expression.

'Have you got an accountant?' he said.

'Well, no, as a matter of fact.'

'Will this theft be treated as income or capital?'

'I haven't really thought like that. The Horde doesn't pay taxes.'

'What? Not to *anyone*?'

'No. It's funny, but they never seem to keep their money for long. It seems to disappear on drink and women and high living. I suppose, from a heroing point of view, they may count as taxes.'

There was a 'pop' as Six Beneficent Winds uncorked a small bottle of ink and licked his writing brush.

'But those sort of things probably count as allowable expenses for a barbarian hero,' he said. 'They are part of the job specification. And then of course there is wear and tear on weaponry, protective clothing . . . They could certainly claim for at least one new loin-cloth a year—'

'I don't think they've claimed for one per century.'

'And there's pensions, of course.'

'Ah. Don't use that word. They think it's a dirty word. But in a way *that* is what they're here for. This is their last adventure.'

'When they've stolen this very valuable thing that you won't tell me about.'

'That's right. You'd be very welcome to join us. You could perhaps be a barbarian . . . to push beans . . . a length of knotted string . . . *ah* . . . accountant. Have you ever killed anyone?'

'Not outright. But I've always thought you can do considerable damage with a well-placed Final Demand.'

Mr Saveloy beamed. 'Ah, yes,' he said. 'Civilization.'

The last ninja was upright, but only just; Hamish had run his wheel-chair over his foot. Mr Saveloy patted the taxman's arm. 'Excuse me,' he said. 'I find I often have to intervene at this stage.'

He padded over to the surviving man, who was looking around wildly. Six swords had become interlaced around his neck as though he'd taken part in a rather energetic folk dance.

'Good morning,' said Mr Saveloy. 'I should just point out that Ghenghiz here is, despite appearances, a remarkably honest man. He finds it hard to understand empty bravura. May I venture to suggest therefore that you refrain from phrases like "I would rather die than betray my Emperor" or "Go ahead and do your worst" unless you *really, really* mean them. Should you wish for mercy, a simple hand signal will suffice. I strongly advise you not to attempt to nod.'

The young man looked sideways at Cohen, who gave him an encouraging smile.

Then he waved a hand quickly.

The swords unwove. Truckle hit the ninja over the head with a club.

'It's all right, you don't have to go on about it, I didn't kill him,' he said sulkily.

'Ow!' Boy Willie had been experimenting with a rice flail and had hit his own ear. 'How'd they manage to fight with this rubbish?'

'Whut?'

'These little Hogswatch decoration thingies look the business, though,' said Vincent, picking up a throwing star. 'Aaargh!' He sucked his fingers. 'Useless foreign junk.'

'That bit where that lad sprang backwards right across the room with them axes in his hands was impressive, though.'

'Yeah.'

'You didn't ought to have stuck your sword out like that, I thought.'

'He's learned an important lesson.'

'It won't do him much good now where he's gone.'

'Whut?'

Six Beneficent Winds was half laughing, half shocked.

'But . . . but . . . I've seen these guards fight before!' he said.

'They're *invincible*.'

'No one told *us*.'

'But you beat them all!'

'Yep!'

'And you're just eunuchs!'

There was a scrape of steel. Six Beneficent Winds closed his eyes. He could feel metal touching his neck in at least five places.

'There's that word again,' said the voice of Cohen the Barbarian.

'But . . . you're . . . *dressed* . . . as . . . eunuchs . . .' murmured Six Beneficent Winds, trying not to swallow.

Mr Saveloy backed away, chuckling nervously.

'You see,' he said, speaking fast, 'you're too old to be taken for guards and you don't look like bureaucrats, so I thought it would be, er, a very good disguise to—'

'*Eunuch?*' roared Truckle. 'You mean people've been looking at me and thinking I mince around saying, *Helluo, Saltat?*'

Like many men whose testosterone had always sloshed out of their ears, the Horde had never fine-tuned their approach to the more complex areas of sexuality. A teacher to the core, Mr Saveloy couldn't help correcting them, even at swordpoint.

'That means, "the glutton dances", not, as you seem to think, "hello, sailor", which is *heus nauta*,' he said. 'And eunuchs don't say it. Not as a matter of course. Look, it's an *honour* to be a eunuch in the Forbidden City. Many of them occupy very exalted positions in—'

'Then prepare yourself for high office, teacher!' Truckle shouted. Cohen knocked the sword out of his hand.

'All right, none of that. I don't like it either,' he said, 'but it's just a disguise. Shouldn't mean anything to a man who once bit a bear's head off, should it?'

'Yeah, but . . . you know . . . it's not . . . I mean, when we went past those young ladies back there they all giggled . . .'

'Maybe later you can find them and make them laugh,' said Cohen. 'But you should've told us, Teach.'

'Sorry.'

'Whut? Whatseesay?'

'He said you're a EUNUCH!' Boy Willie bellowed in Hamish's ear.

457

'Yep!' said Hamish happily.

'What?'

'That's me! The one an' only!'

'No, he didn't mean—'

'Whut?'

'Oh, never mind. It's all pretty much the same to you, Hamish.'

Mr Saveloy surveyed the wrecked gym. 'I wonder what time it is?' he said.

'Ah,' gurgled Six Beneficent Winds, happy to lighten things a little. 'Here, you know, we have an amazing demon-powered device that tells you what the time is even when the sun isn't—'

'Clocks,' said Mr Saveloy. 'We've got them in Ankh-Morpork. Only demons evaporate eventually so now they work by—' He paused. 'Interesting. You don't have a word for it. Er. Shaped metal that does work? Toothed wheels?'

The taxman looked frightened. 'Wheels with teeth?'

'What do you call the things that grind corn?'

'Peasants.'

'Yes, but what do they grind corn with?'

'I don't know. Why should I know? Only peasants need to know *that*.'

'Yes, I suppose that says it all, really,' said Mr Saveloy sadly.

'It's a long way off dawn,' said Truckle. 'Why don't we go and kill everyone in their beds?'

'No, no, no!' said Mr Saveloy. 'I keep telling you, we've got to do it *properly*.'

'I could show you the treasure house,' said Six Beneficent Winds helpfully.

'Never a good idea to give a monkey the key to a banana plantation,' said Mr Saveloy. 'Can you think of anything else to keep them amused for an hour?'

Down in the basement, there was a man who was talking about the government. At the top of his voice.

'You can't fight for a cause! A cause is just a thing!'

'Then we are fighting for the peasants,' said Butterfly. She'd backed away. Rincewind's anger was coming off him like steam.

'Oh? Have you ever met them?'

'I – have seen them.'

'Oh, good! And what is it you want to *achieve*?'

'A better life for the people,' said Butterfly coldly.

458

'You think you having some uprising and hanging a few people will do it? Well, I come from Ankh-Morpork and we've had more rebellions and civil wars than you've had . . . lukewarm ducks' feet, and you know what? The rulers are still in charge! They always are!'

They smiled at him in polite and nervous incomprehension.

'Look,' he said, rubbing his forehead. 'All those people out in the fields, the water buffalo people . . . If you have a revolution it'll all be better for them, will it?'

'Of course,' said Butterfly. 'They will no longer be subject to the cruel and capricious whims of the Forbidden City.'

'Oh, that's good,' said Rincewind. 'So they'll sort of be in charge of themselves, will they?'

'Indeed,' said Lotus Blossom.

'By means of the People's Committee,' said Butterfly.

Rincewind pressed both hands to his head.

'My word,' he said. 'I don't know why, but I had this predictive flash!'

They looked impressed.

'I had this sudden feeling,' he went on, 'that there won't be all that many water buffalo string holders on the People's Committee. In fact . . . I get this kind of . . . voice telling me that a lot of the People's Committee, correct me if I'm wrong, are standing in front of me right now?'

'*Initially*, of course,' said Butterfly. 'The peasants can't even read and write.'

'I expect they don't even know how to farm properly,' said Rincewind, gloomily. 'Not after doing it for only three or four thousand years.'

'We certainly believe that there are many improvements that could be made, yes,' said Butterfly. 'If we act collectively.'

'I bet they'll be really glad when you show them,' said Rincewind.

He stared glumly at the floor. He quite liked the job of a water buffalo string holder. It sounded nearly as good as the profession of castaway. He longed for the kind of life where you could really *concentrate* on the squishiness of the mud underfoot, and make up pictures in the clouds; the kind of life where you could let your mind catch up with you and speculate for hours at a time about when your water buffalo was next going to enrich the loam. But it was probably difficult enough as it was without people trying to *improve* it . . .

He wanted to say: how can you be so nice and yet so dumb? The best thing you can do with the peasants is leave them alone. Let

459

them get on with it. When people who can read and write start fighting on behalf of people who can't, you just end up with another kind of stupidity. If you want to help them, build a big library or something somewhere and leave the door open.

But this is Hunghung. You can't think like that in Hunghung. This is where people have learned to do what they're told. The Horde worked that one out.

The Empire's got something worse than whips all right. It's got obedience. Whips in the soul. They obey anyone who tells them what to do. Freedom just means being told what to do by someone different.

You'll all be killed.

I'm a coward. And even *I* know more about fights than you do. I've run away from some really good ones.

'Oh, let's just get out of here,' he said. He gingerly took the sword from a dead guard and held it the right way round on the second attempt. He weighed it for a second, then shook his head and threw it away.

The cadre looked a lot happier.

'But I'm not leading you,' said Rincewind. 'I'm just showing you the way. And it's the way *out*, do you understand?'

They stood wearing rather bruised looks, as people do who've been subject to several minutes' ranting. No one spoke, until Twoflower whispered:

'He often goes on like this, you know. And then he does something very brave.'

Rincewind snorted.

There was another dead guard at the top of the stairs. Sudden death seemed to be catching.

And, leaning against the wall, was a bundle of swords. Tied to it was a scroll.

'The Great Wizard has shown us the way for only two minutes and already we have extra luck,' said Lotus Blossom.

'Don't touch the swords,' said Rincewind.

'But supposing we see more guards? Should we not resist them with every drop of our life's blood?' said Butterfly.

Rincewind looked blank. 'No. Run away.'

'Ah, yes,' said Twoflower. 'And live to fight another day. That is an Ankh-Morpork saying.'

Rincewind had always assumed that the purpose of running away was to be able to run away another day.

'However,' he said, 'people don't usually find themselves mysteriously let out of prison with a bunch of weapons handily close by and all the guards out of action. Ever thought of that?'

'And with a map!' said Butterfly.

Her eyes shone. She flourished the scroll.

'It's a map of the way out?' said Rincewind.

'No! To the Emperor's chambers! Look, it has been marked! That's what Herb used to talk about sometimes! He must be in the palace! We should assassinate the Emperor!'

'More luck!' said Twoflower. 'But look, you know, I'm sure if we talked to him—'

'Haven't you been listening? We are *not* going to see the Emperor!' hissed Rincewind. 'Does it occur to you that guards don't stab themselves? Cells don't suddenly become unlocked? You don't find swords lying around so conveniently and you don't, you really *don't* find maps saying "This Way, Folks"! And anyway, you can't talk to someone who's a plate of prawn crackers short of a Set Meal A for Two!'

'No,' said Butterfly. 'We must make the most of this opportunity.'

'There will be lots of guards!'

'Well, Great Wizard, you'll have a lot of wishing to do.'

'You think I can snap my fingers like *this*, and all the guards would drop dead? Hah! I wish they would!'

'These two out here have,' Lotus Blossom reported, from the entrance to the dungeons. She was already in awe of Rincewind. Now she looked positively terrified.

'Coincidence!'

'Let's be serious,' said Butterfly. 'We have a sympathizer in the palace. Perhaps it is someone risking their lives every moment! We know some of the eunuchs are on our side.'

'They've got nothing left to lose, I suppose.'

'You have a better idea, Great Wizard?'

'Yes. Back into the cells.'

'What?'

'This smells wrong. Would you *really* kill the Emperor? I mean, *really*?'

Butterfly hesitated.

'We've often talked about it. Two Fire Herb said that if we could assassinate the Emperor we would light the torch of freedom . . .'

'Yes. It'd be you, burning. Look, get back in the cells. It's the safest place. I'll lock you in and . . . scout.'

'That's a very brave suggestion,' said Twoflower. 'And typical of the man,' he added proudly.

461

Butterfly gave Rincewind a look he'd come to dread.

'It *is* a good idea,' she said. 'And I will accompany you.'

'Oh, but it's bound to be . . . very dangerous,' said Rincewind quickly.

'No harm can possibly come to me when I'm with the Great Wizard,' said Butterfly.

'Very true. Very true,' said Twoflower. 'No harm ever came to me, I know that.'

'Besides,' his daughter went on, 'I have the map. And it would be dreadful if you lost your way and accidentally strayed out of the Forbidden City, wouldn't it?'

Rincewind gave in. It struck him that Twoflower's late wife must have been a remarkably intelligent woman.

'Oh, all right,' he said. 'But you're not to get in the way. And you're to do what I tell you, okay?'

Butterfly bowed.

'Lead on, O Great Wizard,' she said.

'I knew it!' said Truckle. 'Poison!'

'No, no. You don't eat it. You rub it on your body,' said Mr Saveloy. 'Watch. And you get what we in civilization call *clean*.'

Most of the Horde stood waist-deep in the warm water, every man with his hands chastely wrapped around his body. Hamish had refused to relinquish his wheelchair, so only his head was above the surface.

'It's all prickly,' said Cohen. 'And my skin's peeling off and dissolving.'

'That's *not* skin,' said Mr Saveloy. 'Haven't *any* of you seen a bath before?'

'Oh, I *seen* one,' said Boy Willie. 'I killed the Mad Bishop of Pseudopolis in one. You get' – he furrowed his brow – 'bubbles and stuff. And fifteen naked maidens.'

'Whut?'

'Definitely. Fifteen. Remember it well.'

'That's more *like* it,' said Caleb.

'All *we've* got to rub is this soap stuff.'

'The Emperor is ritually bathed by twenty-two bath women,' said Six Beneficent Winds. 'I could go and check with the harem eunuchs and wake them up, if you like. It's probably allowable under Entertaining.'

The taxman was warming to his new job. He'd worked out that

although the Horde, as individuals, had acquired mountains of cash in their careers as barbarian heroes they'd lost almost all of it engaging in the other activities (he mentally catalogued these as Public Relations) necessary to the profession, and therefore were entitled to quite a considerable rebate.

The fact that they were registered with no revenue collecting authority *anywhere*[*] was entirely a secondary point. It was the principle that counted. And the interest too, of course.

'No, no young women, I insist,' said Mr Saveloy. 'You're having a bath to get clean. Plenty of time for young women later.'

'Gotta date when all this is over,' said Caleb, a little shyly, thinking wistfully of one of the few women he'd ever had a conversation with. 'She's got her own farm, she said. I could be all right for a duck.'

'I bet Teach don't want you to say that,' said Boy Willie. 'I bet he'd say you gotta call it a waterfowl.'

'Huh, huh, hur!'

'Whut?'

Six Beneficent Winds sidled over to the teacher as the Horde experimented with the bath oil, initially by drinking it.

'I've worked out what it is you're going to steal,' he said.

'Oh, yes?' said Mr Saveloy politely. He was watching Caleb who, having had it brought home to him that he might have been adopting the wrong approach all his life, was trying to cut his nails with his sword.

'It's the legendary Diamond Coffin of Schz Yu!' said Six Beneficent Winds.

'No. Wrong again.'

'Oh.'

'Out of the baths, gentlemen,' said the teacher. 'I think . . . yes . . . you've mastered commerce, social intercourse—'

'—hur, hur, hur . . . sorry—'

'—and the principles of taxation,' Mr Saveloy went on.

'Have we done that? What *are* they, then?' said Cohen.

'You take away almost all the money that the merchants have got,' said Six Beneficent Winds, handing him a towel.

'Oh, is that it? I've been doing that for *years*.'

'No, you've been taking away *all* the money,' said Mr Saveloy. 'That's where you go wrong. You kill too many of them, and the ones you don't kill you leave too poor.'

[*] Except on posters with legends like 'Wanted – Dedd'.

463

'Sounds *frightfully* good to me,' said Truckle, excavating the cretaceous contents of an ear. 'Poor merchants, rich us.'

'No, no, no!'

'No, no, no?'

'Yes! That's not *civilized*!'

'It's like with sheep,' Six Beneficent Winds explained. 'You don't tear their skin off all in one go, you just shear them every year.'

The Horde looked blank.

'Hunter-gatherers,' said Mr Saveloy, with a touch of hopelessness. 'Wrong metaphor.'

'It's the marvellous Singing Sword of Wong, isn't it?' whispered Six Beneficent Winds. 'That's what you're going to steal!'

'No. In fact, "steal" is rather the wrong word. Well, anyway, gentlemen . . . you might not yet be civilized but at least you're nice and clean, and many people think this is identical. Time, I think, for . . . action.'

The Horde straightened up. This was back in the area they understood.

'To the Throne Room!' said Ghenghiz Cohen.

Six Beneficent Winds wasn't that fast on the uptake, but at last he put two and two together.

'It's the Emperor!' he said, and raised his hand to his mouth in horror tinged with evil delight. 'You're going to kidnap him!'

Diamonds glittered when Cohen grinned.

There were two dead guards in the corridor leading to the private Imperial apartments.

'Look, how come you were all taken alive?' whispered Rincewind. 'The guards I saw had big swords. How come you're not dead?'

'I suppose they planned to torture us,' said Butterfly. 'We did injure ten of them.'

'Oh? Pasted posters on them, did you? Sang revolutionary songs until they gave in? Listen, someone *wanted* you alive.'

The floors sang in the darkness. Every footstep produced a chorus of squeaks and groans, just like the floorboards at the University. But you didn't expect that sort of thing in a nice shiny palace like this.

'They're called nightingale floors,' said Butterfly. 'The carpenters put little metal collars around the nails so that no one can creep up unawares.'

Rincewind looked down at the corpses. Neither man had drawn his sword. He leaned his weight on his left foot. The floor squeaked. Then he leaned on his right foot. The floor groaned.

'This isn't right, then,' he whispered. 'You can't creep up on someone on a floor like this. So someone they *knew* killed those guards. Let's get out of here . . .'

'We go on,' said Butterfly firmly.

'It's a trap. Someone's using you to do their dirty work.'

She shrugged. 'Turn left by the big jade statue.'

It was four in the morning, an hour before dawn. There were guards in the official staterooms, but not very many. After all, this was well inside the Forbidden City, with its high walls and small gates. It wasn't as though anything was going to happen.

It needed a special type of mind to stand guard over some empty rooms all night. One Big River had such a mind, orbiting gently within the otherwise blissful emptiness of his skull.

They'd happily called him One Big River because he was the same size and moved at the same speed as the Hung. Everyone had expected him to become a *tsimo* wrestler, but he'd failed the intelligence test because he hadn't eaten the table.

It was impossible for him to get bored. He just didn't have the imagination. But, since the visor of his huge helmet registered a permanent expression of metal rage, he'd in any case cultivated the art of going to sleep on his feet.

He was dozing happily now, aware only of an occasional squeaking, like that of a very cautious mouse.

The helmet's visor swung up. A voice said: 'Would you rather die than betray your Emperor?'

A second voice said: 'This is not a trick question.'

One Big River blinked, and then turned his gaze downwards. An apparition in a squeaky-wheeled wheelchair had a very large sword pointing at exactly that inconvenient place where his upper armour didn't quite meet his lower armour.

A third voice said: 'I should add that the last twenty-nine people who answered wrong are . . . dried shredded fish . . . sorry, dead.'

A fourth voice said: 'And we're not eunuchs.'

One Big River rumbled with the effort of thought.

'I tink I rather live,' he said.

A man with diamonds where his teeth should have been gave him a comradely pat on the shoulder. 'Good man,' he said. 'Join the

Horde. We could use a man like you. Maybe as a siege weapon.'

'Who you?' he said.

This is Ghenghiz Cohen,' said Mr Saveloy. 'Doer of mighty deeds. Slayer of dragons. Ravager of cities. He once bought an apple.'

No one laughed. Mr Saveloy had found that the Horde had no concept whatsoever of sarcasm. Probably no one had ever tried it on them.

One Big River had been raised to do what he was told. Everyone had told him what to do, all through his life. He fell in behind the man with diamond teeth because he was the sort of man you followed when he said 'follow'.

'But, you know, there are tens of thousands of men who *would* die rather than betray their Emperor,' whispered Six Beneficent Winds, as they filed through the corridors.

'I hope so.'

'Some of them will be on guard around the Forbidden City. We've avoided them, but they're still there. We'll have to deal with them eventually.'

'Oh, good!' said Cohen.

'Bad,' said Mr Saveloy. 'That business with the ninjas was just high spirits—'

'—high spirits—' murmured Six Beneficent Winds.

'—but you don't want a big fight out in the open. It'll get messy.'

Cohen walked over to the nearest wall, which had a gorgeous pattern of peacocks, and took out his knife.

'Paper,' he said. 'Bloody paper. Paper walls.' He poked his head through. There was a shrill whimper. 'Oops, sorry, ma'am. Official wall inspection.' He extracted his head, grinning.

'But you can't go through walls!' said Six Beneficent Winds.

'Why not?'

'They're – well, they're the *walls*. What would happen if everyone walked through walls? What do you think doors are for?'

'I think they're for other people,' said Cohen. 'Which way's that throne room?'

'Whut?'

'This is lateral thinking,' explained Mr Saveloy, as they followed him. 'Ghenghiz is quite good at a certain kind of lateral thinking.'

'What a lateral?'

'Er. It's a kind of muscle, I believe.'

'Thinking with your muscles . . . Yes. I see,' said Six Beneficent Winds.

*

466

Rincewind sidled into a space between the wall and a statue of a rather jolly dog with its tongue hanging out.

'What now?' said Butterfly.

'How big's the Red Army?'

'We number many thousands,' said Butterfly, defiantly.

'In Hunghung?'

'Oh, no. There is a cadre in every city.'

'You know that, do you? You've met them?'

'That would be dangerous. Only Two Fire Herb knows how to contact them . . .'

'Fancy that. Well, do you know what I think? I think someone *wants* a revolution. And you're all so damn respectful and polite he's having his work cut out trying to organize one! But once you've got rebels you can do *anything*.'

That can't be true . . .'

'The rebels in other cities, they do great revolutionary deeds, do they?'

'We hear reports all the time!'

'From our friend Herb?'

Butterfly frowned.

'Yes . . .'

'You're thinking, aren't you?' said Rincewind. 'The old brain cells are finally banging together, yes? Good. Have I convinced you?'

'I . . . don't know.'

'Now let's go back.'

'No. Now I've got to find out if what you're suggesting is true.'

'Dying to find out, eh? Good grief, you people make me so *angry*. Look, watch this . . .'

Rincewind strode to the end of the corridor. There was a pair of wide doors, flanked by a pair of jade dragons.

He flung them back.

The room inside was low-ceilinged but large. In the centre, under a canopy, was a bed. It was hard to make out the figure lying there, but it had that certain stillness that suggests the kind of sleep from which there is unlikely to be any kind of awakening.

'You see?' he said. 'He's been . . . killed . . . already . . .'

A dozen soldiers were staring at Rincewind in amazement.

Behind him he heard the creaking of the floor and then some whooshing sounds followed by a noise like wet leather being hit against rock.

Rincewind looked at the nearest soldier. The man was holding a sword.

One drop of blood coursed down the blade and, with a brief pause for dramatic effect, fell on to the floor.

Rincewind looked up and raised his hat.

'I do beg your pardon,' he said, brightly. 'Isn't this room 3B?'

And ran for it.

The floors screamed under him, and behind him someone screamed Rincewind's nickname, which was: 'Don't let him get away!'

Let me get away, Rincewind prayed, oh, please, let me get away.

He slipped as he turned the corner, skidded through a paper wall and landed in an ornamental fish pond. But Rincewind in full flight had catlike, even messianic abilities. The water barely rippled under his feet as he bounced off the surface and headed away.

Another wall erupted and he was in what was possibly the same corridor.

Behind him, someone landed heavily on a valuable koi.

Rincewind shot forward again.

From; that was the most important factor in any mindless escape. You were always running *from*. *To* could look after itself.

He cleared a long flight of shallow stone steps, rolled upright at the bottom and set off at random along another corridor.

His legs had sorted themselves out now. First the mad, wild dash to get you out of immediate danger and then the good solid strides to put as much distance as possible between you and it. That was the trick.

History told of a runner who'd run forty miles after a battle to report its successful outcome to those at home. He was tradition-ally regarded as the greatest runner of all time, but if he'd been reporting news of an *impending* battle he'd have been overtaken by Rincewind.

And yet . . . someone was gaining.

A knife poked through the wall of the throne room and cut a hole large enough to afford space for an upright man or one wheelchair.

There was muttering from the Horde.

'Bruce the Hoon never went in the back way.'

'Shut up.'

'Never one for back gates, Bruce the Hoon.'

'Shut up.'

'When Bruce the Hoon attacked Al Khali, he did it right at the main guard tower, with a thousand screaming men on very small horses.'

'Yeah, but . . . last I saw of Bruce the Hoon, his head was on a spike.'

'All right, I'll grant you that. But at least it was over the main gate. I mean, at least he got in.'

'His head did.'

'Oh, my . . .'

Mr Saveloy was gratified. The room they'd stepped into was enough to silence the Horde, if only briefly. It was large, of course, but that hadn't been its only purpose. One Sun Mirror, as he welded the tribes and countries and little island nations together, had wanted a room built which said to chieftains and ambassadors: this is the biggest space you've ever been in, it is more splendid than anything you could ever imagine, and we've got a lot more rooms like this.

He had wanted it to be impressive. He had very clearly wanted it to intimidate mere barbarians so much that they'd give in there and then. Let there be huge statues, he'd said. And vast decorative hangings. Let there be pillars and carvings. Let the visitor be silenced by the sheer magnificence. Let it say to him, 'This is civilization, and you can join it or die. Now drop to your knees or be shortened some other way.'

The Horde gave it the benefit of their inspection.

Finally Truckle said, 'It's all right, I suppose, but not a patch on our chieftain's longhouse back in Skund. It hasn't even got a fire in the middle of the floor, look.'

'Gaudy, to my mind.'

'Whut?'

'Typically foreign.'

'I'd do away with most of this and get some decent straw on the floor, a few shields round the walls.'

'Whut?'

'Mind you, get in a few hundred tables and you could have a helluva carouse in here.'

Cohen walked across the huge expanse towards the throne, which was under a vast ornamental canopy.

''S got 'n umbrella over it, look.'

'Probably the roof leaks. You can't trust tiles. A good reed thatch'll give you forty years bone dry.'

The throne was lacquered wood, but with many precious gems set in it. Cohen sat down.

'Is this it?' he said. 'We've done it, Teach?'

'Yes. Of course, now you have to get away with it,' said Mr Saveloy.

'I'm sorry,' said Six Beneficent Winds. 'What've you done?'

'You know that thing we were here to steal?' said the teacher.

'Yes?'

'It's the Empire.'

The taxman's expression didn't change for a few seconds, and then it flowed into a horrified grin.

'I think some breakfast is called for before we go any further,' said Mr Saveloy. 'Mr Winds, perhaps you would be so good as to summon someone?'

The taxman was still grinning fixedly.

'But . . . but . . . you can't conquer an empire like this!' he managed. 'You've got to have an army, like the warlords! Just walking in like this . . . It's against the rules! And . . . and . . . there are thousands of guards!'

'Yes, but they're all out there,' said Mr Saveloy.

Guarding us,' said Cohen.

'But they're guarding the *real* Emperor!'

'That's me,' said Cohen.

'Oh yeah?' said Truckle. 'Who died and made *you* Emperor?'

'No one has to die,' said Mr Saveloy. 'It's called usurping.'

'That's right,' said Cohen. 'You just say, see here, Gunga Din, you're out on your ear, okay? Piss off to some island somewhere or—'

'Ghenghiz,' said Mr Saveloy gently, 'do you think you could refrain from referring to foreigners in that rather offensive fashion? It's not civilized.'

Cohen shrugged.

'You're still going to have big trouble with the guards and things,' said Six Beneficent Winds.

'Maybe not,' said Cohen. 'Tell 'em, Teach.'

'Have you ever *seen* the, er, former Emperor?' said Mr Saveloy. 'Mr Winds?'

'Of course not. Hardly anyone has seen—'

He stopped.

'There you are, then,' said Mr Saveloy. 'Very quick on the uptake, Mr Winds. As befits the Lord High Chief Tax Gatherer.'

'But it won't work because—' Six Beneficent Winds stopped again. Mr Saveloy's words reached his brain.

'Lord High Chief? Me? The black hat *with* the red ruby button?'

470

'Yes.'

'And a feather in it, if you like,' said Cohen munificently.

The taxman looked in rapt consideration.

'So . . . if there was, say, a mere District Administrator who was incredibly cruel to his staff, particularly to a hard-working deputy, and thoroughly deserving of a good sound thrashing—'

'As the Lord High Chief Tax Gatherer, of course, that would be entirely your affair.'

Six Beneficent Winds' grin now threatened to remove the top of his head.

'On the subject of new taxation,' he said, 'I've often had this thought that fresh air is all too readily available at far below the cost of production—'

'We will listen to your ideas with extreme interest,' said Mr Saveloy. 'In the meantime, please arrange breakfast.'

'And have summoned,' said Cohen, 'all those buggers who think they know what the Emperor looks like.'

The pursuer was closing.

Rincewind skidded around a corner and there, blocking the passageway, were three guards. These were not dead. They were alive, and they had got swords.

Someone cannoned into the back of him, pushed him to the ground, and leapt past.

He shut his eyes.

There were a couple of thumps, a groan, and then a very strange metallic noise.

It was a helmet, spinning round and round on the floor.

He was pulled to his feet.

'Are you going to lie around all day?' said Butterfly. 'Come on. They're not far behind!'

Rincewind glanced at the recumbent guards, and then loped after the girl.

'How many of them are there?' he managed.

'Seven now. But two of them are limping and one's having trouble breathing. Come *on*.'

'You *hit* them?'

'Do you always waste breath like this?'

'Never found anyone who could keep up with me before!'

They turned a corner and almost ran into another guard.

Butterfly didn't even stop. She took a ladylike step, whirled around on one foot, and kicked the man so hard on his ear that he spun on his own axis and landed on his head.

She paused, panted, and tucked a hair back into place.

'We should split up,' she said.

'Oh, no!' said Rincewind. 'I mean, I must protect you!'

'I'll head back to the others. You lead the guards away some-where—'

'Can you *all* do that?'

'Of course,' said Butterfly, testily. 'I *told* you we fought the guards. Now, if we split up one of us is bound to escape. The murderers! We were supposed to take the blame for that!'

'Didn't I try to tell you? I thought you *wanted* him dead!'

'Yes, but we're rebels. They were palace guards!'

'Er—'

'No time. See you in Heaven.'

She darted away.

'Oh.'

Rincewind looked around. It had all gone quiet.

Guards appeared at the end of the corridor, but cautiously, as befitted people who'd just met Butterfly.

'There!'

'Is it her?'

'No, it's him!'

'Get him!'

He accelerated again, rounded a corner, and found that he was in a cul-de-sac that would undoubtedly, given the sounds behind, become a dead end. But there was a pair of doors. He kicked them open, ran inside, and slowed . . .

The space inside was dark, but the sound and air suggested a large space and a certain flatulent component indicated some kind of stable.

There was some light, though, from a fire. Rincewind trotted towards it and saw that it was under a huge cauldron, man-sized, full of boiling rice.

And now that his eyes were accustomed to the gloom he realized that there were shapes lying on slabs along both walls of an enormous room.

They were snoring gently.

They were, in fact, people. They might even have been humans, or at least had humans in their ancestry before someone, hundreds of years ago, had said, 'Let's see how big and fat we can breed people. Let's try for really big bastards.'

Each giant frame was dressed in what looked like a nappy to Rincewind's eyes and was dozing happily alongside a bowl holding enough rice to explode twenty people, just in case it woke up in the night and felt like a light snack.

A couple of his pursuers appeared in the doorway, and stopped. Then they advanced, but very cautiously, carefully watching the gently moving mounds.

'Oi, oi, oi!' shouted Rincewind.

The men stopped and stared at him.

'Wakey wakey! Let's see the rising sons!' He grabbed a mighty ladle and banged it on the rice cauldron.

'Up you get! Hands off-er-whatever you can find and on with socks!'

The sleepers stirred.

'Oooorrrrr?'

'Oooooaaooooooor!'

The room shook as forty tree-trunk legs swung off the slabs. Flesh rearranged itself so that, in the gloom, Rincewind appeared to be being watched by twenty small pyramids.

'Haaaroooooohhhh?'

'Those men,' said Rincewind, pointing desperately at his pursuers, who were slowly backing away, 'those men have a pork sandwich!'

'Oorrryorrraaah?'

'Oooorrrr?'

'With mustard!'

'Oooorrrr!'

Twenty very small heads turned. A total of eighty specialized neurones fired into life.

And the floor shook. The wrestlers started to move hopefully towards the men, in a slow but deliberate run designed to be halted only by collision with another wrestler or a continent.

'Oooorrr!'

Rincewind dashed for the far door and burst through it. A couple of men were sitting in a small room drinking tea and playing *shibo*, watched by a third.

'The wrestlers are wrestless!' he shouted. 'I think you've got a stampede going on!'

A man threw down his *shibo* tiles. 'Blast! And it's been at least an hour since they were fed!'

The men grabbed various nets and prods and items of protective clothing, leaving Rincewind alone.

There was another door. He sashayed through it. He'd never essayed a sashay before, but he reckoned he was due a sashay for quick thinking.

There was another passage. He ran down it, on the basis that absence of pursuit is no reason to stop running.

Lord Hong was folding paper.

He was an expert at it because when he did it he gave it his full attention. Lord Hong had a mind like a knife, although possibly a knife with a curved blade.

The door slid aside. A guard, red in the face from running, threw himself on to the floor.

'O Lord Hong, who is exalted—'

'Yes, indeed,' said Lord Hong distantly, essaying a taxing crease. 'What has gone wrong this time?'

'My lord?'

'I asked you what has gone wrong.'

'Uh . . . we killed the Emperor as directed—'

'By whom?'

'My lord! You commanded it!'

'Did I?' said Lord Hong, folding the paper lengthwise.

The guard shut his eyes. He had a vision, a very short vision, of the future. There was a spike in it. He carried on.

'But the . . . prisoners can't be found anywhere, lord! We heard someone approach and then . . . well, we saw two people, lord. We're chasing them. But the others have vanished.'

'No slogans? No revolutionary posters? No *culprits*?'

'No, lord.'

'I see. Remain here.'

Lord Hong's hands continued with the folding as he looked at the room's other occupant.

'You have something to say, Two Fire Herb?' he said pleasantly.

The revolutionary leader looked sheepish.

'The Red Army has been quite expensive,' said Lord Hong. 'The printing costs alone . . . And you cannot say I have not helped you. We unlocked the doors and killed the guards and gave your wretched people swords and a map, did we not? And now I can hardly claim that they killed the Emperor, may he stay dead for ten thousand years, when there is no sign of them. People will ask too many questions. I can hardly kill *everyone*. And we appear to have some barbarians in the building, too.'

'Something must have gone wrong, my lord.' Herb was hypnotized by the moving hands as they caressed that paper.

'What a pity. I do not like it when things go wrong. Guard? Redeem your miserable self. Take him away. I will have to try a different plan.'

'My lord!'

'Yes, Two Fire Herb?'

'When you . . . when we agreed . . . when it was agreed that the Red Army should be turned over to you, you did promise me indemnity.'

Lord Hong smiled.

'Oh, yes. I recall. I said, did I not, that I would neither say nor write any order for your death? And I must keep my word, otherwise what am I?'

He folded the last crease and opened his hands, putting the little paper decoration on the lacquered table beside him.

Herb and the guard stared at it.

'Guard . . . take him away,' said Lord Hong.

It was a marvellously constructed paper figure of a man.

But there didn't seem to have been enough paper for a head.

The immediate court turned out to be about eighty men, women and eunuchs, in various states of sleeplessness.

They were astonished at what sat on the throne.

The Horde were quite astonished at the court.

'Who're all them vinegar-faced old baggages at the front?' whispered Cohen, who was idly tossing a throwing knife into the air and catching it again. 'I wouldn't even set fire to them.'

'They're the wives of former Emperors,' hissed Six Beneficent Winds.

'We don't have to marry them, do we?'

'I don't think so.'

'Why're their feet so small?' said Cohen. 'I like to see big feet on a woman.'

Six Beneficent Winds told him. Cohen's expression hardened.

'I'm learning a lot about civilization, I am,' he said. 'Long fingernails, crippled feet and servants running around without their family jewels. Huh.'

'What is going on here, pray?' said a middle-aged man. 'Who are you? Who are these old eunuchs?'

'Who're you?' said Cohen. He drew his sword. 'I need to know so's it can be put on your gravestone—'

'I wonder if I might effect some introductions at this point?' said Mr Saveloy. He stepped forward.

'This,' he said, 'is Ghenghiz Cohen – put it away, Ghenghiz – who is technically a barbarian, and this is his Horde. They have overrun your city. And you are—?'

'Barbarian invaders?' said the man haughtily, ignoring him. 'Barbarian invaders come in their thousands! Big screaming men on little horses!'

'I *told* you,' said Truckle. 'But would anyone listen?'

'—and there is fire, terror, rapine, looting and blood in the streets!'

'We haven't had breakfast yet,' said Cohen, tossing his knife into the air again.

'Hah! I would rather die than submit to such as you!'

Cohen shrugged. 'Why didn't you say earlier?'

'Oops,' said Six Beneficent Winds.

It was a very accurate throw.

'Who *was* he, anyway?' said Cohen, as the body folded up. 'Anyone know who he was?'

'Ghenghiz,' said Mr Saveloy, 'I've kept meaning to tell you: when people say they'd rather die, they don't really *mean* they'd rather die. Not always.'

'Why'd they say it, then?'

'It's the done thing.'

'Is this civilization again?'

'I'm afraid so.'

'Let's settle this once and for all, shall we?' said Cohen. He stood up. 'Hands up those who'd rather die than have me as Emperor.'

'Anyone?' said Mr Saveloy.

Rincewind trotted along another passage. Was there no outside to this place? Several times he thought he'd found an exit, but it led only to a courtyard within the huge building, filled with tinkling fountains and willow trees.

And the place was waking up. There were—

—running steps behind him.

A voice shouted, 'Hey—'

He dived for the nearest door.

The room beyond was full of steam. It roiled in great billowing clouds. He could dimly make out a figure toiling at the huge wheel and the words 'torture chamber' crossed his mind until the smell of soap replaced them with the word 'laundry'. Rather wan but incredibly clean figures looked up from their vats and watched him with barely a hint of interest.

They did not look like people in close touch with current events.

He half ran, half sauntered between the bubbling cauldrons.

'Keep it up. Good man. That's it, scrub, scrub, scrub. Let me see those wringers wringing. Well done. Is there another door out of here? Good bubbles there, very good bubbles. Ah . . .'

One of the laundry workers, who appeared to be in charge, gave him a suspicious glare and seemed to be about to say something.

Rincewind dodged through a courtyard crisscrossed with washing lines and stopped, panting, with his back to a wall.

Although it was against his general principles, it was perhaps time to stop and think.

People were chasing him. That is to say, they were chasing a running figure in a faded red robe and a very charred pointy hat.

It took a great effort for Rincewind to come to terms with the idea, but it was just possible that if he was *wearing something else* he might not be chased.

On the line in front of him, shirts and trousers flapped in the breeze. Their construction was to tailoring in the same way that woodchopping is to carpentry. Someone had mastered the art of the tube, and left it at that. They looked just like the clothes nearly everyone wore in Hunghung.

The palace was almost a city in its own right, said the voice of reason. It must be full of people on all sorts of errands, it added.

It would mean . . . taking off our hat, it added.

Rincewind hesitated. It would be hard for a non-wizard to grasp the enormity of the suggestion. A wizard would sooner go without his robe and trousers than forgo his hat. Without his hat, people might think he was an *ordinary person*.

There was shouting in the distance.

The voice of reason could see that if it wasn't careful it was going to end up as dead as the rest of Rincewind and added sarcastically: all right, keep our wretched hat. Our damn hat is why we're in this mess in the first place. Perhaps you think you're going to have a head left to wear it on?

Rincewind's hands, also aware that times were going to be extremely interesting and very short unless they took matters into themselves, reached out slowly and removed a pair of pants and a shirt and rammed them inside his robe.

The door burst open. There were *still* guards behind him, and a couple of the *tsimo* herders had joined in the chase. One of them waved a prod in Rincewind's direction.

He plunged towards an archway and out into a garden.

It had a little pagoda. It had willow trees, and a pretty lady on a bridge feeding the birds.

And a man painting a plate.

Cohen rubbed his hands together.

'No one? Good. That's all sorted, then.'

'Ahem.'

A small man at the front of the crowd made a great play of keeping his hands to himself, but said:

'Excuse me, but . . . what would happen in the hypothetical situation of us calling the guards and denouncing you?'

'We'd kill you all before they were halfway through the door,' said Cohen, matter of factly. 'Any more questions?' he added, to a chorus of gasps.

'Er . . . the Emperor . . . that is to say, the *last* Emperor . . . had some very special guards . . .'

There was a tinkling sound. Something small and multi-pointed rolled down the steps and spun round on the floor. It was a throwing star.

'Met them,' said Boy Willie.

'Fine, fine,' said the little man. 'That all seems in order. Ten Thousand Years to the Emperor!'

The shout was taken up, a little raggedly.

'What's your name, young man?' said Mr Saveloy.

'Four Big Horns, my lord.'

'Very good. Very good. I can see that you will go a long way. What is your job?'

'I am Grand Assistant to the Lord Chamberlain, my lord.'

'Which one of you is the Lord Chamberlain?'

Four Big Horns pointed to the man who had preferred to die.

'There we are, you see?' said Mr Saveloy. 'Promotion comes fast to adaptable people, Lord Chamberlain. And now, the Emperor will breakfast.'

'And what is his pleasure?' said the new Lord Chamberlain, endeavouring to look bright and adaptable.

'All sorts of things. But right now, big lumps of meat and lots of beer. You will find the Emperor very easy to cater for.' Mr Saveloy smiled the knowing little smile he sometimes smiled when he knew he was the only one seeing the joke. 'The Emperor doesn't favour what he calls "fiddly foreign muck full of eyeballs and suchlike" and much prefers simple, wholesome food like sausages, which are made of miscellaneous animal organs minced up in a length of intestine. Ahaha. But if you want to please him, just keep up the big lumps of meat. Isn't that so, my lord?'

Cohen had been gazing at the assembled courtiers. When you've survived for ninety years all the attacks that can be thrown at you by men, women, trolls, dwarfs, giants, green things with lots of legs and, on one occasion, an enraged lobster, you can learn a lot by looking at faces.

'Eh?' said Cohen. 'Oh. Yep. Right enough. Big lumps. Here, Mr Taxman . . . what do these people *do* all day?'

'What would you like them to do?'

'I'd like them to bugger off.'

'Sorry, my lord?'

'[Complicated pictogram],' said Mr Saveloy. The new Lord Chamberlain looked a little startled.

'What, *here*?'

'It's a figure of speech, lad. He just means he wants everyone to go away quickly.'

The court scurried out. A sufficiently complicated pictogram is worth a thousand words.

After the stampede the artist Three Solid Frogs got to his feet, retrieved his brush from his nostril, pulled his easel out of a tree, and tried to think placid thoughts.

The garden was not what it had been.

The willow tree was bent. The pagoda had been demolished by an out-of-control wrestler, who had eaten the roof. The doves had flown. The little bridge had been broken. His model, the concubine Jade Fan, had run off crying after she'd managed to scramble out of the ornamental pond.

And someone had stolen his straw hat.

Three Solid Frogs adjusted what remained of his dress and endeavoured to compose himself.

The plate with his sketch on had been smashed, of course.

He pulled another one out of his bag and reached for his palette.

There was a huge footprint in the middle of it . . .

He wanted to cry. He'd had such a *good* feeling about this picture.

He just *knew* it would be one that people would remember for a long time. And the colours? Did anyone *understand* how much vermilion cost these days?

He pulled himself together. So there was only blue left. Well, he'd show them . . .

He tried to ignore the devastation in front of him and concentrated on the picture in his mind.

'Let me see, now,' he thought. 'Jade Fan being pursued over a bridge by man waving his arms and screaming, "Get out of the way!" followed by man with prod, three guards, five laundry men and a wrestler unable to stop.'

He had to simplify it a bit, of course.

The pursuers rounded a corner, except for the wrestler, who wasn't built for such a difficult manoeuvre.

'Where'd he go?'

They were in a courtyard. There were pigsties on one side, and middens on the other.

And, in the middle of the courtyard, a pointy hat.

One of the guards reached out and grabbed a colleague's arm before the man stepped forward.

'Steady now,' he said.

'It's just a hat.'

'So where's the rest of him? He couldn't have just . . . disappeared . . . into . . .'

They backed away.

'You heard about him too?'

'They said he blew a hole in the wall just by waving his hands!'

'That's nothing! I heard he appeared on an invisible dragon up in the mountains!'

'What shall we tell Lord Hong?'

'I don't want to be blown to pieces!'

'*I* don't want to tell Lord Hong we lost him. We're in enough trouble already. And I've only just paid for this helmet.'

'Well . . . we could take the hat. That'd be evidence.'

'Right. You pick it up.'

'Me? *You* pick it up!'

'It might be surrounded by terrible spells.'

'Really? So it's all right for *me* to touch it? Thank you! Get one of them to pick it up!'

The laundry men backed away, the Hunghungese habit of

obedience evaporating like morning dew. The soldiers weren't the only ones to have heard rumours.

'Not us!'

'Got a rush order for socks!'

The guard turned. A peasant was stumbling out of one of the pigsties, carrying a sack, his face covered by his big straw hat.

'Hey, you!'

The man dropped to his knees and banged his head on the ground.

'Don't kill me!'

The guards exchanged a glance.

'We ain't going to kill you,' said one of them. 'We just want you to try and pick up that hat over there.'

'What hat, o mighty warrior?'

'That hat there! Right now!'

The man crawled crabwise across the cobbles.

'This hat, o great lord?'

'Yes!'

The man's fingers crept over the stones and prodded the hat's ragged brim.

Then he screamed.

'Your wife is a big hippo! My face is melting! My face is meltinnnnggg!'

Rincewind waited until the sound of fleeing sandals had quite faded, and then stood up, dusted off his hat, and put it in the sack.

That had gone a lot better than he'd expected. So there was another valuable thing to know about the Empire: no one looked at peasants. It must be the clothes and the hat. No one but the common people dressed like that, so anyone dressed like that must be a common person. It was the advertising principle of a wizard's hat, but in reverse. You were careful and polite around people in a pointy hat, in case they took a very physical offence, whereas someone in a big straw hat was a suitable target for a 'Hey, you!' and a—

It was at exactly this point that someone behind him shouted, 'Hey, you!' and hit Rincewind across the shoulders with a stick.

The irate face of a servant appeared in front of him. The man waved a finger in front of Rincewind's nose.

'You are late! You are a bad man! Get inside right now!'

'I—'

The stick hit Rincewind again. The servant pointed at a distant doorway.

'Insolence! Shame! Go to work!'

Rincewind's brain prepared the words: Oh, so we think we're Clever-san just because we've got a big stick, do we? Well, I happen to be a great wizard and you know what you can do with your big stick.

Somewhere between the brain and his mouth they became:

'Yessir! Right away!'

The Horde were left alone.

'Well, gentlemen, we did it,' said Mr Saveloy eventually. 'You have the world on a plate.'

'All the treasure we want,' said Truckle.

'That's right.'

'Let's not hang around, then,' said Truckle. 'Let's get some sacks.'

'There's no *point*,' said Mr Saveloy. 'You'd only be stealing from yourselves. This is an *Empire*. You don't just shove it in a bag and divvy it up at the next campfire!'

'How about the ravishing?'

Mr Saveloy sighed. 'There are, I understand, three hundred concubines in the imperial harem. I'm sure they will be very pleased to see you, although matters will be improved if you take your boots off.'

The old men wore the puzzled look such as might be worn by fish trying to understand the concept of the bicycle.

'We ought to take just small stuff,' said Boy Willie at last. 'Rubies and emeralds, for preference.'

'And chuck a match on the place as we go out,' said Vincent. 'These paper walls and all this lacquered wood should go up a treat.'

'No, no, no!' said Mr Saveloy. 'The vases in this room alone are priceless!'

'Nah, too big to carry. Can't get 'em onna horse.'

'But I've shown you civilization!' said Mr Saveloy.

'Yeah. It's all right to visit. Ain't that so, Cohen?'

Cohen was hunched down in the throne, glaring at the far wall.

'What's that?'

'I'm saying we take everything we can carry and head off back home, right?'

'Home . . . yeah . . .'

That was the Plan, yeah?'

Cohen didn't look at Mr Saveloy's face.

'Yeah . . . the Plan . . .' he said.

'It's a good plan,' said Truckle. 'Great idea. You move in as boss?

Fine. Great scam. Saves trouble. None of that fiddling with locks and things. So we'll all be off home, okay? With all the treasure we can carry?'

'What for?' said Cohen.

'What for? It's *treasure*.'

Cohen seemed to reach a decision.

'What did you spend your last haul on, Truckle? You said you got three sacks of gold and gems from that haunted castle.'

Truckle looked puzzled, as if Cohen had asked what purple smelled like.

'Spend it on? *I* dunno. You know how it is. What's it matter what you spend it on? It's *loot*. Anyway . . . what do you spend yours on?'

Cohen sighed.

Truckle gaped at him.

'You're not thinking of *really* staying here?' He glared at Mr Saveloy.

'Have you two been cooking up something?'

Cohen drummed his fingers on the arm of the throne. 'You said go home,' he said. 'Where to?'

'Well . . . wherever . . .'

'And Hamish there—'

'Whut? Whut?'

'I mean . . . he's a hundred and five, right? Time to settle down, maybe?'

'Whut?'

'Settle down?' said Truckle. '*You* tried it once. Stole a farm and said you was goin' to raise pigs! Gave it up after . . . What was it? . . . three hours?'

'Whutzeesayin'? Whutzeesayin'?'

'He said IT'S TIME YOU SETTLED DOWN, Hamish.'

'Bugrthat!'

The kitchens were in uproar. Half the court had ended up there, in most cases for the first time. The place was as crowded as a street market, through which the servants tried to go about their business as best they could.

The fact that one of them seemed a little unclear as to what his business actually consisted of was quite unnoticed in the turmoil.

'Did you *smell* him?' said Lady Two Streams. 'The *stink*!'

'Like a hot day in a pig yard!' said Lady Peach Petal.

'*I'm* pleased to say I have never experienced that,' said Lady Two Streams haughtily.

Lady Jade Night, who was rather younger than the other two, and who had been rather attracted to Cohen's smell of unwashed lion, said nothing.

The head cook said: 'Just that? Big lumps? Why doesn't he just eat a cow while he's about it?'

'You wait till you hear about this devil food called *sausage*,' said the Lord Chamberlain.

'Big lumps.' The cook was almost in tears. 'Where's the skill in big lumps of meat? Not even sauce? I'd rather die than simply heat up big lumps of meat!'

'Ah,' said the new Lord Chamberlain, 'I should think very carefully about that. The new Emperor, may he have a bath for ten thousand years, tends to interpret that as a request—'

The babble of voices stopped. The cause of the sudden silence was one small, sharp noise. It was a cork, popping.

Lord Hong had a Grand Vizier's talent for apparently turning up out of nowhere. His gaze swept the kitchens. It was certainly the only housework that he had ever done.

He stepped forward. He'd taken a small black bottle from out of the sleeve of his robe.

'Bring me the meat,' he said. 'The sauce will take care of itself.'

The assembled people watched with horrified interest. Poison was all part of the Hunghungese court etiquette but people generally did it while hidden from sight somewhere, out of good manners.

'Is there anyone,' said Lord Hong, 'who has anything they would like to say?'

His gaze was like a scythe. As it swung around the room people wavered, and hesitated, and fell.

'Very well,' said Lord Hong. 'I would rather die than see a . . . *barbarian* on the Imperial throne. Let him have his . . . big lumps. Bring me the meat.'

There was movement in the ground, and the sound of shouting and the thump of a stick. A peasant scuttled forward, reluctantly wheeling a huge covered dish on a trolley.

At the sight of Lord Hong he pushed the trolley aside, flung himself forward and grovelled.

'I avert my gaze from your . . . an orchard in a favourable position . . . *damn* . . . countenance, o lord.'

Lord Hong prodded the prone figure with his foot.

'It is good to see the arts of respect maintained,' he observed. 'Remove the lid.'

The man got up and, still bowing and ducking, lifted the cover.

Lord Hong upended the bottle and held it there until the last drop had hissed out. His audience was transfixed.

'And now let it be taken to the barbarians,' he said.

'Certainly, your celestial . . . ink brush . . . willow frond . . . righteousness.'

'Where are you from, peasant?'

'Bes Pelargic, o lord.'

'Ah. I thought so.'

The big bamboo doors slid back. The new Lord Chamberlain stepped in, followed by a caravan of trolleys.

'Breakfast, o lord of a thousand years,' he said. 'Big lumps of pig, big lumps of goat, big lumps of ox and seven fried rice.'

One of the servants lifted the lid of a dish. 'But take my tip and don't go for this pork,' he said. 'It's been poisoned.'

The Chamberlain spun around.

'Insolent pig! You will die for this.'

'It's Rincewind, isn't it?' said Cohen. '*Looks* like Rincewind—'

'Got my hat here somewhere,' said Rincewind. 'Had to stuff it down my trousers—'

'Poison?' said Cohen. 'You sure?'

'Well, okay, it was a black bottle and it had a skull and crossbones on it and when he tipped it out it smoked,' said Rincewind, as Mr Saveloy helped him up. 'Was it anchovy essence? I don't *think* so.'

'Poison,' said Cohen. 'I *hate* poisoners. Just about the worst sort, poisoners. Creeping around, putting muck in a man's grub . . .'

He glared at the Chamberlain.

'Was it you?' He looked at Rincewind and jerked a thumb towards the cowering Chamberlain. 'Was it him? Because if it was he's going to get done to him what I did to the mad Snake Priests of Start, and this time I'll use both thumbs!'

'No,' said Rincewind. 'It was someone they called Lord Hong. But they all watched him do it.'

A little scream erupted from the Lord Chamberlain. He threw himself to the floor and was about to kiss Cohen's foot until he realized that this would have about the same effect as eating the pork.

'Mercy, o celestial being! We are all pawns in the hands of Lord Hong!'

'What's so special about Lord Hong, then?'

'He's . . . a fine man!' the Chamberlain gibbered. 'I won't say a word against Lord Hong! I certainly don't believe it's true that he has spies everywhere! Long life to Lord Hong, that's what I say!'

He risked looking up and found the point of Cohen's sword just in front of his eyes.

'Yeah, but right now who're you more frightened of? Me or this Lord Hong?'

'Uh . . . Lord Hong!'

Cohen raised an eyebrow. 'I'm impressed. Spies everywhere, eh?'

He looked around the huge room and his gaze came to rest on a very large vase. He sauntered over to it and raised the lid.

'You okay in there?'

'Er . . . yes?' said a voice from the depths of the vase.

'Got everythin' you want? Spare notebook? Potty?'

'Er . . . yes?'

'Would you like, oh, let's say about sixty gallons of boiling water?'

'Er . . . no?'

'Would you rather die than betray Lord Hong?'

'Er . . . can I have a moment to think about it, please?'

'No problem. It takes a long time to heat the water in any case. As you were, then.'

He replaced the lid.

'One Big Mother?' he said.

'That's One Big *River*, Ghenghiz,' said Mr Saveloy.

The guard rumbled into life.

'Just you watch this vase and if it moves again you do to it what I once did to the Green Necromancer of the Night, all right?'

'Don't know what that was you did, lord,' said the soldier.

Cohen told him. One Big River beamed. From inside the jar came the noise of someone trying not to be sick.

Cohen strolled back to the throne.

'So tell me a bit more about Lord Hong, then,' he said.

'He's the Grand Vizier,' said the Chamberlain.

Cohen and Rincewind looked at one another.

'That's right. And everyone knows,' said Rincewind, 'that Grand Viziers are *always*—'

'—complete and utter bastards,' said Cohen. 'Dunno why. Give 'em a turban with a point in the middle and their moral wossname

486

just gets eaten away. I always kill 'em soon as I meet 'em. Saves time later on.'

'I *thought* there was something fishy about him as soon as I saw him,' said Rincewind. 'Look, Cohen—'

'That's *Emperor* Cohen to you,' said Truckle. 'I've never trusted wizards, mister. Never trusted any man in a dress.'

'Rincewind's all right—' said Cohen.

'Thank you!' said Rincewind.

'—but a bloody useless wizard.'

'I just happened to risk my neck to save you, thank you so very much,' said Rincewind. 'Look, some friends of mine are in the prison block. Could you . . . *Emperor*?'

'Sort of,' said Cohen.

'Temp'ry,' said Truckle.

'Technically,' said Mr Saveloy.

'Does that mean you can get my friends somewhere safe? I think Lord Hong has murdered the old Emperor and wants them to take the blame. I'm just hoping he won't believe they'll be hiding in the cells.'

'Why in the cells?' said Cohen.

'Because if I had the chance to get away from Lord Hong's cells I would,' said Rincewind, fervently. 'No one in their right minds'd go back inside if they thought they had a chance to get away.'

'Okay,' said Cohen. 'Boy Willie, One Big Mother, go and round up some of your mates and bring those people here.'

'Here?' said Rincewind. 'I wanted them to be somewhere safe!'

'Well, *we're* here,' said Cohen. 'We can protect 'em.'

'Who's going to protect you?'

Cohen ignored this. 'Lord Chamberlain,' he said, 'I don't 'spect Lord Hong'll be around but . . . in the court was a guy with a nose like a badger. A fat bugger, he was, with a big pink hat. And a skinny woman with a face like a hatful of pins.'

'That would be Lord Nine Mountains and Lady Two Streams,' said the Lord Chamberlain. 'Er. You are not angry with me, o lord?'

'Gods bless you, no,' said Cohen. 'In fact, mister, I'm so impressed I'm going to give you extra responsibilities.'

'Lord?'

'Food taster, for a start. And now go and fetch them other two. Didn't like the look of them at *all*.'

Nine Mountains and Two Streams were ushered in a few moments later. Their merest glance from Cohen to the untouched food would have passed entirely unnoticed by those who weren't watching for it.

487

Cohen nodded cheerfully at them. 'Eat it,' he said.

'My lord! I had a large breakfast! I am entirely full!' said Nine Mountains.

'That's a pity,' said Cohen. 'One Big Mother, before you go off just see Mr Nine Mountains over there and make some room in him so he can have another breakfast. The same goes for the lady, too, if I don't hear chomping in the next five seconds. A good mouthful of everything, understand? With lots of sauce.'

One Big River drew his sword.

The two nobles stared fixedly at the glistening mounds.

'Looks good to me,' said Cohen conversationally. 'The way *you're* looking at it, anyone'd think there was something wrong with it.'

Nine Mountains gingerly put a piece of pork into his mouth.

'Extremely good,' he said, indistinctly.

'Now *swallow*,' said Cohen.

The mandarin gulped.

'Marvellous,' he said. 'And now, if your excellency will excuse me, I—'

'Don't rush off,' said Cohen. 'We don't want you accidentally sticking your fingers down your throat or anything like that, do we?'

Nine Mountains hiccuped.

Then he hiccuped again.

Smoke appeared to be rising from the bottom of his robe.

The Horde dived for cover just as the explosion removed an area of floorboards, a circular part of the ceiling and all of Lord Nine Mountains.

A black hat with a ruby button on it spun around on the floor for a moment.

'That's just like me and pickled onions,' said Vincent.

Lady Two Streams was standing with her eyes shut.

'Not hungry?' said Cohen.

She nodded.

Cohen leaned back.

'One Big Mother?'

'It's "River", Cohen,' said Mr Saveloy, as the guard lumbered forward.

'Take her with you and put her in one of the dungeons. See that she has plenty to eat, if you know what I mean.'

'Yes, excellency.'

'And Mr Chamberlain here can push off down to the kitchen

again and tell the chef *he's* going to share what we eat this time, and he's gonna eat it *first*, all right?'

'Yes indeed, excellency.'

'Call this living?' Caleb burst out, as the Lord Chamberlain scuttled away. 'This is being Emperor, is it? Can't even trust the food? We'll probably be murdered in our beds!'

'Can't see *you* being murdered in your bed,' said Truckle.

'Yeah, 'cos you're never in it,' said Cohen.

He walked over to the big jar and gave it a kick.

'You getting all this?'

'Yessir,' said the jar.

There was some laughter. But it had an edge of nervousness. Mr Saveloy realized that the Horde weren't used to this. If a true barbarian wanted to kill someone during a meal, he'd invite him in with all his henchmen, sit them down, get them drunk and sleepy and then summon his own men from hiding places to massacre them instantly in a straightforward, no-nonsense and honourable manner. It was completely fair. The 'get them drunk and butcher the lot of them' stratagem was the oldest trick in the book, or would have been if barbarians bothered with books. Anyone falling for it would be doing the world a favour by being slaughtered over the pudding. But at least you could trust the *food*. Barbarians didn't poison food. You never knew when you might be short of a mouthful yourself.

'Excuse me, your excellency,' said Six Beneficent Winds, who had been hovering, 'I think Lord Truckle is right. Er. I know a little history. The correct method of succession is to wade to the throne through seas of blood. That is what Lord Hong is planning to do.'

'You say? Seas of blood, right?'

'Or over a mountain of skulls. That's an option, too.'

'But . . . but . . . I thought the Imperial crown was handed down from father to son,' said Mr Saveloy.

'Well, yes,' said Six Beneficent Winds. 'I suppose that could happen in theory.'

'You said once we were at the top of the pyramid everyone'd do what we said,' said Cohen to Mr Saveloy.

Truckle looked from one to the other. 'You two *planned* this?' he said accusingly. 'This is what it's all been about, isn't it? All that learnin' to be civilized? And right at the start you just said it was going to be a really big theft! Eh? I thought we were just going to nick a load of stuff and push off! Loot and pillage, that's the way—'

'Oh, loot and pillage, loot and pillage, I've had it up to here with loot and pillage!' said Mr Saveloy. 'Is that all you can think of, looting and pillaging?'

'Well, there used to be ravishing, too,' said Vincent wistfully.

'I hate to tell you, but they've got a point, Teach,' said Cohen. 'Fightin' and lootin' . . . that's what we do. I ain't happy with all this bowing and scraping business. I ain't sure if I was cut out for civilization.'

Mr Saveloy rolled his eyes. 'Even you, Cohen? You're all so . . . *dim-witted*!' he snapped. 'I don't know why I bother! I mean, look at you! You know what you are? You're legends!'

The Horde stepped back. No one had ever seen Teach lose his temper before.

'From *legendum*, which means "something written down",' said Mr Saveloy. 'Books, you know. Reading and writing. Which incidentally is as alien to you as the Lost City of Ee—'

Truckle's hand went up, a little nervously.

'Actually, I once discovered the Lost City of—'

'Shut up! I'm saying . . . What was I saying? . . . yes . . . you don't read, do you? You never learned to read? Then you've wasted half your life. You could have been accumulating pearls of wisdom instead of rather shoddy gems. It's just as well people read about you and don't meet you face to face because, gentlemen, you are a big disappointment!'

Rincewind watched, fascinated, waiting for Mr Saveloy to have his head cut off. But this didn't seem about to happen. He was possibly too angry to be beheaded.

'What have you actually *done*, gentlemen? And don't tell me about stolen jewels and demon lords. What have you done that's *real*?'

Truckle raised a hand again.

'Well, I once killed all four of the—'

'Yes, yes, yes,' said Mr Saveloy. 'You killed *this* and you stole *that* and you defeated the giant man-eating avocados of somewhere else, but . . . it's all . . . *stuff*. It's just wallpaper, gentlemen! It never changes anything! No one *cares*! Back in Ankh-Morpork I've taught boys who think you are myths. That's what you've achieved. They don't believe you ever really existed. They think someone made you up. You're *stories*, gentlemen. When you die no one will know, because they think you're already dead.'

He paused for breath, and then continued more slowly. 'But here . . . here you *could* be real. You could stop playing at your lives. You could take this ancient and somewhat rotten Empire

490

back into the world. At least . . .' he trailed off. 'That's what I'd hoped. I really thought that, perhaps, we might actually achieve something . . .'

He sat down.

The Horde stood staring at its various feet or wheels.

'Um. Can I say something? The warlords will all be against you,' said Six Beneficent Winds. 'They're out there now, with their armies. Normally they'd fight amongst themselves, but they'll *all* fight you.'

'They'd rather have some poisoner like this Hong instead of me?' said Cohen. 'But he's a bastard!'

'Yes, but . . . he's *their* bastard, you see.'

'We could hold out here. This place has got thick walls,' said Vincent. 'The ones not made of paper, that is.'

'Don't think about that,' said Truckle. 'Not a siege. Sieges are messy. I hate eating boots and rats.'

'Whut?'

'He said WE DON'T WANT A SIEGE WHERE WE HAVE TO EAT BOOTS AND RATS, Hamish.'

'Run outa legs, have we?'

'How many soldiers have they got?' said Cohen.

'I think . . . six or seven hundred thousand,' said the taxman.

'Excuse us,' said Cohen, getting off the throne. 'I have to join my Horde.'

The Horde went into a huddle. There was an occasional 'Whut?' in the hoarse whispered interchanges. Then Cohen turned round.

'Seas of blood, wasn't it?' he said.

'Er. Yes,' said the taxman.

The huddle resumed.

After some further exchanges Truckle's head poked up.

'Did you say *mountain* of skulls?' he said.

'Yes. Yes, I think that's what I said,' said the taxman. He glanced nervously at Rincewind and Mr Saveloy, who shrugged.

Whisper, whisper, Whut . . .

'Excuse me?'

'Yes?'

'About how big a mountain? Skulls don't pile up that well.'

'I don't know how big a mountain! A lot of skulls!'

'Just checking.'

The Horde seemed to reach a decision. They turned to face the other men.

'We're going to fight,' said Cohen.

491

'Yes, you should have said all that about skulls and blood before,' said Truckle.

'We'll show ye whether we'm dead or not!' cackled Hamish.

Mr Saveloy shook his head.

'I think you must have misheard. The odds are a hundred thousand to one!' he said.

'I reckon *that'll* show people we're still alive,' said Caleb.

'Yes, but the whole point of my plan was to show you that you could get to the top of the pyramid without having to fight your way up,' said Mr Saveloy. 'It really is possible in such a stale society. But if you try to fight hundreds of thousands of men you'll *die*.'

And then, to his surprise, he found himself adding: 'Probably.'

The Horde grinned at him.

'Big odds don't frighten us,' said Truckle.

'We like *big* odds,' said Caleb.

'Y' see, Teach, odds of a thousand to one ain't a lot worse than ten to one,' said Cohen. 'The reasons bein'—' He counted on his fingers. 'One, your basic soldier who's fightin' for pay rather than his life ain't goin' to stick *his* neck out when there's all these other blokes around who might as well do the business, and, two, not very many of 'em are goin' to be able to get near us at one time and they'll all be pushin' and shovin', and . . .' He looked at his fingers with an expression of terminal calculation.

' . . . Three . . .' said Mr Saveloy, hypnotized by this logic.

' . . . three, right . . . Half the time when they swings their swords they'll hit one of their mates, savin' us a bit of effort. See?'

'But even if that were true it'd only work for a little while,' Mr Saveloy protested. 'Even if you killed as many as two hundred you'd be tired and there'd be fresh troops attacking you.'

'Oh, they'd be tired too,' said Cohen cheerfully.

'Why?'

'Because by then, to get to us, they'd have to be running uphill.'

'That's logic, that is,' said Truckle, approvingly.

Cohen slapped the shaken teacher on the back.

'Don't you worry about a thing,' he said. 'If we've got the Empire by your kind of plan, we'll keep it by *our* kind of plan. You've shown us civilization, so we'll show you barbarism.'

He walked a few steps and then turned, an evil glint in his eye. 'Barbarism? Hah! When we kills people we do it there and then, lookin' 'em in the eye, and we'd be happy to buy 'em a drink in the next world, no harm done. I never knew a barbarian who cut up people slowly in little rooms, or tortured women to make 'em look

pretty, or put poison in people's grub. Civilization? If that's civilization, you can shove it where the sun don't shine!'

'Whut?'

'He said SHOVE IT WHERE THE SUN DOESN'T SHINE,
Hamish.'

'Ah? Bin there.'

'But there is more to civilization than that!' said Mr Saveloy.
'There's . . . music, and literature, and the concept of justice, and
the ideals of—'

The bamboo doors slid aside. As one man, joints creaking, the
Horde turned with weapons raised.

The men in the doorway were taller and much more richly
dressed than the peasants, and they moved in the manner of people
who are used to there being no one in the way. Ahead of them,
though, was a trembling peasant holding a red flag on a stick. He
was prodded into the room at swordpoint.

'Red flag?' whispered Cohen.

'It means they want to parley,' said Six Beneficent Winds.

'You know . . . it's like our white flag of surrender,' said Mr
Saveloy.

'Never heard of it,' said Cohen.

'It means you mustn't kill anyone until they're ready.'

Mr Saveloy tried to shut out the whispers behind him.

'*Why don't we just invite them to dinner and massacre them all
when they're drunk?*'

'*You heard the man. There's seven hundred thousand of them.*'

'*Ah? So it'd have to be something simple with pasta, then.*'

A couple of the lords strode into the middle of the room. Cohen
and Mr Saveloy went to meet them.

'And you, too,' said Cohen, grabbing Rincewind as he tried to
back away. 'You're a weaselly man with words in a tight spot, so
come on.'

Lord Hong regarded them with the expression of a man whose
ancestry had bequeathed to him the ability to look down on everything.

'My name is Lord Hong. I am the Emperor's Grand Vizier. I order
you to quit these premises immediately and submit to judgement.'

Mr Saveloy turned to Cohen.

'Ain't gonna,' said Cohen.

Mr Saveloy tried to think.

'Um, how shall I phrase this? Ghenghiz Cohen, leader of the
Silver Horde, presents his compliments to Lord Hong but—'

'Tell him he can stuff it,' said Cohen.

'I think, Lord Hong, that perhaps you may have perceived the general flow of opinion here,' said Mr Saveloy.

'Where are the rest of your barbarians, peasant?' he demanded.

Rincewind watched Mr Saveloy. The old teacher seemed at a loss for words this time.

The wizard wanted to run away. But Cohen had been right. Mad as it sounded, it was probably safer to be near him. Running away would put him closer, sooner or later, to Lord Hong.

Who believed that there were *other* barbarians somewhere . . .

'I tell you this, and this only,' said Lord Hong. 'If you quit the Forbidden City now, your deaths, at least, will be quick. And then your heads and significant parts will be paraded through the cities of the Empire so that people will know of the terrible punishment.'

'Punishment?' said Mr Saveloy.

'For killing the Emperor.'

'We ain't killed no Emperor,' said Cohen. 'I've got nothing *against* killing Emperors, but we ain't killed one.'

'He was killed in his bed an hour ago,' said Lord Hong.

'Not by us,' said Mr Saveloy.

'By you,' said Rincewind. 'Only it's against the rules to kill the Emperor so you wanted it to look as though the Red Army did it.'

Lord Hong looked at him as if seeing him for the first time and less than happy about doing so.

'In the circumstances,' said Lord Hong, 'I doubt that anyone will believe you.'

'What will happen if we yield now?' said Mr Saveloy. 'I like to know these things.'

'Then you will die very slowly in . . . interesting ways.'

'That's the saga of my life,' said Cohen. 'I've *always* been dying very slowly in interesting ways. What's it to be? Street fighting? House to house? Free for all or what?'

'In the real world,' said one of the other lords, 'we *battle*. We do not scuffle like barbarians. Our armies will meet on the plain before the city.'

'Before the city what?'

'He means in front of the city, Cohen.'

'Ah. Civilized talk again. When?'

'Dawn tomorrow!'

'Okay,' said Cohen. 'It'll give us an appetite for our breakfast. Anything else we can do for you?'

'How big is your army, barbarian?'

494

'You would not believe how big,' said Cohen, which was probably true. 'We have overrun countries. We have wiped whole cities off the map. Where my army passes, nothing grows.'

'That's true, at least,' said Mr Saveloy.

'We have not heard of you!' said the warlord.

'Yeah,' said Cohen. '*That's* how good we are.'

'There is one other thing about his army, actually,' said someone.

They all turned to Rincewind, who'd been almost as surprised as they were to hear his voice. But a train of thought had just reached the terminus . . .

'Yes?'

'You may have been wondering why you have only seen the . . . generals,' Rincewind went on, slowly, as if working it out as he went along. 'That is because, you see, the men themselves are . . . invisible. Er. Yes. Ghosts, in fact. Everyone knows this, don't they?'

Cohen gaped at him in astonishment.

'Blood-sucking ghosts, as a matter of fact,' said Rincewind. 'After all, everyone knows that's what you get beyond the Wall, don't they?'

Lord Hong sneered. But the warlords stared at Rincewind with the expressions of people who strongly suspected that the people beyond the Wall were flesh and blood but who also relied on millions of people not believing that this was so.

'Ridiculous! *You* are not invisible blood-sucking ghosts,' said one of them.

Cohen opened his mouth so that the diamond teeth glinted.

''S right,' he said. 'Fact is . . . we're the *visible* sort.'

'Hah! A pathetic attempt!' said Lord Hong. 'Ghosts or no ghosts, we will beat you!'

'Well, that went better than I expected,' Mr Saveloy remarked as the warlords strode out. 'Was that an attempt at a little bit of psychological warfare there, Mr Rincewind?'

'Is that what it was? I know about that kind of stuff,' said Cohen. 'It's where you bang your shield all night before the fight so's the enemy can't get any sleep and you sing, "We're gonna *cut* yer *tonkers* off," and stuff like that.'

'Similar,' said Mr Saveloy, diplomatically. 'But it failed to work, I'm afraid. Lord Hong and his generals are rather too sophisticated. It's a great shame you couldn't try it on the common soldiers.'

There was a faint squeak of rabbit behind them. They turned, and looked at the somewhat under-age cadre of the Red Army that was being ushered in. Butterfly was with them. She even gave Rincewind a very faint smile.

Rincewind had always relied on running away. But sometimes, perhaps, you had to stand and fight, if only because there was nowhere left to run.

But he was no good at all with weapons.

At least, the normal sort.

'Um,' he said, 'if we leave the palace now, we'll be killed, right?'

'I doubt it,' said Mr Saveloy. 'It's become a matter of the Art of War now. Someone like Hong would probably slit our throats, but now war is declared things have to be done according to custom.'

Rincewind took a deep breath.

'It's a million-to-one chance,' he said, 'but it might just work . . .'

The Four Horsemen whose Ride presages the end of the world are known to be Death, War, Famine and Pestilence. But even less significant events have their own Horsemen. For example, the Four Horsemen of the Common Cold are Sniffles, Chesty, Nostril and Lack of Tissues; the Four Horsemen whose appearance foreshadows any public holiday are Storm, Gales, Sleet and Contra-flow.

Among the armies encamped in the broad alluvial plain around Hunghung, the invisible horsemen known as Misinformation, Rumour and Gossip saddled up . . .

A large army encamped has all the tedious problems of a city without any of the advantages. Its watchfires and picket lines are, after a while, open to local civilians, especially if they have anything to sell and even more so if they are women whose virtue has a certain commercial element and even, sometimes, if they appear to be selling food which is a break from the monotonous army diet. The food currently on sale was certainly such a break.

'Pork balls! Pork balls! Get them while they're . . .' There was a pause as the vendor mentally tried out ways of ending the sentence, and gave up. 'Pork balls! Onna stick! How about you, shogun, you look like – Here, aren't you the—?'

'Shutupshutupshutup!'

Rincewind pulled D. M. H. Dibhala into the shadows by a tent.

The trader looked at the anguished face framed between a eunuch outfit and a big straw hat.

'It's the Wizard, isn't it? How are—?'

'You know how you seriously wanted to become very rich in international trade?' Rincewind said.

496

'Yes? Can we start?'

'Soon. Soon. But there's something you must do. You know this rumour about the army of invisible vampire ghosts that's heading this way?'

D. M. H. Dibhala's eyes swivelled nervously. But it was part of his stock in trade never to appear to be ignorant of anything except, perhaps, how to give correct change.

'Yes?' he said.

'The one about there being millions of them?' said Rincewind. 'And very hungry on account of not having eaten on the way? And made specially fierce by the Great Wizard?'

'Um . . . yes?'

'Well, it's *not true*.'

'It's not?'

'You don't believe me? After all, I ought to know.'

'Good point.'

'And we don't want people to panic, do we?'

'Very bad for business, panic,' said D. M. H., nodding uncomfortably.

'So make sure you tell people there's no truth in this rumour, will you? Set their minds at rest.'

'Good idea. Er. These invisible vampire ghosts . . . Do they carry money of any sort?'

'No. Because they don't exist.'

'Ah, yes. I forgot.'

'And there are not 2,300,009 of them,' said Rincewind. He was rather proud of this little detail.

'Not 2,300,009 of them . . .' said D. M. H., a little glassy-eyed.

'Absolutely not. There are *not* 2,300,009 of them, no matter what anyone says. Nor has the Great Wizard made them twice as big as normal. Good man. Now I'd better be off—'

Rincewind hurried away.

The trader stood in thought for a while. It stole over him that he'd probably sold enough things for now, and he might as well go home and spend a quiet night in a barrel in the root cellar with a sack over his head.

His route led him through quite a large part of the camp. He made sure that soldiers he met knew there was no truth in the rumour, even though this invariably meant that, first of all, he had to tell them what the rumour actually *was*.

*

A toy rabbit squeaked nervously.

'And I'm afraid of the big inwisible wampire ghosts!' sobbed Favourite Pearl.

The soldiers around this particular campfire tried to comfort her but, unfortunately, there was no one to comfort them.

'An' I heard they alweady et some men!'

One or two soldiers looked over their shoulders. There was nothing to be seen in the darkness. This wasn't, however, a reassuring sign.

The Red Army moved obliquely from campfire to campfire.

Rincewind had been very specific. He'd spent all his adult life – at least, those parts of it where he wasn't being chased by things with more legs than teeth – in Unseen University, and he felt he knew what he was talking about here. Don't tell people anything, he said. Don't *tell* them. You didn't get to survive as a wizard in UU by believing what people told you. You believed what you were *not* told.

Don't tell them. *Ask* them. Ask them if it's true. You can beg them to tell you it's *not* true. Or you can even tell them you've been told to tell them it's not true, and that is the best of all.

Because Rincewind knew very well that when the Four rather small and nasty Horsemen of Panic ride out there is a good job done by Misinformation, Rumour and Gossip, but they are as nothing compared to the fourth horseman, whose name is Denial.

After an hour Rincewind felt quite unnecessary.

There were conversations breaking out everywhere, particularly in those areas on the edge of the camps, where the night stretched away so big and dark and, so very obviously, empty.

'All right, so how come they're saying there's not 2,300,009 of them, eh? If there's none of them, then why's there a number?'

'Look, there's no such thing as invisible vampire ghosts, all right?'

'Oh yeah? How do you know? Have you ever seen any?'

'Listen, I went and asked the captain and he says he's certain there's no invisible ghosts out there.'

'How can he be certain if he can't see them?'

'He says there's no such things as invisible vampire ghosts at all.'

'Oh? How come he's saying that all of a sudden? My grandfather told me there's millions of them outside the—'

'Hold on . . . What's that out there . . .?'

'What?'

'Could've sworn I heard something . . .'

'*I* can't see anything.'

'Oh, *no*!'

Things must have filtered through to High Command because, getting on towards midnight, trumpets were sounded around the camps and a special proclamation was read out.

It confirmed the reality of vampire ghosts in general but denied their existence in any specific, here-and-now sense. It was a masterpiece of its type, particularly since it brought the whole subject to the ears of soldiers the Red Army hadn't been able to reach yet.

An hour later the situation had reached the point of criticality and Rincewind was hearing things he personally hadn't made up and, on the whole, would much rather not hear.

He'd chat with a couple of soldiers and say: 'I'm sure there's no huge hungry army of vampire ghosts' and get told, 'No, there's seven old men.'

'Just seven old men?'

'I heard they're *very* old,' said a soldier. 'Like, too old to die. I heard from someone at the palace that they can walk through walls and make themselves invisible.'

'Oh, come *on*,' said Rincewind. 'Seven old men fighting this whole army?'

'Makes you think, eh? Corporal Toshi says the Great Wizard is helping them. Stands to reason. I wouldn't be fighting a whole army if I didn't have a lot of magic on my side.'

'Er. Anyone know what the Great Wizard looks like?' said Rincewind.

'They say he's taller than a house and got three heads.'

Rincewind nodded encouragingly.

'I heard,' said a soldier, 'that the Red Army is going to fight on their side, too.'

'So what? Corporal Toshi says they're just a bunch of kids.'

'No, I heard . . . the *real* Red Army . . . you know . . .'

'The Red Army ain't gonna side with barbarian invaders! Anyway, there's no such thing as the Red Army. That's just a myth.'

'Like the invisible vampire ghosts,' said Rincewind, giving the clockwork of anxiety another little turn.

'Er . . . yeah.'

He left them arguing.

No one was deserting. Running off into a night full of non-specific terrors was worse than staying in camp. But that was all to the good, he decided. It meant that the really frightened people were staying put and seeking reassurance from their comrades. And there was nothing like someone repeating 'I'm *sure* there's no vampire wizards' and going to the latrine four times an hour to put backbone into a platoon.

Rincewind crept back towards the city, rounded a tent in the shadows, and collided with a horse, which trod heavily on his foot.

'Your wife is a big hippo!'

SORRY.

Rincewind froze, both hands clutching his aching foot. He knew only one person with a voice like a cemetery in midwinter.

He tried to hop backwards, and collided with another horse.

RINCEWIND, ISN'T IT? said Death. YES. GOOD EVENING. I DON'T BELIEVE YOU HAVE MET WAR. RINCEWIND, WAR. WAR, RINCEWIND.

War touched his helmet in salute.

'Pleasure's all mine,' he said. He indicated the other three riders. 'Like to introduce you to m'sons, Terror and Panic. And m'daughter, Clancy.'

The children chorused a 'hello'. Clancy was scowling, looked about seven years old and was wearing a hard hat and a Pony Club badge.

I WASN'T EXPECTING TO SEE *YOU* HERE, RINCEWIND.

'Oh. Good.'

Death pulled an hourglass out of his robe, held it up to the moonlight, and sighed. Rincewind craned to see how much sand was left.

HOWEVER, I COULD—

'Don't you make any special arrangement just on my account,' said Rincewind hurriedly. 'I, er . . . I expect you're all here for the battle?'

YES. IT PROMISES TO BE EXTREMELY – SHORT.

'Who's going to win?'

NOW, YOU KNOW I WOULDN'T TELL YOU THAT, EVEN IF I KNEW.

'Even if you knew?' said Rincewind. 'I thought you were supposed to know everything!'

Death held up a finger. Something fluttered down through the night. Rincewind thought it was a moth, although it looked less fluffy and had a strange speckled pattern on its wings.

It settled on the extended digit for a moment, and then flew up and away again.

ON A NIGHT LIKE THIS, said Death, THE ONLY CERTAIN THING IS UNCERTAINTY. TRITE, I KNOW, BUT TRUE.

Somewhere on the horizon, thunder rumbled.

'I'll, er, just be sort of going, then,' said Rincewind.

DON'T BE A STRANGER, said Death, as the wizard hurried off.

'Odd person,' said War.

WITH HIM HERE, EVEN UNCERTAINTY IS UNCERTAIN. AND I'M NOT SURE EVEN ABOUT THAT.

War pulled a large paper-wrapped package out of his saddlebag.

'We've got . . . let's see now . . . Egg and Cress, Chicken Tikka, and Mature Cheese with Crunchy Pickle, I think.'

THEY DO SUCH MARVELLOUS THINGS WITH SANDWICHES THESE DAYS.

'Oh . . . and Bacon Surprise.'

REALLY? WHAT IS SO SURPRISING ABOUT BACON?

'I don't know. I suppose it comes as something of a shock to the pig.'

Ridcully had been having a long wrestle with himself, and had won.

'We're going to bring him back,' he said. 'It's been four days. And then we can send them back their bloody tube thing. It gives me the willies.'

The senior wizards looked at one another. No one was very keen on a university with a Rincewind component, but the metal dog *did* give them the willies. No one had wanted to go near it. They'd piled some tables around it and tried to pretend it wasn't there.

'All right,' said the Dean. 'But Stibbons kept going on about things weighing the same, right? If we send that back, won't it mean Rincewind arrives here going very fast?'

'Mr Stibbons says he's working on the spell,' said Ridcully. 'Or we could pile some mattresses up at one end of the hall or something.'

The Bursar raised a hand.

'Yes, Bursar?' said Ridcully encouragingly.

'Ho, landlord, a pint of your finest ale!' said the Bursar.

'Good,' said Ridcully. 'That's settled, then. I've already told Mr Stibbons to start looking . . .'

'On that demonic device?'

'Yes.'

'Then nothing can *possibly* go wrong,' said the Dean sourly.

'A trumpet of lobsters, if you would be so good.'

'And the Bursar agrees.'

*

The warlords had gathered in Lord Hong's chambers. They carefully kept a distance from one another, as befitted enemies who were in the most shaky of alliances. Once the barbarians were dealt with, the battle might still continue. But they wanted assurance on one particular point.

'No!' said Lord Hong. 'Let me make this absolutely clear! There is *no* invisible army of blood-sucking ghosts, do you understand? The people beyond the Wall are just like us – except vastly inferior in every respect, of course. But totally visible.'

One or two of the lords did not look convinced.

'And all this talk about the Red Army?' said one of them.

'The Red Army, Lord Tang, is an undisciplined rabble that shall be put down with resolute force!'

'You know what Red Army the peasants are talking about,' said Lord Tang. 'They say that thousands of years ago it—'

'They say that thousands of years ago a wizard who did not exist took mud and lightning and made soldiers that couldn't die,' said Lord Hong. 'Yes. It's a *story*, Lord Tang. A story made up by peasants who did not understand what really happened. One Sun Mirror's army just had' – Lord Hong waved a hand vaguely – 'better armour, better discipline. I am not frightened of ghosts and I am *certainly* not afraid of a legend that probably never existed.'

'Yes, but—'

'Soothsayer!' snapped Lord Hong. The soothsayer, who hadn't been expecting it, gave a start.

'Yes, my lord?'

'How're those entrails coming along?'

'Er – they're about ready, my lord,' said the soothsayer.

The soothsayer was rather worried. This must have been the wrong kind of bird, he told himself. About the only thing the entrails were telling him was that if he got out of this alive he, the soothsayer, might be lucky enough to enjoy a nice chicken dinner. But Lord Hong sounded like a man with the most dangerous kind of impatience.

'And what do they tell you?'

'Er – the future is . . . the future is . . .'

Chicken entrails had never looked like this. For a moment he thought they were moving.

'Er . . . it is uncertain,' he hazarded.

'*Be* certain,' said Lord Hong. 'Who will win in the morning?'

Shadows flickered across the table.

Something was fluttering around the light.

It looked like an undistinguished yellow moth, with black patterns on its wings.

The soothsayer's precognitive abilities, which were considerably more powerful than he believed, told him: this is not a good time to be a clairvoyant.

On the other hand, there was never a good time to be horribly executed, so . . .

'Without a shadow of doubt,' he said, 'the enemy will be most emphatically beaten.'

'How can you be so certain?' said Lord McSweeney.

The soothsayer bridled.

'You see this wobbly bit near the kidneys? You want to argue with this green trickly thing? You know all about liver suddenly? All right?'

'So there you are,' said Lord Hong. 'Fate smiles upon us.'

'Even so—' Lord Tang began. 'The men are very—'

'You can tell the men—' Lord Hong began. He stopped. He smiled.

'You can tell the men,' he said, 'that there *is* a huge army of invisible vampire ghosts.'

'What?'

'Yes!' Lord Hong began to stride up and down, snapping his fingers. 'Yes, there is a terrible army of foreign ghosts. And this has so enraged our *own* ghosts . . . yes, a thousand generations of our ancestors are riding on the wind to repel this barbaric invasion! The ghosts of the Empire are arising! Millions and millions of them! Even our demons are furious at this intrusion! They will descend like a mist of claws and teeth to – Yes, Lord Sung?'

The warlords were looking at one another nervously.

'Are you *sure*, Lord Hong?'

Lord Hong's eyes gleamed behind his tiny spectacles.

'Make the necessary proclamations,' he said.

'But only a few hours ago we told the men there were no—'

'Tell them differently!'

'But will they believe that there—'

'They will believe what they are told!' shouted Lord Hong. 'If the enemy thinks his strength lies in deccit, then we will use their deceit against them. Tell the men that behind them will be a billion ghosts of the Empire!'

The other warlords tried to avoid his gaze. No one was actually going to suggest that your average soldier would not be totally happy with ghosts front and rear, especially given the capricious-ness of ghosts.

'Good,' said Lord Hong. He looked down.

'Are you *still* here?' he said.

'Just clearing up my giblets, my lord!' squealed the soothsayer.

He picked up the remains of his stricken chicken and ran for it.

After all, he told himself as he pelted back home, it's not as though I said *whose* enemy.

Lord Hong was left alone.

He realized he was shaking. It was probably fury. But perhaps . . . perhaps things could be turned to his advantage, even so. Barbarians came from outside, and to most people everywhere outside was the same. Yes. The barbarians were a minute detail, easily disposed of, but carefully managed, perhaps, might figure in his overall strategy.

He was breathing heavily, too.

He walked into his private study and shut the door.

He pulled out the key.

He opened the box.

There was a few minutes' silence, except for the rustle of cloth.

Then Lord Hong looked at himself in the mirror.

He'd gone to great lengths to achieve this. He had used several agents, none of whom knew the whole plan. But the Ankh-Morpork tailor had been good at his work and the measurements had been followed exactly. From pointy boots to hose to doublet, cloak and hat with a feather in it, Lord Hong knew he was a perfect Ankh-Morpork gentleman. The cloak was lined with silk.

The clothes felt uncomfortable and touched him in unfamiliar ways, but those were minor details. This was how a man looked in a society that breathed, that moved, that could go somewhere . . .

He'd walk through the city on that first great day and the people would be silent when they saw their natural leader.

It never crossed his mind that anyone would say, ''Ere, wot a toff! 'Eave 'arf a brick at 'im!'

The ants scurried. The thing that went 'parp' went parp.

The wizards stood back. There wasn't much else to do when Hex was working at full speed, except watch the fish and oil the wheels from time to time. There were occasional flashes of octarine from the tubes.

Hex was spelling several hundred times a minute. It was as simple as that. It would take a human more than an hour to do an ordinary finding spell. But Hex could do them faster. Over and over again. It was netting the whole occult sea in the search for one slippery fish.

It achieved, after ninety-three minutes, what would otherwise have taken the faculty several months.

'You see?' said Ponder, his voice shaking a little as he took the line of blocks out of the hopper. 'I *said* he could do it.'

'Who's he?' said Ridcully.

'Hex.'

'Oh, you mean *it*.'

'That's what I said, sir . . . er . . . yes.'

Another thing about the Horde, Mr Saveloy had noticed, was their ability to relax. The old men had the catlike ability to do nothing when there was nothing to do.

They'd sharpened their swords. They'd had a meal – big lumps of meat for most of them, and some kind of gruel for Mad Hamish, who'd dribbled most of it down his beard – and assured its wholesomeness by dragging the cook in, nailing him to the floor by his apron, and suspending a large axe on a rope that crossed a beam in the roof and was held at the other end by Cohen, while he ate.

Then they'd sharpened their swords again, out of habit, and . . . stopped.

Occasionally one of them would whistle a snatch of a tune, through what remained of his teeth, or search a bodily crevice for a particularly fretful louse. Mainly, though, they just sat and stared at nothing.

After a long while, Caleb said, 'Y'know, I've never been to XXXX. Been everywhere else. Often wondered what it's like.'

'Got shipwrecked there once,' said Vincent. 'Weird place. Lousy with magic. There's beavers with beaks and giant rats with long tails that hops around the place and boxes with one another. Black fellas wanderin' around all over the place. They say they're in a dream. Bright, though. Show 'em a bit of desert with one dead tree in it, next minute they've found a three-course meal with fruits and nuts to follow. Beer's good, too.'

'Sounds like it.'

There was another long pause.

Then:

'I suppose they've *got* minstrels here? Be a bit of a bloody waste, wouldn't it, if we all got killed and no one made up any songs about it.'

'Bound to have loads of minstrels, a city like this.'

'No problem there, then.'

'No.'

'No.'

There was another lengthy pause.

'Not that we're going to get killed.'

'Right. I don't intend to start getting killed at my time of life, haha.'

Another pause.

'Cohen?'

'Yep?'

'You a religious man at all?'

'Well, I've robbed loads of temples and killed a few mad priests in my time. Don't know if that counts.'

'What do your tribe believe happens to you when you die in battle?'

'Oh, these big fat women in horned helmets take you off to the halls of Io where there is fighting and carousing and quaffing for ever.'

Another pause.

'You mean, like, *really* for ever?'

'S'pose so.'

''Cos generally you get fed up even with turkey by about day four.'

'All right, what do *your* lot believe?'

'I think we go off to Hell in a boat made of toenail clippings. Something like that, anyway.'

Another pause.

'But it's not worth talking about 'cos we're not going to get killed today.'

'You said it.'

'Hah, it's not worth dying if all you've got to look forward to is leftover meat and floating around in a boat smelling of your socks, is it, eh?'

'Haha.'

Another pause.

'Down in Klatch they believe if you lead a good life you're rewarded by being sent to a paradise with lots of young women.'

'That's your reward, is it?'

'Dunno. Maybe it's their punishment. But I do remember you eat sherbet all day.'

'Hah. When I was a lad we had proper sherbet, in little tube things and a liquorice straw to suck it up with. You don't get that sort of thing today. People're too busy rushin' about.'

'Sounds a lot better than quaffing toenails, though.'

Another pause.

'Did you ever believe that business about every enemy you killed becoming your servant in the next world?'

'Dunno.'

'How many you killed?'

'What? Oh. Maybe two, three thousand. Not counting dwarfs and trolls, o' course.'

'Definitely not going to be short of a hairbrush or someone to open doors for you after you're dead, then.'

A pause.

'We're definitely not going to die, right?'

'Right.'

'I mean, odds of 100,000 to one . . . hah. The difference is just a lot of zeroes, right?'

'Right.'

'I mean, stout comrades at our side, a strong right arm . . . What more could we want?'

Pause.

'A volcano'd be favourite.'

Pause.

'We're going to die, aren't we?'

'Yep.'

The Horde looked at one another.

'Still, to look on the bright side, I recall I still owe Fafa the dwarf fifty dollars for this sword,' said Boy Willie. 'Looks as though I could end up ahead of the game.'

Mr Saveloy put his head in his hands.

'I'm really sorry,' he said.

'Don't worry about it,' said Cohen.

The grey light of dawn was just visible in the high windows.

'Look,' said Mr Saveloy, 'you don't *have* to die. We could . . . well, we could sneak out. Back along the pipe, maybe. Perhaps we could carry Hamish. People are coming and going all the time. I'm sure we could get out of . . . the city . . . without . . . any . . .'

His voice faded away. No voice could keep going under the pressure of those stares. Even Hamish, whose gaze was generally focused on some point about eighty years away, was glaring at him.

'Ain't gonna run,' said Hamish.

507

'It's not running away,' he managed. 'It's a sensible withdrawal. Tactics. Good grief, it's common sense!'

'Ain't gonna run.'

'Look, even barbarians can count! And you've admitted you're going to die!'

'Ain't gonna run.'

Cohen leaned forward and patted Mr Saveloy on the hand.

'It's the heroing, see,' he said. 'Who's ever heard of a hero running away? All them kids you was telling us about . . . you know, the ones who think we're stories . . . you reckon they'd believe we ran away? Well, then. No, it's not part of the whole deal, running away. Let someone else do the running.'

'Besides,' said Truckle, 'where'd we get another chance like this? Six against five armies! That's bl— that's fantastic! We're not talking legends here, I reckon we've got a good crack at some mythology as well.'

'But . . . you'll . . . *die*.'

'Oh, that's part of it, I'll grant you, that's part of it. But what a way to go, eh?'

Mr Saveloy looked at them and realised that they were speaking another language in another world. It was one he had no key to, no map for. You could teach them to wear interesting pants and handle money but something in their soul stayed exactly the same.

'Do teachers go anywhere special when they die?' said Cohen.

'I don't think so,' said Mr Saveloy gloomily. He wondered for a moment whether there really *was* a great Free Period in the sky. It didn't sound very likely. Probably there would be some marking to do.

'Well, whatever happens, when you're dead, if you ever feel like a good quaff, you're welcome to drop in at any time,' said Cohen. 'It's been *fun*. That's the important thing. And it's been an education, hasn't it, boys?'

There was a general murmur of assent.

'Amazing, all those long words.'

'And learnin' to buy things.'

'And social intercourse, hur, hur . . . sorry.'

'Whut?'

'Shame it didn't work out, but I've never been one for plans,' said Cohen.

Mr Saveloy stood up.

'I'm going to join you,' he said grimly.

'What, to fight?'

'Yes.'

'Do you know how to handle a sword?' said Truckle.

'Er. No.'

'Then you've wasted *all* your life.'

Mr Saveloy looked offended at this.

'I expect I'll get the hang of it as we go along,' he said.

'Get the hang of it? It's a *sword*!'

'Yes, but . . . when you're a teacher, you have to pick things up fast.' Mr Saveloy smiled nervously. 'I once taught practical alchemy for a whole term when Mr Schism was off sick after blowing himself up, and up until then I'd never seen a crucible.'

'Here.' Boy Willie handed the teacher a spare sword. He hefted it.

'Er. I expect there's a manual, or something?'

'Manual? No. You hold the blunt end and poke the other end at people.'

'Ah? Really? Well, that seems quite straightforward. I thought there was rather more to it than that.'

'You *sure* you want to come with us?' said Cohen.

Mr Saveloy looked firm. 'Absolutely. I very much doubt if I'll survive if you lose and . . . well, it seems that you heroes get a better class of Heaven. I must say I rather suspect you get a better class of life, too. And I really don't know where teachers go when they're dead, but I've got a horrible suspicion it'll be full of sports masters.'

'It's just that I don't know if you could really go properly berserk,' said Cohen. 'Have you ever had the red mist come down and woke up to find you'd bitten twenty people to death?'

'I used to be reckoned a pretty ratty man if people made too much noise in class,' said Mr Saveloy. 'And something of a dead shot with a piece of chalk, too.'

'How about you, taxman?'

Six Beneficent Winds backed away hurriedly.

'I . . . I think I'm probably more cut out for undermining the system from within,' he said.

'Fair enough.' Cohen looked at the others. 'I've never done this official sort of warring before,' he said. 'How's it supposed to go?'

'I think you just line up in front of one another and then charge,' said Mr Saveloy.

'Seems straightforward enough. All right, let's go.'

They strode, or in one case wheeled and in another case moved at Mr Saveloy's gentle trot, down the hall. The taxman trailed after them.

'Mr Saveloy!' he shouted. 'You know what's going to happen! Have you lost your senses?'

'Yes,' said the teacher, 'but I may have found some better ones.'

He grinned to himself. The whole of his life, so far, had been complicated. There had been timetables and lists and a whole basket of things he must do and things he shouldn't do, and the life of Mr Saveloy had been this little wriggly thing trying to survive in the middle of it all. But now it had suddenly all become very simple. You held one end and you poked the other into people. A man could live his whole life by a maxim like that. And, afterwards, get a very interesting afterlife—

'Here, you'll need this too,' said Caleb, poking something round at him as they stepped into the grey light. 'It's a shield.'

'Ah. It's to protect myself, yes?'

'If you really need to, bite the edge.'

'Oh, I know about that,' said Mr Saveloy. 'That's when you go berserk, right?'

'Could be, could be,' said Caleb. 'That's why a lot of fighters do it. But personally *I* do it 'cos it's made of chocolate.'

'Chocolate?'

'You can never get a proper meal in these battles.'

And this is me, thought Mr Saveloy, marching down the street with *heroes*. They are the great fi—

'And when in doubt, take all your clothes off,' said Caleb.

'What for?'

'Sign of a good berserk, taking all your clothes off. Frightens the hell out of the enemy. If anyone starts laughing, stab 'em one.'

There was a movement among the blankets in the wheelchair.

'Whut?'

'I said, STAB 'EM ONE, Hamish.'

Hamish waved an arm that looked like bone with skin on it, and apparently far too thin to hold the axe it was in fact holding.

'That's right! Right in the nadgers!'

Mr Saveloy nudged Caleb.

'I ought to be writing this down,' he said. 'Where exactly are the nadgers?'

'Small range of mountains near the Hub.'

'Fascinating.'

The citizens of Hunghung were ranged along the city walls. It was not every day you saw a fight like this.

Rincewind elbowed and kicked his way through the people until he reached the cadre, who'd managed to occupy a prime position over the main gate.

'What're you hanging around here for?' he said. 'You could be miles away!'

'We want to see what happens, of course,' said Twoflower, his spectacles gleaming.

'I know what happens! The Horde will be instantly slaughtered!' said Rincewind. 'What did you *expect* to happen?'

'Ah, but you're forgetting the invisible vampire ghosts,' said Twoflower.

Rincewind looked at him.

'What?'

'Their secret army. I heard that *we've* got some, too. Should be interesting to watch.'

'Twoflower, there are *no* invisible vampire ghosts.'

'Ah, yes, everyone's going round denying it,' said Lotus Blossom. 'So there must be some truth in it.'

'But I made it up!'

'Ah, you may *think* you made it up,' said Twoflower. 'But perhaps you are a pawn of Fate.'

'Listen, there's no—'

'Same old Rincewind,' said Twoflower, in a jolly way. 'You always were so pessimistic about everything, but it always worked out all right in the end.'

'There are no ghosts, there are no magic armies,' said Rincewind. 'There's just—'

'When seven men go out to fight an army 100,000 times bigger there's only one way it can end,' said Twoflower.

'Right. I'm glad you see sense.'

'They'll win,' said Twoflower. 'They've got to. Otherwise the world's just not working properly.'

'You look educated,' said Rincewind to Butterfly. 'Explain to him why he's wrong. It's because of a little thing we have in our country. I don't know if you've ever heard of it – it's called *mathematics*.'

The girl smiled at him.

'You don't believe me, do you?' said Rincewind flatly. 'You're just like him. What d'you think this is, homeopathic warfare? The smaller your side the more likely you are to win? Well, it's not like that. I wish it *was* like that, but it isn't. Nothing is. There are no amazing strokes of luck, no magic solutions, and the good people

511

don't win because they're small and plucky!' He waved his hand irritably at something.

'*You* always survived,' said Twoflower. 'We had amazing adventures and you always survived.'

'That was just coincidence.'

'You kept *on* surviving.'

'And you got us safely out of prison,' said Lotus Blossom.

'There were just a lot of coinci— *Will you go away!*'

A butterfly skittered away from his flailing hand.

'Damn things,' he mumbled. And added: 'Well, that's it. I'm off. I can't watch. I've got things to do. Besides, afterwards I think nasty people are going to be looking for me.'

And then he realised there were tears in Lotus Blossom's eyes.

'We . . . we thought you would do something,' she said.

'Me? I can't do anything! Especially not magic! I'm famous for it! Don't go around believing that Great Wizards solve all your problems, because there aren't any and they don't and I should know because I'm not one!'

He backed away. 'This is always happening to me! I'm just minding my own business and everything goes wrong and suddenly everyone's relying on me and saying, "Oh, Rincewind, what are you going to do about it?" Well, what Mrs Rincewind's little boy, if she was a Mrs Rincewind of course, what he's going to do about it is nothing, right? You have to sort it all out yourselves! No mysterious magical armies are going to— Will you stop looking at me like that? I don't see why it's *my* fault! I've got other things to do! It's not my business!'

And then he turned and ran.

The crowds didn't take much notice of him.

The streets were deserted by Hunghung standards, which meant you could quite often see the cobbles. Rincewind pushed and shoved his way along the alleys nearest the Wall, looking for another gateway with guards too busy to ask questions.

There were footsteps behind him.

'Look,' he said, spinning round, 'I told you, you can all—'

It was the Luggage. It contrived to look a little ashamed of itself.

'Oh, turned up at last, have we?' said Rincewind savagely. 'What happened to the following-master-everywhere thing?'

The Luggage shuffled its feet. From out of an alleyway came a slightly larger and far more ornate version of itself. Its lid was inset with decorative wood and, it seemed to Rincewind, its feet were rather more dainty than the horny-nailed, calloused ones of the Luggage. Besides, the toenails had been painted.

'Oh,' he said. 'Well. Good grief. Fair enough, I suppose. Really? I mean . . . yes. Well. Come on, then.'

He reached the end of the alley and turned round. The Luggage was gently bumping the larger chest, urging it to follow him.

Rincewind's own sexual experiences were not excessive although he had seen diagrams. He hadn't the faintest idea about how it applied to travel accessories. Did they say things like 'What a chest!' or 'Get a load of the hinges on that one!'?

If it came to that, he had no real reason for considering that the Luggage was male. Admittedly it had a homicidal nature, but so had a lot of the women that Rincewind had met, and they had often become a little more homicidal as a result of meeting him. Capacity for violence, Rincewind had heard, was unisexual. He wasn't certain what unisex was, but expected that it was what he normally experienced.

There was a small gate ahead. It seemed to be unguarded.

Despite his fear he walked through it, and refrained from running. Authority always noticed a running man. The time to start running was around about the 'e' in 'Hey, you!'

No one paid him any attention. The attention of the people along the Wall was all on the armies.

'Look at them,' he said bitterly, to the generality of the universe. '*Stupid*. If it was seven against seventy, everyone'd *know* who'd lose. Just because it's seven against 700,000, everyone's not sure. As though suddenly numbers don't mean anything any more. Huh! Why should *I* do anything? It's not as if I even know the guy all that well. Admittedly he saved my life a couple of times, but that's no reason to die horribly just because he can't count. So you can stop looking at me like that!'

The Luggage backed away a little. The *other* Luggage . . .

. . . Rincewind supposed it just *looked* female. Women had bigger luggage than men, didn't they? Because of the - he moved into unknown territory - extra frills and stuff. It was just one of those things, like the fact that they had smaller handkerchiefs than men even though their noses were generally the same size. The Luggage had always been *the* Luggage. Rincewind wasn't mentally prepared for there to be more than one. There was the Luggage and . . . the *other* Luggage.

'Come on, both of you,' he said. 'We're getting out of here. I've done what I can. I just don't care any more. It's nothing to do with me. I don't see why everyone depends on me. I'm not dependable. Even *I* don't depend on me, and I'm me.'

Cohen looked at the horizon. Grey-blue clouds were piling up.

'There's a storm coming,' he said.

'It's a mercy that we won't be alive to get wet, then,' said Boy Willie, cheerfully.

'Funny thing, though. It looks like it's coming from every direction at once.'

'Filthy foreign weather. You can't trust it.'

Cohen turned his attention to the armies of the five warlords.

There seemed to have been some agreement.

They'd arranged themselves around the position that Cohen had taken up. The tactic seemed quite clear. It was simply to advance. The Horde could see the commanders riding up and down in front of their legions.

'How's it supposed to start?' said Cohen, the rising wind whipping at what remained of his hair. 'Does someone blow a whistle or something? Or do we just scream and charge?'

'Commencement is generally by agreement,' said Mr Saveloy.

'Oh.'

Cohen looked at the forest of lances and pennants. Hundreds of thousands of men looked like quite a lot of men when you saw them close to.

'I suppose,' he said, slowly, 'that none of you has got some amazing plan you've been keeping quiet about?'

'We thought *you* had one,' said Truckle.

Several riders had now left each army and approached the Horde in a group. They stopped a little more than a spear's throw away, and sat and watched.

'All right, then,' said Cohen. 'I hate to say this, but perhaps we should talk about surrender.'

'No!' said Mr Saveloy, and then stopped in embarrassment at the loudness of his own voice. 'No,' he repeated, a little more quietly. 'You won't live if you surrender. You just won't die immediately.'

Cohen scratched his nose. 'What's that flag . . . you know . . . when you want to talk to them without them killing you?'

'It's got to be red,' said Mr Saveloy. 'But look, it's no good you—'

'I don't know, red for surrender, white for funerals . . .' muttered Cohen. 'All right. Anyone got something red?'

'I've got a handkerchief,' said Mr Saveloy, 'but it's white and anyway—'

'Give it here.'

The barbarian teacher very reluctantly handed it over.

Cohen pulled a small, worn knife from his belt.

'I don't believe this!' said Mr Saveloy. He was nearly in tears. 'Cohen the Barbarian talking surrender with people like that!'

'Influence of civilization,' said Cohen. ''S probably made me go soft in the head.'

He pulled the knife over his arm, and then clamped the handkerchief over the cut.

'There we are,' he said. 'Soon have a nice red flag.'

The Horde nodded approvingly. It was an amazingly symbolic, dramatic and above all stupid gesture, in the finest traditions of barbarian heroing. It didn't seem to be lost on some of the nearer soldiers, either.

'Now,' Cohen went on, 'I reckon you, Teach, and you, Truckle . . . you two come with me and we'll go and talk to these people.'

'They'll drag you off to their dungeons!' said Mr Saveloy. 'They've got torturers that can keep you alive for *years*!'

'Whut? Whutzeesay?'

'He said THEY CAN KEEP YOU ALIVE FOR YEARS IN THEIR DUNGEONS, Hamish.'

'Good! Fine by me!'

'Oh, dear,' said Mr Saveloy.

He trailed after the other two towards the warlords.

Lord Hong raised his visor and stared down his nose at them as they approached.

'Red flag, look,' said Cohen, waving the rather damp object on the end of his sword.

'Yes,' said Lord Hong. 'We saw that little show. It may impress the common soldiers but it does not impress me, barbarian.'

'Please yourself,' said Cohen. 'We've come to talk about surrender.'

Mr Saveloy noticed some of the lesser lords relax a little. Then he thought: a real soldier probably doesn't like this sort of thing. You don't want to go to soldier Heaven or wherever you go and say, I once led an army against seven old men. It wasn't medal-winning material.

'Ah. Of course. So much for bravado,' said Lord Hong. 'Then lay down your arms and you will be escorted back to the palace.'

Cohen and Truckle looked at one another.

'Sorry?' said Cohen.

'Lay down your arms.' Lord Hong snorted. 'That means put down your weapons.'

Cohen gave him a puzzled look. 'Why should we put down our weapons?'

'Are we not talking about your surrender?'

'*Our* surrender?'

Mr Saveloy's mouth opened in a mad, slow grin.

Lord Hong stared at Cohen.

'Hah! You can hardly expect me to believe that you have come to ask *us* . . .'

He leaned from the saddle and glared at them.

'You do, don't you?' he said. 'You mindless little barbarians. Is it true that you can only count up to five?'

'We just thought that it might save people getting hurt,' said Cohen.

'You thought it would save *you* getting hurt,' said the warlord.

'I daresay a few of yours might get hurt, too,'

'They're peasants,' said the warlord.

'Oh, yes. I was forgetting that,' said Cohen. 'And you're their chief, right? It's like your game of chess, right?'

'I am their lord,' said Lord Hong. 'They will die at my bidding, if necessary.'

Cohen gave him a big, dangerous grin.

'When do we start?' he said.

'Return to your . . . band,' said Lord Hong. 'And then I think we shall start . . . shortly.'

He glared at Truckle, who was unfolding his bit of paper. The barbarian's lips moved awkwardly and he ran a horny finger across the page.

'Misbegotten . . . wretch, so you are,' he said.

'My word,' said Mr Saveloy, who'd created the look-up table.

As the three returned to the Horde Mr Saveloy was aware of a grinding sound. Cohen was wearing several carats off his teeth.

'"Die at my bidding",' he said. 'The bugger doesn't even know what a chief is meant to be, the bastard! Him and his horse!'

Mr Saveloy looked around. There seemed to be some arguing among the warlords.

'You know,' he said, 'they probably will try to take us alive. I used to have a headmaster like him. He liked to make people's lives a misery.'

'You mean they'll be trying not to kill us?' said Truckle.

'Yes.'

'Does that mean we have to try not to kill them?'

'No, I don't think so.'

'Sounds okay to me.'

'What do we do now?' said Mr Saveloy. 'Do we do a battle chant or something?'

'We just wait,' said Cohen.

'There's a lot of waiting in warfare,' said Boy Willie.

'Ah, yes,' said Mr Saveloy. 'I've heard people say that. They say there's long periods of boredom followed by short periods of excitement.'

'Not really,' said Cohen. 'It's more like short periods of waiting followed by long periods of being dead.'

'Blast.'

The fields were crisscrossed with drainage ditches. There seemed to be no straight path anywhere. And the ditches were too wide to jump; they *looked* shallow enough to wade, but only because eighteen inches of water overlay a suffocating depth of rich thick mud. Mr Saveloy said that the Empire owed its prosperity to the mud of the plains, and right now Rincewind was feeling extremely rich.

He was also quite close to the big hill that dominated the city. It really was rounded, with a precision apparently far too accurate for mere natural causes; Saveloy had said that hills like that were drumlins, great piles of topsoil left behind by glaciers. Trees covered the lower slopes of this one, and there was a small building on the top.

Cover. Now, *that* was a good word. It was a big plain and the armies weren't too far away. The hill looked curiously peaceful, as if it belonged to a different world. It was strange that the Agateans, who otherwise seemed to farm absolutely everywhere a water buffalo could stand, had left it alone.

Someone was watching him.

It *was* a water buffalo.

It would be wrong to say it watched him with interest. It just watched him, because its eyes were open and had to be facing in some direction, and it had randomly chosen one which included Rincewind.

Its face held the completely serene expression of a creature that had long ago realized that it was, fundamentally, a tube on legs and had been installed in the universe to, broadly speaking, achieve throughput.

At the other end of the string was a man, ankle-deep in the mud of the field. He had a broad straw hat, like every other buffalo holder. He had the basic pyjama suit of the Agatean man-in-the-field. And he had an expression not of idiocy, but of preoccupation. He was looking at Rincewind. As with the buffalo, this was only because his eyes had to be doing something.

Despite the pressing dangers, Rincewind found himself overcome by a sudden curiosity.

'Er. Good morning,' he said.

The man gave him a nod. The water buffalo made the sound of regurgitating cud. 'Er. Sorry if this is a personal question,' said Rincewind, 'but . . . I can't help wondering . . . why do you stand out in the fields all day with the water buffalo?'

The man thought about it.

'Good for soil,' he said eventually.

'But doesn't it waste a lot of time?' said Rincewind.

The man gave this due appraisal also.

'What's time to a cow?' he said.

Rincewind reversed back on to the highway of reality. 'You see those armies over there?' he said.

The buffalo holder concentrated his gaze.

'Yes,' he decided.

'They're fighting for you.' The man did not appear moved by this. The water buffalo burped gently.

'Some want to see you enslaved and some want you to run the country, or at least to let them run the country while telling you it's you doing it really,' said Rincewind. 'There's going to be a terrible battle. I can't help wondering . . . What do *you* want?'

The buffalo holder absorbed this one for consideration, too. And it seemed to Rincewind that the slowness of the thought process wasn't due to native stupidity, but more to do with the sheer size of the question. He could feel it spreading out so that it incorporated the soil and the grass and the sun and headed on out into the universe.

Finally the man said:

'A longer piece of string would be nice.'

'Ah. Really? Well, well. There's a thing,' said Rincewind. 'Talking to you has been an education. Goodbye.'

The man watched him go. Beside him, the buffalo relaxed some muscles and contracted others and lifted its tail and made the world, in a very small way, a better place.

Rincewind headed on towards the hill. Random as the animal tracks and occasional plank bridges were, they seemed to head right for it. If Rincewind had been thinking clearly, an activity he last remembered doing around the age of twelve, he might have wondered about that.

The trees of the lower slopes were sapient pears, and he didn't even think about *that*. Their leaves turned to watch him as he scrambled past. What he needed now was a cave or a handy—

He paused.

'Oh, no,' he said. 'No, no, no. You don't catch *me* like that. I'll go into a handy cave and there'll be a little door or some wise old man or something and I'll be dragged back into events. Right. Stay out in the open, that's the style.'

He half climbed, half walked to the rounded top of the hill, which rose above the trees like a dome. Now he was closer he could see that it wasn't as smooth as it looked from below. Weather had worn gullies and channels in the soil, and bushes had colonized every sheltered slope.

The building on the top was, to Rincewind's surprise, rusty. It had been made of iron – pointed iron roof, iron walls, iron doorway. There were a few old nests and some debris on the floor, but it was otherwise empty. And not a good place to hide. It'd be the first place anyone would look.

There was a cloud wall around the world now. Lightning crackled in its heart, and there was the sound of thunder – not the gentle rumble of summer thunder but the crackackack of splitting sky.

And yet the heat wrapped the plain like a blanket. The air felt thick. In a minute it was going to rain cats and food.

'Find somewhere where I won't be noticed,' he muttered. 'Keep head down. Only way. Why should I care? Other people's problem.'

Panting in the oppressive heat, he wandered on.

Lord Hong was enraged. Those who knew him could tell, by the way he spoke more slowly and smiled continuously. 'And how do the men know the lightning dragons are *angry*?' he said. 'It may be mere high spirits.'

'Not with a sky that colour,' said Lord Tang. 'That is not an

519

auspicious colour for a sky. It looks like a bruise. A sky like that is portentous.'

'And what, pray, do you think it portends?'

'It's just *generally* portentous.'

'I know what's behind this,' Lord Hong snarled. 'You're too frightened to fight seven old men, is that it?'

'The men say they're the legendary Seven Indestructible Sages,' said Lord Fang. He tried to smile. 'You know how superstitious they are . . .'

'What Seven Sages?' said Lord Hong. 'I am extremely familiar with the history of the world and there are no legendary Seven Indestructible Sages.'

'Er . . . not *yet*,' said Lord Fang. 'Uh. But . . . a day like this . . . Perhaps legends have to *start* somewhere . . .'

'They're barbarians! Oh, gods! Seven men! Can I believe we're afraid of seven men?'

'It feels wrong,' said Lord McSweeney. He added, quickly, 'That's what the men say.'

'You have made the proclamation about our celestial army of ghosts? All of you?'

The warlords tried to avoid his gaze.

'Er . . . yes,' said Lord Fang.

'That must have improved morale.'

'Uh. Not . . . entirely . . .'

'What do you mean, man?'

'Uh. Many men have deserted. Uh. They've been saying that foreign ghosts were bad enough, but . . .'

'But what?'

'They are *soldiers*, Lord Hong,' said Lord Tang sharply. 'They all have people they do not want to meet. Don't you?'

Just for a second, there was the suggestion of a twitch on Lord Hong's cheek. It was only for a second, but those who saw it took note. Lord Hong's renowned glaze had shown a crack.

'What would you do, Lord Tang? Let these insolent barbarians go?'

'Of course not. But . . . you don't need an army against seven men. Seven ancient old men. The peasants say . . . they say . . .'

Lord Hong's voice was slightly higher.

'Come on, man who talks to peasants. I'm sure you're going to tell us what they say about these foolish and foolhardy old men?'

'Well, that's it, you see. They say, if they're so foolish and foolhardy . . . how did they manage to become so old?'

'Luck!'

It was the wrong word. Even Lord Hong realized it. He'd never believed in luck. He'd always taken pains, usually those of other people, to fill life with certainties. But he knew that others believed in luck. It was a foible he'd always been happy to make use of. And now it was turning and stinging him on the hand.

'There is nothing in the Art of War to tell us how five armies attack seven old men,' said Lord Tang. 'Ghosts or no ghosts. And this, Lord Hong, is because no one ever thought such a thing would be done.'

'If you feel so frightened I'll ride out against them with my mere 250,000 men,' he said.

'I am not frightened,' said Lord Tang. 'I am ashamed.'

'Each man armed with two swords,' Lord Hong went on, ignoring him. 'And I shall see how lucky these . . . sages . . . are. Because, my lords, I will only have to be lucky once. They will have to be lucky a quarter of a million times.'

He lowered his visor.

'How lucky do you feel, my lords?'

The other four warlords avoided one another's gaze.

Lord Hong noticed their resigned silence.

'Very well, then,' he said. 'Let the gongs be sounded and the fire-crackers lit – to ensure good luck, of course.'

There were a large number of ranks in the armies of the Empire, and many of them were untranslatable. Three Pink Pig and Five White Fang were, loosely speaking, privates, and not just because they were pale, vulnerable and inclined to curl up and hide when danger threatened.

In fact they were so private as to be downright secretive. Even the army's mules ranked higher than them, because good mules were hard to come by whereas men like Pink Pig and White Fang are found in every army, somewhere where a latrine is in need of cleaning.

They were so insignificant that they had, privately, decided that it would be a waste of an invisible foreign blood-sucking ghost's valuable time to attack them. They felt it only fair, after it had come all this way, to give it the chance of fiendishly killing someone superior.

They had therefore hospitably decamped just before dawn and were now hiding out. Of course, if victory threatened they could always *recamp*. It was unlikely that they'd be missed in all the excitement, and both men were somewhat expert at turning up on battlefields in time to join in the victory celebrations. They lay in the long grass, watching the armies manoeuvre.

From this height, it looked like an impressive war. The army on one side was so small as to be invisible. Of course, if you accepted the very strong denials of last night, it was so *invisible* as to be invisible.

It was also their elevation which meant that they were the first to notice the ring around the sky.

It was just above the thunderous wall on the horizon. Where stray shafts of sunlight hit it, it glowed golden. Elsewhere it was merely yellow. But it was continuous, and thin as a thread.

'Funny-looking cloud,' said White Fang.

'Yeah,' said Pink Pig. 'So what?'

It was while they were thus engaged, and sharing a small bottle of rice wine liberated by Pink Pig from an unsuspecting comrade the previous evening, that they heard a groan.

'Oooooohhhhhh . . .'

Their drinks froze in their throats.

'Did you hear that?' said Pink Pig.

'You mean the—'

'Ooooohhhh . . .'

'That's it!'

They turned, very slowly.

Something had pulled itself out of a gully behind them. It was humanoid, more or less. Red mud dripped from it. Strange noises issued from its mouth.

'Oooooohhhhhshit!'

Pink Pig grabbed White Fang's arm.

'It's an invisible blood-sucking ghost!'

'But I can see it!'

Pink Pig squinted.

'It's the Red Army! They've come up outa the earth like every-body says!'

White Fang, who had several brain cells more than Pink Pig, and more importantly was only on his second cup of wine, took a closer look.

'It could be just one ordinary man with mud all over him,' he suggested. He raised his voice. 'Hey, you!'

The figure turned and tried to run.

Pink Pig nudged his friend.

'Is he one of ours?'

'Looking like that?'

'Let's get him!'

'Why?'

''Cos he's running away!'

'Let him run.'

'Maybe he's got money. Anyway, what's he running away for?'

Rincewind slid down into another gully. Of all the luck! Soldiers should be where they were expected to be. What had happened to duty and honour and stuff like that?

The gully had dead grass and moss in the bottom.

He stood still and listened to the voices of the two men.

The air was stifling. It was as if the oncoming storm was pushing all the hot air in front of it, turning the plain into a pressure cooker.

And then the ground creaked, and sagged suddenly.

The faces of the absentee soldiers appeared over the edge of the gully.

There was another creak and the ground sank another inch or two. Rincewind didn't dare breathe in, in case the extra weight of air made him too heavy. And it was very clear that the least activity, such as jumping, was going to make things worse . . .

Very carefully, he looked down.

The dead moss had given way. He seemed to be standing on a baulk of timber buried in the ground, but dirt pouring around it suggested that there was a hole beneath.

It was going to give way any second n—

Rincewind threw himself forward. The ground fell away underneath so that, instead of standing on a slowly breaking piece of timber, he was hanging with his arms over what felt like another concealed log and, by the feel of it, one which was as riddled with rot as the first one.

This one, possibly out of a desire to conform, began to sag.

And then jolted to a stop.

The faces of the soldiers vanished backwards as the sides of the gully began to slide. Dry earth and small stones slid past Rincewind. He could feel them rattle on his boots and drop away.

He felt, as an expert in these things, that he was over a depth. From his point of view, it was also a height.

The log began to shift again.

This left Rincewind with, as he saw it, two options. He could let go and plunge to an uncertain fate in the darkness, or he could hang on until the timber gave way, and then plunge to an uncertain fate in the darkness.

And then, to his delight, there was a third option. The toe of his boot touched something, a root, a protruding rock. It didn't matter. It took some of his weight. It took at least enough to put him in precarious equilibrium – not exactly safe, not exactly falling. Of course, it was only a temporary measure, but Rincewind had always considered that life was no more than a series of temporary measures strung together.

A pale yellow butterfly with interesting patterns on its wings fluttered along the gully and settled on the only bit of colour available, which turned out to be Rincewind's hat.

The wood sagged slightly.

'Push off!' said Rincewind, trying not to use heavy language. 'Go away!'

The butterfly flattened its wings and sunned itself.

Rincewind pursed his lips and tried to blow up his own nostrils.

Startled, the creature skittered into the air . . .

'Hah!' said Rincewind.

. . . and, in response to its instincts in the face of a threat, moved its wings like *this* and *this*.

The bushes shivered. And around the sky, the towering clouds curved into unusual patterns.

Another cloud formed. It was about the size of an angry grey balloon.

And it started to rain. Not rain generally, but specifically. Specifically on about a square foot of ground which contained Rincewind; specifically, on his hat.

A very small bolt of lightning stung Rincewind on the nose.

'Ah! So we have' – Pink Pig, appearing around the curve of the gully, hesitated a bit before continuing slightly more thoughtfully – 'a head in a hole . . . with a very small thunderstorm above it.'

And then it dawned on him that, storm or no storm, nothing was preventing him from cutting off significant parts. The only significant part available was a head, but that was fine by him.

At which point, Rincewind's hat having absorbed enough moisture, the ancient wood gave way under the strain and plunged him to an uncertain fate in the darkness.

*

It was utterly dark.

There had been a painful confusion of tunnels and sliding dirt. Rince-wind assumed – or the small part of him that was not sobbing with fear assumed – that the earth had caved in after him. Cave. That was a significant word. He was in a cave. Reaching out carefully, in case he felt something, he felt for something to feel.

There was a straight edge. It led to three more straight edges, going off at right angles. So . . . this meant slab.

The darkness was still a choking velvet shroud.

Slab meant that there was some other entrance, some proper entrance. Even now guards were probably hurrying towards him.

Perhaps the Luggage was hurrying towards *them*. It had been acting very funny lately, that was for certain. He was probably better off without it. Probably.

He patted his pockets, saying the mantra that even non-wizards invoke in order to find matches; that is, he said, 'Matches, matches, matches,' madly to himself, under his breath.

He found some, and scratched one desperately with his thumb-nail.

'Ow!'

The smoky yellow flame lit nothing except Rincewind's hand and part of his sleeve.

He ventured a few steps before it burned his fingers, and when it died it left a blue afterglow in the darkness of his vision.

There were no sounds of vengeful feet. There were no sounds at all. In theory there should be the drip of water, but the air felt quite dry.

He tried another match, and this time raised it as high as he could and peered ahead.

A seven-foot warrior smiled at him.

Cohen looked up again.

'It's going to piss down in a minute,' he said. 'Will you look at that sky?'

There were hints of purple and red in the mass, and the occasional momentary glow of lightning somewhere inside the clouds.

'Teach?'

'Yes?'

'You know everything. Why's that cloud looking like that?'

Mr Saveloy looked where Cohen was pointing. There was a

yellowish cloud low on the horizon. Right around the horizon – one thin streak, as though the sun was trying to find a way through.

'Could be the lining?' said Boy Willie.

'What lining?'

'Every cloud's supposed to have a silver one.'

'Yeah, but that's more like gold.'

'Well, gold's cheaper here.'

'Is it me,' said Mr Saveloy, 'or is it getting wider?'

Caleb was staring at the enemy lines.

'There's been a lot of blokes galloping about on their little horses,' he said. 'I hope they get a move on. We don't want to be here all day.'

'I vote we rushes 'em while they're not expectin' it,' said Hamish.

'Hold on . . . hold on . . .' said Truckle. There was the sound of many gongs being beaten, and the crackling of fireworks. 'Looks like the bas— the lovechilds are moving.'

'Thank goodness for that,' said Cohen. He stood up and stubbed out his cigarette.

Mr Saveloy trembled with excitement.

'Do we sing a song for the gods before we go into battle?' he said.

'You can if you like,' said Cohen.

'Well, do we say any heathen chants or prayers?'

'Shouldn't think so,' said Cohen. He glanced up at the horizon-girdling band. It was unsettling him far more than the approaching enemy. It was wider now, but slightly paler. For just a moment he found himself wishing that there was one god or goddess somewhere whose temple he hadn't violated, robbed or burned down.

'Don't we bang our swords on our shields and utter defiance?' said the teacher hopefully.

'Too late for that, really,' said Cohen.

Mr Saveloy looked so crestfallen at the lack of pagan splendour that the ancient barbarian was, to his own surprise, moved to add: 'But feel free, if that's what you want.'

The Horde drew their various swords. In Hamish's case, another axe was produced from under his rug.

'See you in Heaven!' said Mr Saveloy excitedly.

'Yeah, right,' said Caleb, eyeing the line of approaching soldiers.

'Where there's feasting and young ladies and so forth!'

'Yeah, yeah,' said Boy Willie, testing the blade of his sword.

'And carousing and quaffing, I believe!'

'Could be,' said Vincent, trying to ease the tendonitis in his arm.

'And we'll do that thing, you know, where you throw the axes and cut ladies' plaits off!'

'Yeah, if you like.'

'But—'

'Whut?'

'The actual feasting . . . Do they do anything vegetarian?'

And the advancing army screamed and charged.

They rushed at the Horde, almost as fast as the clouds boiling in from every direction.

Rincewind's brain unfroze slowly, in the darkness and silence of the hill.

It's a statue, he told himself. That's all it is. No problem there. Not even a particularly good one. Just a big statue of a man in armour. Look, there's a couple more, you can just see them at the edge of the light . . .

'Ow!'

He dropped the match and sucked his fingers.

What he needed now was a wall. Walls had exits. True, they could also be entrances, but now there did not seem much danger of any guards hurrying in here. The air had an ancient smell, with a hint of fox and a slight trace of thunderstorms, but above all it tasted unused.

He crept forward, testing each step with his foot.

Then there *was* light. A small blue spark jumped off Rincewind's finger.

Cohen grabbed at his beard. It was straining away from his face.

Mr Saveloy's fringe of hair stood out from his head and sparked at the ends.

'Static discharges!' he shouted, above the crackle.

Ahead of them the spears of the enemy glowed at the tips. The charge faltered. There was the occasional shriek as sparks leaped from man to man.

Cohen looked up.

'Oh, my,' he said. 'Will you look at *that*!'

Tiny sparks flickered around Rincewind as he eased himself over the unseen floor.

The word *tomb* had presented itself for his consideration, and one thing Rincewind knew about large tombs was that their builders were often jolly inventive in the traps and spikes department. They also put in things like paintings and statues, possibly so that the dead had something to look at if they became bored.

Rincewind's hand touched stone, and he moved carefully sideways. Now and again his feet touched something yielding and soft. He very much hoped it was mud.

And then, right at hand height, was a lever. It stuck out fully two feet.

Now . . . it *could* be a trap. But traps were generally, well, traps. The first you knew about them was when your head was rolling along the corridor several yards away. And trap builders tended to be straightforwardly homicidal and seldom required victims to actively participate in their own destruction.

Rincewind pulled it.

The yellow cloud sailed overhead in its millions, moving much faster on the wind they'd created than the slow beating of their wings would suggest. Behind them came the storm.

Mr Saveloy blinked.

'*Butterflies?*'

Both sides stopped as the creatures sleeted past. It was even possible to hear the rustle of their wings.

'All right, Teach,' said Cohen. 'Explain *this* one.'

'It, it, it could be a natural phenomenon,' said Mr Saveloy. 'Er . . . Monarch butterflies, for example, have been known to . . . er . . . to tell you the truth, I don't know . . .'

The cloud swarmed on towards the hill.

'Not some kind of sign?' said Cohen. 'There must have been *some* temple I didn't rob.'

'The trouble with signs and portents,' said Boy Willie, 'is you never know who they're for. This'n could be a nice one for Hong and his pals.'

'Then I'm nicking it,' said Cohen.

'You can't steal a message from the gods!' said Mr Saveloy.

'Can you see it nailed down anywhere? No? Sure? Right. So it's mine.'

He raised his sword as the stragglers fluttered past overhead.

'The gods smile on us!' he bellowed. 'Hahaha!'

'Hahaha?' whispered Mr Saveloy.

'Just to worry 'em,' said Cohen.

He glanced at the other members of the Horde. Each man nodded, very slightly.

'All right, lads,' he said quietly. 'This is it.'

'Er . . . what do I do?' said Mr Saveloy.

'Think of something to make yourself good and angry. That gets the ole blood boiling. Imagine the enemy is everything you hate.'

'Head teachers,' said Mr Saveloy.

'Good.'

'Sports masters!' shouted Mr Saveloy.

'Yep.'

'Boys who chew gum!' screamed Mr Saveloy.

'Look at him, steam coming out of his ears already,' said Cohen. 'First one to the afterlife gets 'em in. Charge!'

The yellow cloud thronged up the slopes of the hill and then, carried on the uprising wind, rose.

Above it the storm rose too, piling up and up and spreading into a shape something like a hammer—

It struck.

Lightning hit the iron pagoda so hard that it exploded into white-hot fragments.

It is confusing for an entire army to be attacked by seven old men. No book of tactics is up to the task of offering advice. There is a tendency towards bafflement.

The soldiers backed away in the face of the rush and then, driven by currents in the great mass of men, closed in behind.

A solid circle of shields surrounded the Horde. It buckled and swayed under the press of men, and also under the blows rained on it by Mr Saveloy's sword.

'Come on, fight!' he shouted. 'Smoke pipes at me, would you? You! That boy there! Answer me back, eh! Take that!'

Cohen looked at Caleb, who shrugged. He'd seen berserk rages in his time, but nothing quite so incandescent as Mr Saveloy.

The circle broke as a couple of men tried to dart backwards and cannoned into the rank behind and then rebounded on to the swords of the Horde. One of Hamish's wheels caught a soldier a vicious blow on the knee and, as he bent over, one of Hamish's axes met him coming the other way.

It wasn't speed. The Horde couldn't move very fast. But it *was* economy. Mr Saveloy had remarked on it. They were simply always where they wanted to be, which was never where someone's sword was. They let everyone else do the running around. A soldier would risk a slash in the direction of Truckle and find Cohen rising in front of him, grinning and swinging, or Boy Willie giving him a nod of acknowledgement and a stab. Occasionally one of the Horde took time to parry a blow aimed at Mr Saveloy, who was far too excited to defend himself.

'Pull back, you bloody fools!'

Lord Hong appeared behind the throng, his horse rearing, his helmet visor flung back.

The soldiers tried to obey. Finally, the press eased a little, and then opened. The Horde were left in a widening ring of shields. There was something like silence, broken only by the endless thunder and the crackle of lightning on the hill.

And then, pushing their way angrily through the soldiers, came an altogether different breed of warrior. They were taller, and heavier armoured, with splendid helmets and moustaches that looked like a declaration of war in themselves.

One of them glared at Cohen.

'*Orrrr! Itiyorshu! Yutimishu!*'

'Wassat?' said Cohen.

'He's a samurai,' said Mr Saveloy, wiping his forehead. 'The warrior caste. I think that's their formal challenge. Er. Would you like me to fight him?'

One samurai glared at Cohen. He pulled a scrap of silk out of his armour and tossed it into the air. His other hand grabbed the hilt of his long, thin sword . . .

There was hardly even a hiss, but three shreds of silk tumbled gently to the ground.

'Get back, Teach,' said Cohen slowly. 'I reckon this one's mine. Got another hanky? Thanks.'

The samurai looked at Cohen's sword. It was long, heavy and had so many notches it could have been used as a saw.

'You'll never do it,' he said. 'With that sword? Never.'

Cohen blew his nose noisily.

'You say?' he said. 'Watch this.'

The handkerchief soared into the air. Cohen gripped his sword . . .

He'd beheaded three upward-staring samurai before the hand-kerchief started to tumble. Other members of the Horde, who

530

tended to think in much the same way as their leader, had accounted for half a dozen more.

'Got the idea from Caleb,' said Cohen. 'And the message is: either fight or muck about, it's up to you.'

'Have you no honour?' screamed Lord Hong. 'Are you just a ruffian?'

'I'm a barbarian,' shouted Cohen. 'And the honour I got, see, is mine. I didn't steal it off'f someone else.'

'I had wanted to take you alive,' said Lord Hong. 'However, I see no reason to stick to this policy.'

He drew his sword.

'Back, you scum!' he screamed. 'Right back! Let the bombardiers come forward!' He looked back at Cohen. His face was flushed. His spectacles were askew.

Lord Hong had lost his temper. And, as is always the case when a dam bursts, it engulfs whole countries.

The soldiers pulled back.

The Horde were, once again, in a widening circle.

'What's a bombardier?' said Boy Willie.

'Er, I believe it must mean people who fire some sort of projectile,' said Mr Saveloy. 'The word derives from—'

'Oh, archers,' said Boy Willie, and spat.

'Whut?'

'He said THEY'RE GOING TO USE ARCHERS, Hamish!'

'Heheh, we never let archers stop us at the Battle of Koom Valley!' cackled the antique barbarian.

Boy Willie sighed.

'That was between dwarfs and trolls, Hamish,' he said. 'And you ain't either. So whose side were you on?'

'Whut?'

'I said WHOSE SIDE WERE YOU ON?'

'I were on the side of being paid money to fight,' said Hamish. 'Best side there is.'

Rincewind lay on the floor with his hands over his ears.

The sound of thunder filled the underground chamber. Blue and purple light shone so brightly that he could see it through his eyelids.

Finally the cacophony subsided. There were still the sounds of the storm outside, but the light had faded to a blue-white glow, and the sound into a steady humming.

531

Rincewind risked rolling over and opening his eyes.

Hanging from rusted chains in the roof were big glass globes. Each one was the size of a man, and lightning crackled and sizzled inside, stabbing at the glass, seeking a way out.

At one time there must have been many more. But dozens of the big globes had fallen down over the years, and lay in pieces on the floor. There were still scores up there, swaying gently on their chains as the imprisoned thunderstorms fought for their freedom.

The air felt greasy. Sparks crawled over the floor and crackled on each angle.

Rincewind stood up. His beard streamed out as a mass of individual hairs.

The lightning globes shone down on a round lake of, to judge from the ripples, pure quicksilver. In the centre was a low, five-sided island. As Rincewind stared, a boat came drifting gently around to his side of the pool, making little *slupslup* noises as it moved through the mercury.

It was not a lot larger than a rowing boat and, lying on its tiny deck, was a figure in armour. Or possibly just the armour. If it *was* just empty armour, then it was lying in the arms-folded position of a suit of armour that has passed away.

Rincewind sidled around the silver lake until he reached a slab of what looked very much like gold, set in the floor in front of a statue.

He knew you got inscriptions in tombs, although he was never sure who it was who was supposed to read them. The gods, possibly, although surely they knew everything already? He'd never considered that they'd cluster round and say things like, 'Gosh, "Dearly Beloved" was he? I never knew that.'

This one simply said, in pictograms: One Sun Mirror.

There wasn't anything about mighty conquests. There was no list of his tremendous achievements. There was nothing down there about wisdom or being the father of his people. There was no *explanation*. Whoever knows this name, it seemed to say, knows everything. And there was no admitting the possibility that anyone getting this far would not have heard the name of One Sun Mirror.

The statue looked like porcelain. It had been painted quite realistically. One Sun Mirror seemed an ordinary sort of man. You would not have pointed him out in a crowd as Emperor material. But this man, with his little round hat and little round shield and little round men on little round ponies, had glued together a thousand warring factions into one great Empire, often using their own blood to do it.

Rincewind looked closer. Of course, it was just an impression, but around the set of the mouth and the look of the eyes there was an expression he'd last seen on the face of Ghenghiz Cohen.

It was the expression of someone who was absolutely and totally unafraid of anything.

The little boat headed towards the far side of the lake.

One of the globes flickered a little and then faded to red. It winked out. Another followed it.

He had to get out.

There was something else, though. At the foot of the statue, lying as if they'd just been dropped there, were a helmet, a pair of gauntlets, and two heavy-looking boots.

Rincewind picked up the helmet. It didn't look very strong, but it did look quite light. Normally he didn't bother with protective clothing, reasoning that the best defence against threatening danger was to be on another continent, but right now the idea of armour had its attractions.

He removed his hat, put the helmet on, pulled down the visor, and then wedged the hat on top of the helmet.

There was a flicker in front of his eyes and Rincewind was staring at the back of his own head. It was a grainy picture, and it was in shades of green rather than proper colours, but it was definitely the back of his own head he was looking at. People had told him what it looked like.

He raised the visor and blinked.

The pool was still in front of him.

He lowered the visor.

There he was, about fifty feet away, with this helmet on his head.

He waved a hand up and down.

The figure in the visor waved a hand up and down.

He turned around and faced himself. Yep. That was him.

Okay, he thought. A magic helmet. It lets you see yourself a long way away. Great. You can have fun watching yourself fall into holes you can't see because they're right up close.

He turned around again, raised the visor and inspected the gloves. They seemed as light as the helmet but quite clumsy. You could hold a sword, but not much else.

He tried one on. Immediately, with a faint sizzling noise, a row of little pictures lit up on the wide cuff. They showed soldiers. Soldiers digging, soldiers fighting, soldiers climbing . . .

Ah. So . . . *magic* armour. Perfectly normal magic armour. It had never been very popular in Ankh-Morpork. Of course, it was light.

533

You could make it as thin as cloth. But it tended to lose its magic without warning. Many an ancient lord's last words had been, 'You can't kill me because I've got magic aaargh.'

Rincewind looked at the boots, with suspicious recollection of the trouble there had been with the University's prototype Seven League Boots. Footwear which tried to make you take steps twenty-one miles long imposed unfortunate groinal strains; they'd got the things off the student just in time, but he'd still had to wear a special device for several months, and ate standing up.

All right, but even *old* magic armour would be useful now. It wasn't as if it weighed much, and the mud of Hunghung hadn't improved what was left of his own boots. He put his feet into them.

He thought: Well, so what is supposed to happen now?

He straightened up.

And behind him, with the sound of seven thousand flower pots smashing together, the lightning still crackling over them, the Red Army came to attention.

Hex had grown a bit during the night. Adrian Turnipseed, who had been on duty to feed the mice and rewind the clockwork and clean out the dead ants, had sworn that he'd done nothing else and that no one had come in.

But now, where there had been the big clumsy arrangement of blocks so that the results could be read, was a quill pen in the middle of a network of pulleys and levers.

'Watch,' said Adrian, nervously tapping out a very simple problem. 'It's come up with this after doing all those spells at suppertime . . .'

The ants scuttled. The clockwork spun. The springs and levers jerked so sharply that Ponder took a step back.

The quill pen wobbled over to an inkwell, dipped, returned to the sheet of paper Adrian had put under the levers, and began to write.

'It blots a bit,' he said, in a helpless tone of voice. 'What's *happening*?'

Ponder had been thinking further about this. The latest conclusions hadn't been comforting.

'Well . . . we know that books containing magic become a little bit . . . sapient . . .' he began. 'And we've made a *machine* for . . .'

'You mean it's *alive*?'

'Come on, let's not get all occult about this,' said Ponder, trying to sound jovial. 'We're wizards, after all.'

'Listen, you know that long problem in thaumic fields you wanted me to put in?'

'Yes. Well?'

'It gave me the answer at midnight,' said Adrian, his face pale.

'Good.'

'Yes, good, except that I didn't actually *give* it the problem until half past one, Ponder.'

'You're telling me you got the answer before you asked the question?'

'Yes!'

'Why *did* you ask the question, then?'

'I thought about it, and I thought maybe I had to. I mean, it couldn't have known what the answer was going to be if I didn't give it the problem, yes?'

'Good point. Er. You waited ninety minutes, though.'

Adrian looked at his pointy boots.

'I . . . was hiding in the privy. Well, Redo from Start could—'

'All right, all right. Go and have something to eat.'

'Are we meddling with things we don't understand, Ponder?'

Ponder looked up at the gnomic bulk of the machine. It didn't seem threatening, merely . . . *other*.

He thought: meddle first, understand later. You had to meddle a *bit* before you had anything to try to understand. And the thing was never, ever, to go back and hide in the Lavatory of Unreason. You have to try to get your mind around the Universe before you can give it a twist.

Perhaps we shouldn't have given you a name. We didn't think about that. It was a joke. But we should have remembered that names are important. A thing with a name is a bit more than a thing.

'Off you go, Adrian,' he said firmly.

He sat down and carefully typed:

Hello.

Things whirred.

The quill wrote:

+++ ?????? +++ Hello +++ Redo From Start +++

Far above, a butterfly – its wings an undistinguished yellow, with black markings – fluttered through an open window.

Ponder began the calculations for the transfer between Hunghung and Ankh-Morpork.

The butterfly alighted for a moment on the maze of glass pipes. When it rose again, it left behind a very small blob of nectar.

Ponder typed carefully, far below.

A small but significant ant, one of the scurrying thousands, emerged from a break in the tube and spent a few seconds sucking at the sweet liquid before going back to work.

After a while, Hex gave an answer. Apart from one small but significant point, it was entirely correct.

Rincewind turned around.

With an echoing chorus of creaks and groans, the Red Army turned around too.

And it *was* red. It was the same colour, Rincewind realized, as the soil.

He'd bumped into a few statues in the darkness. He hadn't realized that there were *this* many. They stretched, rank on rank, into the distant shadows.

Experimentally, he turned around. Behind him, there was another chorus of stampings.

After a few false starts he found that the only way to end up facing them was to take off the boots, turn, and put the boots on again.

He lowered the visor for a moment, and saw himself lowering the visor for a moment.

He stuck up an arm. They stuck out their arms. He jumped up and down. They jumped up and down, with a crash that made the globes swing. Lightning sizzled from their boots.

He felt a sudden hysterical urge to laugh.

He touched his nose. They touched their noses. He made, with terrible glee, the traditional gesture for the dismissal of demons. Seven thousand terracotta middle fingers stabbed towards the ceiling.

He tried to calm down.

The word his mind had been groping for finally surfaced, and it was *golem*.

There were one or two of them, even in Ankh-Morpork. You were bound to get them in any area where you had wizards or priests of an experimental turn of mind. They were usually just figures made out of clay and animated with some suitable spell or prayer. They pottered about doing simple odd jobs, but they were not very fashionable these days. The problem was not putting them to work but stopping them from working; if you set a golem to digging the garden and then forgot about it, you'd come back to find it'd planted a row of beans 1500 miles long.

Rincewind looked down at one of the gloves.

He cautiously touched the little picture of a fighting soldier.

The sound of seven thousand swords being simultaneously unsheathed was like the tearing of a thick sheet of steel. Seven thousand points were pointed right at Rincewind.

He took a step back. So did the army.

He was in a place with thousands of artificial soldiers wearing swords. The fact that he appeared to have control of them was no great comfort. He'd theoretically had control of Rincewind for the whole of his life, and look what had happened to him.

He looked at the little pictures again. One of them showed a soldier with two heads. When he touched it, the army turned about smartly. Ah.

Now to get out of here . . .

The Horde watched the bustle among Lord Hong's men. Objects were being dragged to the front line.

They don't look like archers to me,' said Boy Willie.

'Those things are Barking Dogs,' said Cohen. 'I should know. Seen 'em before. They're like a barrel full of fireworks, and when the fireworks are lit a big stone comes rushing out of the other end.'

'Why?'

'Well, would you hang around if someone had just lit a firework by your arse?'

'Here, Teach, he said "arse",' complained Truckle. 'Look, on my bit of paper here it says you mustn't say—'

'We've got shields, haven't we?' said Mr Saveloy. 'I'm sure if we keep close together and put the shields over our heads we'll be as right as rain.'

'The stone's about a foot across and going very fast and it's red hot.'

'Not shields, then?'

'No,' said Cohen. 'Truckle, you push Hamish—'

'We won't get fifty yards, Ghenghiz,' said Caleb.

'Better fifty yards now than six feet in a minute, yes?' said Cohen.

'Bravo!' said Mr Saveloy.

'Whut?'

Lord Hong watched them. He saw the Horde hang their shields around the wheelchair to form a crude travelling wall, and saw the wheels begin to turn.

He raised his sword.

'Fire!'

'Still tamping the charges, o lord!'

'I said *fire!*'

'Got to prime the Dogs, o lord!'

The bombardiers worked feverishly, spurred on less by terror of Lord Hong than by the onrushing Horde.

Mr Saveloy's hair streamed in the wind. He bounded through the dust, waving his sword and screaming.

He'd never been so happy in all his life.

So this was the secret at the heart of it all: to look death right in the face and charge . . . It made everything so utterly simple.

Lord Hong threw down his helmet. 'Fire, you wretched peasants! You scum of the earth! Why must I ask twice! Give me that torch!'

He pushed a bombardier aside, crouched down beside a Dog, heaved on it so that the barrel was pointing at the oncoming Cohen, lifted the torch—

The earth heaved. The Dog reared and rolled sideways.

A round red head, smiling faintly, rose out of the ground.

There were screams in the ranks as the soldiers looked down at the moving dirt under their boots, tried to run on a surface that was just shifting soil, and disappeared in the rising cloud of dust.

The ground caved in.

Then it caved out again as stricken soldiers climbed up one another to escape because, rising gently through the turmoil, was the soil in human shape.

The Horde skidded to a halt.

'What're they? Trolls?' said Cohen. Ten of the figures were visible now, industriously digging at the air.

Then they stopped. One of them turned its gently smiling head this way and that.

A sergeant must have screamed a handful of archers into line, because a few arrows shattered on the terracotta armour, with absolutely no effect.

Other red warriors were climbing up behind the former diggers. They collided with them, with a sound of crockery. Then, as one man – or troll, or demon – they drew their swords, turned around, and headed towards Lord Hong's army.

A few soldiers tried to fight them simply because there was too great a crowd behind them to run away. They died.

It wasn't that the red guards were good fighters. They were very mechanical, each one performing the same thrust, parry, slash, regardless of what their opponent was doing. But they were simply unstoppable. If their opponent escaped one of the blows but didn't get out of the way then he was just trodden on – and by the looks of things, the warriors were extremely heavy.

And it was the way the things *smiled* all the time that added to the terror.

'Well, now, there's a thing,' Cohen said, feeling for his tobacco pouch.

'Never seen trolls fight like that,' said Truckle. Rank after rank was walking up out of the hole, stabbing happily at the air.

The front row were moving in a cloud of dust and screams. It is hard for a big army to do anything quickly, and divisions trying to move forward to see what the trouble was were getting in the way of fleeing individuals seeking a hole to hide in and permanent civilian status. Gongs were banging and men were trying to shout orders, but no one knew what the gongs were meant to mean or how the orders should be obeyed, because there didn't seem to be enough time.

Cohen finished rolling his cigarette, and struck a match on his chin.

'Right,' he said, to the world in general. 'Let's get that bloody Hong.'

The clouds overhead were less fearsome now. There was less lightning. But there were still a lot of them, greeny-black, heavy with rain.

'But this is *amazing*!' said Mr Saveloy.

A few drops hit the ground, leaving wide craters in the dirt.

'Yeah, right,' said Cohen.

'A most strange phenomenon! Warriors rising out of the ground!'

The craters joined up. It felt as though the drops were joining up as well. The rain began to pour down.

'Dunno,' said Cohen, watching a ragged platoon flee past. 'Never been here before. P'raps this happens a lot.'

'I mean, it's just like that myth about the man who sowed dragons' teeth and terrible fighting skeletons came up!'

'I don't believe *that*,' said Caleb, as they jogged after Cohen.

'Why not?'

'If you sow dragons' teeth, you should get dragons. Not fighting skeletons. What did it say on the packet?'

'I don't know! The myth never said anything about them coming in a packet!'

'Should've said "Comes up Dragons" on the packet.'

'You can't believe myths,' said Cohen. 'I should know. Right . . .
there he is . . .' he added, pointing to a distant horseman.

The whole plain was in turmoil now. The red warriors were only
the start. The alliance of the five warlords was glass fragile in any
case, and panicky flight was instantly interpreted as sneak attack.
No one paid any attention to the Horde. They didn't have any
coloured pennants or gongs. They weren't traditional enemies.
And, besides, the soil was now mud, and the mud flew, and everyone from the waist down was the same colour and this was rising.

'What're we doing, Ghenghiz?' said Mr Saveloy.

'We're heading back for the palace.'

'Why?'

''Cos that's where Hong's gone.'

'But there's this astonishing—'

'Look, Teach, I've seen walking trees and spider gods and big
green things with teeth,' said Cohen. 'It's no good goin' around
saying "astonishing" all the time, ain't that so, Truckle?'

'Right. D'you know, when I went after that Five-Headed Vampire
Goat over in Skund they said I shouldn't on account of it being an
endangered species? I said, yes, that was down to me. Were they
grateful?'

'Huh,' said Caleb. 'Should've thanked you, giving them all those
endangered species to worry about. Turn around and go home right
now, soldier boy!'

A group of soldiers, fighting to get away from the red warriors,
skidded in the mud, stared in terror at the Horde, and headed off in a
new direction.

Truckle stopped for breath, rain streaming off his beard.

'I can't be having with this running, though,' he said. 'Not and
push Hamish's wheelchair in all this mud. Let's have a breather.'

'Whut?'

'Stopping for a breather?' said Cohen. 'My gods! I never thought
I'd see the day! A *hero* having a rest? Did Voltan the Indestructible
have a bit of a rest?'

'He's having one now. He's dead, Ghenghiz,' said Caleb.

Cohen hesitated.

'What, old Voltan?'

'Didn't you know? And the Immortal Jenkins.'

'Jenkins isn't dead, I saw him only last year.'

'But he's dead now. All the heroes are dead, 'cept us. And I ain't
too sure about me, too.'

Cohen splashed forward and snatched Caleb upright by his shirt.

'What about Hrun? He can't be dead. He's half our age!'

'Last I heard he got a job. Sergeant of the Guard somewhere.'

'Sergeant of the *Guard*?' said Cohen. 'What, for *pay*?'

'Yep.'

'But . . . what, like, for *pay*?'

'He told me he might make Captain next year. He said . . . he said it's a job with a pension.'

Cohen released his grip.

'There's not many of us now, Cohen,' said Truckle.

Cohen spun around.

'All right, but there's never been many of us! And I ain't dyin'! Not if it means the world's taken over by bastards like Hong, who don't know what a chieftain is. Scum. That's what he called his soldiers. Scum. It's like that bloody civilized game you showed us, Teach!'

'Chess?'

'Right. The prawns are just there to be slaughtered by the other side! While the king just hangs around at the back.'

'Yeah, but the other side's *you*, Cohen.'

'Right! Right . . . well, *yes*, that's fine when I'm the *enemy*. But I don't shove men in front of me to get killed instead of me. And I never use bows and them dog things. When I kill someone it's up close and personal. Armies? Bloody tactics? There's only one way to fight, and that's everyone charging all at once, waving their swords and shouting! Now on your feet and let's get after him!'

'It's been a long morning, Ghenghiz,' said Boy Willie.

'Don't give me that!'

'I could do with the lavatory. It's all this rain.'

'Let's get Hong first.'

'If he's hiding in the privy that's fine by me.'

They reached the city gates. They had been shut. Hundreds of people, citizens as well as guards, watched them from the walls.

Cohen waved a finger at them.

'Now I ain't gonna say this twice,' he said. 'I'm coming in, okay? It can be the easy way, or it can be the hard way.'

Impassive faces looked down at the skinny old man, and up at the plain, where the armies of the warlords fought one another and, in terror, the terracotta warriors. Down. Up. Down. Up.

'Right,' said Cohen. 'Don't say afterwards I didn't *warn* youse.'

He raised his sword and prepared to charge.

'Wait,' said Mr Saveloy. 'Listen . . .'

There was shouting behind the walls, and some confused orders, and then more shouting. And then a couple of screams.

The gates swung open, pulled by dozens of citizens.

Cohen lowered his sword.

'Ah,' he said, 'they've seen reason, have they?'

Wheezing a little, the Horde limped through the gates. The crowd watched them in silence. Several guards lay dead. Rather more had removed their helmets and decided to opt for a bright new future in Civvy Street, where you were less likely to get beaten to death by an angry mob.

Every face watched Cohen, turning to follow him as flowers follow the sun.

He ignored them.

'Crowdie the Strong?' he said to Caleb.

'Dead.'

'Can't be. He was a picture of health when I saw him a coupla months ago. Going on a new quest and everything.'

'Dead.'

'What happened?'

'You know the Terrible Man-eating Sloth of Clup?'

'The one they say guards the giant ruby of the mad snake god?'

'The very same. Well . . . it was.'

The crowd parted to let the Horde through. One or two people tried a cheer, but were shushed into silence. It was a silence that Mr Saveloy had only heard before in the most devout of temples.[*]

There was a whispering, though, growing out of that watchful silence like bubbles in a pot of water on a hot fire.

It went like this.

The Red Army. The Red Army.

'How about Organdy Sloggo? Still going strong down in Howondaland, last I heard.'

'Dead. Metal poisoning.'

'How?'

'Three swords through the stomach.'

The Red Army!

'Slasher Mungo?'

'Presumed dead in Skund.'

---

[*] The only sound the Horde had ever heard in temples was people shouting 'Infidel! He has stolen the Jewelled Eye of – your wife is a big hippo!'

'Presumed?'

'Well, they only found his head.'

The Red Army!

The Horde approached the inner gates of the Forbidden City. The crowd followed them at a distance.

These gates were shut, too. A couple of heavy-set guards were standing in front of them. They wore the expressions of men who'd been told to guard the gates and were going to guard the gates come what may. The military depends on people who will guard gates or bridges or passes come what may and there are often heroic poems written in their honour, invariably posthumously.

'Gosbar the Wake?'

'Died in bed, I heard.'

'Not old Gosbar!'

'Everyone's got to sleep some time.'

'That's not the only thing they've got to do, mister,' said Boy Willie. 'I *really* need the wossname.'

'Well, there's the Wall.'

'Not with everyone watching! That ain't . . . civilized.'

Cohen strode up to the guards.

'I'm not mucking about,' he said. 'Okay? Would you rather die than betray your Emperor?'

The guards stared ahead.

'Right, fair enough.' Cohen drew his sword. A thought seemed to strike him.

'Nurker?' he said. 'Big Nurker? Tough as old boots, him.'

'Fishbone,' said Caleb.

'Nurker? He once killed six trolls with a—'

'Choked on a fishbone in his gruel. I thought you knew. Sorry.'

Cohen stared at him. And then at his sword. And then at the guards. For a moment there was silence, broken only by the sound of the rain.

'Y'know, lads,' he said, in a voice so suddenly full of weariness that Mr Saveloy felt a pit opening up, here, at the moment of triumph, 'I was goin' to chop your heads off. But . . . what's the point, eh? I mean, when you get right down to it, why bother? What sort of difference does it make?'

The guards still stared straight ahead. But their eyes were widening.

Mr Saveloy turned.

543

'You'll end up dead anyway, sooner or later,' Cohen went on. 'Well, that's about it. You live your life best way you can and then it don't actually matter, 'cos you're dead—'

'Er. Cohen?' said Mr Saveloy.

'I mean, look at me. Been chopping heads off my whole life and what've I got to show for it?'

'Cohen . . .'

The guards weren't just staring now. Their faces were dragging themselves into very creditable grimaces of fear.

'Cohen?'

'Yeah, what?'

'I think you should look round, Cohen.'

Cohen turned.

Half a dozen red warriors were advancing up the street. The crowd had pulled right back and were watching in silent terror.

Then a voice shouted: 'Extended Duration To The Red Army!'

Cries rose up here and there in the crowd. A young woman raised her hand in a clenched fist.

'Advance Necessarily With The People While Retaining Due Regard For Traditions!'

Others joined her.

'Deserved Correction To Enemies!'

'I've lost Mr Bunny!'

The red giants clonked to a halt.

'Look at them!' said Mr Saveloy. 'They're not trolls! They move like some kind of engine! Doesn't that interest you?'

'No,' said Cohen, vacantly. 'Abstract thinking is not a major aspect of the barbarian mental process. Now then, where was I?' He sighed. 'Oh, yes. You two . . . you'd rather die than betray your Emperor, would you?'

The two men were rigid with fear now.

Cohen raised his sword.

Mr Saveloy took a deep breath, grabbed Cohen's sword arm and shouted:

'Then open the gates and let him through!'

There was a moment of utter silence.

Mr Saveloy nudged Cohen.

'Go on,' he hissed. 'Act like an Emperor!'

'What . . . you mean giggle, have people tortured, that sort of thing? Blow that!'

'No! Act like an Emperor ought to act!'

Cohen glared at Saveloy. Then he turned to the guards.

'Well done,' he said. 'Your loyalty does you . . . wossname . . . credit. Keep on like this and I can see it's promotion for both of you. Now let us all go inside or I will have my flowerpot men chop off your feet so you'll have to kneel in the gutter while you're looking for your head.'

The men looked at one another, threw down their swords and tried to kowtow.

'And you can bloody well get up, too,' said Cohen, in a slightly nicer tone of voice. 'Mr Saveloy?'

'Yes?'

'I'm Emperor now, am I?'

'The . . . earth soldiers seem to be on our side. The *people* think you've won. We're all alive. I'd say we've won, yes.'

'If I'm Emperor, I can tell everyone what to do, right?'

'Oh, indeed.'

'Properly. You know. Scrolls and stuff. Buggers in uniform blowing trumpets and saying, "This is what he wants you to do."'

'Ah. You want to make a proclamation.'

'Yeah. No more of this bloody kowtowing. It makes me squirm. No kowtowing by anyone to anyone, all right? If anyone sees me they can salute, or maybe give me some money. But none of this banging your head on the ground stuff. It gives me the willies. Now, dress that up in proper writing.'

'Right away. And—'

'Hang on, haven't finished yet.' Cohen bit his lip in unaccustomed cogitation, as the red warriors lurched to a stop. 'Yeah. You can add that I'm letting all prisoners go free, unless they've done something really bad. Like attempted poisoning, for a start. You can work out the details. All torturers to have their heads cut off. And every peasant can have a free pig, something like that. I'll leave you to put in all the proper curly bits about "by order" and stuff.'

Cohen looked down at the guards.

'Get *up*, I said. I swear, the next bastard that kisses the ground in front of me is gonna get kicked in the antique chicken coops. Okay? Now open the gates.'

The crowd cheered. As the Horde stepped inside the Forbidden City they followed, in a sort of cross between a revolutionary charge and a respectful walk.

The red warriors stood outside. One of them raised a terracotta foot, which groaned a little, and walked towards the Wall until it bumped into it.

The warrior staggered drunkenly for a while and then managed to get within a yard or two of the Wall without colliding with it.

It raised a finger and wrote, shakily, in red dust that turned to a kind of paint on the wet plaster:

HELP HELP ITS ME IM OUT HERE ON THEE PLAIN
HELP I CANT GET THIS BLODY ARMER OFF.

The crowd surged along behind Cohen, shouting and singing. If he'd had a surfboard, he could have ridden on it. The rain drummed heavily on the roof and poured into the courtyards.

'Why're they all so excited?' he said.

'They think you're going to sack the palace,' said Mr Saveloy. 'They've heard about barbarians, you see. They want some of it. Anyway, they like the idea about the pig.'

'Hey, you!' shouted Cohen to a boy struggling past under the weight of a huge vase. 'Get your thieving paws off my stuff! That's valuable, that is! It's a . . . a . . .'

'It's S'ang Dynasty,' said Mr Saveloy.

'That's right,' said the vase.

'That's a S'ang Dynasty, that is! Put it back! And you lot back there—' He turned and waved his sword. 'Get those shoes off! You're scratching the floor! Look at the state of it already!'

'You never bothered about the floor yesterday,' Truckle grumbled.

''Tweren't my floor then.'

'Yes, it was,' said Mr Saveloy.

'Not properly,' said Cohen. '*Rite* of conquest, that's the thing. Blood. People understand blood. You just walk in and take over and no one takes it seriously. But seas of blood . . . Everyone understands that.'

'Mountains of skulls,' said Truckle approvingly.

'Look at history,' said Cohen. 'Whenever you— Hey, you, the man with the hat, that's my . . .'

'Inlaid mahogany *Shibo Yangcong-san* table,' murmured Mr Saveloy.

'—so put it back, d'you hear? Yes, whenever you comes across a king where everyone says, "Oo, he was a good king all right," you can bet your sandals he was a great big bearded bastard who broke heads a lot and laughed about it. Hey? But some king who just passed decent little laws and read books and tried to look intelligent . . . "Oh," they say, "oh, he was all right, a bit wet, not what I'd call a proper king." That's people for you.'

Mr Saveloy sighed.

Cohen grinned at him and slapped him on the back so hard he stumbled into two women trying to carry off a bronze statue of Ly Tin Wheedle.

'Can't quite face it, Teach, can you? Can't get your mind round it? Don't worry about it. Basically, you ain't a barbarian. *Put the damn statue back, missus, or you'll feel the flat of my sword, so you will!*'

'But I thought we could do it without anyone getting hurt. By using our brains.'

'Can't. History don't work like that. Blood first, then brains.'

'Mountains of skulls,' said Truckle.

'There's got to be a better way than fighting,' said Mr Saveloy.

'Yep. Lots of 'em. Only none of 'em work. Caleb, take those . . . those . . .'

'—fine Bhong jade miniatures—' muttered Mr Saveloy.

'—take them off that feller. He's got one under his hat.'

Another set of carved doors was swung open. This room was already crowded, but the people shuffled backwards as the doors parted and tried to look keen while avoiding catching Cohen's eye.

As they pulled away they left Six Beneficent Winds standing all alone. The court had become very good at this manoeuvre.

'Mountains of skulls,' said Truckle, not a man to let go in a hurry.

'Er. We saw the Red Army rise out of the ground, er, just as the legend foretold. Er. Truly you are the preincarnation of One Sun Mirror.'

The little taxman had the decency to look embarrassed. As speeches went it was on a dramatic level with the one that traditionally began, 'As you know, your father – the king—' Besides, he'd never believed in legends up to now – not even the one about the peasant who every year filed a scrupulously honest tax return.

'Yeah, right,' said Cohen.

He strode to the throne and stuck his sword in the floor, where it vibrated.

'Some of you are going to get your heads cut off for your own good,' he said. 'But I haven't decided who yet. And someone show Boy Willie where the privy is.'

'No need,' said Boy Willie. 'Not after them big red statues turned up behind me so sudden.'

'Mountains of—' Truckle began.

'Dunno about mountains,' said Cohen.

'And where,' said Six Beneficent Winds tremulously, 'is the Great Wizard?'

'Great Wizard,' said Cohen.

'Yes, the Great Wizard who summoned the Red Army from the earth,' said the taxman.

'Don't know anything about *him*,' said Cohen.

The crowd staggered forward as more people piled into the room.

'They're coming!'

A terracotta warrior clomped its way into the room, its face still wearing a very faint smile.

It stopped, rocking a little, while water dripped off it.

People had crouched back in terror. Except the Horde, Mr Saveloy noticed. Faced with unknown yet terrible dangers, the Horde were either angry or puzzled.

Then he cheered up. They weren't better, just different. They're all right facing huge terrible creatures, he told himself, but ask them to go down the street and buy a bag of rice and they go all to pieces . . .

'What's my move now, Teach?' Cohen whispered.

'Well, you're Emperor,' said Mr Saveloy. 'I think you talk to it.'

'Okay.'

Cohen stood up and nodded cheerfully at the terracotta giant.

''Morning,' he said. 'Nice bit of work out there. You and the rest of your lads can have the day off to plant geraniums in yourselves or whatever you do. Er. You got a Number One giant I ought to speak to?'

The terracotta warrior creaked as it raised one finger.

Then it pressed two fingers against one forearm, then raised a finger again.

Everyone in the crowd started talking at once.

The giant tugged one vestigial ear with two fingers.

'What can this mean?' said Six Beneficent Winds.

'I find this a little hard to credit,' said Mr Saveloy, 'but it is an ancient method of communication used in the land of blood-sucking vampire ghosts.'

'You can understand it?'

'Oh, yes. I think so. You have to try to guess the word or phrase. It's trying to tell us . . . er . . . one word, two syllables. First syllable sounds like . . .'

The giant cupped one hand and made circular, handle-turning motions with the other alongside it.

'Turning,' said Mr Saveloy. 'Winding? Reeling? Revolve? Grind? Grind? Chop? Mince—'

The giant tapped its nose hurriedly and did a very heavy, noisy dance, bits of terracotta armour clanking.

'Sounds like mince,' said Mr Saveloy. 'First syllable sounds like mince.'

'Er . . .'

A ragged figure pushed its way through the crowd. It wore glasses, one lens of which was cracked.

'Er,' it said, 'I've got an idea about that . . .'

Lord Fang and some of his more trusted warriors had clustered on the side of the hills. A good general always knows when to leave the battlefield, and as far as Lord Fang was concerned, it was when he saw the enemy coming towards him.

The men were shaken. They hadn't tried to face the Red Army. Those who had were dead.

'We . . . regroup,' panted Lord Fang. 'And then we'll wait until nightfall and— What's that?'

There was a rhythmic noise coming from the bushes further up the slope, where sliding earth had left another bush-filled ravine.

'Sounds like a carpenter, m'lord,' said one of the soldiers.

'Up here? In the middle of a war? Go and see what it is!'

The man scrambled away. After a while there was a pause in the sawing noise. Then it started again.

Lord Fang had been trying to work out a fresh battle plan according to the Nine Useful Principles. He threw down his map.

'Why is that still going on? Where is Captain Nong?'

'Hasn't come back, m'lord.'

'Then go and see what has happened to him!'

Lord Fang tried to remember if the great military sage had ever had anything to say about fighting giant invulnerable statues. He—

The sawing paused. Then it was replaced by the sound of hammering.

Lord Fang looked around.

'Can I have an order obeyed around here?' he bellowed.

He picked up his sword and scrambled up the muddy slope. The

549

bushes parted ahead of him. There was a clearing. There was a rushing shape, on hundreds of little le—

There was a snap.

The rain was coming down so fast that the drops were having to queue.

The red earth was hundreds of feet deep in places. It produced two or three crops a year. It was rich. It was fecund. It was, when wet, extremely sticky.

The surviving armies had squelched from the field of battle, as red from head to toe as the terracotta men. Not counting those merely trodden on, the Red Army had not in fact killed very many people. Terror had done most of *their* work. Rather more soldiers had been killed in the brief inter-army battles and, in the scramble to escape, by their own sides.[*]

The terracotta army had the field to itself. It was celebrating victory in various ways. Many guards were walking around in circles, wading through the clinging mud as if it was so much dirty air. A number were digging a trench, the sides of which were washing in on them in the thundering rain. A few were trying to climb walls that weren't there. Several, possibly as a result of the exertion following centuries of zero maintenance, had spontaneously exploded in a shower of blue sparks, the red-hot clay shrapnel being a major factor in the opposition's death count.

And all the time the rain fell, a solid curtain of water. It didn't look natural. It was as though the sea had decided to reclaim the land by air drop.

Rincewind shut his eyes. Mud covered the armour. He couldn't make out the pictures any more, and that was something of a relief because he was pretty certain he was messing things up. You could see what any warrior was seeing – at least, presumably you could, if you knew what some of the odder pictures actually did and how to press them in the right order. Rincewind didn't, and in any case whoever had made the magic armour hadn't assumed it would be used in knee-deep mud during a vertical river. Every now and again it sizzled. One of the boots was getting hot.

It had started out so well! But there had been what he was coming to think of as the Rincewind factor. Probably some other wizard would have marched the army out and wouldn't have been rained

[*] 'Friendly stab', as it is formally known.

550

on and even now would be parading through the streets of Hunghung while people threw flowers and said, 'My word, there's a Great Wizard and no mistake.'

Some *other* wizard wouldn't have pressed the wrong picture and started the things digging.

He realized he was wallowing in self-pity. Rather more pertinently, he was also wallowing in mud. And he was sinking. Trying to pull a foot out was no use – it didn't work, and the other foot only went deeper, and got hotter.

Lightning struck the ground nearby. He heard it sizzle, saw the steam, felt the tingle of electricity and tasted the taste of burning tin.

Another bolt hit a warrior. Its torso exploded, raining a sticky black tar. The legs kept going for a few steps, and then stopped.

Water poured past him, thick and red now that the river Hung was overflowing. And the mud continued to suck on his feet like a hollow tooth.

Something swirled past on the muddy water. It looked like a scrap of paper.

Rincewind hesitated, then reached out awkwardly with a gloved hand and scooped it up.

It was, as he'd expected, a butterfly.

'Thank you very much,' he said, bitterly.

The water drained through his fingers.

He half closed his hand and then sighed and, as gently as he could, manoeuvred the creature on to a finger. Its wings hung damply.

He shielded it with his other hand and blew on the wings a few times.

'Go on, push off.'

The butterfly turned. Its multi-faceted eyes glinted green for a moment and then it flapped its wings experimentally.

It stopped raining.

It started to snow, but only where Rincewind was.

'Oh, yes,' said Rincewind. 'Yes indeed. Oh, thank you so very much.'

Life was, he had heard, like a bird which flies out of the darkness and across a crowded hall and then through another window into the endless night again. In Rincewind's case it had managed to do something incontinent in his dinner.

The snow stopped. The clouds pulled back from the dome of the sky with astonishing speed, letting in hot sunlight which almost immediately made the mud steam.

'There you are! We've been looking everywhere!'

Rincewind tried to turn, but the mud made that impossible. There was a wooden thump, as of a plank being laid down on wet ooze.

'Snow on his head? In bright sunshine? I said to myself, that's him all right.'

There was the thump of another plank.

A small avalanche slid off the helmet and slid down Rincewind's neck.

Another thump, and a plank squelched into the mud beside him.

'It's me, Twoflower. Are you all right, old friend?'

'I think my foot is being cooked, but apart from that I'm as happy as anything.'

'I knew it would be you doing the charades,' said Twoflower, sticking his hands under the wizard's shoulders and hauling.

'You got the "Wind" syllable?' said Rincewind. 'That was very hard to do, by remote control.'

'Oh, none of us got that,' said Twoflower, 'but when it did "ohshitohshitohshit I'm going to die" everyone got *that* first go. Very inventive. Er. You seem to be stuck.'

'I think it's the magic boots.'

'Can't you wiggle them off? This mud dries like – well, like terracotta in the sun. Someone can come along and dig them out afterwards.'

Rincewind tried to move his feet. There was some sub-mud bubblings and lie felt his feet come free, with a muffled slurping noise.

Finally, with considerable effort, he was sitting on the plank.

'Sorry about the warriors,' he said. 'It looked so simple when I started out, and then I got confused with all the pictures and it was impossible to stop some of them doing things—'

'But it was a famous victory!' said Twoflower.

'Was it?'

'Mr Cohen's been made Emperor!'

'He has?'

'Well, not made, no one made him, he just came along and took it. And everyone says he's the preincarnation of the first Emperor and he says if you want to be the Great Wizard that's fine by him.'

'Sorry? You lost me there . . .'

'You led the Red Army, didn't you? You made them rise up in the Empire's hour of need?'

'Well, I wouldn't exactly say that I—'

'So the Emperor wants to reward you. Isn't that nice?'

'How do you mean, reward?' said Rincewind, with deep suspicion.

'Not sure, really. Actually, what he said was . . .' Twoflower's eyes glazed as he tried to recall. 'He said, "You go and find Rincewind and say he might be a bit of a pillock but at least he's straight so he can be Chief Wizard of the Empire or whatever he wants to call it, 'cos I don't trust you foreign . . ."' Twoflower squinted upwards as he tried to remember Cohen's precise words '" . . . house of auspicious aspect . . . scent of pine trees . . . buggers."'

The words trickled into Rincewind's ear, slid up into his brain, and started to bang on the walls.

'Chief Wizard?' he said.

'That's what he said. Well . . . actually what he said was he wanted you to be a blob of swallow's vomit, but that was because he used the low sad tone rather than the high questioning one. He definitely *meant* wizard.'

'Of the whole Empire?'

Rincewind stood up.

'Something very bad is about to happen,' he said flatly.

The sky was quite blue now. A few citizens had ventured on to the battlefield to tend the wounded and retrieve the dead. Terracotta warriors stood at various angles, motionless as rocks.

'Any minute now,' said Rincewind.

'Shouldn't we get back?'

'Probably a meteorite strike,' said Rincewind.

Twoflower looked up at the peaceful sky.

'You know me,' said Rincewind. 'Just when I'm getting a grip on something Fate comes along and jumps on my fingers.'

'I don't *see* any meteorites,' said Twoflower. 'How long do we wait?'

'It'll be something else, then,' said Rincewind. 'Someone will come leaping out, or there'll be an earthquake, or *something*.'

'If you insist,' said Twoflower, politely. 'Um. Do you want to wait for something horrible here or would you like to go back to the palace and have a bath and change your clothes and then see what happens?'

Rincewind conceded that he might as well await a dreadful fate in comfort.

'There's going to be a feast,' said Twoflower. 'The Emperor says he's going to teach everyone how to quaff.'

They made their way, plank by plank, back towards the city.

'You know, I swear you never told me that you were married.'

'I'm sure I did.'

'I was, er, I was sorry to hear that your wife, er—'

'Things happen in war. I have two dutiful daughters.'

Rincewind opened his mouth to say something but Twoflower's bright, brittle smile froze the words in his throat.

They worked without speaking, picking up the planks behind them and extending the walkway in front.

'Looking on the bright side,' said Twoflower, breaking the silence, 'the Emperor said you could start your own University, if you wanted.'

'No! No! Someone hit me with an iron bar, please!'

'He said he's well in favour of education provided no one makes him have one. He's been making proclamations like mad. The eunuchs have threatened to go on strike.'

Rincewind's plank dropped on to the mud.

'What is it that eunuchs do,' he said, 'that they stop doing when they go on strike?'

'Serve food, make the beds, things like that.'

'Oh.'

'They run the Forbidden City, really. But the Emperor talked them round to his point of view.'

'Really?'

'He said if they didn't get cracking right now he'd cut off everything else. Um, I think the ground's firm enough now.'

His own University. That'd make him . . . Archchancellor. Rincewind the Archchancellor pictured himself visiting Unseen University. He could have a hat with a really big point. He'd be able to be rude to everyone. He'd—

He tried to stop himself from thinking like that. It'd all go wrong.

'Of course,' said Twoflower, 'it might be that the bad things have already happened to you. Have you considered that? Perhaps you're due something nice?'

'Don't give me any of that karma stuff,' said Rincewind. 'The wheel of fortune has lost a few spokes where I'm concerned.'

'It's worth considering, though,' said Twoflower.

'What, that the rest of my life will be peaceful and enjoyable? Sorry. No. You wait. When my back's turned and – bang!'

Twoflower looked around with some interest.

'I don't know why you think your life has been so bad,' he said. 'We had a lot of fun when we were younger. Hey, do you remember the time when we went over the edge of the world?'

'Often,' said Rincewind. 'Usually around 3 a.m.'

'And that time we were on a dragon and it disappeared in mid-air?'

'You know,' said Rincewind, 'sometimes a whole hour will go by when I *don't* remember that.'

'And that time we were attacked by those people who wanted to kill us?'

'Which of those one hundred and forty-nine occasions are you referring to?'

'Character building, that sort of thing,' said Twoflower, happily. 'Made me what I am today.'

'Oh, yes,' said Rincewind. It was no effort, talking to Twoflower. The little man's trusting nature had no concept of sarcasm and a keen ability not to hear things that might upset him. 'Yes, I can definitely say it was that sort of thing that made me what I am today, too.'

They stepped inside the city. The streets were practically empty. Most people had flocked to the huge square in front of the palace. New Emperors tended towards displays of generosity. Besides, the news had got around that this one was different and was giving away free pigs.

'I heard him talking about sending envoys to Ankh-Morpork,' said Twoflower, as they dripped up the street. 'I expect there's going to be a bit of a fuss about that.'

'Was that man Disembowel-Meself-Honourably present at the time?' said Rincewind.

'Yes, as a matter of fact.'

'When you visited Ankh-Morpork, did you ever meet a man called Dibbler?'

'Oh, yes.'

'If those two ever shake hands I think there might be some sort of explosion.'

'But you could go back, I'm sure,' said Twoflower. 'I mean, your new University will need all sorts of things and, well, I seem to recall that people in Ankh-Morpork were very keen on gold.'

Rincewind gritted his teeth. The image wouldn't go away – of Archchancellor Rincewind buying the Tower of Art and getting them to number all the stones and send it back to Hunghung, of

Archchancellor Rincewind hiring all the faculty as college porters, of Archchancellor Rincewi . . .

'No!'

'Pardon?'

'Don't encourage me to think like that! The moment I think that it's all going to be worthwhile something dreadful will happen!'

There was a movement behind him, and a knife suddenly pressed against his throat.

'The Great Blob of Swallow's Vomit?' said a voice by his ear.

'There,' said Rincewind. 'You see? Run away! Don't stand there, you bloody idiot! *Run!*'

Twoflower stared for a moment and then turned and scampered away.

'Let him go,' said the voice. 'He doesn't matter.'

Hands pulled him into the alley. He had a vague impression of armour, and mud; his captors were skilled in the way of dragging a prisoner so that he had no chance to get a foothold anywhere.

Then he was flung on to the cobbles.

'He does not look so great to me,' said an imperious voice. 'Look up, Great Wizard!'

There was some nervous laughter from the soldiers.

'You fools!' raged Lord Hong. 'He is just a man! Look at him! Does he look so powerful? He is just a man who has found some old trickery! And we will find out how great he is without his arms and legs.'

'Oh,' said Rincewind.

Lord Hong leaned down. There was mud on his face and a wild glint in his eyes. 'We shall see what your barbarian Emperor can do *then*, won't we?' He indicated the sullen group of mud-encrusted soldiers. 'You know, they half believe you really *are* a great wizard? That's superstition, I'm afraid. Very useful most of the time, damn inconvenient on occasion. But when we march you into the square and show them how great you really are, I think your barbarian will not have so very long left. What are these?'

He snatched the gloves off Rincewind's hands.

'Toys,' he said. 'Made things. The Red Army are just machines, like mills and pumps. There's no magic there.'

He tossed them aside and nodded at one of the guards.

'And now,' said Lord Hong, 'let us go to the Imperial Square.'

*

'How'd you like to be governor of Bhangbhangduc and all these islands around here?' said Cohen, as the Horde pored over a map of the Empire. 'You like the seaside, Hamish?'

'Whut?'

The doors of the Throne Room were flung open. Twoflower scuttled in, trailed by One Big River.

'Lord Hong's got Rincewind! He's going to kill him!'

Cohen looked up.

'He can wizard himself out of it, can't he?'

'No! He hasn't got the Red Army any more! He's going to *kill* him! You've got to *do* something!'

'Ach, well, you know how it is with wizards,' said Truckle. 'There's too many of 'em as it is—'

'No.' Cohen picked up his sword and sighed.

'Come on,' he said.

'But, Cohen—'

'I said *come on*. We ain't like Hong. Rincewind's a weasel, but he's *our* weasel. So are you coming or what?'

Lord Hong and his group of soldiers had almost reached the bottom of the wide steps to the palace when the Horde emerged. The crowd surrounded them, held back by the soldiers.

Lord Hong held Rincewind tightly, a knife at his throat.

'Ah, Emperor,' he said, in Ankh-Morporkian. 'We meet again. Check, I think.'

'What's he mean?' Cohen whispered.

'He thinks he has you cornered,' said Mr Saveloy.

'How's he know I won't just let the wizard die?'

'Psychology of the individual, I'm afraid.'

'It doesn't make any sense!' Cohen shouted. 'If you kill him, you'll be dead yourself in seconds. I shall see to it pers'nally!'

'Indeed, no,' said Lord Hong. 'When your . . . Great Wizard . . . is dead, when people see how easily he dies . . . how long will you be Emperor? You won by trickery!'

'What are your terms?' said Mr Saveloy.

'There are none. You can give me nothing I cannot take myself.' Lord Hong grabbed Rincewind's hat from one of the guards and rammed it on to Rincewind's head.

'This is yours,' he hissed. ' "Wizzard" hah! You can't even spell! Well, *wizzard*? Aren't you going to say something?'

'Oh, no!'

557

Lord Hong smiled. 'Ah, that's better,' he said.

'Oh, noooooo!'

'Very good!'

'Aarrgh!'

Lord Hong blinked. For a moment the figure in front of him appeared to stretch to twice its height and then have its feet snap up under its chin.

And then it disappeared, with a small thunderclap.

There was silence in the square, except for the sound of several thousand people being astonished.

Lord Hong waved his hand vaguely in the air.

'Lord Hong?'

He turned. There was a short man behind him, covered in grime and mud. He wore a pair of spectacles, one lens of which was cracked.

Lord Hong hardly glanced at him. He prodded the air again, unwilling to believe his own senses.

'Excuse me, Lord Hong,' said the apparition, 'but do you by any chance remember Bes Pelargic? About six years ago? I think you were quarrelling with Lord Tang? There was something of a skirmish. A few streets destroyed. Nothing very major.'

Lord Hong blinked.

'How dare you address me!' he managed.

'It doesn't really matter,' said Twoflower. 'But it's just that I'd have liked you to have remembered. I got . . . quite angry about it. Er. I want to fight you.'

'*You* want to fight *me*? Do you know who you are talking to? Have you any *idea*?'

'Er. Yes. Oh, yes,' said Twoflower.

Lord Hong's attention finally focused. It had not been a good day.

'You foolish, stupid little man! You don't even have a sword!'

'Oi! Four-eyes!'

They both turned. Cohen threw his sword. Twoflower caught it clumsily and was almost knocked over by the weight.

'Why did you do that?' said Mr Saveloy.

'Man wants to be a hero. That's fine by me,' said Cohen.

'He'll be slaughtered!'

'Might do. Might do. Might do. He might do that, certainly,' Cohen conceded. 'That's not up to me.'

'Father!'

Lotus Blossom grabbed Twoflower's arm.

'He *will* kill you! Come away!'

'No.'

Butterfly took her father's other arm.

'No good purpose will be served,' she said. 'Come on. We can find a better time—'

'He killed your mother,' said Twoflower flatly.

'His soldiers did.'

'That makes it worse. He didn't even know. Please get back, both of you.'

'Look, Father—'

'If you don't both do what you're told I shall get angry.'

Lord Hong drew his long sword. The blade gleamed.

'Do you know *anything* about fighting, clerk?'

'No, not really,' said Twoflower. 'But the important thing is that someone should stand up to you. Whatever happens to them afterwards.'

The Horde were watching with considerable interest. Hardened as they were, they had a soft spot for pointless bravery.

'Yes,' said Lord Hong, looking around at the silent crowd. 'Let *everyone* see what happens.'

He raised his sword.

The air crackled.

The Barking Dog dropped on to the flagstones in front of him.

It was very hot. Its string was alight.

There was a brief sizzle.

Then the world went white.

After some time, Twoflower picked himself up. He seemed to be the first one upright; those people who hadn't flung themselves to the ground had fled.

All that remained of Lord Hong was one shoe, which was smouldering. But there was a smoking trail all the way up the steps behind it.

Staggering a little, Twoflower followed the trail.

A wheelchair was on its side, one wheel spinning.

He peered over it.

'You all right, Mr Hamish?'

'Whut?'

'Good.'

The rest of the Horde were crouched in a circle at the top of the steps. Smoke billowed around them. In its continuing passage, the ball had set fire to part of the palace.

'Can you hear me, Teach?' Cohen was saying.

''Course he can't hear you! How can he hear you, looking like that?' said Truckle.

'He could still be alive,' said Cohen defiantly.

'He is *dead*, Cohen. Really, really *dead*. Alive people have more *body*.'

'But you're all alive?' said Twoflower. 'I saw it bark straight at you!'

'We got out of the way,' said Boy Willie. 'We're good at getting out of the way.'

'Poor ole Teach didn't have our experience of not dyin',' said Caleb. Cohen stood up.

'Where's Hong?' he said grimly. 'I'm going to—'

'He's dead too, Mr Cohen,' said Twoflower.

Cohen nodded, as if this was all perfectly normal.

'We owe it to ole Teach,' he said.

'He was a good sort,' Truckle conceded. 'Funny ideas about swearing, mind you.'

'He had brains. He cared about stuff! And he might not have lived like a barbarian, but he's bloody well going to be buried like one, all right?'

'In a longship, set on fire,' suggested Boy Willie.

'My word,' said Mr Saveloy.

'In a big pit, on top of the bodies of his enemies,' suggested Caleb.

'Good heavens, all of 4B?' said Mr Saveloy.

'In a burial mound,' suggested Vincent.

'Really, I wouldn't put you to the trouble,' said Mr Saveloy.

'*In* a longship set on fire, *on top* of a heap of the bodies of his enemies, *under* a burial mound,' said Cohen flatly. 'Nothing's too good for ole Teach.'

'But I assure you, I feel fine,' said Mr Saveloy. 'Really, I—er . . . Oh . . .'

RONALD SAVELOY?

Mr Saveloy turned.

'Ah,' he said. 'Yes. I see.'

IF YOU WOULD CARE TO STEP THIS WAY?

The palace and the Horde froze and faded gently, like a dream.

'It's funny,' said Mr Saveloy, as he followed Death. 'I didn't expect it to be this way.'

FEW PEOPLE EVER EXPECT IT TO BE ANY WAY.

Gritty black sand crunched under what Mr Saveloy supposed he should still call his feet.

'Where is this?'

THE DESERT.

It was brilliantly lit, and yet the sky was midnight-black. He stared at the horizon.

'How big is it?'

FOR SOME, VERY BIG. FOR LORD HONG, FOR INSTANCE, IT CONTAINS A LOT OF IMPATIENT GHOSTS.

'I thought Lord Hong didn't believe in ghosts.'

HE MAY DO SO NOW. A LOT OF GHOSTS BELIEVE IN LORD HONG.

'Oh. Er. What happens now?'

'Come on, come on, haven't got all day! Step lively, man!'

Mr Saveloy turned around and looked up at the woman on the horse. It was a big horse but, then, it was a big woman. She had plaits, a hat with horns on it, and a breastplate that must have been a week's work for an experienced panelbeater. She gave him a look that was not unkind but had impatience in every line.

'I'm sorry?' he said.

'Says here Ronald Saveloy,' she said. 'The what?'

'The what?'

'Everyone I pick up,' said the woman, leaning down, 'is called "Someone *the* Something". What *the* are you?'

'I'm sorry, I—'

'I'll put you down as Ronald the Apologetic, then. Come on, hop up, there's a war on, got to be going.'

'Where to?'

'Says here quaffing, carousing, throwing axes at young women's hair?'

'Ah, er, I think perhaps there's been a bit of a—'

'Look, old chap, are you coming or what?'

Mr Saveloy looked around at the black desert. He was totally alone. Death had gone about his essential business.

He let her pull him up behind her.

'Have they got a library, perhaps?' he asked hopefully, as the horse rose into the dark sky.

'Don't know. No one's ever asked.'

'Evening classes, perhaps. I could start evening classes?'

'What in?'

'Um. Anything, really. Table manners, perhaps. Is that allowed?'

'I suppose so. I don't think anyone's ever asked that, either.' The Valkyrie turned in the saddle.

'You *sure* you're coming to the right afterlife?'

561

Mr Saveloy considered the possibilities.

'On the whole,' he said, 'I think it's worth a try.'

The crowd in the square were getting to their feet.

They looked at all that remained of Lord Hong, and at the Horde.

Butterfly and Lotus Blossom joined their father. Butterfly ran her hand over the cannon, looking for the trick.

'You see,' said Twoflower, a little indistinctly because he couldn't quite hear the sound of his own voice yet, 'I *told* you he was the Great Wizard.'

Butterfly tapped him on the shoulder.

'What about those?' she said.

A small procession was picking its way through the square. In front, Twoflower recognized, was something he'd once owned.

'It was a very cheap one,' he said, to no one in particular. 'I always thought there was something a little warped about it, to tell you the truth.'

It was followed by a slightly larger Luggage. And then, in descending order of size, four little chests, the smallest being about the size of a lady's handbag. As it passed a prone Hunghungese who'd been too stunned to flee, it paused to kick him in the ear before hurrying after the others.

Twoflower looked at his daughters.

'Can they do that?' he said. 'Make new ones? I thought it needed carpenters.'

'I suppose it learned many things in Ankh-More-Pork,' said Butterfly.

The Luggages clustered together in front of the steps. Then *the* Luggage turned around and, after one or two sad backward glances, or what might have been glances if it had eyes, cantered away. By the time it reached the far side of the square it was a blur.

'Hey, you! Four-eyes!'

Twoflower turned. Cohen was advancing down the steps.

'I remember you,' he said. 'D'you know anything about Grand Viziering?'

'Not a thing, Mr Emperor Cohen.'

'Good. The job's yours. Get cracking. First thing, I want a cup of tea. Thick enough to float a horseshoe. Three sugars. In five minutes. Right?'

'A cup of tea in *five minutes*?' said Twoflower. 'But that's not long enough for even a short ceremony!'

Cohen put a companionable arm around the little man's shoulders.

'There's a *new* ceremony,' he said. 'It goes: "Tea up, luv. Milk? Sugar? Doughnut? Want another one?" And you could tell the eunuchs,' he added, 'that the Emperor is a lit'ral-minded man and used the phrase "heads will roll".'

Twoflower's eyes gleamed behind his cracked glasses. Somehow, he liked the sound of that.

It looked as though he was living in interesting times—

The Luggages sat quietly, and waited.

Fate sat back.

The gods relaxed.

'A draw,' he announced. 'Oh, yes. You have appeared to win in Hunghung *but* you have had to lose your most valuable piece, is that not so?'

'I'm sorry?' said the Lady. 'I don't quite follow you.'

'Insofar as I understand this . . . physics . . .' said Fate, 'I cannot believe that anything could be materialised in the University without dying almost instantly. It is one thing to hit a snowdrift, but quite another to hit a wall.'

'I never sacrifice a pawn,' said the Lady.

'How can you hope to win without sacrificing the occasional pawn?'

'Oh, I never play to win.' She smiled. 'But I do play not to lose. Watch . . .'

The Council of Wizards gathered in front of the wall at the far end of the Great Hall and stared up at the thing which now covered half of it.

'Interesting effect,' said Ridcully, eventually. 'How fast do you think it was going?'

'About five hundred miles an hour,' said Ponder. 'I think perhaps we were a little enthusiastic. Hex says—'

'From a standing start to five hundred miles an hour?' said the Lecturer in Recent Runes. 'That must have come as a shock.'

'Yes,' said Ridcully, 'but I suppose it's a mercy for the poor creature that it was such a brief one.'

'And, of course, we must all be thankful that it wasn't Rincewind.'

A couple of the wizards coughed.

The Dean stood back.

'But what *is* it?' he said.

'Was,' said Ponder Stibbons.

'We could have a look in the Bestiaries,' said Ridcully. 'Shouldn't be hard to find. Grey. Long hind feet like a clown's boots. Rabbit ears. Tail long and pointy. And, of course, not many creatures are twenty feet across, one inch thick and deep fried, so that narrows it down a bit.'

'I don't want to cast a shadow on things,' said the Dean, 'but if this isn't Rincewind, then where is he?'

'I'm sure Mr Stibbons can give us an explanation as to why his calculations went wrong,' said Ridcully.

Ponder's mouth dropped open.

Then he said, as sourly as he dared, 'I probably forgot to take into account that there's three right angles in a triangle, didn't I? Er. I'll have to try and work everything back, but I think that somehow a lateral component was introduced into what should have been a bidirectional sortilegic transfer. It's probably that this was most pronounced at the effective median point, causing an extra node to appear in the transfers at a point equidistant to the other two as prediction in Flume's Third Equation, and Turffe's Law would see to it that the distortion would stabilise in such a way as to create three separate points, each moving a roughly equal mass one jump around the triangle. I'm not sure why the third mass arrived here at such speed, but I think the increased velocity might have been caused by the sudden creation of the node. Of course, it might have been going quite fast anyway. But I shouldn't think it is cooked in its natural state.'

'Do you know,' said Ridcully, 'I think I actually understood some of that? Certainly some of the shorter words.'

'Oh, it's perfectly simple,' said the Bursar brightly. 'We sent the . . . dog thing to Hunghung. Rincewind was sent to some other place. And this creature was sent here. Just like Pass the Parcel.'

'You see?' said Ridcully to Stibbons. 'You're using language the *Bursar* can understand. And *he's* been chasing the dried frog all morning.'

The Librarian staggered into the hall under the weight of a large atlas.

'Oook.'

'At least you can show us where you think our man is,' said Ridcully.

Ponder took a ruler and a pair of compasses out of his hat.

'Well, if we assume Rincewind was in the middle of the Counterweight Continent,' he said, 'then all we need do is draw—'

'Oook!'

'I assure you, I was only going to use pencil—'

'*Eeek.*'

'All we have to do is *imagine*, all right, a third point equidistant from the other two . . . er . . . that looks like somewhere in the Rim Ocean to me, or probably over the Edge.'

'Can't see that thing in the sea,' said Ridcully, glancing up at the recently laminated corpse.

'In that case, it must have been in the other direction—'

The wizards crowded round.

There *was* something there.

''S not even properly drawn in,' said the Dean.

'That's because no one's sure it really exists,' said the Senior Wrangler.

It floated in the middle of the sea, a tiny continent by Discworld standards.

' "XXXX",' Ponder read.

'They only put that on the map because no one knows what it's really called,' said Ridcully.

'And we've sent him there,' said Ponder. 'A place that we're not even certain *exists*?'

'Oh, we know it exists now,' said Ridcully. 'Must do. Must do. Must be a pretty rich land, too, if the rats grow that big.'

'I'll go and see if we can bring—' Ponder began.

'Oh, no,' said Ridcully firmly. 'No, thank you very much. Next time it might be an elephant whizzing over our heads, and those things make a splash. No. Give the poor chap a rest. We'll have to think of something else . . .'

He rubbed his hands together. 'Time for dinner, I feel,' he said.

'Um,' said the Senior Wrangler. 'Do you think we were wise to light that string when we sent the thing back?'

'Certainly,' said Ridcully, as they strolled away. 'No one could say we didn't return it in exactly the same state as it arrived . . .'

Hex dreamed gently in its room.

The wizards were right. Hex couldn't think.

There weren't words, yet, for what it could do.

Even Hex didn't know what it could do.

565

But it was going to find out.

The quill pen scritched and blotted its way over a fresh sheet of paper and drew, for no good reason, a calendar for the year surmounted by a rather angular picture of a beagle, standing on its hind legs.

The ground was red, just like at Hunghung. But whereas that was a kind of clay so rich that leaving a chair on the lawn meant that you had four small trees by nightfall, this ground was sand that looked as if it had got red by being baked in a million-year summer.

There were occasional clumps of yellowed grass and low stands of grey-green trees. But what there was everywhere was heat.

This was especially noticeable in the pond under the ghost gums. It was steaming.

A figure emerged from the clouds, absentmindedly picking the burnt bits off his beard.

Rincewind waited until his own personal world had stopped spinning and concentrated on the four men who were watching him.

They were black with lines and whorls painted on their faces and had, between them, about two square feet of clothing.

There were three reasons why Rincewind was no racist. He'd ended up in too many places too suddenly to develop that kind of mind. Besides, if he'd thought about it much, most of the really dreadful things that had happened to him had been done by quite pale people with big wardrobes. Those were two of the reasons.

The third was that these men, who were just rising from a half-crouching position, were all holding spears pointing at Rincewind and there is something about the sight of four spears aimed at your throat that causes no end of respect and the word 'sir' to arise spontaneously in the mind.

One of the men shrugged, and lowered his spear.

'G'day, bloke,' he said.

This meant only three spears, which was an improvement.

'Er. This isn't Unseen University, is it, sir?' said Rincewind.

The other spears stopped pointing at him. The men grinned. They had very white teeth.

'Klatch? Howondaland? It looks like Howondaland,' said Rincewind hopefully.

'Don't know them blokes, bloke,' said one of the men.

The other three clustered around him.

'What'll we call him?'

'He's Kangaroo Bloke. No worries there. One minute a kangaroo, next minute a bloke. The old blokes say that sort of thing used to happen all the time, back in the Dream.'

'I reckoned he'd look better than that.'

'Yeah.'

'One way to tell.'

The man who was apparently the leader of the group advanced on Rincewind with the kind of grin reserved for imbeciles and people holding guns, and held out a stick.

It was flat, and had a bend in the middle. Someone had spent a long time making rather nice designs on it in little coloured dots. Somehow, Rincewind wasn't at all surprised to see a butterfly among them.

The hunters watched him expectantly.

'Er, yes,' he said. 'Very good. Very good workmanship, yes. Interesting pointillistic effect. Shame you couldn't find a straighter bit of wood.'

One of the men laid down his spear, and squatted down and picked up a long wooden tube, covered with the same designs. He blew into it. The effect was not unpleasant. It sounded like bees would sound if they'd invented full orchestration.

'Um,' said Rincewind. 'Yes.'

It was a test, obviously. They'd given him this bent piece of wood. He had to do something with it. It was clearly very important. He'd—

Oh, no. He'd say something or do something, wouldn't he, and then they'd say, yes, you are the Great Bloke or something, and they'd drag him off and it'd be the start of another Adventure, i.e., a period of horror and unpleasantness. Life was full of tricks like that.

Well, this time Rincewind wasn't going to fall for it.

'I want to go home,' he said. 'I want to go back home to the Library where it was nice and quiet. And I don't know where I am. And I don't care what you do to me, right? I'm not going to have any kind of adventure or start saving the world again and you can't trick me into it with mysterious bits of wood.'

He gripped the stick and flung it away from him with all the force he could still muster.

They stared at him as he folded his arms.

'I'm not playing,' he said. 'I'm stopping right here.'

They were still staring. And now they were grinning, too, at something behind him.

He felt himself getting quite annoyed.

'Do you understand? Are you listening?' he said. 'That's the last time the universe is going to trick Rincewi—'